MATHILDA AND OTHER STORIES

Mary Shelley

MATHILDA
and Other Stories

◆

Mary Shelley

with an Introduction and Notes by
JENNY DIPLACIDI

WORDSWORTH CLASSICS

For my husband
ANTHONY JOHN RANSON
with love from your wife, the publisher.
Eternally grateful for your unconditional love.

Readers who are interested in other titles from
Wordsworth Editions are invited to visit our website at
www.wordsworth-editions.com

For our latest list and a full mail-order service, contact
Bibliophile Books, 5 Datapoint, South Crescent, London E16 4TL
TEL: +44 (0)20 7474 2474 FAX: +44 (0)20 7474 8589
ORDERS: orders@bibliophilebooks.com
WEBSITE: www.bibliophilebooks.com

First published in 2013 by Wordsworth Editions Limited
8B East Street, Ware, Hertfordshire SG12 9HJ

ISBN 978 1 84022 697 3

Text © Wordsworth Editions Limited, 2013
Introduction and Notes © Jenny DiPlacidi 2013

Wordsworth® is a registered trademark of
Wordsworth Editions Limited

Wordsworth Editions
is the company founded in 1987 by
MICHAEL TRAYLER

Typeset in Great Britain
Printed and bound by Clays Ltd, St Ives plc

CONTENTS

GENERAL INTRODUCTION

Wordsworth Classics are inexpensive editions designed to appeal to the general reader and students. We commissioned teachers and specialists to write wide ranging, jargon-free Introductions and to provide Notes that would assist the understanding of our readers rather than interpret the stories for them. In the same spirit, because the pleasures of reading are inseparable from the surprises, secrets and revelations that all narratives contain, we strongly advise you to enjoy this book before turning to the Introduction.

KEITH CARABINE
General Adviser
Rutherford College, University of Kent at Canterbury

INTRODUCTION

I

A Brief Sketch of Mary Shelley's Life

From the beginning of her literary career Mary Wollstonecraft Godwin Shelley's works have been read as compulsively autobiographical and as projections of herself and those closest to her. Her remarkable parentage and experiences during the Romantic period have made it inevitable that both her contemporary and modern readers viewed her as the heroine of her own fiction and searched her life for explanations of her works. Mary was born 30 August 1797 to the radical philosopher William Godwin and the pioneering feminist Mary Wollstonecraft, who died on 10 September from complications in childbirth.[1] William

---

1 William Godwin was a philosophical anarchist who published his political views in the lengthy treatise *Enquiry Concerning Political Justice and its Influence on Morals and Happiness* (1793). Mary Wollstonecraft was a philosopher and proponent of women's rights most famous for her work *A Vindication of the Rights of Woman* (1792).

Godwin subsequently raised Mary and her half-sister Fanny Imlay (Mary Wollstonecraft's first and illegitimate daughter by her lover, American businessman Gilbert Imlay) and he remarried in December 1801. Godwin's second wife, Mary Jane Clairmont, brought with her two children, Charles and Jane (later known as Claire), close in age to Fanny and Mary, and they later had a son together, William Godwin, Jr. The new additions to the family brought increased financial pressures and personality clashes; in particular, Mary had a strong aversion to her stepmother, who was generally thought to be disagreeable.[2]

Godwin ensured that Mary's education was diverse and he 'instructed the older children as a little class in mythology, Roman and English history, followed by the Greek', and she met and dined with some of the most famous writers, artists and scientists of the day (Sunstein, p. 39).[3] In her adolescence, however, her relationship with her stepmother deteriorated and in June 1812 Mary was sent to live with friends of the family near Dundee, Scotland, where she would spend a combined total of some sixteen months. Mary thrived in the stark and imposing scenery of the windswept Grampian Mountains, the nearby beach of the Firth, and views of the fifteenth-century Broughty Castle, and revelled in a newfound freedom from domestic discord (Mellor, p. 16). This period of solitude in nature was fundamental to shaping her voice and inspiring her literary output, as it was here that 'her imagination soared' (Spark, p. 17). Subsequently, her fictions drew upon images of such Romantic landscapes to convey the intense emotions of her characters.

On her return to London in 1814 Mary saw more of Percy Bysshe Shelley, whom she had met briefly in 1812, as he frequently visited Godwin and viewed him as a mentor. Percy, who was already married to and separated from Harriet Westbrook, fell deeply in love with Mary, the daughter of the two radical thinkers he most revered. The two read poetry and visited her mother's grave together; ten years later in her journal Mary would reflect on their developing mutual love: 'such, my loved Shelley, now ten years ago, at this season, did we first meet, and there were the very scenes – that churchyard, with its sacred

2   Sunstein, pp. 26–35, provides a detailed account of the second Mrs Godwin and the family dynamics. For full details of this and other references, see the Bibliography that follows this Introduction. In subsequent references, wherever possible, the surname and page number will follow in parentheses after the quotation.

3   Shelley's works are steeped in Greek and Roman mythology, demonstrating the breadth of her reading. See the notes to this volume for an account of her wide range of mythological, historical and literary references.

tomb, was the spot where love first shone in your dear eyes' (*Journal*, p. 194).[4] Threads of Mary Shelley's account of their bourgeoning love can be seen in her story 'Euphrasia, A Tale of Greece' (1838) in which a pair of orphaned siblings often 'spent the night beside the revered tomb of their lost friend, talking of the hopes and aspirations he had implanted. The young can form such sublime, such beautiful dreams. No disappointment, no evil, no bad passion shadows their glorious visions' (p. 373). While Mary's later journals and letters may idealise the young love that would quickly become a romantic drama tinged with tragedy, there is no doubt that she and Percy influenced and inspired each other's writings.

When Percy and Mary declared their mutual love for each other, the situation was fraught with difficulties – Harriet refused to agree to a legal separation and Godwin reacted badly to Percy's proposal that he and Mary live together as unmarried partners. Godwin attempted to reason with his daughter who eventually agreed not to see Percy, but the pair still communicated. Percy, afraid that Mary would be removed from London or kept from corresponding with him, stormed into the Godwin household. Emily W. Sunstein draws from a melodramatic letter from Mrs Godwin to Lady Mount Cashell that describes how Percy, 'rumpled, red-eyed, distraught, shrill' pushed her aside to approach Mary: ' "They wish to separate us, my beloved; but Death shall unite us," and offered her a bottle of laudanum. "By this you can escape from tyranny; and this," taking a small pistol from his pocket, "shall reunite me to you" ' (Sunstein, pp. 77–8). Mary calmed him down only to be woken later in the night with news of his attempted suicide and shortly afterwards she agreed to flee with him to the Continent (Sunstein, pp. 75–9). Already, Mary and Percy were being written about as characters in an intensely Romantic story.

Their relationship and flight, accompanied by Mary's stepsister, Claire Clairmont, scandalised English society, and when the couple and Claire summered with Lord Byron in Switzerland in 1816, 'League of Incest' rumours circulated, insinuating that Byron and Percy shared Claire and Mary between them (Marchand, pp. 76, 82, 126). Further gossip surrounding the pair included the suicide of Percy's wife Harriet in December 1816 while pregnant, his marriage to Mary two weeks later, the court case that denied Percy custody of his children with Harriet, and the perception of Percy as an immoral

---

4 The tombstone survives in the graveyard of old St Pancras Church, along-side St Pancras Station.

atheist.[5] The vitriolic public response to Godwin's candid revelations of Mary Wollstonecraft's affair with the married Gilbert Imlay in *Memoirs of the Author of A Vindication of the Rights of Woman* (1798) resurfaced in the condemnatory reaction towards Mary's relationship with Percy: 'The best believed of Mary Shelley was that he [Percy] had suborned her, the worst that she was the vicious heir of Wollstonecraft and Godwin, Byron's mistress, atheist, and so on' (Sunstein, p. 140). Clearly, public perception and interest in Mary Shelley's life revolved not only around her actions but also those of her infamous family and friends, and greatly influenced how her works were received, read and reviewed.

2

The Lost Manuscript

Mathilda, an epistolary novel describing the unconsummated incestuous passion between Mathilda and her unnamed father, was first published in 1959 after the discovery of Mary Shelley's copy of the manuscript. It appears that Mary Shelley originally sent her edited manuscript of *Mathilda* to William Godwin via Maria Gisborne, a family friend and one-time love interest of Godwin (Nitchie, p. xvi). E. J. Clery notes that 'Mary's desire to push further the exploration of emotional and moral extremes' marks her as an innovator who 'did not herself foresee the dangers of publishing *Matilda*' (Clery, p. 134). But while Gisborne enjoyed the novel, Godwin found the subject matter of incest 'disgusting and detestable' and, in spite of repeated requests from his daughter, never returned the manuscript (Todd, p. xvii). What happened to his copy remains unknown. Why Mary Shelley, who appears to have retained at least one copy, did not herself approach a publisher, has never been satisfactorily explained.[6] The novel's theme of father–daughter incest and Mary Shelley's father's reaction generated, inevitably, a range of autobiographical and psycho-biographical readings.[7]

Not surprisingly, Elizabeth Nitchie, who first located the manuscript of *Mathilda*, positioned it as an autobiographical project and until

---

5 Lord Eldon's custody decision stated that Percy Shelley could not inculcate his children's morals.

6 A possible explanation is her view of the manuscript as a premonition of her husband's death (Todd, p. xvii; Sunstein, p. 230).

7 Mellor argues that Godwin probably 'perceived, beneath the surface story of incest, his daughter's portrait of his own equally horrendous failure as a loving, supportive parent' (p. 255).

recently much of the subsequent scholarship understood the work in terms of Mary Shelley's relationships and emotional crises. Nitchie argued that: 'In this story, as in all Mary Shelley's writing, there is much that is autobiographical: it would be hard to find a more self-revealing work,' and that: 'The biographical elements are clear: Mathilda is certainly Mary herself; Mathilda's father is Godwin; Woodville is an idealized Shelley' (Nitchie, pp. vii, xii). She furthers details the similarities between Mathilda and Mary:

> Like Mathilda, Mary was a woman of strong passions and affections which she often hid from the world under a placid appearance. Like Mathilda's, Mary's mother had died a few days after giving her birth. Like Mathilda, she spent part of her girlhood in Scotland. Like Mathilda, she met and loved a poet of 'exceeding beauty', and – also like Mathilda – in that sad year she had treated him ill, having become 'captious and unreasonable' in her sorrow [. . .] This story was the outlet for her emotions in 1819.   [Nitchie, p. xiii]

Perhaps more than any other factor, it is this haunting spectre of maternity that has contributed to keeping Mary Shelley's writings firmly entrenched in autobiographical approaches. The novel has been identified as a type of therapy for a mother in mourning because it was written in 1819 following the death of her son William, an idea substantiated by Mary Shelley's journal in which she points to the manuscript's composition as providing her with something on which to focus (Sunstein, p. 177). Many critics view its production as burdened by an albatross of grief that inhibits, and even denies, Mary Shelley's own creative agency.[8]

Mary Shelley in her lifetime objected to readings of her fiction through her relationships and experiences: 'I did not make myself the heroine of my tales. Life appeared to me too commonplace an affair as regarded myself.'[9] When Edward John Trelawney proposed to include a biography of Percy Shelley in his own autobiography, she protested: 'Far from wishing to stand forward to assert myself in any way, now that I am alone in the world, [I] have but the desire to wrap night and the obscurity of insignificance around me. This is weakness – but I cannot help it – to be in print – the subject of men's observations – of

---

8 Harpold, for example, focuses on Mary Shelley's psychological state to understand the novel, whereas Clery, Todd and others note her editing and revision process.

9 Mary Shelley makes this claim regarding her early adolescent Scottish writings in her 1831 Introduction to *Frankenstein* (*Frankenstein*, p. 169).

the bitter hard world's commentaries, to be attacked or defended!' (*Letters* 2, p. 72). While some scholars use such passages as proof of Mary Shelley's 'acceptance of cultural stereotypes' or to describe her as a conservative, they more explicitly articulate a desire to avoid judgments based on representations of herself and Shelley, especially when not written by her (Newlyn, p. 226).[10] Mary Shelley was keenly aware of the dangers associated with male observations of women; Sunstein noting the 'three years of atrocious abuse' that followed Godwin's publication of his memoirs on Wollstonecraft (Sunstein, p. 20). Mary Shelley had no interest in having her life read and reviled by an audience who would attack or defend her, who would position her as the mistress of Shelley or his angelic devotee.

Reading *Mathilda* as 'autobiography projected into fiction' (Williams, p. 95) implies a lack of agency and design on Mary Shelley's part, promoting a vision of the suffering writer gripped by influences beyond her control and understanding, and mitigating the control and care taken by her as a professional writer producing a carefully edited manuscript. Critics will continue to read *Mathilda* 'as an uncontrolled expression of Mary Shelley's psychological anxieties' but we need to rely less on such conclusions and instead examine 'her self-consciousness as a literary artist' (Clemit, p. 37). Mary Shelley's unconventional representation of incest in *Mathilda* is rendered through her skilful blend of forms, tropes and allusions that invest the language with images of unruly and intense desires and portray a heroine at once desiring, victim, outcast, survivor and initiator.[11] Mary Shelley would return repeatedly to *Mathilda* throughout her literary career, making use of the richness of its thematic content and deploying a range of contradictory images and ideas to represent and explore the paradoxes of incestuous desire.

10 See also Poovey's description of Mary Shelley's journals as evidencing 'stereotypical feminine reticence' (p. 115). Myers provides an excellent analysis of such readings of Mary Shelley in 'The Female Author Between Public and Private Spheres'.

11 See Clery, Clemit and Miller, in particular, for readings that examine Mary Shelley's blend of genres.

Reading Mathilda

The novel opens in *medias res* with the first-person narrator, Mathilda, writing: 'It is only four o'clock; but it is winter and the sun has already set' (p. 3). The use of the present tense and the narrator's acknowledgement of the day's premature close lend both urgency and a sense of futility to the narrative. The sun's setting signals Mathilda's impending death and is representative of Mary Shelley's use of the imagery of nature to access emotional states throughout the remainder of her account. The anticipation of her imminent death persuades Mathilda to 'begin to write my tragic history' (p. 3) to Woodville, a young poet who met and befriended her after the events she relates in the lengthy letter, which forms the body of the novel. Mary Shelley's narrative draws from the confessional tradition of Rousseau, Godwin and Wollstonecraft in deploying the autobiographical in fiction while making use of the epistolary form.[12] Popularised in the eighteenth century, the epistolary form was a potentially subversive style of writing that dramatised private exchanges (Epstein, pp. 50–1). By embedding Mathilda's private and sexual confession within a letter, Mary Shelley creates a male gaze for Mathilda's confession; an audience that after her father's suicide she lacked in life. The unification of the epistolary and confessional modes of writing bring together Mathilda's two goals, to explain to Woodville her 'impenetrable and unkind silence' (p. 4) during their friendship, and to relate the incestuous desires shared between her father and herself.

Mary Shelley immediately calls into question the presumed privacy of the letter by demonstrating Mathilda's awareness that it may, in fact, be subject to perusal by a wider audience than Woodville alone. Not only does Mathilda realise the possibility of her 'tragic history' finding a more public reception, but she also imagines and desires it: 'I do not know that any will peruse these pages except you, my friend, who will receive them at my death. I do not address them to you alone because it will give me pleasure to dwell upon our friendship in a way that would be needless if you alone read what I shall write. I shall relate my tale

12 Rousseau's *Emile, or On Education* (1762) draws heavily from his own life while his later *Confessions* (1782–9) provides a detailed account of the experiences that shaped him and his philosophy. Godwin's *Caleb Williams* (1794) and Wollstonecraft's *Mary* (1788) and *The Wrongs of Woman: or, Maria* (1798) combine autobiographical and confessional elements.

therefore as if I wrote for strangers' (pp. 3–4). Mathilda's desire for a
wider audience and acknowledgment that writing for Woodville 'alone'
would be 'needless' destabilises the epistolary framework by actively
seeking an imaginary audience of strangers. Rather than create a sense
of voyeurism on the reader's part, Mary Shelley instead positions
Mathilda as 'a powerful actress or artist rather than as a submissive
victim' (Miller, p. 292) who demands that her story be read:

> Perhaps a history such as mine had better die with me, but a feeling
> that I cannot define leads me on and I am too weak both in body and
> mind to resist the slightest impulse. While life was strong within me I
> thought indeed that there was a sacred horror in my tale that rendered
> it unfit for utterance, and now about to die I pollute its mystic terrors.
> [p. 3]

Ultimately she cannot resist the need to disclose her tale. Mathilda's
'impulse' transgresses the bounds society has proscribed as the performance renders visible the tale that is 'unfit for utterance'. The writing
of the letter is thus analogous to the incestuous desire itself; Mathilda's
need to write that which should remain unwritten is a substitutive act
for the irresistible incestuous desire that led to first her father's suicide
and then her longing for death to reunite them. The 'sacred horror'
of incest to which Mathilda refers incorporates Christian imagery to
position her letter as disclosing a blasphemous secret – one that she
will, in defiance of custom, relate. Mary Shelley employs the oxy-
moronic term to unite the Romantic 'sacred' and the Gothic 'horror' in
a description of incest as at once spiritual and terrifying, reconfiguring
oppositional elements as uncomfortably closely related.

Incest, a familiar theme in works of the Romantic era, was used to
signal a variety of social and psychological conflicts and was often a
means by which characters rebelled against religious and legal
institutions.[13] Byron's Gothic and Romantic dramatic poem *Manfred*
(1817), for example, depicts sibling incest as a consequence of narcissism
and dangerous pursuits at once generated by and productive of social
ostracism. Gothic novels such as those by Ann Radcliffe employ
incestuous desires to articulate the dangerous consequences of
patrimony, to drive female action, and to criticise patriarchy's
appropriation of both female bodies and freedom. Gothic works

---

13 For accounts of incest in Romantic and eighteenth-century literature, see
    the Bibliography that follows this Introduction, particularly Perry, Pollak,
    Punter & Byron, and Richardson.

frequently isolate and/or imprison the heroine who, threatened with unreciprocated incestuous desires, must fight against the double bind in which she is persecuted by figures of authority who, while forbidden by society to commit incest, are endowed with the ability to do so due to their positions of power in that society. Godwin himself made use of the incest theme in his novel *Mandeville* (1817) in which 'he allows that the individual could be thwarted as much by psychological impulse – in this case, the repressed passion of sibling incest – as by unfavorable historical circumstances'; a 'dark vision' that Pamela Clemit argues Mary Shelley appropriated and transformed in *Mathilda* (Clemit, p. 41). Mary Shelley draws upon multiple literary traditions in her treatment of the theme that, as Clery demonstrates, enabled her to study individual subjectivity and psychology because of incest's ability to 'produce violent extremes of passion. No "natural" (as opposed to supernatural) device could do this so effectively as incest, regarded as the ultimate crime against nature' (Clery, p. 135). Clery's argument is essential to understanding Mary Shelley's representation of incest and its potential for producing emotional extremes as a transgressive rewriting of the role of nature and the sublime in Romantic and Gothic fiction.

Mary Shelley's use of the term 'sacred horror' to describe incest is rooted in the Romantic deployment of the sublime. Edmund Burke argued that the sublime was capable of inspiring awe and terror in the imagination and was productive of intense emotion, and Immanuel Kant noted that the sublime was without boundaries (Burke, pp. 110, 130–2; Kant, p. 61). Many Romantic writers depicted the sublime as being experienced through nature and affording a state of spiritual or mental greatness, and in the Gothic its attainment through the contemplation of nature often functioned as an anodyne to imprisoned or terrified characters. Following upon her mother's death and her father's departure Mathilda draws on this use of the sublime in her descriptions of the countryside surrounding her aunt's remote estate in Scotland:

My greatest pleasure was the enjoyment of a serene sky amidst these verdant woods: yet I loved all the changes of nature; and rain, and storm, and the beautiful clouds of heaven brought their delights with them. When rocked by the waves of the lake my spirits rose in triumph [. . .]

But my pleasures arose from the contemplation of nature alone, I had no companion: my warm affections finding no return from any other human heart were forced to run waste on inanimate objects.

[p. 11]

The triumph of Mathilda's spirit via her contemplation of and experiences in nature corresponds to a tradition of characters who are exalted and restored through 'wild scenery' (p. 11). The 'beautiful clouds of heaven' are aligned with the sacred and the pleasure in variety found in 'all the changes of nature' encompasses the depths of Mathilda's emotions. In first resorting to the Romantic and Gothic uses of the sublime in nature, Mary Shelley lays the foundations for the subsequent revelation of their inadequacies in accounting for the range of human emotion.

The reunion between Mathilda and her father that occurs when she is sixteen is productive of perfect happiness for both for some time. He states that, like Mathilda, he imagined their eventual reunion: 'as grief wore off and hope again revisited me I could only turn to her, and amidst cities and deserts her little fairy form, such as I imagined it, forever flitted before me. The northern breeze as it refreshed me was sweeter and more balmy for it seemed to carry some of your spirit along with it. I often thought that I would instantly return and take you along with me to some fertile island where we should live at peace for ever' (p. 14). It is a vision of a utopia, much like that of the creature's vision in *Frankenstein* of his life with a bride in 'the wilds of South America' where 'my companion will be of the same nature as myself [. . .] the sun will shine on us as on man, and will ripen our food. The picture I present to you is peaceful and human' (*Frankenstein*, p. 99). The descriptions of the imagined fertile and restorative locations represent the characters' expectations of emotional peace and happiness, linking the external environment to the internal psychological states – a conjunction that renders them equivalent. And, indeed, the father–daughter reunion produces the imagined paradise: 'I approached the shore, my father held the boat, I leapt lightly out, and in a moment was in his arms. And now I began to live. All around me was changed from a dull uniformity to the brightest scene of joy and delight.' (p. 14). This reunion is Mathilda's rebirth; she only begins to live once she is in her father's embrace, which is equally her awakening and arousal. Mary Shelley reproduces the earlier presentation of emotional extremes in nature to relocate Mathilda's source of joy within her father's presence. Mathilda no longer recalls her previous description of 'all the changes of nature'; rather, she describes her environment before her father's arrival as a 'dull uniformity'. His presence in her world eclipses the role that nature previously held, although she still makes use of the language and imagery associated with it to express her intense joy.

Mathilda's description of the period of joy with her father employs mythological allusions: 'Like Psyche I lived for awhile in an enchanted palace, amidst odours, and music, and every luxurious delight' (p. 17). The reference transforms her ecstatic musings from the filial to the erotic by comparing her happiness to Psyche's pleasures in the enchanted palace where she consummated her love with Cupid. Like a lover, Mathilda jealously guards time alone with her father: 'it was a subject of regret to me whenever we were joined by a third person, yet if I turned with a disturbed look towards my father, his eyes fixed on me and beaming with tenderness instantly restored joy to my heart. O, hours of intense delight!' (p. 17). Any disruption of their intimacy is perceived as an intrusion and causes distress. Mary Shelley uses the language of romantic affection and desire rather than that of a daughter's devotion to describe Mathilda's emotions towards her father. Her 'intense delight' is only restored through her father's gaze; he secures her joy by focusing on her rather than the interloper. This situation is intensified when the unwelcome presence of a suitor exhibits Mathilda's desirability as a romantic partner and prompts her father's discovery of his incestuous desires, provoking his withdrawal from her. When he offers no explanation for his sudden coldness Mathilda is plunged into misery. In pleading for her father to explain his behaviour Mathilda deftly manipulates his confession; it is, as Kathleen A. Miller notes, a scene carefully directed by Mathilda (Miller, pp. 293–4). She incites his incestuous confession by throwing herself at his feet and crying, ' "I know it – I see it – you hate me!" ' (p. 27), prompting his words: ' "My daughter, I love you!" ' (p. 27). Mathilda sinks to the ground, 'almost dead with excess of sickness and fear' (p. 27). Her reaction to her father's declaration of love makes sense only if she reciprocates his passion, otherwise the words 'I love you' would surely not have filled her with fear. She knows her father's love is incestuous because she shares it.

In a letter written to Mathilda stating that he is leaving for ever, the father attempts partially to explain his desires, hoping that Mathilda, his 'angelic judge', can forgive him (p. 32). He limits descriptions of his desires: 'Let a veil be drawn over the unimaginable sensations of a guilty father; the secrets of so agonised a heart may not be made vulgar' (p. 34). His letter also differs from Mathilda's deployment of the epistolary confession; her motivation for writing articulates a need to bring to light, in spite of censure, the incestuous desires – to 'record' her misfortunes for others (p. 4). The claim to veil the 'unimaginable sensations' compels the reader to imagine them and aligns the reader with Mathilda as her father's judge. In spite of his attempt at concealment,

Mary Shelley infiltrates a vocabulary that exposes the sexual nature of his desires: 'if I enjoyed from your looks, and words, and most innocent caresses a rapture usually excluded from the feelings of a parent towards his child, yet no uneasiness, no wish, no casual idea awoke me to a sense of guilt' (p. 34). The confession does not make explicit if the 'rapture' was a purely emotional response or a physical reaction to his daughter's caresses. While he clarifies that his feelings are excluded from the emotional range of other fathers, he immediately denies that they caused him guilt. The language obfuscates his awareness of loving Mathilda incestuously. The word 'rapture' seems to indicate a strictly psychological state – that of ecstasy or bliss – but the fact that it is paired with 'innocent caresses' points to a physical ecstasy. His 'sinless passion' (p. 34) is so because it lacks deliberation; he is unaware of the sexual element underlying his ecstasy and so it is guiltless. Considering the meaning of 'rapture' as the conveyance of a person to heaven and the father's experience of this through his daughter's touch, his words suggest that unwitting incestuous desires are the pathway to nirvana. Mary Shelley uses both the religious and psychological meanings of 'rapture' to distort the binaries of sanctity and sin, rendering the representation of incest here a spiritual sublime.

The contrasting images used to describe the father's realisation that his love is sexual are characteristic of Mary Shelley's Romantic sensibility and use of language:

> Perhaps also my passion was lulled to content by the deep and exclusive affection you felt for me. But when I saw you become the object of another's love; when I imagined that you might be loved otherwise than as a sacred type and image of loveliness and excellence; or that you might love another with a more ardent affection than that which you bore to me, then the fiend awoke within me.   [p. 34]

Prior to jealousy forcing his awareness that Mathilda can be loved erotically he was able to enjoy a 'sinless passion' because he viewed her as a 'sacred type'. His lack of knowledge regarding the sexual nature of his desires absolved him of guilt, but once aware, he becomes a 'fiend'. There is no intermediate in such descriptions; the change in the father is conveyed through a dramatic shift in language, from the supplicant to the fiend. Emotions and people are accounted for in starkly oppositional language and images. Such dichotomies are reiterated in the father's attempt to justify consummating their love based on the belief that Mathilda's body houses her mother's spirit: 'in my madness I dared say to myself – Diana died to give her birth; her mother's spirit was transferred into her frame, and she ought to be as Diana to me. With every effort to cast it off, this love clings closer, this guilty love more unnatural than hate, that withers your hopes and destroys me for ever' (pp. 34–5). Mary Shelley employs the same rhetorical language in the father's confession as she does in Mathilda's initial disclosure, presenting his 'guilty love' as akin to Mathilda's 'sacred horror'. The father recognises that his assertion regarding Mathilda and Diana as one spirit was 'madness', an attempt to free himself from blame that was ultimately fruitless. His belief that he will be unable to rid himself of the 'guilty love' drives him to suicide. But Mathilda's understanding of guilt and innocence is more complex than her father's. Although she is described as horrified and certain that she can never see her father again, Mathilda's intense love for him, called by her father 'the deep and exclusive affection you felt for me' (p. 34), overcomes her vow to remain for ever separated from him.

Mathilda creates a fantasy to justify an eventual reunion with her father, envisioning a future with him after he passes sixteen years wandering the world: 'Might he not many, many years hence, when age had quenched the burning sensations that he now experienced, might he not then be again a father to me?' (p. 29). The physical effects of the passage of time are presented as allowing Mathilda to be with her father without consummating the incestuous desires. It demonstrates a naïve (or possibly wilfully self-deluding) belief that in sixteen years her now vigorous thirty-eight-year-old father will be rendered either impotent or free of sexual urges. Unlike her father, Mathilda does not recognise that her plan is 'madness'; rather, she elaborates and expands upon it:

> Be thy limbs worn and thy heart chilled, and all youth be dead within thee! Let thy hairs be as snow; thy walk trembling and thy voice have lost its mellow tones! Let the liquid luster of thine eyes be quenched; and then return to me, return to thy Mathilda, thy child, who may then be clasped in thy loved arms, while thy heart beats with sinless emotion. Go, Devoted One, and return thus! – This is my curse, a daughter's curse: go, and return pure to thy child, who will never love aught but thee.   [p. 30]

She fixates on the intervening years producing a substantial physical change that will render her father 'pure' and thus enable their reunion. For Mathilda, what is at issue is the physical ability to act out the incestuous desire, not the desire itself; thus, if her father can 'return pure' he will have 'sinless emotion'. In spite of placing the onus of

desire on her father by arguing that his passions must be extinguished
before they can reunite, her preoccupation with his body in this vision
exposes the physical nature of her desire for him. Her focus hyperbolises
the changes that will be wrought by time, foreseeing her father's 'limbs
worn' and his hair 'as snow' in juxtaposition to the 'mellow tones' of his
voice and 'liquid lustre' of his eyes as they are. The contrast discloses
the dangerous attractions he holds for her now. Only once he is altered
can she again be clasped in his 'loved arms'; it is not only to remove his
desires but also her own that necessitates a sixteen-year separation.
Mathilda deliberately overlooks the incestuous nature of the love that
exists regardless of its consummation and that makes futile any attempt
at a 'pure' reunion.

Her father, however, knows that he can never 'return pure' to a
daughter who 'will never love aught but thee'. This awareness causes
him to look towards a reunion with her only in death: 'My child, if after
this life I am permitted to see you again, if pain can purify the heart,
mine will be pure: if remorse may expiate guilt, I shall be guiltless'
(p. 35). Because he believes sin is caused by the knowledge of the desire,
his expectation of a reunion after death is doubtful. He cannot so easily
separate the physical and emotional aspects of their incestuous love; he
perceives that it is guilty regardless of its consummation. This belief
causes him to flee their home and, in the letter, he bids Mathilda not to
follow him. The pursuit scene here has much in common with the
pursuit in *Frankenstein*, both formally and thematically. Clemit notes
that the pursuit in *Frankenstein* is used to 'destabilize conventional moral
values: [. . .] the abandoned creature returns to confront his "monstrous"
father, and the pair act out a drama of enticement and threat that leads
to widespread social destruction' (Clemit, p. 32). Similarly, Mathilda's
dramatic pursuit of her father is very much a drama of enticement;
Mathilda reads her father's letter as a coded confession of imminent
suicide that overtly bids her to stay away while revealing his flight is
more than it appears. Like the creature and Victor, Mathilda's con-
frontation with her 'monstrous' father (Mathilda's father refers to his
'monstrous passion') never transpires. His suicide before she reaches
him is an act of ultimate self-castration engendered by his fear of
Mathilda's power over him and his desire for her.

Mathilda's desolation after her father's declaration and suicide is
united with a description of her joy at their reunion in a passage that
discloses these intense emotions through the imagery of nature. The
schism between the (physical) external and (emotional) internal is thus
dissolved:

my father returned and I could pour my warm affections on a human heart; there was a new sun and a new earth created to me; the waters of existence sparkled: joy! joy! but, alas! what grief! My bliss was more rapid than the progress of a sunbeam on a mountain, which discloses its glades and woods, and then leaves it dark and blank; to my happiness followed madness and agony, closed by despair.

[p. 67]

Mathilda's commandeering of the 'new sun' and 'new earth' to express the intense joy of her father's transforming presence is startlingly ecstatic, but unlike God's (permanent) creation, her earthly 'bliss' is rendered fleeting. Her subsequent inability to find happiness in the natural world is fundamental to reading Mary Shelley's uniquely transgressive representation of incest because it portrays the loss of Mathilda's father as destructive of this newly created world. The description of their life together as edenic is reinforced by Mathilda's description of its termination: 'I lament now, I must ever lament, those few short months of Paradisiacal bliss; I disobeyed no command, I ate no apple, and yet I was ruthlessly driven from it. Alas! My companion did, and I was precipitated in his fall' (p. 16). Mary Shelley uses the allusion to Eden to underscore the sublimity of their relationship during its period of ignorant innocence whilst questioning Mathilda's claim that she is blameless in its destruction. Without his presence there is only darkness and despair, a casting out from the garden. Mathilda's life after her father's death

was very unlike my early life [. . .] Then I bounded across the fields; my spirit often seemed to ride upon the winds, and to mingle in joyful sympathy with the ambient air [. . .] But now my walk was slow – my eyes were seldom raised and often filled with tears; no song, no smiles; no careless motion that might bespeak a mind intent on what surrounded it – I was gathered into myself – a selfish solitary creature.

[p. 45]

Mathilda is unable to engage with nature and benefit from it as she did previously; the freedom and exultation she once accessed through the physical world are irrevocably lost. Mary Shelley draws upon the extremes of emotion and the sacred that were previously associated with 'the beautiful clouds of heaven' but have since been transferred to Mathilda's description of incest as a 'sacred horror.' Incest, in producing violent extremes, usurps the role of nature in inspiring what Burke calls 'the strongest emotion which the mind is capable of feeling'

(Burke, p. 111). It is Mathilda's contemplation of her father's incestuous declaration that now has more power than nature to evoke her emotional responses. Mary Shelley's language thus draws on what David Morris characterises as incest's position as 'the new and often unspoken terror at the heart of Gothic sublimity' (Morris, p. 305) but also employs the Romantic treatment of the sublime in nature and biblical imagery. The seemingly oppositional treatment at once divests incest of its terror while endowing it with natural and spiritual greatness, creating incest as a form of the sublime.

Unable to bear the attentions of distant relations and society after her father's suicide, Mathilda fakes her own death and retreats to rural seclusion where she meets Woodville. In her cottage she leads a largely solitary existence, and begins 'to read history, and to lose my individuality among the crowd that had existed before me. Thus perhaps, as the sensation of immediate suffering wore off, I became more human' (p. 46). Mathilda reads history and undergoes self-education to relieve suffering as do both Mary Shelley and *Frankenstein*'s creature. Mary Shelley recorded in her journal that 'study has become more necessary to me than the air I breathe. In the questioning and searching turn it gives to my thoughts, I find some relief to wild reverie; in the self-satisfaction I feel in commanding myself, I find present solace' (*Journal*, p. 189). In *Frankenstein* the creature's education in history makes him question the morality of society: 'Was man, indeed, at once so powerful, so virtuous, and magnificent, yet so vicious and base? [. . .] The words induced me to turn towards myself' (*Frankenstein*, p. 80). The creature's understanding of history and the world causes him to turn inward while Mathilda views it as a way to lose her own identity, but the results are not so different; it strengthens the creature's sense of his alienation which is what Mathilda desires – to become lost from herself just as the creature becomes lost from the world. Like Mary Shelley's use of study for solace, all are attempts to grasp at humanity. The creature's understanding of the paradoxical differences found in the extremes of qualities that make up mankind renders him unfit for the world. Likewise, Mathilda's incestuous love is marked by her struggle with reconciling the contradictions inherent in the desire that has supplanted all her prior pleasures in the natural world.

Without her father Mathilda feels that 'there was no joy, no hope; that death however bitter would be the welcome seal to all my pangs; death the skeleton was to be as beautiful as love' (p. 55). The external and physical world that is incapable of affording joy to Mathilda must be transcended in order for her to again experience the heightened emotions of pleasure and joy.[14] She looks forward to her death that will be 'as beautiful as love' because death is the means to reunite her with her father, her love. This familial reunion in death is reworked in 'Euphrasia, A Tale of Greece' in which a loving brother 'died in the dear hope of meeting his sister, and her image had shed peace over the last moment of life' (p. 378). Mathilda reflects on her impending death: 'In truth I am in love with death; no maiden ever took more pleasure in the contemplation of her bridal attire than I in fancying my limbs already enwrapped in their shroud: is it not my marriage dress? Alone it will unite me to my father when in an eternal mental reunion we shall never part' (pp. 66–7). Mary Shelley eroticises Mathilda's reflections by imbuing them with references to a future spiritual state alongside the 'pleasure in the contemplation of her bridal attire' that reworks her earlier claim that 'my pleasures arose from the contemplation of nature alone' (p. 11). Her Romantic pleasure in nature has been superseded by her contemplation of incest as such, an inversion of the understanding of Gothic incest as 'unspoken terror' (Morris, p. 305) through both her pleasure in and articulation of it. Her huge claim that she takes 'more pleasure' in the contemplation of the shroud/ wedding gown than any other woman morbidly rejects life's possibilities while pointing to the emotionally extreme state her 'wild reverie' of death allows her to achieve.[15] Mathilda's attention to her bridal shroud recalls the white dress she wore during her reunion with her father in Scotland and reveals a preoccupation with her physical appearance at the future moment of 'eternal mental reunion'. This fancied 'mental' reunion is, like the one she allowed herself to imagine could occur in life after a sixteen-year separation, an attempt to deny its sexual nature. She projects the realisation of her marriage to her father into the afterlife while at once focusing on and denying its physicality, suggesting her belief in a sexually innocent incest is, in fact, chimerical. As her father's

14 Mary Shelley here again works against what Morris characterises as the Gothic's pursuit of 'a version of the sublime utterly without transcendence' (p. 306) and its treatment of death that is 'not absorbed into the beauty of sentimental fictions about natural goodness but rather invested with contradictory emotions of desire and loathing. It is sublime because it remains a terrifying mystery, not simply unknowable but linked with human desires that we wish to keep unknown' (p. 309). Mary Shelley, rather, shows the sublime as experienced through incestuous desires known through a transcendent death.

15 Bennett argues that Mary Shelley 'uses the epistolary form to dramatise the heroine's desperate melancholy' (p. 218).

'rapture' in her 'innocent caresses' elucidated, knowledge and desire preclude purity; the paradox elides any easy designation of their passion as purely emotional.

The physical nature of their reunion is compounded by allusions to the Nicene Creed's 'I look for the resurrection of the dead, and the life of the world to come'[16] in Mathilda's assertion 'I go from this world where he is no longer and soon I shall meet him in another' (p. 67).[17] Mary Shelley displaces the traditional Christian heaven with an alternate vision of incestuous desire; a 'sacred horror' as eternity. The blasphemous appropriation of religious tenets allows Mathilda to look forward to a corporeal resurrection in which she will experience incest as a spiritually sublime state. The paradox of the 'guilty passion' that Mathilda seeks to indulge via 'sinless emotion' is thus resolved only through Mary Shelley's configuration of the incestuous sublime in a physical and mental ecstasy in which Mathilda's father replaces the holy father; incest is sublime to the point of religious ecstasy. The evocation of the sublime through the contemplation of natural imagery without boundaries is, in a sense, most fully realised in Mary Shelley's remobilisation of it here. The future world, the only place free of the social and religious restrictions on the incestuous desires designated as unnatural by society, is eternally without such restraints. Mathilda's incestuous sublime is similarly without boundaries, in terms of either limits or distinctions between binary opposites. Mary Shelley's depiction of incestuous desires culminating in an eternal union between father and daughter deploys and explores the paradoxes created through oxymorons and competing images and ideas to illuminate and transgress socially imposed boundaries on relationships and desire.

16 The Nicene Creed in *The Book of Common Prayer* has been in use in the Anglican Church, unchanged, since 1662.
17 The reported pleas of Percy to Mary to commit suicide with him so they can be together in the afterlife is similarly part of the Romantic fixation on immortality found in works like Byron's *Manfred* and Keats's 'Odes'.

Short Fiction for the Annuals

After Percy's death in 1822 Mary Shelley's financial difficulties were exacerbated by his father Sir Timothy's failure to provide adequate support for his grandson as well as Godwin's ongoing demands for financial assistance. Mary Shelley provided for her son and family by writing for the lucrative market of the annual gift books. Charlotte Sussman notes that the pretty silk-bound gift books and beautiful engravings were associated with the female consumerism of light literature and that this caused their included works to be derided as sham literature, not proper masculine artwork and genius, but trifles that 'appealed to middle-class women' (Sussman, pp. 165–6). These annuals and Mary Shelley's tales, however, were widely read and popular, and, importantly, their reception aligned Mary Shelley with such renowned Romantic writers as Joanne Baillie, Felicia Hemans and William Wordsworth.[18]

The gift-book format dictated the length of the tales, a restriction of which Mary Shelley was keenly aware ('I am worried to death to make my things shorter & shorter'; *Letters* 2, p. 245), and required dexterous experimentation and innovation on her part. She made use of narrative devices to minimise length, such as abrupt introductions ('The Evil Eye'), second- or even third-hand stories ('Euphrasia, A Tale of Greece') and the use of archetypes ('Transformation'). The gift books' illustrations frequently preceded the writing of the stories, and Mary Shelley and other authors were asked at times to tailor their stories to the engravings (Robinson, p. xvi). Mary Shelley avoided allowing the illustrations to dictate content and frequently wrote stories that either paid little attention to the engraving ('The Sisters of Albano') or invested seemingly peaceful or beautiful illustrations with mournful, dangerous, and Gothic themes ('The Mourner', 'The Dream' and 'The Elder Son'). The magazines favoured the sentimental and the Gothic genres, which allowed Mary Shelley to work primarily within the Gothic and make use of its potential to subvert institutional authority and normative desires.[19] Sussman argues that Mary Shelley's stories of women

18 *Athenaeum*, No. 55 (1828), review of *The Keepsake* (1829), cited in Sunstein, pp. 290, 446, note 37

19 See particularly Anolik, Clery, Haggerty, Mulvey-Roberts and Sussman.

experiencing disaster and poverty within the static form of the gift books 'take up this gendered intersection of the human form and the commodity form' to provide social criticism (Sussman, p. 167). In these tales she revisited and substantially reworked the themes of forbidden desire, knowledge and alienation central to *Mathilda* and *Frankenstein* and deployed the Gothic tropes of inheritance, incest, murder, imprisonment and the transcendence of boundaries.

Mary Shelley's writings for the annuals offer intensely emotionally accounts of subjugated and oppressed individuals who access surprising resources of physical and psychological strength to reveal their potential to transform or abandon archaic institutions, obsolete customs and dissolute people. Her story 'The Mourner' (1829) has received critical attention for its clear reworking of *Mathilda* [20] but the story of the self-described parricide who loved her father intensely is more interesting for the anti-establishment sentiments of the gentle and kind narrator, Horace Neville. The story is revealed via a frame narrative in which a visit to a secluded grave provokes Neville's disclosure of how his friendship with the deceased Ellen (the titular mourner) followed his flight from Eton. Neville's confessions regarding Eton reveal the intensity of his character:

> I was fag to a hard taskmaster [. . .] it was his delight to put me to shame, and, finding that I had too much of my mother in my blood, to endeavour to compel me to acts of cruelty from which my nature revolted – I refused to obey. Speak of West Indian slavery! [. . .] the tender years of aristocratic childhood were yielded up to a capricious, unrelenting, cruel bondage, far beyond the measured despotism of Jamaica.   [p. 164–5]

Neville's deployment of abolitionist rhetoric and the imagery of maternity, slavery and bondage link him with female sufferers of male oppression in such works as Wollstonecraft's Gothic/philosophical treatise *Maria, or, the Wrongs of Woman*. Neville's 'cruel bondage' of slavery is rendered all the worse because he has too much of the maternal in him. Sandra Gilbert and Susan Gubar point to women during the eighteenth and nineteenth centuries as being likened to the deformed or diseased; their biology and behaviour not conforming to either the ideal male body or masculine ideals of femininity causing them to be signified as outsiders (Gilbert and Gubar, p. 79). Such feminist analysis usefully reminds us that Mary Shelley describes the

20 Todd, p. xxi; Sussman, p. 171

'hard taskmaster' as identifying the presence of the maternal within Neville as an infection to be routed out. This 'biological' femininity, a disease in the blood inherited from the mother, is equally found in Neville's performance of acts that his tormentor views as too feminine to be tolerated.

Neville's rescue and taming of a bullfinch, for example, enrages the older boy who orders him to kill it; when he refuses the boy strangles the bird before him and throws it at his feet. Neville describes his response as follows:

> Never before – never may I again feel the same swelling, boiling fury in my bursting heart; the sight of my nursling expiring at my feet – my desire of vengeance – my impotence, created a Vesuvius within me that no tears flowed to quench. Could I have uttered – acted – my passion, it would have been less torturous: it was so when I burst into a torrent of abuse and imprecation. My vocabulary – it must have been a choice collection – was supplied by him against whom it was levelled. But words were air – I desired to give more substantial proof of my resentment – I destroyed everything in the room belonging to him; I tore them to pieces, I stamped on them, crushed them with more than childish strength.   [p. 165]

Mary Shelley presents a resistance to tyranny – to the cruel oppression of what is viewed as 'other' – which is here the oppressor's recognition that the oppressed does not ascribe to the socially constructed definitions of masculinity. Neville's resistance is answered by an act of violence that concretises his subordinate position and the rage he feels within. He is thus positioned as a Gothic heroine who employs an exaggerated language of sensibility emphasising feeling and physical manifestations of emotion. The boy, representative of institutionalised privilege and power, effaces Neville's maternal sympathies by violently destroying the object of his 'female' nurturing. Neville's rage in response discloses the powerlessness and the muteness with which subordinate positions are invested. Mary Shelley's silencing of his fury within a scene of unjust tyranny signals that the inability to speak stems from his position as oppressed other. When he does explode into speech his recognition that his 'words were air' highlights the inadequacy of the available discourse verbally to translate his rage; the tyrant cannot understand the oppressed even when his own vocabulary is employed. Yet, Neville's confusion of speech and deed – 'Could I have uttered – acted – my passion' – demonstrates an awareness that words and acts are not so easily distinguished. Hence, when language proves inadequate it is through a systematic, physical destruction of the bully's possessions (signifiers of his position of power) that the subordinated other is able to reassert an identity.

The portrayal of Neville's rejection of a silenced, subordinate and enforced position is representative of much of Mary Shelley's fiction in the annuals. The tales engage with contemporary social concerns while being packaged for consumption by a largely conservative audience. By making use of abolitionist, revolutionary and feminist rhetoric associated with resistances to authority, Mary Shelley portrays the potential for reversal, destruction and change in the most seemingly fixed forms.

5

Experimenting with Convention: Gothic and Resistance

Mary Shelley's experiments with convention can most clearly be seen in her stories that rework the tropes of the Gothic genre or combine elements of the historical novel with the language of unruly desire often found in the Gothic. In stories such as 'The Heir of Mundolfo' (1877) and 'A Tale of the Passions; or, The Death of Despina' (1822), Mary Shelley focuses on the extremes of passions and delineates, through a combination of religious, spiritual, sexual and natural imagery, the inability of society fully to restrict relationships and desire. By reworking Gothic models, such as imprisoned mothers and implacable villains, and through depicting paradoxically sexual yet pure desires, Mary Shelley resists conforming to social and literary conventions. The Gothic and Romantic worlds Mary Shelley creates are hermetic; the characters' wild reveries and their freedom from the intrusions of the outside world are deliberately claustrophobic. Her fixation with characters on the social and emotional edges in such environments has the effect of not only isolating the characters but also dislocates the reader.[21] The unfamiliar territory experienced by both exposes the artificiality of constructions, literary and social, challenging what is professed to be natural and proscribed as unnatural.

'The Heir of Mundolfo' (1877), although the last published, was one of Mary Shelley's earlier stories, probably written prior to the mid-

21 Clery notes the importance of the effect of isolation on Shelley's characters (p. 135).

1820s and her work for the annuals (Robinson, p. 395). The story, told
in the third-person, revolves around a younger son, Ludovico, and his
love for a destitute peasant, Viola, and ostensibly concerns an
objectionable love interest located in a Gothic setting, alongside generic
conventions such as a castle, a threatening and dangerous patriarch, a
kidnapping, imprisonment and a daring escape. Unusually for a Gothic
tale, it is Viola who first recognises her love for Ludovico, and translates
his promises of familial protection into passion:

> She could not see his eyes bent in gentleness on her – his mouth
> lighted by its tender smile – or listen to his voice as he bade her trust
> in him, for that he would be father, brother, all to her, without
> deeply, passionately loving him. He became the sun of her day, the
> breath of her life – her hope, joy, and sole possession. She watched
> for his coming, she watched him as he went, and for a long time she
> was happy.   [p. 387]

There is a disjunction between Ludovico's self-description as a
fraternal or paternal figure in Viola's life and her passionate response
to his self-fashioning. This disjunction is characteristic of Mary
Shelley's Romantic sensibility, her insistence that the language of
kinship is frequently bound up in the language of romantic love. Mary
Shelley experiments with the gender implications of this familiar trope
to portray the female as correctly interpreting the language of kinship
as belonging to the language of passion, and it is the female whose gaze
is fixed on an object of 'familial' desire. It is also the female who sees
her 'relative' as her possession, which, given the status of women at the
time as belonging to first their fathers and then their husbands, radically
contests the established order of both gender and social relations. This
will not be the last time that Viola upends familiar Gothic conventions:
after marrying Ludovico in secret (something Gothic heroines rarely
consent to, no matter how pressing their lovers) and bearing his child,
Fernando discovers their amour, and furious at his son's choice, has
Viola and child abducted and imprisoned.

While many Gothic escapes from imprisonment involve unmarried
and virginal heroines in flight from patriarchal figures intent on either
raping or stealing from them, mothers rarely, if ever, initiate their own
escapes. The prevalence in Gothic fiction of imprisoned or missing
mothers is noted by Ruth Bienstock Anolik, who argues that the erasure
of the maternal body in the genre is a literalisation of British women's
status in marriage as civilly dead (Anolik, pp. 26–7). Mary Shelley
breaks with this tradition and reverses the paradigm, remobilising the

figure of the mother. Thus, Viola does not, like Radcliffe's Olivia or
Louisa in *The Italian* (1797) and *A Sicilian Romance* (1790), await rescue
or assistance; rather, she gathers courage, displays heroism and
ingenuity, and effects her escape in the midst of a raging storm:

> [. . .] it struck her that her person would pass between the iron grates
> of her window. It was not high from the ground; the cloak, fastened
> to one of the staunchions, promised a safe descent [. . .] with darkness
> came rain that poured in torrents, accompanied by thunder and
> lightning that drove every creature to shelter. Viola shuddered. Could
> she expose her child during such a night? Yet again she gathered
> courage. It only made her meditate on some plan by which she might
> get the cloak as a shelter for her boy after it had served for their
> descent. [. . .] She fastened the cloak by means of her long veil which,
> hanging to the ground, was tied by a slipknot and would give way
> when pulled. She took her child in her arms and, having got without
> the bars, bound him with her sash and to her waist; and then without
> accident she reached the ground.   [pp. 397]

Here, maternity inspires rather than inhibits agency and spurs her
desire for freedom. Moreover, the Gothic symbol of the veil, so often
endowed with mystery and terror, so often 'lifted only to disclose
another illusion' (Spooner, p. 6), is another generic convention that
Mary Shelley manipulates deftly. Rather than being deployed as an
instrument of immaterial terror or obscurity, her veil becomes a prosaic
tool ushering the mother and child to freedom.

Paternal tyranny, on which so many Gothic works focus, is shown in
all of its oppression:

> Fernando hated his son. From his earliest boyhood he had felt the
> sentiment of aversion, which, far from endeavouring to quell, he
> allowed to take deep root until Ludovico's most innocent action
> became a crime; and a system of denial and resistance was introduced,
> that called forth all of sinister that there was in the youth's character,
> and engendered an active spirit of detestation in his father's mind.
> Thus Ludovico grew hated and hating; brought together through
> their common situation, the father and son, lord and vassal, oppressor
> and oppressed, the one was continually ready to exert his power of
> inflicting evil – the other perpetually on the alert to resist even the
> shadow of tyranny.   [p. 380]

Mary Shelley weights the description with allusions to the justice
system, natural or innate qualities thwarted by conditioning (a

Godwinian notion) and feudal imagery.[22] The passage thus makes use of the Gothic convention of overbearing fathers to incorporate philosophical questions regarding the degradation of character at the hands of society and the transformation from innocence to hatred through unjust treatment (an idea she had already explored at length in *Frankenstein*). At the same time, she examines the concepts of perception and reality, denials and resistances alongside a chain of oppositional identifiers such as the feudal 'lord and vassal', rendering resistance to tyranny as both natural and inevitable.

These questions of tyranny and resistance are also found in 'A Tale of the Passions; or, The Death of Despina' (1822), which grew out of Mary Shelley's historical research on medieval Italy.[23] The heroine, Despina, served as an attendant to King Manfred's wife Sibilla, and in this role she fell in love with Manfred. She was unaware of the nature of her feelings until Lostendardo, one of Manfred's supporters, professed his love for her: ' "You said that you loved me, and reflected in too faithful a mirror my own emotions: I saw myself and shuddered. But the profound and eternal nature of my passion saved me" ' (p. 84). Despina believes that her love for the married Manfred is, while illicit, nonetheless guiltless because the depth of her emotion equates to an almost religious devotion. Mary Shelley reworks representations of transgressive love in *Mathilda* and 'Mondolfo' to endow Despina, a figure noble to the point of saintliness, with a love at once pure and passionate. Unlike Mathilda's father, Despina reconciles herself to her forbidden desires even after she becomes aware of them because she ' "never in thought or dream degraded the purity of my affection towards him" ' (p. 84). Although Lostendardo subsequently kills Manfred out of jealousy and turns traitor, Despina attempts to persuade him to offer support to Manfred's nephew hoping that her words will transform him.

Mary Shelley's characterisation of Despina as desiring and pure reveals that binaries thought contradictory are not so easily demarcated. Here, as in Viola's reflection in 'Mondolfo' that Ludovico 'was a god; she might adore him; and it were blasphemy to hope for more than a benign acceptation of her worship' (p. 387), Mary Shelley conflates the spiritual with the sexual. Despina views Manfred similarly: ' "My spirit worshipped Manfred as a saint, and my pulses ceased to beat when his

22 Godwin's *Caleb Williams* exemplifies this notion.
23 This conflict between the Guelphs and Ghibbelines, factions fighting for political control and allied with the papacy (Guelphs) or Holy Roman Empire (Ghibbelines), would be used in her 1823 novel *Valperga*.

eye fell upon me [. . .] I loved Manfred. I loved the sun because it enlightened him; I loved the air that fed him; I deified myself for that my heart was the temple in which he resided" ' (p. 84). Despina palpably engineers Manfred as a saint in order to justify her love of a married man and to claim that it is never 'degraded' by sexual or erotic desire. But her assertion that this kind of sanctified love forbids desire is problematic because, as we have seen, in spite of Viola's fear that Ludovico's return of her love would be blasphemous she marries him and bears his son. For Viola, desire trumps fear of sacrilege. The passions Despina accesses through the natural imagery (' "I loved the sun [. . .]" ') and the physical sensations she experiences from his gaze (' "my pulses ceased to beat [. . .]" ') reveal that her love is both religious and erotic. Despina's self-deification that allows Manfred to reside in the temple of her heart does not exclude passion; rather, it glorifies it until extramarital love becomes holy. It is clear that Despina's love is sexual because she is forced to keep it in check: ' "I loved but knew not what love was, and circumscribing my passion in narrow bounds, I adored the being of Manfred as I might love an effigy of stone" ' (p. 84–5). She knows that her passion includes desire, and social custom dictates that she confine it within 'narrow bounds' of purity, worshipping Manfred as an idol rather than a man of flesh and blood. Like Mathilda's vision of her aged father, Despina attempts to create a way to love without the danger of transgressive sex, but the attempts are fantasy only. Such 'circumscribing' does not eliminate desire and no one – including Despina, Lostendardo, and the reader – is convinced that it has done so.

Despina's speech to Lostendardo, an attempt to reform him by proving the purity of her love for Manfred and appealing to his better nature, fails:

'Manfred died, and you thought that I had then forgotten him. But love would indeed be a mockery if death were not the most barefaced cheat. How can he die who is immortalised in my thoughts – my thoughts, that comprehend the universe, and contain eternity in their graspings? What though his earthly vesture is thrown as a despised weed beside the verde, he lives in my soul as lovely, as noble, as entire, as when his voice awoke the mute air: nay, his life is more entire, more true. For before, that small shrine that encased his spirit was all that existed of him; but now, he is a part of all things; his spirit surrounds me, interpenetrates; and divided from him during his life, his death has united me to him for ever.'   [p. 84]

The language displays a Romantic sensibility that draws upon elements of pantheism, a system of belief that identifies the universe and nature with God. Pantheism grew out of the work of the philosopher Baruch Spinoza (1632–77), who claimed that 'the human mind cannot be absolutely destroyed with the body, but there remains of it something which is eternal' (Spinoza, p. 213). The Romantics were strongly influenced by such ideas,[24] and Mary Shelley draws upon them in Despina's speech that describes Manfred's death as enabling their eternal union that was impossible in life.[25] Rather than death being final, it frees the spirit from the body and allows it to become a part of the universe and everything else within it; 'a system of living, active, interrelated forces' (Lamm, p. 173). Despina's claim that Manfred's murder resulted in his spirit surrounding and interpenetrating her, causing their eternal unification, is surely unwise considering her audience; her lofty and philosophical monologue is high-minded and passionate but, of course, she says all the wrong things to the man who killed in order to gain her love. Despina's philosophy and Romantic language, similar to Neville's inability effectively to use his tyrant's vocabulary, fail to persuade and, indeed, evince a near suicidal recklessness.[26]

Lostendardo replies to her words furiously: ' "Your arguments, eloquent Despina," he said, "are indeed unanswerable [. . .] you have sharpened my dagger; and before the air of another night rust it, I may by deeds have repaid your insulting words" ' (p. 84). Lostendardo is infuriated by her because he identifies in her words a subtext, a taunt that his actions have been in vain; have, in fact, facilitated her union with Manfred. Her subordinate position as a female and a captive in enemy territory seems to provide little chance of defeating her tyrannical opponent, but her words are still able to drive Lostendardo to rage. He acknowledges Despina's power over his actions ('you have sharpened my dagger') but because he ultimately privileges deeds over words he overlooks the subversive potential of language. Despina

24 Lamm locates the shifts in interpretations regarding Spinoza's work that allowed it to take on a variety of meanings for different Romantic writers. William Blake, Percy Shelley, Samuel Coleridge Taylor and William Wordsworth were among the Romantic poets who expressed elements of pantheism in their works.

25 Such pantheistic influences are evident in Percy Shelley's note, taken from his pamphlet *The Necessity of Atheism* (1811), to his poem *Queen Mab* (1813) that 'The hypothesis of a pervading Spirit co-eternal with the universe remains unshaken' (p. 124, note to canto vii).

26 Conger argues that Despina is a 'model of pyrrhic heroism' to whom Mary Shelley offers 'a heroic death for a public, political cause' (p. 92).

manipulates the intensity of his emotions and his inability to comprehend her speech, ensuring one form of success or another: Lostendardo will either be persuaded into reformation or driven to her murder. As her love for Manfred functions as Despina's religion, a death at Lostendardo's hands for refusing to renounce her love (religion) would offer her a victorious martyrdom that would unite her with Manfred. After Despina concludes, Lostendardo responds: 'For one moment – as she, having ceased to speak, gazed upon the star – he felt impelled to throw himself at her feet, to confess the diabolical scheme he had forged, and to commit himself body and soul to her guidance, to obey, to serve, to worship her' (p. 87). Ironically, it is only when she ceases to speak that he is fleetingly moved. While Despina's words fail to soften him, her 'angelic' face almost succeeds (p. 87), and that his reaction is to worship her as she did Manfred confirms the concurrence of sexual and sacred passion.

Despina's speech is also richly intertextual and embeds a line from Byron's *Manfred* (1817) in which Manfred describes his sister/lover Astarte as, like him, having 'a mind/ to comprehend the universe' (*Manfred*, 2, 2, 117–18). She also draws from William Blake's poem 'Visions of the Daughters of Albion' (1793) in which the imprisoned Oothoon describes the effects of a patriarchal society: 'And they inclos'd my infinite brain into a narrow circle' ('Visions', 2, 32). The incorporation of Byron's dramatic poem and Blake's feminist and abolitionist work display an innovative amalgamation of poetry and historical narrative laden with Gothic overtones and spiritual and sexual imagery that creates in Despina a knowing, desiring female subject who is, none the less, still positioned as pure and noble. Mary Shelley's use of Byron's poem is a deliberate reference to a work situated around the protagonist's guilt over an incestuous love and the consequences of knowledge; and the explicit nod towards a work concerned with sexual and universal knowledge has further resonance in the Gothic which frequently presents female curiosity as linked to increased sexual knowledge that is productive of danger (Mulvey-Roberts, pp. 100–3). The allusion to Blake's works demonstrates the stunting consequences of society on an 'infinite brain' that only in death can 'comprehend the universe'. As we have seen in *Mathilda*, the heroine's desire to know her father's secret instigates the disclosure of incestuous desires; the knowledge sought and revealed works both with and against its Gothic predecessors by endowing the female with power while destroying the patriarch. That Despina is imprisoned by Lostendardo and dies after she 'endured much' (p. 95) clarifies both his belief that her love for

Manfred was less (or more) than pure, and also that his own position as a usurper of power demands that he crush Despina's female sexuality that defies his desires. 'A Tale of the Passions', like many of her stories, reveals Mary Shelley's commitment to focusing on political and social issues often embedded in complex personal relationships. These deeply reflective and introspective stories are essential additions to her oeuvre because they offer perceptive examinations of the dangers of familial and social bonds, depicting characters who challenge and transgress convention and institutional authority in order, like Mathilda, to escape from the binds of society that 'weighed on me like iron' (p. 43).

DR JENNY DIPLACIDI
School of English, University of Kent

BIBLIOGRAPHY

Work Cited

Dante Alighieri, *The Divine Comedy of Dante Alighieri, A Verse Translation*, Allen Mandelbaum (ed. and trans.), University of California Press, 1982

Ruth Bienstock Anolik, 'The Missing Mother: The Meanings of Maternal Absence in the Gothic Mode', in *Modern Language Studies*, Vol. 33, No. 1/2, 2003, pp. 24–43

Francis Beaumont and John Fletcher, *The Works of Beaumont and Fletcher in Fourteen Volumes: With an Introduction and Explanatory Notes by Henry Weber, Esq.*, Vols 7–9, James Ballantyne and Company, Edinburgh, 1812

Betty T. Bennett, 'Mary Shelley's Letters: The Public/Private Self', in Esther Schor (ed.), *The Cambridge Companion to Mary Shelley*, Cambridge University Press, 2003, pp. 211–25

——— (ed.), *The Letters of Mary Wollstonecraft Shelley: 'Treading in unknown paths'*, Vol. 2, Johns Hopkins University Press, Baltimore and London, 1983

——— and Stuart Curran (eds), *Mary Shelley in Her Times*, Johns Hopkins University Press, Baltimore, 2000

William Blake, 'Visions of the Daughters of Albion', in David V. Erdman (ed.), *The Complete Poetry and Prose of William Blake*, University of California Press, 2008 [1965]

Edmund Burke, *A Philosophical Enquiry into the Origin of Our Ideas on the Sublime and Beautiful* in *The Works of the Right Honourable Edmund Burke*, Vol. 1, John C. Nimmo, London, 1887 [1759]

Lord Byron, *Lord Byron: The Complete Poetical Works*, Jerome J. McGann (ed.), 7 vols, Clarendon Press, Oxford, 1980–93

Pamela Clemit, '*Frankenstein, Matilda*, and the legacies of Godwin and Wollstonecraft', in Esther Schor (ed.), *The Cambridge Companion to Mary Shelley*, Cambridge University Press, 2003, pp. 26–44

E. J. Clery, *Women's Gothic: From Clara Reeve to Mary Shelley*, Northcote House, Devon, 2000

Syndy M. Conger, Frederick S. Frank, Gregory O'Dea (eds), *Iconoclastic Departures: Mary Shelley After Frankenstein: Essays in Honor of the Bicentenary of Mary Shelley's Birth*, Fairleigh Dickinson University Press, Cranberry, NJ and London, 1997

———— 'Mary Shelley's Women in Prison', in Syndy M. Conger, Frederick S. Frank, Gregory O'Dea (eds), *Iconoclastic Departures: Mary Shelley After Frankenstein: Essays in Honor of the Bicentenary of Mary Shelley's Birth*, Fairleigh Dickinson University Press, Cranberry, NJ and London, 1997, pp. 81–97

Richard Cumberland, *Memoirs of Richard Cumberland Written by Himself*, Vol. 1, Lackington, Allen & Co., London, 1807

Julia Epstein, *The Iron Pen: Frances Burney and the Politics of Women's Writing*, Bristol Classical Press, Bristol, 1989

Sandra Gilbert and Susan Gubar, *The Madwoman in the Attic: The Woman Writer and the Nineteenth-Century Literary Imagination*, Yale University Press, 1984 [1979]

George Haggerty, *Queer Gothic*, University of Illinois Press, Urbana, 2006

Terence Harpold, ' "Did you get Mathilda from Papa?" Seduction Fantasy and the Circulation of Mary Shelley's *Mathilda*', in *Studies in Romanticism*, Vol. 28, No. 1, 1989, pp. 49–67

Frederick L. Jones (ed.), *Mary Shelley's Journal*, University of Oklahoma Press, Norman, 1947

Immanuel Kant, *Critique of Judgment* (1790), Cosimo Inc., New York, 2007

Julia A. Lamm, 'Romanticism and Pantheism' in David A. Fergusson (ed.), *The Blackwell Companion to Nineteenth-Century Theology*, Blackwell Publishing, Singapore, 2010, pp. 165–86

Leslie A. Marchand (ed.), *'The Flesh is Frail': Byron's Letters and Journals*, Vol. 6, 1818–1819, Belknap Press of Harvard University Press, 1976

Anne K. Mellor, *Mary Shelley: Her Life, Her Fiction, Her Monsters*, Routledge, New York and London, 1988

Owen Meredith, *Serbski Pesme; or, National Songs of Serbia*, Chapman and Hall, London, 1861

Kathleen A. Miller, ' "The Remembrance Haunts Me Like a Crime": Narrative Control, the Dramatic, and the Female Gothic in Mary Wollstonecraft Shelley's *Mathilda*', in *Tulsa Studies in Women's Literature*, Vol. 27, No. 2, 2008, pp. 291–308

David B. Morris, 'Gothic Sublimity', in *New Literary History*, Vol. 16, No. 2, 1985, pp. 299–319

Marie Mulvey-Roberts, 'From Bluebeard's Bloody Chamber to Demonic Stigmatic', in Diana Wallace and Andrew Smith (eds), *The Female Gothic: New Directions*, Palgrave Macmillan, Basingstoke, 2009, pp. 98–114

Mitzi Myers, 'Mary Wollstonecraft Godwin Shelley: The Female Author Between Public and Private Spheres', in Betty T. Bennett and Stuart Curran (eds), *Mary Shelley in Her Times*, Johns Hopkins University Press, Baltimore, 2000, pp. 160–72

Lucy Newlyn, *Reading, Writing and Romanticism: The Anxiety of Reception*, Oxford University Press, 2003 [2000]

Elizabeth Nitchie, Introduction and Notes to *Mathilda*, in *Studies in Philology*, Vol. 56, No. 3, University of North Carolina Press, Chapel Hill, NC, 1959, pp. vii–xv, 81–9

Ruth Perry, *Novel Relations: The Transformation of Kinship in English Literature and Culture 1748–1818*, Cambridge University Press, 2004

Ellen Pollak, *Incest and The English Novel, 1684–1814*, Johns Hopkins University Press, Baltimore, 2003

Mary Poovey, *The Proper Lady and the Woman Writer: Ideology as Style in the Works of Mary Wollstonecraft, Mary Shelley and Jane Austen*, University of Chicago Press, Chicago, 1984

David Punter and Glennis Byron, *The Gothic*, Blackwell Publishing, Oxford, 2004

Alan Richardson, 'Rethinking Romantic Incest: Human Universals, Literary Representations and the Biology of Mind', in *New Literary History*, Vol. 31, No. 3, 2000, pp. 553–72

Charles E. Robinson, Introduction and Notes to *Mary Shelley: Collected Tales and Stories*, Johns Hopkins University Press, Baltimore and London, 1976

Esther Schor (ed.), *The Cambridge Companion to Mary Shelley*, Cambridge University Press, 2003

Mary Shelley, *Frankenstein: or, The Modern Prometheus*, J. Paul Hunter (ed.), W.W. Norton & Co., New York, 1995

Percy Bysshe Shelley, *Queen Mab*, R. Carlile, London, 1822 [1813]

Muriel Spark, *Mary Shelley: A Biography*, Constable, London, 1988 [1987]

Baruch Spinoza, *Ethics: Treatise on the Emendation of the Intellect and Selected Letters*, Seymour Feldman (ed.), Samuel Shirley (trans.), Hackett Publishing, Indianapolis, IN, 1992

Catherine Spooner, *Fashioning Gothic Bodies*, Manchester University Press, 2004

Emily W. Sunstein, *Mary Shelley: Romance and Reality*, Johns Hopkins University Press, Baltimore, 1991 [1989]

Charlotte Sussman, 'Stories for the *Keepsake*', in Esther Schor (ed.), *The Cambridge Companion to Mary Shelley*, Cambridge University Press, 2003, pp. 163–79

Frederika J. Teute, 'The Loves of the Plants; or, the Cross-Fertilization of Science and Desire at the End of the Eighteenth Century', in *The Huntington Library Quarterly*, Vol. 63, No. 3, 2000, pp. 319–45

Janet Todd, Introduction and Notes to *Matilda*, Penguin Classics, London, 1992 [1991]

John Williams, *Mary Shelley: A Literary Life*, Macmillan Press, Basingstoke, 2000

Mary Wollstonecraft, *Maria; or, The Wrongs of Woman*, Janet Todd (ed.), Penguin Classics, London, 1992 [1991]

Further Reading: Mary Shelley and Her Contexts

Chris Baldick, *In Frankenstein's Shadow: Myth, Monstrosity and Nineteenth-Century Writing*, Oxford University Press, 1987

Betty T. Bennett and Charles E. Robinson (eds), *The Mary Shelley Reader*, Oxford University Press, New York and London, 1990

Ranita Chatterjee, '*Mathilda*: Mary Shelley, William Godwin, and the Ideologies of Incest', in Syndy M. Conger, Frederick S. Frank, Gregory O'Dea (eds), *Iconoclastic Departures: Mary Shelley After Frankenstein: Essays in Honor of the Bicentenary of Mary Shelley's Birth*, Fairleigh Dickinson University Press, Cranberry, NJ and London, 1997, pp. 130–49

Pamela Clemit, 'From *The Fields of Fancy* to *Matilda*: Mary Shelley's Changing Conception of her Novella', in Betty T. Bennett and Stuart Curran (eds), *Mary Shelley in Her Times*, Johns Hopkins University Press, Baltimore, 2000, pp. 64–75

Jean Dunbabin, *Charles I of Anjou: Power, Kingship and State-Making in Thirteenth-Century Europe*, Longman, London and New York, 1998

Paula R. Feldman and Diana Scott-Kilvert (eds), *The Journals of Mary Shelley, 1814–1844*, 2 vols, Clarendon Press, Oxford, 1987

Paul A. Harrison, *Elements of Pantheism: Religious Reverence of Nature and the Universe*, Llumina Press, Coral Springs, FL, 2004 [1999]

A. A. Markley ' "The Truth in Masquerade": Cross-Dressing and Disguise in Mary Shelley's Short Stories', in Michael Eberle-Sinatra (ed.), *Mary Shelley's Fictions: From Frankenstein to Falkner*, St Martin's Press, New York, 2000, pp. 109–26

Thomas McFarland, *Coleridge and the Pantheist Tradition*, Clarendon Press, Oxford, 1969

Lucy Morrison and Staci L. Stone, *A Mary Shelley Encyclopedia*, Greenwood Press, Westport, CT, 2003

Gregory O'Dea, ' "Perhaps a Tale You'll Make it": Mary Shelley's Tales for the *Keepsake*', in Syndy M. Conger, Frederick S. Frank, Gregory O'Dea (eds), *Iconoclastic Departures: Mary Shelley After Frankenstein: Essays in Honor of the Bicentenary of Mary Shelley's Birth*, Fairleigh Dickinson University Press, Cranberry, NJ and London, 1997, pp. 62–78

Judith Pascoe, 'Poetry as Souvenir: Mary Shelley in the Annuals', in Betty T. Bennett and Stuart Curran (eds), *Mary Shelley in Her Times*, Johns Hopkins University Press, Baltimore, 2000, pp. 173–84

———— '*Proserpine* and *Midas*', in Esther Schor (ed.), *The Cambridge Companion to Mary Shelley*, Cambridge University Press, 2003, pp. 180–90

Miranda Seymour, *Mary Shelley*, John Murray, London, 2000

MATHILDA AND OTHER STORIES

Mathilda

Florence
November 9th 1819

IT is only four o'clock; but it is winter and the sun has already set: there are no clouds in the clear, frosty sky to reflect its slant beams, but the air itself is tinged with a slight roseate colour which is again reflected on the snow that covers the ground. I live in a lone cottage on a solitary, wide heath: no voice of life reaches me. I see the desolate plain covered with white, save a few black patches that the noonday sun has made at the top of those sharp pointed hillocks from which the snow, sliding as it fell, lay thinner than on the plain ground: a few birds are pecking at the hard ice that covers the pools – for the frost has been of long continuance.

I am in a strange state of mind. I am alone – quite alone – in the world – the blight of misfortune has passed over me and withered me; I know that I am about to die and I feel happy – joyous. I feel my pulse: it beats fast; I place my thin hand on my cheek: it burns; there is a slight, quick spirit within me which is now emitting its last sparks. I shall never see the snows of another winter – I do believe that I shall never again feel the vivifying warmth of another summer sun; and it is in this persuasion that I begin to write my tragic history. Perhaps a history such as mine had better die with me, but a feeling that I cannot define leads me on and I am too weak both in body and mind to resist the slightest impulse. While life was strong within me I thought indeed that there was a sacred horror in my tale that rendered it unfit for utterance, and now about to die I pollute its mystic terrors. It is as the wood of the Eumenides none but the dying may enter; and Oedipus is about to die.[1]

What am I writing? – I must collect my thoughts. I do not know that any will peruse these pages except you, my friend, who will receive them at my death. I do not address them to you alone because it will give me pleasure to dwell upon our friendship in a way that would be needless if you alone read what I shall write. I shall relate my tale therefore as if I wrote for strangers. You have often asked me the cause of my solitary life; my tears; and above all of my impenetrable and unkind silence. In life I dared not; in death I unveil the mystery. Others will toss these pages lightly over; to you, Woodville, kind, affectionate friend, they will be dear – the precious memorials of a heart-broken girl who, dying, is still warmed by gratitude towards you: your tears will fall on the words that record my misfortunes; I know they will – and while I have life I thank you for your sympathy.

But enough of this. I will begin my tale: it is my last task, and I hope I have strength sufficient to fulfil it. I record no crimes; my faults may easily be pardoned; for they proceeded not from evil motive but from want of judgement; and I believe few would say that they could, by a different conduct and superior wisdom, have avoided the misfortunes to which I am the victim. My fate has been governed by necessity, a hideous necessity. It required hands stronger than mine, stronger I do believe than any human force, to break the thick, adamantine[2] chain that has bound me – once breathing nothing but joy, ever possessed by a warm love and delight in goodness – to misery only to be ended, and now about to be ended, in death. But I forget myself, my tale is yet untold. I will pause a few moments, wipe my dim eyes, and endeavour to lose the present obscure but heavy feeling of unhappiness in the more acute emotions of the past.

I was born in England. My father was a man of rank: he had lost his father early, and was educated by a weak mother with all the indulgence she thought due to a nobleman of wealth. He was sent to Eton and afterwards to college; and allowed from childhood the free use of large sums of money; thus enjoying from his earliest youth the independence which a boy with these advantages always acquires at a public school.

Under the influence of these circumstances his passions found a deep soil wherein they might strike their roots and flourish either as flowers or weeds as was their nature. By being always allowed to act for himself his character became strongly and early marked and exhibited a various surface on which a quick sighted observer might see the seeds of virtues and of misfortunes. His careless extravagance, which made him squander immense sums of money to satisfy passing whims, which from their apparent energy he dignified with the name of passions, often displayed itself in unbounded generosity. Yet while he earnestly occupied himself about the wants of others his own desires were gratified to their fullest extent. He gave his money, but none of his own wishes were sacrificed to his gifts; he gave his time, which he did not value, and his affections which he was happy in any manner to have called into action.

I do not say that if his own desires had been put in competition with those of others that he would have displayed undue selfishness, but this trial was never made. He was nurtured in prosperity and attended by all its advantages; everyone loved him and wished to gratify him. He was ever employed in promoting the pleasures of his companions – but their pleasures were his; and if he bestowed more attention upon the feelings of others than is usual with schoolboys it was because his social temper could never enjoy itself if every brow was not as free from care as his own.

While at school, emulation and his own natural abilities made him hold a conspicuous rank in the forms among his equals; at college he discarded books; he believed that he had other lessons to learn than those which they could teach him. He was now to enter into life and he was still young enough to consider study as a schoolboy shackle, employed merely to keep the unruly out of mischief but as having no real connection with life – whose wisdom of riding, gaming, etc., he considered with far deeper interest. So he quickly entered into all college follies although his heart was too well moulded to be contaminated by them – it might be light but it was never cold. He was a sincere and sympathising friend – but he had met with none who superior or equal to himself could aid him in unfolding his mind, or make him seek for fresh stores of thought by exhausting the old ones. He felt himself superior in quickness of judgement to those around him: his talents, his rank and wealth made him the chief of his party, and in that station he rested not only contented but glorying, conceiving it to be the only ambition worthy for him to aim at in the world.

By a strange narrowness of ideas he viewed all the world in connection only as it was or was not related to his little society. He considered queer and out of fashion all opinions that were exploded by his circle of intimates, and he became at the same time dogmatic and yet fearful of not coinciding with the only sentiments he could consider orthodox. To the generality of spectators he appeared careless of censure, and with high disdain to throw aside all dependence on public prejudices; but at the same time that he strode with a triumphant stride over the rest of the world, he cowered, with self-disguised lowliness, to his own party, and although its chief never dared express an opinion or a feeling until he was assured that it would meet with the approbation of his companions.

Yet he had one secret hidden from these dear friends; a secret he had nurtured from his earliest years, and although he loved his fellow collegiates he would not trust it to the delicacy or sympathy of any one among them. He loved. He feared that the intensity of his passion might become the subject of their ridicule; and he could not bear that they should blaspheme it by considering that trivial and transitory which he felt was the life of his life.

There was a gentleman of small fortune who lived near his family mansion who had three lovely daughters. The eldest was far the most beautiful, but her beauty was only an addition to her other qualities – her understanding was clear and strong and her disposition angelically gentle. She and my father had been playmates from infancy: Diana even in her childhood had been a favourite with his mother; this partiality increased with the years of this beautiful and lively girl and thus during his school and college vacations they were perpetually together. Novels and all the various methods by which youth in civilised life are led to a knowledge of the existence of passions before they really feel them, had produced a strong effect on him who was so peculiarly susceptible of every impression. At eleven years of age Diana was his favourite playmate but he already talked the language of love. Although she was elder than he by nearly two years the nature of her education made her more childish at least in the knowledge and expression of feeling; she received his warm protestations with innocence, and returned them unknowing of what they meant. She had read no novels and associated only with her younger sisters, what could she know of the difference between love and friendship? And when the development of her understanding disclosed the true nature of this intercourse to her, her affections were already engaged to her friend, and all she feared was lest other attractions and fickleness might make him break his infant vows.

But they became every day more ardent and tender. It was a passion that had grown with his growth; it had become entwined with every faculty and every sentiment and only to be lost with life. None knew of their love except their own two hearts; yet although in all things else, and even in this he dreaded the censure of his companions, for thus truly loving one inferior to him in fortune, nothing was ever able for a moment to shake his purpose of uniting himself to her as soon as he could muster courage sufficient to meet those difficulties he was determined to surmount.

Diana was fully worthy of his deepest affection. There were few who could boast of so pure a heart, and so much real humbleness of soul joined to a firm reliance on her own integrity and a belief in that of others. She had from her birth lived a retired life. She had lost her mother when very young, but her father had devoted himself to the care of her education. He had many peculiar ideas which influenced the system he had adopted with regard to her. She was well acquainted with the heroes of Greece and Rome or with those of England who had lived some hundred years ago, while she was nearly ignorant of the passing events of the day: she had read few authors who had written during at least the last fifty years but her reading with this exception was very extensive. Thus although she appeared to be less initiated in the mysteries of life and society than he her knowledge was of a deeper kind and laid on firmer foundations; and if even her beauty and sweetness had not fascinated him her understanding would ever have held his in thrall. He looked up to her as his guide, and such was his adoration that he delighted to augment to his own mind the sense of inferiority with which she sometimes impressed him.

When he was nineteen his mother died. He left college on this event and shaking off for a while his old friends he retired to the neighbour-hood of his Diana and received all his consolation from her sweet voice and dearer caresses. This short separation from his companions gave him courage to assert his independence. He had a feeling that however they might express ridicule of his intended marriage they would not dare display it when it had taken place; therefore seeking the consent of his guardian which with some difficulty he obtained, and of the father of his mistress which was more easily given, without acquainting any one else of his intention, by the time he had attained his twentieth birthday he had become the husband of Diana.

He loved her with passion and her tenderness had a charm for him that would not permit him to think of aught but her. He invited some of his college friends to see him but their frivolity disgusted him. Diana had torn the veil which had before kept him in his boyhood: he was become a man and he was surprised how he could ever have joined in the cant words and ideas of his fellow collegiates or how for a moment he had feared the censure of such as these. He discarded his old friend-ships not from fickleness but because they were indeed unworthy of him. Diana filled up all his heart: he felt as if by his union with her he had received a new and better soul. She was his monitress as he learned what were the true ends of life. It was through her beloved lessons that he cast off his old pursuits and gradually formed himself to become one among his fellow men; a distinguished member of society, a Patriot; and an enlightened lover of truth and virtue. He loved her for her beauty and for her amiable disposition but he seemed to love her more for what he considered her superior wisdom. They studied, they rode together; they were never separate and seldom admitted a third to their society.

Thus my father, born in affluence, and always prosperous, climbed without the difficulty and various disappointments that all human beings seem destined to encounter to the very topmost pinnacle of happiness. Around him was sunshine, and clouds whose shapes of beauty made the prospect divine concealed from him the barren reality which lay hidden below them. From this dizzy point he was dashed at once as he unawares congratulated himself on his felicity. Fifteen months after their marriage I was born, and my mother died a few days after my birth.

A sister of my father was with him at this period. She was nearly fifteen years older than he, and was the offspring of a former marriage of his father. When the latter died this sister was taken by her maternal relations: they had seldom seen one another, and were quite unlike in disposition. This aunt, to whose care I was afterwards consigned, has often related to me the effect that this catastrophe had on my father's strong and susceptible character. From the moment of my mother's death until his departure she never heard him utter a single word: buried in the deepest melancholy he took no notice of anyone; often for hours his eyes streamed tears or a more fearful gloom overpowered him. All outward things seemed to have lost their existence relatively to him and only one circumstance could in any degree recall him from his motionless and mute despair: he would never see me. He seemed insensible to the presence of anyone else, but if, as a trial to awaken his sensibility, my aunt brought me into the room he would instantly rush out with every symptom of fury and distraction. At the end of a month he suddenly quitted his house and, unattended by any servant, departed from that part of the country without by word or writing informing anyone of his intentions. My aunt was only relieved of her anxiety concerning his fate by a letter from him dated Hamburg.

How often have I wept over that letter which until I was sixteen was the only relic I had to remind me of my parents. 'Pardon me,' it said, 'for the uneasiness I have unavoidably given you: but while in that unhappy island, where everything breathes *her* spirit whom I have lost for ever, a spell held me. It is broken: I have quitted England for many years, perhaps for ever. But to convince you that selfish feeling does not entirely engross me I shall remain in this town until you have made by letter every arrangement that you judge necessary. When I leave this place do not expect to hear from me: I must break all ties that at present exist. I shall become a wanderer, a miserable outcast – alone! alone!' In another part of the letter he mentioned me – 'As for that

MATHILDA

unhappy little being whom I could not see, and hardly dare mention, I leave her under your protection. Take care of her and cherish her: one day I may claim her at your hands; but futurity is dark, make the present happy to her.'

My father remained three months at Hamburg; when he quitted it he changed his name; my aunt could never discover that which he adopted and only by faint hints could conjecture that he had taken the road of Germany and Hungary to Turkey.

Thus this towering spirit who had excited interest and high expectation in all who knew and could value him became at once, as it were, extinct. He existed from this moment for himself only. His friends remembered him as a brilliant vision which would never again return to them. The memory of what he had been faded away as years passed; and he who before had been as a part of themselves and of their hopes was now no longer counted among the living.

CHAPTER 2

I now come to my own story. During the early part of my life there is little to relate, and I will be brief; but I must be allowed to dwell a little on the years of my childhood that it may be apparent how when one hope failed all life was to be a blank; and how when the only affection I was permitted to cherish was blasted my existence was extinguished with it.

I have said that my aunt was very unlike my father. I believe that without the slightest tinge of a bad heart she had the coldest that ever filled a human breast: it was totally incapable of any affection. She took me under her protection because she considered it her duty; but she had too long lived alone and undisturbed by the noise and prattle of children to allow that I should disturb her quiet. She had never been married; and for the last five years had lived perfectly alone on an estate, that had descended to her through her mother, on the shores of Loch Lomond in Scotland. My father had expressed a wish in his letters that she should reside with me at his family mansion which was situated in a beautiful country near Richmond in Yorkshire. She would not consent to this proposition, but as soon as she had arranged the affairs which her brother's departure had caused to fall to her care, she quitted England and took me with her to her Scotch estate.

The care of me while a baby and afterwards until I had reached my eighth year devolved on a servant of my mother's, who had accompanied us in our retirement for that purpose. I was placed in a remote part of the house, and only saw my aunt at stated hours. These occurred twice a day; once about noon she came to my nursery, and once after her dinner I was taken to her. She never caressed me, and seemed all the time I stayed in the room to fear that I should annoy her by some childish freak. My good nurse always schooled me with the greatest care before she ventured into the parlour – and the awe my aunt's cold looks and few constrained words inspired was so great that I seldom disgraced her lessons or was betrayed from the exemplary stillness which I was taught to observe during these short visits.

Under my good nurse's care I ran wild about our park and the neighbouring fields. The offspring of the deepest love I displayed from my earliest years the greatest sensibility of disposition. I cannot say with what passion I loved everything, even the inanimate objects that surrounded me. I believe that I bore an individual attachment to every tree in our park; every animal that inhabited it knew me and I loved them. Their occasional deaths filled my infant heart with anguish. I cannot number the birds that I have saved during the long and severe winters of that climate; or the hares and rabbits that I have defended from the attacks of our dogs, or have nursed when accidentally wounded.

When I was seven years of age my nurse left me. I now forget the cause of her departure if indeed I ever knew it. She returned to England, and the bitter tears she shed at parting were the last I saw flow for love of me for many years. My grief was terrible: I had no friend but her in the whole world. By degrees I became reconciled to solitude but no one supplied her place in my affections. I lived in a desolate country where 'there were none to praise/And very few to love'.[3]

It is true that I now saw a little more of my aunt, but she was in every way an unsocial being; and to a timid child she was as a plant beneath a thick covering of ice; I should cut my hands in endeavouring to get at it. So I was entirely thrown upon my own resources. The neighbouring minister was engaged to give me lessons in reading, writing and French, but he was without family and his manners even to me were always perfectly characteristic of the profession in the exercise of whose functions he chiefly shone, that of a schoolmaster. I sometimes strove to form friendships with the most attractive of the girls who inhabited the neighbouring village; but I believe I should never have succeeded even had not my aunt interposed her authority to prevent all intercourse between me and the peasantry; for she was fearful lest I should acquire the Scotch accent and dialect; a little of it I had, although great pains was taken that my tongue should not disgrace my English origin.

As I grew older my liberty increased with my desires, and my wanderings extended from our park to the neighbouring country. Our house was situated on the shores of the lake and the lawn came down to the water's edge. I rambled amidst the wild scenery of this lovely country and became a complete mountaineer. I passed hours on the steep brow of a mountain that overhung a waterfall or rowed myself in a little skiff to some one of the islands. I wandered forever about these lovely solitudes, gathering flower after flower – 'ond' era pinta tutta la mia via'[4] – singing as I might the wild melodies of the country, or occupied by pleasant daydreams. My greatest pleasure was the enjoyment of a serene sky amidst these verdant woods: yet I loved all the changes of nature; and rain, and storm, and the beautiful clouds of heaven brought their delights with them. When rocked by the waves of the lake my spirits rose in triumph as a horseman feels with pride the motions of his high fed steed.

But my pleasures arose from the contemplation of nature alone, I had no companion: my warm affections finding no return from any other human heart were forced to run waste on inanimate objects. Sometimes indeed I wept when my aunt received my caresses with repulsive coldness, and when I looked round and found none to love; but I quickly dried my tears. As I grew older books in some degree supplied the place of human intercourse; the library of my aunt was very small: Shakespeare, Milton, Pope and Cowper were the strangely assorted poets of her collection; and among the prose authors a translation of Livy and Rollin's *Ancient History*[5] were my chief favourites, although as I emerged from childhood I found others highly interesting which I had before neglected as dull.

When I was twelve years old it occurred to my aunt that I ought to learn music; she herself played upon the harp. It was with great hesitation that she persuaded herself to undertake my instruction; yet believing this accomplishment a necessary part of my education, and balancing the evils of this measure or of having someone in the house to instruct me she submitted to the inconvenience. A harp was sent for that my playing might not interfere with hers, and I began: she found me a docile and when I had conquered the first rudiments a very apt scholar. I had acquired in my harp a companion in rainy days; a sweet soother of my feelings when any untoward accident ruffled them: I often addressed it as my only friend; I could pour forth to it my hopes and loves, and I fancied that its sweet accents answered me. I have now mentioned all my studies.

I was a solitary being, and from my infant years, ever since my dear nurse left me, I had been a dreamer. I brought Rosalind and Miranda and the lady of *Comus*[6] to life to be my companions, or on my isle acted over their parts imagining myself to be in their situations. Then I wandered from the fancies of others and formed affections and intimacies with the aerial creations of my own brain – but still clinging to reality I gave a name to these conceptions and nursed them in the hope of realisation. I clung to the memory of my parents: my mother I should never see, she was dead; but the idea of my unhappy, wandering father was the idol of my imagination. I bestowed on him all my affections; there was a miniature of him that I gazed on continually; I copied his last letter and read it again and again. Sometimes it made me weep; and at other times I repeated with transport those words, – 'One day I may claim her at your hands.' I was to be his consoler, his companion in after years. My favourite vision was that when I grew up I would leave my aunt, whose coldness lulled my conscience, and disguised like a boy I would seek my father through the world. My imagination hung upon the scene of recognition; his miniature, which I should continually wear exposed on my breast, would be the means and I imaged the moment to my mind a thousand and a thousand times, perpetually varying the circumstances. Sometimes it would be in a desert; in a populous city; at a ball; we should perhaps meet in a vessel; and his first words constantly were, 'My daughter, I love thee.' What ecstatic moments have I passed in these dreams! How many tears I have shed; how often have I laughed aloud.

This was my life for sixteen years. At fourteen and fifteen I often thought that the time was come when I should commence my pilgrimage, which I had cheated my own mind into believing was my imperious duty: but a reluctance to quit my aunt; a remorse for the grief which, I could not conceal from myself, I should occasion her for ever withheld me. Sometimes when I had planned the next morning for my escape a word of more than usual affection from her lips made me postpone my resolution. I reproached myself bitterly for what I called a culpable weakness; but this weakness returned upon me whenever the critical moment approached, and I never found courage to depart.

CHAPTER 3

It was on my sixteenth birthday that my aunt received a letter from my father. I cannot describe the tumult of emotions that arose within me as I read it. It was dated from London; he had returned! I could only relieve my transports by tears, tears of unmingled joy. He had returned, and he wrote to know whether my aunt would come to London or whether he should visit her in Scotland. How delicious to me were the words of his letter that concerned me: 'I cannot tell you,' it said, 'how ardently I desire to see my Mathilda. I look on her as the creature who will form the happiness of my future life: she is all that exists on earth that interests me. I can hardly prevent myself from hastening immediately to you but I am necessarily detained a week and I write because if you come here I may see you somewhat sooner.' I read these words with devouring eyes; I kissed them, wept over them and exclaimed, 'He will love me!'

My aunt would not undertake so long a journey, and in a fortnight we had another letter from my father, it was dated Edinburgh: he wrote that he should be with us in three days. 'As he approached his desire of seeing me,' he said, 'became more and more ardent, and he felt that the moment when he should first clasp me in his arms would be the happiest of his life.'

How irksome were these three days to me! All sleep and appetite fled from me; I could only read and reread his letter, and in the solitude of the woods imagine the moment of our meeting. On the eve of the third day I retired early to my room; I could not sleep but paced all night about my chamber and, as you may in Scotland at midsummer, watched the crimson track of the sun as it almost skirted the northern horizon. At daybreak I hastened to the woods; the hours passed on while I indulged in wild dreams that gave wings to the slothful steps of time, and beguiled my eager impatience. My father was expected at noon but when I wished to return to meet him I found that I had lost my way: it seemed that in every attempt to find it I only became more involved in the intricacies of the woods, and the trees hid all trace by which I might be guided. I grew impatient, I wept and wrung my hands but still I could not discover my path.

It was past two o'clock when by a sudden turn I found myself close to the lake near a cove where a little skiff was moored. It was not far from our house and I saw my father and aunt walking on the lawn. I jumped into the boat, and well accustomed to such feats, I pushed it from shore, and exerted all my strength to row swiftly across. As I came, dressed in white, covered only by my tartan *rachan*,[7] my hair streaming on my shoulders, and shooting across with greater speed that it could be supposed I could give to my boat, my father has often told me that I looked more like a spirit than a human maid. I approached the shore, my father held the boat, I leapt lightly out, and in a moment was in his arms.

And now I began to live. All around me was changed from a dull uniformity to the brightest scene of joy and delight. The happiness I enjoyed in the company of my father far exceeded my sanguine expectations. We were forever together; and the subjects of our conversations were inexhaustible. He had passed the sixteen years of absence among nations nearly unknown to Europe; he had wandered through Persia, Arabia and the north of India and had penetrated among the habitations of the natives with a freedom permitted to few Europeans. His relations of their manners, his anecdotes and descriptions of scenery whiled away delicious hours, when we were tired of talking of our own plans of future life.

The voice of affection was so new to me that I hung with delight upon his words when he told me what he had felt concerning me during these long years of apparent forgetfulness. 'At first' – said he, 'I could not bear to think of my poor little girl; but afterwards as grief wore off and hope again revisited me I could only turn to her, and amidst cities and deserts her little fairy form, such as I imagined it, forever flitted before me. The northern breeze as it refreshed me was sweeter and more balmy for it seemed to carry some of your spirit along with it. I often thought that I would instantly return and take you along with me to some fertile island where we should live at peace for ever. As I returned my fervent hopes were dashed by so many fears; my impatience became in the highest degree painful. I dared not think that the sun should shine and the moon rise not on your living form but on your grave. But, no, it is not so; I have my Mathilda, my consolation, and my hope.'

My father was very little changed from what he described himself to be before his misfortunes. It is intercourse with civilised society; it is the disappointment of cherished hopes, the falsehood of friends, or the perpetual clash of mean passions that changes the heart and damps the ardour of youthful feelings; lonely wanderings in a wild country among people of simple or savage manners may inure the body but will not tame the soul, or extinguish the ardour and freshness of feeling incident to youth. The burning sun of India, and the freedom from all restraint had rather increased the energy of his character: before he bowed under, now he was impatient of any censure except that of his own mind. He had seen so many customs and witnessed so great a variety of moral creeds that he had been obliged to form an independent one for himself which had no relation to the peculiar notions of any one country: his early prejudices of course influenced his judgement in the formation of his principles, and some raw college ideas were strangely mingled with the deepest deductions of his penetrating mind.

The vacuity his heart endured of any deep interest in life during his long absence from his native country had had a singular effect upon his ideas. There was a curious feeling of unreality attached by him to his foreign life in comparison with the years of his youth. All the time he had passed out of England was as a dream, and all the interest of his soul, all his affections belonged to events which had happened and persons who had existed sixteen years before. It was strange when you heard him talk to see how he passed over this lapse of time as a night of visions; while the remembrances of his youth standing separate as they did from his after life had lost none of their vigour. He talked of my Mother as if she had lived but a few weeks before; not that he expressed poignant grief, but his discription of her person, and his relation of all anecdotes connected with her was thus fervent and vivid.

In all this there was a strangeness that attracted and enchanted me. He was, as it were, now awakened from his long, visionary sleep, and he felt somewhat like one of the seven sleepers, or like Nourjahad,[8] in that sweet imitation of an eastern tale: Diana was gone; his friends were changed or dead, and now on his awakening I was all that he had to love on earth.

How dear to me were the waters, and mountains, and woods of Loch Lomond now that I had so beloved a companion for my rambles. I visited with my father every delightful spot, either on the islands, or by the side of the tree-sheltered waterfalls; every shady path, or dingle[9] entangled with underwood and fern. My ideas were enlarged by his conversation. I felt as if I were recreated and had about me all the freshness and life of a new being: I was, as it were, transported since his arrival from a narrow spot of earth into a universe boundless to the imagination and the understanding. My life had been before as a pleasing country rill, never destined to leave its native fields, but when its task was fulfilled quietly to be absorbed, and leave no trace. Now it seemed to me to be as a various river flowing through a fertile and lovely landscape, ever changing and ever beautiful. Alas! I knew not the desert it was about to reach; the rocks that would tear its waters, and the hideous scene that would be reflected in a more distorted manner in its waves. Life was then brilliant; I began to learn to hope and what brings a more bitter despair to the heart than hope destroyed?

Is it not strange that grief should quickly follow so divine a happiness? I drank of an enchanted cup[10] but gall was at the bottom of its long drawn sweetness. My heart was full of deep affection, but it was calm from its very depth and fullness. I had no idea that misery could arise from love, and this lesson that all at last must learn was taught me in a manner few are obliged to receive it. I lament now, I must ever lament, those few short months of Paradisaical bliss; I disobeyed no command, I ate no apple, and yet I was ruthlessly driven from it. Alas! my companion did, and I was precipitated in his fall. But I wander from my relation – let woe come at its appointed time; I may at this stage of my story still talk of happiness.

Three months passed away in this delightful intercourse, when my aunt fell ill. I passed a whole month in her chamber nursing her, but her disease was mortal and she died, leaving me for some time inconsolable, Death is so dreadful to the living; the chains of habit are so strong even when affection does not link them that the heart must be agonised when they break. But my father was beside me to console me and to drive away bitter memories by bright hopes: methought that it was sweet to grieve that he might dry my tears.

Then again he distracted my thoughts from my sorrow by comparing it with his despair when he lost my mother. Even at that time I shuddered at the picture he drew of his passions: he had the imagination of a poet, and when he described the whirlwind that then tore his feelings he gave his words the impress of life so vividly that I believed while I trembled. I wondered how he could ever again have entered into the offices of life after his wild thoughts seemed to have given him affinity with the unearthly; while he spoke so tremendous were the ideas which he conveyed that it appeared as if the human heart were far too bounded for their conception. His feelings seemed better fitted for a spirit whose habitation is the earthquake and the volcano[11] than for one confined to a mortal body and human lineaments. But these were merely memories; he was changed since then. He was now all love, all softness; and when I raised my eyes in wonder at him as he spoke, the smile on his lips told me that his heart was possessed by the gentlest passions.

Two months after my aunt's death we removed to London where I was led by my father to attend to deeper studies than had before occupied me. My improvement was his delight; he was with me during all my studies and assisted or joined with me in every lesson. We saw a great deal of society, and no day passed that my father did not endeavour to embellish by some new enjoyment. The tender attachment that he bore me, and the love and veneration with which I returned it cast a charm over every moment. The hours were slow for each minute was employed; we lived more in one week than many do in the course of several months and the variety and novelty of our pleasures gave zest to each.

We perpetually made excursions together. And whether it were to visit beautiful scenery, or to see fine pictures, or sometimes for no object but to seek amusement as it might chance to arise, I was always happy when near my father. It was a subject of regret to me whenever we were joined by a third person, yet if I turned with a disturbed look towards my father, his eyes fixed on me and beaming with tenderness instantly restored joy to my heart. O, hours of intense delight! Short as ye were ye are made as long to me as a whole life when looked back upon through the mist of grief that rose immediately after as if to shut ye from my view. Alas! ye were the last of happiness that I ever enjoyed; a few, a very few weeks and all was destroyed. Like Psyche[12] I lived for a while in an enchanted palace, amidst odours, and music, and every luxurious delight; when suddenly I was left on a barren rock; a wide ocean of despair rolled around me: above all was black, and my eyes closed while I still inhabited a universal death. Still I would not hurry on; I would pause for ever on the recollections of these happy weeks; I would repeat every word, and how many do I remember, record every enchantment of the fairy habitation. But, no, my tale must not pause; it must be as rapid as was my fate – I can only describe in short although strong expressions my precipitate and irremediable change from happiness to despair.

CHAPTER 4

Among our most assiduous visitors was a young man of rank, well informed, and agreeable in his person. After we had spent a few weeks in London his attentions towards me became marked and his visits more frequent. I was too much taken up by my own occupations and feelings to attend much to this, and then indeed I hardly noticed more than the bare surface of events as they passed around me; but I now remember that my father was restless and uneasy whenever this person visited us, and when we talked together watched us with the greatest apparent anxiety although he himself maintained a profound silence. At length these obnoxious visits suddenly ceased altogether, but from that moment I must date the change of my father: a change that to remember makes me shudder and then filled me with the deepest grief. There were no degrees which could break my fall from happiness to misery; it was as the stroke of lightning – sudden and entire. Alas! I now met frowns where before I had been welcomed only with smiles: he, my beloved father, shunned me, and either treated me with harshness or a more heart-breaking coldness. We took no more sweet counsel together; and when I tried to win him again to me, his anger, and the terrible emotions that he exhibited drove me to silence and tears.[13]

And this was sudden. The day before we had passed alone together in the country; I remember we had talked of future travels that we should undertake together. There was an eager delight in our tones and gestures that could only spring from deep and mutual love joined to the most unrestrained confidence; and now the next day, the next hour, I saw his brows contracted, his eyes fixed in sullen fierceness on the ground, and his voice so gentle and so dear made me shiver when he addressed me. Often, when my wandering fancy brought by its various images now consolation and now aggravation of grief to my heart, I have compared myself to Proserpine who was gaily and heedlessly gathering flowers on the sweet plain of Enna when the King of Hell snatched her away to the abodes of death and misery.[14] Alas! I who so lately knew of nought but the joy of life; who had slept only to dream sweet dreams and awoke to incomparable happiness, I now passed my days and nights in tears. I who sought and had found joy in the love-breathing countenance of my father now when I dared fix on him a supplicating look it was ever answered by an angry frown. I dared not speak to him; and when sometimes I had worked up courage to meet him and to ask an explanation, one glance at his face where a chaos of mighty passion seemed forever struggling made me tremble and shrink to silence. I was dashed down from heaven to earth as a silly sparrow when pounced on by a hawk; my eyes swam and my head was bewildered by the sudden apparition of grief. Day after day passed marked only by my complaints and my tears; often I lifted my soul in vain prayer for a softer descent from joy to woe, or if that were denied me that I might be allowed to die, and fade for ever under the cruel blast that swept over me,

> for what should I do here,
> Like a decaying flower, still withering
> Under his bitter words, whose kindly heat
> Should give my poor heart life?[15]

Sometimes I said to myself, this is an enchantment, and I must strive against it. My father is blinded by some malignant vision which I must remove. And then, like David, I would try music to win the evil spirit[16] from him; and once while singing I lifted my eyes towards him and saw his fixed on me and filled with tears; all his muscles seemed relaxed to softness. I sprang towards him with a cry of joy and would have thrown myself into his arms, but he pushed me roughly from him and left me. And even from this slight incident he contracted fresh gloom and an additional severity of manner.

There are many incidents that I might relate which showed the diseased yet incomprehensible state of his mind; but I will mention one that occurred while we were in company with several other persons. On this occasion I chanced to say that I thought *Myrrha* the best of Alfieri's tragedies;[17] as I said this I chanced to cast my eyes on my father and met his: for the first time the expression of those beloved eyes displeased me, and I saw with affright that his whole frame shook with some concealed emotion that in spite of his efforts half conquered him: as this tempest faded from his soul he became melancholy and silent. Every day some new scene occurred and displayed in him a mind working as it were with an unknown horror that now he could master but which at times threatened to overturn his reason, and to throw the bright seat of his intelligence into a perpetual chaos.

I will not dwell longer than I need on these disastrous circumstances. I might waste days in describing how anxiously I watched every change of fleeting circumstance that promised better days, and with what despair I found that each effort of mine aggravated his seeming madness. To tell all my grief I might as well attempt to count the tears that have fallen from these eyes, or every sign that has torn my heart. I will be brief for there is in all this a horror that will not bear many words, and I sink almost a second time to death while I recall these sad scenes to my memory. Oh, my beloved father! Indeed you made me miserable beyond all words, but how truly did I even then forgive you, and how entirely did you possess my whole heart while I endeavoured, as a rainbow gleams upon a cataract, to soften thy tremendous sorrows.[18]

Thus did this change come about. I seem perhaps to have dashed too suddenly into the description, but thus suddenly did it happen. In one sentence I have passed from the idea of unspeakable happiness to that of unspeakable grief but they were thus closely linked together. We had remained five months in London three of joy and two of sorrow. My father and I were now seldom alone or if we were he generally kept silence with his eyes fixed on the ground – the dark full orbs in which before I delighted to read all sweet and gentle feeling shadowed from my sight by their lids and the long lashes that fringed them. When we were in company he affected gaiety but I wept to hear his hollow laugh – begun by an empty smile and often ending in a bitter sneer such as never before this fatal period had wrinkled his lips. When others were there he often spoke to me and his eyes perpetually followed my slightest motion. His accents whenever he addressed me were cold and constrained although his voice would tremble when he perceived that my full heart choked the answer to words proffered with a mien yet new to me.

But days of peaceful melancholy were of rare occurrence: they were often broken in upon by gusts of passion that drove me as a weak boat on a stormy sea to seek a cove for shelter; but the winds blew from my native harbour and I was cast far, far out until shattered I perished when the tempest had passed and the sea was apparently calm. I do not know that I can describe his emotions: sometimes he only betrayed them by a word or gesture, and then retired to his chamber and I crept as near it as I dared and listened with fear to every sound, yet still more dreading a sudden silence – dreading I knew not what, but ever full of fear.

It was after one tremendous day when his eyes had glared on me like lightning – and his voice sharp and broken seemed unable to express the extent of his emotion – that in the evening when I was alone he joined me with a calm countenance, and not noticing my tears which I quickly dried when he approached, told me that in three days he intended to remove with me to his estate in Yorkshire, and bidding me prepare left me hastily as if afraid of being questioned.

This determination on his part indeed surprised me. This estate was that which he had inhabited in childhood and near which my mother resided while a girl; this was the scene of their youthful loves and where they had lived after their marriage; in happier days my father had often told me that however he might appear weaned from his widow sorrow, and free from bitter recollections elsewhere, yet he would never dare visit the spot where he had enjoyed her society or trust himself to see the rooms that so many years ago they had inhabited together; her favourite walks and the gardens the flowers of which she had delighted to cultivate. And now while he suffered intense misery he determined to plunge into still more intense, and strove for greater emotion than that which already tore him. I was perplexed, and most anxious to know what this portended; ah, what could it portend but ruin!

I saw little of my father during this interval, but he appeared calmer although not less unhappy than before. On the morning of the third day he informed me that he had determined to go to Yorkshire first alone, and that I should follow him in a fortnight unless I heard any thing from him in the meantime that should contradict this command. He departed the same day, and four days afterwards I received a letter from his steward telling me in his name to join him with as little delay as possible. After travelling day and night I arrived with an anxious, yet a hoping heart, for why should he send for me if it were only to avoid me and to treat me with the apparent aversion that he had in London. I met him at the distance of thirty miles from our mansion. His demeanour was sad; for a moment he appeared glad to see me and then he checked himself as if unwilling to betray his feelings. He was silent during our ride, yet his manner was kinder than before and I thought I beheld a softness in his eyes that gave me hope.

When we arrived, after a little rest, he led me over the house and pointed out to me the rooms which my mother had inhabited. Although more than sixteen years had passed since her death nothing had been changed; her work box, her writing desk were still there and in her room a book lay open on the table as she had left it. My father pointed out these circumstances with a serious and unaltered mien, only now and then fixing his deep and liquid eyes upon me; there was something strange and awful in his look that overcame me, and in spite of myself I wept, nor did he attempt to console me, but I saw his lips quiver and the muscles of his countenance seemed convulsed.

We walked together in the gardens and in the evening when I would have retired he asked me to stay and read to him; and first said, 'When I was last here your mother read Dante to me; you shall go on where she left off.' And then in a moment he said, 'No, that must not be; you must not read Dante. Do you choose a book.' I took up Spencer and read the descent of Sir Guyon to the halls of Avarice;[19] while he listened his eyes fixed on me in sad profound silence.

I heard the next morning from the steward that upon his arrival he had been in a most terrible state of mind: he had passed the first night in the garden lying on the damp grass; he did not sleep but groaned perpetually. 'Alas!' said the old man, who gave me this account with tears in his eyes, 'it wrings my heart to see my lord in this state; when I heard that he was coming down here with you, my young lady, I thought we should have the happy days over again that we enjoyed during the short life of my lady your mother – But that would be too much happiness for us poor creatures born to tears – and that was why she was taken from us so soon; she was too beautiful and good for us. It was a happy day as we all thought it when my lord married her: I knew her when she was a child and many a good turn has she done for me in my old lady's time – You are like her although there is more of my lord in you – But has he been thus ever since his return? All my joy turned to sorrow when I first beheld him with that melancholy countenance enter these doors as it were the day after my lady's funeral. He seemed to recover himself a little after he had bidden me write to you – but still it is a woeful thing to see him so unhappy.' These were the feelings of an old, faithful servant: what must be those of an affectionate daughter. Alas! Even then my heart was almost broken.

We spent two months together in this house. My father spent the greater part of his time with me; he accompanied me in my walks, listened to my music, and leant over me as I read or painted. When he conversed with me his manner was cold and constrained; his eyes only seemed to speak, and as he turned their black, full lustre towards me they expressed a living sadness. There was something in those dark deep orbs so liquid and intense that even in happiness I could never meet their full gaze that mine did not overflow. Yet it was with sweet tears; now there was a depth of affliction in their gentle appeal that rent my heart with sympathy; they seemed to desire peace for me; for himself a heart patient to suffer; a craving for sympathy, yet a perpetual self-denial. It was only when he was absent from me that his passion subdued him – that he clinched his hands – knit his brows – and with haggard looks called for death to his despair, raving wildly, until exhausted he sank down nor was revived until I joined him.

While we were in London there was a harshness and sullenness in his sorrow which had now entirely disappeared. There I shrank and fled from him, now I only wished to be with him that I might soothe him to peace. When he was silent I tried to divert him, and when sometimes I stole to him during the energy of his passion I wept but did not desire to leave him. Yet he suffered fearful agony; during the day he was more calm, but at night when I could not be with him he seemed to give the reins to his grief: he often passed his nights either on the floor in my mother's room, or in the garden; and when in the morning he saw me view with poignant grief his exhausted frame, and his person languid almost to death with watching, he wept; but during all this time he spoke no word by which I might guess the cause of his unhappiness. If I ventured to enquire he would either leave me or press his finger on his lips, and with a deprecating look that I could not resist, turn away. If I wept he would gaze on me in silence but he was no longer harsh and although he repulsed every caress yet it was with gentleness.

He seemed to cherish a mild grief and softer emotions although sad as a relief from despair. He contrived in many ways to nurse his melancholy as an antidote to wilder passion. He perpetually frequented the walks that had been favourites with him when he and my mother wandered together talking of love and happiness; he collected every relic that remained of her and always sat opposite her picture which hung in the room fixing on it a look of sad despair – and all this was done in a mystic and awful silence. If his passion subdued him he locked himself in his room; and at night when he wandered restlessly about the house, it was when every other creature slept.

It may easily be imagined that I wearied myself with conjecture to guess the cause of his sorrow. The solution that seemed to me the most probable was that during his residence in London he had fallen in love with some unworthy person, and that his passion mastered him although he would not gratify it; he loved me too well to sacrifice me to this inclination, and that he had now visited this house that by reviving the memory of my mother whom he so passionately adored he might weaken the present impression. This was possible; but it was a mere conjecture unfounded on any fact. Could there be guilt in it? He was too upright and noble to *do* aught that his conscience would not approve; I did not yet know of the crime there may be in involuntary feeling and therefore ascribed his tumultuous starts and gloomy looks wholly to the struggles of his mind and not any as they were partly due to the worst fiend of all – remorse.

But still do I flatter myself that this would have passed away. His paroxysms of passion were terrific but his soul bore him through them triumphant, though almost destroyed by victory; but the day would finally have been won had not I, foolish and presumptuous wretch! hurried him on until there was no recall, no hope. My rashness gave the victory in this dreadful fight to the enemy who triumphed over him as he lay fallen and vanquished. I! I alone was the cause of his defeat and justly did I pay the fearful penalty. I said to myself, let him receive sympathy and these struggles will cease. Let him confide his misery to another heart and half the weight of it will be lightened. I will win him to me; he shall not deny his grief to me and when I know his secret then will I pour a balm into his soul and again I shall enjoy the ravishing delight of beholding his smile, and of again seeing his

eyes beam if not with pleasure at least with gentle love and thankfulness. This will I do, I said. Half I accomplished; I gained his secret and
we were both lost for ever.

CHAPTER 5

Nearly a year had passed since my father's return, and the seasons had
almost finished their round – It was now the end of May; the woods
were clothed in their freshest verdure, and the sweet smell of the new
mown grass was in the fields. I thought that the balmy air and the lovely
face of nature might aid me in inspiring him with mild sensations, and
give him gentle feelings of peace and love preparatory to the confidence
I determined to win from him.

I chose therefore the evening of one of these days for my attempt. I
invited him to walk with me, and led him to a neighbouring wood of
beech trees whose light shade shielded us from the slant and dazzling
beams of the descending sun – After walking for some time in silence I
seated myself with him on a mossy hillock – It is strange but even now I
seem to see the spot – the slim and smooth trunks were many of
them wound round by ivy whose shining leaves of the darkest green
contrasted with the white bark and the light leaves of the young sprouts
of beech that grew from their parent trunks – the short grass was
mingled with moss and was partly covered by the dead leaves of the last
autumn that driven by the winds had here and there collected in little
hillocks – there were a few moss-grown stumps about – The leaves were
gently moved by the breeze and through their green canopy you could
see the bright blue sky – As evening came on the distant trunks were
reddened by the sun and the wind died entirely away while a few birds
flew past us to their evening rest.

Well it was here we sat together, and when you hear all that passed –
all that of terrible tore our souls even in this placid spot, which but for
strange passions might have been a paradise to us, you will not wonder
that I remember it as I looked on it that its calm might give me calm,
and inspire me not only with courage but with persuasive words. I saw
all these things and in a vacant manner noted them in my mind while I
endeavoured to arrange my thoughts in fitting order for my attempt.
My heart beat fast as I worked myself up to speak to him, for I was
determined not to be repulsed, but I trembled to imagine what effect
my words might have on him; at length, with much hesitation I began:

'Your kindness to me, my dearest father, and the affection – the excessive affection – that you had for me when you first returned will I hope excuse me in your eyes that I dare speak to you, although with the tender affection of a daughter, yet also with the freedom of a friend and equal. But pardon me, I entreat you, and listen to me: do not turn away from me; do not be impatient; you may easily intimidate me into silence, but my heart is bursting, nor can I willingly consent to endure for one moment longer the agony of uncertitude which for the last four months has been my portion.

'Listen to me, dearest friend, and permit me to gain your confidence. Are the happy days of mutual love which have passed to be to me as a dream never to return? Alas! You have a secret grief that destroys us both: but you must permit me to win this secret from you. Tell me, can I do nothing? You well know that on the whole earth there is no sacrifice that I would not make, no labour that I would not undergo with the mere hope that I might bring you ease. But if no endeavour on my part can contribute to your happiness, let me at least know your sorrow, and surely my earnest love and deep sympathy must soothe your despair.

'I fear that I speak in a constrained manner: my heart is overflowing with the ardent desire I have of bringing calm once more to your thoughts and looks; but I fear to aggravate your grief, or to raise that in you which is death to me, anger and distaste. Do not then continue to fix your eyes on the earth; raise them on me for I can read your soul in them: speak to me, and pardon my presumption. Alas! I am a most unhappy creature!'

I was breathless with emotion, and I paused fixing my earnest eyes on my father, after I had dashed away the intrusive tears that dimmed them. He did not raise his, but after a short silence he replied to me in a low voice: 'You are indeed presumptuous, Mathilda, presumptuous and very rash. In the heart of one like me there are secret thoughts working, and secret tortures which you ought not to seek to discover. I cannot tell you how it adds to my grief to know that I am the cause of uneasiness to you; but this will pass away, and I hope that soon we shall be as we were a few months ago. Restrain your impatience or you may mar what you attempt to alleviate. Do not again speak to me in this strain; but wait in submissive patience the event of what is passing around you.'

'Oh, yes!' I passionately replied, 'I will be very patient; I will not be rash or presumptuous: I will see the agonies, and tears, and despair of my father, my only friend, my hope, my shelter, I will see it all with folded arms and downcast eyes. You do not treat me with candour; it is not true what you say; this will not soon pass away, it will last for ever if you deign not to speak to me; to admit my consolations.

'Dearest, dearest father, pity me and pardon me: I entreat you do not drive me to despair; indeed I must not be repulsed; there is one thing that although it may torture me to know, yet that you must tell me. I demand, and most solemnly I demand if in any way I am the cause of your unhappiness. Do you not see my tears which I in vain strive against – You hear unmoved my voice broken by sobs – Feel how my hand trembles: my whole heart is in the words I speak and you must not endeavour to silence me by mere words barren of meaning: the agony of my doubt hurries me on, and you must reply. I beseech you; by your former love for me now lost, I adjure you to answer that one question. Am I the cause of your grief?'

He raised his eyes from the ground, but still turning them away from me, said: 'Besought by that plea I will answer your rash question. Yes, you are the sole, the agonising cause of all I suffer, of all I must suffer until I die. Now, beware! Be silent! Do not urge me to your destruction. I am struck by the storm, rooted up, laid waste; but you can stand against it; you are young and your passions are at peace. One word I might speak and then you would be implicated in my destruction; yet that word is hovering on my lips. Oh! There is a fearful chasm; but I adjure you to beware!'

'Ah, dearest friend!' I cried, 'do not fear! Speak that word; it will bring peace, not death. If there is a chasm our mutual love will give us wings to pass it, and we shall find flowers, and verdure, and delight on the other side.'[20] I threw myself at his feet, and took his hand, 'Yes, speak, and we shall be happy; there will no longer be doubt, no dreadful uncertainty; trust me, my affection will soothe your sorrow; speak that word and all danger will be past, and we shall love each other as before, and for ever.'

He snatched his hand from me, and rose in violent disorder: 'What do you mean? You know not what you mean. Why do you bring me out, and torture me, and tempt me, and kill me – Much happier would it be for you and for me if in your frantic curiosity you tore my heart from my breast and tried to read its secrets in it as its life's blood was dropping from it. Thus you may console me by reducing me to nothing – but your words I cannot bear; soon they will make me mad, quite mad, and then I shall utter strange words, and you will believe them, and we shall be both lost for ever. I tell you I am on the very verge of insanity; why, cruel girl, do you drive me on? You will repent and I shall die.'

When I repeat his words I wonder at my pertinacious folly; I hardly know what feelings resistlessly impelled me. I believe it was that coming out with a determination not to be repulsed I went right forward to my object without well weighing his replies: I was led by passion and drew him with frantic heedlessness into the abyss that he so fearfully avoided – I replied to his terrific words: 'You fill me with affright it is true, dearest father, but you only confirm my resolution to put an end to this state of doubt. I will not be put off thus: do you think that I can live thus fearfully from day to day – the sword in my bosom yet kept from its mortal wound by a hair – a word! – I demand that dreadful word; though it be as a flash of lightning to destroy me, speak it.

'Alas! Alas! What am I become? But a few months have elapsed since I believed that I was all the world to you; and that there was no happiness or grief for you on earth unshared by your Mathilda – your child: that happy time is no longer, and what I most dreaded in this world is come upon me. In the despair of my heart I see what you cannot conceal: you no longer love me. I adjure you, my father, has not an unnatural passion seized upon your heart? Am I not the most miserable worm that crawls? Do I not embrace your knees, and you most cruelly repulse me? I know it – I see it – you hate me!'

I was transported by violent emotion, and rising from his feet, at which I had thrown myself, I leant against a tree, wildly raising my eyes to heaven. He began to answer with violence: 'Yes, yes, I hate you! You are my bane, my poison, my disgust! Oh! No!' And then his manner changed, and fixing his eyes on me with an expression that convulsed every nerve and member of my frame – 'you are none of all these; you are my light, my only one, my life. My daughter, I love you!' The last words died away in a hoarse whisper, but I heard them and sank on the ground, covering my face and almost dead with excess of sickness and fear: a cold perspiration covered my forehead and I shivered in every limb.

But he continued, clasping his hands with a frantic gesture: 'Now I have dashed from the top of the rock to the bottom! Now I have precipitated myself down the fearful chasm! The danger is over; she is alive! Oh, Mathilda, lift up those dear eyes in the light of which I live. Let me hear the sweet tones of your beloved voice in peace and calm. Monster as I am, you are still, as you ever were, lovely, beautiful beyond expression. What I have become since this last moment I know not; perhaps I am changed in mien as the fallen archangel.[21] I do believe I am for I have surely a new soul within me, and my blood riots through my veins: I am burnt up with fever. But these are precious moments; devil as I am become, yet that is my Mathilda before me whom I love as one was never before loved: and she knows it now; she listens to these words which I thought, fool as I was, would blast her to death. Come, come, the worst is past: no more grief, tears or despair; were not those the words you uttered? – We have leapt the chasm I told you of, and now, mark me, Mathilda, we are to find flowers, and verdure, and delight; or is it hell, and fire, and tortures? Oh! Beloved One, I am borne away; I can no longer sustain myself; surely this is death that is coming. Let me lay my head near your heart; let me die in your arms!' – He sank to the earth fainting, while I, nearly as lifeless, gazed on him in despair.

Yes it was despair I felt; for the first time that phantom seized me; the first and only time for it has never since left me – After the first moments of speechless agony I felt her fangs on my heart: I tore my hair; I raved aloud; at one moment in pity for his sufferings I would have clasped my father in my arms; and then starting back with horror I spurned him with my foot; I felt as if stung by a serpent, as if scourged by a whip of scorpions[22] which drove me – Ah! Whither – Whither?

Well, this could not last. One idea rushed on my mind; never, never may I speak to him again. As this terrible conviction came upon me it melted my soul to tenderness and love – I gazed on him as to take my last farewell; he lay insensible – his eyes closed and his cheeks deathly pale. Above, the leaves of the beechwood cast a flickering shadow on his face, and waved in mournful melody over him – I saw all these things and said, 'Aye, this is his grave!' And then I wept aloud, and raised my eyes to heaven to entreat for a respite to my despair and an alleviation of his unnatural suffering – the tears that gushed in a warm and healing stream from my eyes relieved the burthen that oppressed my heart almost to madness. I wept for a long time until I saw him about to revive, when horror and misery again recurred, and the tide of my sensations rolled back to their former channel: with a terror I could not restrain, I sprang up and fled, with winged speed, along the paths of the wood and across the fields until nearly dead I reached our house, and just ordering the servants to seek my father at the spot I indicated, I shut myself up in my own room.

CHAPTER 6

My chamber was in a retired part of the house, and looked upon the garden so that no sound of the other inhabitants could reach it; and here in perfect solitude I wept for several hours. When a servant came to ask me if I would take food I learnt from him that my father had returned, and was apparently well and this relieved me from a load of anxiety, yet I did not cease to weep bitterly. At first, as the memory of former happiness contrasted with my present despair came across me, I gave relief to the oppression of heart that I felt by words, and groans, and heart-rending sighs: but nature became wearied, and this more violent grief gave place to a passionate but mute flood of tears: my whole soul seemed to dissolve in them. I did not wring my hands, or tear my hair, or utter wild exclamations, but as Boccaccio describes the intense and quiet grief of Sigismunda over the heart of Guiscardo,[23] I sat with my hands folded, silently letting fall a perpetual stream from my eyes. Such was the depth of my emotion that I had no feeling of what caused my distress, my thoughts even wandered to many in-different objects; but still neither moving limb or feature my tears fell until, as if the fountains were exhausted, they gradually subsided, and I awoke to life as from a dream.

When I had ceased to weep, reason and memory returned upon me, and I began to reflect with greater calmness on what had happened, and how it became me to act. A few hours only had passed but a mighty revolution had taken place with regard to me – the natural work of years had been transacted since the morning: my father was as dead to me, and I felt for a moment as if he with white hairs were laid in his coffin and I – youth vanished in approaching age, were weeping at his timely dissolution. But it was not so, I was yet young, Oh! far too young, nor was he dead to others; but I, most miserable, must never see or speak to him again. I must fly from him with more earnestness than from my greatest enemy: in solitude or in cities I must never more behold him. That consideration made me breathless with anguish, and impressing itself on my imagination I was unable for a time to follow up any train of ideas. Ever after this, I thought, I would live in the most dreary seclusion. I would retire to the Continent and become a nun; not for religion's sake, for I was not a Catholic, but that I might be for ever shut out from the world. I should there find solitude where I might weep, and the voices of life might never reach me.

But my father; my beloved and most wretched father? Would he die? Would he never overcome the fierce passion that now held pitiless dominion over him? Might he not many, many years hence, when age had quenched the burning sensations that he now experienced, might he not then be again a father to me? This reflection unwrinkled my brow, and I could feel (and I wept to feel it) a half-melancholy smile draw from my lips their expression of suffering: I dared indulge better hopes for my future life; years must pass but they would speed lightly away winged by hope, or if they passed heavily, still they would pass and I had not lost my father for ever. Let him spend another sixteen years of desolate wandering; let him once more utter his wild complaints to the vast woods and the tremendous cataracts of another clime; let him again undergo fearful danger and soul-quelling hardships; let the hot sun of the south again burn his passion-worn cheeks and the cold night-rains fall on him and chill his blood.

To this life, miserable father, I devote thee! – Go! – Be thy days passed with savages, and thy nights under the cope of heaven! Be thy limbs worn and thy heart chilled, and all youth be dead within thee! Let thy hairs be as snow; thy walk trembling and thy voice have lost its mellow tones! Let the liquid lustre of thine eyes be quenched; and then return to me, return to thy Mathilda, thy child, who may then be clasped in thy loved arms, while thy heart beats with sinless emotion. Go, Devoted One, and return thus! – This is my curse, a daughter's curse: go, and return pure to thy child, who will never love aught but thee.

These were my thoughts; and with trembling hands I prepared to begin a letter to my unhappy parent. I had now spent many hours in tears and mournful meditation; it was past twelve o'clock; all was at peace in the house, and the gentle air that stole in at my window did not rustle the leaves of the twining plants that shadowed it. I felt the entire tranquillity of the hour when my own breath and involuntary sobs were all the sounds that struck upon the air. On a sudden I heard a gentle step ascending the stairs; I paused breathless, and as it approached glided into an obscure corner of the room; the steps paused at my door, but after a few moments they again receded, descended the stairs and I heard no more.

This slight incident gave rise in me to the most painful reflections; nor do I now dare express the emotions I felt. That he should be restless I understood; that he should wander as an unlaid ghost and find no quiet from the burning hell that consumed his heart. But why approach my chamber? Was not that sacred? I felt almost ready to faint while he had stood there, but I had not betrayed my wakefulness by the slightest motion, although I had heard my own heart beat with violent fear. He had withdrawn. Oh, never, never, may I see him again! Tomorrow night the same roof may not cover us; he or I must depart. The mutual link of our destinies is broken; we must be divided by seas – by land. The stars and the sun must not rise at the same period to us: he must not say, looking at the setting crescent of the moon, 'Mathilda now watches its fall.' – No, all must be changed. Be it light with him when it is darkness with me! Let him feel the sun of summer while I am chilled by the snows of winter! Let there be the distance of the antipodes[24] between us!

At length the east began to brighten, and the comfortable light of morning streamed into my room. I was weary with watching and for some time I had combated with the heavy sleep that weighed down my eyelids; but now, no longer fearful, I threw myself on my bed. I sought for repose although I did not hope for forgetfulness; I knew I should be pursued by dreams, but did not dread the frightful one that I really had. I thought that I had risen and went to seek my father to inform him of my determination to separate myself from him. I sought him in the house, in the park, and then in the fields and the woods, but I could not find him. At length I saw him at some distance, seated under a tree, and when he perceived me he waved his hand several times, beckoning me to approach; there was something unearthly in his mien that awed and chilled me, but I drew near. When at a short distance from him I saw that he was dead-lily pale, and clothed in flowing garments of white. Suddenly he started up and fled from me; I pursued him: we sped over the fields, and by the skirts of woods, and on the banks of rivers; he flew fast and I followed. We came at last, methought, to the brow of a huge cliff that overhung the sea which, troubled by the winds, dashed against its base at a distance. I heard the roar of the waters; he held his course right on towards the brink and I became breathless with fear lest he should plunge down the dreadful precipice; I tried to augment my speed, but my knees failed beneath me, yet I had just reached him, just caught a part of his flowing robe, when he leapt down and I awoke with a violent scream. I was trembling and my pillow was wet with my tears; for a few moments my heart beat hard, but the bright beams of the sun and the chirping of the birds quickly restored me to myself, and I rose with a languid spirit, yet wondering what events the day would bring forth. Some time passed before I summoned courage to ring the bell for my servant, and when she came I still dared not utter my father's name. I ordered her to bring my breakfast to my room, and was again left alone – yet still I could make no resolve, but only thought that I might write a note to my father to beg his permission to pay a visit to a relation who lived about thirty miles off, and who had before invited me to her house, but I had refused for then I could not quit my suffering father. When the servant came back she gave me a letter.

'From whom is this letter?' I asked trembling.

'Your father left it, madam, with his servant, to be given to you when you should rise.'

'My father left it! Where is he? Is he not here?'

'No; he quitted the house before four this morning.'

'Good God! He is gone! But tell how this was; speak quick!'

Her relation was short. He had gone in the carriage to the nearest town where he took a post-chaise and horses with orders for the London road. He dismissed his servants there, only telling them that he had a sudden call of business and that they were to obey me as their mistress until his return.

CHAPTER 7

With a beating heart and fearful, I knew not why, I dismissed the servant and locking my door, sat down to read my father's letter. These are the words that it contained.

'My dear child –

'I have betrayed your confidence; I have endeavoured to pollute your mind, and have made your innocent heart acquainted with the looks and language of unlawful and monstrous passion. I must expiate these crimes, and must endeavour in some degree to proportionate my punishment to my guilt. You are I doubt not prepared for what I am about to announce; we must separate and be divided for ever.

'I deprive you of your parent and only friend. You are cast out shelter-less on the world: your hopes are blasted; the peace and security of your pure mind destroyed; memory will bring to you frightful images of guilt, and the anguish of innocent love betrayed. Yet I who draw down all this misery upon you; I who cast you forth and remorselessly have set the seal of distrust and agony on the heart and brow of my own child, who with devilish levity have endeavoured to steal away her loveliness to place in its stead the foul deformity of sin; I, in the overflowing anguish of my heart, supplicate you to forgive me.

'I do not ask your pity: you must and do abhor me; but pardon me, Mathilda, and let not your thoughts follow me in my banishment with unrelenting anger. I must never more behold you; never more hear your voice; but the soft whisperings of your forgiveness will reach me and cool the burning of my disordered brain and heart; I am sure I should feel it even in my grave. And I dare enforce this request by relating how miserably I was betrayed into this net of fiery anguish and all my struggles to release myself: indeed if your soul were less pure and bright I would not attempt to exculpate myself to you; I should fear that if I led you to regard me with less abhorrence you might hate vice less: but in addressing you I feel as if I appealed to an angelic judge. I cannot depart without your forgiveness and I must endeavour to gain it, or I must despair. I conjure you therefore to listen to my words, and if with the good guilt may be in any degree extenuated by sharp agony and remorse that rends the brain as madness, perhaps you may think, though I dare not, that I have some claim to your compassion.

'I entreat you to call to your remembrance our first happy life on the shores of Loch Lomond. I had arrived from a weary wandering of sixteen years, during which, although I had gone through many dangers and misfortunes, my affections had been an entire blank. If I grieved it was for your mother, if I loved it was your image; these sole emotions filled my heart in quietness. The human creatures around me excited in me no sympathy and I thought that the mighty change that the death of your mother had wrought within me had rendered me callous to any future impression. I saw the lovely and I did not love, I imagined therefore that all warmth was extinguished in my heart except that which led me ever to dwell on your then infantine image.

'It is a strange link in my fate that without having seen you I should passionately love you. During my wanderings I never slept without first calling down gentle dreams on your head. If I saw a lovely woman, I thought, does my Mathilda resemble her? All delightful things, sublime scenery, soft breezes, exquisite music seemed to me associated with you and only through you to be pleasant to me. At length I saw you. You appeared as the deity of a lovely region, the ministering angel of a paradise to which of all human kind you admitted only me. I dared hardly consider you as my daughter; your beauty, artlessness and untaught wisdom seemed to belong to a higher order of beings; your voice breathed forth only words of love: if there was aught of earthly in you it was only what you derived from the beauty of the world; you seemed to have gained a grace from the mountain breezes – the waterfalls and the lake; and this was all of earthly except your affections that you had; there was no dross, no bad feeling in the composition. You yet even have not seen enough of the world to know the stupendous difference that exists between the women we meet in daily life and a nymph of the woods such as you were, in whose eyes alone mankind may study for centuries and grow wiser and purer. Those divine lights which shone on me as did those of Beatrice upon Dante, and well might I say with him yet with what different feelings – "E quasi mi perdei gli occhi chini".[25] Can you wonder, Mathilda, that I dwelt on your looks, your words, your motions, and drank in unmixed delight?

'But I am afraid that I wander from my purpose. I must be more brief for night draws on apace and all my hours in this house are counted. Well, we removed to London, and still I felt only the peace of sinless passion. You were ever with me, and I desired no more than to gaze on your countenance, and to know that I was all the world to you; I was lapped in a fool's paradise of enjoyment and security. Was my love blamable? If it was I was ignorant of it; I desired only that which I possessed, and if I enjoyed from your looks, and words, and most innocent caresses a rapture usually excluded from the feelings of a parent towards his child, yet no uneasiness, no wish, no casual idea awoke me to a sense of guilt. I loved you as a human father might be supposed to love a daughter borne to him by a heavenly mother; as Anchises might have regarded the child of Venus if the sex had been changed;[26] love mingled with respect and adoration. Perhaps also my passion was lulled to content by the deep and exclusive affection you felt for me.

'But when I saw you become the object of another's love; when I imagined that you might be loved otherwise than as a sacred type and image of loveliness and excellence; or that you might love another with a more ardent affection than that which you bore to me, then the fiend awoke within me; I dismissed your lover; and from that moment I have known no peace. I have sought in vain for sleep and rest; my lids refused to close, and my blood was for ever in a tumult. I awoke to a new life as one who dies in hope might wake in Hell. I will not sully your imagination by recounting my combats, my self-anger and my despair. Let a veil be drawn over the unimaginable sensations of a guilty father; the secrets of so agonised a heart may not be made vulgar. All was uproar, crime, remorse and hate, yet still the tenderest love; and what first awoke me to the firm resolve of conquering my passion and of restoring her father to my child was the sight of your bitter and sympathising sorrows. It was this that led me here: I thought that if I could again awaken in my heart the grief I had felt at the loss of your mother, and the many associations with her memory which had been laid to sleep for seventeen years, that all love for her child would become extinct. In a fit of heroism I determined to go alone; to quit you, the life of my life, and not to see you again until I might guiltlessly. But it would not do: I rated my fortitude too high, or my love too low. I should certainly have died if you had not hastened to me. Would that I had been indeed extinguished!

'And now, Mathilda I must make you my last confession. I have been miserably mistaken in imagining that I could conquer my love for you; I never can. The sight of this house, these fields and woods which my first love inhabited seems to have increased it: in my madness I dared say to myself – Diana died to give her birth; her mother's spirit was transferred into her frame, and she ought to be as Diana to me. With every effort to cast it off, this love clings closer, this guilty love more unnatural than hate, that withers your hopes and destroys me for ever. "Better have loved despair, and safer kissed her."[27]

'No time or space can tear from my soul that which makes a part of it. Since my arrival here I have not for a moment ceased to feel the hell of passion which has been implanted in me to burn until all be cold, and stiff, and dead. Yet I will not die; alas! how dare I go where I may meet Diana, when I have disobeyed her last request; her last words said in a faint voice when all feeling but love, which survives all things else, was already dead, she then bade me make her child happy: that thought alone gives a double sting to death. I will wander away from you, away from all life – in the solitude I shall seek I alone shall breathe of human kind. I must endure life; and as it is my duty so I shall until the grave, dreaded yet desired, receive me free from pain: for while I feel it will be pain that must make up the whole sum of my sensations. Is not this a fearful curse that I labour under? Do I not look forward to a miserable future? My child, if after this life I am permitted to see you again, if pain can purify the heart, mine will be pure; if remorse may expiate guilt, I shall be guiltless.

*   *   *

'I have been at the door of your chamber: everything is silent. You sleep. Do you indeed sleep, Mathilda? Spirits of Good, behold the tears of my earnest prayer! Bless my child! Protect her from the selfish among her fellow creatures; protect her from the agonies of passion, and the despair of disappointment! Peace, Hope and Love be thy guardians, oh, thou soul of my soul: thou in whom I breathe!

*   *   *

'I dare not read my letter over for I have no time to write another, and yet I fear that some expressions in it might displease me. Since I last saw you I have been constantly employed in writing letters, and have several more to write; for I do not intend that anyone shall hear of me after I depart. I need not conjure you to look upon me as one of whom all links that once existed between us are broken. Your own delicacy will not allow you, I am convinced, to attempt to trace me. It is far better for your peace that you should be ignorant of my destination. You will not follow me, for when I banish myself would you nourish guilt by obtruding yourself upon me? You will not do this, I know you will not.

You must forget me and all the evil that I have taught you. Cast off the only gift that I have bestowed upon you, your grief, and rise from under my blighting influence as no flower so sweet ever did rise from beneath so much evil.

'You will never hear from me again: receive these then as the last words of mine that will ever reach you; and although I have forfeited your filial love, yet regard them I conjure you as a father's command. Resolutely shake off the wretchedness that this first misfortune in early life must occasion you. Bear boldly up against the storm: continue wise and mild, but believe it, and indeed it is, your duty to be happy. You are very young; let not this check for more than a moment retard your glorious course; hold on, beloved one. The sun of youth is not set for you; it will restore vigour and life to you; do not resist with obstinate grief its beneficent influence, oh, my child! bless me with the hope that I have not utterly destroyed you.

'Farewell, Mathilda. I go with the belief that I have your pardon. Your gentle nature would not permit you to hate your greatest enemy and though I be he, although I have rent happiness from your grasp; though I have passed over your young love and hopes as the angel of destruction, finding beauty and joy, and leaving blight and despair, yet you will forgive me, and with eyes overflowing with tears I thank you; my beloved one, I accept your pardon with a gratitude that will never die, and that will, indeed it will, outlive guilt and remorse.

'Farewell for ever!'

The moment I finished this letter I ordered the carriage and prepared to follow my father. The words of his letter by which he had dissuaded me from this step were those that determined me. Why did he write them? He must know that if I believed that his intention was merely to absent himself from me that instead of opposing him it would be that which I should myself require – or if he thought that any lurking feeling, yet he could not think that, should lead me to him would he endeavour to overthrow the only hope he could have of ever seeing me again; a lover, there was madness in the thought, yet he was my lover, would not act thus. No, he had determined to die, and he wished to spare me the misery of knowing it. The few ineffectual words he had said concerning his duty were to me a further proof – and the more I studied the letter the more did I perceive a thousand slight expressions that could only indicate a knowledge that life was now over for him. He was about to die! My blood froze at the thought: a sickening feeling of horror came over me that allowed not of tears. As I waited for the carriage I walked up and down with a quick pace; then kneeling and passionately clasping my hands I tried to pray but my voice was choked by convulsive sobs – Oh the sun shone, the air was balmy – he must yet live for if he were dead all would surely be black as night to me!

The motion of the carriage knowing that it carried me towards him and that I might perhaps find him alive somewhat revived my courage: yet I had a dreadful ride. Hope only supported me, the hope that I should not be too late. I did not weep, but I wiped the perspiration from my brow, and tried to still my brain and heart beating almost to madness. Oh! I must not be mad when I see him; or perhaps it were as well that I should be, my distraction might calm his, and recall him to the endurance of life. Yet until I find him I must force reason to keep her seat, and I pressed my forehead hard with my hands – Oh do not leave me; or I shall forget what I am about – instead of driving on as we ought with the speed of lightning they will attend to me, and we shall be too late. Oh! God help me! Let him be alive! It is all dark; in my abject misery I demand no more: no hope, no good: only passion, and guilt, and horror; but alive! Alive! My sensations choked me – No tears fell yet I sobbed, and breathed short and hard; one only thought possessed me, and I could only utter one word, that half screaming was perpetually on my lips: Alive! Alive! –

I had taken the steward with me for he, much better than I, could make the requisite enquiries – the poor old man could not restrain his tears as he saw my deep distress and knew the cause – he sometimes uttered a few broken words of consolation: in moments like these the mistress and servant become in a manner equals and when I saw his old dim eyes wet with sympathising tears, his grey hair thinly scattered on an age-wrinkled brow, I thought oh if my father were as he is – decrepit and hoary – then I should be spared this pain –

When I had arrived at the nearest town I took post-horses and followed the road my father had taken. At every inn where we changed horses we heard of him, and I was possessed by alternate hope and fear. At length I found that he had altered his route; at first he had followed the London road, but now he changed it, and upon enquiry I found that the one which he now pursued led *towards the sea*. My dream recurred to my thoughts; I was not usually superstitious but in wretchedness everyone is so. The sea was fifty miles off, yet it was towards it that he fled. The idea was terrible to my half-crazed imagination, and almost overturned the little self-possession that still remained to me. I journeyed all day; every moment my misery increased and the fever of my blood became intolerable. The summer sun shone in an unclouded sky; the air was close but all was cool to me except my own scorching skin. Towards evening dark thunder clouds arose above the horizon and I heard its distant roll – after sunset they darkened the whole sky and it began to rain, the lightning lighted up the whole country and the thunder drowned the noise of our carriage. At the next inn my father had not taken horses; he had left a box there saying he would return, and had walked over the fields to the town of —, a seacoast town eight miles off.

For a moment I was almost paralysed by fear; but my energy returned and I demanded a guide to accompany me in following his steps. The night was tempestuous but my bribe was high and I easily procured a countryman. We passed through many lanes and over fields and wild downs; the rain poured down in torrents; and the loud thunder broke in terrible crashes over our heads. Oh! What a night it was! And I passed on with quick steps among the high, dank grass, amid the rain and tempest. My dream was forever in my thoughts, and with a kind of half insanity that often possesses the mind in despair, I said aloud: 'Courage! We are not near the sea; we are yet several miles from the ocean' – Yet it was towards the sea that our direction lay and that heightened the confusion of my ideas. Once, overcome by fatigue, I sank on the wet earth; about two hundred yards distant, alone in a large meadow stood a magnificent oak; the lightning showed its myriad boughs torn by the storm. A strange idea seized me; a person must have felt all the agonies of doubt concerning the life and death of one who is the whole world to them before they can enter into my feelings – for in that state, the mind working unrestrained by the will makes strange and fanciful combinations with outward circumstances and weaves the chances and changes of nature into an immediate connection with the event they dread. It was with this feeling that I turned to the old steward who stood pale and trembling beside me: 'Mark, Gaspar, if the next flash of lightning rend not that oak my father will be alive.'

I had scarcely uttered these words than a flash instantly followed by a tremendous peal of thunder descended on it; and when my eyes recovered their sight after the dazzling light, the oak no longer stood in the meadow – The old man uttered a wild exclamation of horror when he saw so sudden an interpretation given to my prophesy. I started up, my strength returned with my terror; I cried, 'Oh, God! Is this thy decree? Yet perhaps I shall not be too late.'

Although still several miles distant we continued to approach the sea. We came at last to the road that led to the town of — and at an inn there we heard that my father had passed by somewhat before sunset; he had observed the approaching storm and had hired a horse for the next town which was situated a mile from the sea that he might arrive there before it should commence; this town was five miles off. We hired a chaise here, and with four horses drove with speed through the storm. My garments were wet and clung around me, and my hair hung in straight locks on my neck when not blown aside by the wind. I shivered, yet my pulse was high with fever. Great God! What agony I endured. I shed no tears but my eyes wild and inflamed were starting from my head; I could hardly support the weight that pressed upon my brain. We arrived at the town of — in a little more than half an hour. When my father had arrived the storm had already begun, but he had refused to stop and leaving his horse there he walked on – *towards the sea*. Alas! it was double cruelty in him to have chosen the sea for his fatal resolve; it was adding madness to my despair.

The poor old servant who was with me endeavoured to persuade me to remain here and to let him go alone – I shook my head silently and sadly; sick almost to death I leant upon his arm, and as there was no road for a chaise dragged my weary steps across the desolate downs to meet my fate, now too certain for the agony of doubt. Almost fainting I slowly approached the fatal waters; when we had quitted the town we heard their roaring. I whispered to myself in a muttering voice – 'The sound is the same as that which I heard in my dream. It is the knell of my father which I hear.'

The rain had ceased; there was no more thunder and lightning; the wind had paused. My heart no longer beat wildly; I did not feel any fever: but I was chilled; my knees sank under me – I almost slept as I walked with excess of weariness; every limb trembled. I was silent: all was silent except the roaring of the sea which became louder and more dreadful. Yet we advanced slowly: sometimes I thought that we should never arrive; that the sound of waves would still allure us, and that we should walk on for ever and ever: field succeeding field, never would our weary journey cease, nor night nor day, but still we should hear the dashing of the sea, and to all this there would be no end. Wild beyond the imagination of the happy are the thoughts bred by misery and despair.

At length we reached the overhanging beach; a cottage stood beside the path; we knocked at the door and it was opened: the bed within instantly caught my eye; something stiff and straight lay on it, covered by a sheet; the cottagers looked aghast. The first words that they uttered confirmed what I before knew. I did not feel shocked or overcome. I believe that I asked one or two questions and listened to the answers. I hardly know, but in a few moments I sank lifeless to the ground; and so would that then all had been at an end!

CHAPTER 8

I was carried to the next town: fever succeeded to convulsions and faintings, and for some weeks my unhappy spirit hovered on the very verge of death. But life was yet strong within me; I recovered: nor did it a little aid my returning health that my recollections were at first vague, and that I was too weak to feel any violent emotion. I often said to myself, my father is dead. He loved me with a guilty passion, and stung by remorse and despair he killed himself. Why is it that I feel no horror? Are these circumstances not dreadful? Is it not enough that I shall never more meet the eyes of my beloved father; never more hear his voice; no caress, no look? All cold, and stiff, and dead! Alas! I am quite callous: the night I was out in was fearful and the cold rain that fell about my heart has acted like the waters of the cavern of Antiparos[28] and has changed it to stone. I do not weep or sigh; but I must reason with myself, and force myself to feel sorrow and despair. This is not resignation that I feel, for I am dead to all regret.

I communed in this manner with myself, but I was silent to all around me. I hardly replied to the slightest question, and was uneasy when I saw a human creature near me. I was surrounded by my female relations, but they were all of them nearly strangers to me: I did not listen to their consolations; and so little did they work their designed effect that they seemed to me to be spoken in an unknown tongue. I found if sorrow was dead within me, so was love and desire of sympathy. Yet sorrow only slept to revive more fierce, but love never woke again – its ghost, ever hovering over my father's grave, alone survived – since his death all the world was to me a blank except where woe had stamped its burning words telling me to smile no more – the living were not fit companions for me, and I was ever meditating by what means I might shake them all off, and never be heard of again.

My convalescence rapidly advanced, yet this was the thought that haunted me, and I was forever forming plans how I might hereafter contrive to escape the tortures that were prepared for me when I should mix in society, and to find that solitude which alone could suit one whom an untold grief separated from her fellow creatures. Who can be more solitary even in a crowd than one whose history and the never-ending feelings and remembrances arising from it is known to no living soul. There was too deep a horror in my tale for confidence; I was on earth the sole depository of my own secret. I might tell it to the winds and to the desert heaths but I must never among my fellow creatures, either by word or look, give allowance to the smallest conjecture of the dread reality; I must shrink before the eye of man lest he should read my father's guilt in my glazed eyes; I must be silent lest my faltering voice should betray unimagined horrors. Over the deep grave of my secret I must heap an impenetrable heap of false smiles and words: cunning frauds, treacherous laughter and a mixture of all light deceits would form a mist to blind others and be as the poisonous simoon[29] to me. I, the offspring of love, the child of the woods, the nursling of nature's bright self was to submit to this? I dared not.

How must I escape? I was rich and young, and had a guardian appointed for me; and all about me would act as if I were one of their great society, while I must keep the secret that I really was cut off from them for ever. If I fled I should be pursued; in life there was no escape for me: why then I must die. I shuddered; I dared not die even though the cold grave held all I loved; although I might say with Job:

> Where is now my hope? For my hope who shall see it?
> They shall go down together to the bars of the pit,
> when our rest together is in the dust – [30]

Yes my hope was corruption and dust and all to which death brings us. – Or after life – No, no, I will not persuade myself to die, I may not, dare not. And then I wept; yes, warm tears once more struggled into my eyes soothing yet bitter; and after I had wept much and called with unavailing anguish, with outstretched arms, for my cruel father; after my weak frame was exhausted by all variety of plaint, I sank once more into reverie, and once more reflected on how I might find that which I most desired; dear to me if aught were dear, a deathlike solitude.

I dared not die, but I might feign death, and thus escape from my comforters: they will believe me united to my father, and so indeed I shall be. For alone, when no voice can disturb my dream, and no cold eye meet mine to check its fire, then I may commune with his spirit; on a lone heath, at noon or at midnight, still I should be near him. His last injunction to me was that I should be happy; perhaps he did not mean the shadowy happiness that I promised myself, yet it was that alone which I could taste. He did not conceive that never again could I make one of the smiling hunters that go coursing after bubbles that break to nothing when caught, and then after a new one with brighter colours; my hope also had proved a bubble, but it had been so lovely, so adorned that I saw none that could attract me after it; besides I was wearied with the pursuit, nearly dead with weariness.

I would feign to die; my contented heirs would seize upon my wealth, and I should purchase freedom. But then my plan must be laid with art; I would not be left destitute, I must secure some money. Alas! to what loathsome shifts must I be driven? Yet a whole life of falsehood was otherwise my portion; and when remorse at being the contriver of any cheat made me shrink from my design I was irresistibly led back and confirmed in it by the visit of some aunt or cousin, who would tell me that death was the end of all men. And then say that my father had surely lost his wits ever since my mother's death; that he was mad and that I was fortunate, for in one of his fits he might have killed me instead of destroying his own crazed being. And all this, to be sure, was delicately put; not in broad words for my feelings might be hurt but:

> Whispered so and so
> In dark hint soft and low[31]

with downcast eyes, and sympathising smiles or whimpers; and I listened with quiet countenance while every nerve trembled; I that dared not utter aye or no to all this blasphemy. Oh, this was a delicious life quite void of guile! I with my dove's look and fox's heart: for indeed I felt only the degradation of falsehood, and not any sacred sentiment of conscious innocence that might redeem it. I who had before clothed myself in the bright garb of sincerity must now borrow one of divers colours; it might sit awkwardly at first, but use would enable me to place it in elegant folds, to lie with grace. Aye, I might dye my soul with falsehood until I had quite hid its native colour. Oh, beloved father! Accept the pure heart of your unhappy daughter; permit me to join you unspotted as I was or you will not recognise my altered semblance. As grief might change Constance[32] so would deceit change me until in heaven you would say, 'This is not my child' – My father, to be happy both now and when again we meet I must fly from all this life which is mockery to one like me. In solitude only shall I be myself; in solitude I shall be thine.

Alas! I even now look back with disgust at my artifices and contrivances by which, after many painful struggles, I effected my retreat. I might enter into a long detail of the means I used, first to secure myself a slight maintenance for the remainder of my life, and afterwards to ensure the conviction of my death; I might, but I will not. I even now blush at the falsehoods I uttered; my heart sickens: I will leave this complication of what I hope I may in a manner call innocent deceit to be imagined by the reader. The remembrance haunts me like a crime – I know that if I were to endeavour to relate it my tale would at length remain unfinished. I was led to London, and had to endure for some weeks cold looks, cold words and colder consolations; but I escaped; they tried to bind me with fetters that they thought silken, yet which weighed on me like iron, although I broke them more easily than a girth formed of a single straw and fled to freedom.

The few weeks that I spent in London were the most miserable of my life: a great city is a frightful habitation to one sorrowing. The sunset and the gentle moon, the blessed motion of the leaves and the murmuring of waters are all sweet physicians to a distempered mind. The soul is expanded and drinks in quiet, a lulling medicine – to me it was as the sight of the lovely water-snakes to the bewitched mariner – in loving and blessing nature I unawares called down a blessing on my own soul.[33] But in a city all is closed shut like a prison, a wiry prison from which you can peep at the sky only. I cannot describe to you what the frantic nature of my sensations were while I resided there; I was often on the verge of madness. Nay, when I look back on many of my wild thoughts, thoughts with which actions sometimes endeavoured to keep pace; when I tossed my hands high calling down the cope of heaven to fall on me and bury me; when I tore my hair and throwing it to the winds cried, 'Ye are free, go seek my father!' And then, like the unfortunate Constance, catching at them again and tying them up, that nought might find him if I might not.[34] How, on my knees I have fancied myself close to my father's grave and struck the ground in anger that it should cover him from me. Oft when I have listened with gasping attention for the sound of the ocean mingled with my father's groans; and then wept until my strength was gone and I was calm and faint. When I have recollected all this I have asked myself if this were not madness. While in London these and many other dreadful thoughts too harrowing for words were my portion. I lost all this suffering when I was free; when I saw the wild heath around me, and the evening star in the west, then I could weep, gently weep, and be at peace.

Do not mistake me; I never was really mad. I was always conscious of my state when my wild thoughts seemed to drive me to insanity, and never betrayed them to aught but silence and solitude. The people around me saw nothing of all this. They only saw a poor girl broken in spirit, who spoke in a low and gentle voice, and from underneath whose downcast lids tears would sometimes steal which she strove to hide. One who loved to be alone, and shrank from observation; who never smiled; oh, no! I never smiled – and that was all.

Well, I escaped. I left my guardian's house and I was never heard of again; it was believed from the letters that I left and other circumstances that I planned that I had destroyed myself. I was sought after therefore with less care than would otherwise have been the case; and soon all trace and memory of me was lost. I left London in a small vessel bound for a port in the north of England. And now, having succeeded in my attempt and being quite alone, peace returned to me. The sea was calm and the vessel moved gently onwards. I sat upon deck under the open canopy of heaven and methought I was an altered creature. Not the wild, raving and most miserable Mathilda but a youthful hermitess dedicated to seclusion and whose bosom she must strive to keep free from all tumult and unholy despair. The fanciful nunlike dress that I had adopted; the knowledge that my very existence was a secret known only to myself; the solitude to which I was for ever hereafter destined, all nursed gentle thoughts in my wounded heart. The breeze that played in my hair revived me, and I watched with quiet eyes the sunbeams that glittered on the waves, and the birds that coursed each other over the waters just brushing them with their plumes. I slept too undisturbed by dreams; and awoke refreshed again to enjoy my tranquil freedom.

In four days we arrived at the harbour to which we were bound. I would not remain on the sea coast, but proceeded immediately inland. I had already planned the situation where I would live. It should be a solitary house on a wide plain near no other habitation, where I could behold the whole horizon, and wander far without molestation from the sight of my fellow creatures. I was not misanthropic, but I felt that the gentle current of my feelings depended upon my being alone. I fixed myself on a wide solitude, on a dreary heath bestrewn with stones, among which short grass grew and here and there a few rushes beside a little pool. Not far from my cottage was a small cluster of pines, the only trees to be seen for many miles: I had a path cut through the furze from my door to this little wood, from whose topmost branches the birds saluted the rising sun and awoke me to my daily meditation. My view was bounded only by the horizon except on one side where a distant wood made a black spot on the heath; everywhere else stretched out its faint hues as far as the eye could reach, wide and very desolate. Here I could mark the network of the clouds as they wove themselves into thick masses: I could watch the slow rise of the heavy thunder clouds and could see the rack[35] as it was driven across the heavens, or under the pine trees I could enjoy the stillness of the azure sky.

My life was very peaceful. I had one female servant who spent the greater part of the day at a village two miles off. My amusements were simple and very innocent; I fed the birds who built on the pines or among the ivy that covered the wall of my little garden, and they soon knew me: the bolder ones pecked the crumbs from my hands and perched on my fingers to sing their thankfulness. When I had lived here some time other animals visited me and a fox came every day for a portion of food appropriated for him and would suffer me to pat his head. I had besides many books and a harp with which when despairing I could soothe my spirits, and raise myself to sympathy and love.

Love! What had I to love? Oh many things: there was the moonshine, and the bright stars; the breezes and the refreshing rains; there was the whole earth and the sky that covers it: all lovely forms that visited my imagination, all memories of heroism and virtue. Yet this was very unlike my early life although as then I was confined to nature and books. Then I bounded across the fields; my spirit often seemed to ride upon the winds, and to mingle in joyful sympathy with the ambient air. Then if I wandered slowly I cheered myself with a sweet song or sweeter daydreams. I felt a holy rapture spring from all I saw. I drank in joy with life; my steps were light; my eyes, clear from the love that animated them, sought the heavens, and with my long hair loosened to the winds I gave my body and my mind to sympathy and delight. But now my walk was slow – my eyes were seldom raised and often filled with tears; no song; no smiles; no careless motion that might bespeak a mind intent on what surrounded it – I was gathered up into myself – a selfish solitary creature ever pondering on my regrets and faded hopes.

Mine was an idle, useless life; it was so; but say not to the lily laid prostrate by the storm, 'Arise, and bloom as before.' My heart was bleeding from its death's wound; I could live no otherwise. Often amid apparent calm I was visited by despair and melancholy; gloom that nought could dissipate or overcome; a hatred of life; a carelessness of beauty; all these would by fits hold me nearly annihilated by their powers. Never for one moment when most placid did I cease to pray for death. I could be found in no state of mind which I would not willingly have exchanged for nothingness. And morning and evening, my tearful eyes raised to heaven, my hands clasped tight in the energy of prayer, I have repeated with the poet:

> 'Before I see another day
> Oh, let this body die away!' [36]

Let me not be reproached then with inutility; I believed that by suicide I should violate a divine law of nature, and I thought that I sufficiently fulfilled my part in submitting to the hard task of enduring the crawling hours and minutes – in bearing the load of time that weighed miserably upon me – and that in abstaining from what I in my calm moments considered a crime, I deserved the reward of virtue. There were periods,

dreadful ones, during which I despaired – and doubted the existence of
all duty and the reality of crime – but I shudder, and turn from the
remembrance.

CHAPTER 9

Thus I passed two years. Day after day so many hundreds wore on;
they brought no outward changes with them, but some few slowly
operated on my mind as I glided on towards death. I began to study
more; to sympathise more in the thoughts of others as expressed in
books; to read history, and to lose my individuality among the crowd
that had existed before me. Thus perhaps, as the sensation of immediate
suffering wore off, I became more human. Solitude also lost for me
some of its charms: I began again to wish for sympathy; not that I was
ever tempted to seek the crowd, but I wished for one friend to love me.
You will say perhaps that I gradually became fitted to return to society.
I do not think so. For the sympathy that I desired must be so pure, so
divested of influence from outward circumstances, that in the world I
could not fail of being balked by the gross materials that perpetually
mingle even with its best feelings. Believe me, I was then less fitted for
any communion with my fellow creatures than before. When I left
them they had tormented me but it was in the same way as pain and
sickness may torment; something extraneous to the mind that galled it,
and that I wished to cast aside. But now I should have desired sympathy;
I should wish to knit my soul to some one of theirs, and should have
prepared for myself plentiful draughts of disappointment and suffering;
for I was tender as the sensitive plant, all nerve. I did not desire sympathy
and aid in ambition or wisdom, but sweet and mutual affection; smiles
to cheer me and gentle words of comfort. I wished for one heart in
which I could pour unrestrained my plaints, and by the heavenly nature
of the soil blessed fruit might spring from such bad seed. Yet how could
I find this? The love that is the soul of friendship is a soft spirit seldom
found except when two amiable creatures are knit from early youth, or
when bound by mutual suffering and pursuits; it comes to some of the
elect unsought and unaware; it descends as gentle dew on chosen spots
which however barren they were before become under its benign
influence fertile in all sweet plants; but when desired it flies; it scoffs at
the prayers of its votaries; it will bestow, but not be sought.

I knew all this and did not go to seek sympathy; but there on my
solitary heath, under my lowly roof where all around was desert, it came

to me as a sunbeam in winter to adorn while it helps to dissolve the drifted snow. – Alas the sun shone on blighted fruit; I did not revive under its radiance for I was too utterly undone to feel its kindly power. My father had been and his memory was the life of my life. I might feel gratitude to another but I never more could love or hope as I had done; it was all suffering; even my pleasures were endured, not enjoyed. I was as a solitary spot among mountains, shut in on all sides by steep black precipices, where no ray of heat could penetrate; and from which there was no outlet to sunnier fields. And thus it was that although the spirit of friendship soothed me for a while it could not restore me. It came as some gentle visitation; it went and I hardly felt the loss. The spirit of existence was dead within me; be not surprised therefore that when it came I welcomed not more gladly, or when it departed I lamented not more bitterly the best gift of heaven – a friend.

The name of my friend was Woodville. I will briefly relate his history that you may judge how cold my heart must have been not to be warmed by his eloquent words and tender sympathy; and how he also being most unhappy we were well fitted to be a mutual consolation to each other, if I had not been hardened to stone by the Medusa head of Misery. The misfortunes of Woodville were not of the heart's core like mine; his was a natural grief, not to destroy but to purify the heart and from which he might, when its shadow had passed from over him, shine forth brighter and happier than before.

Woodville was the son of a poor clergyman and had received a classical education. He was one of those very few whom fortune favours from their birth; on whom she bestows all gifts of intellect and person with a profusion that knew no bounds, and whom under her peculiar protection, no imperfection however slight or disappointment however transitory has leave to touch. She seemed to have formed his mind of that excellence which no dross can tarnish, and his understanding was such that no error could pervert. His genius was transcendent, and when it rose as a bright star in the east all eyes were turned towards it in admiration. He was a poet. That name has so often been degraded that it will not convey the idea of all that he was. He was like a poet of old whom the Muses had crowned in his cradle, and on whose lips bees had fed.[37] As he walked among other men he seemed encompassed with a heavenly halo that divided him from and lifted him above them. It was his surpassing beauty, the dazzling fire of his eyes, and his words whose rich accents wrapped the listener in mute and ecstatic wonder, that made him transcend all others so that before him they appeared only formed to minister to his superior excellence.

He was glorious from his youth. Everyone loved him; no shadow of envy or hate cast even from the meanest mind ever fell upon him. He was, as one the peculiar delight of the gods, railed and fenced in by his own divinity, so that nought but love and admiration could approach him. His heart was simple like a child, unstained by arrogance or vanity. He mingled in society unknowing of his superiority over his companions, not because he undervalued himself but because he did not perceive the inferiority of others. He seemed incapable of con-ceiving of the full extent of the power that selfishness and vice possesses in the world: when I knew him, although he had suffered dis-appoint-ment in his dearest hopes, he had not experienced any that arose from the meanness and self-love of men: his station was too high to allow of his suffering through their hard-heartedness, and too low for him to have experienced ingratitude and encroaching selfishness; it is one of the blessings of a moderate fortune, that by preventing the possessor from conferring pecuniary favours it prevents him also from diving into the arcana of human weakness or malice. To bestow on your fellow men is a godlike attribute – so indeed it is and as such not one fit for mortality; the giver, like Adam and Prometheus, must pay the penalty of rising above his nature by being the martyr to his own excellence. Woodville was free from all these evils; and if slight examples did come across him he did not notice them but passed on in his course as an angel with winged feet might glide along the earth unimpeded by all those little obstacles over which we of earthly origin stumble. He was a believer in the divinity of genius and always opposed a stern disbelief to the objections of those petty cavillers and minor critics who wish to reduce all men to their own miserable level. 'I will make a scientific simile,' he would say, 'in the manner, if you will, of Dr Darwin[38] – I consider the alleged errors of a man of genius as the aberrations of the fixed stars. It is our distance from them and our imperfect means of communication that makes them appear to move; in truth they always remain stationary, a glorious centre, giving us a fine lesson of modesty if we would thus receive it.'

I have said that he was a poet: when he was three and twenty years of age he first published a poem, and it was hailed by the whole nation with enthusiasm and delight. His good star perpetually shone upon him; a reputation had never before been made so rapidly; it was universal. The multitude extolled the same poems that formed the wonder of the sage in his closet: there was not one dissentient voice.

It was at this time, in the height of his glory, that he became acquainted with Elinor. She was a young heiress of exquisite beauty who lived under the care of her guardian; from the moment they were seen together they appeared formed for each other. Elinor had not the genius of Woodville but she was generous and noble, and exalted by her youth and the love that she everywhere excited above the knowledge of aught but virtue and excellence. She was lovely; her manners were frank and simple; her deep blue eyes swam in a lustre which could only be given by sensibility joined to wisdom.

They were formed for one another and they soon loved. Woodville for the first time felt the delight of love; and Elinor was enraptured in possessing the heart of one so beautiful and glorious among his fellow men. Could anything but unmixed joy flow from such a union?

Woodville was a poet – he was sought for by every society and all eyes were turned on him alone when he appeared; but he was the son of a poor clergyman and Elinor was a rich heiress. Her guardian was not displeased with their mutual affection: the merit of Woodville was too eminent to admit of cavil on account of his inferior wealth; but the dying will of her father did not allow her to marry before she was of age and her fortune depended upon her obeying this injunction. She had just entered her twentieth year, and she and her lover were obliged to submit to this delay. But they were ever together and their happiness seemed that of paradise: they studied together, formed plans of future occupations, and drinking in love and joy from each other's eyes and words they hardly repined at the delay to their entire union. Woodville for ever rose in glory; and Elinor become more lovely and wise under the lessons of her accomplished lover.

In two months Elinor would be twenty-one; everything was prepared for their union. How shall I relate the catastrophe to so much joy? But the earth would not be the earth it is covered with blight and sorrow if one such pair as these angelic creatures had been suffered to exist for one another; search through the world and you will not find the perfect happiness which their marriage would have caused them to enjoy; there must have been a revolution in the order of things as established among us miserable earth-dwellers to have admitted of such consummate joy. The chain of necessity ever bringing misery must have been broken and the malignant fate that presides over it would not permit this breach of her eternal laws. But why should I repine at this? Misery was my element, and nothing but what was miserable could approach me; if Woodville had been happy I should never have known him. And can I who for many years was fed by tears, and nourished under the dew of grief, can I pause to relate a tale of woe and death?

Woodville was obliged to make a journey into the country and was detained from day to day in irksome absence from his lovely bride. He received a letter from her to say that she was slightly ill, but telling him to hasten to her, that from his eyes she would receive health and that his company would be her surest medicine. He was detained three days longer and then he hastened to her. His heart, he knew not why prognosticated misfortune; he had not heard from her again; he feared she might be worse and this fear made him impatient and restless for the moment of beholding her once more stand before him arrayed in health and beauty; for a sinister voice seemed always to whisper to him, 'You will never more behold her as she was.'

When he arrived at her habitation all was silent in it; he made his way through several rooms; in one he saw a servant weeping bitterly: he was faint with fear and could hardly ask, 'Is she dead?' and just listened to the dreadful answer, 'Not yet.' These astounding words came on him as of less fearful import than those which he had expected; and to learn that she was still in being and that he might still hope was an alleviation to him. He remembered the words of her letter and he indulged the wild idea that his kisses breathing warm love and life would infuse new spirit into her, and that with him near her she could not die; that his presence was the talisman of her life.

He hastened to her sickroom; she lay, her cheeks burning with fever, yet her eyes were closed and she was seemingly senseless. He wrapped her in his arms; he imprinted breathless kisses on her burning lips; he called to her in a voice of subdued anguish by the tenderest names: 'Return, Elinor; I am with you; your life, your love. Return, dearest one, you promised me this boon, that I should bring you health. Let your sweet spirit revive; you cannot die near me: What is death? To see you no more? To part with what is a part of myself; without whom I have no memory and no futurity? Elinor die! This is frenzy and the most miserable despair: you cannot die while I am near.'

And again he kissed her eyes and lips, and hung over her inanimate form in agony, gazing on her countenance still lovely although changed, watching every slight convulsion and varying colour which denoted life still lingering although about to depart. Once for a moment she revived and recognised his voice; a smile, a last lovely smile, played upon her lips. He watched beside her for twelve hours and then she died.

CHAPTER 10

It was six months after this miserable conclusion to his long nursed hopes that I first saw him. He had retired to a part of the country where he was not known that he might peacefully indulge his grief. All the world, by the death of his beloved Elinor, was changed to him, and he could no longer remain in any spot where he had seen her or where her image mingled with the most rapturous hopes had brightened all around with a light of joy which would now be transformed to a darkness blacker than midnight since she, the sun of his life, was set for ever.

He lived for some time never looking on the light of heaven but shrouding his eyes in a perpetual darkness far from all that could remind him of what he had been; but as time softened his grief, like a true child of nature he sought in the enjoyment of her beauties for a consolation in his unhappiness. He came to a part of the country where he was entirely unknown and where in the deepest solitude he could converse only with his own heart. He found a relief to his impatient grief in the breezes of heaven and in the sound of waters and woods. He became fond of riding; this exercise distracted his mind and elevated his spirits; on a swift horse he could for a moment gain respite from the image that else for ever followed him: Elinor on her deathbed, her sweet features changed, and the soft spirit that animated her gradually waning into extinction. For many months Woodville had in vain endeavoured to cast off this terrible remembrance; it still hung on him until memory was too great a burthen for his loaded soul, but when on horseback the spell that seemingly held him to this idea was snapped; then if he thought of his lost bride he pictured her radiant in beauty; he could hear her voice, and fancy her 'a sylvan huntress by his side',[39] while his eyes brightened as he thought he gazed on her cherished form. I had several times seen him ride across the heath and felt angry that my solitude should be disturbed. It was so long since I had spoken to any but peasants that I felt a disagreeable sensation at being gazed on by one of superior rank. I feared also that it might be someone who had seen me before: I might be recognised, my impostures discovered and I dragged back to a life of worse torture than that I had before endured. These were dreadful fears and they even haunted my dreams.

I was one day seated on the verge of the clump of pines when Woodville rode past. As soon as I perceived him I suddenly rose to escape from his observation by entering among the trees. My rising startled his horse; he reared and plunged and the rider was at length thrown. The horse then galloped swiftly across the heath and the stranger remained on the ground stunned by his fall. He was not materially hurt, a little fresh water soon recovered him. I was struck by his exceeding beauty, and as he spoke to thank me the sweet but melancholy cadence of his voice brought tears into my eyes.

A short conversation passed between us, but the next day he again stopped at my cottage and by degrees an intimacy grew between us. It was strange to him to see a female in extreme youth, I was not yet twenty, evidently belonging to the first classes of society and possessing every accomplishment an excellent education could bestow, living alone on a desolate heath – one on whose forehead the impress of grief was strongly marked, and whose words and motions betrayed that her thoughts did not follow them but were intent on far other ideas; bitter and overwhelming miseries. I was dressed also in a whimsical nunlike habit which denoted that I did not retire to solitude from necessity, but that I might indulge in a luxury of grief and fanciful seclusion.

He soon took great interest in me, and sometimes forgot his own grief to sit beside me and endeavour to cheer me. He could not fail to interest even one who had shut herself from the whole world, whose hope was death, and who lived only with the departed. His personal beauty; his conversation which glowed with imagination and sensibility; the poetry that seemed to hang upon his lips and to make the very air mute to listen to him were charms that no one could resist. He was younger, less worn, more passionless than my father and in no degree reminded me of him: he suffered under immediate grief yet its gentle influence instead of calling feelings otherwise dormant into action, seemed only to veil that which otherwise would have been too dazzling for me. When we were together I spoke little yet my selfish mind was sometimes borne away by the rapid course of his ideas; I would lift my eyes with momentary brilliancy until memories that never died and seldom slept would recur, and a tear would dim them.

Woodville forever tried to lead me to the contemplation of what is beautiful and happy in the world. His own mind was constitutionally bent to a former belief in good rather than in evil and this feeling which must even exhilarate the hopeless ever shone forth in his words. He would talk of the wonderful powers of man, of their present state and of their hopes; of what they had been and what they were, and when reason could no longer guide him, his imagination as if inspired shed light on the obscurity that veils the past and the future. He loved to dwell on what might have been the state of the earth before man lived on it, and how he first arose and gradually became the strange, complicated, but as he said, the glorious creature he now is. Covering the earth with their creations and forming by the power of their minds another world more lovely than the visible frame of things, even all the world that we find in their writings. A beautiful creation, he would say, which may claim this superiority to its model, that good and evil are more easily separated: the good rewarded in the way they themselves desire; the evil punished as all things evil ought to be punished, not by pain which is revolting to all philanthropy to consider but by quiet obscurity, which simply deprives them of their harmful qualities; why kill the serpent when you have extracted his fangs?

The poetry of his language and ideas which my words ill convey held me enchained to his discourses. It was a melancholy pleasure to me to listen to his inspired words; to catch for a moment the light of his eyes; to feel a transient sympathy and then to awaken from the delusion, again to know that all this was nothing – a dream – a shadow for which there was no reality for me; my father had for ever deserted me, leaving me only memories which set an eternal barrier between me and my fellow creatures. I was indeed fellow to none. He – Woodville, mourned the loss of his bride; others wept the various forms of misery as they visited them; but infamy and guilt were mingled with my portion; unlawful and detestable passion had poured its poison into my ears and changed all my blood, so that it was no longer the kindly stream that supports life but a cold fountain of bitterness corrupted in its very source. It must be the excess of madness that could make me imagine that I could ever be aught but one alone; struck off from humanity; bearing no affinity to man or woman; a wretch on whom nature had set her ban.

Sometimes Woodville talked to me of himself. He related his history brief in happiness and woe and dwelt with passion on his and Elinor's mutual love. 'She was,' he said, 'the brightest vision that ever came upon the earth: there was something in her frank countenance, in her voice, and in every motion of her graceful form that overpowered me, as if it were a celestial creature that deigned to mingle with me in intercourse more sweet than man had ever before enjoyed. Sorrow fled before her; and her smile seemed to possess an influence like light to irradiate all mental darkness. It was not like a human loveliness that these gentle smiles went and came, but as a sunbeam on a lake, now light and now obscure, flitting before as you strove to catch them, and fold them for ever to your heart. I saw this smile fade for ever. Alas! I could never have believed that it was indeed Elinor that died if once when I spoke she had not lifted her almost benighted eyes, and for one moment like nought beside on earth, more lovely than a sunbeam, slighter, quicker than the waving plumage of a bird, dazzling as lightning and like it giving day to night, yet mild and faint, that smile came; it went, and then there was an end of all joy to me.'

Thus his own sorrows, or the shapes copied from nature that dwelt in his mind with beauty greater than their own, occupied our talk while I railed in my own griefs with cautious secrecy. If for a moment he showed curiosity, my eyes fell, my voice died away and my evident suffering made him quickly endeavour to banish the ideas he had awakened; yet he forever mingled consolation in his talk, and tried to soften my despair by demonstrations of deep sympathy and compassion. 'We are both unhappy – ' he would say to me; 'I have told you my melancholy tale and we have wept together the loss of that lovely spirit that has so cruelly deserted me; but you hide your griefs. I do not ask you to disclose them, but tell me if I may not console you. It seems to me a wild adventure to find in this desert one like you quite solitary: you are young and lovely; your manners are refined and attractive; yet there is in your settled melancholy, and something, I know not what, in your expressive eyes that seems to separate you from your kind; you shudder; pardon me, I entreat you, but I cannot help expressing this once at least the lively interest I feel in your destiny.

'You never smile; your voice is low, and you utter your words as if you were afraid of the slight sound they would produce; the expression of awful and intense sorrow never for a moment fades from your countenance. I have lost for ever the loveliest companion that any man could ever have possessed, one who rather appears to have been a superior spirit who by some strange accident wandered among us earthly creatures than as belonging to our kind. Yet I smile, and sometimes I speak almost forgetful of the change I have endured. But your sad mien never alters; your pulses beat and you breathe, yet you seem already to belong to another world; and sometimes, pray pardon my wild thoughts, when you touch my hand I am surprised to find your hand warm when all the fire of life seems extinct within you.

'When I look upon you, the tears you shed, the soft deprecating look with which you withstand enquiry; the deep sympathy your voice expresses when I speak of my lesser sorrows add to my interest for you. You stand here shelterless. You have cast yourself from among us and you wither on this wild plain forlorn and helpless: some dreadful calamity must have befallen you. Do not turn from me; I do not ask you to reveal it; I only entreat you to listen to me and to become familiar with the voice of consolation and kindness. If pity, and admiration, and gentle affection can wean you from despair let me attempt the task. I cannot see your look of deep grief without endeavouring to restore you to happier feelings. Unbend your brow; relax the stern melancholy of your regard; permit a friend, a sincere, affectionate friend, I will be one, to convey some relief, some momentary pause to your sufferings.

'Do not think that I would intrude upon your confidence: I only ask your patience. Do not forever look sorrow and never speak it; utter one word of bitter complaint and I will reprove it with gentle exhortation and pour on you the balm of compassion. You must not shut me from all communion with you: do not tell me why you grieve but only say the words, 'I am unhappy,' and you will feel relieved as if for some time excluded from all intercourse by some magic spell you should suddenly enter again the pale of human sympathy. I entreat you to believe in my most sincere professions and to treat me as an old and tried friend; promise me never to forget me, never causelessly to banish me; but try to love me as one who would devote all his energies to make you happy. Give me the name of friend: I will fulfil its duties; and if for a moment complaint and sorrow would shape themselves into words let me be near to speak peace to your vexed soul.'

I repeat his persuasions in faint terms and cannot give you at the same time the tone and gesture that animated them. Like a refreshing shower on an arid soil they revived me, and although I still kept their cause secret he led me to pour forth my bitter complaints and to clothe my woe in words of gall and fire. With all the energy of desperate grief I told him how I had fallen at once from bliss to misery; how that for me there was no joy, no hope; that death however bitter would be the welcome seal to all my pangs; death the skeleton was to be beautiful as love. I know not why but I found it sweet to utter these words to human ears; and though I derided all consolation, yet I was pleased to see it offered me with gentleness and kindness. I listened quietly, and when he paused would again pour out my misery in expressions that showed how far too deep my wounds were for any cure.

But now also I began to reap the fruits of my perfect solitude. I had become unfit for any intercourse, even with Woodville the most gentle and sympathising creature that existed. I had become captious and unreasonable: my temper was utterly spoilt. I called him my friend but I viewed all he did with jealous eyes. If he did not visit me at the appointed hour I was angry, very angry, and told him that if indeed he did feel interest in me it was cold, and could not be fitted for me, a poor worn creature, whose deep unhappiness demanded much more than his worldly heart could give. When for a moment I imagined that his manner was cold I would fretfully say to him – 'I was at peace before you came; why have you disturbed me? You have given me new wants and now you trifle with me as if my heart were as whole as yours, as if I were not in truth a shorn lamb thrust out on the bleak hillside, tortured by every blast. I wished for no friend, no sympathy. I avoided you, you know I did, but you forced yourself upon me and gave me those wants which you see with triumph give you power over me. Oh, the brave power of the bitter north wind which freezes the tears it has caused to be shed! But I will not bear this; go! the sun will rise and set as before you came, and I shall sit among the pines or wander on the heath weeping and complaining without wishing for you to listen. You are cruel, very cruel, to treat me who bleed at every pore in this rough manner.'[40]

And then, when in answer to my peevish words, I saw his countenance bent with living pity on me, when I saw him

> Gli occhi drizzo ver me con quel sembiante
> Che madre fa sopra figlioul deliro,[41]

I wept and said, 'Oh, pardon me! You are good and kind but I am not fit for life. Why am I obliged to live? To drag hour after hour, to see the trees wave their branches restlessly, to feel the air, and to suffer in all I feel keenest agony. My frame is strong, but my soul sinks beneath this endurance of living anguish. Death is the goal that I would attain, but, alas! I do not even see the end of the course. Do you, my compassionate friend, tell me how to die peacefully and innocently and I will bless you: all that I, poor wretch, can desire is a painless death.'

But Woodville's words had magic in them, when beginning with the sweetest pity, he would raise me by degrees out of myself and my sorrows until I wondered at my own selfishness; but he left me and despair returned; the work of consolation was ever to begin anew. I often desired his entire absence; for I found that I was grown out of the ways of life and that by long seclusion, although I could support my accustomed grief, and drink the bitter daily draught with some degree of patience, yet I had become unfit for the slightest novelty of feeling. Expectation, and hopes, and affection were all too much for me. I knew this, but at other times I was unreasonable and laid the blame upon him, who was most blameless, and peevishly thought that if his gentle soul were more gentle, if his intense sympathy were more intense, he could drive the fiend from my soul and make me more human. I am, I thought, a tragedy; a character that he comes to see act; now and then he gives me my cue that I may make a speech more to his purpose: perhaps he is already planning a poem in which I am to figure. I am a farce and play to him, but to me this is all dreary reality; he takes all the profit and I bear all the burthen.

CHAPTER 11

It is a strange circumstance but it often occurs that blessings by their use turn to curses; and that I who in solitude had desired sympathy as the only relief I could enjoy should now find it an additional torture to me. During my father's lifetime I had always been of an affectionate and forbearing disposition, but since those days of joy alas! I was much changed. I had become arrogant, peevish, and above all suspicious. Although the real interest of my narration is now ended and I ought quickly to wind up its melancholy catastrophe, yet I will relate one instance of my sad suspicion and despair and how Woodville, with the goodness and almost the power of an angel, softened my rugged feelings and led me back to gentleness.

He had promised to spend some hours with me one afternoon but a violent and continual rain prevented him. I was alone the whole evening. I had passed two whole years alone unrepining, but now I was miserable. He could not really care for me, I thought, for if he did the storm would rather have made him come even if I had not expected him, than, as it did, prevent a promised visit. He would well know that this drear sky and gloomy rain would load my spirit almost to madness: if the weather had been fine I should not have regretted his absence as heavily as I necessarily must shut up in this miserable cottage with no companions but my own wretched thoughts. If he were truly my friend he would have calculated all this; and let me now calculate this boasted friendship, and discover its real worth. He got over his grief for Elinor, and the country became dull to him, so he was glad to find even me for amusement; and when he does not know what else to do he passes his lazy hours here, and calls this friendship. It is true that his presence is a consolation to me, and that his words are sweet, and when he will he can pour forth thoughts that win me from despair. His words are sweet – and so, truly, is the honey of the bee, but the bee has a sting, and unkindness is a worse smart than that received from an insect's venom. I will put him to the proof. He says all hope is dead to him, and I know that it is dead to me, so we are both equally fitted for death. Let me try if he will die with me; and as I fear to die alone, if he will accompany me to cheer me, then thus he can shew himself my friend in the only manner my misery will permit.

It was madness I believe, but I so worked myself up to this idea that I could think of nothing else. If he dies with me it is well, and there will be an end of two miserable beings; and if he will not, then will I scoff at his friendship and drink the poison before him to shame his cowardice. I planned the whole scene with an earnest heart and frantically set my soul on this project. I procured laudanum and placing it in two glasses on the table, filled my room with flowers and decorated the last scene of my tragedy with the nicest care. As the hour for his coming approached my heart softened and I wept; not that I gave up my plan, but even when resolved the mind must undergo several revolutions of feeling before it can drink its death.

Now all was ready and Woodville came. I received him at the door of my cottage and leading him solemnly into the room, I said: 'My friend, I wish to die. I am quite weary of enduring the misery which hourly I do endure, and I will throw it off. What slave will not, if he may, escape from his chains? Look, I weep; for more than two years I have never enjoyed one moment free from anguish. I have often desired to die; but I am a very coward. It is hard for one so young who was once so happy, as I was, voluntarily to divest themselves of all sensation and to go alone to the dreary grave; I dare not. I must die, yet my fear chills me; I pause and shudder and then for months I endure my excess of wretchedness. But now the time is come when I may quit life. I have a friend who will not refuse to accompany me in this dark journey; such is my request: earnestly do I entreat and implore you to die with me. Then we shall find Elinor and what I have lost. Look, I am prepared; there is the death draught, let us drink it together and willingly and joyfully quit this hated round of daily life.

'You turn from me; yet before you deny me reflect, Woodville, how sweet it were to cast off the load of tears and misery under which we now labour: and surely we shall find light after we have passed the dark valley. That drink will plunge us in a sweet slumber, and when we awaken what joy will be ours to find all our sorrows and fears past. *A little patience, and all will be over*;[42] aye, a very little patience; for, look, there is the key of our prison; we hold it in our own hands, and are we more debased than slaves to cast it away and give ourselves up to voluntary bondage? Even now if we had courage we might be free. Behold, my cheek is flushed with pleasure at the imagination of death; all that we love are dead. Come, give me your hand, one look of joyous sympathy and we will go together and seek them; a lulling journey;

where our arrival will bring bliss and our waking be that of angels. Do you delay? Are you a coward, Woodville? Oh fie! Cast off this blank look of human melancholy. Oh! that I had words to express the luxury of death that I might win you. I tell you we are no longer miserable mortals; we are about to become gods; spirits free and happy as gods. What fool on a bleak shore, seeing a flowery isle on the other side with his lost love beckoning to him from it, would pause because the wave is dark and turbid?

> What if some little payne the passage have
> That makes frayle flesh to fear the bitter wave?
> Is not short payne well borne that brings long ease,
> And lays the soul to sleep in quiet grave?[43]

'Do you mark my words; I have learned the language of despair: I have it all by heart, for I am Despair; and a strange being am I, joyous, triumphant Despair. But those words are false, for the wave may be dark but it is not bitter. We lie down, and close our eyes with a gentle good night, and when we wake, we are free. Come then, no more delay, thou tardy one! Behold the pleasant potion! Look, I am a spirit of good, and not a human maid that invites thee, and with winning accents (oh, that they would win thee!) says, "Come and drink." '

As I spoke I fixed my eyes upon his countenance, and his exquisite beauty, the heavenly compassion that beamed from his eyes, his gentle yet earnest look of deprecation and wonder even before he spoke wrought a change in my high-strained feelings, taking from me all the sternness of despair and filling me only with the softest grief. I saw his eyes humid also as he took both my hands in his; and sitting down near me, he said: 'This is a sad deed to which you would lead me, dearest friend, and your woe must indeed be deep that could fill you with these unhappy thoughts. You long for death and yet you fear it and wish me to be your companion. But I have less courage than you and even thus accompanied I dare not die. Listen to me, and then reflect if you ought to win me to your project, even if with the overbearing eloquence of despair you could make black death so inviting that the fair heaven should appear darkness. Listen I entreat you to the words of one who has himself nurtured desperate thoughts, and longed with impatient desire for death, but who has at length trampled the phantom under foot, and crushed his sting. Come, as you have played Despair with me I will play the part of Una with you and bring you hurtless from his dark cavern. Listen to me, and let yourself be softened by words in which no selfish passion lingers.

'We know not what all this wide world means; its strange mixture of good and evil. But we have been placed here and bid live and hope. I know not what we are to hope; but there is some good beyond us that we must seek; and that is our earthly task. If misfortune come against us we must fight with her; we must cast her aside, and still go on to find out that which it is our nature to desire. Whether this prospect of future good be the preparation for another existence I know not; or whether that it is merely that we, as workmen in God's vineyard, must lend a hand to smooth the way for our posterity. If it indeed be that; if the efforts of the virtuous now, are to make the future inhabitants of this fair world more happy; if the labours of those who cast aside selfishness, and try to know the truth of things, are to free the men of ages, now far distant but which will one day come, from the burthen under which those who now live groan, and like you weep bitterly; if they free them but from one of what are now the necessary evils of life, truly I will not fail but will with my whole soul aid the work. From my youth I have said I will be virtuous; I will dedicate my life for the good of others; I will do my best to extirpate evil and if the spirit who protects ill should so influence circumstances that I should suffer through my endeavour, yet while there is hope, and hope there ever must be, of success, cheerfully do I gird myself to my task.

'I have powers; my countrymen think well of them. Do you think I sow my seed in the barren air, and have no end in what I do? Believe me, I will never desert life until this last hope is torn from my bosom, that in some way my labours may form a link in the chain of gold with which we ought all to strive to drag Happiness from where she sits enthroned above the clouds, now far beyond our reach, to inhabit the earth with us. Let us suppose that Socrates, or Shakespeare, or Rousseau had been seized with despair and died in youth when they were as young as I am; do you think that we and all the world should not have lost incalculable improvement in our good feelings and our happiness through their destruction. I am not like one of these; they influenced millions: but if I can influence but a hundred, but ten, but one solitary individual, so as in any way to lead him from ill to good, that will be a joy to repay me for all my sufferings, though they were a million times multiplied; and that hope will support me to bear them.

'And those who do not work for posterity; or working, as may be my case, will not be known by it; yet they, believe me, have also their duties. You grieve because you are unhappy; it is happiness you seek but you despair of obtaining it. But if you can bestow happiness on another; if you can give one other person only one hour of joy ought you not to live to do it? And everyone has it in their power to do that. The inhabitants of this world suffer so much pain. In crowded cities, among cultivated plains or on the desert mountains, pain is thickly sown, and if we can tear up but one of these noxious weeds, or more, if in its stead we can sow one seed of corn, or plant one fair flower, let that be motive sufficient against suicide. Let us not desert our task while there is the slightest hope that we may in a future day do this.

'Indeed I dare not die. I have a mother whose support and hope I am. I have a friend who loves me as his life, and in whose breast I should infix a mortal sting if I ungratefully left him. So I will not die. Nor shall you, my friend; cheer up; cease to weep, I entreat you. Are you not young, and fair, and good? Why should you despair? Or if you must for yourself, why for others? If you can never be happy, can you never bestow happiness? Oh! believe me, if you beheld on lips pale with grief one smile of joy and gratitude, and knew that you were parent of that smile, and that without you it had never been, you would feel so pure and warm a happiness that you would wish to live for ever again and again to enjoy the same pleasure.

'Come, I see that you have already cast aside the sad thoughts you before frantically indulged. Look in that mirror; when I came your brow was contracted, your eyes deep sunk in your head, your lips quivering; your hands trembled violently when I took them; but now all is tranquil and soft. You are grieved and there is grief in the expression of your countenance but it is gentle and sweet. You allow me to throw away this cursed drink; you smile. Oh! Congratulate me, hope is triumphant, and I have done some good.'

These words are shadowy as I repeat them but they were indeed words of fire and produced a warm hope in me (I, miserable wretch, to hope!) that tingled like pleasure in my veins. He did not leave me for many hours; not until he had improved the spark that he had kindled, and with an angelic hand fostered the return of something that seemed like joy. He left me but I still was calm, and after I had saluted the starry sky and dewy earth with eyes of love and a contented good-night, I slept sweetly, visited by dreams, the first of pleasure I had had for many long months.

But this was only a momentary relief and my old habits of feeling returned; for I was doomed while in life to grieve, and to the natural sorrow of my father's death and its most terrific cause, imagination added a tenfold weight of woe. I believed myself to be polluted by the unnatural love I had inspired, and that I was a creature cursed and set apart by nature. I thought that like another Cain, I had a mark set on my forehead to show mankind that there was a barrier between me and them. Woodville had told me that there was in my countenance an expression as if I belonged to another world; so he had seen that sign: and there it lay a gloomy mark to tell the world that there was that within my soul that no silence could render sufficiently obscure. Why when Fate drove me to become this outcast from human feeling; this monster with whom none might mingle in converse and love; why had she not from that fatal and most accursed moment, shrouded me in thick mists and placed real darkness between me and my fellows so that I might never more be seen, and as I passed, like a murky cloud loaded with blight, they might only perceive me by the cold chill I should cast upon them; telling them, how truly, that something unholy was near? Then I should have lived upon this dreary heath unvisited, and blasting none by my unhallowed gaze. Alas! I verily believe that if the near prospect of death did not dull and soften my bitter feelings, if for a few months longer I had continued to live as I then lived, strong in body, but my soul corrupted to its core by a deadly cancer, if day after day I had dwelt on these dreadful sentiments, I should have become mad, and should have fancied myself a living pestilence: so horrible to my own solitary thoughts did this form, this voice, and all this wretched self appear; for had it not been the source of guilt that wants a name?

This was superstition. I did not feel thus frantically when first I knew that the holy name of father was become a curse to me; but my lonely life inspired me with wild thoughts; and then when I saw Woodville and day after day he tried to win my confidence and I never dared give words to my dark tale, I was impressed more strongly with the withering fear that I was in truth a marked creature, a pariah, only fit for death.

CHAPTER 12

As I was perpetually haunted by these ideas, you may imagine that the influence of Woodville's words was very temporary; and that although I did not again accuse him of unkindness, yet I soon became as unhappy as before. Soon after this incident we parted. He heard that his mother was ill, and he hastened to her. He came to take leave of me, and we walked together on the heath for the last time. He promised that he would come and see me again; and bade me take cheer, and to encourage what happy thoughts I could, until time and fortitude should overcome my misery, and I could again mingle in society.

'Above all other admonition on my part,' he said, 'cherish and follow this one: do not despair. That is the most dangerous gulf on which you perpetually totter; but you must reassure your steps, and take hope to guide you. Hope, and your wounds will be already half healed; but if you obstinately despair, there never more will be comfort for you. Believe me, my dearest friend, that there is a joy that the sun and earth and all its beauties can bestow that you will one day feel. The refreshing bliss of love will again visit your heart, and undo the spell that binds you to woe, until you wonder how your eyes could be closed in the long night that burthens you. I dare not hope that I have inspired you with sufficient interest that the thought of me, and the affection that I shall ever bear you, will soften your melancholy and decrease the bitterness of your tears. But if my friendship can make you look on life with less disgust, beware how you injure it with suspicion. Love is a delicate sprite and easily hurt by rough jealousy. Guard, I entreat you, a firm persuasion of my sincerity in the inmost recesses of your heart out of the reach of the casual winds that may disturb its surface. Your temper is made unequal by suffering, and the tenor of your mind is, I fear, sometimes shaken by unworthy causes; but let your confidence in my sympathy and love be deeper far, and incapable of being reached by these agitations that come and go, and if they touch not your affections leave you uninjured.'

These were some of Woodville's last lessons. I wept as I listened to him; and after we had taken an affectionate farewell, I followed him far with my eyes until they saw the last of my earthly comforter. I had insisted on accompanying him across the heath towards the town where he dwelt: the sun was yet high when he left me, and I turned my steps towards my cottage. It was at the latter end of the month of September when the nights have become chill. But the weather was serene, and as I walked on I fell into no unpleasing reveries. I thought of Woodville with gratitude and kindness and did not, I know not why, regret his departure with any bitterness. It seemed that after one great shock all other change was trivial to me; and I walked on wondering when the time would come when we should all four, my dearest father restored to me, meet in some sweet paradise. I pictured to myself a lovely river such as that on whose banks Dante describes Matilda gathering flowers, which ever flows

> . . . bruna, bruna,
> Sotto l'ombra perpetua, che mai
> Raggiar non lascia sole ivi, nè Luna.[44]

And then I repeated to myself all that lovely passage that relates the entrance of Dante into the terrestrial Paradise; and thought it would be sweet when I wandered on those lovely banks to see the car of light descend with my long lost parent to be restored to me. As I waited there in expectation of that moment, I thought how, of the lovely flowers that grew there, I would wind myself a chaplet and crown myself for joy: I would sing *sul margine d'un rio*,[45] my father's favourite song, and that my voice gliding through the windless air would announce to him in whatever bower he sat expecting the moment of our union, that his daughter was come. Then the mark of misery would have faded from my brow, and I should raise my eyes fearlessly to meet his, which ever beamed with the soft lustre of innocent love. When I reflected on the magic look of those deep eyes I wept, but gently, lest my sobs should disturb the fairy scene.

I was so entirely wrapped in this reverie that I wandered on, taking no heed of my steps until I actually stooped down to gather a flower for my wreath on that bleak plain where no flower grew,[46] when I awoke from my daydream and found myself I knew not where.

The sun had set and the roseate hue which the clouds had caught from him in his descent had nearly died away. A wind swept across the plain. I looked around me and saw no object that told me where I was; I had lost myself, and in vain attempted to find my path. I wandered on, and the coming darkness made every trace indistinct by which I might be guided. At length all was veiled in the deep obscurity of blackest night; I became weary and knowing that my servant was to sleep that night at the neighbouring village, so that my absence would alarm no one, and that I was safe in this wild spot from every intruder, I resolved to spend the night where I was. Indeed I was too weary to walk farther; the air was chill but I was careless of bodily inconvenience, and I thought that I was well inured to the weather during my two years of solitude, when no change of seasons prevented my perpetual wanderings.

I lay upon the grass surrounded by a darkness which not the slightest beam of light penetrated – There was no sound for the deep night had laid to sleep the insects, the only creatures that lived on the lone spot where no tree or shrub could afford shelter to aught else – There was a wondrous silence in the air that calmed my senses yet which enlivened my soul; my mind hurried from image to image and seemed to grasp an eternity. All in my heart was shadowy yet calm, until my ideas became confused and at length died away in sleep.

When I awoke it rained: I was already quite wet, and my limbs were stiff and my head giddy with the chill of night. It was a drizzling, penetrating shower; as my dank hair clung to my neck and partly covered my face, I had hardly strength to part with my fingers the long straight locks that fell before my eyes. The darkness was much dissipated and in the east where the clouds were least dense the moon was visible behind the thin grey cloud:

> The moon is behind, and at the full,
> and yet she looks both small and dull.[47]

Its presence gave me a hope that by its means I might find my home. But I was languid and many hours passed before I could reach the cottage, dragging as I did my slow steps, and often resting on the wet earth unable to proceed.

I particularly mark this night, for it was that which has hurried on the last scene of my tragedy, which else might have dwindled on through long years of listless sorrow. I was very ill when I arrived and quite incapable of taking off my wet clothes that clung about me. In the morning, on her return, my servant found me almost lifeless: possessed by a high fever I was lying on the floor of my room.

I was very ill for a long time, and when I recovered from the immediate danger of fever, every symptom of a rapid consumption declared itself. I was for some time ignorant of this and thought that my excessive weakness was the consequence of the fever. But my strength became less and less; as winter came on I had a cough; and my sunken cheek, before pale, burned with a hectic fever. One by one these symptoms struck me, and I became convinced that the moment I had so much desired was about to arrive and that I was dying. I was sitting by my fire, the physician who had attended me ever since my fever had just left me, and I looked over his prescription in which digitalis was the prominent medicine. 'Yes,' I said, 'I see how this is, and it is strange that I should have deceived myself so long; I am about to die an innocent death, and it will be sweeter even than that which the opium promised.'

I rose and walked slowly to the window; the wide heath was covered by snow which sparkled under the beams of the sun that shone brightly through the pure, frosty air; a few birds were pecking some crumbs under my window. I smiled with quiet joy; and in my thoughts, which through long habit would forever connect themselves into one train, as if I shaped them into words, I thus addressed the scene before me:

'I salute thee, beautiful Sun, and thou, white Earth, fair and cold! Perhaps I shall never see thee again covered with green, and the sweet flowers of the coming spring will blossom on my grave. I am about to leave thee; soon this living spirit which is ever busy among strange shapes and ideas, which belong not to thee, soon it will have flown to other regions and this emaciated body will rest insensate on thy bosom

> Rolled round in earth's diurnal course
> with rocks, and stones, and trees.[48]

'For it will be the same with thee, who art called our Universal Mother, when I am gone. I have loved thee; and in my days both of happiness and sorrow I have peopled your solitudes with wild fancies of my own creation. The woods, and lakes, and mountains which I have loved, have for me a thousand associations; and thou, O Sun! hast smiled upon and borne your part in many imaginations that sprang to life in my soul alone, and which will die with me. Your solitudes, sweet land, your trees and waters will still exist, moved by your winds, or still beneath the eye of noon, though what I have felt about ye, and all my dreams which have often strangely deformed thee, will die with me. You will exist to reflect other images in other minds, and ever will remain the same, although your reflected semblance vary in a thousand ways, changeable as the hearts of those who view thee. One of these fragile mirrors, that ever doted on thine image, is about to be broken, crumbled to dust. But ever teeming nature will create another and another, and thou wilt lose nought by my destruction.

'Thou wilt ever be the same. Receive then the grateful farewell of a fleeting shadow who is about to disappear, who joyfully leaves thee, yet with a last look of affectionate thankfulness. Farewell! Sky and fields and woods; the lovely flowers that grow on thee; thy mountains and thy rivers; to the balmy air and the strong wind of the north, to all, a last farewell. I shall shed no more tears for my task is almost fulfilled, and I am about to be rewarded for long and most burthensome suffering. Bless thy child even in death, as I bless thee; and let me sleep at peace in my quiet grave.'

I feel death to be near at hand and I am calm. I no longer despair, but look on all around me with placid affection. I find it sweet to watch the progressive decay of my strength, and to repeat to myself, another day and yet another, but again I shall not see the red leaves of autumn; before that time I shall be with my father. I am glad Woodville is not with me for perhaps he would grieve, and I desire to see smiles alone during the last scene of my life; when I last wrote to him I told him of my ill health but not of its mortal tendency, lest he should conceive it to be his duty to come to me for I fear lest the tears of friendship should destroy the blessed calm of my mind. I take pleasure in arranging all the little details which will occur when I shall no longer be. In truth I am in love with death; no maiden ever took more pleasure in the contemplation of her bridal attire than I in fancying my limbs already enwrapped in their shroud: is it not my marriage dress? Alone it will unite me to my father when in an eternal mental union we shall never part.

I will not dwell on the last changes that I feel in the final decay of nature. It is rapid but without pain; I feel a strange pleasure in it. For long years these are the first days of peace that have visited me. I no longer exhaust my miserable heart by bitter tears and frantic complaints; I no longer reproach the sun, the earth, the air, for pain and wretchedness. I wait in quiet expectation for the closing hours of a life which has been to me most sweet and bitter. I do not die not having enjoyed life: for sixteen years I was happy; during the first months of my father's return I enjoyed ages of pleasure; now indeed I am grown old in grief; my steps are feeble like those of age; I have become peevish and unfit for life; so having passed little more than twenty years upon the earth I am more fit for my narrow grave than many are when they reach the natural term of their lives.

Again and again I have passed over in my remembrance the different scenes of my short life: if the world is a stage and I merely an actor on it my part has been strange, and, alas! tragical. Almost from infancy I was deprived of all the testimonies of affection which children generally receive; I was thrown entirely upon my own resources, and I enjoyed what I may almost call unnatural pleasures, for they were dreams and not realities. The earth was to me a magic lantern[49] and I a gazer, and a listener but no actor; but then came the transporting and soul-reviving era of my existence: my father returned and I could pour my warm affections on a human heart; there was a new sun and a new earth created to me; the waters of existence sparkled: joy! joy! but, alas! what grief! My bliss was more rapid than the progress of a sunbeam on a mountain, which discloses its glades and woods, and then leaves it dark and blank; to my happiness followed madness and agony, closed by despair.

This was the drama of my life which I have now depicted upon paper. During three months I have been employed in this task. The memory of sorrow has brought tears; the memory of happiness a warm glow the lively shadow of that joy. Now my tears are dried; the glow has faded from my cheeks, and with a few words of farewell to you, Woodville, I close my work: the last that I shall perform.

Farewell, my only living friend; you are the sole tie that binds me to existence, and now I break it. It gives me no pain to leave you; nor can our separation give you much. You never regarded me as one of this world, but rather as a being who for some penance was sent from the Kingdom of Shadows; and she passed a few days weeping on the earth and longing to return to her native soil.[50] You will weep but they will be tears of gentleness. I would, if I thought that it would lessen your regret, tell you to smile and congratulate me on my departure from the misery you beheld me endure. I would say: Woodville, rejoice with your friend. I triumph now and am most happy. But I check these expressions; these may not be the consolations of the living; they weep for their own misery, and not for that of the being they have lost. No; shed a few natural tears due to my memory, and if you ever visit my grave, pluck from thence a flower, and lay it to your heart; for your heart is the only tomb in which my memory will be interred.

My death is rapidly approaching and you are not near to watch the flitting and vanishing of my spirit. Do not regret this; for death is too terrible an object for the living. It is one of those adversities which hurt instead of purifying the heart; for it is so intense a misery that it hardens and dulls the feelings. Dreadful as the time was when I pursued my father towards the ocean, and found there only his lifeless corpse; yet for my own sake I should prefer that to the watching one by one his senses fade; his pulse weaken – and sleeplessly as it were devour his life in gazing. To see life in his limbs and to know that soon life would no longer be there; to see the warm breath issue from his lips and to know they would soon be chill – I will not continue to trace this frightful picture; you suffered this torture once; I never did. And the remembrance fills your heart sometimes with bitter despair when otherwise your feelings would have melted into soft sorrow.

So day by day I become weaker, and life flickers in my wasting form, as a lamp about to loose it vivifying oil. I now behold the glad sun of May. It was May, four years ago, that I first saw my beloved father; it was in May, three years ago that my folly destroyed the only being I was doomed to love. May is returned, and I die. Three days ago, the anniversary of our meeting; and, alas! of our eternal separation, after a day of killing emotion, I caused myself to be led once more to behold the face of nature. I caused myself to be carried to some meadows some miles distant from my cottage; the grass was being mowed, and there was the scent of hay in the fields; all the earth looked fresh and its inhabitants happy. Evening approached and I beheld the sun set. Three years ago and on that day and hour it shone through the branches and leaves of the beech wood and its beams flickered upon the countenance of him whom I then beheld for the last time. I now saw that divine orb, gilding all the clouds with unwonted splendour, sink behind the horizon; it disappeared from a world where he whom I would seek exists not; it approached a world where he exists not. Why do I weep so bitterly? Why does my heart heave with vain endeavour to cast aside the bitter anguish that covers it 'as the waters cover the sea'.[51] I go from this world where he is no longer and soon I shall meet him in another.

Farewell, Woodville, the turf will soon be green on my grave; and the violets will bloom on it. *There* is my hope and my expectation; yours are in this world; may they be fulfilled.

A Tale of the Passions

or, The Death of Despina

AFTER the death of Manfred, King of Naples, the Ghibellines lost their ascendency throughout Italy. The exiled Guelphs returned to their native cities; and not contented with resuming the reins of government, they prosecuted their triumph until the Ghibellines in their turn were obliged to fly, and to mourn in banishment over the violent party spirit which had before occasioned their bloody victories, and now their irretrievable defeat. After an obstinate contest the Florentine Ghibellines were forced to quit their native town; their estates were confiscated; their attempts to reinstate themselves frustrated; and receding from castle to castle, they at length took refuge in Lucca, and awaited with impatience the arrival of Corradino[52] from Germany, through whose influence they hoped again to establish the imperial supremacy.

The first of May was ever a day of rejoicing and festivity at Florence. The youth of both sexes, of the highest rank, paraded the streets, crowned with flowers, and singing the *canzonets* of the day. In the evening they assembled in the Piazza del Duomo,[53] and spent the hours in dancing. The Carroccio[54] was led through the principal streets, the ringing of its bell drowned in the peals that rang from every belfry in the city, and in the music of fifes and drums which made a part of the procession that followed it. The triumph of the reigning party in Florence caused them to celebrate the anniversary of the first of May, 1268,[55] with peculiar splendour. They had indeed hoped that Charles d'Anjou, King of Naples, the head of the Guelphs in Italy, and then Vicare[56] of their republic, would have been there to adorn the festival by his presence. But the expectation of Corradino had caused the greater part of his newly conquered and oppressed kingdom to revolt, and he had hastily quitted Tuscany to secure by his presence those conquests of which his avarice and cruelty endangered the loss. But although Charles somewhat feared the approaching contest with Corradino, the

Florentine Guelphs, newly reinstated in their city and possessions, did not permit a fear to cloud their triumph. The principal families vied with each other in the display of their magnificence during the festival. The knights followed the Carroccio on horseback, and the windows were filled with ladies who leant upon gold-inwoven carpets, while their own dresses, at once simple and elegant, their only ornaments flowers, contrasted with the glittering tapestry and the brilliant colours of the flags of the various communities. The whole population of Florence poured into the principal streets, and none were left at home, except the decrepit and sick, unless it were some discontented Ghibelline, whose fear, poverty or avarice had caused him to conceal his party when it had been banished from the city.

It was not the feeling of discontent which prevented Monna Gegia de' Becari from being among the first of the revellers; and she looked angrily on what she called her 'Ghibelline leg', which fixed her to her chair on such a day of triumph. The sun shone in all its glory in an unclouded sky, and caused the fair Florentines to draw their *fazioles*[57] over their dark eyes, and to bereave the youth of those beams more vivifying than the sun's rays. The same sun poured its full light into the lonely apartment of Monna Gegia, and almost extinguished the fire which was lighted in the middle of the room, over which hung the pot of *minestra*,[58] the dinner of the dame and her husband. But she had deserted the fire and was seated by her window, holding her beads in her hand, while every now and then she peeped from her lattice (five storeys high) into the narrow lane below – but no creature passed. She looked at the opposite window; a cat slept there beside a pot of helio-trope, but no human being was heard or seen – they had all gone to the Piazza del Duomo.[59]

Monna Gegia was an old woman, and her dress of green *coloratio*[60] showed that she belonged to one of the Arti Minori.[61] Her head was covered by a red kerchief, which, folded triangularly, hung loosely over it; her grey hairs were combed back from her high and wrinkled brow. The quickness of her eye spoke the activity of her mind, and the slight irritability that lingered about the corners of her lips might be occasioned by the continual war maintained between her bodily and mental faculties.

'Now, by St John!' she said, 'I would give my gold cross to make one of them; though by giving that I should appear on a *festa*[62] without that which no *festa* yet ever found me wanting.'

And as she spoke she looked with great complacency on a large but thin gold cross which was tied round her withered neck by a ribbon, once black, now of a rusty brown.

'Methinks this leg of mine is bewitched; and it may well be that my Ghibelline husband has used the black art to hinder me from following the Carroccio with the best of them.' A slight sound as of footsteps in the street far below interrupted the good woman's soliloquy. 'Perhaps it is Monna Lisabetta, or Messer Giani dei Agli, the weaver, who mounted the breach first when the castle of Pagibonzi was taken.'[63]

She looked down, but could see no one, and was about to relapse into her old train of thoughts, when her attention was again attracted by the sound of steps ascending the stairs: they were slow and heavy, but she did not doubt who her visitant was when a key was applied to the hole of the door; the latch was lifted up, and a moment after, with an unassured mien and downcast eyes, her husband entered.

He was a short stunted man, more than sixty years of age; his shoulders were broad and high; his legs short; his lank hair, though it grew now only on the back of his head, was still coal-black; his brows were overhanging and bushy; his eyes black and quick; his complexion dark and weather-beaten; his lips as it were contradicted the sternness of the upper part of his face, for their gentle curve betokened even delicacy of sentiment, and his smile was inexpressibly sweet, although a short, bushy, grey beard somewhat spoiled the expression of his countenance. His dress consisted of leather trousers and a kind of short, coarse, cloth tunic, confined at the waist by a leathern girdle. He had on a low-crowned, red cloth cap, which he drew over his eyes, and seating himself on a low bench by the fire, he heaved a deep sigh. He appeared disinclined to enter into any conversation, but Monna Gegia, looking on him with a smile of ineffable contempt, was resolved that he should not enjoy his melancholy mood uninterrupted.

'Have you been to mass, Cincolo?' she asked; beginning with a question sufficiently removed from the point she longed to approach.

He shrugged his shoulders uneasily, but did not reply.

'You are too early for your dinner,' continued Gegia; 'Do you not go out again?'

Cincolo answered, 'No!' in an accent that denoted his disinclination to further questioning. But this very impatience only served to feed the spirit of contention that was fermenting in the bosom of Gegia.

'You are not used,' she said, 'to pass your May days under your chimney.'

No answer.

'Well,' she continued, 'if you will not speak, I have done!' meaning that she intended to begin, 'but by that lengthened face of thine I see that some good news is stirring abroad, and I bless the Virgin for it, whatever it may be. Come, if thou be not too cursed, tell me what happy tidings make thee so woebegone.'

Cincolo remained silent for awhile, then turning half round but not looking at his wife, he replied, 'What if old Marzio the lion[64] be dead?'

Gegia turned pale at the idea, but a smile that lurked in the good-natured mouth of her husband reassured her. 'Nay, St John defend us!' she began; 'but that is not true. Old Marzio's death would not drive you within these four walls, except it were to triumph over your old wife. By the blessing of St John, not one of our lions has died since the eve of the battle of Monte Aperto;[65] and I doubt not that they were poisoned; for Mari, who fed them that night, was more than half a Ghibelline in his heart. Besides, the bells are still ringing, and the drums still beating, and all would be silent enough if old Marzio were to die. On the first of May too! Santa Reparata is too good to us to allow such ill luck; and she has more favour, I trust, in the seventh heaven than all the Ghibelline saints in your calendar. No, good Cincolo, Marzio is not dead, nor the Holy Father, nor Messer Carlo of Naples; but I would bet my gold cross against the wealth of your banished men that Pisa is taken – or Corradino – or – '

'And I here! No, Gegia, old as I am, and much as you need my help (and that last is why I am here at all), Pisa would not be taken while this old body could stand in the breach; or Corradino die, till this lazy blood were colder on the ground than it is in my body. Ask no more questions, and do not rouse me; there is no news, no good or ill luck, that I know. But when I saw the Neri, the Pulci, the Buondelmonti, and the rest of them, ride like kings through the streets, whose very hands are hardly dry from the blood of my kindred; when I saw their daughter crowned with flowers, and thought how the daughter of Arrigo dei Elisei was mourning for her murdered father, with ashes on her head, by the hearth of a stranger – my spirit must be more dead than it is if such a sight did not make me wish to drive among them; and methought I could scatter their pomp with my awl for a sword. But I remembered thee, and am here unstained with blood.'

'That thou wilt never be!' cried Monna Gegia, the colour rising in her wrinkled cheeks: – 'Since the battle of Monte Aperto, thou hast never been well washed of that shed by thee and thy confederates; and how could ye? for the Arno has never since run clear of the blood then spilt.'

'And if the sea were red with that blood, still while there is any of the Guelphs' to spill, I am ready to spill it, were it not for thee. Thou dost well to mention Monte Aperto, and thou wouldst do better to remember over whom its grass now grows.'

'Peace, Cincolo; a mother's heart has more memory in it than thou thinkest; and I well recollect who spurned me as I knelt, and dragged my only child, but sixteen years of age, to die in the cause of that misbeliever Manfred. Let us indeed speak no more. Woe was the day when I married thee! but those were happy times when there was neither Guelph nor Ghibelline – they will never return.'

'Never – until, as thou sayest, the Arno run clear of the blood shed on its banks; never while I can pierce the heart of a Guelph; never till both parties are cold under one bier.'

'And thou and I, Cincolo?'

'Are two old fools, and shall be more at peace under ground than above it. Rank Guelph as thou art, I married thee before I was a Ghibelline; so now I must eat from the same platter with the enemy of Manfred, and make shoes for Guelphs, instead of following the fortunes of Corradino, and sending them, my battleaxe in my hand, to buy their shoes in Bologna.'

'Hush! hush! good man, talk not so loud of thy party; hearest thou not that someone knocks?'

Cincolo went to open the door with the air of a man who thinks himself ill used at being interrupted in his discourse, and is disposed to be angry with the intruder, however innocent he might be of any intention of breaking in upon his eloquent complaint. The appearance of his visitor calmed his indignant feelings. He was a youth whose countenance and person showed that he could not be more than sixteen, but there was a self-possession in his demeanour and a dignity in his physiognomy that belonged to a more advanced age. His figure though not tall was slight; and his countenance though of wonderful beauty and regularity of feature, was pale as monumental marble; the thick and curling locks of his chestnut hair clustered over his brow and round his fair throat; his cap was drawn far down on his forehead. Cincolo was about to usher him with deference into his humble room, but the youth stayed him with his hand, and uttered the words, 'Swabia, Cavalieri!' the words by which the Ghibellines were accustomed to recognise each other. He continued in a low and hurried tone: 'Your wife is within?'

'She is.'

'Enough; although I am a stranger to you, I come from an old friend. Harbour me until nightfall; we will then go out, and I will explain to you the motives of my intrusion. Call me Ricciardo de' Rossini of Milan, travelling to Rome. I leave Florence this evening.'

Having said these words, without giving Cincolo time to reply, he motioned that they should enter the room. Monna Gegia had fixed her eyes on the door from the moment he had opened it with a look of impatient curiosity; when she saw the youth enter she could not refrain from exclaiming, 'Gesu Maria!' – so different was he from anyone she had expected to see.

'A friend from Milan,' said Cincolo.

'More likely from Lucca,' replied his wife, gazing on her visitant. 'You are doubtless one of the banished men, and you are more daring than wise to enter this town: however, if you be not a spy, you are safe with me.'

Ricciardo smiled and thanked her in a low, sweet voice. 'If you do not turn me out,' he said, 'I shall remain under your roof nearly all the time I remain in Florence, and I leave it soon after dusk.'

Gegia again gazed on her guest, nor did Cincolo scrutinise him with less curiosity. His black cloth tunic reached below his knees and was confined by a black leather girdle at the waist. He had on trousers of coarse scarlet stuff, over which were drawn short boots, such as are now seen on the stage only; a cloak of common fox's fur, unlined, hung from his shoulder. But although his dress was thus simple, it was such as was then worn by the young Florentine nobility. At that time the Italians were simple in their private habits; the French army led by Charles d'Anjou into Italy first introduced luxury into the palaces of the Cis-alpines.[66] Manfred was a magnificent prince, but it was his saintly rival who was the author of that trifling foppery of dress and ornaments, which degrades a nation, and is a sure precursor of their downfall. But of Ricciardo – his countenance had all the regularity of a Grecian head; and his blue eyes, shaded by very long, dark eyelashes, were soft, yet full of expression: when he looked up, the heavy lids, as it were, unveiled the gentle light beneath, and then again closed over them, as shading what was too brilliant to behold. His lips expressed the deepest sensibility, and something perhaps of timidity, had not the placid confidence of his demeanour forbidden such an idea. His appearance was extraordinary, for he was young and delicate of frame, while the decision of his manner prevented the feeling of pity from arising in the spectator's mind: you might love him, but he rose above compassion.

His host and hostess were at first silent; but he asked some natural questions about the buildings of their city, and by degrees led them into discourse. When midday struck, Cincolo looked towards his pot of *minestra*, and Ricciardo, following his look, asked if that was not the dinner. 'You must entertain me,' he said, 'for I have not eaten today.' A table was drawn near the window, and the *minestra* poured out into one plate was placed in the middle of it, a spoon was given to each, and a jug of wine filled from a barrel. Ricciardo looked at the two old people, and seemed somewhat to smile at the idea of eating from the same plate with them; he ate, however, though sparingly, and drank of the wine, though with still greater moderation. Cincolo, however, under pretence of serving his guest, filled his jug a second time, and was about to rise for the third measure, when Ricciardo, placing his small white hand on his arm, said, 'Are you a German, my friend, that you cease not after so many draughts? I have heard that you Florentines were a sober people.'

Cincolo was not much pleased with this reproof; but he felt that it was timely; so, conceding the point, he sat down again, and somewhat heated with what he had already drank, he asked his guest the news from Germany, and what hopes for the good cause? Monna Gegia bridled at these words, and Ricciardo replied, 'Many reports are abroad, and high hopes entertained, especially in the North of Italy, for the success of our expedition. Corradino is arrived at Genoa, and it is hoped that although the ranks of his army were much thinned by the desertion of his German troops they will be quickly filled by Italians, braver and truer than those foreigners, who, strangers to our soil, could not fight for his cause with our ardour.'

'And how does he bear himself?'

'As beseems one of the house of Swabia, and the nephew of Manfred. He is inexperienced and young, even to childishness. He is not more than sixteen. His mother would hardly consent to this expedition, but wept with agony at the fear of all he might endure: for he has been bred in a palace, nursed in every luxury, and habituated to all the flattering attentions of courtiers, and the tender care of a woman, who, although she be a princess, has waited on him with the anxious solicitude of a cottager for her infant. But Corradino is of good heart; docile, but courageous; obedient to his wiser friends, gentle to his inferiors, but noble of soul. The spirit of Manfred seems to animate his unfolding mind; and surely, if that glorious prince now enjoys the reward of his surpassing virtues, he looks down with joy and approbation on him who is, I trust, destined to fill his throne.'

The enthusiasm with which Ricciardo spoke suffused his pale countenance with a slight blush, while his eyes swam in the lustre of the dew that filled them. Monna Gegia was little pleased with his harangue, but curiosity kept her silent, while her husband proceeded to question his guest. 'You seem to be well acquainted with Corradino?'

'I saw him at Milan, and was closely connected with his most intimate friend there. As I have said, he has arrived at Genoa, and perhaps has even now landed at Pisa: he will find many friends in that town?' 'Every

man there will be his friend. But during his journey southward he will
have to contend with our Florentine army, commanded by the marshals
of the usurper Charles, and assisted by his troops. Charles himself has
left us, and is gone to Naples to prepare for this war. But he is detested
there, as a tyrant and a robber, and Corradino will be received in the
Regno as a saviour: so that if he once surmount the obstacles which
oppose his entrance, I do not doubt his success, and trust that he will be
crowned within a month at Rome, and the week after sit on the throne
of his ancestors in Naples.'

'And who will crown him?' cried Gegia, unable to contain herself:
'Italy contains no heretic base enough to do such a deed, unless it be
a Jew; or he send to Constantinople for a Greek, or to Egypt for a
Mahometan. Cursed may the race of the Frederics ever be! Thrice
cursed one who has affinity to that miscreant Manfred! And little do
you please me, young man, by holding such discourse in my house.'

Cincolo looked at Ricciardo, as if he feared that so violent a partisan
for the house of Swabia would be irritated at his wife's attack; but he was
looking on the aged woman with a regard of the most serene benignity;
no contempt even was mingled with the gentle smile that played round
his lips. 'I will restrain myself,' he said; and turning to Cincolo, he
conversed on more general subjects, describing the various cities of Italy
that he had visited; discussing their modes of government, and relating
anecdotes concerning their inhabitants, with an air of experience that,
contrasted with his youthful appearance, greatly impressed Cincolo, who
looked on him at once with admiration and respect. Evening came on.
The sound of bells died away after the *Ave Maria*[67] had ceased to ring;
but the distant sound of music was wafted to them by the night air, and
its quick time indicated that the music was already begun.

Ricciardo was about to address Cincolo, when a knocking at the gate
interrupted him. It was Buzeccha, the Saracen, a famous chess-player,
who was used to parade about under the colonnades of the Duomo,
and challenge the young nobles to play; and sometimes much stress
was laid on these games, and the gain and loss became the talk of
Florence. Buzeccha was a tall ungainly man, with all that good-natured
consequence of manner which the fame he had acquired by his pro-
ficiency in so trifling a science, and the familiarity with which he was
permitted to treat those superior to him in rank, who were pleased to
measure their forces with him, might well bestow. He was beginning
with, 'Eh, messere!' when perceiving Ricciardo, he cried, 'Who have
we here?'

'A friend to good men,' replied Ricciardo, smiling.

'Then, by Mahomet, thou art my friend, my stripling.'

'Thou shouldst be a Saracen, by thy speech?' said Ricciardo.

'And through the help of the Prophet, so am I. One who in Manfred's time – but no more of that. We won't talk of Manfred, eh, Monna Gegia? I am Buzeccha, the chess-player, at your service, Messer lo Forestiere.'

The introduction thus made, they began to talk of the procession of the day. After a while, Buzeccha introduced his favourite subject of chess playing; he recounted some wonderfully good strokes he had achieved, and related to Ricciardo how before the Palagio del Popolo,[68] in the presence of Count Guido Novello de' Giudi, then Vicare of the city, he had played an hour at three chessboards with three of the best chessplayers in Florence, playing two by memory, and one by sight; and out of three games which made the board, he had won two. This account was wound up by a proposal to play with his host. 'Thou art a hard-headed fellow, Cincolo, and make better play than the nobles. I would swear that thou thinkest of chess only as thou cobblest thy shoes; every hole of your awl is a square of the board, every stitch a move, and a finished pair, paid for, checkmate to your adversary; eh! Cincolo? Bring out the field of battle, man.'

Ricciardo interposed, 'I leave Florence in two hours, and before I go, Messer Cincolo promised to conduct me to the Piazza del Duomo.'

'Plenty of time, good youth,' cried Buzeccha, arranging his men; 'I only claim one game, and my games never last more than a quarter of an hour; and then we will both escort you, and you shall dance a set into the bargain with a black-eyed Houri, all Nazarene as thou art. So stand out of my light, good youth, and shut the window, if you have heeding, that the torch flare not so.'

Ricciardo seemed amused by the authoritative tone of the chess-player; he shut the window and trimmed the torch, which, stuck against the wall, was the only light they had, and stood by the table, overlooking the game. Monna Gegia had replaced the pot for supper, and sat some-what uneasily, as if she were displeased that her guest did not talk with her. Cincolo and Buzeccha were deeply intent on their game, when a knock was heard at the door. Cincolo was about to rise and open it, but Ricciardo saying, 'Do not disturb yourself,' opened it himself, with the manner of one who does humble offices as if ennobling them, so that no one action can be more humble to them than another.

The visitant was welcomed by Gegia alone, with, 'Ah! Messer Beppe, this is kind, on May Day night.'

Ricciardo glanced slightly on him, and then resumed his stand by the players. There was little in Messer Beppe to attract a favourable regard. He was short, thin and dry; his face long-drawn and liney; his eyes deep-set and scowling; his lips straight, his nose hooked, and his head covered by a close scullcap, his hair cut close all round. He sat down near Gegia, and began to discourse in a whining, servile voice, complimenting her on her good looks, launching forth into praise of the magnificence of certain Guelph Florentines, and concluded by declaring that he was hungry and tired.

'Hungry, Beppe?' said Gegia, 'that should have been your first word, friend. Cincolo, wilt thou give thy guest to eat? Cincolo, art thou deaf? Art thou blind? Dost thou not hear? Wilt thou not see? – Here is Messer Giuseppe de' Bosticchi.'

Cincolo slowly, his eyes still fixed on the board, was about to rise. But the name of the visitant seemed to have the effect of magic on Ricciardo. 'Bosticchi!' he cried – 'Giuseppe Bosticchi! I did not expect to find that man beneath thy roof, Cincolo, all Guelph as thy wife is – for she also has eaten of the bread of the Elisei. Farewell! thou wilt find me in the street below; follow me quickly.'

He was about to go, but Bosticchi placed himself before the door, saying in a tone whose whine expressed mingled rage and servility, 'In what have I offended this young gentleman? Will he not tell me my offence?'

'Dare not to stop my way,' cried Ricciardo, passing his hand before his eyes, 'nor force me again to look on thee – Begone!'

Cincolo stopped him: 'Thou art too hasty, and far too passionate, my noble guest,' said he: 'however this man may have offended thee, thou art too violent.'

'Violent!' cried Ricciardo, almost suffocated by passionate emotion – 'Aye, draw thy knife, and show the blood of Arrigo dei Elisei with which it is still stained.'

A dead silence followed. Bosticchi slunk out of the room; Ricciardo hid his face in his hands and wept. But soon he calmed his passion and said: 'This is indeed childish. Pardon me; that man is gone; excuse and forget my violence. Resume thy game, Cincolo, but conclude it quickly, for time gains on us – Hark! an hour of night sounds from the Campanile.'

'The game is already concluded,' said Buzeccha, sorrowfully, 'thy cloak overthrew the best checkmate this head ever planned – so God forgive thee!'

'Checkmate!' cried the indignant Cincolo, 'Checkmate! and my queen mowing you down, rank and file!'

'Let us begone,' exclaimed Ricciardo: 'Messer Buzeccha, you will play out your game with Monna Gegia. Cincolo will return ere long.' So taking his host by the arm, he drew him out of the room, and descended the narrow high stairs with the air of one to whom those stairs were not unknown.

When in the street he slackened his pace, and first looking round to assure himself that none overheard their conversation, he addressed Cincolo: 'Pardon me, my dear friend; I am hasty, and the sight of that man made every drop of my blood cry aloud in my veins. But I do not come here to indulge in private sorrows or private revenge, and my design ought alone to engross me. It is necessary for me to see, speedily and secretly, Messer Guielmo Lostendardo, the Neapolitan commander. I bear a message to him from the Countess Elizabeth, the mother of Corradino, and I have some hope that its import may induce him to take at least a neutral part during the impending conflict. I have chosen you, Cincolo, to aid me in this, for not only are you of that little note in your town that you may act for me without attracting observation, but you are brave and true, and I may confide to your known worth. Lostendardo resides at the Palagio del Governo;[69] when I enter its doors I am in the hands of my enemies, and its dungeons may alone know the secret of my destiny. I hope better things. But if after two hours I do not appear or let you hear of my welfare, carry this packet to Corradino at Pisa: you will then learn who I am, and if you feel any indignation at my fate, let that feeling attach you still more strongly to the cause for which I live and die.'

As Ricciardo spoke he still walked on; and Cincolo observed that without his guidance he directed his steps towards the Palagio del Governo. 'I do not understand this,' said the old man; – 'by what argument, unless you bring one from the other world, do you hope to induce Messer Guielmo to aid Corradino? He is so bitter an enemy of Manfred that although that prince is dead yet when he mentions his name he grasps the air as it were a dagger. I have heard him with horrible imprecations curse the whole house of Swabia.'

A tremor shook the frame of Ricciardo, but he replied, 'Lostendardo was once the firmest support of that house and the friend of Manfred. Strange circumstances gave birth in his mind to this unnatural hatred, and he became a traitor. But perhaps now that Manfred is in Paradise, the youth, the virtues and the inexperience of Corradino may inspire him with more generous feelings and reawaken his ancient faith. At least I must make this last trial. This cause is too holy, too sacred, to admit of common forms of reasoning or action. The nephew of Manfred must sit upon the throne of his ancestors; and to achieve that I will endure what I am about to endure.'

They entered the Palace of Government. Messer Guielmo was carousing in the great hall. 'Bear this ring to him, good Cincolo, and say that I wait. Be speedy, that my courage, my life, do not desert me at the moment of trial.'

Cincolo, casting one more inquisitive glance on his extraordinary companion, obeyed his orders, while the youth leant against one of the pillars of the court and passionately cast up his eyes to the clear firmament. 'Oh, ye stars!' he cried in a smothered voice, 'ye are eternal; let my purpose, my will, be as constant as ye!' Then, more calm, he folded his arms in his cloak, and with strong inward struggle endeavoured to repress his emotion. Several servants approached him and bade him follow them. Again he looked at the sky and said, 'Manfred,' and then he walked on with slow but firm steps. They led him through several halls and corridors to a large apartment hung with tapestry, and well lighted by numerous torches; the marble of the floor reflected their glare, and the arched roof echoed the footsteps of one who paced the apartment as Ricciardo entered. It was Lostendardo. He made a sign that the servants should retire; the heavy door closed behind them, and Ricciardo stood alone with Messer Guielmo; his countenance pale but composed, his eyes cast down as in expectation, not in fear; and but for the convulsive motion of his lips, you would have guessed that every faculty was almost suspended by intense agitation.

Lostendardo approached. He was a man in the prime of life, tall and athletic; he seemed capable with a single exertion to crush the frail being of Ricciardo. Every feature of his countenance spoke of the struggle of passions, and the terrible egotism of one who would sacrifice even himself to the establishment of his will: his black eyebrows were scattered, his grey eyes deep-set and scowling, his look at once stern and haggard. A smile seemed never to have disturbed the settled scorn which his lips expressed; his high forehead, already becoming bald, was marked by a thousand contradictory lines. His voice was studiously restrained as he said: 'Wherefore do you bring that ring?'

Ricciardo looked up and met his eye, which glanced fire as he exclaimed: 'Despina!' He seized her hand with a giant's grasp: 'I have prayed for this night and day, and thou art now here! Nay, do not struggle; you are mine; for by my salvation I swear that thou shalt never again escape me.' Despina replied calmly: 'Thou mayst well believe that in thus placing myself in thy power I do not dread any injury thou canst inflict upon me, or I were not here. I do not fear thee, for I do not fear death. Loosen then thy hold, and listen to me. I come in the name of those virtues that were once thine; I come in the name of all noble sentiment, generosity, and ancient faith; and I trust that in listening to me your heroic nature will second my voice, and that Lostendardo will no longer rank with those whom the good and great never name but to condemn.'

Lostendardo appeared to attend little to what she said. He gazed on her with triumph and malignant pride; and if he still held her, his motive appeared rather the delight he felt in displaying his power over her, than any fear that she would escape. You might read in her pale cheek and glazed eye that if she feared it was herself alone that she mistrusted; that her design lifted her above mortal dread, and that she was as impassive as the marble she resembled to any event that did not either advance or injure the object for which she came. They were both silent, until Lostendardo leading her to a seat, and then standing opposite to her, his arms folded, every feature dilated by triumph, and his voice sharpened by agitation, he said: 'Well, speak! What wouldst thou with me?'

'I come to request that if you cannot be induced to assist Prince Corradino in the present struggle, you will at least stand neutral, and not oppose his advance to the kingdom of his ancestors.'

Lostendardo laughed. The vaulted roof repeated the sound, but the harsh echo, though it resembled the sharp cry of an animal of prey whose paw is on the heart of its enemy, was not so discordant and dishuman as the laugh itself. 'How,' he asked, 'dost thou pretend to induce me to comply? This dagger,' and he touched the hilt of one that was half concealed in his vesture, 'is yet stained by the blood of Manfred; ere long it will be sheathed in the heart of that foolish boy.'

Despina conquered the feeling of horror these words inspired, and replied: 'Will you give me a few minutes' patient hearing?'

'I will give you a few minutes' hearing, and if I be not so patient as in the Palagio Reale, fair Despina must excuse me. Forbearance is not a virtue to which I aspire.'

'Yes, it was in the Palagio Reale at Naples, the palace of Manfred, that you first saw me. You were then the bosom friend of Manfred, selected by that choice specimen of humanity as his confidant and counsellor. Why did you become a traitor? Start not at that word: if you could hear the united voice of Italy, and even of those who call themselves your friends, they would echo that name. Why did you thus degrade and belie yourself? You call me the cause, yet I am most innocent. You saw me at the court of your master, an attendant on

Queen Sibilla, and one who unknown to herself had already parted with her heart, her soul, her will, her entire being, an involuntary sacrifice at the shrine of all that is noble and divine in human nature. My spirit worshipped Manfred as a saint, and my pulses ceased to beat when his eye fell upon me. I felt this, but I knew it not. You awoke me from my dream. You said that you loved me, and you reflected in too faithful a mirror my own emotions: I saw myself and shuddered. But the profound and eternal nature of my passion saved me. I loved Manfred. I loved the sun because it enlightened him; I loved the air that fed him; I deified myself for that my heart was the temple in which he resided. I devoted myself to Sibilla, for she was his wife, and never in thought or dream degraded the purity of my affection towards him. For this you hated him. He was ignorant of my passion: my heart contained it as a treasure which you having discovered came to rifle. You could more easily deprive me of life than my devotion for your king, and therefore you were a traitor.

'Manfred died, and you thought that I had then forgotten him. But love would indeed be a mockery if death were not the most barefaced cheat. How can he die who is immortalised in my thoughts – my thoughts, that comprehend the universe, and contain eternity in their graspings? What though his earthly vesture is thrown as a despised weed beside the verde, he lives in my soul as lovely, as noble, as entire as when his voice awoke the mute air; nay, his life is more entire, more true. For before, that small shrine that encased his spirit was all that existed of him; but now, he is a part of all things; his spirit surrounds me, interpenetrates; and divided from him during his life, his death has united me to him for ever.'

The countenance of Lostendardo darkened fearfully. When she paused, he looked black as the sea before the heavily charged thunder-clouds that canopy it dissolve themselves in rain. The tempest of passion that arose in his heart seemed too mighty to admit of swift manifestation; it came slowly up from the profoundest depths of his soul, and emotion was piled upon emotion before the lightning of his anger sped to its destination. 'Your arguments, eloquent Despina,' he said, 'are indeed unanswerable. They work well for your purpose. Corradino is I hear at Pisa; you have sharpened my dagger, and before the air of another night rust it, I may by deeds have repaid your insulting words.'

'How far do you mistake me! And is praise and love of all heroic excellence insult to you? Lostendardo, when you first knew me, I was an inexperienced girl; I loved but knew not what love was, and circumscribing my passion in narrow bounds, I adored the being of Manfred as I might love an effigy of stone, which, when broken, has no longer an existence. I am now much altered. I might before have treated you with disdain or anger, but now these base feelings have expired in my heart. I am animated but by one feeling – an aspiration to another life, another state of being. All the good depart from this strange earth; and I doubt not that when I am sufficiently elevated above human weaknesses, it will also be my turn to leave this scene of woe. I prepare myself for that moment alone; and in endeavouring to fit myself for a union with all the brave, generous and wise that once adorned humanity, and have now passed from it, I consecrate myself to the service of this most righteous cause. You wrong me, therefore, if you think there is aught of disdain in what I say, or that any degrading feelings are mingled with my devotion of spirit when I come and voluntarily place myself in your power. You can imprison me for ever in the dungeons of this palace, as a returned Ghibelline and spy, and have me executed as a criminal. But before you do this, pause for your own sake; reflect on the choice of glory or ignominy that you are now about to make. Let your old sentiments of love for the house of Swabia have some sway in your heart; reflect that as you are the despised enemy so you may become the chosen friend of its last descendant, and receive from every heart the praise of having restored Corradino to the honours and power to which he was born.

'Compare this prince to the hypocritical, the bloody and mean-spirited Charles. When Manfred died, I went to Germany, and have resided at the court of the Countess Elizabeth;[70] I have, therefore, been an hourly witness of the great and good qualities of Corradino. The bravery of his spirit makes him rise above the weakness of youth and inexperience: he possesses all the nobility of spirit that belongs to the family of Swabia, and, in addition, a purity and gentleness that attracts the respect and love of the old and wary courtiers of Frederic and Conrad. You are brave, and would be generous, did not the fury of your passions, like a consuming fire, destroy in their violence every generous sentiment: how then can you become the tool of Charles? His scowling eyes and sneering lips betoken the selfishness of his mind. Avarice, cruelty, meanness and artifice are the qualities that characterise him, and render him unworthy of the majesty he usurps. Let him return to Provence, and reign with paltry despotism over the luxurious and servile French; the free-born Italians require another Lord. They are not fit to bow to one whose palace is the change-house of moneylenders, whose generals are usurers, whose courtiers are milliners or monks, and who basely vows allegiance to the enemy of freedom and virtue, Clement, the murderer of Manfred. Their king, like them, should be clothed in the armour of valour and simplicity; his ornaments, his shield and spear; his treasury, the possessions of his subjects; his army, their unshaken loves. Charles will treat you as a tool, Corradino as a friend; Charles will make you the detested tyrant of a groaning province, Corradino the governor of a prosperous and happy people.

'I cannot tell by your manner if what I have said has in any degree altered your determination. I cannot forget the scenes that passed between us at Naples. I might then have been disdainful; I am not so now. Your execrations of Manfred excited every angry feeling in my mind; but, as I have said, all but the feeling of love expired in my heart when Manfred died, and methinks that where love is, excellence must be its companion. You said you loved me; and though, in other times, that love was twin-brother to hate – though then, poor prisoner in your heart, jealousy, rage, contempt and cruelty were its handmaids – yet if it were love, methinks that its divinity must have purified your heart from baser feelings; and now that I, the bride of Death, am removed from your sphere, gentler feelings may awaken in your bosom, and you may incline mildly to my voice.

'If indeed you loved me, will you not now be my friend? Shall we not hand in hand pursue the same career? Return to your ancient faith; and now that death and religion have placed the seal upon the past, let Manfred's spirit, looking down, behold his repentant friend the firm ally of his successor, the best and last scion of the house of Swabia.'

She ceased; for the glare of savage triumph, which, as a rising fire at night time, enlightened with growing and fearful radiance the face of Lostendardo, made her pause in her appeal. He did not reply; but when she was silent he quitted the attitude in which he had stood immoveably opposite to her, and pacing the hall with measured steps, his head declined, he seemed to ruminate on some project. Could it be that he weighed her reasonings? If he hesitated, the side of generosity and old fidelity would certainly prevail. Yet she dared not hope; her heart beat fast; she would have knelt, but she feared to move, lest any motion should disturb his thoughts and curb the flow of good feeling which she fondly hoped had arisen within him: she looked up and prayed silently as she sat. Notwithstanding the glare of the torches, the beams of one small star struggled through the dark window pane; her eye resting on it, her thoughts were at once elevated to the eternity and space which that star symbolised: it seemed to her the spirit of Manfred, and she inwardly worshipped it, as she prayed that it would shed its benign influence on the soul of Lostendardo.

Some minutes elapsed in this fearful silence, and then he approached her. 'Despina, allow me to reflect on your words; tomorrow I will answer you. You will remain in this palace until the morning, and then you shall see and judge of my repentance and returning faith.' He spoke with studious gentleness. Despina could not see his face, for the lights shone behind him. When she looked up to reply, the little star twinkled just above his head, and seemed with its gentle lustre to reassure her. Our minds, when highly wrought, are strangely given to superstition, and Despina lived in a superstitious age. She thought that the star bade her comply, and assured her of protection from heaven – from where else could she expect it? She said therefore, 'I consent. Only let me request that you acquaint the man who gave you my ring that I am safe, or he will fear for me.'

'I will do as you desire.'

'And I will confide myself to your care. I cannot, dare not, fear you. If you would betray me, still I trust in the heavenly saints that guard humanity.'

Her countenance was so calm, it beamed with so angelic a self-devotion and a belief in good, that Lostendardo dared not look on her. For one moment – as she, having ceased to speak, gazed upon the star – he felt impelled to throw himself at her feet, to confess the diabolical scheme he had forged, and to commit himself body and soul to her guidance, to obey, to serve, to worship her. The impulse was momentary: the feeling of revenge returned on him. From the moment she had rejected him, the fire of rage had burned in his heart, consuming all healthy feeling, all human sympathies and gentleness of soul. He had sworn never to sleep on a bed, or to drink aught but water, until his first cup of wine was mingled with the blood of Manfred. He had fulfilled this vow. A strange alteration had worked within him from the moment he had drained that unholy cup. The spirit not of a man but of a devil seemed to live within him, urging him to crime from which his long protracted hope of more complete revenge had alone deterred him. But Despina was now in his power, and it seemed to him as if fate had preserved him so long only that he might now wreak his full rage upon her. When she spoke of love, he thought how from that he might extract pain. He formed his plan; and this slight human weakness now conquered, he bent his thoughts to its completion. Yet he feared to stay longer with her; so he quitted her, saying that he would send attendants who would show her an apartment where she might repose. He left her, and several hours passed; but no one came. The torches burnt low, and the stars of heaven could now with twinkling beams conquer their feebler light. One by one these torches went out, and the shadows of the high windows of the hall, before invisible, were thrown upon its marble pavement. Despina looked upon the shade, at first unconsciously, until she found herself counting, one, two, three, the shapes of the iron bars that lay so placidly on the stone. 'Those grates are thick,' she said: 'this room would be a large but secure dungeon.' As by inspiration, she now felt that she was a prisoner. No change, no word, had intervened since she had walked fearlessly in the room, believing herself free. But now no doubt of her situation occurred to her mind; heavy chains seemed to fall around her; the air to feel thick and heavy as that of a prison; and the star-beams that had before cheered her became the dreary messengers of fearful danger to herself, and of the utter defeat of all the hopes she had dared nourish of success to her beloved cause.

Cincolo waited, first with impatience, and then with anxiety, for the return of the youthful stranger. He paced up and down before the gates of the palace; hour after hour passed on; the stars arose and descended, and ever and anon meteors shot along the sky. They were not more frequent than they always are during a clear summer night in Italy; but they appeared strangely numerous to Cincolo, and portentous of change and calamity. Midnight struck, and at that moment a procession of monks passed, bearing a corpse and chaunting a solemn *De Profundis*.[71] Cincolo felt a cold tremor shake his limbs when he reflected how ill an augury this was for the strange adventurer he had guided to that palace. The sombre cowls of the priests, their hollow voices, and the dark burthen they carried, augmented his agitation even to terror: without confessing the cowardice to himself, he was possessed with fear lest he should be included in the evil destiny that evidently awaited his companion. Cincolo was a brave man: he had often been foremost in a perilous assault; but the most courageous among us sometimes feel our hearts fail within us at the dread of unknown and fated danger. He was struck with panic; he looked after the disappearing lights of the procession, and listened to their fading voices; his knees shook, a cold perspiration stood on his brow; until, unable to resist the impulse, he began slowly to withdraw himself from the Palace of Government, and to quit the circle of danger which seemed to hedge him in if he remained on that spot.

He had hardly quitted his post by the gate of the palace when he saw lights issue from it, attendant on a company of men, some of whom were armed, as appeared from the reflection their lances' heads cast; and some of them carried a litter hung with black and closely drawn. Cincolo was rooted to the spot. He could not render himself any reason for his belief, but he felt convinced that the stranger youth was there, about to be carried out to death. Impelled by curiosity and anxiety, he followed the party as they went towards the Porta Romana; they were challenged by the sentinels at the gate; they gave the word and passed. Cincolo dared not follow, but he was agitated by fear and compassion. He remembered the packet confided to his care; he dared not draw it from his bosom, lest any Guelph should be near to overlook and discover that it was addressed to Corradino; he could not read, but he wished to look at the arms of the seal, to see whether they bore the imperial ensigns. He returned back to the Palagio del Governo: all there was dark and silent; he walked up and down before the gates, looking up at the windows, but no sign of life appeared. He could not tell why he was thus agitated, but he felt as if all his future peace depended on the fate of this stranger youth. He thought of Gegia, her helplessness and age; but he could not resist the impulse that impelled him, and he resolved that very night to commence his journey to Pisa, to deliver the packet, to learn who the stranger was, and what hopes he might entertain for his safety.

He returned home, that he might inform Gegia of his journey. This was a painful task, but he could not leave her in doubt. He ascended his narrow stairs with trepidation. At the head of them a lamp twinkled before a picture of the Virgin. Evening after evening it burnt there, guarding through its influence his little household from all earthly or supernatural dangers. The sight of it inspired him with courage; he said an Ave Maria before it; and then looking around him to assure himself that no spy stood on the narrow landing place, he drew the packet from his bosom and examined the seal. All Italians in those days were conversant in heraldry, since from ensigns of the shields of the knights they learned, better than from their faces or persons, to what family and party they belonged. But it required no great knowledge for Cincolo to decipher these arms; he had known them from his childhood; they were those of the Elisei, the family to whom he had been attached as a partisan during all these civil contests. Arrigo dei Elisei had been his patron, and his wife had nursed his only daughter, in those happy days when there was neither Guelph nor Ghibelline. The sight of these arms reawakened all his anxiety. Could this youth belong to that house? The seal showed that he really did; and this discovery confirmed his determination of making every exertion to save him, and inspired him with sufficient courage to encounter the remonstrances and fears of Monna Gegia.

He unlocked his door; the old dame was asleep in her chair, but awoke as he entered. She had slept only to refresh her curiosity, and she asked a thousand questions in a breath, to which Cincolo did not reply: he stood with his arms folded looking at the fire, irresolute how to break the subject of his departure. Monna Gegia continued to talk: 'After you went, we held a consultation concerning this hot-brained youth of this morning; I, Buzeccha, Beppe de' Bosticchi who returned, and Monna Lisa from the Mercato Nuovo. We all agreed that he must be one of two persons; and be it one or the other, if he have not quitted Florence, the Stinchi [72] will be his habitation by sunrise. Eh! Cincolo, man! you do not speak; where did you part with your prince?'

'Prince, Gegia! Are you mad? – what prince?'

'Nay, he is either a prince or a baker; either Corradino himself, or Ricciardo the son of Messer Tommaso de' Manelli; he that lived o'th' Arno, and baked for all that Sesto, when Count Guido de' Giudi was Vicare. By this token, that Messer Tommaso went to Milan with Ubaldo de' Gargalandi, and Ricciardo, who went with his father, must now be sixteen. He had the fame of kneading with as light a hand as his father, but he liked better to follow arms with the Gargalandi: he was a fair, likely youth, they said; and so, to say the truth, was our youngster of this morning. But Monna Lisa will have it that it must be Corradino himself – '

Cincolo listened as if the gossip of two old women could unravel his riddle. He even began to doubt whether the last conjecture, extravagant as it was, had not hit the truth. Every circumstance forbade such an idea; but he thought of the youth and exceeding beauty of the stranger, and he began to doubt. There was none among the Elisei who answered to his appearance. The flower of their youth had fallen at Monte Aperto; the eldest of the new generation was but ten; the other males of that house were of a mature age.

Gegia continued to talk of the anger that Beppe de' Bosticchi evinced at being accused of the murder of Arrigo dei Elisei. 'If he had done that deed,' she cried, 'never more should he have stood on my hearth; but he swore his innocence; and truly, poor man, it would be a sin not to believe him.' Why, if the stranger were not an Elisei, should he have shown such horror on viewing the supposed murderer of the head of that family?

Cincolo turned from the fire; he examined whether his knife hung safely in his girdle, and he exchanged his sandal-like shoes for stronger boots of common undressed fur.

This last act attracted the attention of Gegia. 'What are you about, good man?' she cried. 'This is no hour to change your dress, but to come to bed. Tonight you will not speak; but tomorrow I hope to get it all out from you. What are you about?'

'I am about to leave you, my dear Gegia; and heaven bless and take care of you! I am going to Pisa.'

Gegia uttered a shriek, and was about to remonstrate with great volubility, while the tears rolled down her aged cheeks.

Tears also filled the eyes of Cincolo, as he said, 'I do not go for the cause you suspect. I do not go into the army of Corradino, though my heart will be with it. I go but to carry a letter, and will return without delay.'

'You will never return,' cried the old woman: 'the Commune will never let you enter the gates of this town again if you set foot in that traitorous Pisa. But you shall not go; I will raise the neighbours; I will declare you mad – '

'Gegia, no more of this! Here is all the money I have; before I go, I will send your cousin 'Nunziata to you. I must go. It is not the Ghibelline cause, or Corradino, that obliges me to risk your ease and comforts; but the life of one of the Elisei is at stake; and if I can save him, would you have me rest here, and afterwards curse you and the hour when I was born?'

'What! is he – ? But no; there is none among the Elisei so young as he; and none so lovely, except her whom these arms carried when an infant – but she is a female. No, no; this is a tale trumped up to deceive me and gain my consent; but you shall never have it. Mind that! you will never have it; and I prophecy that if you do go, your journey will be the death of both of us.' She wept bitterly. Cincolo kissed her aged cheek, and mingled his tears with hers; and then recommending her to the care of the Virgin and the saints, he quitted her, while grief choked her utterance, and the name of the Elisei had deprived her of all energy to resist his purpose.

It was four in the morning before the gates of Florence were opened and Cincolo could leave the city. At first he availed himself of the carts of the *contadini*[73] to advance on his journey; but as he drew near Pisa, all modes of conveyance ceased, and he was obliged to take by-roads, and act cautiously, not to fall into the hands of the Florentine outposts, or of some fierce Guelph, who might suspect him, and have him carried before the *podesta*[74] of a village; for if once suspected and searched, the packet addressed to Corradino would convict him, and he would pay for his temerity with his life. Having arrived at Vico Pisano,[75] he found a troop of Pisan horse there on guard: he was known to many of the soldiers, and he obtained a conveyance for Pisa; but it was night before he arrived. He gave the Ghibelline watchword, and was admitted within the gates. He asked for Prince Corradino: he was in the city, at the palace of the Lanfranchi. He crossed the Arno,[76] and was admitted into the palace by the soldiers who guarded the door. Corradino had just returned from a successful skirmish in the Lucchese states, and was reposing; but when Count Gherardo Doneratico, his principal attendant, saw the seal of the packet, he immediately ushered the bearer into a small room, where the prince lay on a fox's skin thrown upon the pavement. The mind of Cincolo had been so bewildered by the rapidity of the events of the preceding night, by fatigue and want of sleep, that he had overwrought himself to believe that the stranger youth was indeed Corradino; and when he had heard that that prince was in Pisa, by a strange disorder of ideas, he still imagined that he and Ricciardo were the same; that the black litter was a phantom, and his fears ungrounded. The first sight of Corradino, his fair hair and round Saxon features, destroyed this idea; it was replaced by a feeling of deep anguish when Count Gherardo, announcing him, said, 'One who brings a letter from Madonna Despina dei Elisei waits upon your highness.'

The old man sprang forward, uncontrolled by the respect he would otherwise have felt for one of so high lineage as Corradino. 'From Despina! Did you say from her? Oh! unsay your words! Not from my beloved, lost, foster-child.'

Tears rolled down his cheeks. Corradino, a youth of fascinating gentleness, but, as Despina had said, 'young, even to childishness', attempted to reassure him. 'Oh! my gracious Lord,' cried Cincolo, 'open that packet, and see if it be from my blessed child – if in the disguise of Ricciardo I led her to destruction.' He wrung his hands. Corradino, pale as death with fear for the destiny of his lovely and adventurous friend, broke the seal. The packet contained an inner envelope, without any direction, and a letter, which Corradino read, while horror convulsed every feature. He gave it to Gherardo. 'It is indeed from her. She says that the bearer can relate all that the world will probably know of her fate. And you, old man, who weep so bitterly, you to whom my best and lovely friend refers me, tell me what you know of her.'

Cincolo told his story in broken accents. 'May these eyes be for ever blinded!' he cried, when he had concluded, 'that knew not Despina in those soft looks and heavenly smiles. Dotard that I am! When my wife railed at your family and princely self, and the sainted Manfred, why did

I not read her secret in her forbearance? Would she have forgiven those words in any but her who had nursed her infancy, and been a mother to her when Madonna Pia died? And when she taxed Bosticchi with her father's death, I, blind fool, did not see the spirit of the Elisei in her eyes. My Lord, I have but one favour to ask you. Let me hear her letter, that I may judge from that what hopes remain; but there are none – none.'

'Read it to him, my dear count,' said the prince; 'I will not fear as he fears. I dare not fear that one so lovely and beloved is sacrificed for my worthless cause.' Gherardo read the letter.

Cincolo de' Becari, my foster-father, will deliver this letter into your hands, my respected and dear Corradino. The Countess Elizabeth has urged me to my present undertaking; I hope nothing from it – except to labour for your cause, and perhaps through its event to quit somewhat earlier a life which is but a grievous trial to my weak mind. I go to endeavour to arouse the feelings of fidelity and generosity in the soul of the traitor Lostendardo; I go to place myself in his hands, and I do not hope to escape from them again. Corradino, my last prayer will be for your success. Mourn not for one who goes home after a long and weary exile. Burn the enclosed packet, without opening it. The Mother of God protect thee!

DESPINA

Corradino had wept as this epistle was reading, but then, starting up, he said – 'To revenge or death! we may yet save her!'

A blight had fallen on the house of Swabia, and all their enterprises were blasted. Beloved by their subjects, noble, and with every advantage of right on their side, except those the church bestowed, they were defeated in every attempt to defend themselves against a foreigner and a tyrant, who ruled by force of arms, and those in the hands of a few only, over an extensive and warlike territory. The young and daring Corradino was also fated to perish in this contest. Having overcome the troops of his adversary in Tuscany, he advanced towards his kingdom with the highest hopes. His arch enemy, Pope Clement IV, had shut himself up in Viterbo,[77] and was guarded by a numerous garrison. Corradino passed in triumph and hope before the town, and proudly drew out his troops before it, to display to the Holy Father his forces, and humiliate him by this show of success. The cardinals, who beheld the lengthened line and good order of the army, hastened to the papal palace. Clement was in his oratory, praying; the frightened monks, with pale looks, related how the excommunicated heretic dared to menace the town where the Holy Father himself resided; adding, that if the insult were carried to the pitch of an assault, it might prove dangerous warfare. The Pope smiled contemptuously. 'Do not fear,' he said; 'the projects of these men will dissipate in smoke.' He then went on the ramparts, and saw Corradino and Frederic of Austria,[78] who had drawn up the line of knights in the plain below. He watched them for a time; then turning to his cardinals, he said, 'They are victims, who permit themselves to be led to sacrifice.'

His words were a prophecy. Notwithstanding the first successes of Corradino, and the superior numbers of his army, he was defeated by the artifice of Charles in a pitched battle. He escaped from the field, and, with a few friends, arrived at a tower called Astura, which belonged to the family of Frangipani, of Rome. Here he hired a vessel, embarked, and put out to sea, directing his course for Sicily, which, having rebelled against Charles, would, he hoped, receive him with joy. They were already under weigh, when one of the family of the Frangipani seeing a vessel filled with Germans making all sail from shore, suspected that they were fugitives from the battle of Tagliacozzo;[79] he followed them in other vessels, and took them all prisoners. The person of Corradino was a rich prey for him; he delivered him into the hands of his rival, and was rewarded by the donation of a fief near Benevento.

The dastardly spirit of Charles instigated him to the basest revenge; and the same tragedy was acted on those shores which has been renewed in our days. A daring and illustrious prince was sacrificed with the mock forms of justice at the sanguinary altar of tyranny and hypocrisy. Corradino was tried. One of his judges alone, a Provençal, dared condemn him, and he paid with his life the forfeit of his baseness. For scarcely had he, solitary among his fellows, pronounced the sentence of death against this prince, than Robert of Flanders, the brother-in-law of Charles himself,[80] struck him on the breast with a staff, crying, 'It behoves not thee, wretch, to condemn to death so noble and worthy a knight.' The judge fell dead in the presence of the king, who dared not avenge his creature.

On the 26th of October, Corradino and his friends were led out to die in the Marketplace of Naples, by the seaside. Charles was present with all his court, and an immense multitude surrounded the triumphant king, and his more royal adversary, about to suffer an ignominious death. The funereal procession approached its destination. Corradino, agitated, but controlling his agitation, was drawn in an open cart. After him came a close litter, hung with black, with no sign to tell who was within. The Duke of Austria and several other illustrious victims followed. The guard that conducted them to the scaffold was headed by Lostendardo; a malicious triumph laughed in his eyes, and he rode near the litter, looking from time to time, first at it and then at Corradino, with the dark look of a tormenting fiend. The procession stopped at the foot of the scaffold, and Corradino looked at the flashing light which every now and then arose from Vesuvius, and threw its reflection on the sea. The sun had not yet risen, but the halo if its approach illuminated the bay of Naples, its mountains and its islands. The summits of the distant hills of Baiae gleamed with its first beams. Corradino thought, 'By the time those rays arrive here, and shadows are cast from the persons of these men – princes and peasants – around me, my living spirit will be shadowless.' Then he turned his eyes on the companions of his fate, and for the first time he saw the silent and dark litter that accompanied them. At first he thought, 'It is my coffin.' But then he recollected the disappearance of Despina, and would have sprung towards it; his guards stopped him; he looked up, and his glance met that of Lostendardo, who smiled – a smile of dread; but the feeling of religion which had before calmed him again descended on him: he thought that her sufferings, as well as his, would soon be over.

They were already over. And the silence of the grave is upon those events which had occurred since Cincolo beheld her carried out of Florence until now, when she was led by her fierce enemy to behold the death of the nephew of Manfred. She must have endured much; for when, as Corradino advanced to the front of the scaffold, the litter being placed opposite to it, Lostendardo ordered the curtains to be withdrawn, the white hand that hung inanimate from the side was thin as a winter leaf, and her fair face, pillowed by the thick knots of her dark hair, was sunken and ashy pale, while you could see the deep blue of her eyes struggle through the closed eyelids. She was still in the attire in which she had presented herself at the house of Cincolo: perhaps her tormentor thought that her appearance as a youth would attract less compassion than if a lovely woman were thus dragged to so unnatural a scene.

Corradino was kneeling and praying when her form was thus exposed. He saw her, and saw that she was dead! About to die himself; about, pure and innocent, to die ignominiously, while his base conqueror, in pomp and glory, was spectator of his death, he did not pity those who were at peace; his compassion belonged to the living alone, and as he rose from his prayer he exclaimed, 'My beloved mother, what profound

sorrow will the news thou art about to hear cause thee!' He looked
upon the living multitude around him, and saw that the hard-visaged
partisans of the usurper wept; he heard the sobs of his oppressed and
conquered subjects; so he drew his glove from his hand and threw
it among the crowd, in token that he still held his cause good, and
submitted his head to the axe.

During many years after those events, Lostendardo enjoyed wealth,
rank and honour. Suddenly, however, while at the summit of glory and
prosperity, he withdrew from the world, took the vows of a severe order
in a convent, in one of the desolate and unhealthy plains by the seashore
in Calabria, and after having gained the character of a saint, through a
life of self-inflicted torture, he died murmuring the names of Corradino,
Manfred and Despina.

The Bride of Modern Italy

My heart is fixt:
This is the sixt.   ELIA [81]

O N a serene winter morning two young ladies, Clorinda and Teresa,
walked up and down the garden of the convent of St S—, at
Rome. If my reader has never seen a convent, or if he has only
seen the better kind, let him dismiss from his mind all he may have
heard or imagined of such abodes, or he can never transport himself into
the garden of St S—. He must figure it to himself as bounded by
a long, low, straggling, whitewashed, weather-stained building, with
grated windows, the lower ones glassless. It is a kitchen garden, but the
refuse of the summer stock alone remained, except a few cabbages, which
perfumed the air with their rank exhalations. The walks were neglected,
yet not overgrown, but strewn with broken earthenware, ashes, cabbage-
stalks, orange peel, bones, and all that marks the vicinity of a much
frequented, but disorderly mansion. The beds were intersected by these
paths, and the whole was surrounded by a high wall. This common
scene was, however, unlike what it would have been in this country. You
saw the decayed and straggling boughs of the passion-flower against the
walls of the convent; here and there a geranium, its luxuriant foliage
starred by scarlet flowers, grew unharmed by frost among the cabbages;
the lemon plants had been removed to shelter, but orange trees were
nailed against the wall, the golden fruit peeping out from amidst the
dark leaves; the wall itself was variegated by a thousand rich hues; and
thick and pointed aloes grew beneath it. Under the highest wall, opposite
the back door of the convent, a corner of ground was enclosed; this was
the burial place of the nuns; and on the path that led from the door to
this enclosure Clorinda and Teresa walked up and down.

'He will never come!' exclaimed Clorinda.

'I fear the dinner bell will ring and interrupt us, if he does come,'
observed Teresa.

'Some cruel obstacle doubtless prevents him,' continued Clorinda, sighing – 'and I have prayed to St Giacomo, and vowed to give him the best flowers and a candle a foot long next Easter.'

Teresa smiled: 'I remember,' she said, 'that at Christmas you fulfilled such a vow to San Francesco – was not that for the sake of Cieco Magni? for you change your saint as your lover changes name; tell me, sweet Clorinda, how many saints have been benefited by your piety?'

Clorinda looked angry, and then sorrowful; the large drops gathered in her dark eyes: 'You are unkind to taunt me thus, Teresina; when did I love truly until now? believe me, never; and if heaven bestows Giacomo upon me – oh! that is his bell! – naughty Teresa, you will cause me to meet him with tears in my eyes.'

Away they ran to the parlour of the convent, and were joined there by an old woman purblind and nearly deaf, who was to be present at the visit of Giacomo de' Tolomei, the brother of Teresa. He kissed the hands of the young ladies, and then they commenced a conversation, which, by the lowness of their tones, and an occasional intermixture of French, was quite incomprehensible to their Argus,[82] who was busily employed in knitting a large green worsted shawl.

'Well?' said Clorinda, in a tone of enquiry.

'Well, dear Clorinda, I have executed our design, though I hope little from it. I have written a proposal of marriage; if you approve of it, I will send it to your parents. Here it is.'

'What is that paper?' cried the Argus.

Teresa bawled in her ear: 'Only the history of the late miracle performed at Asisa' (Italians, male or female, are not great patronisers of truth), 'look at it, dear Eusta.' (Eusta could not read.) 'I will read it to you by and by.' Eusta went on with her knitting.

The two girls looking over one another, read the proposal of marriage which Giacomo de' Tolomei made to the parents of Clorinda Saviani. The paper was divided into two columns, one headed: 'The Proposal', the other: 'Observations to be made thereon', and this latter column was left blank. The proposal itself was divided into several heads and numbered. It premised that a noble family of Sienna wishing to ally themselves to the family of the Saviani of Rome, in the persons of their eldest son and Clorinda, they presented the following considerations to the heads of that house first, that the young man was well-made, good-looking, healthy, studiously inclined and of irreproachable morals. The circumstances of his fortune were then detailed, and the claims of dowry; it concluded by saying that if the parents of Clorinda approved of the terms proposed, the young people might be introduced to each other, and if mutually pleased at their interview, the nuptials might be celebrated in the course of a few months. When Clorinda had finished reading, the tears that had gathered in her eyes fell drop after drop upon the paper.

'Wherefore do you weep?' asked Giacomo, 'why do you distress me thus?'

'This proposal will never be accepted. You have asked twelve thousand crowns in dowry; my parents will not give more than six.'

'And yet,' replied Giacomo, 'I have named a sum to which I am convinced my father will never agree; he will require twenty thousand at least; even if your parents accede I shall have to win his consent; but if prayers and tears can move him, I will not be chary of either.'

The bell rang for dinner, old Eusta arose, and Giacomo retired. Dinner! – what dainty feast of convent-like confectionaries does the reader picture? – Let him see, in truth, a long, brick-paved floor, with long deal tables, and benches ditto; the tables covered with not white cloths; cellars of black salt; bottles of sour wine, and small loaves of bitter bread. Then came the *minestra*,[83] consisting (for it was fast day) of what we call macaroni, water, oil and cheese; then a few vegetables swimming in oil; a concluding dish of eggs fried with garlic, and the repast of one of the most highborn and loveliest girls in Rome was finished. Clorinda Saviani was indeed handsome, and all her fine features expressed the *bisogna d'amare*[84] which ruled her heart. She was just eighteen, and had been five years in this convent, waiting until her father should find a husband of noble birth, who would be content with a slender dowry. During this time she had formed several attachments for various youths, who, under different pretexts, had visited the convent. She had written letters, prayed and wept, and then yielding to insurmountable difficulties she had changed her idol, though she had never ceased to love. The fastidious English must not be disgusted with this picture. It is, perhaps, only a coarse representation of what takes place at every ballroom with us. And if it went beyond, then the nature of the Catholic religion, which crushes the innate conscience by giving a false one in its room; the system of artifice and heartlessness that subsists in a convent; the widely spread maxim in Italy, that dishonour attaches itself to the discovered not the concealed fault – all this forms the excuse why, with a tender heart and much native talent, there was neither constancy in Clorinda's love nor dignity in her conduct.

After their repast the friends retired to Clorinda's cell: a small, though high room, floored with brick, miserably furnished, and neither clean nor orderly. A prie-dieu[85] was beside the little bed with a crucifix over it, together with two or three prints (like our penny children's prints) of saints, among which St Giacomo appeared with the freshest and cleanest face; beside these was a glass (resembling a bird's drinking vessel) containing holy water, rather the worse for long standing; in a closet, with the door ajar, among tattered books and female apparel, hung a glass-case enclosing a waxen Gesu Bambino, and some flowers, gathered for this holy dedication and drooping for want of light, were placed beneath him; some mignionette, basil and heliotrope, weeds o'ergrown, flowered in a wooden trough at the window; a broken looking glass; a leaden ink stand – such was Clorinda's boudoir.

'I despair,' she exclaimed. 'I see no end to my evils and but one road open – flight.'

'Which would ruin my brother.'

'How? – he is of another state.'

'And your honour?'

'Honour in this dungeon! Oh, let me breathe the fresh air of heaven; let me no longer see this prison room; these high walls and all the circumstances of my convent life, and I care not for the rest.'

'But how? You may get people into the convent – but to get out yourself is a different affair.'

'I have many plans; if this proposal of your brother fail, as it will, I will disclose them to him.'

A lay sister now came in to ask the young ladies if they would take coffee with the Superior. They found her alone: a little, squat, snuff-taking old woman; she was in high ill-humour: 'Body of Bacchus!' she began, 'you introduce strange laws in St S—! This coffee is detestable. Your brother, Teresina, is here every day – I detest coffee without rum. Clorinda sees him, and it begins to be talked of; when he comes tomorrow, you only must receive him, and request him to discontinue his visits.'

Clorinda's tears mingled with her coffee. 'The old witch!' she said, when they had retired, 'she is fishing for a present.'

'And must have one; what shall Giacomo bring her?'

'Let him send some rum. Did you not see the faces she made over her coffee? yet she is too niggardly to buy it herself.' A note was hastily dispatched to Giacomo by Teresa, to inform him of the necessary oblation. He came the next day well provided, for the waiter of a neighbouring inn accompanied him bearing six bottles of what bore the name of Romme. Teresa was called and dispatched to solicit the presence of the Superior. She came; Giacomo took off his hat: 'Signora,' said he, 'it is wintertime, and I bring you a wintry gift. Will you favour me by accepting this rum?'

'Signor, you are too courteous.'

'The courtesy is yours, signora, in honouring me by receiving my present. I hope that you will find it good.'

He uncorked a bottle; Teresa ran for a glass; Giacomo filled it, and the Superior emptied it. Clorinda at the same moment tripped into the room. She started with a natural air, and after saluting Giacomo was going away, but he detained her, and they all sat down together, until the Superior was called away to give out bread for supper, and the three young people remained together.

The girls turned to Giacomo with enquiring looks: his were sorrowful. 'My proposal has not been received. Your parents replied that they have proposed you to someone, and cannot break off the treaty.'

'And thus I am to be sacrificed!' cried Clorinda, casting up her beautiful eyes. 'Will you consent?' said Giacomo reproachfully.

'What means have I? I have talked of flight' (Giacomo's countenance fell); 'and that, although difficult, is not impossible.'

'How?'

'Why, my cell adjoins that of the Superior. She is fond of sweet things; on the next holiday I will make some cakes for her, filled with sugar and a little opium. I can then steal away the keys, make an impression on wax (I have a large piece ready), and you can easily get them counterfeited.'

'You would engage my brother in a dangerous enterprise,' said Teresa.

'My dear, dear Clorinda, my sweet friend,' said Giacomo, 'you are ignorant of the world's ways. I would sacrifice my life for you; but you would thus lose your honour, I should be imprisoned, and you would be sent to some dreary convent among the mountains, till forced to marry some boor who would render you miserable for life.'

'What is to be done then?' asked Clorinda, discontentedly.

'It requires thought. Something must, something shall, be done; do you be faithful to me, and refuse your parents' offer, and I do not despair. In the meantime I will set out for Sienna tomorrow and see my father.'

Giacomo had formed an intimacy with a young English artist residing at Rome, and he left the cares of his love in the hands of this gentleman, while he by short daily journeys, and with a heavy heart, proceeded towards Sienna. The following day brought a letter of five pages, in a nearly illegible hand, to be delivered to Clorinda. Our Englishman had been a year in Rome, but he had never yet been within a convent. As he passed the prison-like building of St S—, and measured with his eye the lofty walls of its garden, he had peopled it with nuns of all ages, states, and dispositions: the solemn and demure, the ambitious, the bigoted, and those who, repenting of their vows, wetted their pallet with their midnight tears, and then, prostrate on the damp marble before the crucifix, prayed God to pardon them for being human. And then he thought of the novices fearful as brides, but not so hopeful; and of the boarders who dreamt of the world outside, as we of Paradise beyond the grave. He pictured echoing corridors, painted windows, the impenetrable grate, the religious cloister, and the garden, that most immaculate of asylums, with grassy walks, majestic trees and veiled forms flitting under their shade. Well, thought he, I am now in for it; and if I do not lose my heart, I shall at least gain some excellent hints for my picture of the Profession of Eloisa.[86]

He crossed the outer hall, rang at the bell, and the old tottering portress came towards the door. He asked for 'the Signora Teresa de' Tolomei'. He was shown into the parlour – a vaulted room, the floor bricked, the furniture mean, without fire or chimney, though the cold east wind covered the ground with hoar frost. In a few minutes the two friends tripped into the room, followed by Eusta, who, instead of her knitting, carried a fire-pot filled with wood ashes, over which she held her withered hands and her blue nose, frostbitten. The girls were some-what startled on seeing the stranger, who advanced, and announcing himself as Signor Marcott Alleyn, a friend of the brother of Teresa, delivered a little packet, together with a note which bade his sister confide implicitly in the Englishman.

The conversation became animated. No bashfulness intruded to prevent Clorinda from discoursing eloquently of her passion, especially when she observed the deep interest which her account excited. Alleyn was a man of infinitely pleasing manners; he had a soft tone of voice and eyes full of expression. Italian ladies are not accustomed to the English system of gallantry; since in that country either downright love is made, or the most distant coldness preserved between the sexes. Alleyn's compassion was excited in various ways. He heard that Clorinda had been imprisoned in that convent for five years; he saw the desolate garden, he felt the bitter cold, which was unalleviated by anything except fire-pots; he had a glance at the blank corridors and squalid cells, and he saw in the victim an elegance of manners and a delicate sensitiveness that ill accorded with such dreary privations. Several visits ensued, and Alleyn became a favourite in the convent. He was only seventeen; his spirits were high; he diverted the friends, brought presents of rum and confectionary to the nuns, kissed some of the least ugly, made covert game of the Superior, and established himself with greater freedom in this seclusion in a week than Giacomo had done in a year. At first he sympathised with Clorinda, now he did more – he amused her. If she wept for the absence of Giacomo, he made her laugh at some story told apropos, which diverted her. If she complained of the petty tyranny of the nuns, he laid some plot of droll revenge, which she executed. He introduced a system of English jokes and hoaxes, at which the poor Italians were perfectly aghast, and to which no experience prevented their becoming victims, so utterly unable were they to comprehend the meaning of such machinations; and then, when their loud voices pealed through the arched passages in wonder and anger, they were appeased by soft words and well-timed gifts.

But this sunshine could not last for ever. Clorinda was at first more happy and gay than she had ever been. She in vain endeavoured to lament the absence of her lover. Alleyn prevented every emotion except gaiety from finding a place in her heart. She looked forward with delight for the hour of his visit, and the merriment that he excited left its traces on the rest of the day. Her step was light; and the cold of her cheerless cell was unfelt, since it had been adorned with caricatures of the Superior and nuns; their tyranny was either laid asleep or revenged, and Giacomo was, alas! forgotten. Her love-breathing letters lost their fire, and the writing them became an irksome task; her sighs were changed into smiles – but suddenly these again vanished, and Clorinda became more pensive and sad than ever. She avoided Teresa, and passed most of her time in lonely walks up and down the straight paths of the garden. She was fretful if Alleyn did not come; when he was announced, she would blush, sit silent in his presence, and, if any of his sallies provoked her laughter, it was quickly quenched by her tears. Her devotions even lost their accustomed warmth; Alleyn had no tutelar saint; no Marcott had ever been honoured with canonisation, nor had any of the bones found in the catacombs been baptised with that transalpine name. 'Marry, this is miching Mallecho; it means mischief'[87] – the brief mischief of inconstancy, new love, and all the evils attendant on such a change. Alleyn did not suspect this turn in the tide, till, left tête-à-tête one morning, some slight attentions on his part painted her cheeks with blushes; the confession was not far behind, he heard with mingled surprise and delight, and one kiss sealed their infidelity to the absent Giacomo just as Teresa and Eusta entered.

Alleyn was only seventeen. At that age men look on women as living Edens which they dare not imagine they can ever enjoy; they love, and dream not of being loved; they seek, and their wildest fancies do not picture themselves as sought; so it was small wonder that the heart of Alleyn beat with exultation, that his step was light and his eyes sparkling as he left the convent on that day. His visits were now more frequent; Teresa was confined to her room by illness, and the lovers (though that sacred name is profaned by such an application) were left together unwatched. Clorinda's thoughts turned wholly upon escape, and Alleyn heedlessly fostered such thoughts, until one day she said: 'If I quit the convent this night, will you be under the walls to receive me?'

'My sweet Clorinda, are you serious?'

'Alas! no, I cannot. But in a few nights I trust that I shall be able to execute my project. Look, here is wax with an impression of the keys of the convent; you must get others made from it. The sisters shall sleep well that night, and before morning we will be far on our journey towards your happy country. Fear not; my disguise is ready – all will go well.'

'The devil it will!' thought Alleyn, as he quitted St S—, and carefully placing the waxen impression he had received against a sunny wall, he paced up the Corso; 'and the devil take me if ever I go within those walls again! I have sown a pretty crop, but I am not mad enough to reap it; and, as the fates will have it, here is Tolomei returned to tax me with my false proceedings. I wish all convents and women – '

Tolomei now accosted him. They walked together towards the Coliseum, talking of indifferent things. They climbed to the highest part of the ruin, and then, seated amid leafy shrubs and fragrant violets and wallflowers, looking over the desert lanes and violated Forum of Rome, Giacomo asked, 'What news of Clorinda?' Alleyn wished himself hanged, and, with a look that almost indicated that his wish was about to be fulfilled, replied briefly to his friend's questions, and then began a string himself, that he might escape his keen, lover-like looks – more painful than his words. Giacomo's hopes were nearly dead. His father was inexorable; and he had learnt, besides, that the person selected by her parents as a husband for Clorinda had arrived in Rome, and this accomplished his misery. He shed abundance of tears as he related this, and ended by declaring that if he still found Clorinda faithful and affectionate, the contrariety of his destiny would urge him to some desperate measure. They separated at length, having appointed to go together to St S— on the following day.

Alleyn broke this appointment. He sent an excuse to Giacomo, who accordingly went alone. In the evening he received a note from Clorinda. She lamented his absence; declared her utter aversion for Giacomo; bewailed her hard fate, and having acquainted him that she was to spend the following day with her parents, entreated him to call on the succeeding one. Alleyn passed the intermediate time at Tivoli, that he might avoid his injured friend, and at the appointed hour went to the convent. Teresa and Clorinda were together; they both looked disturbed and angry; when Alleyn appeared, Teresa arose, and casting a disdainful look on the conscious pair, left the parlour. Clorinda burst into tears. 'Oh, my beloved friend,' she cried, 'I have gone through heart-breaking scenes since I last saw you. This cruel Teresa is continually upbraiding me, and Giacomo's silent looks of grief are a still greater reproach. Yet I am innocent. This heart has escaped from my control; its overwhelming sensations defy all the efforts of my reason, and I passionately love without hope, almost without a return – nor is this all.' She then related that during her visit of the day before, she had been introduced to the person on whom her parents had resolved to bestow her. 'At first,' she continued, 'I was ignorant of the design on foot, and saw him with indifference. Presently my mother took me aside; she began with a torrent of reproaches; told me that all my artifices were discovered, and then showed me a letter of mine to Giacomo which had been intercepted by that artful monster the Superior, and concluded by telling me that I must agree instantly to marry the personage to whom I had been introduced. "Not that you shall be forced," she said; "beware therefore of spreading that report; but your conduct necessitates the strongest measures. If you refuse this match, which is in every way suitable to you, you must prepare to be sent to a convent of Carthusian nuns at Benevento, where if you do not take the veil, you will be strictly guarded, and your plots, letters, and lovers, will be of no avail." Without permitting me to reply, this cruel mother led me back to the drawing-room; this personage, whose name is Romani, came near me, and presently took an opportunity of asking whether I agreed to the arrangement of my parents. What could I say? I gave an ungracious assent, and they consider the matter settled. His estate is near Spolcto, and he is gone to prepare for my reception. The writings are drawing up; the time will soon arrive when I shall change my cage and be miserable for life. You alone, Alleyn, you, generous and brave Englishman, can aid me; take me hence; bear me away to freedom and love, and let me not be sacrificed to this unknown bridegroom, whose person I hardly know, and the idea of whom fills my heart with despair.' Alleyn replied as he best might, with expressions of real sorrow, but of small consolation, and the inexorable dinner-bell rang and separated them just as he concluded his reply.

The same evening Alleyn received a note from her. 'My horror of this marriage,' she wrote, 'increases in proportion as the period of its accomplishment approaches. I hear today that my parents have already given my *corrèdo*[88] to Romani, which he is to expend in jewels and dresses for me, and thus my fate is nearly sealed. I shall be banished from Rome and my friends; I shall live with a stranger – I must be miserable. Giacomo is better than this. But as an union with him is impossible, and you refuse to aid me, and to liberate one whom you say you love, listen to a plan I have formed; some years ago I was addressed by one, who at that time gained my heart, and whom I still regard with tenderness. The smallness of my dowry caused his father to break off the treaty; this father is now dead. Go to this gentleman – find out whether he still loves me. Married to him, I should be united to one whose merits I know – I should live at Rome, and there would be some alleviation to my cruel fate. At least come tomorrow to the convent, and endeavour to console your miserable friend.'

Alleyn, as may easily be supposed, did not pay the required visit to the quondam lover of Clorinda. Perhaps she expected this; for the same night she wrote to him herself. Her letter was long and eloquent. Its expressions seemed to proceed from the overflowings of a passionate and loving heart. She referred to Alleyn as a common friend, and urged expedition in every measure that was to be pursued. This letter was intercepted and carried to her parents. On the following day Alleyn received a despairing note, entreating him not to attempt to come to the convent. 'Alas!' she wrote, 'how truly miserable I am! What a fate! I suffer, and am the cause of a thousand griefs to others. Oh, heaven! I were better dead; then I should cease to lament, or at least to occasion wretchedness to others. Now I am hated by others, and even by myself – Oh, my incomparable friend! Angel of my heart! Can I be the cause of misery even to you? See Giacomo, my beloved friend; tell him how deeply I pity him, but counsel him in my name to desist from all further pursuit. He must permit me to obey my parents, and they will never consent. My sole aim now is to escape from this prison.'

Another and another letter came; and she most earnestly begged him not to come to the convent. Thus nearly a month passed, when one morning early Alleyn was surprised by a visit from the Superior of the convent of St S—. The old lady seemed very full of matter. She drank the *rosoglio* presented to her, took snuff, and opened her budget. She talked of the trouble she had ever had with poor Clorinda; inveighed against Giacomo; during her long discourse she praised her own sagacity, the tender affection of Clorinda's parents, and related how she had always opposed the entrance of young men into the convent and their free communication with Clorinda, except his own; but that his politeness and known integrity had in this particular caused her to relax her discipline; and she concluded by inviting him to visit the convent whenever it should be agreeable to him. She then took her leave.

Alleyn was much disturbed. He wished not to go to St S—; he knew that he ought not to see Clorinda again. He resolved not to go out at all, and sat thinking of her beauty, love and unaffected manners, until he resolved to walk that he might get rid of such thoughts. He hurried down the Corso, and before he was aware found himself before the door of the convent of St S—. He paused, again he entered the outer hall – his hand was on the bell, when the door opened and Giacomo came out. Seeing Alleyn, he threw himself into his arms, shedding a torrent of tears. This exordium startled our Englishman; the conclusion was soon told: Clorinda had married Romani the day before, and on the same evening had quitted Rome for Spoleto.

This news sobered Alleyn at once; he shuddered almost to think of the folly he had been about to commit, feeling as one who is stayed by a friendly hand when about to place his foot beyond the brink of a high precipice. They turned from the convent door. 'And yet,' said Alleyn as he walked on, 'are you secure of the truth of your account? The Superior called on me yesterday and invited me to visit St S—. Why should she do this if Clorinda were gone? I have half a mind to go and fathom this mystery.'

'Ay, go by all means,' replied Giacomo bitterly, 'you will be welcome; fill your pockets with sugar plums; dose the old lady with *rosoglio*, and kiss the gentle nuns, the youngest of whom bears the weight of sixty years under the fillet on her brow.[89] They miss your good cheer, and who knows, Clorinda gone, what other nets they may weave to secure so valuable a prize. True, you are an Englishman and a heretic; words which, interpreted into pure Tuscan, mean an untired prodigal, and one, pardon me, whose conscience will no more stickle at violating yon sanctuary than at eating flesh on Fridays. Go by all means, and make the best of your good fortune among these houris.'[90]

'Rather say, take post horses for Spoleto, friend Giacomo. And yet neither – it is all vanity and vexation of spirit. I will go paint my *Profession of Eloisa*.'

Ferdinando Eboli

A Tale

DURING this quiet time of peace, we are fast forgetting the excitements and astonishing events of the last war; and the very names of Europe's conquerors are becoming antiquated to the ears of our children. Those were more romantic days than these; for the revulsions occasioned by revolution or invasion were full of romance; and travellers in those countries in which these scenes had place hear strange and wonderful stories, whose truth so much resembles fiction that while interested in the narration we never give implicit credence to the narrator. Of this kind is a tale I heard at Naples. The fortunes of war perhaps did not influence its actors; yet it appears improbable that any circumstances so out of the usual routine could have had place under the garish daylight that peace sheds upon the world.

When Murat, then called Gioacchino, King of Naples,[91] raised his Italian regiments, several young nobles, who had before been scarcely more than vine-dressers on the soil, were inspired with a love of arms, and presented themselves as candidates for military honours. Among these was the young Count Eboli. The father of this youthful noble had followed Ferdinando to Sicily; but his estates lay principally near Salerno, and he was naturally desirous of preserving them; while the hopes that the French government held out of glory and prosperity to his country made him often regret that he had followed his legitimate but imbecile king to exile. When he died, therefore, he recommended his son to return to Naples, to present himself to his old and tried friend the Marchese Spina, who held a high office in Murat's government, and through his means to reconcile himself to the new king. All this was easily achieved. The young and gallant count was permitted to possess his patrimony; and, as a further pledge of good fortune, he was betrothed to the only child of the Marchese Spina. The nuptials were deferred till the end of the ensuing campaign.

Meanwhile the army was put in motion, and Count Eboli only

obtained such short leave of absence as permitted him to visit for a few hours the villa of his future father-in-law, there to take leave of him and his affianced bride. The villa was situated on one of the Apennines to the north of Salerno, and looked down, over the plain of Calabria, in which Paestum is situated, on to the blue Mediterranean. A precipice on one side, a brawling mountain torrent, and a thick grove of ilex, added beauty to the sublimity of its site. Count Eboli ascended the mountain path in all the joy of youth and hope. His stay was brief. An exhortation and a blessing from the Marchese, a tender farewell, graced by gentle tears, from the fair Adalinda, were the recollections he was to bear with him, to inspire him with courage and hope in danger and absence. The sun had just sunk behind the distant isle of Istria, when, kissing his lady's hand, he said at last, 'Addio,' and with slower steps, and more melancholy mien, rode down the mountain on his road to Naples.

That same night Adalinda retired early to her apartment, dismissing her attendants; and then, restless from mingled fear and hope, she threw open the glass door that led to a balcony looking over the edge of the hill upon the torrent, whose loud rushing often lulled her to sleep; but whose waters were concealed from sight by the ilex trees, which lifted their topmost branches above the guarding parapet of the balcony.

Leaning her check upon her hand, she thought of the dangers her lover would encounter, of her loneliness the while, of his letters, and of his return. A rustling sound now caught her ear: was it the breeze among the ilex trees? her own veil was unwaved by every wind, her tresses even, heavy in their own rich beauty only, were not lifted from her check. Again those sounds. Her blood retreated to her heart, and her limbs trembled. What could it mean? Suddenly the upper branches of the nearest tree were disturbed; they opened, and the faint starlight showed a man's figure among them. He prepared to spring from his hold on to the wall. It was a feat of peril. First the soft voice of her lover bade her, 'Fear not,' and on the next instant he was at her side, calming her terrors, and recalling her spirits, that almost left her gentle frame, from mingled surprise, dread and joy. He encircled her waist with his arm, and pouring forth a thousand passionate expressions of love, she leant on his shoulder, and wept from agitation; while he covered her hands with kisses, and gazed on her with ardent adoration.

Then in calmer mood they sat together; triumph and joy lighted up his eyes, and a modest blush glowed on her cheek; for never before had she sat alone with him, nor heard unrestrained his impassioned assurances of affection. It was indeed Love's own hour. The stars trembled on the roof of his eternal temple; the dashing of the torrent, the mild summer atmosphere, and the mysterious aspect of the darkened scenery, were all in unison, to inspire security and voluptuous hope. They talked of how their hearts, through the medium of divine nature, might hold commune during absence; of the joys of reunion, and of their prospect of perfect happiness.

The moment at last arrived when he must depart. 'One tress of this silken hair,' said he, raising one of the many curls that clustered on her neck. 'I will place it on my heart, a shield to protect me against the swords and balls of the enemy.' He drew his keen-edged dagger from its sheath. 'Ill weapon for so gentle a deed,' he said, severing the lock, and at the same moment many drops of blood fell fast on the fair arm of the lady. He answered her fearful enquiries by showing a gash he had awkwardly inflicted on his left hand. First he insisted on securing his prize, and then he permitted her to bind his wound, which she did half laughing, half in sorrow, winding round his hand a riband loosened from her own arm. 'Now farewell,' he cried; 'I must ride twenty miles ere dawn, and the descending Bear shows that midnight is past.' His descent was difficult, but he achieved it happily, and the stave of a song, whose soft sounds rose like the smoke of incense from an altar, from the dell below, to her impatient ear, assured her of his safety.

As is always the case when an account is gathered from eye-witnesses, I never could ascertain the exact date of these events. They occurred however while Murat was King of Naples, and when he raised his Italian regiments, Count Eboli, as aforesaid, became a junior officer in them, and served with much distinction; though I cannot name either the country, or the battle in which he acted so conspicuous a part that he was on the spot promoted to a troop.

Not long after this event, and while he was stationed in the north of Italy, Gioacchino, sending for him to headquarters late one evening, entrusted him with a confidential mission, across a country occupied by the enemy's troops, to a town possessed by the French. It was necessary to undertake the expedition during the night, and he was expected to return on that succeeding the following day. The king himself gave him his despatches and the word; and the noble youth, with modest firmness, protested that he would succeed, or die, in the fulfilment of his trust.

It was already night, and the crescent moon was low in the west, when Count Ferdinando Eboli mounted his favourite horse and at a quick gallop cleared the streets of the town; and then, following the directions given him, crossed the country among the fields planted with vines, carefully avoiding the main road. It was a beauteous and still night; calm, and sleep, occupied the earth; war, the bloodhound, slumbered; the spirit of love alone had life at that silent hour. Exulting in the hope of glory, our young hero commenced his journey, and visions of aggrandisement and love formed his reveries. A distant sound roused him; he checked his horse and listened; voices approached; recognising the speech of a German, he turned from the path he was following to a still straighter way. But again the tone of an enemy was heard, and the trampling of horses. Eboli did not hesitate; he dismounted, tied his steed to a tree, and, skirting along the enclosure of the field, trusted to escape thus unobserved. He succeeded after an hour's painful progress, and arrived on the borders of a stream, which, as the boundary between two states, was the mark of his having finally escaped danger. Descending the steep bank of the river, which, with his horse, he might perhaps have forded, he now prepared to swim. He held his despatch in one hand, threw away his cloak, and was about to plunge into the water, when from under the dark shade of the *argine*,[92] which had concealed them, he was suddenly arrested by unseen hands, cast on the ground, bound, gagged and blinded, and then placed in a little boat, which was sculled with infinite rapidity down the stream.

There seemed so much of premeditation in the act that it baffled conjecture, yet he must believe himself a prisoner to the Austrian. While, however, he still vainly reflected, the boat was moored, he was lifted out, and the change of atmosphere made him aware that they entered some house. With extreme care and celerity, yet in the utmost silence, he was stripped of his clothes, and the two rings he wore were drawn from his fingers; other habiliments were thrown over him; and then no departing footstep was audible: but soon he heard the splash of a single oar, and he felt himself alone. He lay perfectly unable to move; the only relief his captor or captors had afforded him being the exchange of the gag for a tightly bound handkerchief. For hours he thus remained, with a tortured mind, bursting with rage, impatience and disappointment; now writhing, as well as he could, in his endeavours to free himself, now still, in despair. His despatches were taken away, and the period was swiftly passing when he could by his presence have remedied in some degree this evil. The morning dawned; and though the full glare of the sun could not visit his eyes, he felt it play upon his limbs. As the day advanced, hunger preyed on him, and though amidst the visitation of mightier, he at first disdained this minor evil, towards evening it became, in spite of himself, the predominant sensation. Night approached, and the fear that he should remain, and even starve, in this unvisited solitude had more than once thrilled through his frame, when feminine voices and a child's gay laugh met his ear. He heard persons enter the apartment, and he was asked in his native language, while the ligature was taken from his mouth, the cause of his present situation. He attributed it to *banditti*: his bonds were quickly cut, and his banded eyes restored to sight. It was long before he recovered himself. Water brought from the stream, however, was some refreshment, and by degrees he resumed the use of his senses, and saw that he was in a dilapidated shepherd's cot, with no one near him save the peasant girl and a child who had liberated him. They rubbed his ankles and wrists, and the little fellow offered him some bread and eggs; after which refreshment, and an hour's repose, Ferdinando felt himself sufficiently restored to revolve his adventure in his mind, and to determine on the conduct he was to pursue.

He looked at the dress which had been given him in exchange for that which he had worn. It was of the plainest and meanest description. Still no time was to be lost; and he felt assured that the only step he could take was to return with all speed to the headquarters of the Neapolitan army, and inform the king of his disasters and his loss.

It were long to follow his backward steps, and to tell all of indignation and disappointment that swelled his heart. He walked painfully but resolutely all night, and by three in the morning entered the town where Gioacchino then was. He was challenged by the sentinels; he gave the word confided to him by Murat, and was instantly made prisoner by the soldiers. He declared to them his name and rank, and the necessity he was under of immediately seeing the king. He was taken to the guardhouse, and the officer on duty there listened with contempt to his representations, telling him that Count Ferdinando Eboli had returned three hours before, ordering him to be confined for further examination as a spy. Eboli loudly insisted that some impostor had taken his name; and while he related the story of his capture, another officer came in, who recognised his person; other individuals acquainted with him joined the party; and as the impostor had been seen by none but the officer of the night, his tale gained ground.

A young Frenchman of superior rank, who had orders to attend the king early in the morning, carried a report of what was going forward to Murat himself. The tale was so strange that the king sent for the young count; and then, in spite of having seen and believed in his counterfeit a few hours before, and having received from him an account of his mission, which had been faithfully executed, the appearance of the youth staggered him, and he commanded the presence of him who, as Count Eboli, had appeared before him a few hours previously. As Ferdinando stood beside the king, his eye glanced at a large and splendid mirror.

His matted hair, his bloodshot eyes, his haggard looks and torn and mean dress, derogated from the nobility of his appearance; and still less did he appear like the magnificent Count Eboli, when, to his utter confusion and astonishment, his counterfeit stood beside him.

He was perfect in all the outward signs that denoted high birth; and so like him whom he represented, that it would have been impossible to discern one from the other apart. The same chestnut hair clustered on his brow; the sweet and animated hazel eyes were the same; the one voice was the echo of the other. The composure and dignity of the pretender gained the suffrages of those around. When he was told of the strange appearance of another Count Eboli, he laughed in a frank good-humoured manner, and turning to Ferdinando, said, 'You honour me much in selecting me for your personation; but there are two or three things I like about myself so well that you must excuse my unwillingness to exchange myself for you.' Ferdinando would have answered, but the false count, with greater haughtiness, turning to the king, said, 'Will your majesty decide between us? I cannot bandy words with a fellow of this sort.' Irritated by scorn, Ferdinando demanded leave to challenge the pretender; who said, that if the king and his brother officers did not think that he should degrade himself and disgrace the army by going out with a common vagabond, he was willing to chastise him, even at the peril of his own life. But the king, after a few more questions, feeling assured that the unhappy noble was an impostor, in severe and menacing terms reprehended him for his insolence, and telling him that he owed it to his mercy alone that he was not executed as a spy, ordered him instantly to be conducted without the walls of the town, with threats of weighty punishment if he ever dared to subject his impostures to further trial.

It requires a strong imagination, and the experience of much misery, fully to enter into Ferdinando's feelings. From high rank, glory, hope and love, he was hurled to utter beggary and disgrace. The insulting words of his triumphant rival, and the degrading menaces of his so lately gracious sovereign, rang in his ears; every nerve in his frame writhed with agony. But, fortunately for the endurance of human life, the worst misery in early youth is often but a painful dream, which we cast off when slumber quits our eyes. After a struggle with intolerable anguish, hope and courage revived in his heart. His resolution was quickly made. He would return to Naples, relate his story to the Marchese Spina, and through his influence obtain at least an impartial hearing from the king. It was not, however, in his peculiar situation, an easy task to put his determination into effect. He was pennyless; his dress bespoke poverty; he had neither friend nor kinsman near, but such as would behold in him the most impudent of swindlers. Still his courage did not fail him. The kind Italian soil, in the autumnal season now advanced, furnished him with chestnuts, arbutus berries and grapes. He took the most direct road over the hills, avoiding towns, and indeed every habitation; travelling principally in the night, when, except in cities, the officers of government had retired from their stations. How he succeeded in getting from one end of Italy to the other it is difficult to say; but certain it is that, after the interval of a few weeks, he presented himself at the Villa Spina.

With considerable difficulty he obtained admission to the presence of the marchese, who received him standing, with an enquiring look, not at all recognising the noble youth. Ferdinando requested a private interview, for there were several visitors present. His voice startled the marchese, who complied, taking him into another apartment. Here Ferdinando disclosed himself, and, with rapid and agitated utterance, was relating the history of his misfortunes, when the tramp of horses was heard, the great bell rang, and a domestic announced, 'Count Ferdinando Eboli.' 'It is himself,' cried the youth, turning pale. The words were strange, and they appeared still more so, when the person announced entered; the perfect semblance of the young noble, whose name he assumed, as he had appeared, when last, at his departure, he trod the pavement of the hall. He inclined his head gracefully to the baron, turning with a glance of some surprise, but more disdain, towards Ferdinando, exclaiming, 'Thou here!'

Ferdinando drew himself up to his full height. In spite of fatigue, ill fare and coarse garments, his manner was full of dignity. The marchese looked at him fixedly, and started as he marked his proud mien, and saw in his expressive features the very face of Eboli. But again he was perplexed when he turned and discerned, as in a mirror, the same countenance reflected by the newcomer, who underwent this scrutiny somewhat impatiently. In brief and scornful words, he told the marchese that this was a second attempt in the intruder to impose himself as Count Eboli; that the trick had failed before, and would again; adding, laughing, that it was hard to be brought to prove himself to be himself, against the assertion of a *briccone*,[93] whose likeness to him, and matchless impudence, were his whole stock in trade.

'Why, my good fellow,' continued he, sneeringly, 'you put me out of conceit with myself, to think that one, apparently so like me, should get on no better in the world.'

The blood mounted into Ferdinando's cheeks on his enemy's bitter taunts; with difficulty he restrained himself from closing with his foe, while the words, 'Traitorous impostor!' burst from his lips. The baron commanded the fierce youth to be silent, and, moved by a look that he remembered to be Ferdinando's, he said, gently, 'By your respect for me, I adjure you to be patient; fear not but that I will deal impartially.' Then turning to the pretended Eboli, he added that he could not doubt but that he was the true count, and asked excuse for his previous indecision. At first the latter appeared angry, but at length he burst into a laugh, and then, apologising for his ill breeding, continued laughing heartily at the perplexity of the marchese. It is certain, his gaiety gained more credit with his auditor than the indignant glances of poor Ferdinando. The false count then said that, after the king's menaces, he had entertained no expectation that the farce was to be played over again. He had obtained leave of absence, of which he profited to visit his future father-in-law, after having spent a few days in his own palazzo[94] at Naples.

Until now, Ferdinando had listened silently with a feeling of curiosity, anxious to learn all he could of the actions and motives of his rival; but at these last words he could no longer contain himself. 'What!' cried he, 'hast thou usurped my place in my own father's house, and dared assume my power in my ancestral halls?' A gush of tears overpowered the youth; he hid his face in his hands.

Fierceness and pride lit up the countenance of the pretender. 'By the eternal God and the sacred cross, I swear,' he exclaimed, 'that palace is my father's palace; those halls the halls of my ancestors!'

Ferdinando looked up with surprise. 'And the earth opens not,' he said, 'to swallow the perjured man.' He then, at the call of the marchese, related his adventures, while scorn mantled on the features of his rival.

The marchese, looking at both, could not free himself from doubt. He turned from one to the other: in spite of the wild and disordered appearance of poor Ferdinando, there was something in him that forbade his friend to condemn him as the impostor; but then it was utterly impossible to pronounce such the gallant and noble-looking youth, who could only be acknowledged as the real count by the disbelief of the other's tale. The marchese, calling an attendant, sent for his fair daughter. 'This decision,' said he, 'shall be made over to the subtle judgement of a woman, and the keen penetration of one who loves.' Both the youths now smiled – the same smile; the same expression – that, of anticipated triumph. The baron was more perplexed than ever.

Adalinda had heard of the arrival of Count Eboli, and entered, resplendent in youth and happiness. She turned quickly towards him who resembled most the person she expected to see; when a well-known voice pronounced her name, and she gazed aghast on the double appearance of the lover. Her father, taking her hand, briefly explained the mystery, and bade her assure herself which was her affianced husband.

'Signorina,' said Ferdinando, 'disdain me not because I appear before you thus in disgrace and misery. Your love, your goodness will restore me to prosperity and happiness.'

'I know not by what means,' said the wondering girl, 'but surely you are Count Eboli.'

'Adalinda,' said the rival youth, 'waste not your words on a villain. Lovely and deceived one, I trust, trembling I say it, that I can with one word assure you that I am Eboli.'

'Adalinda,' said Ferdinando, 'I placed the nuptial ring on your finger; before God your vows were given to me.'

The false count approached the lady, and bending one knee, took from his heart a locket, enclosing hair tied with a green riband, which she recognised, and pointed to a slight scar on his left hand. Adalinda blushed deeply and turning to her father said, motioning towards the kneeling youth, 'He is Ferdinando.'

All protestations now from the unhappy Eboli were vain. The marchese would have cast him into a dungeon; but, at the earnest request of his rival, he was not detained, but thrust ignominiously from the villa. The rage of a wild beast newly chained was less than the tempest of indignation that now filled the heart of Ferdinando. Physical suffering, from fatigue and fasting, was added to his internal anguish; for some hours madness, if that were madness which never forgets its ill, possessed him. In a tumult of feelings there was one predominant idea: it was, to take possession of his father's house, and to try, by ameliorating the fortuitous circumstances of his lot, to gain the upper hand of his adversary. He expended his remaining strength in reaching Naples, entered his family palace, and was received and acknowledged by his astonished domestics.

One of his first acts was to take from a cabinet a miniature of his father encircled with jewels, and to invoke the aid of the paternal spirit. Refreshment and a bath restored him to some of his usual strength; and he looked forward with almost childish delight to one night in peace under the roof of his father's house. This was not permitted. Ere midnight the great bell sounded: his rival entered as master, with the Marchese Spina. The result may be divined. The marchese appeared more indignant than the false Eboli. He insisted that the unfortunate youth should be imprisoned. The portrait, whose setting was costly, found on him, proved him guilty of robbery. He was given into the hands of the police, and thrown into a dungeon. I will not dwell on the subsequent scenes. He was tried by the tribunal, condemned as guilty, and sentenced to the galleys for life.

On the eve of the day when he was to be removed from the Neapolitan prison to work on the roads in Calabria, his rival visited him in his dungeon. For some moments both looked at the other in silence. The impostor gazed on the prisoner with mingled pride and compassion: there was evidently a struggle in his heart. The answering glance of Ferdinando was calm, free and dignified. He was not resigned to his hard fate, but he disdained to make an exhibition of despair to his cruel and successful foe. A spasm of pain seemed to wrench the bosom of the false one; and he turned aside, striving to recover the hardness of heart which had hitherto supported him in the prosecution of his guilty enterprise.

Ferdinando spoke first. 'What would the triumphant criminal with his innocent victim?'

His visitant replied haughtily, 'Do not address such epithets to me, or I leave you to your fate: I am that which I say I am.'

'To me this boast!' cried Ferdinando, scornfully; 'but perhaps these walls have ears.'

'Heaven, at least, is not deaf,' said the deceiver; 'favouring heaven, which knows and admits my claim. But a truce to this idle discussion. Compassion – a distaste to see one so very like myself in such ill condition – a foolish whim, perhaps, on which you may congratulate yourself – has led me hither. The bolts of your dungeon are drawn; here is a purse of gold; fulfil one easy condition, and you are free.'

'And that condition?'

'Sign this paper.'

He gave to Ferdinando a writing, containing a confession of his imputed crimes. The hand of the guilty youth trembled as he gave it; there was confusion in his mien, and a restless uneasy rolling of his eye. Ferdinando wished in one mighty word, potent as lightning, loud as thunder, to convey his burning disdain of this proposal; but expression is weak, and calm is more full of power than storm. Without a word, he tore the paper in two pieces, and threw them at the feet of his enemy.

With a sudden change of manner, his visitant conjured him, in voluble and impetuous terms, to comply. Ferdinando answered only by requesting to be left alone. Now and then a half word broke uncontrollably from his lips; but he curbed himself. Yet he could not hide his agitation when, as an argument to make him yield, the false count assured him that he was already married to Adalinda. Bitter agony thrilled poor Ferdinando's frame; but he preserved a calm mien, and an unaltered resolution. Having exhausted every menace and every persuasion, his rival left him, the purpose for which he came unaccomplished. On the morrow, with many others, the refuse of mankind, Count Ferdinando Eboli was led in chains to the unwholesome plains of Calabria, to work there at the roads.

I must hurry over some of the subsequent events; for a detailed account of them would fill volumes. The assertion of the usurper of Ferdinando's right, that he was already married to Adalinda, was, like all else he said, false. The day was, however, fixed for their union, when the illness and the subsequent death of the Marchese Spina delayed its celebration. Adalinda retired, during the first months of mourning, to a castle belonging to her father not far from Arpino, a town of the kingdom of Naples, in the midst of the Apennines, about fifty miles from the capital. Before she went, the deceiver tried to persuade her to consent to a private marriage. He was probably afraid that, in the long interval that was about to ensue before he could secure her, she would discover his imposture. Besides, a rumour had gone abroad that one of the fellow-prisoners of Ferdinando, a noted bandit, had escaped, and that the young count was his companion in flight. Adalinda, however, refused to comply with her lover's entreaties, and retired to her seclusion with an old aunt, who was blind and deaf, but an excellent *duenna*.[95]

The false Eboli seldom visited his mistress; but he was a master in his art, and subsequent events showed that he must have spent all his time disguised in the vicinity of the castle. He contrived by various means, unsuspected at the moment, to have all Adalinda's servants changed for creatures of his own; so that, without her being aware of the restraint, she was, in fact, a prisoner in her own house. It is impossible to say what first awakened her suspicions concerning the deception put upon her. She was an Italian, with all the habitual quiescence and lassitude of her country-women in the ordinary routine of life, and with all their energy and passion when roused. The moment the doubt darted into her mind, she resolved to be assured; a few questions relative to scenes that had passed between poor Ferdinando and herself sufficed for this. They were asked so suddenly and pointedly that the pretender was thrown off his guard; he looked confused, and stammered in his replies. Their eyes met, he felt that he was detected, and she saw that he perceived her now-confirmed suspicions. A look such as is peculiar to an impostor, a glance that deformed his beauty, and filled his usually noble countenance with the hideous lines of cunning and cruel triumph, completed her faith in her own discernment. 'How,' she thought, 'could I have mistaken this man for my own gentle Eboli?' Again their eyes met: the peculiar expression of his terrified her, and she hastily quitted the apartment.

Her resolution was quickly formed. It was of no use to attempt to explain her situation to her old aunt. She determined to depart immediately for Naples, throw herself at the feet of Gioacchino, and to relate and obtain credit for her strange history. But the time was already lost when she could have executed this design. The contrivances of the deceiver were complete – she found herself a prisoner. Excess of fear gave her boldness, if not courage. She sought her jailor. A few minutes before, she had been a young and thoughtless girl, docile as a child, and as unsuspecting. Now she felt as if she had suddenly grown old in wisdom, and that the experience of years had been gained in that of a few seconds.

During their interview, she was wary and firm; while the instinctive power of innocence over guilt gave majesty to her demeanour. The contriver of her ills for a moment cowered beneath her eye. At first he would by no means allow that he was not the person he pretended to be: but the energy and eloquence of truth bore down his artifice, so that, at length driven into a corner, he turned – a stag at bay. Then it was her turn to quail; for the superior energy of a man gave him the mastery. He declared the truth. He was the elder brother of Ferdinando, a natural son of the old Count Eboli. His mother, who had been wronged, never forgave her injuror, and bred her son in deadly hate for his parent, and a belief that the advantages enjoyed by his more fortunate brother were rightfully his own. His education was rude; but he had an Italian's subtle talents, swiftness of perception and guileful arts.

'It would blanch your cheek,' he said to his trembling auditress, 'could I describe all that I have suffered to achieve my purpose. I would trust to none – I executed all myself. It was a glorious triumph, but due to my perseverance and my fortitude, when I and my usurping brother stood, I, the noble, he, the degraded outcast, before our sovereign.'

Having rapidly detailed his history, he now sought to win the favourable ear of Adalinda, who stood with averted and angry looks. He tried by the varied shows of passion and tenderness to move her heart. Was he not, in truth, the object of her love? Was it not he who scaled her balcony at Villa Spina? He recalled scenes of mutual overflow of feeling to her mind, thus urging arguments the most potent with a delicate woman; pure blushes tinged her cheek, but horror of the deceiver predominated over every other sentiment. He swore that as soon as they should be united he would free Ferdinando, and bestow competency, nay, if so she willed it, half his possessions, on him. She coldly replied that she would rather share the chains of the innocent and misery than link herself with imposture and crime. She demanded her liberty, but the untamed and even ferocious nature that had borne the deceiver through his career of crime now broke forth, and he invoked fearful imprecations on his head if she ever quitted the castle except as his wife. His look of conscious power and unbridled wickedness terrified her; her flashing eyes spoke abhorrence: it would have been far easier for her to have died than have yielded the smallest point to a man who made her feel for one moment his irresistible power, arising from her being an unprotected woman, wholly in his hands. She left him, feeling as if she had just escaped from the impending sword of an assassin.

One hour's deliberation suggested to her a method of escape from her terrible situation. In a wardrobe at the castle lay in their pristine gloss the habiliments of a page of her mother, who had died suddenly, leaving these unworn relics of his station. Dressing herself in these, she tied up her dark shining hair, and even, with a somewhat bitter feeling, girded on the slight sword that appertained to the costume. Then, through a private passage leading from her own apartment to the chapel of the castle, she glided with noiseless steps, long after the Ave Maria[96] sounded at twenty-four o'clock had, on a November night, given token that half an hour had passed since the setting of the sun. She possessed the key of the chapel door – it opened at her touch; she closed it behind her, and she was free. The pathless hills were around her, the starry heavens above, and a cold wintry breeze murmured around the castle walls; but fear of her enemy conquered every other fear, and she tripped lightly on, in a kind of ecstasy, for many a long hour over the stony mountain path – she, who had never before walked more than a mile or two at any time in her life – till her feet were blistered, her slight shoes cut through, her way utterly lost. At morning's dawn she found herself in the midst of the wild ilex-covered Apennines, and neither habitation nor human being apparent.

She was hungry and weary. She had brought gold and jewels with her, but here were no means of exchanging these for food. She remembered stories of *banditti*; but none could be so ruffian-like and cruel as him from whom she fled. This thought, a little rest and a draught of water from a pure mountain spring restored her to some portion of courage, and she continued her journey. Noonday approached; and, in the south of Italy, the noonday sun, when unclouded, even in November, is oppressively warm, especially to an Italian woman who never exposes herself to its beams. Faintness came over her. There appeared recesses in the mountainside along which she was travelling, grown over with bay and arbutus: she entered one of these, there to repose. It was deep, and led to another that opened into a spacious cavern lighted from above; there were cates, grapes and a flagon of wine on a rough-hewn table. She looked fearfully around, but no inhabitant appeared. She placed herself at the table, and, half in dread, ate of the food presented to her, and then sat, her elbow on the table, her head resting on her little snow-white hand; her dark hair shading her brow and clustering round her throat. An appearance of languor and fatigue diffused through her attitude, while her soft black eyes filled at intervals with large tears, as pitying herself, she recurred to the cruel circumstances of her lot. Her fanciful but elegant dress, her feminine form, her beauty and her grace, as she sat pensive and alone in the rough unhewn cavern, formed a picture a poet would describe with delight, an artist love to paint.

'She seemed a being of another world; a seraph, all light and beauty; a Ganymede, escaped from his thrall above to his natal Ida.[97] It was long before I recognised, looking down on her from the opening hill, my lost Adalinda.' Thus spoke the young Count Eboli, when he related this story; for its end was as romantic as its commencement.

When Ferdinando had arrived a galley-slave in Calabria, he found himself coupled with a bandit, a brave fellow, who abhorred his chains, from love of freedom, as much as his fellow-prisoner did, from all the combination of disgrace and misery they brought upon him. Together they devised a plan of escape, and succeeded in effecting it. On their road, Ferdinando related his story to the outlaw, who encouraged him to hope a favourable turn of fate; and meanwhile invited and persuaded the desperate man to share his fortunes as a robber among the wild hills of Calabria.

The cavern where Adalinda had taken refuge was one of their fastnesses, whither they betook themselves at periods of imminent danger for safety only, as no booty could be collected in that unpeopled solitude; and there, one afternoon, returning from the chase, they found the wandering, fearful, solitary, fugitive girl; and never was lighthouse more welcome to tempest-tossed sailor than was her own Ferdinando to his lady-love.

Fortune, now tired of persecuting the young noble, favoured him still further. The story of the lovers interested the bandit chief, and promise of reward secured him. Ferdinando persuaded Adalinda to remain one night in the cave, and on the following morning they prepared to

Adalinda

proceed to Naples; but at the moment of their departure they were surprised by an unexpected visitant: the robbers brought in a prisoner – it was the impostor. Missing on the morrow her who was the pledge of his safety and success, but assured that she could not have wandered far, he dispatched emissaries in all directions to seek her; and himself, joining in the pursuit, followed the road she had taken and was captured by these lawless men, who expected rich ransom from one whose appearance denoted rank and wealth. When they discovered who their prisoner was, they generously delivered him up into his brother's hands.

Ferdinando and Adalinda proceeded to Naples. On their arrival, she presented herself to Queen Caroline; and, through her, Murat heard with astonishment the device that had been practised on him. The young count was restored to his honours and possessions, and within a few months afterwards was united to his betrothed bride.

The compassionate nature of the count and countess led them to interest themselves warmly in the fate of Ludovico, whose subsequent career was more honourable but less fortunate. At the intercession of his relative, Gioacchino permitted him to enter the army, where he distinguished himself, and obtained promotion. The brothers were at Moscow together, and mutually assisted each other during the horrors of the retreat. At one time overcome by drowsiness, the mortal symptom resulting from excessive cold, Ferdinando lingered behind his comrades; but Ludovico refusing to leave him, dragged him on in spite of himself, till, entering a village, food and fire restored him, and his life was saved. On another evening, when wind and sleet added to the horror of their situation, Ludovico, after many ineffective struggles, slid from his horse lifeless; Ferdinando was at his side, and, dismounting, endeavoured by every means in his power to bring back pulsation to his stagnant blood. His comrades went forward, and the young count was left alone with his dying brother in the white boundless waste. Once Ludovico opened his eyes and recognised him; he pressed his hand, and his lips moved to utter a blessing as he died. At that moment the welcome sounds of the enemy's approach roused Ferdinando from the despair into which his dreadful situation had plunged him. He was taken prisoner, and his life was thus saved. When Napoleon went to Elba, he, with many others of his countrymen, was liberated, and returned to Naples.

The Sisters of Albano

And near Albano's scarce divided waves
Shine from a sister valley; and afar
The Tiber winds, and the broad ocean laves
The Latian coast where sprang the Epic war,
'Arms and the Man,' whose re-ascending star
Rose o'er an empire; but beneath thy right
Tully reposed from Rome; and where yon bar
Of girdling mountains intercepts the sight
The Sabine farm was till'd, the weary bard's delight.[98]

IT was to see this beautiful lake that I made my last excursion before quitting Rome. The spring had nearly grown into summer, the trees were all in full but fresh green foliage, the vine-dresser was singing, perched among them, training his vines; the cicala[99] had not yet begun her song, the heats therefore had not commenced; but at evening the fireflies gleamed among the hills, and the cooing aziola[100] assured us of what in that country needs no assurance, fine weather for the morrow. We set out early in the morning to avoid the heats, breakfasted at Albano, and till ten o'clock passed our time in visiting the Mosaic, the villa of Cicero, and other curiosities of the place. We reposed during the middle of the day in a tent elevated for us at the hilltop, whence we looked on the hill-embosomed lake, and the distant eminence crowned by a town with its church. Other villages and cottages were scattered among the foldings of mountains, and beyond we saw the deep blue sea of the southern poets, which received the swift and immortal Tiber, rocking it to repose among its devouring waves. The Coliseum falls and the Pantheon decays – the very hills of Rome are perishing, but the Tiber lives for ever, flows for ever – and forever feeds the land-encircling Mediterranean with fresh waters.

Our summer and pleasure-seeking party consisted of many; to me the most interesting person was the Countess Atanasia D— , who was as beautiful as an imagination of Raphael, and good as the ideal of a poet.

Two of her children accompanied her, with animated looks and gentle manners, quiet, yet enjoying. I sat near her, watching the changing shadows of the landscape before us. As the sun descended, it poured a tide of light into the valley of the lake, deluging the deep bank formed by the mountain with liquid gold. The domes and turrets of the far town flashed and gleamed, the trees were dyed in splendour; two or three slight clouds, which had drunk the radiance till it became their essence, floated golden islets in the lustrous empyrean. The waters, reflecting the brilliancy of the sky and the fire-tinted banks, beamed a second heaven, a second irradiated earth, at our feet. The Mediterranean gazing on the sun – as the eyes of a mortal bride fail and are dimmed when reflecting her lover's glance – was lost, mixed in his light, till it had become one with him. Long (our souls, like the sea, the hills and lake, drinking in the supreme loveliness) we gazed, till the too full cup overflowed, and we turned away with a sigh.

At our feet there was a knoll of ground that formed the foreground of our picture; two trees lay basking against the sky, glittering with the golden light, which like dew seemed to hang amid their branches – a rock closed the prospect on the other side, twined round by creepers, and redolent with blooming myrtle – a brook crossed by huge stones gushed through the turf, and on the fragments of rock that lay about sat two or three persons, peasants, who attracted our attention. One was a hunter, as his gun, lying on a bank not far off, demonstrated, yet he was a tiller of the soil; his rough straw hat, and his picturesque but coarse dress, belonged to that class. The other was some *contadina*,[101] in the costume of her country, returning, her basket on her arm, from the village to her cottage home. They were regarding the stores of a pedlar, who with doffed hat stood near: some of these consisted of pictures and prints – views of the country, and portraits of the Madonna. Our peasants regarded these with pleased attention.

'One might easily make out a story for that pair,' I said: 'his gun is a help to the imagination, and we may fancy him a bandit with his contadina love, the terror of all the neighbourhood, except of her, the most defenceless being in it.'

'You speak lightly of such a combination,' said the lovely countess at my side, 'as if it must not in its nature be the cause of dreadful tragedies. The mingling of love with crime is a dread conjunction, and lawless pursuits are never followed without bringing on the criminal, and all allied to him, ineffable misery. I speak with emotion, for your observation reminds me of an unfortunate girl, now one of the Sisters of Charity in the convent of Santa Chiara at Rome, whose unhappy passion

Lake Albano

for a man, such as you mention, spread destruction and sorrow widely around her.'

I entreated my lovely friend to relate the history of the nun: for a long time she resisted my entreaties, as not willing to depress the spirit of a party of pleasure by a tale of sorrow. But I urged her, and she yielded. Her sweet Italian phraseology now rings in my ears, and her beautiful countenance is before me. As she spoke, the sun set, and the moon bent her silver horn in the ebbing tide of glory he had left. The lake changed from purple to silver, and the trees, before so splendid, now in dark masses, just reflected from their tops the mild moonlight. The fireflies flashed among the rocks; the bats circled round us. Meanwhile, thus commenced the Countess Atanasia:

The nun of whom I speak had a sister older than herself; I can remember them when as children they brought eggs and fruit to my father's villa. Maria and Anina were constantly together. With their large straw hats to shield them from the scorching sun, they were at work in their father's *podere*[102] all day, and in the evening, when Maria, who was the elder by four years, went to the fountain for water, Anina ran at her side. Their cot – the folding of the hill conceals it – is at the lakeside opposite; and about a quarter of a mile up the hill is the rustic fountain of which I speak. Maria was serious, gentle, and considerate; Anina was a laughing, merry little creature, with the face of a cherub.

When Maria was fifteen, their mother fell ill, and was nursed at the convent of Santa Chiara at Rome. Maria attended her, never leaving her bedside day or night. The nuns thought her an angel, she deemed them saints; her mother died, and they persuaded her to make one of them; her father could not but acquiesce in her holy intention, and she became one of the Sisters of Charity, the nun-nurses of Santa Chiara. Once or twice a year she visited her home, gave sage and kind advice to Anina, and sometimes wept to part from her; but her piety and her active employments for the sick reconciled her to her fate. Anina was more sorry to lose her sister's society. The other girls of the village did not please her; she was a good child, and worked hard for her father, and her sweetest recompense was the report he made of her to Maria, and the fond praises and caresses the latter bestowed on her when they met.

It was not until she was fifteen that Anina showed any diminution of affection for her sister. Yet I cannot call it diminution, for she loved her perhaps more than ever, though her holy calling and sage lectures prevented her from reposing confidence, and made her tremble lest the nun, devoted to heaven and good works, should read in her eyes, and disapprove of the earthly passion that occupied her. Perhaps a part of her reluctance arose from the reports that were current against her lover's character, and certainly from the disapprobation and even hatred of him that her father frequently expressed. Ill-fated Anina! I know not if in the north your peasants love as ours; but the passion of Anina was entwined with the roots of her being, it was herself: she could die, but not cease to love. The dislike of her father for Domenico made their intercourse clandestine. He was always at the fountain to fill her pitcher, and lift it on her head. He attended the same mass; and when her father went to Albano, Velletri or Rome, he seemed to learn by instinct the exact moment of his departure, and joined her in the *podere*, labouring with her and for her, till the old man was seen descending the mountain-path on his return. He said he worked for a *contadino*[103] near Nemi. Anina sometimes wondered that he could spare so much time for her; but his excuses were plausible, and the result too delightful not to blind the innocent girl to its obvious cause.

Poor Domenico! the reports spread against him were too well founded; his sole excuse was that his father had been a robber before him, and he had spent his early years among these lawless men. He had better things in his nature, and yearned for the peace of the guiltless. Yet he could hardly be called guilty, for no dread crime stained him; nevertheless, he was an outlaw and a bandit, and now that he loved Anina these names were the stings of an adder to pierce his soul. He would have fled from his comrades to a far country, but Anina dwelt amid their very haunts. At this period also, the police established by the French government, which then possessed Rome, made these bands more alive to the conduct of their members, and rumours of active measures to be taken against those who occupied the hills near Albano, Nemi and Velletri caused them to draw together in tighter bonds. Domenico would not, if he could, desert his friends in the hour of danger.

On a *festa*[104] at this time – it was towards the end of October – Anina strolled with her father among the villagers, who all over Italy make holiday by congregating and walking in one place. Their talk was entirely of the *ladri*[105] and the French, and many terrible stories were related of the extirpation of *banditti* in the kingdom of Naples, and the mode by which the French succeeded in their undertaking was minutely described. The troops scoured the country, visiting one haunt of the robbers after the other, and dislodging them, tracked them, as in those countries they hunt the wild beasts of the forest, till drawing the circle narrower, they enclosed them in one spot. They then drew a cordon round the place, which they guarded with the utmost vigilance, forbidding any to enter it with provisions on pain of instant death. And as this menace was rigorously executed, in a short time the besieged bandits were starved into a surrender. The French troops were now daily expected, for they had been seen at Velletri and Nemi; at the same time it was affirmed that several outlaws had taken up their abode at Rocca Giovane, a deserted village on the summit of one of these hills, and it was supposed that they would make that place the scene of their final retreat.

The next day, as Anina worked in the *podere*, a party of French horse passed by along the road that separated her garden from the lake. Curiosity made her look at them; and her beauty was too great not to attract: their observations and address soon drove her away – for a woman in love consecrates herself to her lover, and deems the admiration of others to be profanation. She spoke to her father of the impertinence of these men, and he answered by rejoicing at their arrival, and the destruction of the lawless bands that would ensue. When, in the evening, Anina went to the fountain, she looked timidly around, and hoped that Domenico would be at his accustomed post, for the arrival of the French destroyed her feeling of security. She went rather later than usual, and a cloudy evening made it seem already dark; the wind roared among the trees, bending hither and thither even the stately cypresses; the waters of the lake were agitated into high waves and dark masses of thundercloud lowered over the hilltops, giving a lurid tinge to the landscape. Anina passed quickly up the mountain path; when she came in sight of the fountain, which was rudely hewn in the living rock, she saw Domenico leaning against a projection of the hill, his hat drawn over his eyes, his *tabarro*[106] fallen from his shoulders, his arms folded in an attitude of dejection. He started when he saw her; his voice and phrases were broken and un-connected; yet he never gazed on her with such ardent love, nor solicited her to delay her departure with such impassioned tenderness.

'How glad I am to find you here!' she said: 'I was fearful of meeting one of the French soldiers: I dread them even more than the *banditti*.'

Domenico cast a look of eager enquiry on her, and then turned away, saying, 'Sorry am I that I shall not be here to protect you. I am obliged to go to Rome for a week or two. You will be faithful, Anina mia; you will love me, though I never see you more?'

The interview, under these circumstances, was longer than usual; he led her down the path till they nearly came in sight of her cottage; still they lingered: a low whistle was heard among the myrtle underwood at the lakeside; he started; it was repeated, and he answered it by a similar note; Anina, terrified, was about to ask what this meant, when, for the first time, he pressed her to his heart, kissed her roseate lips, and, with a muttered, 'Carissima, addio,'[107] left her, springing down the bank; and as she gazed in wonder, she thought she saw a boat cross a line of light made by the opening of a cloud. She stood long absorbed in reverie, wondering and remembering with thrilling pleasure the quick embrace and impassioned farewell of her lover. She delayed so long that her father came to seek her.

Each evening after this, Anina visited the fountain at the Ave Maria; he was not there; each day seemed an age; and incomprehensible fears occupied her heart. About a fortnight after, letters arrived from Maria. They came to say that she had been ill of the malaria fever, that she was now convalescent, but that change of air was necessary for her recovery, and that she had obtained leave to spend a month at home at Albano. She asked her father to come the next day to fetch her. These were pleasant tidings for Anina; she resolved to disclose everything to her sister, and during her long visit she doubted not but that she would contrive her happiness. Old Andrea departed the following morning, and the whole day was spent by the sweet girl in dreams of future bliss. In the evening Maria arrived, weak and wan, with all the marks of that dread illness about her; yet, as she assured her sister, feeling quite well.

As they sat at their frugal supper, several villagers came in to enquire for Maria; but all their talk was of the French soldiers and the robbers, of whom a band of at least twenty was collected in Rocca Giovane, strictly watched by the military.

'We may be grateful to the French,' said Andrea, 'for this good deed: the country will be rid of these ruffians.'

'True, friend,' said another; 'but it is horrible to think what these men suffer: they have, it appears, exhausted all the food they brought with them to the village, and are literally starving. They have not an ounce of macaroni among them; and a poor fellow, who was taken and executed yesterday, was a mere anatomy; you could tell every bone in his skin.'

'There was a sad story the other day,' said another, 'of an old man from Nemi, whose son, they say, is among them at Rocca Giovane: he was found within the lines with some *baccalà* under his *pastrano*,[108] and shot on the spot.'

'There is not a more desperate gang,' observed the first speaker, 'in the states and the regno put together. They have sworn never to yield but upon good terms; to secure these, their plan is to waylay passengers and make prisoners, whom they keep as hostages for mild treatment from the government. But the French are merciless; they are better pleased that the bandits wreak their vengeance on these poor creatures than spare one of their lives.'

'They have captured two persons already,' said another; 'and there is old Betta Tossi half frantic, for she is sure her son is taken: he has not been at home these ten days.'

'I should rather guess,' said an old man, 'that he went there with good will: the young scape-grace[109] kept company with Domenico Baldi of Nemi.'

'No worse company could he have kept in the whole country,' said Andrea. 'Domenico is the bad son of a bad race. Is he in the village with the rest?'

'My own eyes assured me of that,' replied the other. 'When I was up the hill with eggs and fowls to the picket there, I saw the branches of an ilex move; the poor fellow was weak perhaps, and could not keep his hold; presently he dropped to the ground; every musket was levelled at him, but he started up and was away like a hare among the rocks. Once he turned, and then I saw Domenico as plainly, though thinner, poor lad, by much than he was, as plainly as I now see – Santa Virgine! what is the matter with Nina?'

She had fainted; the company broke up, and she was left to her sister's care. When the poor child came to herself she was fully aware of her situation, and said nothing, except expressing a wish to retire to rest. Maria was in high spirits at the prospect of her long holiday at home, but the illness of her sister made her refrain from talking that night, and blessing her, as she said good-night, she soon slept. Domenico starving! – Domenico trying to escape and dying through hunger, was the vision of horror that wholly possessed poor Anina. At another time, the discovery that her lover was a robber might have inflicted pangs as keen as those which she now felt; but this, at present, made a faint impression, obscured by worse wretchedness. Maria was in a deep and tranquil sleep. Anina rose, dressed herself silently, and crept downstairs. She stored her market basket with what food there was in the house, and, unlatching the cottage-door, issued forth, resolved to reach Rocca Giovane, and to administer to her lover's dreadful wants. The night was dark, but this was favourable, for she knew every path and turn of the hills; every bush and knoll of ground between her home and the deserted village which occupies the summit of that hill: you may see the dark outline of some of its houses about two hours' walk from her cottage. The night was dark, but still; the *libeccio*[110] brought the clouds below the mountain-tops, and veiled the horizon in mist; not a leaf stirred; her footsteps sounded loud in her ears, but resolution overcame fear. She had entered yon ilex grove, her spirits rising with her success, when suddenly she was challenged by a sentinel; no time for escape; fear chilled her blood; her basket dropped from her arm, its contents rolled out on the ground; the soldier fired his gun and brought several others round him; she was made prisoner.

In the morning, when Maria awoke, she missed her sister from her side. I have overslept myself, she thought, and Nina would not disturb me. But when she came downstairs and met her father, and Anina did not appear, they began to wonder. She was not in the *podere*; two hours passed, and then Andrea went to seek her. Entering the near village, he saw the *contadini* crowding together, and a stifled exclamation of, 'Ecco il padre!'[111] told him that some evil had betided. His first impression was that his daughter was drowned; but the truth, that she had been taken by the French carrying provisions within the forbidden line, was still more terrible. He returned in frantic desperation to his cottage, first to acquaint Maria with what had happened, and then to ascend the hill to save his child from her impending fate. Maria heard his tale with horror; but a hospital is a school in which to learn self-possession and presence of mind. 'Do you remain, my father,' she said: 'I will go. My holy character will awe these men, my tears move them: trust me; I swear that I will save my sister.' Andrea yielded to her superior courage and energy.

The nuns of Santa Chiara when out of their convent do not usually wear their monastic habit, but dress simply in a black gown. Maria, however, had brought her nun's habiliments with her, and thinking thus to impress the soldiers with respect, she now put it on. She received her father's benediction, and asking that of the Virgin and the saints, she departed on her expedition. Ascending the hill, she was soon stopped by the sentinels. She asked to see their commanding officer, and being conducted to him, she announced herself as the sister of the unfortunate girl who had been captured the night before. The officer, who had received her with carelessness, now changed countenance: his serious look frightened Maria, who clasped her hands, exclaiming, 'You have not injured the child! she is safe?'

'She is safe – now,' he replied with hesitation; 'but there is no hope of pardon.'

'Holy Virgin, have mercy on her! what will be done to her?'

'I have received strict orders; in two hours she dies.'

'No! no!' exclaimed Maria impetuously, 'that cannot be! You cannot be so wicked as to murder a child like her.'

'She is old enough, madame,' said the officer, 'to know that she ought not to disobey orders; mine are so strict, that were she but nine years old, she dies.'

These terrible words stung Maria to fresh resolution: she entreated for mercy; she knelt; she vowed that she would not depart without her sister; she appealed to heaven and the saints. The officer, though cold-hearted, was good-natured and courteous, and he assured her with the utmost gentleness that her supplications were of no avail; that were the criminal his own daughter he must enforce his orders. As a sole con-cession, he permitted her to see her sister. Despair inspired the nun with energy: she almost ran up the hill, out-speeding her guide; they crossed a folding of the hills to a little sheep-cot, where sentinels paraded before the door. There was no glass to the windows, so the shutters were shut, and when Maria first went in from the bright daylight she hardly saw the slight figure of her sister leaning against the wall, her dark hair fallen below her waist, her head sunk on her bosom, over which her arms were folded. She started wildly as the door opened, saw her sister, and sprang with a piercing shriek into her arms.

They were left alone together: Anina uttered a thousand frantic exclamations, beseeching her sister to save her, and shuddering at the near approach of her fate. Maria had felt herself, since their mother's death, the natural protectress and support of her sister, and she never deemed herself so called on to fulfil this character as now that the trembling girl clasped her neck, her tears falling on her cheeks and her choked voice entreating her to save her. The thought – Oh, could I suffer instead of you! was in her heart, and she was about to express it, when it suggested another idea, on which she was resolved to act. First she soothed Anina by her promises, then glanced round the cot: they were quite alone; she went to the window, and through a crevice saw the soldiers conversing at some distance. 'Yes, dearest sister,' she cried, 'I will – I can save you – quick – we must change dresses – there is no time to be lost! – you must escape in my habit.'

'And you remain to die?'

'They dare not murder the innocent, a nun! Fear not for me – I am safe.'

Anina easily yielded to her sister, but her fingers trembled; every string she touched she entangled. Maria was perfectly self-possessed, pale, but calm. She tied up her sister's long hair, and adjusted her veil over it so as to conceal it; she unlaced her bodice, and arranged the folds of her own habit on her with the greatest care – then more hastily she assumed the dress of her sister, putting on, after a lapse of many years, her native *contadina* costume. Anina stood by, weeping and helpless, hardly hearing her sister's injunctions to return speedily to their father, and under his guidance to seek sanctuary. The guard now opened the door. Anina clung to her sister in terror, while she, in soothing tones, entreated her to calm herself.

The soldier said, they must delay no longer, for the priest had arrived to confess the prisoner.

To Anina the idea of confession associated with death was terrible; to Maria it brought hope. She whispered, in a smothered voice, 'The priest will protect me – fear not – hasten to our father!'

Anina almost mechanically obeyed: weeping, with her handkerchief placed unaffectedly before her face, she passed the soldiers; they closed the door on the prisoner, who hastened to the window, and saw her sister descend the hill with tottering steps, till she was lost behind some rising ground. The nun fell on her knees – cold dew bathed her brow; instinctively she feared: the French had shown small respect for the monastic character; they destroyed the convents and desecrated the churches. Would they be merciful to her, and spare the innocent! Alas! was not Anina innocent also? Her sole crime had been disobeying an arbitrary command, and she had done the same.

'Courage!' cried Maria; 'perhaps I am fitter to die than my sister is. Gesu, pardon me my sins, but I do not believe that I shall outlive this day!'

In the meantime, Anina descended the hill slowly and tremblingly. She feared discovery – she feared for her sister – and above all at the present moment, she feared the reproaches and anger of her father. By dwelling on this last idea, it became exaggerated into excessive terror, and she determined, instead of returning to her home, to make a circuit among the hills and to find her way by herself to Albano, where she trusted to find protection from her pastor and confessor. She avoided the open paths, and following rather the direction she wished to pursue than any beaten road, she passed along nearer to Rocca Giovane than she anticipated. She looked up at its ruined houses and bell-less steeple, straining her eyes to catch a glimpse of him, the author of all her ills. A low but distinct whistle reached her ear, not far off; she started – she remembered that on the night when she last saw Domenico a note like that had called him from her side; the sound was echoed and re-echoed from other quarters; she stood aghast, her bosom heaving, her hands clasped. First she saw a dark and ragged head of hair, shadowing two fiercely gleaming eyes, rise from beneath a bush. She screamed, but before she could repeat her scream three men leapt from behind a rock, secured her arms, threw a cloth over her face, and hurried her up the acclivity. Their talk, as she went along, informed her of the horror and danger of her situation.

Pity, they said, that the holy father and some of his red stockings[112] did not command the troops: with a nun in their hands, they might obtain any terms. Coarse jests passed as they dragged their victim towards their ruined village. The paving of the street told her when they arrived at Rocca Giovane, and the change of atmosphere that they entered a house. They unbandaged her eyes: the scene was squalid and miserable, the walls ragged and black with smoke, the floor strewn with offals and dirt; a rude table and broken bench was all the furniture; and the leaves of Indian corn, heaped high in one corner, served, it seemed, for a bed, for a man lay on it, his head buried in his folded arms. Anina looked round on her savage hosts: their countenances expressed every variety of brutal ferocity, now rendered more dreadful from gaunt famine and suffering.

'Oh, there is none who will save me!' she cried. The voice startled the man who was lying on the floor; he leapt up – it was Domenico: Domenico, so changed, with sunk cheeks and eyes, matted hair, and looks whose wildness and desperation differed little from the dark countenances around him. Could this be her lover?

His recognition and surprise at her dress led to an explanation. When the robbers first heard that their prey was no prize, they were

mortified and angry; but when she related the danger she had incurred
by endeavouring to bring them food, they swore with horrid oaths
that no harm should befall her, but that if she liked she might make
one of them in all honour and equality. The innocent girl shuddered.
'Let me go,' she cried; 'let me only escape and hide myself in a convent
for ever!'

Domenico looked at her in agony. 'Yes, poor child,' he said; 'go, save
yourself. God grant no evil befall you; the ruin is too wide already.'
Then turning eagerly to his comrades, he continued – 'You hear her
story. She was to have been shot for bringing food to us: her sister has
substituted herself in her place. We know the French; one victim is to
them as good as another: Maria dies in their hands. Let us save her.
Our time is up; we must fall like men, or starve like dogs; we have still
ammunition, still some strength left. To arms! let us rush on the
poltroons,[113] free their prisoner, and escape or die!'

There needed but an impulse like this to urge the outlaws to desperate
resolves. They prepared their arms with looks of ferocious determination. Domenico, meanwhile, led Anina out of the house to the verge
of the hill, enquiring whither she intended to go. On her saying to
Albano, he observed, 'That were hardly safe; be guided by me, I entreat
you: take these piastres, hire the first conveyance you find, hasten to
Rome, to the convent of Santa Chiara; for pity's sake, do not linger in
this neighbourhood.'

'I will obey your injunctions, Domenico,' she replied, 'but I cannot
take your money; it has cost you too dear; fear not, I shall arrive safely at
Rome without that ill-fated silver.'

Domenico's comrades now called loudly to him: he had no time to
urge his request; he threw the despised dollars at her feet.

'Nina, adieu for ever,' he said. 'May you love again more happily!'

'Never!' she replied. 'God has saved me in this dress; it were sacrilege
to change it: I shall never quit Santa Chiara.'

Domenico had led her a part of the way down the rock; his comrades
appeared at the top, calling to him.

'Gesu save you!' cried he: 'reach the convent – Maria shall join you
there before night. Farewell!' He hastily kissed her hand, and sprang up
the acclivity to rejoin his impatient friends.

The unfortunate Andrea had waited long for the return of his children.
The leafless trees and bright clear atmosphere permitted every object
to be visible, but he saw no trace of them on the hillside; the shadows
of the dial showed noon to be passed, when, with uncontrollable
impatience, he began to climb the hill, towards the spot where Anina

had been taken. The path he pursued was in part the same that this unhappy girl had taken on her way to Rome. The father and daughter met: the old man saw the nun's dress, and saw her unaccompanied; she covered her face with her hands in a transport of fear and shame; but when, mistaking her for Maria, he asked in a tone of anguish for his youngest darling, her arms fell; she dared not raise her eyes, which streamed with tears.

'Unhappy girl!' exclaimed Andrea, 'where is your sister?'

She pointed to the cottage prison, now discernible near the summit of a steep acclivity. 'She is safe,' she replied: 'she saved me; but they dare not murder her.'

'Heaven bless her for this good deed!' exclaimed the old man, fervently; 'but you hasten on your way, and I will go in search of her.'

Each proceeded on an opposite path. The old man wound up the hill, now in view and now losing sight of the hut where his child was captive: he was aged, and the way was steep. Once, when the closing of the hill hid the point towards which he for ever strained his eyes, a single shot was fired in that direction: his staff fell from his hands, his knees trembled and failed him; several minutes of dead silence elapsed before he recovered himself sufficiently to proceed; full of fears he went on, and at the next turn saw the cot again. A party of soldiers were on the open space before it, drawn up in a line as if expecting an attack. In a few moments from above them shots were fired, which they returned, and the whole was enveloped and veiled in smoke. Still Andrea climbed the hill, eager to discover what had become of his child; the firing continued quick and hot. Now and then, in the pauses of musquetry and the answering echoes of the mountains, he heard a funereal chant; presently, before he was aware, at a turning of the hill, he met a company of priests and *contadini*, carrying a large cross and a bier. The miserable father rushed forward with frantic impatience; the awestruck peasants set down their load – the face was uncovered, and the wretched man fell senseless on the corpse of his murdered child.

The Countess Atanasia paused, overcome by the emotions inspired by the history she related. A long pause ensued; at length one of the party observed, 'Maria, then, was the sacrifice to her goodness.'

'The French,' said the countess, 'did not venerate her holy vocation; one peasant girl to them was the same as another. The immolation of any victim suited their purpose of awe-striking the peasantry. Scarcely, however, had the shot entered her heart, and her blameless spirit been received by the saints in Paradise, when Domenico and his followers rushed down the hill to avenge her and themselves. The contest was

furious and bloody; twenty French soldiers fell, and not one of the
banditti escaped; Domenico, the foremost of the assailants, being the
first to fall.'

I asked, 'And where are now Anina and her father?'

'You may see them, if you will,' said the countess, 'on your return to
Rome. She is a nun of Santa Chiara. Constant acts of benevolence and
piety have inspired her with calm and resignation. Her prayers are daily
put up for Domenico's soul, and she hopes, through the intercession of
the Virgin, to rejoin him in the other world.

'Andrea is very old; he has outlived the memory of his sufferings; but
he derives comfort from the filial attentions of his surviving daughter.
But when I look at his cottage on this lake, and remember the happy
laughing face of Anina among the vines, I shudder at the recollection
of the passion that has made her cheeks pale, her thoughts forever
conversant with death, her only wish to find repose in the grave.'

The Evil Eye

The wild Albanian kirtled to his knee,
With shawl-girt head, and ornamented gun,
And gold-embroider'd garments, fair to see;
The crimson-scarfed man of Macedon – [114]

LORD BYRON

THE Moreot,[115] Katusthius Ziani, travelled wearily, and in fear of its robber-inhabitants, through the pashalik of Yannina;[116] yet he had no cause for dread. Did he arrive, tired and hungry, in a solitary village – did he find himself in the uninhabited wilds suddenly surrounded by a band of Klephts[117] – or in the larger towns did he shrink at finding himself sole of his race among the savage mountaineers and despotic Turk – as soon as he announced himself the *pobratimo*[118] of Dmitri of the Evil Eye, every hand was held out, every voice spoke welcome.

The Albanian, Dmitri, was a native of the village of Korvo. Among the savage mountains of the district between Yannina and Tepellenè,[119] the deep broad stream of Argyro-Castro flows; bastioned to the west by abrupt wood-covered precipices, shadowed to the east by elevated mountains. The highest among these is Mount Trebucci; and in a romantic folding of that hill, distinct with minarets, crowned by a dome rising from out a group of pyramidal cypresses, is the picturesque village of Korvo. Sheep and goats form the apparent treasure of its inhabitants; their guns and *yataghans*,[120] their warlike habits, and, with them, the noble profession of robbery, are sources of still greater wealth. Among a race renowned for dauntless courage and sanguinary enterprise, Dmitri was distinguished.

It was said that in his youth, this Klepht was remarkable for a gentler disposition and more refined taste than is usual with his countrymen. He had been a wanderer, and had learned European arts, of which he was not a little proud. He could read and write Greek, and a book was often stowed beside his pistols in his girdle. He had spent several years in Scio,[121] the most civilised of the Greek islands, and had married a Sciote girl. The Albanians are characterised as despisers of women; but Dmitri, in becoming the husband of Helena, enlisted under a more chivalrous rule, and became the proselyte of a better creed. Often he returned to his native hills, and fought under the banner of the renowned Ali, and then came back to his island home. The love of the tamed barbarian was concentrated, burning, and something beyond this – it was a portion of his living, beating heart – the nobler part of himself – the diviner mould in which his rugged nature had been recast.

On his return from one of his Albanian expeditions, he found his home ravaged by the Mainotes.[122] Helena – they pointed to her tomb, but dared not tell him how she died; his only child, his lovely infant daughter, was stolen; his treasure-house of love and happiness was rifled, its gold-excelling wealth changed to blank desolation. Dmitri spent three years in endeavours to recover his lost offspring. He was exposed to a thousand dangers – underwent incredible hardships: he dared the wild beast in his lair, the Mainote in his port of refuge; he attacked, and was attacked by them. He wore the badge of his daring in a deep gash across his eyebrow and cheek. On this occasion he had died, but that Katusthius, seeing a scuffle on shore and a man left for dead, disembarked from a Moreot *sacoleva*,[123] carried him away, tended and cured him. They exchanged vows of friendship, and for some time the Albanian shared his brother's toils; but they were too pacific to suit his taste, and he returned to Korvo.

Who in the mutilated savage could recognise the handsomest amongst the Arnaoots?[124] His habits kept pace with his change of physiognomy – he grew ferocious and hard-hearted – he only smiled when engaged in dangerous enterprise; he had arrived at that worst state of ruffian feeling, the taking delight in blood. He grew old in these occupations; his mind became reckless, his countenance more dark; men trembled before his glance, women and children exclaimed in terror, 'The Evil Eye!' The opinion became prevalent – he shared it himself – he gloried in the dread privilege; and when his victim shivered and withered beneath the mortal influence, the fiendish laugh with, which he hailed this demonstration of his power struck with worse dismay the failing heart of the fascinated person. But Dmitri could command the arrows of his sight; and his comrades respected him the more for his supernatural attribute, since they did not fear the exercise of it on themselves.

Dmitri had just returned from an expedition beyond Prevesa. He and his comrades were laden with spoil. They killed and roasted a goat whole for their repast; they drank dry several wineskins; then, round the fire in the court, they abandoned themselves to the delights of the kerchief dance, roaring out the chorus, as they dropped upon and then rebounded from their knees, and whirled round and round with an activity all their own. The heart of Dmitri was heavy; he refused to dance, and sat apart, at first joining in the song with his voice and lute, till the air changed to one that reminded him of better days; his voice died away – his instrument dropped from his hands – and his head sank upon his breast.

At the sound of stranger footsteps he started up; in the form before him he surely recognised a friend – he was not mistaken. With a joyful exclamation he welcomed Katusthius Ziani, clasping his hand, and kissing him on his cheek. The traveller was weary, so they retired to Dmitri's own home: a neatly plastered, whitewashed cottage, whose earthen floor was perfectly dry and clean, and the walls hung with arms, some richly ornamented, and other trophies of his Klephtic triumphs. A fire was kindled by his aged female attendant; the friends reposed on mats of white rushes, while she prepared the pilaf and seethed flesh of kid. She placed a bright tin tray on a block of wood before them, and heaped upon it cakes of Indian corn, goat's milk cheese, eggs and olives; a jar of water from their purest spring, and skin of wine, served to refresh and cheer the thirsty traveller.

After supper, the guest spoke of the object of his visit. 'I come to my *pobratimo*,' he said, 'to claim the performance of his vow. When I rescued you from the savage Kakovougnis of Boularias, you pledged to me your gratitude and faith; do you disclaim the debt?'

Dmitri's brow darkened. 'My brother,' he cried, 'need not remind me of what I owe. Command my life – in what can the mountain Klepht aid the son of the wealthy Ziani?'

'The son of Ziani is a beggar,' rejoined Katusthius, 'and must perish, if his brother deny his assistance.'

The Moreot then told his tale. He had been brought up as the only son of a rich merchant of Corinth. He had often sailed as *caravokeiri*[125] of his father's vessels to Stamboul, and even to Calabria. Some years before, he had been boarded and taken by a Barbary corsair.[126] His life since then had been adventurous, he said; in truth, it had been a guilty one – he had become a renegade – and won regard from his new allies, not by his superior courage, for he was cowardly, but by the frauds that make men wealthy. In the midst of this career some superstition had influenced him, and he had returned to his ancient religion. He escaped from Africa, wandered through Syria, crossed to Europe, found occupation in Constantinople; and thus years passed. At last, as he was on the point of marriage with a Fanariote beauty,[127] he fell again into poverty, and he returned to Corinth to see if his father's fortunes had prospered during his long wanderings. He found that while these had improved to a wonder, they were lost to him for ever. His father, during his protracted absence, acknowledged another son as his; and dying a year before, had left all to him. Katusthius found this unknown kinsman, with his wife and child, in possession of his expected inheritance. Cyril divided with him, it is true, their parent's property; but Katusthius grasped at all, and resolved to obtain it. He brooded over a thousand schemes of murder and revenge; yet the blood of a brother was sacred to him; and Cyril, beloved and respected at Corinth, could only be attacked with considerable risk. Then his child was a fresh obstacle. As the best plan that presented itself, he hastily embarked for Butrinto, and came to claim the advice and assistance of the Arnaoot whose life he had saved, whose *pobratimo* he was. Not thus, barely, did he tell his tale, but glossed it over; so that had Dmitri needed the incitement of justice, which was not at all a desideratum with him, he would have been satisfied that Cyril was a base interloper, and that the whole transaction was one of imposture and villainy.

All night these men discussed a variety of projects whose aim was that the deceased Ziani's wealth should pass undivided into his elder son's hands. At morning's dawn Katusthius departed, and two days afterwards Dmitri quitted his mountain home. His first care had been to purchase a horse, long coveted by him on account of its beauty and fleetness; he provided cartridges, and replenished his powder-horn. His accoutrements were rich, his dress gay; his arms glittered in the sun. His long hair fell straight from under the shawl twisted round his cap, even to his waist; a shaggy white *capote* hung from his shoulder; his face wrinkled and puckered by exposure to the seasons; his brow furrowed with care; his mustachios long and jet black; his scarred face; his wild, savage eyes; his whole appearance, not deficient in barbaric grace, but stamped chiefly with ferocity and bandit pride, inspired, and we need not wonder, the superstitious Greek with a belief that a supernatural spirit of evil dwelt in his aspect, blasting and destroying. Now prepared for his journey, he departed from Korvo, crossing the woods of Acarnania, on his way to the Morea.[128]

*   *   *

'Wherefore does Zella tremble, and press her boy to her bosom, as if fearful of evil?' Thus asked Cyril Ziani, returning from the city of

Corinth to his own rural abode. It was a home of beauty. The abruptly broken hills covered with olives, or brighter plantations of orange-trees, overlooked the blue waves of the Gulf of Aegina. A myrtle underwood spread sweet scent around, and dipped its dark shining leaves into the sea itself. The low-roofed house was shaded by two enormous fig trees, while vineyards and cornland stretched along the gentle upland to the north. When Zella saw her husband, she smiled, though her cheek was still pale and her lips quivering – 'Now you are near to guard us,' she said, 'I dismiss fear; but danger threatens our Constans, and I shudder to remember that an Evil Eye has been upon him.'

Cyril caught up his child – 'By my head!' he cried, 'thou speakest of an ill thing. The Franks call this superstition; but let us beware. His cheek is still rosy; his tresses flowing gold – Speak, Constans, hail thy father, my brave fellow!'

It was but a short-lived fear; no ill ensued, and they soon forgot an incident which had causelessly made their hearts to quail. A week afterwards Cyril returned, as he was wont, from shipping a cargo of currants, to his retreat on the coast. It was a beautiful summer evening; the creaking water-wheel, which produced the irrigation of the land, chimed in with the last song of the noisy cicala;[129] the rippling waves spent themselves almost silently among the shingles. This was his home; but where its lovely flower? Zella did not come forth to welcome him. A domestic pointed to a chapel on a neighbouring acclivity, and there he found her; his child (nearly three years of age) was in his nurse's arms; his wife was praying fervently, while the tears streamed down her cheeks. Cyril demanded anxiously the meaning of this scene; but the nurse sobbed; Zella continued to pray and weep; and the boy, from sympathy, began to cry. This was too much for man to endure. Cyril left the chapel; he leant against a walnut tree: his first exclamation was a customary Greek one – 'Welcome this misfortune, so that it come single!' But what was the ill that had occurred? Unapparent was it yet; but the spirit of evil is most fatal when unseen. He was happy – a lovely wife, a blooming child, a peaceful home, competence, and the prospect of wealth; these blessings were his: yet how often does Fortune use such as her decoys? He was a slave in an enslaved land, a mortal subject to the high destinies, and ten thousand were the envenomed darts which might be hurled at his devoted head. Now timid and trembling, Zella came from the chapel: her explanation did not calm his fears. Again the Evil Eye had been on his child, and deep malignity lurked surely under this second visitation. The same man, an Arnaoot, with glittering arms, gay attire, mounted on a black steed, came from the neighbouring ilex grove, and, riding furiously up to the door, suddenly checked and reined in his horse at the very threshold. The child ran towards him: the Arnaoot bent his sinister eyes upon him. 'Lovely art thou, bright infant,' he cried; 'thy blue eyes are beaming, thy golden tresses fair to see; but thou art a vision fleeting as beautiful. Look at me!' The innocent looked up, uttered a shriek, and fell gasping on the ground. The women rushed forward to seize him; the Albanian put spurs to his horse, and galloping swiftly across the little plain, up the wooded hillside, he was soon lost to sight. Zella and the nurse bore the child to the chapel, they sprinkled him with holy water, and, as he revived, besought the Panagia with earnest prayers to save him from the menaced ill.

Several weeks elapsed; little Constans grew in intelligence and beauty; no blight had visited the flower of love, and its parents dismissed fear. Sometimes Cyril indulged in a joke at the expense of the Evil Eye; but Zella thought it unlucky to laugh, and crossed herself whenever the event was alluded to. At this time Katusthius visited their abode. 'He was on his way,' he said, 'to Stamboul, and he came to know whether he could serve his brother in any of his transactions in the capital.' Cyril and Zella received him with cordial affection: they rejoiced to perceive that fraternal love was beginning to warm his heart. He seemed full of ambition and hope; the brothers discussed his prospects, the politics of Europe and the intrigues of the Fanar;[130] the petty affairs of Corinth even were made subjects of discourse, and the probability that in a short time, young as he was, Cyril would be named Codja-Bashee[131] of the province. On the morrow, Katusthius prepared to depart – 'One favour does the voluntary exile ask: will my brother and sister accompany me some hours on my way to Napoli, whence I embark?'

Zella was unwilling to quit her home, even for a short interval; but she suffered herself to be persuaded, and they proceeded all together for several miles towards the capital of the Morea. At noontide they made a repast under the shadow of a grove of oaks, and then separated. Returning homeward, the wedded pair congratulated themselves on their tranquil life and peaceful happiness, contrasted with the wanderer's lonely and homeless pleasures. These feelings increased in intensity as they drew nearer their dwelling, and anticipated the lisped welcome of their idolised child. From an eminence they looked upon the fertile vale which was their home; it was situated on the southern side of the isthmus, and looked upon the Gulf of Aegina: all was verdant, tranquil and beautiful. They descended into the plain; there a singular appearance attracted their attention. A plough with its yoke of oxen had been deserted midway in the furrow; the animals had dragged it to the side of the field, and endeavoured to repose as well as their conjunction permitted. The sun already touched its western bourne, and the summits of the trees were gilded by its parting beams. All was silent; even the eternal water-wheel was still; no menials appeared at their usual rustic labours. From the house the voice of wailing was too plainly heard. 'My child!' Zella exclaimed. Cyril began to reassure her; but another lament arose, and he hurried on. She dismounted, and would have followed him, but sank on the road's side. Her husband returned. 'Courage, my beloved,' he cried; 'I will not repose night or day until Constans is restored to us – trust to me – farewell!' With these words he rode swiftly on. Her worst fears were thus confirmed; her maternal heart, late so joyous, became the abode of despair, while the nurse's narration of the sad occurrence tended but to add worse fear to fear. Thus it was: the same stranger of the Evil Eye had appeared, not as before, bearing down on them with eagle speed, but as if from a long journey; his horse lame and with drooping head; the Arnaoot himself covered with dust, apparently scarcely able to keep his seat. 'By the life of your child,' he said, 'give a cup of water to one who faints with thirst.' The nurse, with Constans in her arms, got a bowl of the desired liquid, and presented it. Ere the parched lips of the stranger touched the wave, the vessel fell from his hands. The women started back, while he, at the same moment darting forward, tore with strong arm the child from her embrace. Already both were gone – with arrowy speed they traversed the plain, while her shrieks, and cries for assistance, called together all the domestics. They followed on the track of the ravisher and none had yet returned. Now, as night closed in, one by one they came back; they had nothing to relate; they had scoured the woods, crossed the hills – they could not even discover the route which the Albanian had taken.

On the following day Cyril returned, jaded, haggard, miserable; he had obtained no tidings of his son. On the morrow he again departed on his quest, nor came back for several days. Zella passed her time wearily – now sitting in hopeless despondency, now climbing the near hill to see whether she could perceive the approach of her husband. She was not allowed to remain long thus tranquil: the trembling domestics, left in guard, warned her that the savage forms of several Arnaoots had been seen prowling about: she herself saw a tall figure, clad in a shaggy white *capote*, steal round the promontory, and on seeing her, shrink back; once at night the snorting and trampling of a horse roused her, not from slumber, but from her sense of security. Wretched as the bereft mother was, she felt personally almost reckless of danger; but she was not her own, she belonged to one beyond expression dear; and duty, as well as affection for him, enjoined self-preservation. He, Cyril, again returned: he was gloomier, sadder than before; but there was more resolution on his brow, more energy in his motions; he had obtained a clue, yet it might only lead him to the depths of despair.

He discovered that Katusthius had not embarked at Napoli. He had joined a band of Arnaoots lurking about Vasilico, and had proceeded to Patras with the Protoklepht; thence they put off together in a *mono-xylon*[132] for the northern shores of the Gulf of Lepanto: nor were they alone; they bore a child with them wrapped in a heavy torpid sleep. Poor Cyril's blood ran cold when he thought of the spells and witch-craft which had probably been put in practice on his boy. He would have followed close upon the robbers but for the report that reached him that the remainder of the Albanians had proceeded southward towards Corinth. He could not enter upon a long wandering search among the pathless wilds of Epirus leaving Zella exposed to the attacks of these bandits. He returned to consult with her, to devise some plan of action which at once ensured her safety and promised success to his endeavours.

After some hesitation and discussion, it was decided that he should first conduct her to her native home, consult with her father as to his present enterprise, and be guided by his warlike experience before he rushed into the very focus of danger. The seizure of his child might only be a lure, and it were not well for him, sole protector of that child and its mother, to rush inadvisably into the toils.

Zella, strange to say, for her blue eyes and brilliant complexion belied her birth, was the daughter of a Mainote; yet dreaded and abhorred by the rest of the world as are the inhabitants of Cape Taenarus, they are celebrated for their domestic virtues and the strength of their private attachments. Zella loved her father, and the memory of her rugged rocky home, from which she had been torn in an adverse hour. Near neighbours of the Mainotes, dwelling in the ruder and most incult portion of Maina, are the Kakovougnis, a dark suspicious race, of squat and stunted form, strongly contrasted with the tranquil cast of countenance characteristic of the Mainote. The two tribes are em-broiled in perpetual quarrels; the narrow sea-girt abode which they share affords at once a secure place of refuge from the foreign enemy, and all the facilities of internal mountain warfare. Cyril had once, during a coasting voyage, been driven by stress of weather into the little bay on whose shores is placed the small town of Kardamyla. The crew at first dreaded to be captured by the pirates; but they were reassured on finding them fully occupied by their domestic dissensions. A band of Kakovougnis were besieging the castellated rock overlooking Kardamyla, blockading the fortress in which the Mainote capitano and his family had taken refuge. Two days passed thus, while furious contrary winds detained Cyril in the bay. On the third evening the western gale subsided, and a land breeze promised to emancipate them from their perilous condition; however, in the night, as they were about to put off in a boat from shore, they were hailed by a party of Mainotes, and one, an old man of commanding figure, demanded a parley. He was the capitano of Kardamyla, the chief of the fortress, now attacked by his implacable enemies; he saw no escape – he must fall – and his chief desire was to save his treasure and his family from the hands of his enemies. Cyril consented to receive them on board: the latter consisted of an old mother, a *paramana*,[133] and a young and beautiful girl, his daughter. Cyril conducted them in safety to Napoli. Soon after, the capitano's mother and *paramana* returned to their native town, while, with her father's consent, fair Zella became the wife of her preserver. The fortunes of the Mainote had prospered since then, and he stood first in rank, the chief of a large tribe, the capitano of Kardamyla.

Thither then the hapless parents repaired; they embarked on board a small *sacoleva*, which dropped down the Gulf of Aegina, weathering the islands of Skyllo and Cerigo and the extreme point of Taenarus; favoured by prosperous gales, they made the desired port and arrived at the hospitable mansion of old Camaraz. He heard their tale with indignation; swore by his beard to dip his poniard in the best blood of Katusthius, and insisted upon accompanying his son-in-law on his expedition to Albania. No time was lost – the grey-headed mariner, still full of energy, hastened every preparation. Cyril and Zella parted; a thousand fears, a thousand hours of misery rose between the pair, late sharers in perfect happiness. The boisterous sea and distant lands were the smallest of the obstacles that divided them; they would not fear the worst; yet hope, a sickly plant, faded in their hearts as they tore themselves asunder after a last embrace.

Zella returned from the fertile district of Corinth to her barren native rocks. She felt all joy expire as she viewed from the rugged shore the lessening sails of the *sacoleva*. Days and weeks passed, and still she remained in solitary and sad expectation: she never joined in the dance, nor made one in the assemblies of her country-women, who met together at eveningtide to sing, tell stories and while away the time in dance and gaiety. She secluded herself in the most lonely part of her father's house, and gazed unceasingly from the lattice upon the sea beneath, or wandered on the rocky beach; and when tempest darkened the sky, and each precipitous promontory grew purple under the shadows of the wide-winged clouds, when the roar of the surges was on the shore, and the white crests of the waves, seen afar upon the ocean-plain, showed like flocks of new-shorn sheep scattered along wide-extended downs, she felt neither gale nor inclement cold, nor returned home till recalled by her attendants. In obedience to them she sought the shelter of her abode, but not to remain long, for the wild winds spoke to her, and the stormy ocean reproached her tranquillity. Unable to control the impulse, she would rush from her habitation on the cliff, nor remember, till she reached the shore, that her *papooshes*[134] were left midway on the mountain path, and that her forgotten veil and disordered dress were unmeet for such a scene. Often the unnumbered hours sped on, while this orphaned child of happiness leant on a cold dark rock; the low-browed crags beetled over her, the surges broke at her feet, her fair limbs were stained by spray, her tresses dishevelled by the gale. Hopelessly she wept until a sail appeared on the horizon; and then she dried her fast flowing tears, fixing her large eyes upon the nearing hull or fading topsail. Meanwhile the storm tossed the clouds into a thousand gigantic shapes, and the tumultuous sea grew blacker and more wild; her natural gloom was heightened by superstitious horror; the Moirae, the old Fates of her native Grecian soil, howled in the breezes; apparitions, which told of her child pining under the influence of the Evil Eye, and of her husband, the prey of some Thracian witchcraft, such as still is practised in the dread neighbourhood of Larissa, haunted her broken slumbers, and stalked like dire shadows across her waking thoughts. Her bloom was gone, her eyes lost their lustre, her limbs their round full beauty; her strength failed her, as she tottered to the accustomed spot to watch – vainly, yet for ever to watch.

What is there so fearful as the expectation of evil tidings delayed? Sometimes in the midst of tears, or worse, amidst the convulsive gaspings of despair, we reproach ourselves for influencing the eternal fates by our gloomy anticipations: then, if a smile wreathe the mourner's quivering lip, it is arrested by a throb of agony. Alas! are not the dark tresses of the young, painted grey; the full cheek of beauty, delved with sad lines by the spirits of such hours? Misery is a more welcome visitant, when she comes in her darkest guise, and wraps us in perpetual black, for then the heart no longer sickens with disappointed hope.

Cyril and old Camaraz had found great difficulty in doubling the many capes of the Morea as they made a coasting expedition from Kardamyla to the Gulf of Arta, north of Cefalonia and St Mauro.

Zella

During their voyage they had time to arrange their plans. As a number of Moreots travelling together might attract too much attention, they resolved to land their comrades at different points, and travel separately into the interior of Albania; Yannina was their first place of rendezvous. Cyril and his father-in-law disembarked in one of the most secluded of the many creeks which diversify the winding and precipitous shores of the gulf. Six others, chosen from the crew, would, by other routes, join them at the capital. They did not fear for themselves; alone, but well armed, and secure in the courage of despair, they penetrated the fastnesses of Epirus. No success cheered them; they arrived at Yannina without having made the slightest discovery. There they were joined by their comrades, whom they directed to remain three days in the town, and then separately to proceed to Tepellenè, whither they immediately directed their steps. At the first village on their way thither, at 'monastic Zitza',[135] they obtained some information not to direct but to encourage their endeavours. They sought refreshment and hospitality in the monastery which is situated on a green eminence, crowned by a grove of oak trees, immediately behind the village. Perhaps there is not in the world a more beautiful or more romantic spot, sheltered itself by clustering trees, looking out on one widespread landscape of hill and dale, enriched by vineyards, dotted with frequent flocks; while the Calamas in the depth of the vale gives life to the scene, and the far blue mountains of Zoumerkas, Sagori, Sulli and Acroccraunia, to the east, west, north and south, close in the various prospects. Cyril half envied the Caloyers[136] their inert tranquillity. They received the travellers gladly, and were cordial though simple in their manners. When questioned concerning the object of their journey, they warmly sympathised with the father's anxiety, and eagerly told all they knew. Two weeks before, an Arnaoot, well known to them as Dmitri of the Evil Eye, a famous Klepht of Korvo, and a Moreot, arrived, bringing with them a child, a bold, spirited, beautiful boy, who, with firmness beyond his years, claimed the protection of the Caloyers, and accused his companions of having carried him off by force from his parents. 'By my head!' cried the Albanian, 'a brave Palikar:[137] he keeps his word, brother; he swore by the Panagia, in spite of our threats of throwing him down a precipice, food for the vulture, to accuse us to the first good men he saw: he neither pines under the Evil Eye, nor quails beneath our menaces.' Katusthius frowned at these praises, and it became evident during their stay at the monastery that the Albanian and the Moreot quarrelled as to the disposal of the child. The rugged mountaineer threw off all his sternness as he gazed upon the boy. When little

Constans slept, he hung over him, fanning away, with a woman's care, the flies and gnats. When he spoke, he answered with expressions of fondness, winning him with gifts, teaching him, all baby as he was, a mimicry of warlike exercises. When the boy knelt and besought the Panagia to restore him to his parents, his infant voice quivering, and tears running down his cheeks, the eyes of Dmitri overflowed; he cast his cloak over his face; his heart whispered to him – 'Thus, perhaps, my child prayed. Heaven was deaf – alas! where is she now?' – Encouraged by such signs of compassion, which children are quick to perceive, Constans twined his arms round his neck, telling him that he loved him, and that he would fight for him when a man, if he would take him back to Corinth. At such words Dmitri would rush forth, seek Katusthius, remonstrate with him, till the unrelenting man checked him by reminding him of his vow. Still he swore that no hair of the child's head should be injured; while the uncle, unvisited by compunction, meditated his destruction. The quarrels which thence arose were frequent and violent, till Katusthius, weary of opposition, had recourse to craft to obtain his purpose. One night he secretly left the monastery, bearing the child with him. When Dmitri heard of his evasion, it was a fearful thing to the good Caloyers only to look upon him; they instinctively clutched hold of every bit of iron on which they could lay their hands, so to avert the Evil Eye which glared with native and untamed fierceness. In their panic a whole score of them had rushed to the iron-plated door which led out of their abode; with the strength of a lion, Dmitri tore them away, threw back the portal, and, with the swiftness of a torrent fed by the thawing of the snows in spring, he dashed down the steep hill: the flight of an eagle not more rapid; the course of a wild beast not more resolved.

Such was the clue afforded to Cyril. It were too long to follow him in his subsequent search; he, with old Camaraz, wandered through the vale of Argyro-Castro, and climbed Mount Trebucci to Korvo. Dmitri had returned; he had gathered together a score of faithful comrades, and sallied forth again; various were the reports of his destination, and the enterprise which he meditated. One of these led our adventurers to Tepellenè, and hence back towards Yannina: and now chance again favoured them. They rested one night in the habitation of a priest at the little village of Mosme, about three leagues to the north of Zitza; and here they found an Arnaoot who had been disabled by a fall from his horse; this man was to have made one of Dmitri's band; they learned from him that the Arnaoot had tracked Katusthius, following him close and forcing him to take refuge in the monastery of the Prophet Elias, which stands on an elevated peak of the mountains of Sagori, eight leagues from Yannina. Dmitri had followed him, and demanded the child. The Caloyers refused to give it up, and the Klepht, roused to mad indignation, was now besieging and battering the monastery to obtain by force this object of his newly-awakened affections.

At Yannina, Camaraz and Cyril collected their comrades, and departed to join their unconscious ally. He, more impetuous than a mountain stream or ocean's fiercest waves, struck terror into the hearts of the recluses by his ceaseless and dauntless attacks. To encourage them to further resistance, Katusthius, leaving the child behind in the monastery, departed for the nearest town of Sagori, to entreat its Belouk-Bashee[138] to come to their aid. The Sagorians are a mild, amiable, social people; they are gay, frank, clever; their bravery is universally acknowledged, even by the more uncivilised mountaineers of Zoumerkas; yet robbery, murder, and other acts of violence, are unknown among them. These good people were not a little indignant when they heard that a band of Arnaoots was besieging and battering the sacred retreat of their favourite Caloyers. They assembled in a gallant troop, and taking Katusthius with them, hastened to drive the insolent Klephts back to their ruder fastnesses. They came too late. At midnight, while the monks prayed fervently to be delivered from their enemies, Dmitri and his followers tore down their iron-plated door and entered the holy precincts. The Protoklepht strode up to the gates of the sanctuary, and placing his hands upon it, swore that he came to save, not to destroy. Constans saw him. With a cry of delight he disengaged himself from the Caloyer who held him, and rushed into his arms: this was sufficient triumph. With assurances of sincere regret for having disturbed them, the Klepht quitted the chapel with his followers, taking his prize with him.

Katusthius returned some hours after, and so well did the traitor plead his cause with the kind Sagorians, bewailing the fate of his little nephew among these evil men, that they offered to follow, and, superior as their numbers were, to rescue the boy from their destructive hands. Katusthius, delighted with the proposition, urged their immediate departure. At dawn they began to climb the mountain summits, already trodden by the Zoumerkians.

Delighted with repossessing his little favourite, Dmitri placed him before him on his horse, and, followed by his comrades, made his way over the elevated mountains, clothed with old Dodona's oaks or, in higher summits, by dark gigantic pines. They proceeded for some hours, and at length dismounted to repose. The spot they chose was the depth of a dark ravine, whose gloom was increased by the broad shadows of dark ilexes; an entangled underwood, and a sprinkling of craggy isolated rocks, made it difficult for the horses to keep their footing. They dismounted, and sat by the little stream. Their simple fare was spread, and Dmitri enticed the boy to eat by a thousand caresses. Suddenly one of his men, set as a guard, brought intelligence that a troop of Sagorians, with Katusthius as their guide, was advancing from the monastery of St Elias; while another man gave the alarm of the approach of six or eight well-armed Moreots, who were advancing on the road from Yannina; in a moment every sign of encampment had disappeared. The Arnaoots began to climb the hills, getting under cover of the rocks, and behind the large trunks of the forest trees, keeping concealed till their invaders should be in the very midst of them. Soon the Moreots appeared, turning round the defile, in a path that only allowed them to proceed two by two; they were unaware of danger, and walked carelessly, until a shot that whizzed over the head of one, striking the bough of a tree, recalled them from their security. The Greeks, accustomed to the same mode of warfare, betook themselves also to the safeguards of the rocks, firing from behind them, striving with their adversaries which should get to the most elevated station; jumping from crag to crag, and dropping down and firing as quickly as they could load; one old man alone remained on the pathway. The mariner, Camaraz, had often encountered the enemy on the deck of his caique, and would still have rushed foremost at a boarding, but this warfare required too much activity. Cyril called on him to shelter himself beneath a low, broad stone; the Mainote waved his hand. 'Fear not for me,' he cried; 'I know how to die!'

The brave love the brave. Dmitri saw the old man stand, unflinching, a mark for all the balls, and he started from behind his rocky screen, calling on his men to cease. Then addressing his enemy, he cried, 'Who art thou? wherefore art thou here? If ye come in peace, proceed on your way. Answer, and fear not!'

The old man drew himself up, saying, 'I am a Mainote, and cannot fear. All Hellas trembles before the pirates of Cape Matapan, and I am one of these! I do not come in peace! Behold! you have in your arms the cause of our dissension! I am the grandsire of that child – give him to me!'

Dmitri, had he held a snake, which he felt awakening in his bosom, could not so suddenly have changed his tone – 'The offspring of a Mainote!' – he relaxed his grasp; Constans would have fallen had he not clung to his neck. Meanwhile each party had descended from their rocky station and were grouped together in the pathway below. Dmitri tore the child from his neck; he felt as if he could, with savage delight, dash him down the precipice – when, as he paused and trembled from excess of passion, Katusthius, and the foremost Sagorians, came down upon them.

'Stand!' cried the infuriated Arnaoot. 'Behold Katusthius! behold, friend, whom I, driven by the resistless fates, madly and wickedly forswore! I now perform thy wish – the Mainote child dies! the son of the accursed race shall be the victim of my just revenge!'

Cyril, in a transport of fear, rushed up the rock; he levelled his musket, but he feared to sacrifice his child. The old Mainote, less timid and more desperate, took a steady aim; Dmitri saw the act, and hurled the dagger, already raised against the child, at him – it entered his side – while Constans, feeling his late protector's grasp relax, sprang from it into his father's arms.

Camaraz had fallen, yet his wound was slight. He saw the Arnaoots and Sagorians close round him; he saw his own followers made prisoners. Dmitri and Katusthius had both thrown themselves upon Cyril, struggling to repossess themselves of the screaming boy. The Mainote raised himself – he was feeble of limb, but his heart was strong; he threw himself before the father and child; he caught the upraised arm of Dmitri. 'On me,' he cried, 'fall all thy vengeance! I of the evil race! For the child, he is innocent of such parentage! Maina cannot boast him for a son!'

'Man of lies!' commenced the infuriated Arnaoot, 'this falsehood shall not stead thee!'

'Nay, by the souls of those you have loved, listen!' continued Camaraz, 'and if I make not good my words, may I and my children die! The boy's father is a Corinthian, his mother, a Sciote girl!'

'Scio!' the very word made the blood recede to Dmitri's heart. 'Villain!' he cried, dashing aside Katusthius's arm, which was raised against poor Constans, 'I guard this child – dare not to injure him! Speak, old man, and fear not, so that thou speakest the truth.'

'Fifteen years ago,' said Camaraz, 'I hovered with my caique, in search of prey, on the coast of Scio. A cottage stood on the borders of a chestnut wood, it was the habitation of the widow of a wealthy islander – she dwelt in it with her only daughter, married to an Albanian, then absent; the good woman was reported to have a concealed treasure in her house and the girl herself would be rich spoil – it was an adventure worth the risk. We ran our vessel up a shady creek, and, on the going down of the moon, landed, stealing under the covert of night towards the lonely abode of these women.'

Dmitri grasped at his dagger's hilt – it was no longer there; he half drew a pistol from his girdle – little Constans, again confiding in his former friend, stretched out his infant hands and clung to his arm; the Klepht looked on him, half yielded to his desire to embrace him, half feared to be deceived; so he turned away, throwing his capote[139] over his face, veiling his anguish, controlling his emotions, till all should be told.

Camaraz continued: 'It became a worse tragedy than I had contemplated. The girl had a child – she feared for its life, and struggled with the men like a tigress defending her young. I was in another room seeking for the hidden store, when a piercing shriek rent the air – I never knew what compassion was before – this cry went to my heart – but it was too late, the poor girl had sunk to the ground, the life-tide oozing from her bosom. I know not why, but I turned woman in my regret for the slain beauty. I meant to have carried her and her child on board, to see if aught could be done to save her, but she died ere we left the shore. I thought she would like her island grave best, and truly feared that she might turn vampire to haunt me, did I carry her away; so we left her corse for the priests to bury, and carried off the child, then about two years old. She could say few words except her own name, that was Zella, and she is the mother of this boy!'

*   *   *

A succession of arrivals in the bay of Kardamyla had kept poor Zella watching for many nights. Her attendant had, in despair of ever seeing her sleep again, drugged with opium the few cates she persuaded her to eat, but the poor woman did not calculate on the power of mind over body, of love over every enemy, physical or moral, arrayed against it. Zella lay on her couch, her spirit somewhat subdued, but her heart alive, her eyes unclosed. In the night, led by some unexplained impulse, she crawled to her lattice, and saw a little *sacoleva* enter the bay; it ran in swiftly, under favour of the wind, and was lost to her sight under a jutting crag. Lightly she trod the marble floor of her chamber; she drew a large shawl close round her; she descended the rocky pathway, and reached, with swift steps, the beach – still the vessel was invisible, and she was half inclined to think that it was the offspring of her excited imagination – yet she lingered. She felt a sickness at her very heart whenever she attempted to move, and her eyelids weighed down in spite of herself. The desire of sleep at last became irresistible; she lay down on the shingles, reposed her head on the cold, hard pillow, folded her shawl still closer, and gave herself up to forgetfulness.

So profoundly did she slumber under the influence of the opiate, that for many hours she was insensible of any change in her situation. By degrees only she awoke, by degrees only became aware of the objects around her; the breeze felt fresh and free – so was it ever on the wave-beaten coast; the waters rippled near, their dash had been in her ears as she yielded to repose; but this was not her stony couch, that canopy, not the dark overhanging cliff. Suddenly she lifted up her head – she was on the deck of a small vessel, which was skimming swiftly over the ocean waves; a cloak of sables pillowed her head; the shores of Cape Matapan were to her left, and they steered right towards the noonday sun. Wonder rather than fear possessed her: with a quick hand she drew aside the sail that veiled her from the crew – the dreaded Albanian was sitting close at her side, her Constans cradled in his arms – she uttered a cry – Cyril turned at the sound, and in a moment she was folded in his embrace.

The False Rhyme

Come, tell me where the maid is found
Whose heart can love without deceit,
And I will range the world around
To sigh one moment at her feet.[140]

THOMAS MOORE

O N a fine July day, the fair Margaret, Queen of Navarre, then on a visit to her royal brother, had arranged a rural feast for the morning following, which Francis declined attending. He was melancholy, and the cause was said to be some lover's quarrel with a favourite dame. The morrow came, and dark rain and murky clouds destroyed at once the schemes of the courtly throng. Margaret was angry, and she grew weary; her only hope for amusement was in Francis, and he had shut himself up – an excellent reason why she should the more desire to see him. She entered his apartment: he was standing at the casement, against which the noisy shower beat, writing with a diamond on the glass. Two beautiful dogs were his sole companions. As Queen Margaret entered, he hastily let down the silken curtain before the window, and looked a little confused.

'What treason is this, my liege,' said the queen, 'which crimsons your check? I must see the same.'

'It is treason,' replied the king, 'and therefore, sweet sister, thou mayest not see it.'

This the more excited Margaret's curiosity, and a playful contest ensued. Francis at last yielded; he threw himself on a huge high-backed settee; and as the lady drew back the curtain with an arch smile, he grew grave and sentimental as he reflected on the cause which had inspired his libel against all womankind.

'What have we here?' cried Margaret: 'nay, this is *lèse-majesté* –

> Souvent femme varie,
> Bien fou qui s'y fie![141]

Very little change would greatly amend your couplet. Would it not run better thus –

> Souvent homme varie,
> Bien folle qui s'y fie![142]

I could tell you twenty stories of man's inconstancy.'

'I will be content with one true tale of woman's fidelity,' said Francis, drily; 'but do not provoke me. I would fain be at peace with the soft mutabilities, for thy dear sake.'

'I defy your grace,' replied Margaret, rashly, 'to instance the falsehood of one noble and well-reputed dame.'

'Not even Emilie de Lagny?' asked the king.

This was a sore subject for the queen. Emilie had been brought up in her own household, the most beautiful and the most virtuous of her maids of honour. She had long loved the Sire de Lagny, and their nuptials were celebrated with rejoicings but little ominous of the result. De Lagny was accused but a year after of traitorously yielding to the emperor a fortress under his command, and he was condemned to perpetual imprisonment. For some time Emilie seemed inconsolable, often visiting the miserable dungeon of her husband, and suffering on her return, from witnessing his wretchedness, such paroxysms of grief as threatened her life. Suddenly, in the midst of her sorrow, she disappeared and enquiry only divulged the disgraceful fact that she had escaped from France, bearing her jewels with her, and accompanied by her page, Robinet Leroux. It was whispered that, during their journey, the lady and the stripling often occupied one chamber; and Margaret, enraged at these discoveries, commanded that no further quest should be made for her lost favourite.

Taunted now by her brother, she defended Emilie, declaring that she believed her to be guiltless, even going so far as to boast that within a month she would bring proof of her innocence.

'Robinet was a pretty boy,' said Francis, laughing.

'Let us make a bet,' cried Margaret: 'if I lose, I will bear this vile rhyme of thine as a motto to my shame to my grave; if I win – '

'I will break my window, and grant thee whatever boon thou askest.'

The result of this bet was long sung by troubadour and minstrel. The queen employed a hundred emissaries – published rewards for any intelligence of Emilie – all in vain. The month was expiring, and Margaret would have given many bright jewels to redeem her word. On the eve of the fatal day, the jailor of the prison in which the Sire de

Francis I and Margaret his sister

Lagny was confined sought an audience of the queen; he brought her a message from the knight to say that if the Lady Margaret would ask his pardon as her boon, and obtain from her royal brother that he might be brought before him, her bet was won. Fair Margaret was very joyful, and readily made the desired promise. Francis was unwilling to see his false servant, but he was in high good humour, for a cavalier had that morning brought intelligence of a victory over the Imperialists. The messenger himself was lauded in the despatches as the most fearless and bravest knight in France. The king loaded him with presents, only regretting that a vow prevented the soldier from raising his visor or declaring his name.

That same evening as the setting sun shone on the lattice on which the ungallant rhyme was traced, Francis reposed on the same settee, and the beautiful Queen of Navarre, with triumph in her bright eyes, sat beside him. Attended by guards, the prisoner was brought in: his frame was attenuated by privation, and he walked with tottering steps. He knelt at the feet of Francis, and uncovered his head; a quantity of rich golden hair then escaping, fell over the sunken cheeks and pallid brow of the suppliant. 'We have treason here!' cried the king: 'sir jailor, where is your prisoner?'

'Sire, blame him not,' said the soft faltering voice of Emilie; 'wiser men than he have been deceived by women. My dear lord was guiltless of the crime for which he suffered. There was but one mode to save him: I assumed his chains – he escaped with poor Robinet Leroux in my attire – he joined your army; the young and gallant cavalier who delivered the despatches to your grace, whom you overwhelmed with honours and reward, is my own Enguerrard de Lagny. I waited but for his arrival with testimonials of his innocence to declare myself to my lady, the queen. Has she not won her bet? And the boon she asks – '

'Is de Lagny's pardon,' said Margaret, as she also knelt to the king; 'spare your faithful vassal, sire, and reward this lady's truth.'

Francis first broke the false-speaking window, then he raised the ladies from their supplicatory posture.

In the tournament given to celebrate this 'Triumph of Ladies', the Sire de Lagny bore off every prize; and surely there was more loveliness in Emilie's faded cheek and more grace in her emaciated form, type as they were of truest affection, than in the prouder bearing and fresher complexion of the most brilliant beauty in attendance on the courtly festival.

The Mourner

One fatal remembrance, one sorrow that throws
Its bleak shade alike o'er our joys and our woes,
To which life nothing darker or brighter can bring,
For which joy has no balm, and affliction no sting![143]

MOORE

A GORGEOUS scene of kingly pride is the prospect now before us! The offspring of art, the nursling of nature – where can the eye rest on a landscape more deliciously lovely than the fair expanse of Virginia Water, now an open mirror to the sky, now shaded by umbrageous banks, which wind into dark recesses or are rounded into soft promontories? Looking down on it, now that the sun is low in the west, the eye is dazzled, the soul oppressed, by excess of beauty. Earth, water, air, drink to overflowing the radiance that streams from yonder well of light: the foliage of the trees seems dripping with the golden flood; while the lake, filled with no earthly dew, appears but an im-basining of the sun-tinctured atmosphere; and trees and gay pavilion float in its depth, more clear, more distinct, than their twins in the upper air. Nor is the scene silent: strains more sweet than those that lull Venus to her balmy rest, more inspiring than the song of Tiresias which awoke Alexander to the deed of ruin,[144] more solemn than the chantings of St Cecilia, float along the waves and mingle with the lagging breeze, which ruffles not the lake. Strange, that a few dark scores should be the key to this fountain of sound; the unconscious link between unregarded noise, and harmonies which unclose paradise to our entranced senses!

The sun touches the extreme boundary, and a softer, milder light mingles a roseate tinge with the fiery glow. Our boat has floated long on the broad expanse; now let it approach the umbrageous bank. The green tresses of the graceful willow dip into the waters, which are checked by them into a ripple. The startled teal dart from their recess, skimming the waves with splashing wing. The stately swans float onward; while innumerable water fowl cluster together out of the way of the oars. The twilight is blotted by no dark shades; it is one subdued, equal receding of the great tide of day, which leaves the shingles bare, but not deformed. We may disembark and wander yet amid the glades, long before the thickening shadows speak of night. The plantations are formed of every English tree, with an old oak or two standing out in the walks. There the glancing foliage obscures heaven, as the silken texture of a veil a woman's lovely features: beneath such fretwork we may indulge in light-hearted thoughts; or, if sadder meditations lead us to seek darker shades, we may pass the cascade towards the large groves of pine, with their vast undergrowth of laurel, reaching up to the Belvidere;[145] or, on the opposite side of the water, sit under the shadow of the silver-stemmed birch, or beneath the leafy pavilions of those fine old beeches, whose high fantastic roots seem formed in nature's sport; and the near jungle of sweet-smelling myrica leaves no sense unvisited by pleasant ministration.

Now this splendid scene is reserved for the royal possessor; but in past years, while the lodge was called the Regent's Cottage, or before, when the under ranger inhabited it, the mazy paths of Chapel Wood were open, and the iron gates enclosing the plantations and Virginia Water were guarded by no Cerberus untamable by sops.[146] It was here, on a summer's evening, that Horace Neville and his two fair cousins floated idly on the placid lake,

> In that sweet mood when pleasant thoughts
> Bring sad thoughts to the mind.[147]

Neville had been eloquent in praise of English scenery. 'In distant climes,' he said, 'we may find landscapes grand in barbaric wildness, or rich in the luxuriant vegetation of the south, or sublime in Alpine magnificence. We may lament, though it is ungrateful to say so on such a night as this, the want of a more genial sky; but where find scenery to be compared to the verdant, well-wooded, well-watered groves of our native land; the clustering cottages, shadowed by fine old elms; each garden blooming with early flowers, each lattice gay with geraniums and roses; the blue-eyed child devouring his white bread, while he drives a cow to graze; the hedge redolent with summer blooms; the enclosed cornfields, seas of golden grain, weltering in the breeze; the stile, the track across the meadow, leading through the copse, under which the path winds, and the meeting branches overhead, which give, by their dimming tracery, a cathedral-like solemnity to the scene; the river, winding "with sweet inland murmur";[148] and, as additional graces, spots like these – oases of taste – gardens of Eden – the works of wealth,

Virginia Water

which evince at once the greatest power and the greatest will to create beauty?

'And yet,' continued Neville, 'it was with difficulty that I persuaded myself to reap the best fruits of my uncle's will, and to inhabit this spot, familiar to my boyhood, associated with unavailing regrets and recollected pain.'

Horace Neville was a man of birth – of wealth; but he could hardly be termed a man of the world. There was in his nature a gentleness, a sweetness, a winning sensibility, allied to talent and personal distinction, that gave weight to his simplest expressions, and excited sympathy for all his emotions. His younger cousin, his junior by several years, was attached to him by the tenderest sentiments – secret long – but they were now betrothed to each other – a lovely, happy pair. She looked enquiringly; but he turned away. 'No more of this,' he said; and giving a swifter impulse to their boat, they speedily reached the shore, landed, and walked through the long extent of Chapel Wood. It was dark night before they met their carriage at Bishopsgate.[149]

A week or two after, Horace received letters to call him to a distant part of the country: it even seemed possible that he might be obliged to visit an estate in the north of Ireland. A few days before his departure, he requested his cousin to walk with him. They bent their steps across several meadows to Old Windsor churchyard. At first he did not deviate from the usual path; and as they went they talked cheerfully – gaily: the beauteous sunny day might well exhilarate them; the dancing waves sped onwards at their feet, the country church lifted its rustic spire into the bright pure sky. There was nothing in their conversation that could induce his cousin to think that Neville had led her hither for any saddening purpose; but when they were about to quit the churchyard, Horace, as if he had suddenly recollected himself, turned from the path, crossed the greensward, and paused beside a grave near the river. No stone was there to commemorate the being who reposed beneath – it was thickly grown with rich grass, starred by a luxuriant growth of humble daisies; a few dead leaves, a broken bramble twig, defaced its neatness; Neville removed these, and then said, 'Juliet, I commit this sacred spot to your keeping while I am away.

'There is no monument,' he continued; 'for her commands were implicitly obeyed by the two beings to whom she addressed them. One day another may lie near, and his name will be her epitaph. – I do not mean myself,' he said, half smiling at the terror his cousin's countenance expressed; 'but promise me, Juliet, to preserve this grave from every violation. I do not wish to sadden you by the story; yet, if I have excited your curiosity – your interest, I should say – I will satisfy it; but not now – not here.'

Leaving the churchyard, they found their horses in attendance, and they prolonged their ride across Bishopsgate Heath. Neville's mind was full of the events to which he had alluded; he began the tale, and then abruptly broke off. It was not till the following day, when, in company with her sister, they again visited Virginia Water, that, seated under the shadow of its pines, whose melodious swinging in the wind breathed unearthly harmony, and looking down upon the water, association of place, and its extreme beauty, reviving, yet soothing, the recollections of the past, unasked by his companions, Neville at once commenced his story.

'I was sent to Eton at eleven years of age. I will not dwell upon my sufferings there; I would hardly refer to them, did they not make a part of my present narration. I was a fag to a hard taskmaster: every labour he could invent – and the youthful tyrant was ingenious – he devised for my annoyance; early and late, I was forced to be in attendance, to the neglect of my school duties, so incurring punishment. There were worse things to bear than these: it was his delight to put me to shame, and, finding that I had too much of my mother in my blood, to endeavour to compel me to acts of cruelty from which my nature revolted – I refused to obey. Speak of West Indian slavery! I hope things may be better now; in my days, the tender years of aristocratic childhood were yielded up to a capricious, unrelenting, cruel bondage, far beyond the measured despotism of Jamaica.

'One day – I had been two years at school, and was nearly thirteen – my tyrant, I will give him no other name, issued a command, in the wantonness of power, for me to destroy a poor little bullfinch I had tamed and caged. In a hapless hour he found it in my room, and was indignant that I should dare to appropriate a single pleasure. I refused, stubbornly, dauntlessly, though the consequence of my disobedience was immediate and terrible. At this moment a message came from my tormentor's tutor – his father had arrived. "Well, old lad," he cried, "I shall pay you off some day!" Seizing my pet at the same time, he wrung its neck, threw it at my feet, and, with a laugh of derision, quitted the room.

'Never before – never may I again feel the same swelling, boiling fury in my bursting heart; the sight of my nursling expiring at my feet – my desire for vengeance – my impotence, created a Vesuvius within me that no tears flowed to quench. Could I have uttered – acted – my passion, it would have been less torturous: it was so when I burst into a torrent of abuse and imprecation. My vocabulary – it must have been a choice collection – was supplied by him against whom it was levelled. But words were air – I desired to give more substantial proof of my resentment – I destroyed everything in the room belonging to him; I tore them to pieces, I stamped on them, crushed them with more than childish strength. My last act was to seize a timepiece, on which my tyrant infinitely prided himself, and to dash it to the ground. The sight of this, as it lay shattered at my feet, recalled me to my senses, and something like an emotion of fear allayed the tumult in my heart. I began to meditate an escape: I got out of the house, ran down a lane and across some meadows, far out of bounds, above Eton. I was seen by an elder boy, a friend of my tormentor. He called to me, thinking at first that I was performing some errand for him; but seeing that I shirked, he repeated his "*Come up!*" in an authoritative voice. It put wings to my heels; he did not deem it necessary to pursue.

But I grow tedious, my dear Juliet; enough that fears, the most intense, of punishment both from my masters and the upper boys made me resolve to run away. I reached the banks of the Thames, tied my clothes over my head, swam across, and, traversing several fields, entered Windsor Forest, with a vague childish feeling of being able to hide myself for ever in the unexplored obscurity of its immeasurable wilds. It was early autumn; the weather was mild, even warm; the forest oaks yet showed no sign of winter change, though the fern beneath wore a yellowy tinge. I got within Chapel Wood; I fed upon chestnuts and beechnuts; I continued to hide myself from the gamekeepers and wood-men. I lived thus two days.

'But chestnuts and beechnuts were sorry fare to a growing lad of thirteen years old. A day's rain occurred, and I began to think myself the most unfortunate boy on record. I had a distant, obscure idea of starvation: I thought of the Children in the Wood, of their leafy shroud, gift of the pious robin; this brought my poor bullfinch to my mind, and tears streamed in torrents down my cheeks. I thought of my father and mother; of you, then my little baby cousin and playmate; and I cried with renewed fervour, till, quite exhausted, I curled myself up under a huge oak among some dry leaves, the relics of a hundred summers, and fell asleep.

'I ramble on in my narration as if I had a story to tell; yet I have little except a portrait – a sketch – to present, for your amusement or interest. When I awoke, the first object that met my opening eyes was a little foot, delicately clad in silk and soft kid. I looked up in dismay, expecting to behold some gaily dressed appendage to this indication of high-bred elegance; but I saw a girl, perhaps seventeen, simply clad in a dark cotton dress, her face shaded by a large very coarse straw hat; she was pale even to marmoreal whiteness; her chestnut-coloured hair was parted in plain tresses across a brow which wore traces of extreme suffering; her eyes were blue, full, large, melancholy, often even suffused with tears; but her mouth had an infantine sweetness and innocence in its expression that softened the otherwise sad expression of her countenance.

'She spoke to me. I was too hungry, too exhausted, too unhappy, to resist her kindness, and gladly permitted her to lead me to her home. We passed out of the wood by some broken palings on to Bishopsgate Heath, and after no long walk arrived at her habitation. It was a solitary, dreary-looking cottage; the palings were in disrepair, the garden waste, the lattices unadorned by flowers or creepers; within, all was neat, but sombre, and even mean. The diminutiveness of a cottage requires an appearance of cheerfulness and elegance to make it pleasing; the bare floor – clean, it is true – the rush chairs, deal table, checked curtains of this cot, were beneath even a peasant's rusticity; yet it was the dwelling of my lovely guide, whose little white hand, delicately gloved, contrasted with her unadorned attire, as did her gentle self with the clumsy appurtenances of her too humble dwelling.

'Poor child! she had meant entirely to hide her origin, to degrade herself to a peasant's state, and little thought that she forever betrayed herself by the strangest incongruities. Thus, the arrangements of her table were mean, her fare meagre for a hermit; but the linen was match-lessly fine, and wax lights stood in candlesticks which a beggar would almost have disdained to own. But I talk of circumstances I observed afterwards; then I was chiefly aware of the plentiful breakfast she caused her single attendant, a young girl, to place before me, and of the sweet soothing voice of my hostess, which spoke a kindness with which lately I had been little conversant. When my hunger was appeased, she drew my story from me, encouraged me to write to my father, and kept me at her abode till, after a few days, I returned to school pardoned. No long time elapsed before I got into the upper forms, and my woeful slavery ended.

'Whenever I was able, I visited my disguised nymph. I no longer associated with my schoolfellows; their diversions, their pursuits, appeared vulgar and stupid to me; I had but one object in view – to accomplish my lessons and to steal to the cottage of Ellen Burnet.

'Do not look grave, love! true, others as young as I then was have loved, and I might also; but not Ellen. Her profound, her intense melancholy, sister to despair – her serious, sad discourse – her mind, estranged from all worldly concerns, forbade that; but there was an enchantment in her sorrow, a fascination in her converse, that lifted me above commonplace existence; she created a magic circle, which I entered as holy ground: it was not akin to heaven, for grief was the presiding spirit; but there was an exaltation of sentiment, an enthusiasm, a view beyond the grave, which made it unearthly, singular, wild, en-thralling. You have often observed that I strangely differ from all other men; I mingle with them, make one in their occupations and diversions, but I have a portion of my being sacred from them: a living well, sealed up from their contamination, lies deep in my heart – it is of little use, but there it is; Ellen opened the spring, and it has flowed ever since.

'Of what did she talk? She recited no past adventures, alluded to no past intercourse with friend or relative; she spoke of the various woes that wait on humanity, on the intricate mazes of life, on the miseries of passion, of love, remorse and death, and that which we may hope or fear beyond the tomb; she spoke of the sensation of wretchedness alive in her own broken heart, and then she grew fearfully eloquent, till, suddenly pausing, she reproached herself for making me familiar with such wordless misery. "I do you harm," she often said; "I unfit you for society; I have tried, seeing you thrown upon yonder distorted miniature of a bad world, to estrange you from its evil contagion; I fear that I shall be the cause of greater harm to you than could spring from association with your fellow creatures in the ordinary course of things. This is not well – avoid the stricken deer."[150]

'There were darker shades in the picture than those which I have already developed. Ellen was more miserable than the imagination of one like you, dear girl, unacquainted with woe, can portray. Sometimes she gave words to her despair – it was so great as to confuse the boundary between physical and mental sensation – and every pulsation of her heart was a throb of pain. She has suddenly broken off in talking of her sorrows, with a cry of agony – bidding me leave her – hiding her face on her arms, shivering with the anguish some thought awoke. The idea that chiefly haunted her, though she earnestly endeavoured to put it aside, was self-destruction – to snap the silver cord that bound together so much grace, wisdom and sweetness – to rob the world of a creation made to be its ornament. Sometimes her piety checked her; oftener a sense of unendurable suffering made her brood with pleasure over the dread resolve. She spoke of it to me as being wicked; yet I often fancied this was done rather to prevent her example from being of ill effect to me, than from any conviction that the Father of all, would regard angrily the last act of his miserable child. Once she had prepared the mortal beverage; it was on the table before her when I entered; she did not deny its nature, she did not attempt to justify herself; she only besought me not to hate her and to sooth by my kindness her last moments. – "I cannot live!" was all her explanation, all her excuse; and it was spoken with such fervent wretchedness that it seemed wrong to attempt to persuade her to prolong the sense of pain. I did not act like a boy; I wonder I did not; I made one simple request, to which she instantly acceded, that she should walk with me to this Belvidere. It was a glorious sunset; beauty and the spirit of love breathed in the wind, and hovered over the softened hues of the landscape. "Look, Ellen," I cried, "if only such loveliness of nature existed, it were worth living for!"

' "True, if a latent feeling did not blot this glorious scene with murky shadows. Beauty is as we see it – my eyes view all things deformed and evil." She closed them as she said this; but, young and sensitive, the visitings of the soft breeze already began to minister consolation.

' "Dearest Ellen," I continued, "what do I not owe to you? I am your boy, your pupil; I might have gone on blindly as others do, but you opened my eyes; you have given me a sense of the just, the good, the beautiful – and have you done this merely for my misfortune? If you leave me, what can become of me?" The last words came from my heart, and tears gushed from my eyes. "Do not leave me, Ellen," I said; "I cannot live without you – and I cannot die, for I have a mother – a father." She turned quickly round, saying, "You are blessed sufficiently." Her voice struck me as unnatural; she grew deadly pale as she spoke, and was obliged to sit down. Still I clung to her, prayed, cried; till she – I had never seen her shed a tear before – burst into passionate weeping. After this she seemed to forget her resolve. We returned by moonlight, and our talk was even more calm and cheerful than usual. When in her cottage, I poured away the fatal draught. Her, "Good-night," bore with it no traces of her late agitation; and the next day she said, "I have thoughtlessly, even wickedly, created a new duty to myself, even at a time when I had forsworn all; but I will be true to it. Pardon me for making you familiar with emotions and scenes so dire; I will behave better – I will preserve myself, if I can, till the link between us is loosened, or broken, and I am free again."

'One little incident alone occurred during our intercourse that appeared at all to connect her with the world. Sometimes I brought her a newspaper, for those were stirring times; and though, before I knew her, she had forgotten all except the world her own heart enclosed, yet, to please me, she would talk of Napoleon – Russia, from whence the emperor now returned overthrown – and the prospect of his final defeat. The paper lay one day on her table; some words caught her eye; she bent eagerly down to read them, and her bosom heaved with violent palpitation; but she subdued herself, and after a few moments told me to take the paper away. Then, indeed, I did feel an emotion of even impertinent inquisitiveness; I found nothing to satisfy it – though afterwards I became aware that it contained a singular advertisement, saying,

If these lines meet the eye of any one of the passengers who were on board the *St Mary*, bound for Liverpool from Barbados, which sailed on the third of May last, and was destroyed by fire on the high seas, a part of the crew only having been saved by his majesty's frigate the *Bellerophon*, they are entreated to communicate with the advertiser; and if anyone be acquainted with the particulars of the Hon. Miss Eversham's fate and present abode, they are earnestly requested to disclose them, directing to L. E., Stratton Street, Park Lane.

'It was after this event, as winter came on, that symptoms of decided ill health declared themselves in the delicate frame of my poor Ellen. I have often suspected that, without positively attempting her life, she did many things that tended to abridge it and to produce mortal disease. Now, when really ill, she refused all medical attendance; but she got better again, and I thought her nearly well when I saw her for the last time, before going home for the Christmas holidays. Her manner was full of affection: she relied, she said, on the continuation of my friend-ship; she made me promise never to forget her, though she refused to write to me, and forbade any letters from me.

'Even now I see her standing at her humble doorway. If an appearance of illness and suffering can ever be termed lovely, it was in her. Still she was to be viewed as the wreck of beauty. What must she not have been in happier days, with her angel expression of face, her nymph-like figure, her voice, whose tones were music? "So young – so lost!" was the sentiment that burst even from me, a young lad, as I waved my hand to her as a last adieu. She hardly looked more than fifteen, but none could doubt that her very soul was impressed by the sad lines of sorrow that rested so unceasingly on her fair brow. Away from her, her figure forever floated before my eyes; I put my hands before them, still she was there; my day, my night, dreams were filled by my recollections of her.

'During the winter holidays, on a fine soft day, I went out to hunt: you, dear Juliet, will remember the sad catastrophe; I fell and broke my leg. The only person who saw me fall was a young man who rode one of the most beautiful horses I ever saw, and I believe it was by watching him as he took a leap that I incurred my disaster; he dismounted, and was at my side in a minute. My own animal had fled; he called his; it obeyed his voice; with ease he lifted my light figure on to the saddle, contriving to support my leg, and so conducted me a short distance to a lodge situated in the woody recesses of Elmore Park, the seat of the Earl of D—, whose second son my preserver was. He was my sole nurse for a day or two, and during the whole of my illness passed many hours of each day by my bedside. As I lay gazing on him, while he read to me, or talked, narrating a thousand strange adventures which had occurred during his service in the Peninsula, I thought, Is it for ever to be my fate to fall in with the highly gifted and excessively unhappy?

'The immediate neighbour of Lewis's family was Lord Eversham. He had married in very early youth, and became a widower young. After this misfortune, which passed like a deadly blight over his prospects and possessions, leaving the gay view utterly sterile and bare, he left his surviving infant daughter under the care of Lewis's mother, and travelled for many years in far distant lands. He returned when Clarice was about ten, a lovely sweet child, the pride and delight of all connected with her. Lord Eversham, on his return – he was then hardly more than thirty – devoted himself to her education. They were never separate: he was a good musician, and she became a proficient under his tutoring. They rode – walked – read together. When a father is all that a father may be, the sentiments of filial piety, entire dependence and perfect confidence being united, the love of a daughter is one of the deepest and strongest, as it is the purest passion of which our natures are capable. Clarice worshipped her parent, who came, during the transition from mere childhood to the period when reflection and observation awaken, to adorn a commonplace existence with all the brilliant adjuncts which enlightened and devoted affection can bestow. He appeared to her like an especial gift of providence, a guardian angel – but far dearer, as being akin to her own nature. She grew, under his eye, in loveliness and refinement both of intellect and heart. These feelings were not divided – almost strengthened, by the engagement that had place between her and Lewis: – Lewis was destined for the army, and, after a few years' service, they were to be united.

'It is hard, when all is fair and tranquil, when the world, opening before the ardent gaze of youth, looks like a well-kept demesne, un-incumbered by let or hinderance for the annoyance of the young traveller, that we should voluntarily stray into desert wilds and tempest-visited districts. Lewis Elmore was ordered to Spain; and, at the same time, Lord Eversham found it necessary to visit some estates he possessed in Barbados. He was not sorry to revisit a scene, which had dwelt in his memory as an earthly paradise, nor to show to his daughter a new and strange world, so to form her understanding and enlarge her mind. They were to return in three months, and departed as on a summer tour. Clarice was glad that, while her lover gathered experience and knowledge in a distant land, she should not remain in idleness – she was glad that there would be some diversion for her anxiety during his perilous absence; and in every way she enjoyed the idea of travelling with her beloved father, who would fill every hour, and adorn every new scene, with pleasure and delight. They sailed. Clarice wrote home, with enthusiastic expressions of rapture and delight, from Madeira – yet without her father, she said, the fair scene had been blank to her. More than half her letter was filled by the expressions of her gratitude and affection for her adored and revered parent. While he, in his, with fewer words, perhaps, but with no less energy, spoke of his satisfaction in her improvement, his pride in her beauty, and his grateful sense of her love and kindness.

'Such were they, a matchless example of happiness in the dearest connection in life, as resulting from the exercise of their reciprocal duties and affections. A father and daughter: the one all care, gentleness and sympathy, consecrating his life to her happiness; the other, fond, duteous, grateful. Such had they been – but where were they now – the noble, kind, respected parent and the beloved and loving child? They had departed from England as on a pleasure voyage down an inland stream; but the ruthless car of destiny had overtaken them on their unsuspecting way, crushing them under its heavy wheels – scattering love, hope and joy as the bellowing avalanche overwhelms and grinds to mere spray the streamlet of the valley. They were gone: but whither? Mystery hung over the fate of the most helpless victim; and my friend's anxiety was to penetrate the clouds that hid poor Clarice from his sight.

'After an absence of a few months, they had written, fixing their departure in the *St Mary*, to sail from Barbados in a few days. Lewis, at the same time, returned from Spain: he was invalided, in his very first action, by a bad wound in his side. He arrived, and each day expected to hear of the landing of his friends, until that common messenger, the newspaper, brought him tidings to fill him with more than anxiety – with fear and agonising doubt. The *St Mary* had caught fire and had burned in the open sea. A frigate, the *Bellerophon*, had saved a part of the crew. In spite of illness and a physician's commands, Lewis set out the same day for London, to ascertain as speedily as possible the fate of her he loved. There he heard that the frigate was expected in the Downs. Without alighting from his travelling chaise, he posted thither, arriving in a burning fever. He went on board, saw the commander, and spoke with the crew. They could give him few particulars as to whom they had saved; they had touched at Liverpool, and left there most of the persons, including all the passengers rescued from the *St Mary*. Physical suffering for a while disabled Mr Elmore; he was confined by his wound and consequent fever, and only recovered to give himself up to his exertions to discover the fate of his friends; – they did not appear nor write; and all Lewis' enquiries only tended to confirm his worst fears; yet still he hoped, and still continued indefatigable in his perquisitions. He visited Liverpool, and Ireland, whither some of the passengers had gone, and learnt only scattered, incongruous details of the fearful tragedy that told nothing of Miss Eversham's present abode; though much that confirmed his suspicion that she still lived.

'The fire on board the *St Mary* had raged long and fearfully before the *Bellerophon* hove in sight, and boats came off for the rescue of the crew. The women were to be first embarked; but Clarice clung to her father, and refused to go till he should accompany her. Some fearful presentiment that, if she were saved, he would remain and die, gave such energy to her resolve that not the entreaties of her father, nor the angry expostulations of the captain, could shake it. Lewis saw this man, after the lapse of two or three months, and he threw most light on the dark scene. He well remembered that, transported with anger by her woman's obstinacy, he had said to her, "You will cause your father's death – and be as much a parricide as if you put poison into his cup; you are not the first girl who has murdered her father in her wilful mood." Still Clarice passionately refused to go – there was no time for long parley – the point was yielded, and she remained pale, but firm, near her parent, whose arm was around her, supporting her during the awful interval. It was no period for regular action and calm order: a tempest was rising, the scorching flames blew this way and that, making a fearful day of the night which veiled all except the burning ship. The boats returned with difficulty, and one only could contrive to approach; it was nearly full; Lord Eversham and his daughter advanced to the deck's edge to get in. "We can only take one of you," vociferated the sailors: "keep back on your life! throw the girl to us – we will come back for you if we can." Lord Eversham cast with a strong arm his daughter, who had now entirely lost her self-possession, into the boat; she was alive again in a minute, she called to her father, held out her arms to him, and would have thrown herself into the sea, but was held back by the sailors. Meanwhile Lord Eversham feeling that no boat could again approach the lost vessel, contrived to heave a spar overboard, and threw himself into the sea, clinging to it. The boat, tossed by the huge waves, with difficulty made its way to the frigate; and as it rose from the trough of the sea, Clarice saw her father struggling with his fate – battling with the death that at last became the victor; the spar floated by, his arms had fallen from it – were those his pallid features? She neither wept nor fainted, but her limbs grew rigid, her face colourless, and she was lifted as a log on to the deck of the frigate.

'The captain allowed that on her homeward voyage, the people had rather a horror of her, as having caused her father's death; her own servants had perished, few people remembered who she was; but they talked together with no careful voices as they passed her, and a hundred times she must have heard herself accused of having destroyed her parent. She spoke to no one, or only in brief reply when addressed; to avoid the rough remonstrances of those around, she appeared at table, ate as well as she could; but there was a settled wretchedness in her face that never changed. When they landed at Liverpool, the captain conducted her to a hotel; he left her, meaning to return, but an opportunity of sailing that night for the Downs occurred, of which he availed himself, without again visiting her. He knew, he said, and truly, that she was in her native country, where she had but to write a letter to gather crowds of friends about her; and where can greater civility be found than at an English hotel, if it is known that you are perfectly able to pay your bill?

'This was all that Mr Elmore could learn, and it took many months to gather together these few particulars. He went to the hotel at Liverpool. It seemed that as soon as there appeared some hope of rescue from the frigate, Lord Eversham had given his pocketbook to his daughter's care, containing bills on a banking-house at Liverpool to the amount of a few hundred pounds. On the second day after Clarice's arrival there, she had sent for the master of the hotel, and showed him these. He got the cash for her; and the next day, she quitted Liverpool in a little coasting vessel. In vain Lewis endeavoured to trace her. Apparently she had crossed to Ireland; but whatever she had done, wherever she had gone, she had taken infinite pains to conceal, and all clue was speedily lost.

'Lewis had not yet despaired; he was even now perpetually making journeys, sending emissaries, employing every possible means for her discovery. From the moment he told me this story, we talked of nothing else. I became deeply interested, and we ceaselessly discussed the probabilities of the case, and where she might be concealed; that she did not meditate suicide was evident from her having possessed herself of money; yet, unused to the world, young, lovely and inexperienced, what could be her plan? What might not have been her fate?

'Meanwhile I continued for nearly three months confined by the fracture of my limb; before the lapse of that time, I had begun to crawl about the ground, and now I considered myself as nearly recovered. It had been settled that I should not return to Eton, but be entered at Oxford; and this leap from boyhood to man's estate elated me considerably. Yet still I thought of my poor Ellen, and was angry at her obstinate silence. Once or twice I had, disobeying her command, written to her, mentioning my accident, and the kind attentions of Mr Elmore: still she wrote not; and I began to fear that her illness might have had a fatal termination. She had made me vow so solemnly never to mention her name, never to enquire about her during my absence, that, considering obedience the first duty of a young inexperienced boy to one older than himself, I resisted each suggestion of my affection or my fears to transgress her orders.

'And now spring came, with its gift of opening buds, odoriferous flowers and sunny genial days. I returned home, and found my family on the eve of their departure for London; my long confinement had weakened me – it was deemed inadvisable for me to encounter the bad air and fatigues of the metropolis, and I remained to rusticate. I rode and hunted, and thought of Ellen; missing the excitement of her conversation, and feeling a vacancy in my heart which she had filled.

I began to think of riding across the country from Shropshire to Berkshire for the purpose of seeing her. The whole landscape haunted my imagination – the fields round Eton – the silver Thames – the majestic forest – this lovely scene of Virginia Water – the heath and her desolate cottage – she herself pale, slightly bending from weakness of health, awakening from dark abstraction to bestow on me a kind smile of welcome. It grew into a passionate desire of my heart to behold her, to cheer her as I might by my affectionate attentions, to hear her, and to hang upon her accents of inconsolable despair, as if it had been celestial harmony. As I meditated on these things, a voice seemed forever to repeat, Now go, or it will be too late; while another yet more mournful tone responded, You can never see her more!

'I was occupied by these thoughts as, on a summer moonlight night, I loitered in the shrubbery, unable to quit a scene of entrancing beauty, when I was startled at hearing myself called by Mr Elmore. He came on his way to the coast; he had received a letter from Ireland, which made him think that Miss Eversham was residing near Enniscorthy: a strange place for her to select, but as concealment was evidently her object, not an improbable one. Yet his hopes were not high; on the contrary, he performed this journey more from the resolve to leave nothing undone than in expectation of a happy result. He asked me if I would accompany him; I was delighted with the offer, and we departed together on the following morning.

'We arrived at Milford Haven, where we were to take our passage. The packet was to sail early in the morning – we walked on the beach, and beguiled the time by talk. I had never mentioned Ellen to Lewis; I felt now strongly inclined to break my vow, and to relate my whole adventure with her; but restrained myself, and we spoke only of the unhappy Clarice – of the despair that must have been hers, of her remorse and unavailing regret.

'We retired to rest, and early in the morning I was called to prepare for going on board. I got ready, and then knocked at Lewis's door; he admitted me, for he was dressed, though a few of his things were still unpacked, and scattered about the room. The morocco case of a miniature was on his table; I took it up – "Did I never show you that?" said Elmore; "poor dear Clarice! she was very happy when that was painted!"

'I opened it. Rich luxuriant curls clustered on her brow and the snow-white throat; there was a light zephyr appearance in the figure; an expression of unalloyed exuberant happiness in the countenance; but those large dove's eyes, the innocence that dwelt on her mouth, could not be mistaken, and the name of Ellen Burnet burst from my lips.

'There was no doubt: why had I ever doubted? the thing was so plain! who but the survivor of such a parent, and she the apparent cause of his death, could be so miserable as Ellen? A torrent of explanation followed, and a thousand minute circumstances, forgotten before, now assured us that my sad hermitess was the beloved of Elmore. No more sea voyage – not a second of delay – our chaise, the horses' heads turned to the east, rolled on with lightning rapidity, yet far too slowly to satisfy our impatience. It was not until we arrived at Worcester that the tide of expectation, flowing all one way, ebbed. Suddenly, even while I was telling Elmore some anecdote to prove that, in spite of all, she would be accessible to consolation, I remembered her ill health and my fears. Lewis saw the change my countenance underwent; for some time I could not command my voice; and when at last I spoke, my gloomy anticipations passed like an electric shock into my friend's soul.

'When we arrived at Oxford, we halted for an hour or two, unable to proceed; yet we did not converse on the subject so near our hearts, nor until we arrived in sight of Windsor did a word pass between us; then Elmore said, "Tomorrow morning, dear Neville, you shall visit Clarice; we must not be too precipitate."

'The morrow came. I arose with that intolerable weight at my breast which it is grief's worst heritage to feel. A sunny day it was; yet the atmosphere looked black to me; my heart was dead within me. We sat at the breakfast table, but neither ate, and after some restless indecision, we left our inn, and (to protract the interval) walked to Bishopsgate. Our conversation belied our feelings; we spoke as if we expected all to be well, we felt that there was no hope. We crossed the heath along the accustomed path. On one side was the luxuriant foliage of the forest; on the other, the widespread moor; her cottage was situated at one extremity and could hardly be distinguished until we should arrive close to it. When we drew near, Lewis bade me go on alone, he would wait my return; I obeyed, and reluctantly approached the confirmation of my fears. At length it stood before me, the lonely cot and desolate garden; the unfastened wicket swung in the breeze; every shutter was closed.

'To stand motionless and gaze on these symbols of my worst forebodings was all that I could do. My heart seemed to me to call aloud for Ellen – for such was she to me (her other name might be a fiction), but silent as her own life-deserted lips were mine. Lewis grew impatient, and advanced – my stay had occasioned a transient ray of hope to enter his mind – it vanished when he saw me, and her deserted dwelling. Slowly we turned away, and were directing our steps back again, when my name was called by a child. A little girl came running across some fields towards us, whom at last I recognised as having seen before with Ellen. "Mr Neville, there is a letter for you!" cried the child.

' "A letter – where? – who?"

' "The lady left a letter for you. You must go to Old Windsor, to Mr Cooke's; he has got it for you."

'She had left a letter – was she then departed on an earthly journey? "I will go for it immediately. Mr Cooke! Old Windsor! Where shall I find him? Who is he?"

' "Oh, sir, every body knows him," said the child; "he lives close to the churchyard; he is the sexton. After the burial, Nancy gave him the letter to take care of."

'Had we hoped? had we for a moment indulged the expectation of ever again seeing our miserable friend? Never! Oh, never! Our hearts had told us that the sufferer was at peace – the unhappy orphan with her father in the abode of spirits! Why then were we here? Why had a smile dwelt on our lips, now wreathed into the expression of anguish? Our full hearts demanded one consolation – to weep upon her grave, her sole link now with us, her mourners. There at last my boy's grief found vent in tears, in lamentation. You saw the spot; the grassy mound rests lightly on the bosom of fair Clarice, of my own poor Ellen. Stretched upon this, kissing the scarcely springing turf, for many hours no thought visited me but the wretched one – that she had lived – and was lost to me for ever!

'If Lewis had ever doubted the identity of my friend with her he loved, the letter put into our hands undeceived him; the handwriting was Miss Eversham's, it was directed to me, and contained words like these:

April 11

I have vowed never to mention certain beloved names, never to communicate with beings who cherished me once, to whom my deepest gratitude is due; and, as well as poor bankrupt can, is paid. Perhaps it is a mere prevarication to write to you, dear Horace, concerning them; but, heaven pardon me! my disrobed spirit would not repose, I fear, if I did not thus imperfectly bid them a last farewell.

You know him: Neville; and know that he forever laments her whom he has lost. Describe your poor Ellen to him, and he will speedily see that *she* died on the waves of the murderous Atlantic. Ellen had nothing in common with *her*, save love for and interest in him. Tell him, it had been well for him, perhaps, to have united himself to the child of prosperity, the nursling of deep love; but it had been destruction, even could he have meditated such an act, to wed the parrici –

I will not write that word. Sickness and near death have taken the sting from my despair. The agony of woe, which you witnessed, is melted into tender affliction and pious hope. I am not miserable now. Now! When you read these words, the hand that writes, the eye that sees, will be a little dust, becoming one with the earth around it. You, perhaps he, will visit my quiet retreat, bestow a few tears on my fate, but let them be secret; they may make green my grave, but do not let a misplaced feeling adorn it with any other tribute. It is my last request; let no stone, no name, mark that spot.

Farewell, dear Horace! Farewell, to one other whom I may not name. May the God to whom I am about to resign my spirit in confidence and hope bless your earthly career! Blindly, perhaps, you will regret me for your own sakes; but for mine, you will be grateful to the providence which has snapped the heavy chain binding me to unutterable sorrow, and which permits me from my lowly grass-grown tomb to say to you, I am at peace.

ELLEN

The Swiss Peasant

WHY is the mind of man so apt to be swayed by contraries? Why does the imagination forever paint the impossible in glittering tints, and the hearts of wayward mortals cling, with the greatest tenacity, to what, eel-like, is bent on escaping from their grasp? Why – to bring the matter home – is solitude abhorrent to me, now that I enjoy it in perfection? I have apostrophised the coy nymph in ball-rooms, when the bright lamps of heaven were shamed by brighter earth-stars, and lamented her absence at a picnic party, where the nightingale was silenced by the fiddle, and the flowery turf was strewn with the impertinent finery of ugly old women, and the greenwood shade made redolent with the fumes of roasted fowls.

And now, O solitude! I abjure thee, in thy fitting temple – in Switzerland – among cloud-piercing mountains, by the resounding waves of the isle-surrounding lake. I am beside the waters of Uri – where Tell lived – in Brunnen, where the Swiss patriots swore to die for freedom.[151] It rains – magic word to destroy the spell to which these words give rise – the clouds envelop the hills – the white mists veil the ravines – there is a roar and a splash in my ears – and now, and then, the vapours break and scatter themselves, and I see something dark between, which is the hoar side of a dark precipice, but which might as well be the turf stack or old wall that bounded Cumberland's view as he wrote *The Wheel of Fortune*.[152]

The sole book that I possess is *The Prisoner of Chillon*.[153] I have read it through three times within an hour. Its noble author composed it to beguile weary hours like these when he remained rain-bound for three days in a little inn on the shores of the Lake of Geneva; and cannot I, following with unequal steps, so cheat the minutes in this dim spot? I never, by the by, could invent the commonest incident. As a man of honour, of course I never lie; but, as a nursery child and schoolboy, I never did; simply, as I remember, because I never could concoct one – but a true tale was lately narrated to me by its very heroine, the incidents of which haunt my memory, adorned as they were by her animated looks and soft silvery accent. Let me try to record them, stripped though they must be of their greatest charm.

I was, but a week ago, travelling with my friend Ashburn in a *coupée*,[154] in the district of Subiaco, in the ecclesiastical territory. We were jolted along a rough ravine, through which the River Anio sped, and beetling mountains and shady trees, a distant convent and a picturesque cell on a hill, formed a view which so awoke the pictorial propensities of my friend that he stopped the *coupée* (though we were assured that we should never reach our inn by nightfall, and that the road was dangerous in the dark), took out his portfolio and began to sketch. As he drew I continued to speak in support of an argument we had entered upon before. I had been complaining of the commonplace and ennui of life. Ashburn insisted that our existence was only too full of variety and change – tragic variety and wondrous incredible change. 'Even,' said the painter, 'as sky, and earth and water seem forever the same to the vulgar eye, and yet to the gifted one assume a thousand various guises and hues – now robed in purple – now shrouded in black – now resplendent with living gold – and anon sinking into sober and unobtrusive grey, so do our mortal lives change and vary. No living being among us but could tell a tale of soul-subduing joys and heart-consuming woes, worthy, had they their poet, of the imagination of Shakspeare or Goethe. The veriest weather-worn cabin is a study for colouring, and the meanest peasant will offer all the acts of a drama in the apparently dull routine of his humble life.'

'This is pure romance,' I replied; 'put it to the test. Let us take, for example, yonder woman descending the mountain path.'

'What a figure!' cried Ashburn; 'oh that she would stay thus but one quarter of an hour! – she has come down to bathe her child – her upturned face – her dark hair – her picturesque costume – the little plump fellow bestriding her – the rude scenery around – '

'And the romantic tale she has to tell.'

'I would wager a louis[155] that hers has been no common fate. She steps a goddess – her attitude – her looks, are all filled with majesty.'

I laughed at his enthusiasm, and accepted his bet. We hurried to join our fair peasantess, and thus formed acquaintance with Fanny Chaumont. A sudden storm, as we were engaged conversing with her, came, driven down from the tempest-bearing hills, and she gave us a cordial invitation to her cottage.

It was situated on a sunny slope, yet sheltered from the winds. There was a look of cheerfulness and *aisance*[156] about it, beyond what is usually met in that part of Switzerland, reminding me of the cottages of the

Fanny

inhabitants of the free states. There, also, we found her husband. I always feel curious to know on whom a woman, who bears the stamp of superior intellect and who is beautiful and refined – for peasant as she was, Fanny was both – has been induced to bestow herself.

Louis Chaumont was considerably older than his wife; he was handsome, with brown lively eyes, curly chesnut hair, a visage embrowned by the sun, bearing every mark of having led an active, even an adventurous life; there was, besides, an expression which, if it were not ferocity, resembled it nearly, in his vivacious glances, and in the sternness of his deeply-lined forehead; while she, in spite of her finely-formed brow, her majestic person, and her large expressive eyes, looked softness and patience itself. There was something incongruous in the pair, and more strangely matched they seemed when we heard their story. It lost me my louis, but proved Fanny at once to be a fitting heroine for romance, and was a lesson, moreover, to teach the strange pranks love can play with us, mingling fire and water, blending in one harmonious concord the harsh base and melodious tenor of two differently stringed instruments. Though their child was five years old, Fanny and her husband were attached to each other with the tenderness and passion of early love; they were happy – his faults were tempered by her angel disposition, and her too melancholy and feeling-fraught spirit was enlivened and made plastic to the purposes of this world by his energy and activity.

Fanny was a Bernese by birth: she was the child of humble cottagers, one among a large family. They lived on the brow of one summit and at the foot of another. The snowy mountains were piled about them; thaw-fed torrents brawled around; during the night a sound like thunder, a crash among the tempest-beaten pines would tell of an avalanche; or the snowdrift, whirring past the lattice, threatened to bury the little fabric. Winter was the season of peace in the deep vales, not so in the higher district. The peasant was often kept waking by the soft-falling snow which threatened insidiously to encroach on and to overwhelm his habitation; or a straying cow would lead him far into the depths of the stormy hills, and his fearful family would count in agony the hours of his absence. Perpetual hardship and danger, however, rather brutify than exalt the soul of man; and those of the Swiss who are most deeply planted among the rocky wilds are often stultified and sullen.

Fanny opened her youthful eyes and observation on this scene. She was one of those lovely children only to be seen in Switzerland, whose beauty is heartfelt but indescribable: hers was the smooth candid brow, the large hazel eyes, half soft, half wild; the round dimpled cheek, the full sensitive mouth, the pointed chin, and (as framework to the picture) the luxuriant curly chesnut hair, and voice which is sweetest music. The exceeding beauty of little Fanny gained her the observation of the wife of the governor of the château which overlooked and commanded the district, and at ten years of age she became a frequent visitor there. Fanny's little soul was love, so she soon twined herself round the kind lady's heart, became a pet with the governor and the favourite playmate of their only son.

One fête day Fanny had dined at the château. It had been fine warm spring weather, but wind and storm came on with the setting sun; the snow began to fall thickly, and it was decided that Fanny must pass the night in the château. She had been unusually eager to return home; and when the tempest came on, she crept near her protectress, and begged to be sent to her mother. *C'est impossible* – Fanny pressed no further, but she clambered to a window, and looked out wistfully to where, hidden by the hills, her parents' cottage stood. It was a fatal night for her: the thunders of frequent avalanches, the roaring of torrents, the crash of trees, spoke of devastation, and her home was its chief prey. Father, mother, brothers and sisters, not one survived. Where, the day before, cottage and outhouse and flower-adorned garden had stood, the little lawn where she played, and the grove that sheltered her, there was now a monumental pile of snow, and the rocky path of a torrent; no trace remained, not one survivor to tell the tale. From that night Fanny became a constant inmate of the château.

It was Madame de Marville's project to give her a bourgeois education, which would raise her from the hardships of a peasant's life, and yet not elevate her above her natural position in society. She was brought up kindly, but humbly; it was the virtues of her disposition which raised her in the eyes of all around her, not any ill-judged favour of her benefactress. The night of the destruction of her family never passed away from her memory; it set a seal of untimely serious-ness on her childish brow, awoke deep thoughts in her infant heart, and a strong resolve that while she lived, her beloved friends should find her, as far as her humble powers admitted, a source of good alone – a reason to rejoice that they had saved her from the destruction that had overwhelmed her family.

Thus Fanny grew up in beauty and in virtue. Her smiles were as the rainbows of her native torrents; her voice, her caresses, her light step, her unalterable sweetness and ceaseless devotion to the wishes of others, made her the idol of the family. Henry, the only child of her protectors, was of her own age, or but a few months her senior. Every time Henry returned from school to visit his parents, he found Fanny more beautiful, more kind, more attractive than before; and the first passion his youthful heart knew was for the lovely peasant girl, whose virtues sanctified his home. A look, a gesture betrayed his secret to his mother; she turned a hasty glance on Fanny, and saw on her countenance innocence and confidence alone. Half reassured, yet still fearful, Madame de Marville began to reflect on some cure for the threatened evil. She could not bear to send away Fanny; she was solicitous that her son should for the present reside in his home. The lovely girl was perfectly unconscious of the sentiments of the young seigneur; but would she always continue so? and was the burning heart that warmed her gentle bosom to be forever insensible to the despotic and absorbing emotions of love?

It was with wonder, and a curious mixture of disappointed maternal pride and real gladness, that the lady, at length, discovered a passion dawning in fair Fanny's heart for Louis Chaumont, a peasant some ten years older than herself. It was natural that one with such high wrought feelings as our heroine should love one to whom she could look up, and on whom to depend, rather than her childhood's playmate – the gay thoughtless Henry. Louis's family had been the victim of a moral ruin, as hers of a physical one. They had been oppressed, reduced to poverty, driven from their homes by some feudal tyrant, and had come poor and forlorn from a distant district. His mother, accustomed to a bourgeois life, died broken-hearted; his father, a man of violent passions, nourished in his own and in his son's heart, sentiments of hatred and revenge against the 'proud oppressors of the land'.[157] They were obliged to labour hard, yet in the intervals of work, father and son would read or discourse concerning the ills attendant on humanity, and they traced all to the social system, which made the few the tyrants of the many.

Louis was handsome, bold and active; he excelled his compeers in every hardy exercise; his resolution, his eloquence, his daring, made him, in spite of his poverty, a kind of leader among them. He had many faults: he was too full of passion, of the spirit of resistance and revenge; but his heart was kind; his understanding, when not thwarted, strong; and the very depth of his feelings made him keenly susceptible to love. Fanny, in her simple but majestic beauty, in her soft kindness of manner, mingled with the profoundest sensibility, made a deep impression on the young man's heart. His converse, so different and so superior to those of his fellows, won her attention.

Hitherto Fanny had never given utterance to the secrets of her soul. Habitual respect held her silent with Madame, and Henry, as spirited and as heedless as a chamois,[158] could ill understand her; but Louis became the depositary of the many feelings which, piled up in secrecy and silence, were half awful to herself; he brought reason, or what he deemed such, to direct her heart-born conclusions. To have heard them talk of life and death, and all its shows, you would have wondered by what freak philosophy had dressed herself in youth and a peasant's garb and wandered from the schools to these untaught wilds.

Madame de Marville saw and encouraged this attachment. Louis was not exactly the person she would have selected for Fanny; but he was the only being for whom she had ever evinced a predilection; and, besides, the danger of a misalliance which threatened her own son, rendered her eager to build an insurmountable wall between him and the object of his affections. Thus Fanny enjoyed the heart-gladdening pride of hearing her choice applauded and praised by the person she most respected and loved in the world. As yet, however, love had been covert; the soul but not the apparent body of their intercourse. Louis was kept in awe by this high-minded girl, and Fanny had not yet learned her own secret. It was Henry who made the discovery for them – Henry, who, with all the impetuosity of his vivacious character, contrived a thousand ways to come between them; who, stung by jealousy to injustice, reviled Louis for his ruin, his poverty, his opinions, and brought the spirit of dissension to disquiet a mind entirely bent, as she imagined, on holy and pure thoughts.

Under this clash of passion, the action of the drama rapidly developed itself, and, for nearly a year, a variety of scenes were acted among these secluded mountains of no interest save to the parties themselves, but to them fateful and engrossing. Louis and Fanny exchanged vows; but that sufficed not. Fanny insisted on the right of treating with uniform kindness the son of her best friend, in spite of his injustice and insolence. The young men were often, during the rural festivals, brought into angry collision. Fanny was the peace-maker: but a woman is the worst possible mediator between her rival lovers. Henry was sometimes irritated to complain to his father of Louis's presumption. The spirit of the French Revolution then awakening, rendered a peasant's assumptions peculiarly grating; and it required Madame de Marville's impartial gentleness to prevent Fanny's betrothed, as now he was almost considered, from being further oppressed.

At length it was decided that Henry should absent himself for a time, and visit Paris. He was enraged in the extreme by what he called his banishment. Noble and generous as he naturally was, love was the tyrant of his soul, and drove him almost to crime. He entered into a fierce quarrel with his rival on the very eve of his departure: it ended in a scene of violence and bloodshed. No great real harm was done; but Monsieur de Marville, hitherto scarcely kept back from such a measure by his wife, suddenly obtained an order for Louis (his father had died a year before) to quit the territory within twelve hours. Fanny was commanded, as she valued the favour of her friends, to give him up. The young men were both gone before any intercession could avail; and that kind of peace which resembles desolation took possession of the château.

Aware of the part she had taken in encouraging Fanny's attachment to her peasant-lover, Madame de Marville did not make herself a party to the tyranny of her husband; she requested only of her protégée to defer any decisive step, and not to quit her guardianship until the return of her son, which was to take place the following year. Fanny consented to such a delay, although in doing so, she had to resist the angry representations of her lover, who exacted that she should quit the roof of his oppressors. It was galling to his proud spirit that she should continue to receive benefits from them, and injurious to his love that she should remain where his rival's name was the constant theme of discourse and the object of interest. Fanny in vain represented her debt of gratitude, the absence of Henry, the impossibility that she could feel any undue sentiment towards the young seigneur; not to hate him was a crime in Louis's eyes; yet how, in spite of his ill conduct, could Fanny hate her childhood's playmate – her brother? His violent passions excited to their utmost height – jealousy and the sense of impotent indignation raging in his heart – Louis swore to revenge himself on the Marvilles – to forget and to abhor his mistress! – his last words were a malediction on them, and a violent denunciation of scorn upon her.

'It will all be well yet,' thought Fanny, as she strove to calm the tumultuous and painful emotions to which his intemperate passion gave rise. 'Not only are storms the birth of the wild elements, but of the heart of man, and we can oppose patience and fortitude alone to their destructive violence. A year will pass – I shall quit the château; Louis will acknowledge my truth, and retract his frightful words.'

She continued, therefore, to fulfil her duties cheerfully, not permitting her thoughts to dwell on the idea that, in spite of her struggles, too painfully occupied her – the probability that Louis would in the end renounce or forget her; but committing her cause to the spirit of good, she trusted that its influence would in the end prevail.

She had, however, much to endure; four months passed, and no tidings reached her of Louis. Often she felt sick at heart; often she became the prey of the darkest despair; above all, her tender heart missed the fond attentions of love, the bliss of knowing that she bestowed happiness, and the unrestrained intercourse to which mutual affection had given rise. She cherished hope as a duty, and faith in love, rather than in her unjust and cruelly neglectful lover. It was a hard task, for she had nowhere to turn for consolation or encouragement. Madame de Marville marked with gladness the total separation between them. Now that the danger that threatened her son was averted, she repented having been influential in producing an attachment between Fanny and one whom she deemed unworthy of her. She redoubled her kindness, and, in the true continental fashion, tried to get up a match between her and some one among her many and more prosperous admirers. She failed, but did not despair, till she saw the poor girl's cheek grow pale and her vivacity desert her as month after month passed away and the very name of Louis appeared to be forgotten by all except herself.

The stirring and terrible events that took place at this time in France added to Fanny's distress of mind. She had been familiarised to the discussion of the theories, now attempted to be put in practice, by the conversations of Chaumont. As each fresh account brought information of the guilty and sanguinary acts of men whose opinions were the same as those of her lover, her fears on his account increased. In a few words I shall hurry over this part of her story. Switzerland became agitated by the same commotions as tore the near kingdom. The peasantry rose in tumult; acts of violence and blood were committed; at first at a distance from her retired valley, but gradually approaching its precincts, until at last the tree of liberty was set up in the neighbouring village.[159] Monsieur de Marville was an aristocrat of the most bigoted species. In vain was the danger represented to him, and the unwarlike state of his retinue. He armed them – he hurried down – he came unawares on the crowd who were proclaiming the triumph of liberty, rather by feasting than force. On the first attack, they were dispersed, and one or two among them were wounded; the pole they had gathered round was uprooted, the emblematic cap trampled to the earth. The governor returned victorious to his château.

This act of violence on his part seemed the match to fire a train of organised resistance to his authority, of which none had dreamt before. Strangers from other cantons thronged into the valley; rustic labours were cast aside; popular assemblies were held, and the peasants exercised in the use of arms. One was coming to place himself at their head, it was said, who had been a party in the tumults at Geneva. Louis Chaumont was coming – the champion of liberty, the sworn enemy of M. de Marville. The influence of his presence soon became manifest. The inhabitants of the château were, as it were, besieged. If one ventured beyond a certain limit he was assailed by stones and knives. It was the resolve of Louis that all within its walls should surrender themselves to his mercy. What that might be, the proud curl of his lip and the fire that glanced from his dark eyes rendered scarcely problematic. Fanny would not believe the worst of her lover, but Monsieur and Madame de Marville, no longer restrained by any delicacy, spoke of the leveller in unmeasured terms of abhorrence, comparing him to the monsters who then reigned in France, while the danger they incurred through him added a bitter sting to their words. The peril grew each day; famine began to make its appearance in the château; while the intelligence which some of the more friendly peasants brought was indicative of preparations for a regular attack of the most formidable nature. A summons at last came from the insurgents. They were resolved to destroy the emblem of their slavery – the feudal halls of their tyrants. They declared their intention of firing the château the next day, and called on all within to deliver themselves up, if they would not be buried in its ruins. They offered their lives and free leave to depart to all, save the governor himself, who must place himself unconditionally at the mercy of their leader. 'The wretch,' exclaimed his lady, 'who thirsts for your blood! Fly! if there is yet time for flight; we, you see, are safe. Fly! nor suffer these cruel dastards to boast of having murdered you.'

M. de Marville yielded to these entreaties and representations. He had sent for a military force to aid him – it had been denied; he saw that he himself, as the detested person, was the cause of danger to his family. It was therefore agreed that he should seek a chalet situated on a mountain ten leagues distant, where he might lie concealed till his family joined him. Accordingly, in a base disguise, he quitted at midnight the walls he was unable to defend; a miserable night for the unfortunate beings left behind. The coming day was to witness the destruction of their home; and they, beggars in the world, were to wander through the inhospitable mountains, till, with caution and terror, they could unobserved reach the remote and miserable chalet, and learn the fate of the unhappy fugitive. It was a sleepless night for all. To add to Madame's agony, she knew that her son's life was in danger in Paris – that he had been denounced – and though yet untaken, his escape was still uncertain. From the turret of the castle that, situated high on a rock, commanded the valley below, she sat the livelong night watching for every sound – fearful of some shout, some report of firearms, which would announce the capture of her husband. It was September; the nights were chill; pale and trembling, she saw day break over the hills. Fanny had busied herself during these anxious hours by preparing for their departure; the terrified domestics had already fled; she, the lady, and the old lame gardener were all that remained. At dawn she brought forth the mule, and harnessed him to the rude vehicle which was to convey them to their place of refuge. Whatever was most valuable in the château had already been sent away long before, or was secreted; a few necessaries alone she provided. And now she ascended the turret stairs, and stood before her protectress, announcing that all was ready, and that they must depart. At this last moment, Madame de Marville appeared deprived of strength; she strove to rise – she sank to the ground in a fit. Forgetful of her deserted state, Fanny called aloud for help, and then her heart beat wildly, as a quick, youthful step was heard on the stairs. Who could he be? would *he* come to insult their wretchedness – he, the author of their woe? The first glance changed the object of her terror. Henry flew to his mother's side, and, with broken exclamations and agitated questions, demanded an explanation of what he saw. He had fled for safety to the habitation of his parents – he found it deserted; the first voice he heard was that of Fanny crying for help – the first sight that presented itself was his mother, to all appearance dead, lying on the floor of the turret. Her recovery was followed by brief explanations, and a consultation of how his safety was to be provided for. The name of Chaumont excited his bitterest execrations. With a soldier's haughty resolve, he was for darting from the castle to meet and to wreak vengeance on his rival. His mother threw herself at his feet, clasping his knees, calling wildly on him not to desert her. Fanny's gentle, sweet voice was of more avail to calm his passion. 'Chevalier,' she said, 'it is not thus that you must display your courage or protect the helpless. To encounter yonder infuriated mob would be to run on certain death; you must preserve yourself for your family – you must have pity on your mother, who cannot survive you. Be guided by me, I beseech you.'

Henry yielded to her voice, and a more reasonable arrangement took place. The departure of Madame de Marville and Fanny was expected at the village, and a pledge had been given that they should proceed unmolested. But deeply had the insurgents sworn that if the governor or his son (whose arrival in the château had been suspected) attempted to escape with them, they should be immediately sacrificed to 'justice'. No disguise would suffice – the active observation of their enemies was known. Every inhabitant of the castle had been numbered – the fate of each ascertained, save that of the two most detested – the governor, whose flight had not been discovered, and his son, whose arrival was so unexpected and ill-timed. As still they consulted, a beat to arms was heard in the valley below: it was the signal that the attack on the empty castle walls would soon begin. There was no time for delay or hesitation; Henry placed himself at the bottom of the *charrette*;[160] straw and a variety of articles were heaped upon him; the two women ascended in trepidation; and the old gardener sat in front and held the reins.

In consequence of the disturbed state of the districts through which they were to pass – where the appearance of one of the upper classes excited the fiercest enmity, and frightful insult, if not death, was their sure welcome – Madame and her friend assumed a peasant's garb. And thus they wound their way down the steep; the unhappy lady weeping bitterly – Fanny, with tearless eyes, but with pale cheek and compressed lips, gazing for the last time on the abode which had been her refuge when, in helpless infancy, she was left an orphan – where kindness and benevolence had waited on her, and where her days had passed in innocence and peace. 'And he drives us away! – him, whom I loved – whom I love! – O misery!'

They reached the foot of the eminence on which the château was placed, and proceeded along the road which led directly through the village. With the approach of danger, vain regrets were exchanged for a lively sense of fear in the bosom of the hapless mother, and for the exertion of her courage and forethought in Fanny's more energetic mind. They passed a peasant or two, who uttered a malediction or imprecation on them as they went; then groups of two or three, who were even more violent in gesture and menace; when suddenly the sound of many steps came on their ears, and, at a turn of the road, they met Chaumont with a band of about twenty disciplined men.

'Fear not,' he said to Madame de Marville; 'I will protect you from danger till you are beyond the village.'

With a shriek, the lady, in answer, threw herself in Fanny's arms, crying, 'He is here! – save me! – he will murder us.'

'Fear not, madame – he dares not injure you. Begone, Louis! insult us not by your presence. Begone! I say.'

Fanny spoke angrily. She had not adopted this tone, but that the lady's terror, and the knowledge that even then the young soldier crouched at their feet burnt to spring up and confront his enemy, made her use an authority which a woman always imagines that a lover dare not resist.

'I do not insult you,' repeated Chaumont – 'I save you. I have no quarrel with the lady; tyrants alone need fear me. You are not safe without my escort. Do not you, false girl, irritate me. I have ensured her escape; but yours – you are in my power.'

A violent movement at the bottom of the *charrette* called forth all Fanny's terrors.

'Take me!' she cried; 'do with me what you please; but you dare not, you cannot raise a finger against the innocent. Begone, I say! let me never see you more!'

'You are obeyed. On you fall the consequences.'

Thus, after many months of separation, did Fanny and her lover meet. She had purposed when she should see him to make an appeal to his better nature – his reason; she had meant to use her all-persuasive voice to recall him from the dangerous path he was treading. Several times, indeed, since his arrival in the valley, she had endeavoured to obtain an interview with him, but he dreaded her influence: he had resolved on revenge, and he feared to be turned back. But now the unexpected presence of his rival robbed her of her self-possession, and forced her to change her plans. She saw frightful danger in their meeting, and all her endeavours were directed to the getting rid of her lover.

Louis and his companions proceeded towards the château, while the *charrette* of the fugitives moved on in the opposite direction. They met many a ferocious group, who were rushing forward to aid in the destruction of their home; and glad they were, in that awful hour, that any object had power to divert the minds of their enemies from attention to themselves. The road they pursued wound through the valley; the precipitous mountain on one side, a brawling stream on the other. Now they ascended higher and now again descended in their route, while the road, broken by the fall of rocks, intersected by torrents, which tore their way athwart it, made their progress slow. To get beyond the village was the aim of their desires; when, lo! just as they came upon it, and were in the very midst of its population, which was pouring towards the castle, suddenly the *charrette* sank in a deep rut; it half upset, and every spoke in the wheel giving way rendered the vehicle wholly useless.

'Mais, descendez donc, mesdames,' said a peasant; 'il faut bien marcher.'[161]

Fanny had indeed already sprung to the ground to examine what hope remained: there was none. 'Grand Dieu! nous sommes perdues!'[162] were the first words that escaped her, while her friend stood aghast, trembling, almost insensible, knowing that the hope of her life, the existence of her son, depended on these miserable moments.

A peasant who owed Fanny some kindness now advanced, and in a kind of cavalier way, as if to blemish as much as he could the matter of his offer by its manner, told them that, for the pleasure of getting rid of the aristocrats, he would lend his cart – there it was, let them quickly bestow their lading in it and pursue their way. As he spoke, he caught up a box, and began the transfer from one cart to the other.

'No, no!' cried Madame de Marville, as, with a scream, she sprang forward and grasped the arm of the man as he was in the very act of discovering her son's hiding-place. 'We will accept nothing from our base enemies! – Begone with your offers! we will die here rather than accept anything from such *canaille*.'[163]

The word was electric. The fierce passions of the mob, excited by the mischief they were about to perpetrate, now burst like a stream into this new channel. With violent execrations they rushed upon the unfortunate woman: they would have torn her from the cart, but already her son had sprung from his hiding-place, and striking a violent blow at the foremost assailant, checked for a moment their brutal outrages. Then again, with a yell, such as the savage Indians alone could emulate, they rushed on their prey. Mother and son were torn asunder, and cries of, 'À bas les aristocrats!' – 'À la lanterne!'[164] declared too truly their sanguinary designs.

At this moment, Louis appeared – Louis, whose fears for Fanny had overcome his indignation, and who returned to guard her; while she, perceiving him, with a burst of joy, called on him to rescue her friends. His cry of, 'Arretez-vous!'[165] was loud and distinct amidst the uproar. It was obeyed; and then he caught sight of his rival, his oppressor, his enemy in his power. At first, rage inflamed every feature, to be replaced by an expression of triumph and implacable hatred. Fanny caught the fierce glance of his eye, and grew pale. She trembled as, trying to be calm, she said, 'Yes, you behold he is here. And you must save him – and your own soul. Rescue him from death, and be blest that your evil career enables you at least to perform this one good action.'

For a moment Louis seemed seeking for a word, as a man, meaning to stab, may fumble for his dagger's hilt, unable in his agitation to grasp his weapon.

'My friends,' at length he said, 'let the women depart – we have promised it. Ye may deal with the young aristocrat according to his merits.'

'À la lanterne!' burst in response from a hundred voices.

'Let his mother first depart!'

Could it be Louis that spoke these words, and had she loved this man? To appeal to him was to rouse a tiger from his lair. Another thought darted into Fanny's mind; she scarcely knew what she said or did; but already knives were drawn; already, with a thrill of horror, she thought she saw the blood of her childhood's playmate spilt like water on the earth. She rushed forward – she caught the upraised arm of one – 'He is no aristocrat!' she cried; 'he is my husband! Will you murder one who, forgetting his birth, his duty, his honour, has married a peasant girl – one of yourselves?'

Even this appeal had little effect upon the mob; but it strangely affected her cruel lover. Grasping her arm with iron fingers, he cried, 'Is this tale true? Art thou married to that man – his wife?'

'Even so!' – the words died on her lips as she strove to form them, terrified by their purport, and the effect they might produce. An inexplicable expression passed over Chaumont's face; the fierceness that jealousy had engendered for a moment was exalted almost to madness, and then faded wholly away. The stony heart within him softened at once. A tide of warm, human, and overpowering emotion flowed into his soul: he looked on her he had loved even to guilt and crime, on her whom he had lost for ever, and tears rushed into his eyes, as he saw her gasping, trembling before him – at his mercy.

'Fear not,' at last he said; 'fear neither for him nor yourself. Poor girl! so young, you shall not lose all – so young, you shall not become a widow. He shall be saved!'

Yet it was no easy task, even for him, to stem the awakened passions of the bloodthirsty mob. He had spent many an hour in exciting them against their seigneurs,[166] and now at once to control the violence to which he had given rise seemed impossible. Yet his energy, his strong will overcame all opposition. They should pierce the chevalier's heart, he swore, through his alone. He prevailed – the fugitives were again seated in their cart. He took the rein of their mule, and saying to his comrades, 'Attendez-moi,'[167] he led them out of the village. All were silent; Fanny knew not what to say, and surprise held the others mute. Louis went with them until a turn in the road hid them from the view of the village. What his thoughts were, none could guess; he looked calm as, resigning the rein into the chevalier's hands, he gently wished them, 'Bon voyage,' touching his hat in reply to their salutations. They moved on, and Fanny looked back to catch a last view of her lover: he was standing where they left him, when suddenly, instead of returning on his steps into the village, she saw him with rapid strides ascend the mountainside, taking a well-known path that conducted him away from the scene of his late exploits. His pace was that of a man flying from pursuers – soon he was lost to sight.

Astonishment still kept the fugitives silent, as they pursued their way;

and when at last joy broke forth, and Madame de Marville, rejoicing in their escape, embraced again and again her son, he with the softest tenderness thanked Fanny for his life; she answered not, but withdrawing to the farthest part of the *charrette*, wept bitterly.

Late that night, they reached the destined chalet, and found Monsieur de Marville arrived. It was a half-ruined miserable habitation perched among the snows, cold and bare; food was ill to be obtained, and danger breathed around them. Fanny attended on them with assiduous care, but she never spoke of the scene in the village; and though she strove to look the same, Henry never addressed her but her cheeks grew white, and her voice trembled. She could not divine her distant lover's thoughts, but she knew that he believed her married to another; and that other, earnestly though she strove to rule her feelings, became an object of abhorrence to her.

Three weeks they passed in this wretched abode; three weeks replete with alarm, for the district around was in arms, and the life of Monsieur de Marville loudly threatened. They never slept but they dreaded the approach of the murderers; food they had little, and the inclement season visited them roughly. Fanny seemed to feel no inconvenience; her voice was cheerful; to console, encourage and assist her friends appeared to occupy her whole heart. At length one night they were roused by a violent knocking at the door of their hut. Monsieur de Marville and Henry were on their feet in a moment, seizing their weapons as they rose. It was a domestic of their own, come to communicate the intelligence that the troubles were over, that the legal government had reasserted its authority, and he invited the governor to return to Berne.

They descended from their mountain refuge, and the name of Louis hovered on Fanny's lips, but she spoke it not. He seemed everywhere forgotten. It was not until some time afterwards that she ascertained the fact that he had never been seen or heard of since he had parted from her on the morning of their escape. The villagers had waited for him in vain; they suspended their designs, for they all depended upon him; but he came not.

Monsieur and Madame de Marville returned to their château with their son, but Fanny remained behind. She would not inhabit the same roof as Henry; she recoiled even from receiving further benefits from his parents. What could she do? Louis would doubtless discover the falsehood of her marriage, but he dared not return; and even if he communicated with her, even though yet she loved him, could she unite herself with one accused too truly of the most frightful crimes? At first, these doubts agitated her, but by degrees they faded as oblivion closed over Chaumont's name – and he came not and she heard not of him, and he was as dead to her. Then the memory of the past revived in her heart: her love awoke with her despair; his mysterious flight became the sole occupation of her thoughts; time rolled on and brought its changes. Madame de Marville died – Henry was united to another – Fanny remained, to her own thoughts, alone in the world. A relation, who lived at Subiaco, sent for her, and there she went to take up her abode. In vain she strove to wean herself from the memory of Louis – her love for him haunted her soul.

There was war in Europe, and every man was converted into a soldier; the country was thinned of its inhabitants, and each victory or defeat brought a new conscription. At length peace came again, and its return was celebrated with rejoicing. Many a soldier returned to his home – and one came back who had no home. A man, evidently suffering from recent wounds, way-worn and sick, asked for hospitality at Fanny's cottage; it was readily afforded, and he sat at her cottage fire, and removed his cap from his brows. His person was bent – his cheeks fallen in – yet those eyes of fire, that quick animated look, which almost brought the bright expression of youth back into his face, could never be forgotten. Fanny gazed almost in alarm, and then in joy, and at last, in her own sweet voice, she said, 'Et toi, Louis – tu aussi es de retour.'[168]

Louis had endured many a sorrow and many a hardship, and, most of all, he had been called on to wage battle with his own fierce spirit. The rage and hate which he had sedulously nourished suddenly became his tormentors and his tyrants – at the moment that love, before too closely allied to them, emancipated itself from their control. Love, which is the source of all that is most generous and noble in our nature, of self-devotion and of high intent, separated from the alloy he had blended with it, asserted its undivided power over him – strange that it should be so, at the moment that he believed that he had lost her he loved for ever!

All his plans had been built for revenge. He would destroy the family that oppressed him – unbuild, stone by stone, the proud abode of their inheritance – he would be the sole refuge and support of his mistress in exile and in poverty. He had entered upon his criminal career with this design alone, and with the anticipation of ending all by heaping benefits and the gifts of fortune upon Fanny. The very steps he had taken, he now believed to be those that occasioned his defeat. He had lost her – the lovely and the good – he had lost her by proving unworthy – yet not so unworthy was he as to make her the victim of his crimes. The family he had vowed to ruin was now hers, and every injury that befell them visited her; to save her he must unweave his pernicious webs – to keep her scatheless, his dearest designs must fall to the ground.

A veil seemed rent before his eyes – he had fled, for he would not assist in the destruction of her fortunes – he had not returned, for it was torture to him to know that she lived, the wife of another. He entered the French army – but in every change his altered feelings pursued him, and to prove himself worthy of her he had lost was the constant aim of his ambition. His excellent conduct led to his promotion, and yet mishap still waited on him. He was wounded, even dangerously, and became so incapable of service as to be forced to solicit his dismission. This had occurred at the end of a hard campaign in Germany, and his intention was to pass into Italy, where a friend, with whom he had formed an intimacy in the army, promised to procure him some employment under government. He passed through Subiaco in his way, and, ignorant of its occupiers, had asked for hospitality in his mistress's cottage.

If guilt can be expiated by repentance and reform, as is the best lesson of religion, Louis had expiated his. If constancy in love deserve reward, these lovers deserved that, which they reaped, in the happiness consequent on their union. Her image, side by side with all that is good in our nature, had dwelt in his heart; which thus became a shrine at which he sacrificed every evil passion. It was a greater bliss than he had ever dared to anticipate to find that in so doing he had at the same time been conducing to the welfare of her he loved, and that the lost and idolised being whom he worshipped founded the happiness of her life upon his return to virtue, and the constancy of his affection.

Transformation

Forthwith this frame of mine was wrench'd
    With a woeful agony,
Which forced me to begin my tale,
    And then it set me free.
Since then, at an uncertain hour,
    That agony returns;
And till my ghastly tale is told
This heart within me burns.[169]

COLERIDGE's Ancient Mariner

I HAVE heard it said that when any strange, supernatural and necromantic adventure has occurred to a human being, that being, however desirous he may be to conceal the same, feels at certain periods torn up as it were by an intellectual earthquake and is forced to bare the inner depths of his spirit to another. I am a witness of the truth of this. I have dearly sworn to myself never to reveal to human ears the horrors to which I once, in excess of fiendly pride, delivered myself over. The holy man who heard my confession, and reconciled me to the church, is dead. None knows that once –

Why should it not be thus? Why tell a tale of impious tempting of providence and soul-subduing humiliation? Why? answer me, ye who are wise in the secrets of human nature! I only know that so it is; and in spite of strong resolve – of a pride that too much masters me, of shame, and even of fear, so to render myself odious to my species – I must speak.

Genoa! my birthplace – proud city! looking upon the blue waves of the Mediterranean Sea – dost thou remember me in my boyhood, when thy cliffs and promontories, thy bright sky and gay vineyards, were my world? Happy time! when to the young heart the narrow-bounded universe, which leaves, by its very limitation, free scope to the imagination, enchains our physical energies, and, sole period in our lives, innocence and enjoyment are united. Yet, who can look back to childhood and not remember its sorrows and its harrowing fears? I was born with the most imperious, haughty, tameless spirit, with which ever mortal was gifted. I quailed before my father only; and he, generous and noble, but capricious and tyrannical, at once fostered and checked the wild impetuosity of my character, making obedience necessary, but inspiring no respect for the motives which guided his commands. To be a man, free, independent – or, in better words, insolent and domineering – was the hope and prayer of my rebel heart.

My father had one friend, a wealthy Genoese noble, who in a political tumult was suddenly sentenced to banishment, and his property confiscated. The Marchese Torella went into exile alone. Like my father, he was a widower; he had one child, the almost infant Juliet, who was left under my father's guardianship. I should certainly have been an unkind master to the lovely girl but that I was forced by my position to become her protector. A variety of childish incidents all tended to one point – to make Juliet see in me a rock of refuge; I in her one who must perish through the soft sensibility of her nature too rudely visited, but for my guardian care. We grew up together. The opening rose in May was not more sweet than this dear girl. An irradiation of beauty was spread over her face. Her form, her step, her voice – my heart weeps even now to think of all of relying, gentle, loving and pure that was enshrined in that celestial tenement. When I was eleven and Juliet eight years of age, a cousin of mine, much older than either – he seemed to us a man – took great notice of my playmate; he called her his bride, and asked her to marry him. She refused, and he insisted, drawing her unwillingly towards him. With the countenance and emotions of a maniac I threw myself on him – I strove to draw his sword – I clung to his neck with the ferocious resolve to strangle him: he was obliged to call for assistance to disengage himself from me. On that night I led Juliet to the chapel of our house: I made her touch the sacred relics – I harrowed her child's heart, and profaned her child's lips with an oath, that she would be mine, and mine only.

Well, those days passed away. Torella returned in a few years, and became wealthier and more prosperous than ever. When I was seventeen, my father died; he had been magnificent to prodigality; Torella rejoiced that my minority would afford an opportunity for repairing my fortunes. Juliet and I had been affianced beside my father's deathbed – Torella was to be a second parent to me.

I desired to see the world, and I was indulged. I went to Florence, to Rome, to Naples; thence I passed to Toulon, and at length reached what had long been the bourne of my wishes, Paris. There was wild work in Paris then. The poor king, Charles the Sixth,[170] now sane, now mad, now a monarch, now an abject slave, was the very mockery of humanity. The queen, the dauphin, the Duke of Burgundy, alternately friends and foes – now meeting in prodigal feasts, now shedding blood in rivalry – were blind to the miserable state of their country, and the dangers that impended over it, and gave themselves wholly up to dissolute enjoyment or savage strife. My character still followed me. I was arrogant and self-willed; I loved display, and above all, I threw all control far from me. Who could control me in Paris? My young friends were eager to foster passions which furnished them with pleasures. I was deemed handsome – I was master of every knightly accomplishment. I was disconnected with any political party. I grew a favourite with all: my presumption and arrogance were pardoned in one so young; I became a spoiled child. Who could control me? not the letters and advice of Torella – only strong necessity visiting me in the abhorred shape of an empty purse. But there were means to refill this void. Acre after acre, estate after estate, I sold. My dress, my jewels, my horses and their caparisons,[171] were almost unrivalled in gorgeous Paris, while the lands of my inheritance passed into the possession of others.

The Duke of Orleans was waylaid and murdered by the Duke of Burgundy. Fear and terror possessed all Paris. The dauphin and the queen shut themselves up; every pleasure was suspended.[172] I grew weary of this state of things, and my heart yearned for my boyhood's haunts. I was nearly a beggar, yet still I would go there, claim my bride, and rebuild my fortunes. A few happy ventures as a merchant would make me rich again. Nevertheless, I would not return in humble guise. My last act was to dispose of my remaining estate near Albaro for half its worth, for ready money. Then I despatched all kinds of artificers, arras, furniture of regal splendour, to fit up the last relic of my inheritance, my palace in Genoa. I lingered a little longer yet, ashamed at the part of the prodigal returned, which I feared I should play. I sent my horses. One matchless Spanish jennet[173] I despatched to my promised bride; its caparisons flamed with jewels and cloth of gold. In every part I caused to be entwined the initials of Juliet and her Guido. My present found favour in hers and in her father's eyes.

Still to return a proclaimed spendthrift, the mark of impertinent wonder, perhaps of scorn, and to encounter singly the reproaches or taunts of my fellow-citizens, was no alluring prospect. As a shield between me and censure, I invited some few of the most reckless of my comrades to accompany me; thus I went armed against the world, hiding a rankling feeling, half fear and half penitence, with bravado and an insolent display of satisfied vanity.

I arrived in Genoa. I trod the pavement of my ancestral palace. My proud step was no interpreter of my heart, for I deeply felt that, though surrounded by every luxury, I was a beggar. The first step I took in claiming Juliet must widely declare me such. I read contempt or pity in the looks of all. I fancied, so apt is conscience to imagine what it deserves, that rich and poor, young and old, all regarded me with derision. Torella came not near me. No wonder that my second father should expect a son's deference from me in waiting first on him. But, galled and stung by a sense of my follies and demerit, I strove to throw the blame on others. We kept nightly orgies in Palazzo Carega. To sleepless, riotous nights, followed listless, supine mornings. At the Ave Maria we showed our dainty persons in the streets, scoffing at the sober citizens, casting insolent glances on the shrinking women. Juliet was not among them – no, no; if she had been there, shame would have driven me away, if love had not brought me to her feet.

I grew tired of this. Suddenly I paid the marchese a visit. He was at his villa, one among the many which deck the suburb of San Pietro d'Arena. It was the month of May – a month of May in that garden of the world – the blossoms of the fruit trees were fading among thick, green foliage; the vines were shooting forth; the ground strewn with the fallen olive blooms; the firefly was in the myrtle hedge; heaven and earth wore a mantle of surpassing beauty. Torella welcomed me kindly, though seriously; and even his shade of displeasure soon wore away. Some resemblance to my father – some look and tone of youthful ingenuousness, lurking still in spite of my misdeeds, softened the good old man's heart. He sent for his daughter – he presented me to her as her betrothed. The chamber became hallowed by a holy light as she entered. Hers was that cherub look, those large, soft eyes, full dimpled cheeks, and mouth of infantine sweetness, that expresses the rare union of happiness and love. Admiration first possessed me; she is mine! was the second proud emotion, and my lips curled with haughty triumph. I had not been the *enfant gâté*[174] of the beauties of France not to have learnt the art of pleasing the soft heart of woman. If towards men I was overbearing, the deference I paid to them was the more in contrast. I commenced my courtship by the display of a thousand gallantries to Juliet, who, vowed to me from infancy, had never admitted the devotion of others; and who, though accustomed to expressions of admiration, was uninitiated in the language of lovers.

For a few days all went well. Torella never alluded to my extravagance; he treated me as a favourite son. But the time came, as we discussed the preliminaries to my union with his daughter, when this fair face of things should be overcast. A contract had been drawn up in my father's lifetime. I had rendered this, in fact, void, by having squandered the whole of the wealth which was to have been shared by Juliet and myself. Torella, in consequence, chose to consider this bond as cancelled, and proposed another, in which, though the wealth he bestowed was immeasurably increased, there were so many restrictions as to the mode of spending it that I, who saw independence only in free career being given to my own imperious will, taunted him as taking advantage of my situation, and refused utterly to subscribe to his conditions. The old man mildly strove to recall me to reason. Roused pride became the tyrant of my thought: I listened with indignation – I repelled him with disdain.

'Juliet, thou art mine! Did we not interchange vows in our innocent childhood? are we not one in the sight of God? and shall thy cold-hearted, cold-blooded father divide us? Be generous, my love, be just; take not away a gift, last treasure of thy Guido – retract not thy vows – let us defy the world, and setting at nought the calculations of age, find in our mutual affection a refuge from every ill.'

Fiend I must have been, with such sophistry to endeavour to poison that sanctuary of holy thought and tender love. Juliet shrank from me affrighted. Her father was the best and kindest of men, and she strove to show me how, in obeying him, every good would follow. He would receive my tardy submission with warm affection; and generous pardon would follow my repentance. Profitless words for a young and gentle daughter to use to a man accustomed to make his will law; and to feel in his own heart a despot so terrible and stern that he could yield obedience to nought save his own imperious desires! My resentment grew with resistance; my wild companions were ready to add fuel to the flame. We laid a plan to carry off Juliet. At first it appeared to be crowned with success. Midway, on our return, we were overtaken by the agonised father and his attendants. A conflict ensued. Before the city guard came to decide the victory in favour of our antagonists, two of Torella's servitors were dangerously wounded.

This portion of my history weighs most heavily with me. Changed man as I am, I abhor myself in the recollection. May none who hear this tale ever have felt as I. A horse driven to fury by a rider armed with barbed spurs was not more a slave than I to the violent tyranny of my temper. A fiend possessed my soul, irritating it to madness. I felt the voice of conscience within me; but if I yielded to it for a brief interval, it was only to be a moment after torn, as by a whirlwind, away – borne along on the stream of desperate rage – the plaything of the storms

engendered by pride. I was imprisoned, and, at the instance of Torella,
set free. Again I returned to carry off both him and his child to France;
which hapless country, then preyed on by freebooters and gangs of
lawless soldiery, offered a grateful refuge to a criminal like me. Our
plots were discovered. I was sentenced to banishment; and, as my debts
were already enormous, my remaining property was put in the hands of
commissioners for their payment. Torella again offered his mediation,
requiring only my promise not to renew my abortive attempts on himself and his daughter. I spurned his offers, and fancied that I triumphed
when I was thrust out from Genoa, a solitary and penniless exile. My
companions were gone: they had been dismissed the city some weeks
before, and were already in France. I was alone – friendless; with no
sword at my side, no ducat in my purse.

I wandered along the seashore, a whirlwind of passion possessing
and tearing my soul. It was as if a live coal had been set burning in my
breast. At first I meditated on what I should do. I would join a band of
freebooters. Revenge! – the word seemed balm to me – I hugged it –
caressed it – till, like a serpent, it stung me. Then again I would abjure
and despise Genoa, that little corner of the world. I would return to
Paris, where so many of my friends swarmed; where my services would
be eagerly accepted; where I would carve out fortune with my sword,
and might, through success, make my paltry birthplace, and the false
Torella, rue the day when they drove me, a new Coriolanus,[175] from
her walls. I would return to Paris – thus, on foot – a beggar – and
present myself in my poverty to those I had formerly entertained
sumptuously? There was gall in the mere thought of it.

The reality of things began to dawn upon my mind, bringing despair
in its train. For several months I had been a prisoner: the evils of my
dungeon had whipped my soul to madness, but they had subdued my
corporeal frame. I was weak and wan. Torella had used a thousand
artifices to administer to my comfort; I had detected and scorned them
all – and I reaped the harvest of my obduracy. What was to be done? –
Should I crouch before my foe, and sue for forgiveness? – Die rather
ten thousand deaths! – Never should they obtain that victory! Hate – I
swore eternal hate! Hate from whom? – to whom? – From a wandering
outcast – to a mighty noble. I and my feelings were nothing to them:
already had they forgotten one so unworthy. And Juliet! – her angel-
face and sylph-like form gleamed among the clouds of my despair with
vain beauty; for I had lost her – the glory and flower of the world!
Another will call her his! – that smile of paradise will bless another!

Even now my heart fails within me when I recur to this rout of grim-visaged ideas. Now subdued almost to tears, now raving in my agony, still I wandered along the rocky shore, which grew at each step wilder and more desolate. Hanging rocks and hoar precipices overlooked the tideless ocean; black caverns yawned; and forever, among the sea-worn recesses, murmured and dashed the unfruitful waters. Now my way was almost barred by an abrupt promontory, now rendered nearly impracticable by fragments fallen from the cliff. Evening was at hand, when, seaward, arose, as if on the waving of a wizard's wand, a murky web of clouds, blotting the late azure sky, and darkening and disturbing the till now placid deep. The clouds had strange fantastic shapes; and they changed, and mingled, and seemed to be driven about by a mighty spell. The waves raised their white crests; the thunder first muttered, then roared from across the waste of waters, which took a deep purple dye, flecked with foam. The spot where I stood looked, on one side, to the widespread ocean; on the other, it was barred by a rugged promontory. Round this cape suddenly came, driven by the wind, a vessel. In vain the mariners tried to force a path for her to the open sea – the gale drove her on the rocks. It will perish! – all on board will perish! – Would I were among them! And to my young heart the idea of death came for the first time blended with that of joy. It was an awful sight to behold that vessel struggling with her fate. Hardly could I discern the sailors, but I heard them. It was soon all over! – A rock, just covered by the tossing waves, and so unperceived, lay in wait for its prey. A crash of thunder broke over my head at the moment that, with a frightful shock, the skiff dashed upon her unseen enemy. In a brief space of time she went to pieces. There I stood in safety; and there were my fellow-creatures, battling, how hopelessly, with annihilation. Me-thought I saw them struggling – too truly did I hear their shrieks, conquering the barking surges in their shrill agony. The dark breakers threw hither and thither the fragments of the wreck; soon it disappeared. I had been fascinated to gaze till the end; at last I sank on my knees – I covered my face with my hands. I again looked up; something was floating on the billows towards the shore. It neared and neared. Was that a human form? It grew more distinct; and at last a mighty wave, lifting the whole freight, lodged it upon a rock. A human being be-striding a sea-chest! – A human being! – Yet was it one? Surely never such had existed before – a misshapen dwarf, with squinting eyes, distorted features, and body deformed till it became a horror to behold. My blood, lately warming towards a fellow-being so snatched from a watery tomb, froze in my heart. The dwarf got off his chest; he tossed his straight, straggling hair from his odious visage:

'By St Beelzebub!' he exclaimed, 'I have been well bested.' He looked round and saw me. 'Oh, by the fiend! here is another ally of the mighty one. To what saint did you offer prayers, friend – if not to mine? Yet I remember you not on board.'

I shrank from the monster and his blasphemy. Again he questioned me, and I muttered some inaudible reply.

'Your voice is drowned by this dissonant roar. What a noise the big ocean makes! Schoolboys bursting from their prison are not louder than these waves set free to play. They disturb me. I will no more of their ill-timed brawling. Silence, hoary one! Winds, avaunt! – to your homes! Clouds, fly to the Antipodes, and leave our heaven clear!'

As he spoke, he stretched out his two long lank arms, that looked like spider's claws, and seemed to embrace with them the expanse before him. Was it a miracle? The clouds became broken, and fled; the azure sky first peeped out, and then was spread a calm field of blue above us; the stormy gale was exchanged to the softly breathing west; the sea grew calm; the waves dwindled to riplets.

'I like obedience even in these stupid elements,' said the dwarf. 'How much more in the tameless mind of man! It was a well-got-up storm, you must allow – and all of my own making.'

It was tempting providence to interchange talk with this magician. But power, in all its shapes, is venerable to man. Awe, curiosity, a clinging fascination, drew me towards him.

'Come, don't be frightened, friend,' said the wretch: 'I am good-humoured when pleased; and something does please me in your well-proportioned body and handsome face, though you look a little woe-begone. You have suffered a land wreck – I, a sea wreck. Perhaps I can allay the tempest of your fortunes as I did my own. Shall we be friends?' And he held out his hand; I could not touch it. 'Well, then, com-panions – that will do as well. And now, while I rest after the buffeting I underwent just now, tell me why, young and gallant as you seem, you wander thus alone and downcast on this wild seashore.'

The voice of the wretch was screeching and horrid, and his con-tortions as he spoke were frightful to behold. Yet he did gain a kind of influence over me, which I could not master, and I told him my tale. When it was ended, he laughed long and loud: the rocks echoed back the sound; hell seemed yelling around me.

'Oh, thou cousin of Lucifer!' said he; 'so thou too hast fallen through thy pride; and, though bright as the son of morning,[176] thou art ready to give up thy good looks, thy bride, and thy well-being, rather than submit thee to the tyranny of good. I honour thy choice, by my soul! –

So thou hast fled, and yield the day; and mean to starve on these rocks, and to let the birds peck out thy dead eyes, while thy enemy and thy betrothed rejoice in thy ruin. Thy pride is strangely akin to humility, methinks.'

As he spoke, a thousand fanged thoughts stung me to the heart.

'What would you that I should do?' I cried.

'I! – Oh, nothing, but lie down and say your prayers before you die. But, were I you, I know the deed that should be done.'

I drew near him. His supernatural powers made him an oracle in my eyes; yet a strange unearthly thrill quivered through my frame as I said: 'Speak! – teach me – what act do you advise?'

'Revenge thyself, man! – humble thy enemies! – set thy foot on the old man's neck, and possess thyself of his daughter!'

'To the east and west I turn,' cried I, 'and see no means! Had I gold, much could I achieve; but, poor and single, I am powerless.'

The dwarf had been seated on his chest as he listened to my story. Now he got off; he touched a spring; it flew open! – What a mine of wealth – of blazing jewels, beaming gold and pale silver – was displayed therein. A mad desire to possess this treasure was born within me.

'Doubtless,' I said, 'one so powerful as you could do all things.'

'Nay,' said the monster, humbly, 'I am less omnipotent than I seem. Some things I possess which you may covet; but I would give them all for a small share, or even for a loan of what is yours.'

'My possessions are at your service,' I replied, bitterly – 'my poverty, my exile, my disgrace – I make a free gift of them all.'

'Good! I thank you. Add one other thing to your gift, and my treasure is yours.'

'As nothing is my sole inheritance, what besides nothing would you have?'

'Your comely face and well-made limbs.'

I shivered. Would this all-powerful monster murder me? I had no dagger. I forgot to pray – but I grew pale.

'I ask for a loan, not a gift,' said the frightful thing: 'lend me your body for three days – you shall have mine to cage your soul the while, and, in payment, my chest. What say you to the bargain? – Three short days.'

We are told that it is dangerous to hold unlawful talk; and well do I prove the same. Tamely written down, it may seem incredible that I should lend any ear to this proposition; but, in spite of his unnatural ugliness, there was something fascinating in a being whose voice could govern earth, air and sea. I felt a keen desire to comply; for with that

chest I could command the world. My only hesitation resulted from a
fear that he would not be true to his bargain. Then, I thought, I shall
soon die here on these lonely sands, and the limbs he covets will be
mine no more: it is worth the chance. And, besides, I knew that, by all
the rules of art-magic, there were formulas and oaths which none of
its practisers dared break. I hesitated to reply; and he went on, now
displaying his wealth, now speaking of the petty price he demanded,
till it seemed madness to refuse. Thus is it: place our bark in the
current of the stream, and down, over fall and cataract it is hurried;
give up our conduct to the wild torrent of passion, and we are away,
we know not whither.

He swore many an oath, and I adjured him by many a sacred name;
till I saw this wonder of power, this ruler of the elements, shiver like an
autumn leaf before my words; and as if the spirit spoke unwillingly and
perforce within him, at last, he, with broken voice, revealed the spell
whereby he might be obliged, did he wish to play me false, to render up
the unlawful spoil. Our warm life-blood must mingle to make and to
mar the charm.

Enough of this unholy theme. I was persuaded – the thing was done.
The morrow dawned upon me as I lay upon the shingles, and I knew
not my own shadow as it fell from me. I felt myself changed to a shape
of horror, and cursed my easy faith and blind credulity. The chest was
there – there the gold and precious stones for which I had sold the
frame of flesh which nature had given me. The sight a little stilled my
emotions: three days would soon be gone.

They did pass. The dwarf had supplied me with a plenteous store of
food. At first I could hardly walk, so strange and out of joint were all
my limbs; and my voice – it was that of the fiend. But I kept silent, and
turned my face to the sun, that I might not see my shadow, and
counted the hours, and ruminated on my future conduct. To bring
Torella to my feet – to possess my Juliet in spite of him – all this my
wealth could easily achieve. During dark night I slept, and dreamt of
the accomplishment of my desires. Two suns had set – the third
dawned. I was agitated, fearful. Oh expectation, what a frightful thing
art thou, when kindled more by fear than hope! How dost thou twist
thyself round the heart, torturing its pulsations! How dost thou dart
unknown pangs all through our feeble mechanism, now seeming to
shiver us like broken glass, to nothingness – now giving us a fresh
strength, which can *do* nothing, and so torments us by a sensation,
such as the strong man must feel who cannot break his fetters, though
they bend in his grasp. Slowly paced the bright, bright orb up

the eastern sky; long it lingered in the zenith, and still more slowly wandered down the west; it touched the horizon's verge – it was lost! Its glories were on the summits of the cliff – they grew dun and grey. The evening star shone bright. He will soon be here.

He came not! – By the living heavens, he came not! – and night dragged out its weary length, and, in its decaying age, 'day began to grizzle its dark hair';[177] and the sun rose again on the most miserable wretch that ever upbraided its light. Three days thus I passed. The jewels and the gold – oh, how I abhorred them!

Well, well – I will not blacken these pages with demoniac ravings. All too terrible were the thoughts, the raging tumult of ideas that filled my soul. At the end of that time I slept; I had not before since the third sunset; and I dreamt that I was at Juliet's feet, and she smiled, and then she shrieked – for she saw my transformation – and again she smiled, for still her beautiful lover knelt before her. But it was not I – it was he, the fiend, arrayed in my limbs, speaking with my voice, winning her with my looks of love. I strove to warn her, but my tongue refused its office; I strove to tear him from her, but I was rooted to the ground – I awoke with the agony. There were the solitary hoar precipices – there the plashing sea, the quiet strand, and the blue sky over all. What did it mean? was my dream but a mirror of the truth? was he wooing and winning my betrothed? I would on the instant back to Genoa – but I was banished. I laughed – the dwarf's yell burst from my lips – *I* banished! Oh, no! they had not exiled the foul limbs I wore; I might with these enter, without fear of incurring the threatened penalty of death, my own, my native city.

I began to walk towards Genoa. I was somewhat accustomed to my distorted limbs; none were ever so ill adapted for a straightforward movement; it was with infinite difficulty that I proceeded. Then, too, I desired to avoid all the hamlets strewn here and there on the sea-beach, for I was unwilling to make a display of my hideousness. I was not quite sure that, if seen, the mere boys would not stone me to death as I passed, for a monster; some ungentle salutations I did receive from the few peasants or fishermen I chanced to meet. But it was dark night before I approached Genoa. The weather was so balmy and sweet that it struck me that the marchese and his daughter would very probably have quitted the city for their country retreat. It was from Villa Torella that I had attempted to carry off Juliet; I had spent many an hour reconnoitring the spot, and knew each inch of ground in its vicinity. It was beautifully situated, embosomed in trees, on the margin of a stream. As I drew near, it became evident that my conjecture was right; nay, moreover, that the hours were being then devoted to feasting and merriment. For the house was lighted up; strains of soft and gay music were wafted towards me by the breeze. My heart sank within me. Such was the generous kindness of Torella's heart that I felt sure that he would not have indulged in public manifestations of rejoicing just after my unfortunate banishment, but for a cause I dared not dwell upon.

The country people were all alive and flocking about; it became necessary that I should study to conceal myself; and yet I longed to address someone, or to hear others discourse, or in any way to gain intelligence of what was really going on. At length, entering the walks that were in immediate vicinity to the mansion, I found one dark enough to veil my excessive frightfulness; and yet others as well as I were loitering in its shade. I soon gathered all I wanted to know – all that first made my very heart die with horror, and then boil with indignation. Tomorrow Juliet was to be given to the penitent, reformed, beloved Guido – tomorrow my bride was to pledge her vows to a fiend from hell! And I did this! – my accursed pride – my demoniac violence and wicked self-idolatry had caused this act. For if I had acted as the wretch who had stolen my form had acted – if, with a mien at once yielding and dignified, I had presented myself to Torella, saying, I have done wrong, forgive me; I am unworthy of your angel-child, but permit me to claim her hereafter, when my altered conduct shall manifest that I abjure my vices, and endeavour to become in some sort worthy of her. I go to serve against the infidels; and when my zeal for religion and my true penitence for the past shall appear to you to cancel my crimes, permit me again to call myself your son. Thus had he spoken; and the penitent was welcomed even as the prodigal son of scripture: the fatted calf was killed for him; and he, still pursuing the same path, displayed such open-hearted regret for his follies, so humble a concession of all his rights, and so ardent a resolve to reacquire them by a life of contrition and virtue, that he quickly conquered the kind, old man; and full pardon, and the gift of his lovely child, followed in swift succession.

Oh! had an angel from paradise whispered to me to act thus! But now, what would be the innocent Juliet's fate? Would God permit the foul union – or, some prodigy destroying it, link the dishonoured name of Carega with the worst of crimes? Tomorrow at dawn they were to be married; there was but one way to prevent this – to meet mine enemy, and to enforce the ratification of our agreement. I felt that this could only be done by a mortal struggle. I had no sword – if indeed my distorted arms could wield a soldier's weapon – but I had a dagger, and in that lay my every hope. There was no time for pondering or balancing

Juliet

nicely the question: I might die in the attempt; but besides the burning jealousy and despair of my own heart, honour, mere humanity, demanded that I should fall rather than not destroy the machinations of the fiend.

The guests departed – the lights began to disappear; it was evident that the inhabitants of the villa were seeking repose. I hid myself among the trees – the garden grew desert – the gates were closed – I wandered round and came under a window – ah! well did I know the same! – a soft twilight glimmered in the room – the curtains were half withdrawn. It was the temple of innocence and beauty. Its magnificence was tempered, as it were, by the slight disarrangements occasioned by its being dwelt in, and all the objects scattered around displayed the taste of her who hallowed it by her presence. I saw her enter with a quick light step – I saw her approach the window – she drew back the curtain yet farther, and looked out into the night. Its breezy freshness played among her ringlets, and wafted them from the transparent marble of her brow. She clasped her hands, she raised her eyes to heaven. I heard her voice. 'Guido!' she softly murmured. 'Mine own Guido!' and then, as if overcome by the fullness of her own heart, she sank on her knees: her upraised eyes – her negligent but graceful attitude – the beaming thankfulness that lighted up her face – oh, these are tame words! Heart of mine, thou imagest ever, though thou canst not portray, the celestial beauty of that child of light and love.[178]

I heard a step – a quick firm step along the shady avenue. Soon I saw a cavalier, richly dressed, young and, methought, graceful to look on, advance. I hid myself yet closer. The youth approached; he paused beneath the window. She arose, and again looking out she saw him, and said – I cannot, no, at this distant time I cannot record her terms of soft silver tenderness; to me they were spoken, but they were replied to by him.

'I will not go,' he cried; 'here where you have been, where your memory glides like some heaven-visiting ghost, I will pass the long hours till we meet, never, my Juliet, again, day or night, to part. But do thou, my love, retire; the cold morn and fitful breeze will make thy cheek pale, and fill with languor thy love-lighted eyes. Ah, sweetest! could I press one kiss upon them, I could, methinks, repose.'

And then he approached still nearer, and methought he was about to clamber into her chamber. I had hesitated, not to terrify her; now I was no longer master of myself. I rushed forward – I threw myself on him – I tore him away – I cried, 'Oh loathsome and foul-shaped wretch!'

I need not repeat epithets, all tending, as it appeared, to rail at a person I at present feel some partiality for. A shriek rose from Juliet's lips. I neither heard nor saw – I *felt* only mine enemy, whose throat I grasped, and my dagger's hilt; he struggled, but could not escape; at length hoarsely he breathed these words: 'Do! – strike home! destroy this body – you will still live; may your life be long and merry!'

The descending dagger was arrested at the word, and he, feeling my hold relax, extricated himself and drew his sword, while the uproar in the house, and flying of torches from one room to the other, showed that soon we should be separated – and I – oh! far better die: so that he did not survive, I cared not. In the midst of my frenzy there was much calculation: fall I might, and so that he did not survive, I cared not for the death-blow I might deal against myself. While still, therefore, he thought I paused, and while I saw the villainous resolve to take advantage of my hesitation in the sudden thrust he made at me, I threw myself on his sword, and at the same moment plunged my dagger, with a true desperate aim, in his side. We fell together, rolling over each other, and the tide of blood that flowed from the gaping wound of each mingled on the grass. More I know not – I fainted.

Again I returned to life: weak almost to death, I found myself stretched upon a bed – Juliet was kneeling beside it. Strange! my first broken request was for a mirror. I was so wan and ghastly that my poor girl hesitated, as she told me afterwards; but, by the mass! I thought myself a right proper youth when I saw the dear reflection of my own well-known features. I confess it is a weakness, but I avow it, I do entertain a considerable affection for the countenance and limbs I behold whenever I look at a glass; and have more mirrors in my house and consult them oftener than any beauty in Venice. Before you too much condemn me, permit me to say that no one better knows than I the value of his own body; no one, probably, except myself, ever having had it stolen from him.

Incoherently I at first talked of the dwarf and his crimes, and re-proached Juliet for her too easy admission of his love. She thought me raving, as well she might, and yet it was some time before I could prevail on myself to admit that the Guido whose penitence had won her back for me was myself; and while I cursed bitterly the monstrous dwarf, and blest the well-directed blow that had deprived him of life, I suddenly checked myself when I heard her say – Amen! knowing that him whom she reviled was my very self. A little reflection taught me silence – a little practice enabled me to speak of that frightful night without any very excessive blunder. The wound I had given myself was no mockery of one – it was long before I recovered – and as the benevolent and generous Torella sat beside me, talking such wisdom as might win friends to repentance, and mine own dear Juliet hovered near me, administering to my wants, and cheering me by her smiles, the work of my bodily cure and mental reform went on together. I have never, indeed, wholly recovered my strength – my cheek is paler since – my person a little bent. Juliet sometimes ventures to allude bitterly to the malice that caused this change, but I kiss her on the moment, and tell her all is for the best. I am a fonder and more faithful husband – and true is this – but for that wound, never had I called her mine.

I did not revisit the seashore, nor seek for the fiend's treasure; yet, while I ponder on the past, I often think, and my confessor was not backward in favouring the idea, that it might have been a good rather than an evil spirit, sent by my guardian angel, to show me the folly and misery of pride. So well at least did I learn this lesson, roughly taught as I was, that I am known now by all my friends and fellow-citizens by the name of Guido il Cortese.[179]

The Dream

A Tale

Chi dice mal d'amore
Dice una falsità![180]

Italian song

THE time of the occurrence of the little legend about to be narrated was that of the commencement of the reign of Henry IV of France,[181] whose accession and conversion, while they brought peace to the kingdom whose throne he ascended, were inadequate to heal the deep wounds mutually inflicted by the inimical parties. Private feuds, and the memory of mortal injuries, existed between those now apparently united; and often did the hands that had clasped each other in seeming friendly greeting, involuntarily, as the grasp was released, clasp the dagger's hilt, as fitter spokesman to their passions than the words of courtesy that had just fallen from their lips. Many of the fiercer Catholics retreated to their distant provinces; and while they concealed in solitude their rankling discontent, not less keenly did they long for the day when they might show it openly.

In a large and fortified château built on a rugged steep overlooking the Loire, not far from the town of Nantes, dwelt the last of her race and the heiress of their fortunes, the young and beautiful Countess de Villeneuve. She had spent the preceding year in complete solitude in her secluded abode; and the mourning she wore for a father and two brothers, the victims of the civil wars, was a graceful and good reason why she did not appear at court, and mingle with its festivities. But the orphan countess inherited a high name and broad lands; and it was soon signified to her that the king, her guardian, desired that she should bestow them, together with her hand, upon some noble whose birth and accomplishments should entitle him to the gift. Constance, in reply, expressed her intention of taking vows, and retiring to a convent. The king earnestly and resolutely forbade this act, believing such an idea to be the result of sensibility overwrought by sorrow, and relying on the hope that, after a time, the genial spirit of youth would break through this cloud.

A year passed, and still the countess persisted; and at last Henry, unwilling to exercise compulsion – desirous, too, of judging for himself of the motives that led one so beautiful, young, and gifted with fortune's favours, to desire to bury herself in a cloister – announced his intention, now that the period of her mourning was expired, of visiting her château; and if he brought not with him, the monarch said, inducement sufficient to change her design, he would yield his consent to its fulfilment.

Many a sad hour had Constance passed – many a day of tears, and many a night of restless misery. She had closed her gates against every visitant; and, like the Lady Olivia in *Twelfth Night*, vowed herself to loneliness and weeping.[182] Mistress of herself, she easily silenced the entreaties and remonstrances of underlings, and nursed her grief as it had been the thing she loved. Yet it was too keen, too bitter, too burning, to be a favoured guest. In fact, Constance, young, ardent, and vivacious, battled with it, struggled, and longed to cast it off; but all that was joyful in itself, or fair in outward show, only served to renew it; and she could best support the burthen of her sorrow with patience, when, yielding to it, it oppressed but did not torture her.

Constance had left the castle to wander in the neighbouring grounds. Lofty and extensive as were the apartments of her abode, she felt pent up within their walls, beneath their fretted roofs. The clear sky, the spreading uplands, the antique wood, associated to her with every dear recollection of her past life, enticed her to spend hours and days beneath their leafy coverts. The motion and change eternally working, as the wind stirred among the boughs, or the journeying sun rained its beams through them, soothed and called her out of that dull sorrow which clutched her heart with so unrelenting a pang beneath her castle roof.

There was one spot on the verge of the well-wooded park, one nook of ground, whence she could discern the country extended beyond, yet which was in itself thick set with tall umbrageous trees – a spot which she had forsworn, yet whither unconsciously her steps forever tended, and where now again, for the twentieth time that day, she had unaware found herself. She sat upon a grassy mound, and looked wistfully on the flowers she had herself planted to adorn the verdurous recess – to her the temple of memory and love. She held the letter from the king which was the parent to her of so much despair.

Constance

Dejection sat upon her features, and her gentle heart asked fate why, so young, unprotected and forsaken, she should have to struggle with this new form of wretchedness.

'I but ask,' she thought, 'to live in my father's halls – in the spot familiar to my infancy – to water with my frequent tears the graves of those I loved; and here in these woods, where such a mad dream of happiness was mine, to celebrate for ever the obsequies of hope!'

A rustling among the boughs now met her ear – her heart beat quick – all again was still. 'Foolish girl!' she half muttered: 'dupe of thine own passionate fancy; because here we met; because seated here I have expected, and sounds like these have announced, his dear approach; so now every coney as it stirs, and every bird as it awakens silence, speaks of him. O Gaspar! – mine once – never again will this beloved spot be made glad by thee – never more!'

Again the bushes were stirred, and footsteps were heard in the brake. She rose; her heart beat high; it must be that silly Manon, with her impertinent entreaties for her to return. But the steps were firmer and slower than would be those of her waiting-woman; and now emerging from the shade, she too plainly discerned the intruder. Her first impulse was to fly: but once again to see him – to hear his voice – once again before she placed eternal vows between them to stand together, and find the wide chasm filled which absence had made, could not injure the dead, and would soften the fatal sorrow that made her cheek so pale.

And now he was before her the same beloved one with whom she had exchanged vows of constancy. He, like her, seemed sad, nor could she resist the imploring glance that entreated her for one moment to remain.

'I come, lady,' said the young knight, 'without a hope to bend your inflexible will. I come but once again to see you, and to bid you farewell before I depart for the Holy Land. I come to beseech you not to immure yourself in the dark cloister to avoid one as hateful as myself – one you will never see more. Whether I die or live in Palestine, France and I are parted for ever!'

'Palestine!' said Constance; 'that were fearful, were it true; but King Henry will never so lose his favourite cavalier. The throne you helped to build, you still will guard. Nay, as I ever had power over thought of thine, go not to Palestine.'

'One word of yours could detain me – one smile – Constance – ' and the youthful lover knelt before her; but her harsher purpose was recalled by the image once so dear and familiar, now so strange and so forbidden.

'Linger no longer here!' she cried. 'No smile, no word of mine will ever again be yours. Why are you here – here, where the spirits of the dead wander, and, claiming these shades as their own, curse the false girl who permits their murderer to disturb their sacred repose?'

'When love was young and you were kind,' replied the knight, 'you taught me to thread the intricacies of these woods – you welcomed me to this dear spot, where once you vowed to be my own – even beneath these ancient trees.'

'A wicked sin it was,' said Constance, 'to unbar my father's doors to the son of his enemy, and dearly is it punished!'

The young knight gained courage as she spoke; yet he dared not move, lest she, who, every instant, appeared ready to take flight, should be startled from her momentary tranquillity; but he slowly replied: 'Those were happy days, Constance, full of terror and deep joy, when evening brought me to your feet; and while hate and vengeance were as its atmosphere to yonder frowning castle, this leafy, starlit bower was the shrine of love.'

'*Happy*? – miserable days!' echoed Constance; 'when I imagined good could arise from failing in my duty, and that disobedience would be rewarded of God. Speak not of love, Gaspar! – a sea of blood divides us for ever! Approach me not! The dead and the beloved stand even now between us: their pale shadows warn me of my fault, and menace me for listening to their murderer.'

'That am not I!' exclaimed the youth. 'Behold, Constance, we are each the last of our race. Death has dealt cruelly with us, and we are alone. It was not so when first we loved – when parent, kinsman, brother, nay, my own mother breathed curses on the house of Villeneuve; and in spite of all I bless'd it. I saw thee, my lovely one, and bless'd it. The God of peace planted love in our hearts, and with mystery and secrecy we met during many a summer night in the moonlit dells; and when daylight was abroad, in this sweet recess we fled to avoid its scrutiny, and here, even here, where now I kneel in supplication, we both knelt and made our vows. Shall they be broken?'

Constance wept as her lover recalled the images of happy hours. 'Never,' she exclaimed, 'Oh never! Thou knowest, or wilt soon know, Gaspar, the faith and resolves of one who dare not be yours. Was it for us to talk of love and happiness, when war, and hate, and blood were raging around? The fleeting flowers our young hands strewed were trampled by the deadly encounter of mortal foes. By your father's hand mine died; and little boots it to know whether, as my brother swore, and you deny, your hand did or did not deal the blow that destroyed him. You fought among those by whom he died. Say no more – no other word: it is impiety towards the unreposing dead to hear you. Go, Gaspar; forget me. Under the chivalrous and gallant Henry your career may be glorious; and many a fair girl will listen, as once I did, to your vows, and be made happy by them. Farewell! May the Virgin bless you! In my cell and cloister-home I will not forget the best Christian lesson – to pray for our enemies. Gaspar, farewell!'

She glided hastily from the bower; with swift steps she threaded the glade and sought the castle. Once within the seclusion of her own apartment she gave way to the burst of grief that tore her gentle bosom like a tempest; for hers was that worst sorrow which taints past joys, making remorse wait upon the memory of bliss, and linking love and fancied guilt in such fearful society as that of the tyrant when he bound a living body to a corpse.[183] Suddenly a thought darted into her mind. At first she rejected it as puerile and superstitious; but it would not be driven away. She called hastily for her attendant. 'Manon,' she said, 'didst thou ever sleep on St Catherine's couch?'

Manon crossed herself. 'Heaven forefend! None ever did, since I was born, but two: one fell into the Loire and was drowned; the other only looked upon the narrow bed, and returned to her own home without a word. It is an awful place; and if the votary have not led a pious and good life, woe betide the hour when she rests her head on the holy stone!'

Constance crossed herself also. 'As for our lives, it is only through our Lord and the blessed saints that we can any of us hope for righteousness. I will sleep on that couch tomorrow night!'

'Dear, my lady! and the king arrives tomorrow.'

'The more need that I resolve. It cannot be that misery so intense should dwell in any heart, and no cure be found. I had hoped to be the bringer of peace to our houses; and is the good work to be for me a crown of thorns? Heaven shall direct me. I will rest tomorrow night on St Catherine's bed; and if, as I have heard, the saint deigns to direct her votaries in dreams, I will be guided by her; and believing that I act according to the dictates of heaven, I shall feel resigned even to the worst.'

The king was on his way to Nantes from Paris, and he slept on this night at a castle but a few miles distant. Before dawn a young cavalier was introduced into his chamber. The knight had a serious, nay, a sad aspect; and all beautiful as he was in feature and limb, looked way-worn and haggard. He stood silent in Henry's presence, who, alert and gay, turned his lively blue eyes upon his guest, saying gently, 'So thou foundest her obdurate, Gaspar?'

'I found her resolved on our mutual misery. Alas! my liege, it is not, credit me, the least of my grief, that Constance sacrifices her own happiness when she destroys mine.'

'And thou believest that she will say nay to the gaillard chevalier[184] whom we ourselves present to her?'

'Oh! my liege, think not that thought! it cannot be. My heart deeply, most deeply, thanks you for your generous condescension. But she whom her lover's voice in solitude – whose entreaties, when memory and seclusion aided the spell – could not persuade, will resist even your majesty's commands. She is bent upon entering a cloister; and I, so please you, will now take my leave. I am henceforth a soldier of the cross, and will die in Palestine.'

'Gaspar,' said the monarch, 'I know woman better than thou. It is not by submission nor tearful plaints she is to be won. The death of her relatives naturally sits heavy at the young countess's heart; and nourishing in solitude her regret and her repentance, she fancies that heaven itself forbids your union. Let the voice of the world reach her – the voice of earthly power and earthly kindness – the one commanding, the other pleading, and both finding response in her own heart – and by my fay and the Holy Cross, she will be yours. Let our plan still hold. And now to horse: the morning wears, and the sun is risen.'

The king arrived at the bishop's palace, and proceeded forthwith to mass in the cathedral. A sumptuous dinner succeeded, and it was afternoon before the monarch proceeded through the town beside the Loire to where, a little above Nantes, the Château Villeneuve was situated. The young countess received him at the gate. Henry looked in vain for the cheek blanched by misery, the aspect of downcast despair which he had been taught to expect. Her cheek was flushed, her manner animated, her voice scarce tremulous. 'She loves him not,' thought Henry, 'or already her heart has consented.'

A collation was prepared for the monarch; and after some little hesitation, arising even from the cheerfulness of her mien, he mentioned the name of Gaspar. Constance blushed instead of turning pale, and replied very quickly, 'Tomorrow, good my liege; I ask for a respite but until tomorrow; all will then be decided; tomorrow I am vowed to God – or – '

She looked confused, and the king, at once surprised and pleased, said, 'Then you hate not young De Vaudemont – you forgive him for the inimical blood that warms his veins.'

'We are taught that we should forgive, that we should love our enemies,' the countess replied with some trepidation.

'Now by St Denis that is a right welcome answer for the nonce,' said the king, laughing. 'What ho! my faithful serving-man, Dan Apollo in disguise! Come forward, and thank your lady for her love.'

In such disguise as had concealed him from all, the cavalier had hung behind, and viewed with infinite surprise the demeanour and calm countenance of the lady. He could not hear her words; but was this even she whom he had seen trembling and weeping the evening before? – she whose very heart was torn by conflicting passion? – who saw the pale ghosts of parent and kinsman stand between her and the lover whom more than her life she adored? It was a riddle hard to solve. The king's call was in unison with his impatience, and he sprang forward. He was at her feet; while she, still passion-driven, over-wrought by the very calmness she had assumed, uttered one cry as she recognised him, and sank senseless on the floor.

All this was very unintelligible. Even when her attendants had brought her to life, another fit succeeded, and then passionate floods of tears; while the monarch, waiting in the hall, eyeing the half-eaten collation, and humming some romance in commemoration of woman's way-wardness, knew not how to reply to Vaudemont's look of bitter dis-appointment and anxiety. At length the countess's chief attendant came with an apology: 'Her lady was ill, very ill. The next day she would throw herself at the king's feet, at once to solicit his excuse and to disclose her purpose.'

'Tomorrow – again tomorrow! – Does tomorrow bear some charm, maiden?' said the king. 'Can you read us the riddle, pretty one? What strange tale belongs to tomorrow, that all rests on its advent?'

Manon coloured, looked down, and hesitated. But Henry was no tyro in the art of enticing ladies' attendants to disclose their ladies' counsel. Manon was besides frightened by the countess's scheme, on which she was still obstinately bent, so she was the more readily induced to betray it. To sleep in St Catherine's bed, to rest on a narrow ledge overhanging the deep rapid Loire, and if, as was most probable, the luckless dreamer escaped from falling into it, to take the disturbed visions that such uneasy slumber might produce for the dictate of heaven, was a madness of which even Henry himself could scarcely deem any woman capable. But could Constance, her whose beauty was so highly intellectual, and whom he had heard perpetually praised for her strength of mind and talents, could *she* be so strangely infatuated! And can passion play such freaks with us? – like death, levelling even the aristocracy of the soul, and bringing noble and peasant, the wise and foolish, under one thraldom? It was strange – yet she must have her way. That she hesitated in her decision was much; and it was to be hoped that St Catherine would play no ill-natured part. Should it be otherwise, a purpose to be swayed by a dream might be influenced by other waking thoughts. To the more material kind of danger some safeguard should be brought.

There is no feeling more awful than that which invades a weak human heart bent upon gratifying its ungovernable impulses in contradiction to the dictates of conscience. Forbidden pleasures are said to be the most agreeable; it may be so to rude natures, to those who love to struggle, combat, and contend; who find happiness in a fray, and joy in the conflict of passion. But softer and sweeter was the gentle spirit of Constance; and love and duty contending crushed and tortured her poor heart. To commit her conduct to the inspirations of religion, or, if it was so to be named, of superstition, was a blessed relief. The very perils that threatened her undertaking gave a zest to it; to dare for his sake was happiness; the very difficulty of the way that led to the completion of her wishes at once gratified her love and distracted her thoughts from her despair. Or if it was decreed that she must sacrifice all, the risk of danger and of death were of trifling import in comparison with the anguish which would then be her portion for ever.

The night threatened to be stormy – the raging wind shook the casements – and the trees waved their huge shadowy arms, as giants might in fantastic dance and mortal broil. Constance and Manon, unattended, quitted the château by a postern, and began to descend the hillside. The moon had not yet risen; and though the way was familiar to both, Manon tottered and trembled; while the countess, drawing her silken cloak round her, walked with a firm step down the steep. They came to the river's side, where a small boat was moored, and one man was in waiting. Constance stepped lightly in, and then aided her fearful companion. In a few moments they were in the middle of the stream. The warm, tempestuous, animating, equinoctial wind swept over them. For the first time since her mourning, a thrill of pleasure swelled the bosom of Constance. She hailed the emotion with double joy. It cannot be, she thought, that heaven will forbid me to love one so brave, so generous, and so good as the noble Gaspar. Another I can never love; I shall die if divided from him; and this heart, these limbs, so alive with glowing sensation, are they already predestined to an early grave? Oh, no! life speaks aloud within them. I shall live to love. Do not all things love? – the winds as they whisper to the rushing waters? the waters as they kiss the flowery banks, and speed to mingle with the sea? Heaven and earth are sustained by, live through, love; and shall Constance alone, whose heart has ever been a deep, gushing, overflowing well of true affection, be compelled to set a stone upon the fount to lock it up for ever?

These thoughts bid fair for pleasant dreams; and perhaps the countess, an adept in the blind god's lore,[185] therefore indulged them the more readily. But as thus she was engrossed by soft emotions, Manon caught her arm: 'Lady, look,' she cried; 'it comes – yet the oars have no sound. Now the Virgin shield us! Would we were at home!'

A dark boat glided by them. Four rowers, habited in black cloaks, pulled at oars which, as Manon said, gave no sound; another sat at the helm: like the rest, his person was veiled in a dark mantle, but he wore no cap; and though his face was turned from them, Constance recognised her lover. 'Gaspar,' she cried aloud, 'dost thou live?' – but the figure in the boat neither turned its head nor replied, and quickly it was lost in the shadowy waters.

How changed now was the fair countess's reverie! Already heaven had begun its spell, and unearthly forms were around as she strained her eyes through the gloom. Now she saw and now she lost view of the bark that occasioned her terror; and now it seemed that another was there, which held the spirits of the dead; and her father waved to her from shore, and her brothers frowned on her.

Meanwhile they neared the landing. Her bark was moored in a little cove, and Constance stood upon the bank. Now she trembled, and half yielded to Manon's entreaty to return; till the unwise *suivante*[186] mentioned the king's and De Vaudemont's name, and spoke of the answer to be given tomorrow. What answer, if she turned back from her intent?

She now hurried forward up the broken ground of the bank, and then along its edge, till they came to a hill which abruptly hung over the tide. A small chapel stood near. With trembling fingers the countess drew forth the key and unlocked its door. They entered. It was dark – save that a little lamp, flickering in the wind, showed an uncertain light from before the figure of St Catherine. The two women knelt; they prayed; and then rising, with a cheerful accent the countess bade her attendant good-night. She unlocked a little low iron door. It opened on a narrow cavern. The roar of waters was heard beyond. 'Thou mayest not follow, my poor Manon,' said Constance, 'nor dost thou much desire – this adventure is for me alone.'

It was hardly fair to leave the trembling servant in the chapel alone, who had neither hope nor fear, nor love nor grief, to beguile her; but, in those days, esquires and waiting-women often played the part of sub-alterns in the army, gaining knocks and no fame. Besides, Manon was safe in holy ground. The countess meanwhile pursued her way groping in the dark through the narrow tortuous passage. At length what seemed light to her long-darkened sense gleamed on her. She reached an open cavern in the overhanging hill's side, looking over the rushing tide beneath. She looked out upon the night. The waters of the Loire were speeding, as since that day have they ever sped – changeful, yet the same; the heavens were thickly veiled with clouds, and the wind in the trees was as mournful and ill-omened as if it rushed round a murderer's tomb. Constance shuddered a little, and looked upon her bed – a narrow ledge of earth and a moss-grown stone bordering on the very verge of the precipice. She doffed her mantle – such was one of the conditions of the spell; she bowed her head, and loosened the tresses of her dark hair – she bared her feet – and thus, fully prepared for suffering to the utmost the chill influence of the cold night, she stretched herself on the narrow couch that scarce afforded room for her repose, and whence, if she moved in sleep, she must be precipitated into the cold waters below.

At first it seemed to her as if she never should sleep again. No great wonder that exposure to the blast and her perilous position should forbid her eyelids to close. At length she fell into a reverie so soft and soothing that she wished even to watch – and then by degrees her senses became confused – and now she was on St Catherine's bed – the Loire rushing beneath, and the wild wind sweeping by – and now – O whither? – and what dreams did the saint send, to drive her to despair, or to bid her be blest for ever?

Beneath the rugged hill, upon the dark tide, another watched, who feared a thousand things, and scarce dared hope. He had meant to precede the lady on her way, but when he found that he had outstayed his time, with muffled oars and breathless haste he had shot by the bark that contained his Constance, nor even turned at her voice, fearful to incur her blame, and her command to return. He had seen her emerge from the passage, and shuddered as she leant over the cliff. He saw her step forth, clad as she was in white, and could mark her as she lay on the ledge beetling above. What a vigil did the lovers keep! – she given up to visionary thoughts, he knowing – and the consciousness thrilled his bosom with strange emotion – that love, and love for him, had led her to that perilous couch; and that while dangers surrounded her in every shape, she was alive only to the small still voice that whispered to her heart the dream which was to decide their destinies. She slept perhaps – but he waked and watched; and night wore away, as, now praying, now entranced by alternating hope and fear, he sat in his boat, his eyes fixed on the white garb of the slumberer above.

Morning – was it morning that struggled in the clouds? Would morning ever come to waken her? And had she slept? and what dreams of weal or woe had peopled her sleep?[187] Gaspar grew impatient. He commanded his boatmen still to wait, and he sprang forward, intent on clambering the precipice. In vain they urged the danger, nay, the impossibility of the attempt; he clung to the rugged face of the hill, and found footing where it would seem no footing was. The acclivity, indeed, was not high; the dangers of St Catherine's bed arising from the likelihood that anyone who slept on so narrow a couch would be precipitated into the waters beneath. Up the steep ascent Gaspar continued to toil, and at last reached the roots of a tree that grew near the summit. Aided by its branches, he made good his stand at the very extremity of the ledge, near the pillow on which lay the uncovered head of his beloved. Her hands were folded on her bosom; her dark hair fell round her throat and pillowed her cheek; her face was serene: sleep was there in all its innocence and in all its helplessness; every wilder emotion was hushed, and her bosom heaved in regular breathing. He could see her heart beat as it lifted her fair hands crossed above. No statue hewn of marble in monumental effigy was ever half so fair; and within that surpassing form dwelt a soul true, tender, self-devoted and affectionate as ever warmed a human breast.

With what deep passion did Gaspar gaze, gathering hope from the placidity of her angel countenance! A smile wreathed her lips; and he too involuntarily smiled, as he hailed the happy omen; when suddenly her cheek was flushed, her bosom heaved, a tear stole from her dark lashes, and then a whole shower fell, as starting up she cried, 'No! – he shall not die! – I will unloose his chains! – I will save him!' Gaspar's hand was there. He caught her light form ready to fall from the perilous couch. She opened her eyes and beheld her lover, who had watched over her dream of fate, and who had saved her.

Manon also had slept well, dreaming or not, and was startled in the morning to find that she waked surrounded by a crowd. The little desolate chapel was hung with tapestry – the altar adorned with golden chalices – the priest was chanting mass to a goodly array of kneeling knights. Manon saw that King Henry was there; and she looked for another whom she found not, until the iron door of the cavern passage opened, and Gaspar de Vaudemont entered from it, leading the fair form of Constance; who, in her white robes and dark dishevelled hair, with a face in which smiles and blushes contended with deeper emotion, approached the altar, and kneeling with her lover, pronounced the vows that united them for ever.

It was long before the happy Gaspar could win from his lady the secret of her dream. In spite of the happiness she now enjoyed, she had suffered too much not to look back even with terror to those days when she thought love a crime, and every event connected with them wore an awful aspect. Many a vision, she said, she had that fearful night. She had seen the spirits of her father and brothers in paradise; she had beheld Gaspar victoriously combating among the infidels; she had beheld him in King Henry's court, favoured and beloved, and she herself – now pining in a cloister, now a bride – now grateful to heaven for the full measure of bliss presented to her, now weeping away her sad days – till suddenly she thought herself in Paynim land;[188] and the saint herself, St Catherine, guiding her unseen through the city of the infidels. She entered a palace and beheld the miscreants rejoicing in victory; and then descending to the dungeons beneath, they groped their way through damp vaults, and low mildewed passages, to one cell, darker and more frightful than the rest. On the floor lay one with soiled and tattered garments, with unkempt locks and wild matted beard. His cheek was worn and thin; his eyes had lost their fire; his form was a mere skeleton; the chains hung loosely on the fleshless bones.

'And was it my appearance in that attractive state and winning costume that softened the hard heart of Constance?' asked Gaspar, smiling at this painting of what would never be.

'Even so,' replied Constance; 'for my heart whispered to me that this was my doing; and who could recall the life that waned in your pulses – who restore, save the destroyer? My heart never warmed to my living happy knight as then it did to his wasted image, as it lay, in the visions of night, at my feet. A veil fell from my eyes; a darkness was dispelled from before me. Methought I then knew for the first time what life and what death was. I was bid believe that to make the living happy was not to injure the dead; and I felt how wicked and how vain was that false philosophy which placed virtue and good in hatred and unkindness. You should not die: I would loosen your chains and save you, and bid you live for love. I sprang forward, and the death I deprecated for you would, in my presumption, have been mine – then, when first I felt the real value of life – but that your arm was there to save me, your dear voice to bid me be blest for evermore.'

The Brother and Sister

An Italian Story

IT is well known that the hatred borne by one family against another, and the strife of parties which often led to bloodshed in the Italian cities during the Middle Ages, so vividly described by Shakespeare in *Romeo and Juliet*, was not confined to the Montecchi and Capelletti of Verona, but existed with equal animosity in almost every other town of that beautiful peninsula. The greatest men among them were the victims; and crowds of exiles – families who but the day before were in the full enjoyment of the luxuries of life and the endearing associations of home – were every now and then seen issuing from the gates of their native cities, deprived of every possession, and with melancholy and slow steps dragging their wearied limbs to the nearest asylum offered them, thence to commence a new career of dependence and poverty, to endure to the end of their lives, or until some lucky accident should enable them to change places with their enemies, making those the sufferers who were late the tyrants. In that country, where each town formed an independent state, to change one for the other was to depart from the spot cherished as a country and a home for distant banishment – or worse – for as each city entertained either hatred or contempt for its neighbour, it often happened that the mourning exile was obliged to take up his abode among a people whom he had injured or scoffed. Foreign service offered a resource to the young and bold among the men. But lovely Italy was to be left, the ties of young hearts severed, and all the endearing associations of kin and country broken and scattered for ever. The Italians were always peculiarly susceptible to these misfortunes. They loved their native walls, the abodes of their ancestors, the familiar scenes of youth, with all the passionate fervour characteristic of that clime.

It was therefore no uncommon thing for any one among them, like Foscari of Venice,[189] to prefer destitution and danger in their own city, to a precarious subsistence among strangers in distant lands; or, if compelled to quit the beloved precincts of their native walls, still to hover near, ready to avail themselves of the first occasion that should present itself for reversing the decree that condemned them to misery.

For three days and nights there had been warfare in the streets of Sienna – blood flowed in torrents – yet the cries and groans of the fallen but excited their friends to avenge them – not their foes to spare. On the fourth morning, Ugo Mancini, with a scanty band of followers, was driven from the town: succours from Florence had arrived for his enemies, and he was forced to yield. Burning with rage, writhing with an impotent thirst for vengeance, Ugo went round to the neighbouring villages to rouse them, not against his native town, but the victorious Tolomei. Unsuccessful in these endeavours, he next took the more equivocal step of seeking warlike aid from the Pisans. But Florence kept Pisa in check, and Ugo found only an inglorious refuge where he had hoped to acquire active allies. He had been wounded in these struggles; but, animated by a superhuman spirit, he had forgotten his pain and surmounted his weakness; nor was it until a cold refusal was returned to his energetic representations that he sank beneath his physical sufferings. He was stretched on a bed of torture when he received intelligence that an ediet of perpetual banishment and confiscation of property was passed against him. His two children, beggars now, were sent to him. His wife was dead, and these were all of near relations that he possessed. His bitter feelings were still too paramount for him to receive comfort from their presence; yet these agitated and burning emotions appeared in after-times a remnant of happiness compared to the total loss of every hope – the wasting inaction of sickness and of poverty.

For five years Ugo Mancini lay stretched on his couch, alternating between states of intense pain and overpowering weakness; and then he died. During this interval, the wreck of his fortunes, consisting of the rent of a small farm, and the use of some money lent, scantily supported him. His few relatives and followers were obliged to seek their subsistence elsewhere, and he remained alone with his pain, and with his two children, who yet clung to the paternal side.

Hatred to his foes and love for his native town were the sentiments that possessed his soul, and which he imparted in their full force to the plastic mind of his son, which received like molten metal the stamp he desired to impress. Lorenzo was scarcely twelve years old at the period of his father's exile, and he naturally turned with fondness towards the spot where he had enjoyed every happiness, where each hour had been spent in light-hearted hilarity and the kindness and observance of many attended on his steps. Now, how sad the contrast! – dim penury – a solitude cheered by no encouraging smiles or sunny flatteries – perpetual attendance on his father and untimely cares cast their dark shadows over his altered lot.

Lorenzo was many years older than his sister. Friendless and destitute as was the exile's family, it was he who overlooked its moderate disbursements, who was at once his father's nurse and his sister's guardian, and acted as the head of the family during the incapacity of his parent. But instead of being narrowed or broken in spirit by these burthens, his ardent soul rose to meet them, and grew enlarged and lofty from the very calls made upon it. His look was serious, not careworn – his manner calm, not humble – his voice had all the tenderness of a woman – his eye all the pride and fire of a hero.

Still his unhappy father wasted away, and Lorenzo's hours were entirely spent beside his bed. He was indefatigable in his attentions – weariness never seemed to come near him. His limbs were always alert – his speech inspiriting and kind. His only pastime was during any interval in his parent's sufferings to listen to his eulogiums on his native town, and to the history of the wrongs which, from time immemorial, the Mancini had endured from the Tolomei. Lorenzo, though replete with noble qualities, was still an Italian; and fervent love for his birthplace, and violent hatred towards the foes of his house, were the darling passions of his heart. Nursed in loneliness, they acquired vigour; and the nights he spent in watching his father were varied by musing on the career he should hereafter follow – his return to his beloved Sienna, and the vengeance he would take on his enemies.

Ugo often said, I die because I am an exile: – at length these words were fulfilled, and the unhappy man sank beneath the ills of fortune. Lorenzo saw his beloved father expire – his father, whom he loved as a mother loves a sickly infant which she has led from its birth to an early five-years'-old tomb. He seemed to deposit in his obscure grave all that best deserved reverence and honour in the world; and turning away his steps, he lamented the sad occupation of so many years, and regretted the exchange he made from his father's sickbed to a lonely and unprized freedom.

The first use he made of the liberty he had thus acquired was to return to Sienna with his little sister. He entered his native town as if it were a paradise, and he found it a desert in all save the hues of beauty and delight with which his imagination loved to invest it. There was no one to whom he could draw near in friendship within the whole circuit of its walls. According to the barbarous usage of the times, his father's palace had been razed, and the mournful ruins stood as a tomb to commemorate the fall of his fortunes. Not as such did Lorenzo view them – he often stole out at nightfall, when the stars alone beheld his enthusiasm, and, clambering to the highest part of the massy fragments, spent long hours in mentally rebuilding the desolate walls, and in consecrating once again the weed-grown hearth to family love and hospitable festivity. It seemed to him that the air was more balmy and light, breathed amidst these memorials of the past; and his heart warmed with rapture over the tale they told of what his progenitors had been – what he again would be.

Yet, had he viewed his position sanely, he would have found it full of mortification and pain; and he would have become aware that his native town was perhaps the only place in the world where his ambition would fail in the attainment of its aim. The Tolomei reigned over it. They had led its citizens to conquest, and enriched them with spoils. They were adored; and to flatter them, the populace were prone to revile and scoff at the name of Mancini. Lorenzo did not possess one friend within its walls: he heard the murmur of hatred as he passed along, and beheld his enemies raised to the pinnacle of power and honour; and yet, so strangely framed is the human heart, that he continued to love Sienna, and would not have exchanged his obscure and penurious abode within its walls to become the favoured follower of the German emperor. Such a place, through education and the natural prejudices of man, did Sienna hold in his imagination that a lowly condition there seemed a nobler destiny than to be great in any other spot.

To win back the friendship of its citizens and humble his enemies was the dream that shed so sweet an influence over his darkened hours. He dedicated his whole being to this work, and he did not doubt but that he should succeed. The house of Tolomei had for its chief, a youth but a year or two older than himself – with him, when an opportunity should present itself, he would enter the lists. It seemed the bounty of providence that gave him one so nearly equal with whom to contend; and during the interval that must elapse before they could clash, he was busy in educating himself for the struggle. Count Fabian de' Tolomei bore the reputation of being a youth full of promise and talent; and Lorenzo was glad to anticipate a worthy antagonist. He occupied himself in the practice of arms, and applied with perseverance to the study of the few books that fell in his way. He appeared in the marketplace on public occasions modestly attired; yet his height, his dignified carriage, and the thoughtful cast of his noble countenance, drew the observation of the bystanders – though, such was the prejudice against his name, and the flattery of the triumphant party, that taunts and maledictions followed him. His nobility of appearance was called pride; his affability, meanness; his aspiring views, faction; – and it was declared that it would be a happy day when he should no longer blot their sunshine with his shadow. Lorenzo smiled – he disdained to resent, or even to feel, the mistaken insults of the crowd, who, if fortune changed, would the next day throw up their caps for him. It was only when loftier foes approached that his brow grew dark, that he drew himself up to his full height, repaying their scorn with glances of defiance and hate.

But although he was ready in his own person to encounter the contumely of his townsmen, and walked on with placid mien, regardless of their sneers, he carefully guarded his little sister from such scenes. She was led by him each morning, closely veiled, to hear mass in an obscure church. And when, on feast-days, the public walks were crowded with cavaliers and dames in splendid attire, and with citizens and peasants in their holiday garb, this gentle pair might be seen in some solitary and shady spot, he bending down and smiling on the lovely child, who looked up to him with eyes expressive of unutterable affection. In the whole world, Flora knew none to love except her brother – she was his junior by nearly seven years – she had grown under his eyes from infancy; and while he attended on the sickbed of their father, he was father, brother, tutor, guardian to Flora – the fondest mother could not have been more indulgent; and yet there was mingled a something beyond, pertaining to their difference of sex. Uniformly observant and kind, he treated her as if she had been a high-born damsel, nurtured in her gayest bower.

Her attire was simple – but thus, she was instructed, it befitted every damsel to dress; her needleworks were such as a princess might have emulated; and while she learnt under her brother's tutelage to be reserved, studious of obscurity, and always occupied, she was taught that such were the virtues becoming her sex, and no idea of dependence or penury was raised in her mind. Had he been the sole human being that approached her, she might have believed herself to be on a level with the highest in the land; but coming in contact with dependants and various females in the humble class of life, Flora became acquainted with her true position; and learnt, at the same time, to understand and appreciate the unequalled kindness of her brother, and to regard his virtues as superhuman.

Two years passed while this brother and sister continued, in obscurity and poverty, to cherish the dearest blessings of life, hope, honour and mutual love. If an anxious thought ever crossed Lorenzo, it was for the future destiny of Flora, whose beauty as a child gave promise of perfect loveliness hereafter. For her sake he was anxious to begin the career he had marked out for himself, and resolved no longer to delay his endeavours to revive his party in Sienna, and to seek rather than avoid any contest with the young Count Fabian, on whose overthrow he would rise – Count Fabian, the darling of the citizens, vaunted as a model for a youthful cavalier, overflowing with good qualities, and so adorned by gallantry, subtle wit and gay, winning manners that he stepped by right of nature, as well as birth, on the pedestal which exalted him the idol of all around.

It was on a day of public feasting that Lorenzo first presented himself in rivalship with Fabian. His person was unknown to the count, who, in all the pride of rich dress and splendid accoutrements, looked down with a smile of patronage on the poorly mounted and plainly attired youth, who presented himself to run a tilt with him.[190] But before the challenge was accepted, the name of his antagonist was whispered to Fabian; then, all the bitterness engendered by family feuds; all the spirit of vengeance, which had been taught as a religion, arose at once in the young noble's heart; he wheeled round his steed, and riding rudely up to his competitor, ordered him instantly to retire from the course, nor dare to disturb the revels of the citizens by the hated presence of a Mancini. Lorenzo answered with equal scorn; and Fabian, governed by uncontrollable passion, called together his followers to drive the youth with ignominy from the lists. A fearful array was mustered against the hateful intruder; but had their number been trebled, the towering spirit of Lorenzo had met them all. One fell – another was disabled by his weapon before he was disarmed and made prisoner; but his bravery did not avail to extract admiration from his prejudiced foes: they rather poured execrations on him for its disastrous effects, as they hurried him to a dungeon, and called loudly for his punishment and death.

Far from this scene of turmoil and bloodshed, in her poor but quiet chamber, in a remote and obscure part of the town, sat Flora, occupied by her embroidery, musing, as she worked, on her brother's project, and anticipating his success. Hours passed, and Lorenzo did not return – the day declined, and still he tarried. Flora's busy fancy forged a thousand causes for the delay. Her brother's prowess had awaked the chilly zeal of the partisans of their family – he was doubtless feasting among them, and the first stone was laid for the rebuilding of their house. At last, a rush of steps upon the staircase, and a confused clamour of female voices calling loudly for admittance, made her rise and open the door; in rushed several of the women of the house – dismay was painted on their faces – their words flowed in torrents – their eager gestures helped them to a meaning, and, though not without difficulty amidst the confusion, Flora heard of the disaster and imprisonment of her brother – of the blood shed by his hand, and the fatal issue that such a deed ensured. Flora grew pale as marble. Her young heart was filled with speechless terror; she could form no image of the thing she dreaded, but its indistinct idea was full of fear. Lorenzo was in prison – Count Fabian had placed him there – he was to die! Overwhelmed by such tidings, yet in a moment she rose above their benumbing power, and without proffering a word, or listening to the questions and remonstrances of the women, she rushed past them, down the high staircase, into the street; and then with swift pace to where the public prison was situated. She knew the spot she wished to reach, but she had so seldom quitted her home that she soon got entangled among the streets, and proceeded onwards at random. Breathless, at length, she paused before the lofty portal of a large palace – no one was near – the fast fading twilight of an Italian evening had deepened into absolute darkness. At this moment the glare of flambeaux was thrown upon the street, and a party of horsemen rode up; they were talking and laughing gaily. She heard one addressed as Count Fabian: she involuntarily drew back with instinctive hate; and then rushed forward and threw herself at his horse's feet, exclaiming, 'Save my brother!' The young cavalier reined up shortly his prancing steed, angrily reproving her for her heedlessness, and, without deigning another word, entered the court-yard. He had not, perhaps, heard her prayer; he could not see the suppliant and spoke but in the impatience of the moment; but the poor child, deeply wounded by what had the appearance of a personal insult, turned proudly from the door, repressing the bitter tears that filled her eyes. Still she walked on; but night took from her every chance of finding her way to the prison, and she resolved to return home, to engage one of the women of the house, of which she occupied a part, to accompany her. But even to find her way back became a matter of difficulty; and she wandered on, discovering no clue to guide her, and far too timid to address anyone she might chance to meet. Fatigue and personal fear were added to her other griefs, and tears streamed plentifully down her cheeks as she continued her hopeless journey. At length, at the corner of a street, she recognised an image of the Madonna in a niche, with a lamp burning over it, familiar to her recollection as being near her home. With characteristic piety she knelt before it in thankfulness, and was offering a prayer for Lorenzo when the sound of steps made her start up, and her brother's voice hailed, and her brother's arms encircled her; it seemed a miracle, but he was there, and all her fears were ended.

Lorenzo anxiously asked whither she had been straying; her explanation was soon given; and he in return related the misfortunes of the morning – the fate that impended over him, averted by the generous intercession of young Fabian himself; and yet – he hesitated to unfold the bitter truth – he was not freely pardoned; he stood there a banished man, condemned to die if the morrow's sun found him within the walls of Sienna.

They had arrived, meanwhile, at their home; and with feminine care, Flora placed a simple repast before her brother, and then employed herself very busily in making various packages. Lorenzo paced the room, absorbed in thought; at length he stopped, and kissing the fair girl said, 'Where can I place thee in safety? how preserve thee, my flower of beauty, while we are divided?'

Flora looked up fearfully. 'Do I not go with you?' she asked; 'I was making preparations for our journey.'

'Impossible, dearest; I go to privation and hardship.'

'And I would share them with thee.'

'It may not be, sweet sister,' replied Lorenzo, 'fate divides us, and we must submit. I go to camps – to the society of rude men; to struggle with such fortune as cannot harm me, but which for thee would be fraught with peril and despair. No, my Flora, I must provide safe and honourable guardianship for thee, even in this town.' And again Lorenzo meditated deeply on the part he should take, till suddenly a lightning thought flashed on his mind. 'It is hazardous,' he murmured, 'and yet I do him wrong to call it so. Were our fates reversed, should I not think myself highly honoured by such a trust?' And then he told his sister to don hastily her best attire; to wrap her veil round her, and to come with him. She obeyed – for obedience to her brother was the first and dearest of her duties. But she wept bitterly while her trembling fingers braided her long hair, and she hastily changed her dress.

At length they walked forth again, and proceeded slowly, as Lorenzo employed the precious minutes in consoling and counselling his sister. He promised as speedy a return as he could accomplish; but if he failed to appear as soon as he could wish, yet he vowed solemnly that, if alive and free, she should see him within five years from the moment of parting. Should he not come before, he besought her earnestly to take patience, and to hope for the best till the expiration of that period; and made her promise not to bind herself by any vestal or matrimonial vow in the interim. They had arrived at their destination, and entered the courtyard of a spacious palace. They met no servants, so crossed the court and ascended the ample stairs. Flora had endeavoured to listen to her brother. He had bade her be of good cheer, and he was about to leave her; he told her to hope; and he spoke of an absence to endure five years – an endless term to her childish anticipations. She promised obedience, but her voice was choked by sobs, and her tottering limbs would not have supported her without his aid. She now perceived that they were entering the light and inhabited rooms of a noble dwelling, and tried to restrain her tears, as she drew her veil closely around her. They passed from room to room, in which preparations for festivity were making; the servants ushered them on, as if they had been invited guests, and conducted them into a hall filled with all the nobility and beauty of Sienna. Each eye turned with curiosity and wonder on the pair. Lorenzo's tall person, and the lofty yet sweet expression of his handsome countenance put the ladies in good-humour with him, while the cavaliers tried to peep under Flora's veil.

'It is a mere child,' they said, 'and a sorrowing one – what can this mean?'

The youthful master of the house, however, instantly recognised his uninvited and unexpected guest; but before he could ask the meaning of his coming, Lorenzo had advanced with his sister to the spot where he stood, and addressed him.

'I never thought, Count Fabian, to stand beneath your roof, and much less to approach you as a suitor. But that Supreme Power, to whose decrees we must all bend, has reduced me to such adversity as, if it be his will, may also visit you, notwithstanding the many friends that now surround you, and the sunshine of prosperity in which you bask. I stand here a banished man and a beggar. Nor do I repine at this my fate. Most willing am I that my right arm alone should create my fortunes; and, with the blessing of God, I hope so to direct my course, that we may yet meet upon more equal terms. In this hope, I turn my steps, not unwillingly, from this city; dear as its name is to my heart – and dear the associations which link its proud towers with the memory of my forefathers. I leave it a soldier of fortune; how I may return is written in the page where your unread destiny is traced as well as mine. But my care ends not with myself. My dying father bequeathed to me this child, my orphan sister, whom I have, until now, watched over with a parent's love. I should ill perform the part entrusted to me, were I to drag this tender blossom from its native bower into the rude highways of life. Lord Fabian, I can count no man my friend; for it would seem that your smiles have won the hearts of my fellow-citizens from me; and death and exile have so dealt with my house, through the intervention of yours, that not one of my name exists within the walls of Sienna. To you alone can I intrust this precious charge. Will you accept it until called upon to render it back to me, her brother, or to the juster hands of our Creator, pure and untarnished as I now deliver her to you? I ask you to protect her helplessness, to guard her honour; will you – dare you accept a treasure, with the assurance of restoring it unsoiled, unhurt?'

The deep expressive voice of the noble youth and his earnest eloquence enchained the ears of the whole assembly; and when he ceased, Fabian, proud of the appeal, and nothing loth in the buoyant spirit of youth to undertake a charge which, thus proffered before his assembled kinsmen and friends, became an honour, answered readily – 'I agree, and solemnly before heaven accept your offer. I declare myself the guardian and protector of your sister; she shall dwell in safety beneath my kind mother's care, and if the saints permit your return, she shall be delivered back to you as spotless as she now is.'

Lorenzo bowed his head; something choked his utterance as he thought that he was about to part for ever from his Flora; but he disdained to betray this weakness before his enemies. He took his sister's hand and gazed upon her slight girlish form with a look of earnest fondness, then murmuring a blessing over her, and kissing her brow, he again saluted Count Fabian, and turning away with measured steps and lofty mien, left the hall. Flora, scarcely understanding what had passed, stood trembling and weeping under her veil. She yielded her passive hand to Fabian, who leading her to his mother, said: 'Madam, I ask of your goodness, and the maternal indulgence you have ever shown, to assist me in fulfilling my promise to yonder stripling, by taking under your gracious charge this young orphan.'

'You command here, my son,' said the countess, 'and your will shall be obeyed.' Then in response to a sign to one of her attendants, Flora was conducted from the hall, to where, in solitude and silence, she wept over her brother's departure and her own strange and humiliating position.

Flora thus became an inmate of the dwelling of her ancestral foes, and the ward of her most bitter enemy. Lorenzo was gone she knew not wither, and her only pleasure consisted in reflecting that she was obeying his behests. Her life was uniform and tranquil. Her occupation was working tapestry, in which she displayed taste and skill. Sometimes she had the more mortifying task imposed on her of waiting on the Countess de' Tolomei, who having lost two brothers in the last contest with the Mancini, nourished a deep hatred towards the whole race, and never smiled on the luckless orphan. Flora submitted to every command imposed upon her. She was buoyed up by the reflection that her sufferings were imposed on her by Lorenzo; schooling herself in any moment of impatience by the idea that thus she shared his adversity. No murmur escaped her, though the pride and independence of her nature were often cruelly offended by the taunts and supercilious airs of her patroness or mistress, who was not a bad woman, but who thought it virtue to ill-treat a Mancini. Often, indeed, she neither heard nor heeded these things. Her thoughts were far away, and grief for the loss of her brother's society weighed too heavily on her to allow her to spend more than a passing sigh on her personal injuries.

The countess was unkind and disdainful, but it was not thus with Flora's companions. They were amiable and affectionate girls, either of the bourgeois class, or daughters of dependants of the house of Tolomei. The length of time which had elapsed since the overthrow of the Mancini had erased from their young minds the bitter duty of hatred, and it was impossible for them to live on terms of daily inter-course with the orphan daughter of this ill-fated race and not to become strongly attached to her. She was wholly devoid of selfishness, and content to perform her daily tasks in inoffensive silence. She had no envy, no wish to shine, no desire of pleasure. She was nevertheless ever ready to sympathise with her companions, and glad to have it in her power to administer to their happiness. To help them in the manufacture of some piece of finery; to assist them in their work; and, perfectly prudent and reserved herself, to listen to all their sentimental adventures; to give her best advice, and to aid them in any difficulty, were the simple means she used to win their unsophisticated hearts. They called her an angel; they looked up to her as to a saint, and in their hearts respected her more than the countess herself.

One only subject ever disturbed Flora's serene melancholy. The praises she perpetually heard lavished on Count Fabian, her brother's too successful rival and oppressor, were an unendurable addition to her many griefs. Content with her own obscurity, her ambition, her pride, her aspiring thoughts were spent upon her brother. She hated Count Fabian as Lorenzo's destroyer, and the cause of his unhappy and hazardous exile. His accomplishments she despised as painted vanities; his person she contemned as the opposite of his prototype. His blue eyes, clear and open as day; his fair complexion and light brown hair; his slight elegant person; his voice, whose tones in song won each listener's heart to tenderness and love; his wit, his perpetual flow of spirits and unalterable good-humour, were impertinences and frivolities to her who cherished with such dear worship the recollection of her serious, ardent, noble-hearted brother, whose soul was ever set on high thoughts, and devoted to acts of virtue and self-sacrifice; whose fortitude and affectionate courtesy seemed to her the crown and glory of manhood; how different from the trifling flippancy of the butterfly, Fabian: 'Name an eagle,' she would say, 'and we raise our eyes to heaven, there to behold a creature fashioned in nature's bounty; but it is a degradation to waste one thought on the insect of a day.' Some speech similar to this had been kindly reported to the young count's lady mother, who idolised her son as the ornament and delight of his age and country. She severely reprimanded the incautious Flora, who, for the first time, listened proudly and unyieldingly. From this period her situation grew more irksome; all she could do was to endeavour to withdraw herself entirely from observation, and to brood in deeper secrecy over the perfections, while she lamented yet more feelingly the absence, of her brother.

Two or three years thus flew away, and Flora grew from a childish-looking girl of twelve into the bewitching beauty of fifteen. She unclosed like a flower, whose fairest petals are yet shut, but whose half-veiled loveliness is yet more attractive. It was at this time that on occasion of doing honour to a prince of France, who was passing on to Naples, the Countess Tolomei and her son, with a bevy of friends and followers, went out to meet and to escort the royal traveller on his way. While they were assembled in the hall of the palace, waiting for the arrival of some of their number, Count Fabian went round his mother's circle, saying agreeable and merry things to all. Wherever his cheerful blue eyes lighted, there smiles were awakened and each young heart beat with vanity at his harmless flatteries. After a gallant speech or two he espied Flora, retired behind her companions.

'What flower is this,' he said, 'playing at hide and seek with her beauty?' And then, struck by the modest sweetness of her aspect, her eyes cast down, and a rosy blush mantling over her cheek, he added, 'What fair angel makes one of your company?'

'An angel indeed, my lord,' exclaimed one of the younger girls, who dearly loved her best friend; 'she is Flora Mancini.'

'Mancini!' exclaimed Fabian, while his manner became at once respectful and kind: 'are you the orphan daughter of Ugo – the sister of Lorenzo, committed by him to my care?' For since then, through her careful avoidance, Fabian had never even seen his fair ward. She bowed an assent to his questions, while her swelling heart denied her speech;

and Fabian, going up to his mother, said, 'Madam, I hope for our honour's sake that this has not before happened. The adverse fortune of this young lady may render retirement and obscurity befitting; but it is not for us to turn into a menial one sprung from the best blood in Italy. Let me entreat you not to permit this to occur again. How shall I redeem my pledged honour, or answer to her brother for this unworthy degradation?'

'Would you have me make a friend and a companion of a Mancini?' asked the countess, with raised colour.

'I ask you not, mother, to do aught displeasing to you,' replied the young noble; 'but Flora is my ward, not our servant; permit her to retire; she will probably prefer the privacy of home to making one among the festive crowd of her house's enemies. If not, let the choice be hers. – Say, gentle one, will you go with us or retire?'

She did not speak, but raising her soft eyes, curtsied to him and to his mother, and quitted the room, so tacitly making her selection.

From this time Flora never quitted the more secluded apartments of the palace, nor again saw Fabian. She was unaware that he had been profuse in his eulogium on her beauty; but that while frequently expressing his interest in his ward, he rather avoided the dangerous power of her loveliness. She led rather a prison life, walking only in the palace garden when it was else deserted, but otherwise her time was at her own disposal, and no commands interfered with her freedom. Her labours were all spontaneous. The countess seldom even saw her, and she lived among this lady's attendants like a free boarder in a convent, who cannot quit the walls, but who is not subservient to the rules of the asylum. She was more busy than ever at her tapestry frame, because the countess prized her work; and thus she could in some degree repay the protection afforded her. She never mentioned Fabian, and always imposed silence on her companions when they spoke of him. But she did this in no disrespectful terms. 'He is a generous enemy, I acknowledge,' she would say, 'but still he is my enemy, and while through him my brother is an exile and a wanderer upon earth, it is painful to me to hear his name.'

After the lapse of many months spent in entire seclusion and tranquillity, a change occurred in the tenor of her life. The countess suddenly resolved to pass the Easter festival at Rome. Flora's companions were wild with joy at the prospect of the journey, the novelty, and the entertainment they promised themselves from this visit, and pitied the dignity of their friend, which prevented her from making one in their mistress's train; for it was soon understood that Flora was to be left behind; and she was informed that the interval of the lady's absence was to be passed by her in a villa belonging to the family situated in a sequestered nook among the neighbouring Apennines.

The countess departed in pomp and pride on her so called pilgrimage to the sacred city, and at the same time Flora was conveyed to her rural retreat. The villa was inhabited only by the peasant and his family who cultivated the farm, or *podere*, attached to it, and the old *cassicre* or housekeeper. The cheerfulness and freedom of the country were delightful, and the entire solitude consonant to the habits of the meditative girl, accustomed to the confinement of the city, and the intrusive prattle of her associates. Spring was opening with all the beauty which that season showers upon favoured Italy; while blights and chilling rain usually characterise it in these northern lands. The almond and peach trees were in blossom; and the vine-dresser sang at his work, perched with his pruning-knife among the trees. Blossoms and flowers, in laughing plenty, graced the soil; and the trees, swelling with buds ready to expand into leaves, seemed to feel the life that animated their dark old boughs. Flora was enchanted; the country labours interested her, and the hoarded experience of old Sandra was a treasure-house of wisdom and amusement. Her attention had hitherto been directed to giving the most vivid hues and truest imitation to her transcript with her needle of some picture given her as a model; but here was a novel occupation. She learned the history of the bees, watched the habits of the birds, and enquired into the culture of plants. Sandra was delighted with her new companion; and, though notorious for being cross, yet could wriggle her antique lips into smiles for Flora.

To repay the kindness of her guardian and his mother, she still devoted much time to her needle. This occupation but engaged half her attentions; and while she pursued it, she could give herself up to endless reverie on the subject of Lorenzo's fortunes. Three years had flown since he had left her; and, except a little gold cross brought to her by a pilgrim from Milan, but one month after his departure, she had received no tidings of him. Whether from Milan he had proceeded to France, Germany or the Holy Land, she did not know; by turns her fancy led him to either of these places, and fashioned the course of events that might have befallen him. She figured to herself his toilsome journeys – his life in the camp – his achievements, and the honours showered on him by kings and nobles; her cheek glowed at the praises he received, and her eye kindled with delight as it imaged him standing with modest pride and an erect but gentle mien before them. Then the fair enthusiast paused; it crossed her recollection like a shadow that if all had gone prosperously, he had returned to share his prosperity with her, and her faltering heart turned to sadder scenes to account for his protracted absence.

Sometimes, while thus employed, she brought her work into the trellised arbour of the garden, or, when it was too warm for the open air, she had a favourite shady window, which looked down a deep ravine into a majestic wood, whence the sound of falling water met her ears. One day, while she employed her fingers upon the spirited likeness of a hound which made a part of the hunting-piece she was working for the countess, a sharp, wailing cry suddenly broke on her ear, followed by the trampling of horses and the hurried steps and loud vociferations of men. They entered the villa on the opposite side from that which her window commanded; but the noise continuing, she rose to ask the reason, when Sandra burst into the room, crying, 'O Madonna! he is dead! come and help him; he has been thrown from his horse, and he will never speak more.' Flora, for an instant, could only think of her brother, as if expecting to see him stretched on his bier. She rushed past the old woman, down into the great hall, in which, lying on a rude litter of boughs, she beheld the inanimate body of Count Fabian. He was surrounded by servitors and peasants, who were all clasping their hands and tearing their hair as, with frightful shrieks, they pressed round their lord, not one of them endeavouring to restore him to life. Flora's first impulse was to retire; but, casting a second glance on the livid brow of the young count, she saw his eyelids move, and the blood falling in quick drops from his hair on the pavement; she exclaimed, 'He is not dead – he bleeds! hasten some of you for a leech!' And meanwhile she hurried to get water, sprinkled it on his face, and dispersed the group that hung over him and impeded the free air; the soft breeze playing on his forehead revived him, and he gave manifest tokens of life; so that when the physician arrived, he found that, though he was seriously and even dangerously hurt, every hope might be entertained of his recovery.

Flora undertook the office of his nurse, and fulfilled its duties with unwearied attention. She watched him by night and waited on him by day with that spirit of Christian humility and benevolence which animates a Sister of Charity as she tends the sick. For several days Fabian's soul seemed on the wing to quit its earthly abode; and the state of weakness that followed his insensibility was scarcely less alarming. At length, he recognised and acknowledged the care of Flora, but she alone possessed any power to calm and guide him during the state of irritability and fever that then ensued. Nothing except her presence controlled his impatience; before her he was so lamb-like that she could scarcely have credited the accounts that others gave her of his violence, but that, whenever she returned, after leaving him for any time, she heard his voice far off in anger, and found him with flushed cheeks and flashing eyes, all which demonstrations subsided into meek acquiescence when she drew near.

In a few weeks he was able to quit his room; but the motion of his horse was forbidden him, and any noise or sudden sound drove him almost insane. So loud is an Italian's quietest movements, that Flora was obliged to prevent the approach of any except herself; and her soft voice and noiseless footfall were the sweetest medicine she could administer to her patient. It was painful to her to be in perpetual attendance on Lorenzo's rival and foe, but she subdued her heart to her duty, and custom helped to reconcile her. As he grew better, she could not help remarking the intelligence of his countenance, and the kindness and cordiality of his manners. There was an unobtrusive and delicate attention and care in his intercourse with her that won her to be pleased. When he conversed, his discourse was full of entertainment and variety. His memory was well stored with numerous *fabliaux, novelle*[191] and romances, which he quickly discovered to be highly interesting to her, and so contrived to have one always ready from the exhaustless stock he possessed. These romantic stories reminded her of the imaginary adventures she had invented, in solitude and silence, for her brother; and each tale of foreign countries had a peculiar charm, which animated her face as she listened, so that Fabian could have gone on for ever, only to mark the varying expression of her countenance as he proceeded. Yet she acknowledged these attractions in him as a Catholic nun may the specious virtues of a heretic; and, while he contrived each day to increase the pleasure she derived from his society, she satisfied her conscience with regard to her brother by cherishing in secret a little quiet stock of family hate, and by throwing over her manners, whenever she could recollect so to do, a cold and ceremonious tone, which she had the pleasure of seeing vexed him heartily.

Nearly two months had passed, and he was so well recovered that Flora began to wonder that he did not return to Sienna, and of course to fulfil her duty by wishing that he should; and yet, while his cheek was sunk through past sickness, and his elastic step grown slow, she, as a nurse desirous of completing her good work, felt averse to his entering too soon on the scene of the busy town and its noisy pleasures. At length, two or three of his friends having come over to see him, he agreed to return with them to the city. A significant glance which they cast on his young nurse probably determined him. He parted from her with a grave courtesy and a profusion of thanks, unlike his usual manner, and rode off without alluding to any probability of their meeting again.

She fancied that she was relieved from a burthen when he went, and was surprised to find the days grow tedious, and mortified to perceive that her thoughts no longer spent themselves so spontaneously on her brother and to feel that the occupation of a few weeks could unhinge her mind and dissipate her cherished reveries; thus, while she felt annoyance from the absence of Fabian, she hated him the more for having, in addition to his other misdeeds, invaded the sanctuary of her dearest thoughts. She was beginning to conquer this listlessness, and to return with renewed zest to her usual occupations, when, about a week after his departure, Fabian suddenly returned. He came upon her as she was gathering flowers for the shrine of the Madonna; and, on seeing him, she blushed as rosy red as the roses she held. He looked infinitely worse in health than when he went: his wan cheeks and sunk eyes excited her concern; and her earnest and kind questions somewhat revived him. He kissed her hand, and continued to stand beside her as she finished her nosegay. Had anyone seen the glad, fond look with which he regarded her as she busied herself among the flowers, even old Sandra might have prognosticated his entire recovery under her care.

Flora was totally unaware of the feelings that were excited in Fabian's heart and the struggle he made to overcome a passion too sweet and too seductive, when awakened by so lovely a being, ever to be subdued. He had been struck with her some time ago, and avoided her. It was through his suggestion that she passed the period of the countess's pilgrimage in this secluded villa; nor had he thought of visiting her there; but, riding over one day to enquire concerning a foal rearing for him, his horse had thrown him and caused him that injury which had made him so long the inmate of the same abode. Already prepared to admire her, her kindness, her gentleness and her unwearied patience during his illness easily conquered a heart most ready and yet most unwilling to yield. He had returned to Sienna resolved to forget her; but he came back assured that his life and death were in her hands.

At first Count Fabian had forgot that he had any but his own feelings and prejudices, and those of his mother and kindred, to overcome; but when the tyranny of love vanquished these, he began to fear a more insurmountable impediment in Flora. The first whisper of love fell like mortal sin upon her ear; and disturbed, and even angry, she replied: 'Methinks you wholly forget who I am, and what you are. I speak not of ancient feuds, though there were enough to divide us for ever. Know that I hate you as my brother's murderer. Restore Lorenzo to me – recall him from banishment – erase the memory of all that he has suffered through you – win his love and approbation; and when all this is fulfilled, which never can be, speak a language which now it is as the bitterness of death for me to hear!'

And saying this, she hastily retired, to conceal the floods of tears which this, as she termed it, insult had caused to flow; to lament yet more deeply her brother's absence and her own dependence.

Fabian was not so easily silenced; and Flora had no wish to renew scenes and expressions of violence so foreign to her nature. She imposed a rule on herself, never swerving from which she hoped to destroy the ill-omened love of her protector. She absented herself from him as much as possible; and when with him assumed such chilling indifference of manner, and made apparent in her silence so absolute and cold a rejection of all his persuasions, that had not love with its unvanquishable hopes reigned absolutely in young Fabian's heart, he must have despaired. He ceased to speak of his affection, so to win back her ancient kindness. This was at first difficult; for she was timid as a young bird, whose feet have touched the limed twigs.[192] But naturally credulous, and quite inexperienced, she soon began to believe that her alarm was exaggerated, and to resume those habits of intimacy which had heretofore subsisted between them. By degrees Fabian contrived to insinuate the existence of his attachment – he could not help it. He asked no return – he would wait for Lorenzo's arrival, which he was sure could not be far distant. Her displeasure could not change, nor silence destroy, a sentiment which survived in spite of both. Entrenched in her coldness and her indifference, she could not quarrel with each word he spoke; and hoping to weary him out by her defensive warfare, she fancied that he would soon cease his pursuit in disgust.

The countess had been long away; she had proceeded on to view the feast of San Gennaro at Naples, and had not received tidings of her son's illness. She was now expected back; and Fabian, still lingering at the villa, resolved to return to Sienna in time to receive her. Both he and Flora were therefore surprised one day, when she suddenly entered the apartment where they both were. Flora had long peremptorily insisted that he should not intrude while she was employed on her embroidery frame; but this day he had made so good a pretext that for the first time he was admitted, and then suffered to stay a few minutes – they now neither of them knew how long; she was busy at her work; and he sitting near, gazing unreproved on her unconscious face and graceful figure, felt himself happier than he had ever been before.

The countess was sufficiently surprised, and not a little angry; but before she could do more than utter one exclamation, Fabian interrupted, by entreating her not to spoil all. He drew her away – he made his own explanations, and urged his wishes with resistless persuasion. The countess had been used to indulge him in every wish; it was impossible for her to deny any strongly urged request; his pertinacity – his agitation – his entreaties half won her; and the account of his illness, and his assurances, seconded by those of all the family, that Flora had saved his life, completed the conquest, and she became in her turn a suitor for her son to the orphan daughter of Mancini.

Flora, educated till the age of twelve by one who never consulted his own pleasures and gratifications, but went right on in the path of duty, regardless of pain or disappointment, had no idea of doing aught merely because she or others might wish it. Since that time she had been thrown on her own resources; and jealously cherishing her individuality in the midst of her enemies, every feeling of her heart had been strengthened by solitude and by a sense of mental independence. She was the least likely of anyone to go with the stream, or to yield to the mere influence of circumstances. She felt, she knew, what it became her to do, and that must be done in spite of every argument.

The countess's expostulations and entreaties were of no avail. The promise she had made to her brother of engaging herself by no vow for five years must be observed under every event; it was asked her at the sad and solemn hour of their parting, and was thus rendered doubly sacred. So constituted, indeed, were her feelings, that the slightest wish ever remembered by her having been expressed by Lorenzo had more weight with her than the most urgent prayers of another. He was a part of her religion; reverence and love for him had been moulded into the substance of her soul from infancy; their very separation had tended to render these impressions irradicable. She brooded over them for years; and when no sympathy or generous kindness was afforded her – when the countess treated her like an inferior and a dependant, and Fabian had forgotten her existence, she had lived from month to month, and from year to year, cherishing the image of her brother, and only able to tolerate the annoyances that beset her existence by considering that her patience, her fortitude and her obedience were all offerings at the shrine of her beloved Lorenzo's desires.

It is true that the generous and kindly disposition of Fabian won her to regard him with a feeling nearly approaching tenderness, though this emotion was feeble, the mere ripple of the waves, compared to the mighty tide of affection that set her will all one way, and made her deem everything trivial except Lorenzo's return – Lorenzo's existence – obedience to Lorenzo. She listened to her lover's persuasions so unyieldingly that the countess was provoked by her inflexibility; but she bore her reproaches with such mildness, and smiled so sweetly, that Fabian was the more charmed. She admitted that she owed him a certain submission as the guardian set over her by her brother; Fabian would have gladly exchanged this authority for the pleasure of being commanded by her; but this was an honour he could not attain, so in playful spite he enforced concessions from her. At his desire she appeared in society, dressed as became her rank, and filled in his house the station a sister of his own would have held. She preferred seclusion, but she was averse to contention and it was little that she yielded, while the purpose of her soul was as fixed as ever.

The fifth year of Lorenzo's exile was now drawing to a close, but he did not return, nor had any intelligence been received of him. The decree of his banishment had been repealed, the fortunes of his house restored, and his palace, under Fabian's generous care, rebuilt. These were acts that demanded and excited Flora's gratitude; yet they were performed in an unpretending manner, as if the citizens of Sienna had suddenly become just and wise, without his interference. But these things dwindled into trifles while the continuation of Lorenzo's absence seemed the pledge of her eternal misery; and the tacit appeal made to her kindness, while she had no thought but for her brother, drove her to desperation. She could no longer tolerate the painful anomaly of her situation; she could not endure her suspense for her brother's fate, nor the reproachful glances of Fabian's mother and his friends. He himself was more generous – he read her heart, and, as the termination of the fifth year drew nigh, ceased to allude to his own feelings, and appeared as wrapped as herself in doubt concerning the fate of the noble youth, whom they could scarcely entertain a hope of ever seeing more. This was small comfort to Flora. She had resolved that when the completion of the fifth year assured her that her brother was for ever lost, she would never see Fabian again. At first she had resolved to take refuge in a convent, and in the sanctity of religious vows. But she remembered how averse Lorenzo had always shown himself to this vocation, and that he had preferred to place her beneath the roof of his foe, than within the walls of a nunnery. Besides, young as she was, and despite herself, full of hope, she recoiled from shutting the gates of life upon herself for ever. Notwithstanding her fears and sorrow, she clung to the belief that Lorenzo lived; and this led her to another plan. When she had received her little cross from Milan, it was accompanied by a message that he

Flora

believed he had found a good friend in the archbishop of that place. This prelate, therefore, would know whither Lorenzo had first bent his steps, and to him she resolved to apply. Her scheme was easily formed. She possessed herself of the garb of a pilgrim, and resolved on the day following the completion of the fifth year to depart from Sienna, and bend her steps towards Lombardy, buoyed up by the hope that she should gain some tidings of the object of all her care.

Meanwhile Fabian had formed a similar resolve. He had learnt the fact from Flora, of Lorenzo having first resorted to Milan, and he determined to visit that city, and not to return without certain information. He acquainted his mother with his plan, but begged her not to inform Flora, that she might not be tortured by double doubt during his absence.

The anniversary of the fifth year was come, and with it the eve of these several and separate journeys. Flora had retired to spend the day at the villa before mentioned. She had chosen to retire thither for various reasons. Her escape was more practicable thence than in the town; and she was anxious to avoid seeing both Fabian and his mother, now that she was on the point of inflicting severe pain on them. She spent the day at the villa and in its gardens, musing on her plans, regretting the quiet of her past life – saddened on Fabian's account – grieving bitterly for Lorenzo. She was not alone, for she had been obliged to confide in one of her former companions, and to obtain her assistance. Poor little Angeline was dreadfully frightened with the trust reposed in her, but did not dare expostulate with or betray her friend; and she continued near her during this last day, by turns trying to console and weeping with her. Towards evening they wandered together into the wood contiguous to the villa. Flora had taken her harp with her, but her trembling fingers refused to strike its chords; she left it, she left her companion, and strayed on alone to take leave of a spot consecrated by many a former visit. Here the umbrageous trees gathered about her, and shaded her with their thick and drooping foliage; a torrent dashed down from a neighbouring rock, and fell from a height into a rustic basin, hollowed to receive it; then, overflowing the margin at one spot, it continued falling over successive declivities, till it reached the bottom of a little ravine, when it stole on in a placid and silent course. This had ever been a favourite resort of Flora. The twilight of the wood and the perpetual flow, the thunder, the hurry and the turmoil of the waters, the varied sameness of the eternal elements, accorded with the melancholy of her ideas, and the endless succession of her reveries. She came to it now; she gazed on the limpid cascade – for the last time; a soft sadness glistened in her eyes and her attitude denoted the tender regret that filled her bosom; her long bright tresses streaming in elegant disorder, her light veil and simple, yet rich, attire, were fitfully mirrored in the smooth face of the rushing waters. At this moment the sound of steps more firm and manly than those of Angeline struck her ear, and Fabian himself stood before her; he was unable to bring himself to depart on his journey without seeing her once again. He had ridden over to the villa, and, finding that she had quitted it, sought and found her in the lone recess where they had often spent hours together which had been full of bliss to him. Flora was sorry to see him, for her secret was on her lips, and yet she resolved not to give it utterance. He was ruled by the same feeling. Their interview was therefore short, and neither alluded to what sat nearest the heart of each. They parted with a simple, 'Good-night,' as if certain of meeting the following morning: each deceived the other, and each was in turn deceived. There was more of tenderness in Flora's manner than there had ever been; it cheered his faltering soul, about to quit her, while the anticipation of the blow he was about to receive from her made her regard as venial this momentary softening towards her brother's enemy.

Fabian passed the night at the villa, and early the next morning he departed for Milan. He was impatient to arrive at the end of his journey, and often he thrust his spurs into his horse's sides, and put him to his speed, which even then appeared slow. Yet he was aware that his arrival at Milan might advance him not a jot towards the ultimate object of his journey; and he called Flora cruel and unkind, until the recollection of her kind farewell came across to console and cheer him.

He stopped the first night at Empoli, and, crossing the Arno,[193] began to ascend the Apennines on the northern side. Soon he penetrated their fastnesses, and entered deep into the ilex woods. He journeyed on perseveringly, and yet the obstructions he met with were many, and borne with impatience. At length, on the afternoon of the third day, he arrived at a little rustic inn, hid deep in a wood, which showed signs of seldom being visited by travellers. The burning sun made it a welcome shelter for Fabian; and he deposited his steed in the stable, which he found already partly occupied by a handsome black horse, and then entered the inn to seek refreshment for himself. There seemed some difficulty in obtaining this. The landlady was the sole domestic, and it was long before she made her appearance, and then she was full of trouble and dismay; a sick traveller had arrived – a gentleman to all appearance dying of a malignant fever. His horse, his well-stored purse and rich dress showed that he was a cavalier of consequence – the more the pity. There was no help, nor any means of carrying him forward;

yet half his pain seemed to arise from his regret at being detained – he was so eager to proceed to Sienna. The name of his own town excited the interest of Count Fabian, and he went up to visit the stranger, while the hostess prepared his repast.

Meanwhile Flora awoke with the lark, and with the assistance of Angeline attired herself in her pilgrim's garb. From the stir below, she was surprised to find that Count Fabian had passed the night at the villa, and she lingered till he should have departed, as she believed, on his return to Sienna. Then she embraced her young friend, and taking leave of her with many blessings and thanks, alone, with heaven, as she trusted, for her guide, she quitted Fabian's sheltering roof, and with a heart that maintained its purpose in spite of her feminine timidity, began her pilgrimage. Her journey performed on foot was slow, so that there was no likelihood that she could overtake her lover, already many miles in the advance. Now that she had begun it, her undertaking appeared to her gigantic, and her heart almost failed her. The burning sun scorched her; never having before found herself alone in a highway, a thousand fears assailed her, and she grew so weary that soon she was unable to support herself. By the advice of a landlady at an inn, where she stopped, she purchased a mule to help her on in her long-drawn way. Yet with this help, it was the third night before she arrived at Empoli, and then crossing the Arno, as her lover had done before, her disasters seemed to begin to unfold themselves, and to grow gigantic as she entered the dark woods of the Apennines and found herself amidst the solitude of its vast forests. Her pilgrim's garb inspired some respect, and she rested at convents by the way. The pious sisters held up their hands in admiration of her courage; while her heart beat faintly with the knowledge that she possessed absolutely none. Yet, again and again, she repeated to herself that, the Apennines once passed, the worst would be over. So she toiled on, now weary, now frightened – very slowly, and yet very anxious to get on with speed.

On the evening of the seventh day after her quitting Sienna, she was still entangled in the mazes of these savage hills. She was to sleep at a convent on their summit that night, and the next day arrive at Bologna. This hope had cheered her through the day; but evening approached, the way grew more intricate, and no convent appeared. The sun had set, and she listened anxiously for the bell of the Ave Maria,[194] which would give her hope that the goal she sought was nigh; but all was silent, save the swinging boughs of the vast trees and the timid beating of her own heart; darkness closed around her, and despair came with the increased obscurity, till a twinkling light, revealing itself among the trees, afforded her some relief. She followed this beamy guide till it led her to a little inn, where the sight of a kind-looking woman and the assurance of safe shelter dispelled her terrors and filled her with grateful pleasure.

Seeing her so weary, the considerate hostess hastened to place food before her, and then conducted her to a little low room where her bed was prepared. 'I am sorry, lady,' said the landlady, in a whisper, 'not to be able to accommodate you better; but a sick cavalier occupies my best room – it is next to this – and he sleeps now, and I would not disturb him. Poor gentleman! I never thought he would rise more; and under heaven he owes his life to one who, whether he is related to him or not, I cannot tell, for he did not accompany him. Four days ago he stopped here, and I told him my sorrow – how I had a dying guest, and he charitably saw him, and has since then nursed him more like a twin brother than a stranger.'

The good woman whispered on. Flora heard but little of what she said, and overcome by weariness and sleep, paid no attention to her tale. But having performed her orisons, placed her head on the pillow, and was quickly lapped in the balmy slumber she so much needed.

Early in the morning she was awoken by a murmur of voices in the next room. She started up, and recalling her scattered thoughts, tried to remember the account the hostess had given her the preceding evening. The sick man spoke, but his accent was low, and the words did not reach her; he was answered – could Flora believe her senses? did she not know the voice that spoke these words? – 'Fear nothing, a sweet sleep has done you infinite good; and I rejoice in the belief that you will speedily recover. I have sent to Sienna for your sister, and do indeed expect that Flora will arrive this very day.'

More was said, but Flora heard no more: she had risen, and was hastily dressing herself; in a few minutes she was by her brother's, her Lorenzo's bedside, kissing his wan hand and assuring him that she was indeed Flora.

'These are indeed wonders,' he at last said, 'and if you are mine own Flora, you perhaps can tell me who this noble gentleman is, who day and night has watched beside me, as a mother may by her only child, giving no time to repose but exhausting himself for me.'

'How, dearest brother,' said Flora, 'can I truly answer your question? to mention the name of our benefactor were to speak of a mask and a disguise, not a true thing. He is my protector and guardian, who has watched over and preserved me, while you wandered far; his is the most generous heart in Italy, offering past enmity and family pride as sacrifices at the altar of nobleness and truth. He is the restorer of your fortunes in your native town – '

'And the lover of my sweet sister. I have heard of these things and was on my way to confirm his happiness and to find my own when sickness laid me thus low, and would have destroyed us both for ever but for Fabian Tolomei – '

'Who now exerts his expiring authority to put an end to this scene,' interrupted the young count; 'not till this day has Lorenzo been sufficiently composed to hear any of these explanations, and we risk his returning health by too long a conversation. The history of these things and of his long wanderings, now so happily ended, must be reserved for a future hour; when assembled in our beloved Sienna, exiles and foes no longer, we shall long enjoy the happiness which providence, after so many trials, has bounteously reserved for us.'

The Invisible Girl

THIS slender narrative has no pretensions to the regularity of a story, or the development of situations and feelings; it is but a slight sketch, delivered nearly as it was narrated to me by one of the humblest of the actors concerned; nor will I spin out a circumstance interesting principally from its singularity and truth, but narrate, as concisely as I can, how I was surprised on visiting what seemed a ruined tower, crowning a bleak promontory overhanging the sea that flows between Wales and Ireland, to find that though the exterior preserved all the savage rudeness that betokened many a war with the elements, the interior was fitted up somewhat in the guise of a summerhouse, for it was too small to deserve any other name. It consisted but of the ground floor, which served as an entrance, and one room above, which was reached by a staircase made out of the thickness of the wall. This chamber was floored and carpeted, decorated with elegant furniture; and, above all, to attract the attention and excite curiosity, there hung over the chimney-piece – for to preserve the apartment from damp a fireplace had been built evidently since it had assumed a guise so dissimilar to the object of its construction – a picture simply painted in watercolours, which seemed more than any part of the adornments of the room to be at war with the rudeness of the building, the solitude in which it was placed and the desolation of the surrounding scenery. This drawing represented a lovely girl in the very pride and bloom of youth; her dress was simple, in the fashion of the day – (remember, reader, I write at the beginning of the eighteenth century), her countenance was embellished by a look of mingled innocence and intelligence, to which was added the imprint of serenity of soul and natural cheerfulness. She was reading one of those folio romances which have so long been the delight of the enthusiastic and young; her mandoline was at her feet; her parroquet[195] perched on a huge mirror near her; the arrangement of furniture and hangings gave token of a luxurious dwelling, and her attire also evidently that of home and privacy yet bore with it an appearance of ease and girlish ornament, as if she wished to please. Beneath this picture was inscribed in golden letters, 'The Invisible Girl'.

Rambling about a country nearly uninhabited, having lost my way, and being overtaken by a shower, I had lighted on this dreary looking tenement, which seemed to rock in the blast, and to be hung up there as the very symbol of desolation. I was gazing wistfully and cursing inwardly my stars which led me to a ruin that could afford no shelter, though the storm began to pelt more seriously than before, when I saw an old woman's head popped out from a kind of loophole, and as suddenly withdrawn; a minute after a feminine voice called to me from within, and penetrating a little brambly maze that screened a door which I had not before observed, so skilfully had the planter succeeded in concealing art with nature, I found the good dame standing on the threshold and inviting me to take refuge within. 'I had just come up from our cot hard by,' she said, 'to look after the things, as I do every day, when the rain came on – will ye walk up till it is over?' I was about to observe that the cot hard by, at the venture of a few raindrops, was better than a ruined tower, and to ask my kind hostess whether 'the things' were pigeons or crows that she was come to look after, when the matting of the floor and the carpeting of the staircase struck my eye. I was still more surprised when I saw the room above; and beyond all, the picture and its singular inscription, naming her invisible whom the painter had coloured forth into very agreeable visibility, awakened my most lively curiosity; the result of this, of my exceeding politeness towards the old woman and her own natural garrulity, was a kind of garbled narrative which my imagination eked out, and future enquiries rectified, till it assumed the following form.

Some years before in the afternoon of a September day, which, though tolerably fair, gave many tokens of a tempestuous evening, a gentleman arrived at a little coast town about ten miles from this place; he expressed his desire to hire a boat to carry him to the town of — about fifteen miles further on the coast. The menaces which the sky held forth made the fishermen loth to venture, till at length two – one the father of a numerous family, bribed by the bountiful reward the stranger promised, the other, the son of my hostess, induced by youthful daring – agreed to undertake the voyage. The wind was fair, and they hoped to make good way before nightfall, and to get into port ere the rising of the storm. They pushed off with good cheer, at least the fishermen did; as for the stranger, the deep mourning which he wore was not half so black as the melancholy that wrapped his mind. He looked as if he had never smiled – as if some unutterable thought, dark as night and bitter as death, had built its nest within his bosom, and

The Invisible Girl

brooded therein eternally; he did not mention his name, but one of the villagers recognised him as Henry Vernon, the son of a baronet who possessed a mansion about three miles distant from the town for which he was bound. This mansion was almost abandoned by the family; but Henry had, in a romantic fit, visited it about three years before, and Sir Peter had been down there during the previous spring for about a couple of months.

The boat did not make so much way as was expected; the breeze failed them as they got out to sea, and they were fain with oar as well as sail to try to weather the promontory that jutted out between them and the spot they desired to reach. They were yet far distant when the shifting wind began to exert its strength, and to blow with violent though unequal puffs. Night came on pitchy dark, and the howling waves rose and broke with frightful violence, menacing to overwhelm the tiny bark that dared resist their fury. They were forced to lower every sail, and take to their oars; one man was obliged to bale out the water, and Vernon himself took an oar, and rowing with desperate energy, equalled the force of the more practised boatmen. There had been much talk between the sailors before the tempest came on; now, except a brief command, all were silent. One thought of his wife and children, and silently cursed the caprice of the stranger that endangered in its effects not only his life but their welfare; the other feared less, for he was a daring lad, but he worked hard, and had no time for speech; while Vernon, bitterly regretting the thoughtlessness which had made him cause others to share a peril, unimportant as far as he himself was concerned, now tried to cheer them with a voice full of animation and courage, and now pulled yet more strongly at the oar he held. The only person who did not seem wholly intent on the work he was about was the man who baled; every now and then he gazed intently round, as if the sea held afar off, on its tumultuous waste, some object that he strained his eyes to discern. But all was blank, except as the crests of the high waves showed themselves, or far out on the verge of the horizon, a kind of lifting of the clouds betokened greater violence for the blast. At length he exclaimed, 'Yes, I see it! – the larboard oar! – now! if we can make yonder light, we are saved!' Both the rowers instinctively turned their heads, but cheerless darkness answered their gaze.

'You cannot see it,' cried their companion, 'but we are nearing it; and, please God, we shall outlive this night.' Soon he took the oar from Vernon's hand, who, quite exhausted, was failing in his strokes. He rose and looked for the beacon which promised them safety; it glimmered with so faint a ray, that now he said, 'I see it;' and again, 'It is nothing;'

still, as they made way, it dawned upon his sight, growing more steady and distinct as it beamed across the lurid waters, which themselves became smoother, so that safety seemed to arise from the bosom of the ocean under the influence of that flickering gleam.

'What beacon is it that helps us at our need?' asked Vernon, as the men, now able to manage their oars with greater ease, found breath to answer his question.

'A fairy one, I believe,' replied the elder sailor, 'yet no less a true: it burns in an old tumbledown tower, built on the top of a rock which looks over the sea. We never saw it before this summer; and now each night it is to be seen, at least when it is looked for, for we cannot see it from our village; and it is in such an out-of-the-way place that no one has need to go near it, except through a chance like this. Some say it is burnt by witches, some say by smugglers; but this I know, two parties have been to search, and found nothing but the bare walls of the tower. All is deserted by day, and dark by night; for no light was to be seen while we were there, though it burned sprightly enough when we were out at sea.'

'I have heard say,' observed the younger sailor, 'it is burnt by the ghost of a maiden who lost her sweetheart in these parts; he being wrecked, and his body found at the foot of the tower; she goes by the name among us of the "Invisible Girl". '

The voyagers had now reached the landing-place at the foot of the tower. Vernon cast a glance upward – the light was still burning. With some difficulty, struggling with the breakers and blinded by night, they contrived to get their little bark to shore, and to draw her up on the beach: they then scrambled up the precipitous pathway, overgrown by weeds and underwood, and, guided by the more experienced fisherman, they found the entrance to the tower; door or gate there was none, and all was dark as the tomb, and silent and almost as cold as death.

'This will never do,' said Vernon; 'surely our hostess will show her light, if not herself, and guide our darkling steps by some sign of life and comfort.'

'We will get to the upper chamber,' said the sailor, 'if I can but hit upon the broken-down steps; but you will find no trace of the Invisible Girl nor her light either, I warrant.'

'Truly a romantic adventure of the most disagreeable kind,' muttered Vernon, as he stumbled over the unequal ground; 'she of the beacon-light must be both ugly and old, or she would not be so peevish and inhospitable.'

With considerable difficulty, and, after divers knocks and bruises, the adventurers at length succeeded in reaching the upper storey; but all was blank and bare, and they were fain to stretch themselves on the hard floor, when weariness, both of mind and body, conduced to steep their senses in sleep.

Long and sound were the slumbers of the mariners. Vernon but forgot himself for an hour; then, throwing off drowsiness and finding his rough couch uncongenial to repose, he got up and placed himself at the hole that served for a window, for glass there was none, and there being not even a rough bench, he leant his back against the embrasure, as the only rest he could find. He had forgotten his danger, the mysterious beacon and its invisible guardian; his thoughts were occupied on the horrors of his own fate, and the unspeakable wretchedness that sat like a nightmare on his heart.

It would require a good-sized volume to relate the causes which had changed the once happy Vernon into the most woeful mourner that ever clung to the outer trappings of grief, as slight though cherished symbols of the wretchedness within. Henry was the only child of Sir Peter Vernon, and as much spoiled by his father's idolatry as the old baronet's violent and tyrannical temper would permit. A young orphan was educated in his father's house, who in the same way was treated with generosity and kindness, and yet who lived in deep awe of Sir Peter's authority. He was a widower and these two children were all he had to exert his power over, or to whom to extend his affection. Rosina was a cheerful-tempered girl, a little timid, and careful to avoid displeasing her protector; but so docile, so kind-hearted, and so affectionate, that she felt even less than Henry the discordant spirit of his parent. It is a tale often told; they were playmates and companions in childhood, and lovers in after days. Rosina was frightened to imagine that this secret affection, and the vows they pledged, might be disapproved of by Sir Peter. But sometimes she consoled herself by thinking that perhaps she was in reality her Henry's destined bride, brought up with him under the design of their future union; and Henry, while he felt that this was not the case, resolved to wait only until he was of age to declare and accomplish his wishes in making the sweet Rosina his wife. Meanwhile he was careful to avoid premature discovery of his intentions, so to secure his beloved girl from persecution and insult. The old gentleman was very conveniently blind; he lived always in the country, and the lovers spent their lives together, unrebuked and uncontrolled. It was enough that Rosina played on her mandoline, and sang Sir Peter to sleep every day after dinner; she was the sole female in the house above the rank of a servant, and had her own way in the disposal of her time. Even when Sir Peter frowned, her innocent caresses and sweet voice were powerful to smooth the rough current of his temper. If ever human spirit lived in an earthly paradise, Rosina did at this time: her pure love was made happy by Henry's constant presence; and the confidence they felt in each other, and the security with which they looked forward to the future, rendered their path one of roses under a cloudless sky. Sir Peter was the slight drawback that only rendered their tête-à-tête more delightful, and gave value to the sympathy they each bestowed on the other. All at once an ominous personage made its appearance in Vernon Place, in the shape of a widow sister of Sir Peter, who, having succeeded in killing her husband and children with the effects of her vile temper, came, like a harpy, greedy for new prey, under her brother's roof. She too soon detected the attachment of the unsuspicious pair. She made all speed to impart her discovery to her brother, and at once to restrain and inflame his rage. Through her contrivance Henry was suddenly despatched on his travels abroad, that the coast might be clear for the persecution of Rosina; and then the richest of the lovely girl's many admirers, whom, under Sir Peter's single reign, she was allowed, nay, almost commanded, to dismiss, so desirous was he of keeping her for his own comfort, was selected, and she was ordered to marry him. The scenes of violence to which she was now exposed, the bitter taunts of the odious Mrs Bainbridge and the reckless fury of Sir Peter, were the more frightful and overwhelming from their novelty. To all she could only oppose a silent, tearful, but immutable steadiness of purpose: no threats, no rage could extort from her more than a touching prayer that they would not hate her, because she could not obey.

'There must be something we don't see under all this,' said Mrs Bainbridge, 'take my word for it, brother – she corresponds secretly with Henry. Let us take her down to your seat in Wales, where she will have no pensioned beggars to assist her; and we shall see if her spirit be not bent to our purpose.'

Sir Peter consented, and they all three posted down to —shire, and took up their abode in the solitary and dreary looking house before alluded to as belonging to the family. Here poor Rosina's sufferings grew intolerable: before, surrounded by well-known scenes, and in perpetual intercourse with kind and familiar faces, she had not despaired in the end of conquering by her patience the cruelty of her persecutors; nor had she written to Henry, for his name had not been mentioned by his relatives, nor their attachment alluded to, and she felt an instinctive wish to escape the dangers about her without his being annoyed, or the sacred secret of her love being laid bare, and wronged by the vulgar abuse of his aunt or the bitter curses of his father. But when she was taken to Wales, and made a prisoner in her apartment, when the flinty mountains about her seemed feebly to imitate the stony hearts she had to deal with, her courage began to fail. The only attendant permitted to approach her was Mrs Bainbridge's maid; and under the tutelage of her fiendlike mistress, this woman was used as a decoy to entice the poor prisoner into confidence, and then to betray her. The simple, kind-hearted Rosina was a facile dupe, and at last, in the excess of her despair, wrote to Henry, and gave the letter to this woman to be forwarded. The letter in itself would have softened marble; it did not speak of their mutual vows, it but asked him to intercede with his father, that he would restore her to the kind place she had formerly held in his affections, and cease from a cruelty that would destroy her. 'For I may die,' wrote the hapless girl, 'but marry another – never!' That single word, indeed, had sufficed to betray her secret, had it not been already discovered; as it was, it gave increased fury to Sir Peter, as his sister triumphantly pointed it out to him, for it need hardly be said that while the ink of the address was yet wet, and the seal still warm, Rosina's letter was carried to this lady. The culprit was summoned before them; what ensued none could tell; for their own sakes the cruel pair tried to palliate their part. Voices were high, and the soft murmur of Rosina's tone was lost in the howling of Sir Peter and the snarling of his sister. 'Out of doors you shall go,' roared the old man; 'under my roof you shall not spend another night.' And the words 'infamous seductress', and worse, such as had never met the poor girl's ear before, were caught by listening servants; and to each angry speech of the baronet, Mrs Bainbridge added an envenomed point worse than all.

More dead than alive, Rosina was at last dismissed. Whether guided by despair, whether she took Sir Peter's threats literally, or whether his sister's orders were more decisive, none knew, but Rosina left the house; a servant saw her cross the park, weeping, and wringing her hands as she went. What became of her none could tell; her disappearance was not disclosed to Sir Peter till the following day, and then he showed by his anxiety to trace her steps and to find her that his words had been but idle threats. The truth was that though Sir Peter went to frightful lengths to prevent the marriage of the heir of his house with the portion-less orphan, the object of his charity, yet in his heart he loved Rosina, and half his violence to her rose from anger at himself for treating her so ill. Now remorse began to sting him, as messenger after messenger came back without tidings of his victim; he dared not confess his worst fears to himself; and when his inhuman sister, trying to harden her conscience by angry words, cried, 'The vile hussy has too surely made away with herself out of revenge to us;' an oath, the most tremendous, and a look sufficient to make even her tremble, commanded her silence. Her conjecture, however, appeared too true: a dark and rushing stream that flowed at the extremity of the park had doubtless received the lovely form, and quenched the life of this unfortunate girl. Sir Peter, when his endeavours to find her proved fruitless, returned to town, haunted by the image of his victim, and forced to acknowledge in his own heart that he would willingly lay down his life, could he see her again, even though it were as the bride of his son – his son, before whose questioning he quailed like the veriest coward; for when Henry was told of the death of Rosina, he suddenly returned from abroad to ask the cause – to visit her grave, and mourn her loss in the groves and valleys which had been the scenes of their mutual happiness. He made a thousand enquiries, and an ominous silence alone replied. Growing more earnest and more anxious, at length he drew from servants and dependants, and his odious aunt herself, the whole dreadful truth. From that moment despair struck his heart, and misery named him her own. He fled from his father's presence; and the recollection that one whom he ought to revere was guilty of so dark a crime, haunted him, as of old the Eumenides tormented the souls of men given up to their torturings. His first, his only wish, was to visit Wales, and to learn if any new discovery had been made, and whether it were possible to recover the mortal remains of the lost Rosina, so to satisfy the unquiet longings of his miserable heart. On this expedition was he bound when he made his appearance at the village before named; and now in the deserted tower, his thoughts were busy with images of despair and death, and what his beloved one had suffered before her gentle nature had been goaded to such a deed of woe.

While immersed in gloomy reverie, to which the monotonous roaring of the sea made fit accompaniment, hours flew on, and Vernon was at last aware that the light of morning was creeping from out its eastern retreat and dawning over the wild ocean, which still broke in furious tumult on the rocky beach. His companions now roused themselves and prepared to depart. The food they had brought with them was damaged by sea water, and their hunger, after hard labour and many hours fasting, had become ravenous. It was impossible to put to sea in their shattered boat; but there stood a fisher's cot about two miles off, in a recess in the bay of which the promontory on which the tower stood formed one side, and to this they hastened to repair; they did not spend a second thought on the light which had saved them, nor its cause, but left the ruin in search of a more hospitable asylum. Vernon cast his eyes round as he quitted it, but no vestige of an inhabitant met his eye, and he began to persuade himself that the beacon had been a creation of fancy merely. Arriving at the cottage in question, which was inhabited by a fisherman and his family, they made a homely breakfast, and then prepared to return to the tower, to refit their boat and if possible bring her round. Vernon accompanied them, together with their host and his son. Several questions were asked concerning the Invisible Girl and her light, each agreeing that the apparition was novel, and not one being able to give even an explanation of how the name had become affixed to the unknown cause of this singular appearance; though both of the men of the cottage affirmed that once or twice they had seen a female figure in the adjacent wood, and that now and then a stranger girl made her appearance at another cot a mile off, on the other side of the promontory, and bought bread; they suspected both these to be the same, but could not tell. The inhabitants of the cot, indeed, appeared too stupid even to feel curiosity, and had never made any attempt at discovery. The whole day was spent by the sailors in repairing the boat, and the sound of hammers and the voices of the men at work resounded along the coast and mingled with the dashing of the waves. This was no time to explore the ruin for one who whether human or supernatural so evidently withdrew herself from intercourse with every living being. Vernon, however, went over the tower, and searched every nook in vain; the dingy bare walls bore no token of serving as a shelter; and even a little recess in the wall of the staircase, which he had not before observed, was equally empty and desolate. Quitting the tower, he wandered in the pine wood that surrounded it, and giving up all thought of solving the mystery, was soon engrossed by thoughts that touched his heart more nearly, when suddenly there appeared on the ground at his feet the vision of a slipper. Since Cinderella so tiny a slipper had never been seen; as plain as shoe could speak, it told a tale of elegance, loveliness and youth. Vernon picked it up; he had often admired Rosina's singularly small foot, and his first thought was a question whether this little slipper would have fitted it. It was very strange! – it must belong to the Invisible Girl. Then there was a fairy form that kindled that light, a form of such material substance that its foot needed to be shod; and yet how shod? – with kid so fine[196] and of shape so exquisite that it exactly resembled such as Rosina wore! Again the recurrence of the image of the beloved dead came forcibly across him; and a thousand home-felt associations, childish yet sweet and loverlike though trifling, so filled Vernon's heart that he threw himself his length on the ground and wept more bitterly than ever at the miserable fate of the sweet orphan.

In the evening the men quitted their work, and Vernon returned with them to the cot where they were to sleep, intending to pursue their voyage, weather permitting, the following morning. Vernon said nothing of his slipper, but returned with his rough associates. Often he looked back; but the tower rose darkly over the dim waves, and no light appeared. Preparations had been made in the cot for their accommodation, and the only bed in it was offered Vernon; but he refused to deprive his hostess, and spreading his cloak on a heap of dry leaves, endeavoured to give himself up to repose. He slept for some hours; and when he awoke, all was still, save that the hard breathing of the sleepers in the same room with him interrupted the silence. He rose, and going to the window, looked out over the now placid sea towards the mystic tower; the light was burning there, sending its slender rays across the waves. Congratulating himself on a circumstance he had not anticipated, Vernon softly left the cottage, and, wrapping his cloak round him, walked with a swift pace round the bay towards the tower. He reached it; still the light was burning. To enter and restore the maiden her shoe, would be but an act of courtesy; and Vernon intended to do this with such caution as to come unaware, before its wearer could, with her accustomed arts, withdraw herself from his eyes; but, unluckily, while yet making his way up the narrow pathway, his foot dislodged a loose fragment that fell with crash and sound down the precipice. He sprang forward, on this, to retrieve by speed the advantage he had lost by this unlucky accident. He reached the door; he entered: all was silent, but also all was dark. He paused in the room below; he felt sure that a slight sound met his ear. He ascended the steps, and entered the upper chamber; but blank obscurity met his penetrating gaze, the starless night admitted not even a twilight glimmer through the only aperture. He closed his eyes, to try, on opening them again, to be able to catch some faint, wandering ray on the visual nerve; but it was in vain. He groped round the room; he stood still, and held his breath; and then, listening intently, he felt sure that another occupied the chamber with him, and that its atmosphere was slightly agitated by another's respiration. He remembered the recess in the staircase; but, before he approached it, he spoke, hesitating a moment what to say. 'I must believe,' he said, 'that misfortune alone can cause your seclusion; and if the assistance of a man – of a gentleman – '

An exclamation interrupted him; a voice from the grave spoke his name – the accents of Rosina syllabled, 'Henry! – is it indeed Henry whom I hear?'

He rushed forward, directed by the sound, and clasped in his arms the living form of his own lamented girl – his own Invisible Girl he called her; for even yet, as he felt her heart beat near his, and as he entwined her waist with his arm, supporting her as she almost sank to the ground with agitation, he could not see her; and, as her sobs prevented her speech, no sense, but the instinctive one that filled his heart with tumultuous gladness, told him that the slender, wasted form he pressed so fondly was the living shadow of the Hebe beauty[197] he had adored.

The morning saw this pair thus strangely restored to each other on the tranquil sea, sailing with a fair wind for L—, whence they were to proceed to Sir Peter's seat, which, three months before, Rosina had quitted in such agony and terror. The morning light dispelled the shadows that had veiled her, and disclosed the fair person of the Invisible Girl. Altered indeed she was by suffering and woe, but still the same sweet smile played on her lips, and the tender light of her soft blue eyes were all her own. Vernon drew out the slipper, and showed the cause that had occasioned him to resolve to discover the guardian of the mystic beacon; even now he dared not enquire how she had existed in that desolate spot, or wherefore she had so sedulously avoided observation, when the right thing to have been done was to have sought him immediately, under whose care, protected by whose love, no danger need be feared. But Rosina shrank from him as he spoke, and a deathlike pallor came over her cheek as she faintly whispered, 'Your father's curse – your father's dreadful threats!' It appeared, indeed, that Sir Peter's violence, and the cruelty of Mrs Bainbridge, had succeeded in impressing Rosina with wild and unvanquishable terror. She had fled from their house without plan or forethought – driven by frantic horror and overwhelming fear, she had left it with scarcely any money, and there seemed to her no possibility of either returning or proceeding onward. She had no friend except Henry in the wide world; whither could she go? – to have sought Henry would have sealed their fates to misery; for, with an oath, Sir Peter had declared he would rather see them both in their coffins than married. After wandering about, hiding by day and only venturing forth at night, she had come to this deserted tower, which seemed a place of refuge. How she had lived since then she could hardly tell; she had lingered in the woods by day, or slept in the vault of the tower, an asylum none were acquainted with or had discovered; by night she burned the pine cones of the wood, and night was her dearest time; for it seemed to her as if security came with darkness. She was unaware that Sir Peter had left that part of the country, and was terrified lest her hiding-place should be revealed to him. Her only hope was that Henry would return – that Henry would never rest till he had found her. She confessed that the long interval and the approach of winter had visited her with dismay; she feared that, as her strength was failing and her form wasting to a skeleton, she might die, and never see her own Henry more.

An illness, indeed, in spite of all his care, followed her restoration to security and the comforts of civilised life; many months went by before the bloom revisiting her cheeks, and her limbs regaining their round-ness, she resembled once more the picture drawn of her in her days of bliss, before any visitation of sorrow. It was a copy of this portrait that decorated the tower, the scene of her suffering, in which I had found shelter. Sir Peter, overjoyed to be relieved from the pangs of remorse, and delighted again to see his orphan ward, whom he really loved, was now as eager as before he had been averse to bless her union with his son. Mrs Bainbridge they never saw again. But each year they spent a few months in their Welsh mansion, the scene of their early wedded happiness, and the spot where again poor Rosina had awoken to life and joy after her cruel persecutions. Henry's fond care had fitted up the tower, and decorated it as I saw; and often did he come over, with his 'Invisible Girl', to renew, in the very scene of their occurrence, the remembrance of all the incidents which had led to their meeting again, during the shades of night, in that sequestered ruin.

The Pole [198]

IT was in the early part of the month of February of the year 1831, near the close of day, that a travelling *caleche*,[199] coming from Rome, was seen approaching, at full gallop, towards Mola di Gaeta.[200] The road leading to the inn is rocky and narrow; on one side is an orange grove, extending to the sea; on the other an old Roman wall, overgrown by blossoming shrubs, enormous aloes, floating tangles of vines and a thousand species of parasite plants peculiar to the South. Scarcely had the *caleche* entered this defile, when the careless postilion drove one of the wheels over a protruding ledge of rock and overturned it; and in the next moment, a crowd of people came running to the spot. Not one of them, however, thought of relieving the traveller within the fallen vehicle; but, with violent gestures and loud outcries, began to examine what damage the *caleche* had sustained, and what profit they might derive from it. The wheelwright declared every wheel was shattered; the carpenter that the shafts were splintered; while the blacksmith, passing and repassing under the carriage, tugged at every clamp and screw and nail with all the violence necessary to ensure himself a handsome job. The traveller it contained, having quietly disengaged himself from various cloaks, books and maps, now slowly descended, and for a moment the busy crowd forgot their restlessness to gaze with admiration upon the noble figure of the stranger. He seemed to be scarcely two-and-twenty. In stature he was sufficiently tall to give an idea of superiority to his fellow mortals; and his form was moulded in such perfect proportions that it presented a rare combination of youthful lightness and manly strength. His countenance, had you taken from it its deep thoughtfulness and its expression of calm intrepid bravery, might have belonged to the most lovely woman, so transparently blooming was his complexion, so regular his features, so blond and luxuriant his hair. Of all those present, he seemed the least concerned at the accident; he neither looked at the *caleche*, nor paid any attention to the offers of service that were screamed from a dozen mouths, but, drawing out his watch, asked his servant if the carriage was broken.

'Pann, the shafts are snapped, two of the springs are injured and the linchpin has flown.'

'How long will it take to repair them?'

'Twenty-four hours.'

'It is now four o'clock. See that everything be in order again by tomorrow's daybreak.'

'Pann, with these lazy Italians, I fear it will be impossible – '

'Ja pozwalam,'[201] replied the traveller, coldly, but decidedly. 'Pay double – triple – what you will, but let all be ready for the hour I have mentioned.'

Without another word, he walked towards the inn, followed by the crowd, teasing for alms. A few seconds ago they had all been active and healthy beings, so full of employment they could not afford to mend his *caleche* unless tempted by some extraordinary reward: now the men declared themselves cripples and invalids, the children were orphans the women helpless widows, and they would all die of hunger if his eccellenza did not bestow a few *grani*.[202] 'What a tedious race!' exclaimed the traveller, casting a handful of coins upon the ground, which caused a general scramble and enabled him to proceed unmolested. At the inn new torments awaited him: a fresh crowd, composed of the landlord, the landlady and their waiters and hostlers, gathered round and assailed him with innumerable questions. The landlord hoped none of his limbs were broken, and begged him to consider himself master of the house; the waiters desired to know at what hour he would sup, what fare he chose, how long he intended to stay, where he came from, whither he was going; and the landlady led him, ostentatiously, through all the rooms of the inn, expatiating endlessly upon the peculiar and in-describable advantages of each. Ineffably weary of their officiousness, the traveller at last traversed a long and spacious hall, and took refuge in a balcony that looked upon the Bay of Gaeta.

The inn is built upon the site of Cicero's villa. Beneath the balcony, and on each side, along the whole curve of the bay, stretched a thick grove of orange trees, which sloped down to the very verge of the Mediterranean. Balls of golden fruit, and blossoms faint with odour and fair as stars, studded this amphitheatre of dark foliage; and at its extremity the liquid light of the waves pierced the glossy leaves, mingling their blue splendour with earth's green paradise. Every rock and mountain glowed with a purple hue, so intense and soft they resembled violet vapours dissolving into the pale radiance of the evening sky. Far away in the deep broad flood of the ocean rose the two mountain islands of Ischia and Procida, between which

Vesuvius thrust in his jagged form, and his floating banner of snow-white smoke. The solitary heaven was without sun or moon, without a star or cloud, but smiled in that tender vestal light which speaks of eternal, immutable peace.

It would be difficult to define the feelings of the traveller as he gazed on this scene; his countenance, uplifted to heaven, was animated with a profound and impassioned melancholy, with an expression of an earnest and fervid pleading against some vast and inevitable wrong. He was thinking probably of his country, and while he contrasted its ruined villages and devastated fields with the splendour and glow of the fair land before him, was breathing inwardly a passionate appeal against that blind and cruel destiny which had consigned Poland to the desolating influence of Russian despotism.[203] His reverie was interrupted by the sound of a female voice singing in Polish among the orange trees at his feet. The singer was invisible; but the sweetness of her voice, and the singular reference of the words (the following prose translation conveys their meaning) to the thoughts of his own mind, filled the traveller with surprise:

When thou gazest upon the azure heaven, so mighty in its calm, do not say, O bright enchantment, hast thou no pity, that thou dawnest thus in unattainable loveliness upon my world-wearied eyes?

When the southern wind softly breathes, do not say reproachfully, Thy cradle is the ether of the morning sun, thou drinkest the odorous essence of myrtle and lemon blossoms; thou should'st bear upon thy wings all sweet emotions, all soft desires; why bringest thou then no healing to the anguish I endure?

Neither in the dark hour, when thou thinkest upon thy country and thy friends, say not with grief, They are lost! They are not! Say rather with joy, They were illustrious! and it is bliss to know that they have been!

It were wise in me to obey thy lesson, sweet songstress, thought the traveller; and, revolving in his mind the singularity of the serenade, he continued to gaze upon the trees below: there was no rustling amid their branches, no sound which told a human being was concealed beneath their foliage; nothing was heard beyond the almost imperceptible breathings of the evening air. Did such things exist anywhere but in the imagination of the poet? He could almost have believed that the spirit of that divine scene had assumed a human voice and human words to soothe his melancholy, so floating and airy had been the strain, so deep the silence that succeeded it. One moment more, and there arose from the same spot cries for help uttered in Italian, and shrieks of distress so piercing, they made the traveller fly with the speed of lightning through the great hall, down the staircase into the garden. The first object that met his eyes was the figure of a girl about sixteen, her one arm tightly embracing the stem of a tree, her other angrily repelling a young man who was endeavouring to drag her away.

'I will not go with you – I love you no longer, Giorgio, and go with you, I will not,' shrieked the girl, in tones of mingled violence and fear.

'You must – you shall,' retorted her aggressor, in a voice of thunder. 'I have found you again, and I won't be duped by your fooleries, Marietta . . . And who are you, and who begged you to interfere?' added he, turning fiercely upon the traveller, whose strong grasp had torn him from Marietta. 'An officer, as it should seem by your dress; be pleased to know that I am also an officer, and risk my displeasure no further.'

'No officer would ill-treat a defenceless girl,' the Pole replied, with quiet contempt.

At this taunt Giorgio quivered with rage. His features, handsome and regular as those of Italians generally are, became quite distorted. His hands with convulsive movements sought about his breast for the dagger that was concealed there, his dark flashing eyes fixed intently at the same time upon his adversary, as if he hoped the fiendish spirit that burned within them might previously annihilate him.

'Be on your guard – he is a perfect wretch,' cried Marietta, rushing towards her protector.

The arrival of several servants from the inn dispelled all idea of present danger; they dragged off Giorgio, telling him that, although the girl was his sister, he had no right to separate her from the *corps d'opéra*, with whom she was travelling through Gaeta.

'E vero, è verissimo,'[204] cried Marietta with joyful triumph. 'What is it to him if I like my liberty, and prefer wandering about, singing here and there, to being his unhappy par – '

'Marietta! beware! dare not to speak ill of me!' screamed the retiring Giorgio, looking back over his shoulder, and accompanying his words with a look of such frightful menace as completely subdued his sister.

She watched in anxious silence till he had disappeared, and then, with affectionate humility and a graceful quickness that allowed not of its prevention, knelt lightly down, and pressed the stranger's hand to her lips. 'You have more than repaid me for the song I sang to you,' she said, rising and leading the way to the inn, 'and, if you like it, I will sing others to you while you sup.'

'Are you a Pole?' enquired the traveller.

'A fine demand! how can I be a Pole? Did you not say yourself there was no longer any such country as Poland?'

'I? not that I recollect.'

'If you did not say it, confess at least that you thought it. The Poles are all become Russians, and for nothing in the world, signor, would I be a Russian. Why in all their language they have no word that expresses *honour*. No! rather than be a Russian, much as I hate it, I would go with Giorgio.'

'Are you an Italian?'

'No – not exactly.'

'What are you, then?'

'Um! I am what I am, who can be more? But, signor, one thing I must beg of you, do not ask me any questions about myself, nor any about Giorgio. I will sing to you, talk to you, wait upon you – anything of that kind you please, but I will not answer questions on those subjects.'

Seating herself upon a stool, in a dark corner of the traveller's apartment, as far removed as possible from him, and all other interruptions, Marietta passed the evening in playing on her guitar and singing. She was a most accomplished singer, possessing and managing all the intricacies of the art with perfect ease, but this scarcely excited admiration in comparison with the natural beauty of her voice. There was a profound melancholy in its intense sweetness that dissolved the soul of the traveller in grief. All that was dear to him in the memory of the past, the joys of home and childhood, the tenderness and truth of his first friendships, the glow of patriotism; every cherished hour, every endeared spot, all that he had loved, and all that he had lost upon earth, seemed again to live and again to fade as he listened to her strains. Without paying any attention to him, and apparently without any effort to herself, she breathed forth melody after melody for her own pleasure, like some lone nightingale that, in a home of green leaves, sings to cheer its solitude with sweet sounds. Her countenance and figure would have been beautiful had they been more fully developed. They resembled those sketches of a great artist in which there are only a few lightly-traced lines, but those are so full of spirit and meaning that you easily imagine what a masterpiece it would have been when finished.

The first visit of our traveller, on arriving next day at Naples, was to the Princess Dashkhoff. She was a Russian lady, whose high birth, immense wealth and talents for intrigue had procured for her the intimacy of half the crowned heads of Europe, and had made her all powerful at the Court of St Petersburg. Detesting the cold barbarism of her native country, she had established herself at Naples in a splendid mansion, near the Strada Nuova; and affecting an extravagant admiration for Italy, by her munificent patronage of the arts and artists, and by perpetual exhibitions of her own skill in drawing and singing, dancing and acting, had obtained the name of the Corinna of the North.[205] Her *salon* was the evening resort of the wise, the idle, the witty and the dissipated. Not to know Corinna was to be yourself unknown; and not to frequent her *conversazioni*[206] was, as far as society was concerned, to be banished from all that was fashionable or delightful in Naples.

It was the hour of evening reception. The Pole burned with impatience to speak to the princess, for on her influence, at Petersburg, depended the fate of a brother, the only being in existence he now cared for. A splendid suite of apartments, blazing with lights, crowded with company and furnished with the munificence of an Eastern harem, lay open before him; without allowing himself to be announced he entered them. When a highly imaginative mind is absorbed by some master feeling, all opposing contrasts, all glowing extremes, serve but to add depth and intensity to that feeling. The festal scene of marble columns garlanded by roses, the walls of Venetian mirror, reflecting the light of innumerable tapers, and the forms of lovely women and gay youths floating in the mazy dance seemed to him deceitful shows that veiled some frightful sorrow; and with eager rapid steps, as if borne along by the impulse of his own thoughts, he hurried past them. Scarcely knowing how he had arrived there, he at length found himself standing beside the princess in a marble colonnade open above to the moonlight and the stars of heaven and admitting at its sides the odorous air and blossoming almond trees of the adjacent garden.

'Ladislas!' exclaimed the lady, starting, 'is it possible – to see you here almost exceeds belief.'

After remaining some moments in deep silence, collecting and arranging his thoughts, the Pole replied. A conversation ensued, in so low a voice as to be only audible to themselves; from their attitudes and gestures it might be inferred that Ladislas was relating some tale of deep anguish, mixed with solemn and impressive adjurations to which the princess listened with a consenting tranquillising sympathy.

They issued from the recess, walked up the colonnade and entered a small temple that terminated it. From the centre of its airy dome hung a lighted alabaster lamp of a boat-like shape, beneath which a youthful female was seated alone sketching a range of moonlight hills that appeared between the columns. 'Idalie,' said the princess, 'I have brought you a new subject for your pencil – and such a subject, my love – one whose fame has already made him dear to your imagination; no less a person than the hero of Ostroleka, the Vistula and the Belvedere. So call up one of those brightest, happiest moods of your genius, in which all succeeds to you, and enrich my album with his likeness,' spreading it before her.

It is difficult to refuse any request to a person who has just granted us an important favour. Ladislas suffered himself to be seated, and as soon as the princess had quitted them, the gloom which had shadowed his brow at the names of Ostroleka, the Vistula and the Belvedere vanished. The surpassing beauty of the young artist would have changed the heaviest penance into a pleasure. She was lovely as one of Raphael's Madonnas; and, like them, there was a silent beauty in her presence that struck the most superficial beholder with astonishment and satisfaction. Her hair, of a golden and burnished brown (the colour of the autumnal foliage illuminated by the setting sun), fell in gauzy wavings round her face, throat and shoulders. Her small clear forehead, gleaming with gentle thought; her curved, soft, and rosy lips; the delicate moulding of the lower part of the face, expressing purity and integrity of nature, were all perfectly Grecian. Her hazel eyes, with their arched lids and dark arrowy lashes, pierced the soul with their full and thrilling softness. She was clad in long and graceful drapery, white as snow; but, pure as this garment was, it seemed a rude disguise to the resplendent softness of the limbs it enfolded. The delicate light that gleamed from the alabaster lamp above them was a faint simile of the ineffable spirit of love that burned within Idalie's fair transparent frame; and the one trembling shining star of evening that palpitates responsively to happy lovers, never seemed more divine or more beloved than she did to Ladislas, as she sat there, now fixing a timid but attentive gaze upon his countenance, and then dropping it upon the paper before her. And not alone for Ladislas was this hour the dawn of passionate love. The same spell was felt in the heart of Idalie, veiling the world and lifting her spirit into vast and immeasurable regions of unexplored delight. One moment their eyes met and glanced upon each other, the look of exalted, of eternal love, mute, blessed and inexpressible. Their lids fell and were raised no more. Rapture thrilled their breasts and swelled their full hearts, a rapture felt but not seen; for motionless, and in deep silence, as if every outward faculty were absorbed in reverence, they continued, each inwardly knowing, hearing, seeing nothing but the divine influence and attraction of the other.

I know not if the portrait was finished. I believe it was not. Noiselessly
Idalie arose and departed to seek the princess, and Ladislas followed.
'Who is that lovely being?' enquired an English traveller sometime
afterward, pointing out Idalie from a group of ladies. 'A Polish girl – a
protégée of mine,' was the reply of the princess; 'a daughter of one of
Kosciusko's[207] unfortunate followers, who died here poor and unknown.
She has a great genius for drawing and painting, but she is so different
in her nature from the generality of people that I am afraid she will
never get on in the world. All the family are wild and strange. There is
a brother, who they say is a complete ruffian; brave as a Pole and
unprincipled as an Italian; a villain quite varnished in picturesque, like
one of your Lord Byron's corsairs and giaours. Then there is a younger
sister; the most uncontrollable little creature, who chose to pretend my
house was insupportable, and ran away into Calabria or Campagna, and
set up as a *prima donna*. But these, to be sure, are the children of a
second wife, an Italian; and Idalie, I must confess, has none of their
lawlessness, but is remarkably gentle and steady.'

Disgusted with heartless conversation, which disturbed his mood of
ecstacy, Ladislas hastily quitted the Dashkhoff palace and entered the
Villa Reale, whose embowering trees promised solitude. Not one
straggler of the many gay crowds that frequent this luxurious garden
from morning till midnight was now to be seen. With its straight walks
buried in gloom and shadow; its stone fonts of sleeping water; its marble
statues, its heaven-pointing obelisks, and the tingling silence of its
midnight air, it was holy and calm as a deserted oratory, when the last
strain of the vesper hymn has died away, the last taper has ceased to
burn, the last censer has been flung, and both priests and worshippers
have departed. Ladislas cast himself upon a stone seat in the ilex grove
that skirts the margin of the bay. 'I dreamt not of love,' he exclaimed, 'I
sought her not! I had renounced life and all its train of raptures, hopes
and joys. Cold, and void of every wish, the shadow of death lay upon my
heart; suddenly she stood before me, lovely as an angel that heralds
departed spirits to the kingdom of eternal bliss. Fearless, but mild, she
poured the magic of her gaze upon my soul. I speak the word of the
hour. She shall be mine – or I will die!'

Reclining in the ilex grove, Ladislas passed the remaining hours of
that too-short night, entranced in bliss, as if the bright form of his
beloved were still shining beside him. Gradually, every beauty of
the wondrous and far-famed Bay of Naples impressed itself upon his
attention. The broad and beamless moon sinking behind the tall elms
of Posillipo – the broken starlight on the surface of the waves – their

rippling sound as they broke at his feet – Sorrento's purple promontory, and the gentle wind that blew from it – the solitary grandeur of Capri's mountain-island, rising out of the middle of the bay, a colossal sphinx guarding two baths of azure light – Vesuvius breathing its smoke, and flame, and sparks, into the cloudless ether – all became mingled in inexplicable harmony with his new-born passion, and were indelibly associated with his recollection of that night.

The next morning Idalie was sketching in the Villa Reale. She had seated herself on the outside of a shady alley. Two persons passed behind her, and the childish, petulant voice of one of them drew her attention. That voice, so sweet even in its impatience, certainly belonged to her fugitive sister. 'It is she!' exclaimed Idalie, gliding swift as thought between the trees, and folding the speaker to her bosom. 'Marietta, – my dear little Marietta! at last you are come back again. *Cattivella!*[208] now promise to stay with me. You know not how miserable I have been about you.'

'No! I cannot promise anything of the kind,' replied Marietta, playing with the ribbons of her guitar. 'I choose to have my liberty.'

Idalie's arms sank, and her eyes were cast upon the ground when she heard the cold and decided tone in which this refusal was pronounced. On raising the latter, they glanced upon the companion of her sister, and were filled with unconquerable emotion at discovering Ladislas, the elected of her heart.

'I met your sister here a few minutes ago,' explained he, partaking her feelings; 'and having been so fortunate the other day as to render her a slight service – '

'Oh, yes,' interrupted Marietta; 'I sang for him a whole evening at Gaeta. It was a curious adventure. His carriage was overturned close to the inn. I had arrived there half an hour before, and was walking in an orange grove near the spot, and saw the accident happen, and heard him speak in Polish to his servant. My heart beat with joy to behold one belonging to that heroic nation. He looked wondrous melancholy: I thought it must be about his country, so I crept as softly as a mouse among the trees under his balcony, and sang him a salve-song in Polish. I *improvised* it on the spur of the moment. I do not very well recollect it, but it was about azure heavens, southern winds, myrtle and lemon blossoms, and the illustrious unfortunate; and it ought to have pleased him. Just as I had finished, out starts our blessed brother, Giorgio, from the inn, and began one of his most terrific bothers. Imagine how frightened I was, for I thought he was gone to Sicily with his regiment. However, they got him away, and I followed this stranger into his room, and sang to him the rest of the evening. All my best songs, the 'Mio ben quando verrà', 'Nina pazza per Amore', the 'All' armi' of Generali, the 'Dolce cara patria' from *Tancredi*, the 'Deh calma' from *Otello*[209] – all my whole stock, I assure you.' Thus rattled on Marietta; and then, as if her quick eye had already discovered the secret of their attachment, she added, with an arch smile, 'But don't be frightened, Idalie, though his eyes filled with tears while I sang, as yours often do, not a word of praise did the Sarmatian bestow on me.'

'Then return and live with me, dear Marietta, and I will praise you as much and more than you desire.'

'Santa Maria del Piè di Grotta![210] What a tiresome person you are, Idalie. When you have got an idea into your head, an earthquake would not get it out again. Have I not told you that I will not. If you knew the motive, you would approve my resolution. I said I liked my liberty, and so forth, but that was not the reason of my flight. I do not choose to have anything to do with Giorgio and the princess; for, believe me, dearest Idalie, disgraceful as my present mode of life seems to you, it is innocence itself compared with the crimes they were leading me into.'

'Some suspicion of this did once cross my mind,' her sister replied with a sigh, 'but I rejected it as too horrible. Dear child, think no more about them. Do you not know that I have left the princess's house, and am living by myself in a little pavilion far up on the Strada Nuova. There you need not fear their molestations.'

'Is not Giorgio, then, with you?'

'No, I have not seen him for some time. I doubt if he be in Naples.'

'So, Messer Giorgio, you have deceived me again. But I might have known that, for he never speaks a word of truth. Be assured, however, he is in Naples, for I caught a glimpse of him this morning, mounting the hill that leads to the barracks at Pizzofalcone, and he is as intimate with the princess as ever, though she pretends to disown him. As for me, I am engaged at San Carlos; the writing is signed and sealed, and cannot be broken without forfeiting a heavy sum of money; otherwise I should be happy to live peacefully with you; for you know not, Idalie, all I have had to suffer; how sad and ill-treated I have been! how often pinched with want and hunger; and worse than that, when Giorgio takes it into his head to pursue me, and plants himself in the pit, fixing his horrible looks upon me as I sing! how many times I have rushed out of the theatre, and spent the nights in the great wide Maremma,[211] beset by robbers, buffaloes and wild boars, till I was almost mad with fear and bewilderment. There is a curse upon our family, I think. Did not our father once live in a splendid castle of his own, with a hundred retainers to wait upon him; and do you remember the miserable garret in which he died? But I cannot stay any longer. I am wanted at the rehearsal; so, farewell, dearest Idalie. Be you at least happy, and leave me to fulfil the evil destiny that hangs over our race.'

'No! No!' exclaimed Ladislas, 'that must not be – the writing must be cancelled' – and then, with the affection and unreserve of a brother, he entered into their sentiments; with sweet and persuasive arguments overcame their scruples of receiving a pecuniary obligation from him, and finally, taking Marietta by the hand, led her away to San Carlos in order to cancel her engagement.

And in another hour it was cancelled. Marietta was once more free and joyful; and, affectionate as old friends, the three met again in the little pavilion, which was Idalie's home. It stood alone in a myrtle wood on the last of the green promontories which form the Strada Nuova and separate the Bay of Naples from the Bay of Baia – a lonely hermitage secluded from the noise and turmoil of the city, whose only visitors were the faint winds of morning and evening, the smiles of the fair Italian heaven, its wandering clouds and, perchance, a solitary bird. From every part of the building you could see the Baian Ocean sparkling breathlessly beneath the sun; through the windows and the columns of the portico you beheld the mountains of the distant coast shining on, hour after hour, like amethysts in a thrilling vapour of purple transparent light, so ardent yet halcyon, so bright and unreal, a poet would have chosen it to emblem the radiant atmosphere that glows around Elysian isles of eternal peace and joy. Marietta soon left the building to join some fisher boys who were dancing the tarantella upon the beach below. Idalie took her drawing, which was her daily employment, and furnished her the means of subsistence, and Ladislas sat by her side. There was no sound of rolling carriages, no tramp of men and horse, no distant singing, no one speaking near; the wind awoke no rustling amid the leaves of the myrtle wood, and the wave died without a murmur on the shore. Ladislas's deep but melodious voice alone broke the crystal silence of the noonday air. Italy was around him, robed in two splendours of blue and green; but he was an exile, and the recollections of his native land thronged into his memory, and oppressed him with their numbers and their life. During the three months it had taken him to effect his escape from Warsaw to Naples, his lips had been closed in silence, while his mind had been wrapped in the gloom of the dreadful images that haunted it. In Idalie's countenance there was that expression of innocence and sublimity of soul, of purity and strength, that excited the warmest admiration, and inspired sudden and deep confidence. She looked like some supernatural being that walks through the world untouched by its corruptions; like one that unconsciously, yet with delight, confers pleasure and peace; and Ladislas felt that, in speaking to her of the dark sorrows of his country, they would lose their mortal weight and be resolved into beauty by her sympathy. In glowing terms he described the heroic struggle of Poland for liberty; the triumph and exultation that had filled every bosom during the few months they were free; the hardships and privations they had endured, the deeds of daring bravery of the men, the heroism it had awakened in the women; and then its fall – the return of the Russians; the horrible character of Russian despotism, its sternness and deceit, its pride and selfish ignorance; the loss of public and private integrity, the disbelief of good, the blighted, hopeless, joyless life endured by those whom it crushes beneath its servitude.

Thus passed the hours of the forenoon. Then Ladislas fixing his eyes upon the coast of Baia, and expressing at the same time his impatience to visit that ancient resort of heroes and of emperors, Idalie led the way by a small path down the hill to the beach. There they found a skiff dancing idly to and fro upon the waves, and, unmooring it from its rocky haven, embarked in it. It had been sweet to mark the passage of that light bark freighted with these happy lovers, when borne by its sails it swept through the little ocean-channel that lies between the beaked promontories of the mainland and the closing cliffs of the island of Nisida; and when with gentler motion it glided into the open expanse of the Bay of Baia, and cut its way through the translucent water above the ruins of temples and palaces overgrown by seaweed, on which the rays of the sun were playing, creating a thousand rainbow hues that varied with every wave that flowed over them. In all that plane of blue light it was the only moving thing; and as if it had been the child of the ocean that bore it and the sun that looked down on it, it sped gaily along in their smiles past the fortress where Brutus and Cassius sought shelter after the death of Caesar; past the temples of Jupiter and Neptune; by the ruins of that castle in which three Romans once portioned out the world between them, to the Cumaean hill that enshadows the beloved Linternum of Scipio Africanus,[212] and in which he died. The whole of this coast is a paradise of natural beauty, investing with its own loveliness the time-eaten wrecks with which it is strewn; the mouldering past is mingled with the vivid present; ruin and grey annihilation are decked in eternal spring. The woody windings of the shore reveal, in their deep recesses, the gleaming marble fragments of the abodes of ancient heroes; the verdurous hues of the promontories mingle with the upright columns of shattered temples or clothe, with nature's voluptuous bloom, the pale funereal urns of departed gods; while the foliage and the inland fountains, and the breaking waves upon the shore, were murmuring around their woven minstrelsy of love and joy. Earth, sea and sky blazed like three gods, with tranquil but animated loveliness; with a splendour that did not dazzle – with a richness that could not satiate. The air on that beautiful warm coast was as a field of fragrance; the refreshing sea-breeze seemed to blow from paradise, quickening their senses and bringing to them the odour of a thousand unknown blossoms. 'What world is this?' exclaimed Ladislas, in a tone of rapture that nearly answered its own question. 'I could imagine I had entered an enchanted garden; four heavens surround me; the one above; the pure element beneath me with its waves that shine and tremble as stars; the adorned earth that hangs over it; and the heaven of delight they create within my breast. Morning is here a rose, day a tulip, night a lily; evening is, like morning, again a rose, and life seems a choral hymn of beautiful and glowing sentiments that I go singing to myself as I wander along this perpetual path of flowers.'

It was night ere they again reached the pavilion. It stood dark and deserted in the clear moonshine; the door was locked; the windows and their outer shutters had been closed from within, so securely as to deny all admittance, unless by breaking them open, which the solid nature of the shutters rendered almost impossible. After calling and knocking repeatedly without obtaining any answer, it became evident that Marietta had quitted the dwelling. In the first moment of surprise which this occurrence occasioned, they had not observed a written sheet of paper, of a large size, which lay unfolded and placed directly before the door, as if to attract attention. Idalie took it up and read the following lines, traced by Marietta.

Oh, Idalie! what a fiendish thing is life. But a few hours ago, how calm and secure we were in happiness – now danger and perhaps destruction is our portion. One chance yet remains. The moment you get this, persuade – not only persuade – but compel that adorable stranger to fly instantly from Naples. He is not safe here an instant longer. Do not doubt what I say, or his life may be the forfeit. How can I impress this on your mind. I would not willingly betray anyone, but how else can I save him? Giorgio has been here. Oh! the frightful violence of that man. He raved like an insane person, and let fall such dark and bloody hints as opened worlds of horror to me. I am gone to discover what I can. I know his haunts, and his associates, and shall soon find out if there be any truth in what he threatens. I could not await your return, neither dare I leave the pavilion open. Who knows if, in the interval between my departure and your return, an assassin might not conceal himself within, and your first welcome be to see the stranger fall lifeless at your feet. His every step is watched by spies armed for his destruction. I know not what to do – and yet it seems to me that my going may possibly avert the catastrophe.

MARIETTA

Ladislas listened to these lines unmoved; but the effect they produced on Idalie was dreadful. She gave implicit credence to them, and every word sounded as a knell. She lost all presence of mind; every reflection that might have taught her to avert the stroke she so much dreaded, was swallowed up in anguish, as if the deed that was to be consummated were already done. What task can be more difficult than to describe the overwhelming agony which heavy and unexpected misery produces. To have lived the day that Idalie had just lived – a day in which all the beauty of existence had been unveiled to its very depths; to have dreamt as she had done, a dream of love that steeped her soul in divine, and almost uncommunicable joy; and now to sink from this pinnacle of happiness into a black and lampless cavern, the habitation of death, whose spectral form and chilling spirit was felt through all the air! This is but a feeble metaphor of the sudden transition from rapture to misery which Idalie experienced. She looked upon Ladislas, and beheld him bright and full of life; the roseate hues of health upon his cheek, his eyes beaming with peaceful joy, his noble countenance varying not in the least from that imperturbable and godlike self-possession which was its habitual expression. And as her imagination made present to her the fatal moment when beneath the dagger of the assassin this adored being should sink bleeding, wounded, and then be ever lost in death, her blood rushed to her heart; a deadly pause ensued, from which she awoke in a bewildering mist of horror. The still air and quite moonshine to her seemed brooding mischief; a thousand shadows that proceeded from no one, but were the creatures of her distressed brain, flitted around, and filled the empty space of the portico. Poor Idalie! an eternity of bliss would have been dearly bought at the price of that moment's over-whelming anguish! Ladislas beheld her excess of emotion with pain, in which, however, all was not pain, for it was blended with that triumphant exultation that a lover ever feels when he for the first time becomes assured that he is beloved by the object of his love with an affection tender and intense as his own.

As soon as Idalie recovered some presence of mind, with passionate supplications she entreated Ladislas to leave her, to fly this solitary spot and to seek safety amid the crowded streets of Naples. He would not hear of this; he gently remonstrated with her upon the unreasonableness of her terrors, urging how little probable it was that his passing *rencontre*[213] with Giorgio at Gaeta could have awakened in him such a deadly spirit of revenge as Marietta represented. He viewed the whole thing lightly, attributing it either to the vivacity of Marietta's imagination, which had made her attach a monstrous import to some angry expressions of her brother, or looking upon it as some merry device which she had contrived, in order to frighten them; he tranquillised Idalie by assurances that they would shortly see her wild sister return laughing and full of glee at the success of her plot. In this expectation two hours passed away, but still no Marietta appeared, and it had grown too late to seek another shelter without exposing Idalie to the slander of evil-minded people. They passed the rest of the night therefore in the portico, Idalie sometimes pale and breathless, with recurring fears, and sometimes calm and happy, as Ladislas poured forth his tale of passionate love. His feelings on the contrary were pure and unalloyed. Where Idalie was, there was the whole universe to him; where she was not, there was only a formless void. He had an insatiable thirst for her presence, which only grew intenser with the enjoyment of its own desire; and he blessed the fortunate occurrence that prolonged his bliss during hours which otherwise would have been spent pining in absence from her. No other considerations intruded. Blessings kindled within his eyes as he gazed upon that lovely countenance and faultless form, and angels might have envied the happiness he felt.

Morning came, bright and serene; the sun arose, the ocean and the mountains again resumed their magic splendour; the myrtle-woods and every minuter bloom of the garden shone out beneath the sun, and the whole earth was a happy form made perfect by the power of light. They recollected that they had promised to join the Princess Dashkhoff, and a large party of her friends, at eight o'clock, in an excursion to Paestum. The point of meeting was the shore of the Villa Reale, where the numerous guests were to embark in a steamer which had been engaged for the occasion. In Idalie's present homeless and uncertain condition, this plan offered some advantages. It would enable them to pass the day in each other's society under the auspices of the princess, and it was to be hoped that on their return the mystery of Marietta's disappearance would be unravelled and Idalie would find her home once more open to her. They had scarcely settled to go ere one of those horse *calessini*[214] which ply in the streets of Naples was seen coming towards them. Its driver, a ragged boy, sat on the shaft, singing as he drove; another urchin, all in tatters, stood as lackey behind, and between them sat Marietta; the paleness of fear was on her cheeks, and her eyes had the staggered affrighted look of one who has gazed upon some appalling horror. She hastily descended, and bade the *calessino* retire to some distance, and await further orders. 'Why is he yet here?' said she to her sister. 'You foolish blind Idalie, why did you not mind my letter – too proud I suppose to obey any but yourself; but mark, you would not hear my warnings – we shall lose him, and you will feel them in your heart's core.' She then, with all the violent gesticulation of an Italian, threw herself at the feet of Ladislas, and with a countenance that expressed her own full conviction in what she said, besought him to fly instantly, not only from Naples, but from Italy, for his life would never be safe in that land of assassins and traitors. With entreaties almost as violent as her own, Ladislas and Idalie urged her to explain, but this only threw her into a new frenzy; she wept and tore her hair; she declared the peril was too urgent to admit of explanation – every moment was precious – another's hour's stay in Naples would be his death.

The situation of Ladislas was a curious one. He had served in the Russian campaigns against Persia and Turkey, and had been there daily exposed to the chances of destruction; in the late struggle between Poland and Russia, he had performed actions of such determined and daring bravery as had made his name a glory to his countrymen, and a terror to their enemies. In all these exploits he had devoted himself so unreservedly to death that his escape was considered as a miraculous interposition of heaven. It was not to be expected that this Mars in a human form, this Achilles who had braved death in a thousand shapes, should now consent to fly before the uplifted finger and visionary warnings of a dream-sick girl, for such Marietta appeared to him to be. He pitied her sufferings, endeavoured to soothe her, but asserted he had seen no reason that could induce him to quit Naples.

A full quarter of an hour elapsed before an explanation could be wrung from Marietta. The chaos that reigned in her mind may easily be imagined. She had become possessed of a secret which involved the life of two persons. Ladislas refused to save himself unless she revealed what might place her brother's life in jeopardy. Whichever way she looked, destruction closed the view. Nature had bestowed on her a heart exquisitely alive to the sufferings of others; a mind quick in perceiving the nicest lines of moral rectitude and strenuous in endeavouring to act up to its perceptions. Any deviations in her conduct from these principles had been the work of a fate that, strong and fierce as a tempest, had bent down her weak youth like a reed beneath its force. She had once loved Giorgio; he had played with and caressed her in infancy – with the fond patronage of an elder brother had procured her the only indulgences her orphaned childhood had ever known. Fraternal love called loudly on her not to endanger his life; gratitude as loudly called on her not to allow her benefactor to become his victim. This last idea was too horrible to be endured. The present moment is ever all-powerful with the young, and Marietta related what she knew.

Well might the poor child be wild and disordered. She had passed the night in the catacombs of San Gennaro, under Capo di Monte. In these subterranean galleries were held the nightly meetings of the band of desperate *bravi*[215] of whom Giorgio was in secret the chief. The entrance to the catacombs is in a deserted vineyard, and is overgrown by huge aloes; rooted in stones and sharp rocks, they lift their thorny leaves above the opening, and conceal it effectually. A solitary fig-tree that grows near renders the spot easily recognisable by those already acquainted with the secret. The catacombs themselves are wide winding caves, the burial-place of the dead of past ages. Piles of human bones, white and bleached by time, are heaped along the rocky sides of these caverns. In one of these walks, while they were friends, Giorgio had shown the place to Marietta. In those days he feared not to entrust his mysterious way of life to her; for although in all common concerns she was wild and untractable, yet in all that touched the interests of those few whom she loved, Marietta was silent and reserved as Epicharis[216] herself. The menaces Giorgio let fall in his visit on the preceding forenoon had excited her highest alarm, and she determined, at any risk, to learn the extent of the danger that hung over the stranger. After waiting in vain for Idalie's return till the close of evening, she had hastened to Capo di Monte, entered the catacombs alone and, concealed behind a pile of bones, had awaited the arrival of the confederates. They assembled at midnight. Their first subject of consultation was the stranger. Giorgio acquainted them with his history, which he told them had been communicated to him that very morning by a Russian lady of high consequence, who had likewise charged him with the business he had to unfold to them. He described Ladislas as a fugitive, unprotected by any government; he bore about his person certain papers which had been found in the palace of Warsaw and were the confidential communications of the Russian Autocrat to his brother the Viceroy of

Poland, and were of such a nature as to rouse all Europe in arms against their writer. These papers had been entrusted to Ladislas, whose intention was to proceed to Paris and publish them there. Private business, however, of the greatest importance, had forced him to visit Naples before going to Paris. The Russian government had traced him to Naples, and had empowered a certain Russian lady to take any step, or go any lengths, in order to obtain these papers from Ladislas. This lady had made Giorgio her emissary; her name he carefully concealed, but Marietta averred, from his description, that it could be no other than the Princess Dashkhoff. After much consulting among the band, the assassination of the Pole had been decided upon. This seemed to be the only sure method, for he carried the papers ever about his person, was distinguished for his bravery and if openly attacked would resist to the last. Giorgio was no stickler in the means he employed, and told his companions he had the less reason to be so in this case as he had received assurances from the highest quarter that his crime should go unpunished and the reward be enormous. Ladislas was almost unknown in Naples; the government would not interest itself for a fugitive, without passport, country or name; and what friends had he here to enquire into the circumstances of his destruction or to interest themselves to avenge it?

Such was Marietta's tale, and Ladislas instantly acknowledged the necessity of flight. He was too well acquainted with the perfidy and barbarism of the Russians to doubt that even a lady of a rank so distinguished as the Princess Dashkhoff might be induced to undertake as foul a task as that attributed to her by Marietta. The worldly and artificial manners of this lady in an Italian or a French woman would only have resulted from habits of intrigue; but a Russian, unaccustomed to look on human life as sacred, taught by the government of her own country that cruelty and treachery are venial offences, wholly destitute of a sense of honour, concealed, under such an exterior, vices the most odious, and a callousness to guilt unknown in more civilised lands. Ladislas knew this; and he knew that the badness of the Neapolitan government afforded scope for crime which could not exist elsewhere; and he felt that on every account it were better to withdraw himself immediately from the scene of danger.

While musing on these things, Idalie's beseeching eyes were eloquent in imploring him to fly. He consented; but a condition was annexed to his consent, that Idalie should share his flight. He urged his suit with fervour. It were easy for them on a very brief notice to seek the young lady's confessor, induce him to bestow on them the nuptial benediction, and thus to sanctify their departure together. Marietta seconded the young lover's entreaties, and Idalie, blushing and confused, could only reply, 'My accompanying you could only increase your danger, and facilitate the bravo's means of tracing you. How could I get a passport? How leave this place?'

'I have a plan for all,' replied Ladislas; and he then related that the *Sully* steam-packet lay in the harbour of Naples, ready to sail on the shortest notice; he would engage that for their conveyance, and so speedily bid adieu to the shores of Naples, and all its perils.

'But that boat,' exclaimed Idalie, 'that steam-packet is the very one engaged by the princess for our excursion to Paestum, this morning.'

This, for a time, seemed to disarrange their schemes, but they considered that no danger could happen to Ladislas while one of a party of pleasure with the princess, who from this act of his would be quite unsuspicious of his intended departure. At night, upon their return from Paestum, when the rest of the party should have disembarked at Naples, Ladislas and Idalie would remain on board, and the vessel immediately commence its voyage for France. This plan thus assumed a very feasible appearance, while Ladislas, in accents of fond reproach, asked Idalie wherefore she refused to share his fortunes, and accompany him in his journey; and Marietta, clapping her hands exclaimed, 'She consents! she consents! Do not ask any more, she has already yielded. We will all return to Naples. Ladislas shall proceed immediately to seek out the captain of the *Sully*, and arrange all with him; while, without loss of time, we will proceed to the convent of Father Basil, and get everything ready by the time Ladislas shall join us, which must be with as much speed as he can contrive.'

Idalie silently acquiesced in this arrangement, and Ladislas kissed her hand with warm and overflowing gratitude. They now contrived to stow themselves in the little *calessino*, and as they proceeded on their way, Ladislas said: 'We seem to have forgotten the future destiny of our dear Marietta all this time. The friendless condition in which we shall leave her fills me with anxiety. She is the preserver of my life, and we are both under the deepest obligations to her. What shall you do, Marietta, when we are gone?'

'Fear not for me,' exclaimed the wild girl, 'it is necessary I should remain behind to arrange those things which Idalie's sudden departure will leave in sad disorder; but you will see me soon in Paris, for how can I exist apart from my sister?'

When near to Naples, Ladislas alighted from the *calessino*, and directed his steps towards the port, while the fair girls proceeded on their way to

the convent. What the bashful conscious Idalie would have done without her sister's help, it is difficult to guess. Marietta busied herself
about all: won over the priest to the sudden marriage, contrived to put
up articles of dress for the fair bride's journey, and thinking of everything, with far more watchfulness and care than if her own fate had
depended on the passing hour, seemed the guardian angel of the
lovers. Ladislas arrived at the convent; he had been successful with the
master of the steam-packet, and all was prepared. Marietta heard this
from his own lips, and carried the happy news to Idalie. He did not see
her till they met at the altar, where, kneeling before the venerable
priest, they were united for ever. And now time, as it sped on, gave
them no moment to indulge their various and overpowering feelings.
Idalie embraced her sister again and again, and entreating her to join
them speedily in Paris, made her promise to write, and then, escorted
by her husband, proceeded to the *Sully*, on board of which most of the
party were already assembled.

The smoke lifted its stream of dishevelled tresses to the wind, which
was right aft; the engine began to work, and the wheels to run their
round. The blue wave was disturbed in its tranquil water, and cast back
again in sheeted spray on its brother wave. Farewell to Naples! That
Elysian city, as the poet justly calls it; that favourite of sea, and land,
and sky. The hills that surround it smooth their rugged summits, and
descend into gentle slopes and opening defiles to receive its buildings
and habitations. Temples, domes and marble palaces are ranged round
the crescent form of the bay, and above them arise dark masses and
wooded clefts and fair gardens whose trees are ever vernal. Before it the
mighty sea binds its wild streams, and smoothes them into gentlest
waves, as they kiss the silver, pebbly shore, and linger with dulcet
murmur around the deep-based promontories. The heaven – who has
not heard of an Italian heaven? – one intense diffusion, one serene
omnipresence, forever smiling in inextinguishable beauty above the
boundless sea and forever bending in azure mirth over the flowing
outlines of the distant mountains.

The steamboat proceeded on its equal and swift course along the
shores, each varying in beauty and redolent with sweets. They first
passed Castel-a-Mare, and then the abrupt promontories on which
Sorrento and ancient Amalfi are situated. The sublimity and intense
loveliness of the scene wrapped in delight each bosom not inaccessible
to pure and lofty emotions. The hills, covered with ilex, dark laurel and
bright-leaved myrtle, were mirrored in the pellucid waves, which the
lower branches caressed and kissed as the winds waved them. Behind

arose other hills, also covered with woods; and, more distant, forming the grand background, was sketched the huge ridge of lofty Apennines, which extends even to the foot of Italy. Still proceeding on their way to Paestum, they exchanged the rocky beach for a low and dreary shore. The dusky mountains retired inland, and leaving a waste, the abode of malaria and the haunt of robbers, the landscape assumed a gloomy magnificence in place of the romantic and picturesque loveliness which had before charmed their eyes. Ladislas leaned from the side of the vessel, and gazed upon the beauty of nature with sentiments too disturbed for happiness. He was annoyed by the unpropitious presence of the idle and the gay. He saw Idalie in the midst of them, and did not even wish to join her while thus situated. He shrank into himself, and tried, forgetting the immediate discomforts of his position, to think only of that paradise into which love had led him to compensate for his patriotic sorrows. He strove patiently to endure the tedious hours of this never-ending day, during which he must play a false part, and see his bride engaged by others. While his attention was thus occupied, the voice of the Princess Dashkhoff startled him, and looking up, he wondered how a face that seemed so bland, and a voice that spoke so fair, could hide so much wickedness and deceit. As the hours passed on, his situation became irksome in the extreme. Once or twice he drew near Idalie, and tried to disengage her from the crowd; but each time he saw the princess watching him stealthily, while his young bride, with feminine prudence, avoided every opportunity of conversing apart with him. Ladislas could ill endure this. He began to fancy that he had a thousand things to say, and that their mutual safety depended on his being able to communicate them to her. He wrote a few lines hastily on the back of a letter, with a pencil, conjuring her to find some means of affording him a few minutes' conversation, and telling her that if this could not be done before, he should take occasion, while the rest of the company were otherwise occupied, to steal from them that evening to the larger temple, and there to await her joining him, for that everything depended on his being able to speak to her. He scarcely knew what he meant as he wrote this; but driven by contradiction and impatience, and desirous of learning exactly how she meant to conduct herself on the princess's disembarking at Naples, it seemed to him of the last importance that his request should be complied with. He was folding the paper, when the princess was at his side, and addressed him. 'A sonnet, Count Ladislas; surely a poetic imagination inspires you; may I not see it?' And she held out her hand. Taken unaware, Ladislas darted at her a look of indignation and horror, which made her step back trembling and in surprise. Was she discovered? The idea was fraught with terror. His revenge would surely be as fierce as the wrongs he suffered might well inspire. But Ladislas, perceiving the indiscretion of his conduct, masked his sensations with a smile, and replied, 'They are words of a Polish song, which I wish Idalie to translate for the amusement of your friends;' and stepping forward he gave Idalie the paper, and made his request. All pressed to know what the song was. Idalie glanced at the writing, and changing colour, was scarcely able to command her voice to make such an excuse as the imprudence of her husband rendered necessary. She said that it required time and thought, and that she could not at the moment comply; then crushing the paper between her trembling fingers, began confusedly to talk of something else. The company interchanged smiles, but even the princess only suspected some loverlike compliment to her protégée. 'Nay,' she said, 'we must at least know the subject of these verses: what is it? Tell us, I entreat you.' 'Treachery,' said Ladislas, unable to control his feelings. The Princess became ashy-pale; all her self-possession fled, and she turned from the searching glance of the Pole with a sickness of heart which almost punished her for her crimes.

They were now drawing near their destination. Idalie, grasping the paper, longed to read it before they should reach the shore. She tried to recede from the party, and Ladislas, watching her movements, in order to facilitate her designs entered into conversation with the princess. He had effectually roused her fears and her curiosity, and she eagerly seized the opportunity which he offered her of conversing with him, endeavouring to find out whether he indeed suspected anything, or whether her own guilty conscience suggested the alarm with which his strange expression had filled her. Ladislas thus contrived to engross her entire attention, and led her insensibly towards the stern of the vessel; and as they leant over its side, and gazed on the waters beneath, Idalie was effectually relieved from all observation. She now disengaged herself from the rest of the party, and walking forward, read the lines pencilled by Ladislas. Then, terrified by the secret they contained, and unaccustomed to bear the weight of concealment – she tore the paper, as if fearful that its contents might be guessed, and was about to throw the fragments into the sea, when gazing cautiously round, she perceived the position of the princess and Ladislas, and was aware that the lady's quick eye would soon discern the floating scraps as the boat passed on. Idalie feared the least shadow of danger, so she retreated from the vessel's side, but still anxious to get rid of the perilous papers, she determined to throw them into the hold. She approached it, and looked down. Had the form of a serpent met her eye, she had not been more horror-struck; a shriek hovered on her lips, but with a strong effort she repressed it and, staggering on, leant against the mast, trembling and aghast. She could not be deceived; it was Giorgio's dark and scowling eye that she had encountered; his sinister countenance, upturned, could not be mistaken. Was danger, then, so near, so pressing or so inevitable? How could she convey the fatal intelligence to her husband, and put him on his guard? She remembered his written request, with which she had previously determined in prudence not to comply. But it would now afford her an opportunity, should no other offer, of informing him of the unexpected messmate which the crew had on board.

Thus perfidy, dark hate and trembling fear possessed the hearts of these human beings, who, had a cursory observer seen them as they glided over that sea of beauty, beneath the azure heaven, along that enchanted shore, attended by every luxury, waited on by every obvious blessing of life – he would have imagined that they had been selected from the world for the enjoyment of perfect happiness. But sunny sky and laughing ocean appeared to Idalie only as the haunt and resort of tigers and serpents; a dark mist seemed to blot the splendour of the sky, as the guilty souls of her fellow-creatures cast their deforming shadows over its brightness.

They had now arrived close on the low shore, and horses and two or three light open carriages were at the water's edge to convey them to the temples. They landed. Ladislas presented himself to hand Idalie across the plank from the vessel to the beach. 'Yes?' he asked her, in a voice of entreaty, as he pressed her hand. She softly returned the pressure, and the word, 'Beware,' trembled on her lips, when the young Englishman who had before admired her, and had endeavoured to engross her attention the whole day, was again at her side to tell her that the princess was waiting for her in her carriage and entreated her not to delay.

The party proceeded to where those glorious relics stand, between the mountains and the sea, rising like exhalations from the waste and barren soil, alone on the wide and dusky shore. A few sheep grazed at the base of the columns, and two or three wild-eyed men, clothed in garments of undressed sheepskin, loitered about. Exclamations of wonder and delight burst from all, while Ladislas, stealing away to the more distant one, gladly escaped from the impertinent intrusion of the crowd to indulge in lonely reverie among these ruins. 'What is man in his highest glory?' he thought. 'Had we burst the bonds of

Poland; and had she, in her freedom, emulated the magical achievements of Greece; nevertheless, when time, with insidious serpent windings, had dragged its length through a few more centuries, the monuments we had erected would have fallen like these, and our monuments, a new Paestum, have existed merely to excite the idiot wonder and frivolous curiosity of fools!'

Ladislas was certainly in no good humour while he thus vented his spleen; but was annoyed by two circumstances, sufficient to irritate a young philosopher: he beheld a scene, whose majestic beauty filled his soul with sensibility and awe, in the midst of a crowd of pretenders, more intent on the prospect of their picnic dinner than on regarding the glories of art; and he saw his bride, surrounded by strangers, engrossed by their conversation and flattery, and unable to interchange one word or look of confidence with him. He sighed for the hours passed under the portico of Idalie's solitary pavilion, and the near prospect of their voyage did not reconcile him to the present; for his soul was disturbed by the necessity of interchanging courtesies with his enemy, and haunted by images of treacherous attempts from which his valour could not protect him.

It had been arranged that the party should dine at the archbishop's palace, and not embark again until ten o'clock, when the moon would rise. After a couple of hours spent among the ruins, the servants informed them that their repast was ready; it was now nearly six o'clock, and after they had dined, more than two hours must elapse before they could depart. Night had gathered round the landscape, and its darkness did not invite even the most romantic to wander again among the ruins; the princess, eager to provide for the amusement of her guests, contrived to discover a violin, a flute and a pipe, and with the assistance of this music, which in the hands of Italian rustics was as true to time and expression as if Wieprecht himself had presided,[217] they commenced dancing. Idalie's hand was sought by the Englishman; she looked round the room, Ladislas was not there; he had doubtless repaired to the temples to wait for her, and ignorant of the presence of Giorgio, wholly unsuspicious and off his guard, to what dangers might he not be exposed? Her blood ran cold at the thought; she decidedly refused to dance, and perceiving the princess whirling round in a waltz at a distant part of the room, she dispatched her officious admirer on some feigned errand for refreshment, and hastily quitting the house, hurried along over the grass towards the temples. When she had first emerged into the night, the scene seemed wrapped in impenetrable darkness, but the stars shed their faint rays, and in a few moments she began to distinguish objects, and as she drew near the appointed temple, she saw a man's form moving slowly among the columns: she did not doubt that it was her husband, wrapped in his cloak, awaiting her. She was hurrying towards him, when, leaning against one of the pillars, she saw Ladislas himself, and the other, at the same moment, exchanging his stealthy pace for a tiger-like spring. She saw a dagger flashing in his hand; she darted forward to arrest his arm, and the blow descended on her; with a faint shriek, she fell on the earth, while Ladislas turned and closed with the assassin; a mortal struggle ensued; already had Ladislas wrested the poignard from his grasp when the villain drew another knife. Ladislas warded off the unexpected blow aimed at him with this, and plunged his own stiletto[218] in the bravo's breast; he fell to earth with a heavy groan, and then the silence of the tomb rested on the scene; the white robe of Idalie, who lay fainting on the ground, directed Ladislas to her side. He raised her up in speechless agony – as he beheld the blood which stained her dress; but by this time she had recovered from her swoon; she assured him her wound was slight, that it was nothing; but again sank into his arms insensible. In a moment his plan was formed; ever eager and impetuous, he executed it ere any second thought could change it. He had before resolved not to rejoin the party in the archbishop's palace, but after his interview with Idalie, to hasten on board the steamboat; he had therefore ordered his horse to be saddled, had led it to the temple and fastened it to one of the columns. He lifted the senseless Idalie carefully in his arms, mounted his horse, and turning his steps from the lighted and noisy palace, wound his way to the lonely shore, where he found the captain and his crew already preparing for their homeward voyage. With their help Idalie was taken on board, and Ladislas gave orders for the instant heaving of the anchor, and their immediate departure. The captain asked for the rest of the company. 'They return by land,' said Ladislas. As he spoke the words he felt a slight sensation of remorse, remembering the difficulty they would have to get there; and how, during the darkness of night, they might fear to proceed on their journey on a tract of country haunted by *banditti*; but the senseless and pale form of Idalie dissipated these thoughts: to arrive at Naples, to procure assistance for her, and then if, as he hoped, her wound was slight, to continue their voyage before the Princess Dashkhoff's return, were motives too paramount to allow him to hesitate. The captain of the *Sully* asked no more questions; the anchor was weighed, the wheels set in motion, and a silver light in the east announced the rising of the moon as they stood off from the shore and made their swift way back to Naples. They had not gone far, before the care of Ladislas revived his fair bride. Her wound was in her arm, and had merely grazed the skin. Terror for her husband, horror for the mortal strife which had endangered his life, had caused her to faint more than pain or loss of blood. She bound up her own arm; and then, as there appeared no necessity for medical aid, Ladislas revoked his orders for returning to Naples; instead, stretching out at once to sea, they began their voyage to Marseilles.

Meanwhile, during a pause in the dance, the absence of Ladislas and Idalie was observed by the feasters in the archbishop's palace. It excited some few sarcasms, which as it continued, grew more bitter. The Princess Dashkhoff joined in these, and yet she could not repress the disquietude of her heart. Had Ladislas alone been absent, her knowledge of the presence of Giorgio, and his designs, had sufficiently explained its cause, and its duration, to her; but that Idalie also should not be found might bring a witness to the crime committed, and discover her own guilty share in the deed of blood perpetrated at her instigation. At length the rising of the moon announced the hour when they were to repair to the shore. The horses and carriages were brought to the door, and then it was found that the steed of Ladislas was missing. 'But the Signora Idalie, has she not provided herself with a palfry?'[219] asked the Englishman, sneering. They were now about to mount, when it was proposed to take a last look at the temples by moonlight. The Princess opposed this, but vainly; her conscience made her voice faint, and took from her the usual decision of her manner; so she walked on silently, half fearful that her foot might strike against some object of terror, and at every word spoken by the party, anticipating an exclamation of horror; the fitful moonbeams seemed to disclose here and there ghastly countenances and mangled limbs, and the dew of night appeared to her excited imagination as the slippery moisture of the life-blood of her victim.

They had scarcely entered the temple when a peasant rushed in with the news that the steamboat was gone; he brought back Ladislas's horse, the latter having put the bridle into the man's hands on embarking; and the fellow declared that the fainting Idalie was his companion. Terror at the prospect of their dark ride, indignation at the selfish proceeding of the lovers, raised every voice against them; and the princess, whom conscience had before made the most silent, hearing that the Pole was alive and safe, was now loudest and most bitter in her remarks. As they were thus all gathered together in dismay, debating what was to be done, and the Princess Dashkhoff in no gentle terms railing at the impropriety and ingratitude of Idalie's behaviour, and declaring that

Poles alone could conduct themselves with such mingled deceit and baseness, a figure all bloody arose from the ground at her feet, and as the moon cast its pale rays on his yet paler countenance, she recognised Giorgio; the ladies shrieked, the men rushed towards him, while the princess, desiring the earth to open and swallow her, stood transfixed as by a spell, gazing on the dying man in terror and despair. 'He has escaped, lady,' said Giorgio. 'Ladislas has escaped your plots, and I am become their victim;' he fell as he spoke these words, and when the Englishman drew near to raise and if possible assist him, he found that life had entirely flown.

Thus ended the adventures of the Pole at Naples. The princess returned in her *caleche* alone, for none would bear her company; the next day she left Naples bound for Russia, where her crime was unknown, except to those who had been accomplices in it. Marietta spread the intelligence of her sister's marriage, and thus entirely cleared Idalie's fair fame; and quitting Italy soon after, joined the happy Ladislas and his bride at Paris.

The Mortal Immortal

A Tale

JULY 16, 1833 – this is a memorable anniversary for me; on it I complete my three hundred and twenty-third year! The Wandering Jew?[220] – certainly not. More than eighteen centuries have passed over his head. In comparison with him, I am a very young Immortal. Am I, then, immortal? This is a question which I have asked myself, by day and night for now three hundred and three years, and yet cannot answer it. I detected a grey hair amidst my brown locks this very day – that surely signifies decay. Yet it may have remained concealed there for three hundred years – for some persons have become entirely white-headed before twenty years of age.

I will tell my story, and my reader shall judge for me. I will tell my story, and so contrive to pass some few hours of a long eternity, become so wearisome to me. For ever! Can it be? to live for ever! I have heard of enchantments, in which the victims were plunged into a deep sleep, to wake, after a hundred years, as fresh as ever; I have heard of the Seven Sleepers – thus to be immortal would not be so burthensome; but, oh! the weight of never-ending time – the tedious passage of the still-succeeding hours! How happy was the fabled Nourjahad![221] But to my task.

All the world has heard of Cornelius Agrippa. His memory is as immortal as his arts have made me. All the world has also heard of his scholar, who, unawares, raised the foul fiend during his master's absence, and was destroyed by him.[222] The report, true or false, of this accident, was attended with many inconveniences to the renowned philosopher. All his scholars at once deserted him – his servants disappeared. He had no one near him to put coals on his ever-burning fires while he slept, or to attend to the changeful colours of his medicines while he studied. Experiment after experiment failed, because one pair of hands was insufficient to complete them; the dark spirits laughed at him for not being able to retain a single mortal in his service.

I was then very young – very poor – and very much in love. I had been for about a year the pupil of Cornelius, though I was absent when this accident took place. On my return, my friends implored me not to return to the alchemist's abode. I trembled as I listened to the dire tale they told; I required no second warning; and when Cornelius came and offered me a purse of gold if I would remain under his roof, I felt as if Satan himself tempted me. My teeth chattered – my hair stood on end – I ran off as fast as my trembling knees would permit.

My failing steps were directed whither for two years they had every evening been attracted – a gently bubbling spring of pure living water, beside which lingered a dark-haired girl, whose beaming eyes were fixed on the path I was accustomed each night to tread. I cannot remember the hour when I did not love Bertha; we had been neighbours and playmates from infancy – her parents, like mine, were of humble life, yet respectable – our attachment had been a source of pleasure to them. In an evil hour, a malignant fever carried off both her father and mother, and Bertha became an orphan. She would have found a home beneath my paternal roof, but, unfortunately, the old lady of the near castle, rich, childless and solitary, declared her intention to adopt her. Henceforth Bertha was clad in silk – inhabited a marble palace – and was looked on as being highly favoured by fortune. But in her new situation among her new associates, Bertha remained true to the friend of her humbler days; she often visited the cottage of my father, and when forbidden to go thither, she would stray towards the neighbouring wood, and meet me beside its shady fountain.

She often declared that she owed no duty to her new protectress equal in sanctity to that which bound us. Yet still I was too poor to marry, and she grew weary of being tormented on my account. She had a haughty but an impatient spirit, and grew angry at the obstacles that prevented our union. We met now after an absence, and she had been sorely beset while I was away; she complained bitterly, and almost reproached me for being poor. I replied hastily, 'I am honest, if I am poor! – were I not, I might soon become rich!'

This exclamation produced a thousand questions. I feared to shock her by owning the truth, but she drew it from me; and then, casting a look of disdain on me, she said, 'You pretend to love, yet you fear to face the Devil for my sake!'

I protested that I had only dreaded to offend her – while she dwelt on the magnitude of the reward that I should receive. Thus encouraged – shamed by her – led on by love and hope, laughing at my late fears, with quick steps and a light heart, I returned to accept the offers of the alchemist, and was instantly installed in my post.

A year passed away. I became possessed of no insignificant sum of money. Custom had banished my fears. In spite of the most painful vigilance, I had never detected the trace of a cloven foot; nor was the studious silence of our abode ever disturbed by demoniac howls. I still continued my stolen interviews with Bertha, and hope dawned on me – hope – but not perfect joy; for Bertha fancied that love and security were enemies, and her pleasure was to divide them in my bosom. Though true of heart, she was somewhat of a coquette in manner; and I was jealous as a Turk. She slighted me in a thousand ways, yet would never acknowledge herself to be in the wrong. She would drive me mad with anger, and then force me to beg her pardon. Sometimes she fancied that I was not sufficiently submissive, and then she had some story of a rival, favoured by her protectress. She was surrounded by silk-clad youths – the rich and gay. What chance had the sad-robed scholar of Cornelius compared with these?

On one occasion, the philosopher made such large demands upon my time that I was unable to meet her as I was wont. He was engaged in some mighty work, and I was forced to remain, day and night, feeding his furnaces and watching his chemical preparations. Bertha waited for me in vain at the fountain. Her haughty spirit fired at this neglect; and when at last I stole out during the few short minutes allotted to me for slumber, and hoped to be consoled by her, she received me with disdain, dismissed me in scorn, and vowed that any man should possess her hand rather than he who could not be in two places at once for her sake. She would be revenged! And truly she was. In my dingy retreat I heard that she had been hunting, attended by Albert Hoffer. Albert Hoffer was favoured by her protectress, and the three passed in cavalcade before my smoky window. Methought that they mentioned my name – it was followed by a laugh of derision, as her dark eyes glanced contemptuously towards my abode.

Jealousy, with all its venom, and all its misery, entered my breast. Now I shed a torrent of tears to think that I should never call her mine; and, anon, I imprecated a thousand curses on her inconstancy. Yet, still I must stir the fires of the alchemist, still attend on the changes of his unintelligible medicines.

Cornelius had watched for three days and nights, nor closed his eyes. The progress of his alembics[223] was slower than he expected; in spite of his anxiety, sleep weighed upon his eyelids. Again and again he threw off drowsiness with more than human energy; again and again it stole away his senses. He eyed his crucibles wistfully. 'Not ready yet,' he murmured; 'will another night pass before the work is accomplished?

Winzy, you are vigilant – you are faithful – you have slept, my boy –
you slept last night. Look at that glass vessel. The liquid it contains is of
a soft rose-colour; the moment it begins to change its hue, awaken me –
till then I may close my eyes. First, it will turn white, and then emit
golden flashes; but wait not till then; when the rose-colour fades, rouse
me.' I scarcely heard the last words, muttered, as they were, in sleep.
Even then he did not quite yield to nature. 'Winzy, my boy,' he again
said, 'do not touch the vessel – do not put it to your lips; it is a philtre –
a philtre to cure love; you would not cease to love your Bertha – beware
to drink!'

And he slept. His venerable head sank on his breast, and I scarce
heard his regular breathing. For a few minutes I watched the vessel –
the rosy hue of the liquid remained unchanged. Then my thoughts
wandered – they visited the fountain, and dwelt on a thousand charming
scenes never to be renewed – never! Serpents and adders were in my
heart as the word 'Never!' half formed itself on my lips. False girl! –
false and cruel! Nevermore would she smile on me as that evening she
smiled on Albert. Worthless, detested woman! I would not remain
unrevenged – she should see Albert expire at her feet – she should die
beneath my vengeance. She had smiled in disdain and triumph – she
knew my wretchedness and her power. Yet what power had she? – the
power of exciting my hate – my utter scorn – my – oh, all but indifference!
Could I attain that – could I regard her with careless eyes, transferring
my rejected love to one fairer and more true, that were indeed a victory!

A bright flash darted before my eyes. I had forgotten the medicine of
the adept; I gazed on it with wonder: flashes of admirable beauty, more
bright than those which the diamond emits when the sun's rays are on
it, glanced from the surface of the liquid; an odour the most fragrant
and grateful stole over my sense; the vessel seemed one globe of living
radiance, lovely to the eye and most inviting to the taste. The first
thought, instinctively inspired by the grosser sense, was, I will – I must
drink. I raised the vessel to my lips. 'It will cure me of love – of torture!'
Already I had quaffed half of the most delicious liquor ever tasted by
the palate of man, when the philosopher stirred. I started – I dropped
the glass – the fluid flamed and glanced along the floor, while I felt
Cornelius's grip at my throat as he shrieked aloud, 'Wretch! you have
destroyed the labour of my life!'

The philosopher was totally unaware that I had drunk any portion of
his drug. His idea was, and I gave a tacit assent to it, that I had raised the
vessel from curiosity, and that, frighted at its brightness and the flashes
of intense light it gave forth, I had let it fall. I never undeceived him.

The fire of the medicine was quenched – the fragrance died away – he grew calm, as a philosopher should under the heaviest trials, and dismissed me to rest.

I will not attempt to describe the sleep of glory and bliss which bathed my soul in paradise during the remaining hours of that memorable night. Words would be faint and shallow types of my enjoyment, or of the gladness that possessed my bosom when I woke. I trod air – my thoughts were in heaven. Earth appeared heaven, and my inheritance upon it was to be one trance of delight. 'This it is to be cured of love,' I thought; 'I will see Bertha this day, and she will find her lover cold and regardless; too happy to be disdainful, yet how utterly indifferent to her!'

The hours danced away. The philosopher, secure that he had once succeeded, and believing that he might again, began to concoct the same medicine once more. He was shut up with his books and drugs, and I had a holiday. I dressed myself with care; I looked in an old but polished shield, which served me for a mirror; methought my good looks had wonderfully improved. I hurried beyond the precincts of the town, joy in my soul, the beauty of heaven and earth around me. I turned my steps towards the castle – I could look on its lofty turrets with lightness of heart, for I was cured of love. My Bertha saw me afar off, as I came up the avenue. I know not what sudden impulse animated her bosom, but at the sight, she sprang with a light fawn-like bound down the marble steps, and was hastening towards me. But I had been perceived by another person. The old high-born hag, who called herself her protectress and was her tyrant, had seen me, also; she hobbled, panting, up the terrace; a page, as ugly as herself, held up her train and fanned her as she hurried along; she stopped my fair girl with a, 'How, now, my bold mistress? whither so fast? Back to your cage – hawks are abroad!'

Bertha clasped her hands – her eyes were still bent on my approaching figure. I saw the contest. How I abhorred the old crone who checked the kind impulses of my Bertha's softening heart. Hitherto, respect for her rank had caused me to avoid the lady of the castle; now I disdained such trivial considerations. I was cured of love, and lifted above all human fears; I hastened forward, and soon reached the terrace. How lovely Bertha looked! her eyes flashing fire, her cheeks glowing with impatience and anger, she was a thousand times more graceful and charming than ever. I no longer loved – Oh! no, I adored – worshipped – idolised her!

She had that morning been persecuted, with more than usual vehemence, to consent to an immediate marriage with my rival. She was reproached with the encouragement that she had shown him – she was threatened with being turned out of doors with disgrace and shame. Her proud spirit rose in arms at the threat; but when she remembered the scorn that she had heaped upon me, and how, perhaps, she had thus lost one whom she now regarded as her only friend, she wept with remorse and rage. At that moment I appeared. 'Oh, Winzy!' she exclaimed, 'take me to your mother's cot; swiftly let me leave the detested luxuries and wretchedness of this noble dwelling – take me to poverty and happiness.'

I clasped her in my arms with transport. The old lady was speechless with fury, and broke forth into invective only when we were far on our road to my natal cottage. My mother received the fair fugitive, escaped from a gilt cage to nature and liberty, with tenderness and joy; my father, who loved her, welcomed her heartily; it was a day of rejoicing, which did not need the addition of the celestial potion of the alchemist to steep me in delight.

Soon after this eventful day, I became the husband of Bertha. I ceased to be the scholar of Cornelius, but I continued his friend. I always felt grateful to him for having, unawares, procured me that delicious draught of a divine elixir, which, instead of curing me of love (sad cure! solitary and joyless remedy for evils which seem blessings to the memory), had inspired me with courage and resolution, thus winning for me an inestimable treasure in my Bertha.

I often called to mind that period of trance-like inebriation with wonder. The drink of Cornelius had not fulfilled the task for which he affirmed that it had been prepared, but its effects were more potent and blissful than words can express. They had faded by degrees, yet they lingered long – and painted life in hues of splendour. Bertha often wondered at my lightness of heart and unaccustomed gaiety; for, before, I had been rather serious, or even sad, in my disposition. She loved me the better for my cheerful temper, and our days were winged by joy.

Five years afterwards I was suddenly summoned to the bedside of the dying Cornelius. He had sent for me in haste, conjuring my instant presence. I found him stretched on his pallet, enfeebled even to death; all of life that yet remained animated his piercing eyes, and they were fixed on a glass vessel, full of a roseate liquid.

'Behold,' he said, in a broken and inward voice, 'the vanity of human wishes![224] a second time my hopes are about to be crowned, a second time they are destroyed. Look at that liquor – you remember five years ago I had prepared the same, with the same success; then, as now, my thirsting lips expected to taste the immortal elixir – you dashed it from me! and at present it is too late.'

Bertha intercepted

He spoke with difficulty, and fell back on his pillow. I could not help asking, 'How, revered master, can a cure for love restore you to life?'

A faint smile gleamed across his face as I listened earnestly to his scarcely intelligible answer.

'A cure for love and for all things – the Elixir of Immortality. Ah! if now I might drink, I should live for ever!'

As he spoke, a golden flash gleamed from the fluid; a well-remembered fragrance stole over the air; he raised himself, all weak as he was – strength seemed miraculously to re-enter his frame – he stretched forth his hand – a loud explosion startled me – a ray of fire shot up from the elixir, and the glass vessel which contained it was shivered to atoms! I turned my eyes towards the philosopher; he had fallen back – his eyes were glassy – his features rigid – he was dead!

But I lived, and was to live for ever! So said the unfortunate alchemist, and for a few days I believed his words. I remembered the glorious drunkenness that had followed my stolen draught. I reflected on the change I had felt in my frame – in my soul. The bounding elasticity of the one – the buoyant lightness of the other. I surveyed myself in a mirror and could perceive no change in my features during the space of the five years which had elapsed. I remembered the radiant hues and grateful scent of that delicious beverage – worthy the gift it was capable of bestowing – I was, then, IMMORTAL!

A few days after I laughed at my credulity. The old proverb, that 'a prophet is least regarded in his own country', was true with respect to me and my defunct master. I loved him as a man – I respected him as a sage – but I derided the notion that he could command the powers of darkness, and laughed at the superstitious fears with which he was regarded by the vulgar. He was a wise philosopher, but had no acquaintance with any spirits but those clad in flesh and blood. His science was simply human; and human science, I soon persuaded myself, could never conquer nature's laws so far as to imprison the soul for ever within its carnal habitation. Cornelius had brewed a soul-refreshing drink – more inebriating than wine – sweeter and more fragrant than any fruit; it possessed probably strong medicinal powers, imparting gladness to the heart and vigour to the limbs; but its effects would wear out; already were they diminished in my frame. I was a lucky fellow to have quaffed health and joyous spirits, and perhaps long life, at my master's hands; but my good fortune ended there: longevity was far different from immortality.

I continued to entertain this belief for many years. Sometimes a thought stole across me – Was the alchemist indeed deceived? But my habitual credence was that I should meet the fate of all the children of Adam at my appointed time – a little late, but still at a natural age. Yet it was certain that I retained a wonderfully youthful look. I was laughed at for my vanity in consulting the mirror so often, but I consulted it in vain – my brow was untrenched – my cheeks – my eyes – my whole person continued as untarnished as in my twentieth year.

I was troubled. I looked at the faded beauty of Bertha – I seemed more like her son. By degrees our neighbours began to make similar observations, and I found at last that I went by the name of the Scholar Bewitched. Bertha herself grew uneasy. She became jealous and peevish, and at length she began to question me. We had no children; we were all in all to each other; and though, as she grew older, her vivacious spirit became a little allied to ill-temper, and her beauty sadly diminished, I cherished her in my heart as the mistress I had idolised, the wife I had sought and won with such perfect love.

At last our situation became intolerable: Bertha was fifty – I twenty years of age. I had, in very shame, in some measure adopted the habits of a more advanced age; I no longer mingled in the dance among the young and gay, but my heart bounded along with them while I restrained my feet; and a sorry figure I cut among the Nestors of our village.[225] But before the time I mention, things were altered – we were universally shunned; we were – at least, I was – reported to have kept up an iniquitous acquaintance with some of my former master's supposed friends. Poor Bertha was pitied, but deserted. I was regarded with horror and detestation.

What was to be done? we sat by our winter fire – poverty had made itself felt, for none would buy the produce of my farm; and often I had been forced to journey twenty miles, to some place where I was not known, to dispose of our property. It is true we had saved something for an evil day – that day was come.

We sat by our lone fireside – the old-hearted youth and his antiquated wife. Again Bertha insisted on knowing the truth; she recapitulated all she had ever heard said about me, and added her own observations. She conjured me to cast off the spell; she described how much more comely grey hairs were than my chestnut locks; she descanted on the reverence and respect due to age – how preferable to the slight regard paid to mere children: could I imagine that the despicable gifts of youth and good looks outweighed disgrace, hatred and scorn? Nay, in the end I should be burnt as a dealer in the black art, while she, to whom I had not deigned to communicate any portion of my good fortune, might be stoned as my accomplice. At length she insinuated that I must share my secret with her, and bestow on her like benefits to those I myself enjoyed, or she would denounce me – and then she burst into tears.

Thus beset, methought it was the best way to tell the truth. I revealed it as tenderly as I could, and spoke only of a *very long life*, not of immortality – which representation, indeed, coincided best with my own ideas. When I ended, I rose and said, 'And now, my Bertha, will you denounce the lover of your youth? – You will not, I know. But it is too hard, my poor wife, that you should suffer from my ill-luck and the accursed arts of Cornelius. I will leave you – you have wealth enough, and friends will return in my absence. I will go; young as I seem, and strong as I am, I can work and gain my bread among strangers, unsuspected and unknown. I loved you in youth; God is my witness that I would not desert you in age, but that your safety and happiness require it.'

I took my cap and moved towards the door; in a moment Bertha's arms were round my neck, and her lips were pressed to mine. 'No, my husband, my Winzy,' she said, 'you shall not go alone – take me with you; we will remove from this place, and, as you say, among strangers we shall be unsuspected and safe. I am not so very old as quite to shame you, my Winzy; and I dare say the charm will soon wear off, and, with the blessing of God, you will become more elderly-looking, as is fitting; you shall not leave me.'

I returned the good soul's embrace heartily. 'I will not, my Bertha; but for your sake I had not thought of such a thing. I will be your true, faithful husband while you are spared to me, and do my duty by you to the last.'

The next day we prepared secretly for our emigration. We were obliged to make great pecuniary sacrifices – it could not be helped. We realised a sum sufficient, at least, to maintain us while Bertha lived; and, without saying adieu to anyone, quitted our native country to take refuge in a remote part of western France.

It was a cruel thing to transport poor Bertha from her native village, and the friends of her youth, to a new country, new language, new customs. The strange secret of my destiny rendered this removal immaterial to me; but I compassionated her deeply, and was glad to perceive that she found compensation for her misfortunes in a variety of little ridiculous circumstances. Away from all tell-tale chroniclers, she sought to decrease the apparent disparity of our ages by a thousand feminine arts – rouge, youthful dress and assumed juvenility of manner. I could not be angry – Did not I myself wear a mask? Why quarrel with hers, because it was less successful? I grieved deeply when I remembered that this was my Bertha, whom I had loved so fondly, and won with such transport – the dark-eyed, dark-haired girl, with smiles of enchanting archness and a step like a fawn – this mincing, simpering, jealous old woman. I should have revered her grey locks and withered cheeks; but thus! – It was my work, I knew; but I did not the less deplore this type of human weakness.

Her jealousy never slept. Her chief occupation was to discover that, in spite of outward appearances, I was myself growing old. I verily believe that the poor soul loved me truly in her heart, but never had woman so tormenting a mode of displaying fondness. She would discern wrinkles in my face and decrepitude in my walk, while I bounded along in youthful vigour, the youngest looking of twenty youths. I never dared address another woman: on one occasion, fancying that the belle of the village regarded me with favouring eyes, she bought me a grey wig. Her constant discourse among her acquaintances was that though I looked so young there was ruin at work within my frame; and she affirmed that the worst symptom about me was my apparent health. My youth was a disease, she said, and I ought at all times to prepare, if not for a sudden and awful death, at least to awake some morning white-headed, and bowed down with all the marks of advanced years. I let her talk – I often joined in her conjectures. Her warnings chimed in with my never-ceasing speculations concerning my state, and I took an earnest, though painful, interest in listening to all that her quick wit and excited imagination could say on the subject.

Why dwell on these minute circumstances? We lived on for many long years. Bertha became bed-rid and paralytic: I nursed her as a mother might a child. She grew peevish, and still harped upon one string – of how long I should survive her. It has ever been a source of consolation to me that I performed my duty scrupulously towards her. She had been mine in youth, she was mine in age, and at last, when I heaped the sod over her corpse, I wept to feel that I had lost all that really bound me to humanity.

Since then how many have been my cares and woes, how few and empty my enjoyments! I pause here in my history – I will pursue it no further. A sailor without rudder or compass, tossed on a stormy sea – a traveller lost on a widespread heath, without landmark or star to guide him – such have I been: more lost, more hopeless than either. A nearing ship, a gleam from some far cot, may save them; but I have no beacon except the hope of death.

Death! mysterious, ill-visaged friend of weak humanity! Why alone of all mortals have you cast me from your sheltering fold? Oh, for the peace of the grave! the deep silence of the iron-bound tomb! that thought would cease to work in my brain, and my heart beat no more with emotions varied only by new forms of sadness!

Am I immortal? I return to my first question. In the first place, is it not more probable that the beverage of the alchemist was fraught rather with longevity than eternal life? Such is my hope. And then be it remembered that I only drank *half* of the potion prepared by him. Was not the whole necessary to complete the charm? To have drained half the Elixir of Immortality is but to be half immortal – my forever is thus truncated and null.

But again, who shall number the years of the half of eternity? I often try to imagine by what rule the infinite may be divided. Sometimes I fancy age advancing upon me. One grey hair I have found. Fool! do I lament? Yes, the fear of age and death often creeps coldly into my heart; and the more I live, the more I dread death, even while I abhor life. Such an enigma is man – born to perish – when he wars, as I do, against the established laws of his nature.

But for this anomaly of feeling surely I might die: the medicine of the alchemist would not be proof against fire – sword – and the strangling waters. I have gazed upon the blue depths of many a placid lake, and the tumultuous rushing of many a mighty river, and have said, peace inhabits those waters; yet I have turned my steps away, to live yet another day. I have asked myself, whether suicide would be a crime in one to whom thus only the portals of the other world could be opened. I have done all, except presenting myself as a soldier or duellist, an object of destruction to my – no, *not* my fellow-mortals, and therefore I have shrunk away. They are not my fellows. The inextinguishable power of life in my frame and their ephemeral existence place us wide as the poles asunder. I could not raise a hand against the meanest or the most powerful among them.

Thus I have lived on for many a year – alone, and weary of myself – desirous of death, yet never dying – a mortal immortal. Neither ambition nor avarice can enter my mind, and the ardent love that gnaws at my heart, never to be returned – never to find an equal on which to expend itself – lives there only to torment me.

This very day I conceived a design by which I may end all – without self-slaughter, without making another man a Cain – an expedition, which mortal frame can never survive, even endued with the youth and strength that inhabits mine. Thus I shall put my immortality to the test, and rest for ever – or return, the wonder and benefactor of the human species.

Before I go, a miserable vanity has caused me to pen these pages. I would not die, and leave no name behind. Three centuries have passed since I quaffed the fatal beverage: another year shall not elapse before, encountering gigantic dangers – warring with the powers of frost in their home – beset by famine, toil and tempest – I yield this body, too tenacious a cage for a soul which thirsts for freedom, to the destructive elements of air and water – or, if I survive, my name shall be recorded as one of the most famous among the sons of men; and, my task achieved, I shall adopt more resolute means, and, by scattering and annihilating the atoms that compose my frame, set at liberty the life imprisoned within and so cruelly prevented from soaring from this dim earth to a sphere more congenial to its immortal essence.

The Elder Son

MY father was the second son of a wealthy baronet. As he and his elder brother formed all the family of my grandfather, he inherited the whole of his mother's fortune, which was considerable, and settled on the younger children. He married a lady whom he tenderly loved; and having taken orders, and procured preferment, retired to his deanery in the north of Ireland, and there took up his abode. When I was about ten years old he lost my mother: I was their only child.

My father was something of an ascetic, if such name can be given to a rigid adherence to the precepts of morality which arose from the excess and not the absence of feeling. He adored my mother; he mourned for her to the verge of insanity; but his grief was silent, devouring and gloomy. He never formed another matrimonial engagement: secluding himself entirely from society, and given up to the duties of his sacred calling, he passed his days in solitude, or in works of charity among the poor.

Even now I cannot remember him without awe. He was a tall and, I thought, a venerable-looking man; for he was thin and pale, and he was partly bald. His manners were cold and reserved; he seldom spoke, and when he did it was in such measured phrase, in so calm and solemn a voice, and on such serious topics, as resembled rather oracular enunciation than familiar conversation. He never caressed me; if ever he stroked my head or drew me on his knee, I felt a mingled alarm and delight difficult to describe. Yet, strange to say, my father loved me almost to idolatry; and I knew this and repaid his affection with enthusiastic fondness, notwithstanding his reserve and my awe. He was something greater, and wiser, and better, in my eyes, than any other human being. I was the sole creature he loved; the object of all his thoughts by day and his dreams by night. Abstracted and even severe as he seemed, he has visited my bedside at night, subdued by womanly fears, and hung over me for hours, to assure himself of my life and well-being. He has watched by me in sickness night after night with unwearied assiduity. He never spoke harshly to me, and treated me at once with a distance and gentleness hard to be understood.

When I was eighteen he died. During his last illness the seal was taken from his lips, and his heart threw off that husk within which he had hitherto concealed its true nature. He died of a rapid consumption, which terminated his existence within six months of his being first taken ill. His body wasted under the effects of mortal disease; but his soul assumed new life and energy, and his temper became as soft and demonstrative as it had hitherto been repulsive and concentrated. He became my father, friend and brother, all in one; a thousand dear relationships combined in one stronger than any. This sudden melting, this divine sensibility, which expanded at once, having been so long shut up and hid, was like a miracle. It fascinated and entranced me. I could not believe that I was about to lose him at the moment when we discovered each other's worth: I mean by that expression, as regards myself, all the happiness that he derived from the truth and vivacity of my filial affection.

It were vain to attempt to refer even to our conversations: the sublime morality he inculcated; the tenderness and charity of his expressions; the overflowing and melting eloquence with which he talked of the affections of this world, and his aspirations after a better. He died suddenly at last, as I was playing to him a simple air my mother loved. It was a moment of horror, yet of solemn and pious resignation: his soul had sought its native heaven and congenial companion – might it be blest! Yet I had lost him, and grief immeasurable was the result. The impression of the misery I suffered can never be entirely worn from my mind: I often wonder my heart did not break with the violence of my sorrow.

I had been brought up at the deanery, apart from all acquaintances. I had had a governess, a most worthy woman, who married just before my father was taken ill, and who kindly came to me when all was over, to endeavour to console the inconsolable. One of my father's objects in life had been to accumulate a fortune for me; not for the sake of placing me in the dangerous situation of an heiress, but to render me independent. It thus happened that by his ever-lamented death I inherited considerable wealth. His own fortune, my mother's, and his savings, formed the sum of fifty thousand pounds. He left me under the guardianship of his elder brother, Sir Richard Gray, with only one restriction, that I was not to marry, even with my uncle's consent, till I was twenty-one. He wished thus to secure me freedom of choice, and time for deliberation. To this sagacious clause I owe the happiness of my life.

As soon as my health and the first agony of my grief would permit, I left the deanery. My kind governess accompanied me to Dublin, and Sir Richard Gray came hither himself to fetch me, and to carry me to his seat in England. I was beyond measure surprised when I saw my uncle. He was a year older than my father – my venerable father – and he looked in comparison a boy. He was indeed under fifty, and had at first sight a juvenility of aspect quite astonishing. On examination, the traces of years and care became perceptible; and there was a haggardness in his face which contrasted strangely with its expression of thoughtlessness. No one could be kinder than he was to me, and yet his very kindness was revolting, from the contrast he formed with my lost parent. The world, society and pleasure occupied his time and thoughts. Solitude and misery were synonymous terms with him; and he called everything solitude that did not include the idea of a crowd. He rattled away during our journey, thinking his anecdotes and good stories would enliven me. He was so sorry that it was not the season that I could go to London – he would have invited his daughter, Lady Hythe, to his seat, that he might arrange a party to enliven it for me; but she was on the Continent, and his other married daughter was resident in Scotland. What was to be done? He had engagements himself during the shooting season at various gentlemen's houses and I should be moped to death at Beech Grove. This account of the seclusion of my retreat was all my comfort. I declared that nothing should induce me to go into society for several years. He stared, and then smiled, and in his usual caressing gallant manner said I should do as I liked; he would never contradict me in anything; he only hoped that he should be always able to please and gratify me.

My uncle's story is soon told. He married, very early in life, a girl of inferior rank. His relations were exceedingly enraged, and discarded him. His father died; and his grandfather, fearing that he would sell his expectations and squander the whole property, offered him a large immediate income, upon condition that he would entail the estate upon his eldest son. He consented. A few years after, his grandfather died, and he came into the titles and estate. The new Lady Gray made herself many friends from the extreme propriety of her conduct. They had a large family, but lost many children; and she died in child-bed of her youngest. Five only survived. The eldest son was abroad, two daughters were well married, and the youngest, a girl of only twelve years of age, lived with her governess at the family seat in Hampshire. Sir Richard talked kindly of his children, but chiefly of his eldest son, against whom therefore I conceived a prejudice; because, from his father's description,

I considered him dissipated and worthless. Such, indeed, was my uncle; but I did not dislike him, for by the charm of manner he vanquished aversion, and I transferred to his favourite son the disapprobation he had at first excited. I was glad to hear that my cousin was at Vienna, and that I was not likely to see him.

We arrived at Beech Grove on the 29th August. It was a fine summer day, and the country in all its glory. The house was spacious and elegant, and situated in an extensive park, laid out with infinite taste and kept up with extreme care. All looked so gay and smiling, so unlike the sombre scenes I had left on the shores of the dark northern ocean, that I contemplated my new abode with distaste: such is the force of habit. My uncle had expected that I should be enchanted with the novel beauty of an English park and mansion, and was disappointed at my languid praise. There were no rocks, no sea, no extensive moors. Groves of beech, a river threading verdant wooded banks, a variety of upland and valley, glade and copse, did not command my admiration; so true it is that we seldom admire that which is absolutely new. A few months totally altered this first impression. The cheerfulness of the scene imperceptibly acted on my spirits. I became reconciled to its (to a certain degree) tameness, and learnt at last to love its refined and elegant beauty.

Sir Richard talked of visiting and company. He would have called his neighbours round us, and forced me to accept invitations at the various houses where, in the shooting season, were assembled large parties of the rich and gay. I earnestly assured him that my depressed spirits and deep-rooted sorrow needed tranquillity – that the seclusion which his house promised was its principal attraction – that I was most happy to be alone. He could not believe my assertions – it hurt his feelings to leave me in this desert: he actually delayed his departure for two days, not liking to quit me. At last he went; and speedily, in the pursuit of pleasure, forgot my existence.

I was not absolutely alone in his house; my cousin Marianne inhabited it with me. She was a pretty, agreeable girl of twelve years of age; and we got on very well together. I had recourse to her society when over-weary of thought; and she was so young that I could leave her, and betake myself to my mournful, lonely reveries, whenever I liked, without ceremony.

I had not been at Beech Grove more than a week when late one afternoon, on returning from a drive, we distinguished lights in the dining-room. 'Can it be my brother?' cried Marianne; 'can Clinton have arrived!'

'I hope not,' I said.

'Oh, do not say so,' replied the little girl; 'you would love Clinton; he is so lively and dear – everybody loves him.'

She scarce waited for the steps to be let down, but jumped from the carriage; she returned to me in a minute with an air of disappointment, 'It is only my brother Vernon,' she said.

'And you do not care about him?'

'Oh, yes,' she replied, 'Vernon is very good, and all that; but he is quite different from Clinton; he may stay a month in the house and I not see him twice.'

The habit of solitude had rendered me a little bashful. I had dined early with my cousin, and the newcomer was at dinner. I went into the drawing-room therefore, and made her stay with me, and awaited his entrance with some alarm. He soon joined us. As he entered, I was struck with his being the handsomest man I had ever seen. His complexion was a clear olive; his eyes a dark blue; his head small and well-shaped; his figure scarcely above the middle size, but slender and elegant. I expected the courteous manners of my uncle to correspond with the grace of his appearance; but Vernon had no vivacity, no softness. His words were pregnant with meaning, and his eyes flashed fire as he spoke; but his address was abrupt, his conversation pointed and sarcastic, and a disagreeable ironical smile, in which he indulged, deteriorated greatly from his good looks. Still, he was very handsome, very clever, and very entertaining.

One part of Marianne's description at least was erroneous. He spent every day and all day with us. He rode or walked with us in the morning; read to us in the evening; conversed as we worked or painted; and did all that a person most sedulous to please could do, except turning over the leaves of our music-books. He did not like music – of which my father was so passionately fond – in all else his tastes seemed mine. He gave me Italian lessons; and, except when I drove him away, was never absent from our side. Marianne declared that her brother Vernon was an altered man. I thought that I knew whence the alteration sprang.

What girl of eighteen, just emerged from solitude, could perceive the birth of love in the heart of a young, accomplished and handsome man and not feel her vanity gratified? My peculiar education had prevented my having any of the coquettishness of beauty or the insolence of wealth. I own I felt elated. I became of consequence in my own eyes; and my silly heart swelled with conscious triumph. Vernon grew each day more openly devoted to me, more solicitous to please, more flattering and attentive. He advanced with imperceptible steps to the desired bourne, and no impatience of temper disturbed for a moment his progress. Stealthy as a serpent, and as wily, he became necessary to my comfort; and I had compromised myself by displaying my vain triumph in my conquest, before he betrayed himself by a word.

When I found that he sought a return for his love, I was frightened. I discovered that with all his talents and agreeable qualities I scarcely liked him; and certainly could never feel a sentiment more tender than friendship. I reproached myself for my ingratitude – I felt ashamed of my vacillation. He saw my struggles – he was all humility – he did not deserve better – he was satisfied if I would only be a sister to him – pity him – endure his presence. I agreed, and reassumed my familiarity and good humour.

It is impossible to describe his refined artifice, or the wonderful assiduity with which he watched by his concealed net till I was completely immeshed. He contrived first that I should consent to listen to him talking of his passion; then he excited my pity for his sufferings – he was eloquent in describing them and in exalting my merits. He asked for so little, he seemed so humble – but he was importunate, and never gave up the smallest advantage he had once gained. Forgotten by my uncle, unknown and unregarded by the rest of the world, I was delivered over to his machinations. Day after day he renewed them. He discerned and worked upon every weakness of my character. My fear to do wrong; my alarm at the idea of being the occasion of pain; my desire to preserve my integrity without a flaw – these might be termed virtues; but, distorted and exaggerated by natural conceit and youthful inexperience, they rendered me a too easy prey. At last he extracted from me a promise to marry him when I should be of age. This pledge seemed the only method left me to prove my delicacy and truth. I gave it the more readily because I admired his talents, and believed that he deserved a better wife than I, and that my want of love was a fault in me for which I ought to compensate to him. With all the rashness and inexperience of my age, I confess that I even tried to conceal my latent aversion; so that when, after having obtained my promise, he went away for a week, I willingly assented to his request that I should correspond with him, and my letters were full of affection. I found it easier to write than speak what I did not really feel, and was glad to show my gratitude and my sense of his attachment at an easy rate. At the same time, I consented to keep our engagement secret, that thus I might have an excuse for preserving the reserve of my conduct. I took advantage of this wish on his part to insist on his leaving me for a time. I was glad when he went, yet mortified at the readiness of his obedience.

I must not be unjust. Vernon had many faults, but coldness of feeling was not among them. Vehemence and passion were his characteristics, though he could unite them to a deliberation in design, and a wiliness in execution, without example. He had determined before he saw me to win me and my fortune; but such was the violence of his disposition, that he was unavoidably caught in his own toils; and the project that was founded on self-interest ended in making him the slave of love – of a girl whom he despised. He went when I bade him eagerly; but he fulfilled his aim better by so doing. My letters were to be confirmations strong against me – in case that hereafter, as he too justly feared, I should wish to retract my vows. I heedlessly accomplished his ends, beyond his most sanguine expectations. My letters were those of a betrothed bride; and what they might want in tenderness was made up by their uncompromising acknowledgment of our relative position. Having obtained these testimonies, he returned. I was not sorry. I was too little pleased with myself to be in love with solitude. His presence kept alive the feeling of irresistible fate to which I had yielded; and his society enlivened the monotonous quiet of Beech Grove.

At length Christmas came, and my uncle returned and filled his house with visitors. Then the darker shades of Vernon's character became apparent. He was as jealous as an Italian. His disposition was sombre and averse to sociable pleasures. God knows grief sat too heavy at my heart to allow me to be very vivacious; still, I wished to please my uncle, and thought that I had no right to cloud the good humour of the company; and added to this was the elastic spirit of youth, which sprang eagerly and spontaneously from the gloom and mystery of Vernon's artifices into the more congenial atmosphere of friendly intercourse. He saw me unlike anything he had ever seen in me before – sprightly, and ready to share the amusement of the hour. He groaned in bitterness of spirit. He reproached – reprehended – and became a very taskmaster. I was naturally timid and docile – in vain did my spirit revolt from his injustice: he gained and kept complete ascendency over me. Yet my soul was in arms against him even while I submitted to his control, and dislike began to develop itself in my bosom. I tasked myself severely for my ingratitude. I became in appearance kinder than ever; but every internal struggle and every outward demonstration had unfortunately one result – to alienate my affections more and more from my lover-cousin.

Our guests left us. My uncle went up to town. He told me he hoped I would accompany him there as soon as Lady Hythe returned to chaperone me. But I was more averse than ever to visiting London. Bound to Vernon by my promises, and wishing to keep my faith with him, I did not like to expose myself to the temptation of seeing others I should like better. Besides, the memory of my father was still unfaded, and I resolved not to appear in public till the year of mourning was expired. Vernon accompanied his father to town, but returned again to us almost immediately. We appeared to revert to our former mode of life; but the essence of it was changed. He was moody – I anxious. I almost ventured to accuse him of ill-temper and tyranny, till, reading in my own heart its indifference, I was inclined to consider myself the cause of his discontent. I tried to restore his complacency by kindness, and in some degree succeeded.

One day Sir Richard suddenly appeared at Beech Grove. He seemed surprised to find Vernon, and care and even anxiety clouded his usual hilarity. He told us that he expected Clinton daily, and should, immediately on his arrival, bring him down to Hampshire.

'To celebrate my birthday?' asked Vernon, with a sardonic smile; 'I am of age on Friday.'

'No,' said his father; 'he will not be here so soon.'

'Nor I so honoured,' said Vernon; 'Clinton's coming of age was celebrated by tumultuous rejoicings; but he is the Elder Son.'

Sir Richard gave Vernon, who spoke sneeringly, a quick glance – an indescribable expression of pain crossed his countenance.

'Have you been staying here since Christmas?' he asked at last. Vernon would have replied evasively, but Marianne said: 'Oh yes! he is always here now.'

'You appear to have become very fond of Beech Grove of a sudden,' continued his father. I felt that Sir Richard's eye was fixed on me as he spoke, and I was conscious that not only my cheeks, but my temples and neck were crimsoned with blushes. Some time after I saw my uncle in the shrubbery; he was alone, and the want of society was always so painful to him that I thought it but a mark of duteous kindness to join him. I wondered, as I approached, to see every token of haggard care on a face usually so smiling. He saw me, and smoothed his brow; he began talking of London, of my elder cousin, of his desire that I should conquer my timidity, and consent to be presented this spring. At length he suddenly stopped short, and scrutinising me as he spoke, said: 'Pardon me, dear Ellen, if I annoy you; but I am your guardian, your second father – am I not? Do not be angry, therefore, if I ask you, are you attached to my son Vernon?'

My natural frankness prompted one reply, but a thousand feelings, inexplicable but powerful, hung on my tongue. I answered, stammering: 'No – I believe so – I like him.'

'But you do not love him?'

'What a question, dear uncle!' I replied, covered with confusion.

'Is it even so?' cried Sir Richard; 'and is he to succeed in all?'

'You mistake,' I said; for I had a horror of confessing an attachment which, after all, I did not feel, and so of making our engagement more binding. But I blushed deeply as I spoke, and my uncle looked incredulous and said: 'Yet it would make you very unhappy if he married another.'

'Oh, no!' I cried, 'he has my free leave. I should wish him joy with all my heart.'

The idea – the hope that he was playing me false, and might release me from my trammels, darted through my mind with a quick thrill of delight. Sir Richard saw that I was in earnest, and his countenance cleared.

'What a strange thing is maiden coyness,' he observed; 'you blushed so prettily, Ellen, that I could have sworn you had given your heart to Vernon. But I see I was mistaken; I am glad of it, for he would not suit you.'

No more was said, but I felt conscience-stricken and miserable. I had deceived my uncle, and yet I had not. I had declared that I did not love him to whom I had pledged my hand; and the whole was a mystery and an entanglement that degraded me in my own eyes. I longed to make a full confession; yet then all would be over – we should both be inextricably bound. As it was, some caprice might cause Vernon to transfer his affection to another, and I could give him entire freedom, without any human being knowing how foolishly I had acted.

We had no guests at dinner; Sir Richard was to leave us early the next morning. After dinner I speedily retired to the drawing-room, leaving father and son together; they remained two hours. I was on the point of withdrawing to my own room, to avoid a meeting which alarmed me, I knew not why, when they entered. It seemed as if, in the interval of my absence, they had received sudden intelligence of a dear friend's death; and yet not quite so, for though Vernon looked absorbed in thought, his gloom was strangely interspersed with glances of swelling triumph; his smiles were no longer sneers – yet they did not betray a sunshine of the heart, but rather joy on a bad victory. He looked on me askance, with a kind of greedy satisfaction, and at his father with scorn. I trembled, and turned to my uncle; but sadness and confusion marked his features – he was stamped as with disgrace, and quailed beneath my eye; though presently he rallied, drew a chair near, and was kinder than ever. He told me that he was going up to town on the morrow, and that

Vernon was to accompany him; he asked me if there was anything he could do for me, and testified his affection by a thousand little attentions. Vernon said nothing, and took leave of me so coldly that I thought his manner implied that he expected to see me in the morning. Thinking it right to indulge him, I rose early; but he did not come down till long after Sir Richard, who thanked me for my kindness in disturbing myself on his account. They went away immediately after breakfast, and Vernon's formal adieu again struck me with wonder. Was it possible that he was indeed going to marry another? This doubt was all my comfort, for I was painfully agitated by the false position in which I had entangled myself by the mystery that enveloped my actions, and the falsehood which my lips perpetually implied, if they did not utter.

I was habitually an early riser. On the third morning after the departure of my relations, before I rose and while I was dressing, I thought that pebbles were thrown at my window; but my mind was too engrossed to pay attention, till at last, after my toilette had been leisurely completed, I looked from my window, and saw Vernon below, in the secluded part of the park which it overlooked. I hurried down, my heart palpitating with anxiety.

'I have been waiting for you these two hours,' he said, angrily: 'did you not hear my signal?'

'I know of no signal,' I replied; 'I am not accustomed to clandestine appointments.'

'And yet you can carry on a clandestine engagement excellently well! You told Sir Richard that you did not love me – that you should be glad if I married another.'

An indignant reply was bursting from my lips, but he saw the rising storm and hastened to allay it. He changed his tone at once from reproach to tender protestations.

'It broke my heart to leave you as I did,' he said, 'but I could do no less. Sir Richard insisted on my accompanying him – I was obliged to comply. Even now he believes me to be in town. I have travelled all night. He half suspected me, because I refused to dine with him today; and I was forced to promise to join him at a ball tonight. I need not be there till twelve or one and so can stay two hours with you.'

'But why this hurried journey?' I asked. 'Why do you come?'

He answered by pleading the vehemence of his affection, and spoke of the risk he ran of losing me for ever. 'Do you not know,' he said, 'that my father has set his heart upon your marrying my brother?'

'He is very good,' I replied, disdainfully. 'But I am not a slave, to be bought and sold. My cousin Clinton is the last person in the world whom you need fear.'

'Oh, Ellen, how much do you comfort – transport me, by this generous contempt for wealth and rank! You ask why I am here – it were worth the fatigue, twice ten thousand times told, to have these assurances. I have trembled – I have feared – but you will not love this favoured of fortune – this elder son!'

I cannot describe Vernon's look as he said this. Methought envy, malice and demoniac exultation were all mingled. He laughed aloud – I shrank from him dismayed. He became calmer a moment after.

'My life is in your hands, Ellen,' he said – but why repeat his glossing speeches, in which deceit and truth were so kneaded into one mass that the poison took the guise of the wholesome substance, while the whole was impregnated with destruction. I felt that I liked him less than ever; yet I yielded to his violence. I believed myself the victim of a venial but irreparable mistake of my own. I confirmed my promises, and pledged my faith most solemnly. It is true that I undeceived him as much as I could with regard to the extent of my attachment; at first he was furious at my coldness, then overwhelmed me with entreaties for forgiveness – tears even streamed from his eyes – and then again he haughtily reminded me that I forfeited every virtue of my sex and became a monument of falsehood if I failed him. We separated at last – I promised to write every day, and saw him ride away with a sensation as if relieved from the infliction of the torture.

A week after this scene – my spirits still depressed, and often weeping my dear father's death, which I considered the root of every evil – I was reading, or rather trying to read, in my dressing-room, but in reality brooding over my sorrows, when I heard Marianne's cheerful laugh in the shrubbery, and her voice calling me to join her. I roused myself from my sad reverie, and resolved to cast aside care and misery, while Vernon's absence afforded me a shadow of freedom; and, in fulfilment of this determination, went down to join my young light-hearted cousin. She was not alone. Clinton was with her. There was no resemblance between him and Vernon. His countenance was all sunshine; his light-blue eyes laughed in their own gladness and purity; his beaming smile, his silver-toned voice, his tall manly figure and, above all, his open-hearted engaging manners, were all the reverse of his dark mysterious brother. I saw him, and felt that my prejudices had been ridiculous; we became intimate in a moment. I know not how it was, but we seemed like brother and sister – each feeling, each thought, being laid bare to the other. I was naturally frank, but rendered timid by education;

so that it charmed me doubly when the unreserve of another invited me to indulge in the unguarded confidence of my disposition. How speedily the days now flew! they contained but one drawback, my correspondence with my cousin – not that I felt myself unfaithful towards him; my affection for my new-found relation did not disturb my conscience – that was pure, undisguised, sisterly. We had met from across the ocean of life – two beings who formed a harmonised whole; but the sympathy was too perfect, too untinged by earthly dross, to be compared with the selfish love given and exacted by Vernon. Yet I feared that his jealousy might be awakened, while I felt less inclined than ever to belie my own heart; and with aversion and hesitation penned letters containing the formula of affection and engaged vows.

Sir Richard came down to Beech Grove. He was highly pleased to see the cordial friendship that subsisted between his son and me.

'Did I not tell you that you would like him?' he said.

'Everyone must,' I replied; 'he is formed to win all hearts.'

'And suits you much better than Vernon?'

I did not know what to answer; it was a tender string that he touched; but I resolved not to feel or think. Sir Richard's were all flying visits; he was to leave us in the evening. He had, during the morning, a long conversation with Clinton; and immediately after, he sought for an opportunity to talk to me.

'Ellen,' he said, 'I have not been a wise but I am a fond father. I have done Clinton many injuries, of which he, poor fellow, is wholly unconscious; and I have wished to compensate for all in giving him a wife worthy of him. His temper is generous; his spirit clear and noble. By my soul, I think he has every virtue under heaven; and you alone deserve him. Do not interrupt me, I beseech you; hear me this once. I confess that ever since you became my ward this has been my favourite project. There have been several obstacles; but the most serious ones seem to vanish. You have seen each other, and I flatter myself have each discovered and appreciated the good qualities of the other. Is it so, Ellen? I know not whence my fears arise, and yet they intrude themselves. I fear, while I have been endeavouring to secure my boy's happiness, I may have been adding to the ruin already heaped on his head by my means. I have talked with him today. He has no disguise in his nature, and he avows that he loves you. I know that this confession would come better from himself; but your fortune, your beauty, make him fear to be misinterpreted. Do not mistake – he is wholly unaware of my intention of speaking to you. I see your distress, dear Ellen; have patience but for one word more – do not trifle with Clinton's feelings, as sometimes –

forgive me – it has appeared to me that you have trifled with Vernon's – do not foster hopes not to be fulfilled. Be frank, be honest, despite the bashfulness and coquetry of your sex.'

After these words, fearful of having offended – overcome by more agitation than I could have imagined him capable of feeling – my uncle drew me towards him, pressed me convulsively to his bosom, and then rushed from the room.

I cannot describe the state in which he left me – a spasm of pain passed through my frame; I became sick and faint, till a flood of tears relieved my bursting heart. I wept long – I sobbed in agony – I felt the veriest wretch that ever trod the earth.

My uncle had rent the veil that concealed me from myself. I loved Clinton – he was the whole world to me – all the world of light and joy, and I had shut myself out from him for ever. And he also was my victim. I beheld his dear face beaming with hope; I heard his thrilling voice harmonised by love; and saw the fearless cordiality of his manners, which bespoke his confidence in my sympathy; while I knew that I held a poisoned dagger which I was about to plunge into his heart. Sometimes I thought to treat him coldly; sometimes – oh! I cannot tell the various imaginations that haunted me – some self-sacrificing, others wicked and false – all ended in one way. My uncle departed; we were left together, our full hearts beating to respond to each other without any division or reserve. I felt that every moment might cause Clinton to open his soul to me, and to seek in mine for a feeling too truly and too fondly alive there, but which was sinful and fatal to both. To prevent his confession, my own preceded it. I revealed to him my engagement to Vernon, and declared my resolve not to swerve from my faith. He commended me. I saw despair at losing me painted in his countenance, mingled with horror at supplanting his brother; and alarm that he, the elder born, gifted by fortune with every blessing, should be suspected of the intention of stealing the sole remaining good which Vernon had won by his diligence, perhaps by his deserts. Forbid it, heaven! I saw in the clear mirror of his expressive countenance the struggle of passion and principle, and the triumph of honour and virtue exalted over the truest love that ever warmed man's breast.

Our gaiety was flown; our laughter stilled. We talked sadly and seriously together, neither lamenting our fate nor acknowledging our sufferings; tamed to endurance, and consoling each other by such demonstrations of affection as were permitted to our near relationship. We read clearly in each other's hearts, and supported each other in the joint sacrifice; and this without any direct acknowledgement. Clinton talked of returning to the Continent; I of my seclusion and tranquillity at Beech Grove. The time was distant – two years was an eternity at our age – before Vernon could claim my hand; and we did not advert to that fatal consummation. We gave up each other; and that single misery sufficed without a more cruel addition. I was calm, pale and tearless. I had brought it all on myself, and must submit. I could not cast aside the younger son to select the elder; and if in my secret thoughts I cherished a hope to induce Vernon to forgo his claims, that very circumstance would the more entirely divide me from Clinton. As my brother-in-law, I might see him – in some sort, our fortunes were shared; but as a rival to Vernon, a stream of blood separated us for ever.

The hours of sad sympathy which we passed were very dear to us. We knew that they were brief. Clinton had fixed the day and hour of his departure – each moment it drew nearer. We should never meet again till after my marriage; but till the hour of separation, for two short days, we were all in all to each other, despite the wall of adamant which was raised between us. We tried each to pretend to think and talk of indifferent subjects; and we *never* spoke of that nearest our hearts – but how superfluous are words as interpreters between lovers! As we walked or rode, and spent hours in each other's society, we exchanged thoughts more intimately during long periods of absolute silence than Vernon with his vehemence and eloquence could have conceived. Had we spoken folio volumes, we could have said no more. Our looks – the very casting down of our eyes and mutual tacit avoidance, told our resolve to fulfil our duties and to conquer our love; and yet how, by a glance or a faltering word, when the future was alluded to, did we promise never to forget, but to cherish mutual esteem and tenderness as all that was left of the paradise from which we were so ruthlessly driven! Now and then a playful expression on his part, or a blush on mine, betrayed more feeling than we considered right; the one was checked by a sigh, the other by an assumption of indifference.

It was at this time that Clinton made the sketch copied in the portrait accompanying this tale. I had been spending many hours in tears and anguish, when, resolved to overcome my weakness, and to recover an appearance of serenity before my cousin returned from his ride, I went into Marianne's schoolroom and took up a book. The exhaustion of weeping had calmed me; and I thought of my kinsman – his endearing qualities, and of the tie between us, with softened feelings. As I indulged in reverie, my head resting on my hand, my book falling from my fingers, my eyes closed and I passed from the agitated sense of life and sorrow into the balmy forgetfulness of sleep. Clinton had wished to

Ellen

make a portrait of me, yet had not ventured to ask me to sit, and he came
in at this moment; Marianne, whispering, told him not to disturb me.
He took her drawing materials, and made a hasty sketch, which genius
and love united to render a perfect likeness. I awoke and saw his work; it
was beyond our contract; I asked him for it; he felt that I was right and
gave it. This sacrifice on his part proved that he did not palter with his
sense of right. On the morrow we were to part; and he would preserve
no memorial beyond a remembrance which he could not destroy.

That morrow came. Clinton asked me and his sister to walk through
the park with him, to join his chariot at the farther lodge. We consented; but, at the moment of going, Marianne, who knew nothing
certainly, but who darkly guessed that all was not right, excused herself.
I joined him alone. There was something in his person and manner
that so promised protection and tenderness that I felt it doubly hard to
be torn from him. A dignified reserve, foreign to his usual nature,
founded on a resolve to play only the brother's part, checked me
somewhat; yet I loved him the more for it – while I would have laid
down my existence so that it had only been permitted us to throw aside
the mask but for one short hour, and to use the language of nature and
truth. It could not be; and our conversation was upon indifferent
subjects. When we approached the lodge, we found that the chariot
had not come, and we retreated a little, and sat down on a turfy bank;
then Clinton said a few words, the only ones that at all revealed the
agitation he was enduring: 'I have a little more experience than you,
Ellen,' he said; 'and, besides, I am haunted by strange presentiments;
we seem to know what we ought to do, and what we are to do, and act
accordingly – yet life is a strange, wild thing. I wish to ensure for you a
friend more willing and active than Sir Richard. I have a sister to whom
I am fondly attached; she is now on the Continent, but I shall hasten to
her, and entreat her to afford you a friendship you so richly deserve.
You will love Lady Hythe for her own sake as well as for mine.'

I was desirous of thanking him for this mark of kindness, but my
voice failed me, and I burst into tears, overcome by the excess of anguish
that deluged my heart. I tried to conceal my tears – I could not.

'Do not, Ellen, dear Ellen, I beseech you – command yourself.'

Clinton spoke in a voice so broken, so full of misery, that he inspired
me at once with fear and courage. The tread of a horse roused us – a
horse at swift gallop. I raised my eyes, and uttered a shriek; for, reining
in the animal with a sudden strong pull, Vernon halted close to us. The
most violent passions convulsed his countenance. He threw himself
from the horse, and casting the bridle from him, came up. What he

meant to say or do I cannot tell; perhaps to conceal the workings of his heart – and the quick departure of Clinton would have smoothed all; but I saw the barrel of a pistol peep from the pocket of his coat. I was seized with terror – I shrieked aloud. Clinton, terrified at my alarm, would have supported me, but Vernon pushed him rudely away.

'Dare not to approach or touch her, as you value your life!' he cried.

'My life! you talk idly, Vernon. I value her security – one moment of peace to her – far more.'

'You confess it!' exclaimed Vernon; 'and you, too, false and treacherous girl! Ha! did you think to betray me, and be unpunished? Do you think, if I so chose it, that I would not force you to look on till the blood of one of the brothers flowed at your feet? But there are other punishments in store for you.'

The expressions of menace used towards myself restored my courage, and I exclaimed, 'Beware that you do not break the tie that binds us – at least that bound us a moment ago – perhaps it is already broken.'

'Doubtless,' he cried, grinding his teeth with rage, 'it is broken, and a new one created to bind you to the elder son. Oh, yes! you would fain cast aside the poor miserable beggar, who has vainly fawned on you, and madly loved – you would take the rich, the honourable and honoured Sir Clinton! Base, hollow-hearted fool!'

'Vernon,' said Clinton, 'whatever your claims are on our cousin, I cannot stand by and see her insulted. You forget yourself.'

'The forgetfulness, sir, is on your part; proud in your seniority to rival your brother, to drive him from his all, has been a May-game for you; but know, proud fool or villain – take which name you will – your hour is passed by – your reign at an end! Your station is a fiction, your very existence a disgrace!'

Clinton and I both began to think that Vernon was really mad – a suspicion confirmed by his violent gestures. We looked at each other in alarm.

'Stay!' exclaimed the infuriated man, seizing my arm with a fierce grasp; while, fearful to induce Clinton's interference, I yielded. 'Stay, and listen to what your lover is – or shall I wound your delicate ears? There are soft phrases and silken words to adorn that refuse of the world – a bastard!'

'Vernon, dare not! – beware, sir, and begone!'

Clinton's face crimsoned; his voice, his majestic indignation almost forced the ruffian to quail; he threw my arm from him.

'Take him, fair Ellen! it is true you take what I say – a natural son. Do you think that my information is not correct? Ask our father, for he is yours, Clinton, and our mother is the same; you are the firstborn of Richard Gray and Matilda Towers; but I am the eldest son of Mr and Mrs Gray.'

It could not have been that Vernon would have acted this cowardly and foolish part had he not been driven by a kind of madness. In truth, Sir Richard had, to quench his hopes for ever, with that carelessness of truth – his fatal propensity – affirmed that Clinton and I were acknowledged lovers; and he came goaded by worse than jealousy – by a spirit of hatred and revenge. Seeing us together, obviously engaged by the most engrossing feelings, his temper, which had been worked into fury during his journey, burst forth beyond the bounds he had prescribed for himself. I have called him a serpent, and such he was in every respect: he could crawl and coil, and hide his wily advance; but he could erect his crest, dart out his forked tongue and infix the deadly venom when roused, as he now was. Clinton turned alternately pale and red.

'Be it as you will,' he said: 'my fortunes and yours are of slight moment in comparison to Ellen's safety. If there is any truth in this tale of yours, there will be time enough to discover it and to act upon it. Meanwhile, dear cousin, I see they have brought my chariot to the lodge. You cannot walk home – get into it; it will drive you to the house, and come back for me.'

I looked at him enquiringly.

'Do not fear to be deserted by me,' he said, 'or that I shall do any thing rashly. Vernon must accompany me to town – to our father's presence, there to expiate his foul calumny or to prove it. Be assured he shall not approach you without your leave. I will watch over him, and guard you.'

Clinton spoke aloud, and Vernon became aware that he must yield to this arrangement, and satisfied that he had divided us, Clinton led me to his carriage.

'You will hear soon from some one of us, Ellen,' he said; 'and let me implore you to be patient – to take care of yourself – to fear nothing. I can make no remark – affirm, deny nothing now; but you shall not be kept in suspense. Promise me to be patient and calm.'

'And do you,' I said at last, commanding my trembling voice, 'promise not to be rash; and promise not to leave England without seeing me again.'

'I promise not to leave England for any time without your leave. Oh, trust me, my dear cousin, it is not in such storms as these that you shall be ashamed of me; one sentiment may subdue me, but poverty, disgrace and every angry passion, I can master.'

Vernon did not dare interrupt us. He felt that he had destroyed his carefully woven web through his own rashness and gnawed his lips in silent rage. I looked at him once, and turned away my eyes in contempt. I got into the chariot; it drove me to the house, and went back to take Clinton up to town. Thus we were separated, as we intended; and yet, how differently! Hope was reborn in my heart, out of the very ashes of its despair.

Two mortal days passed, and I was still in my solitude, receiving no intelligence, except, indeed, such as was contained in a letter from Vernon. In this he demanded me as a right, and fiercely insisted that I should keep my faith with him; but he did not allude to the scene in the park, nor to his strange assertions there. I threw the letter from me as unworthy of notice or thought. The third morning brought me one from my uncle. I tore it open with uncontrollable impatience: these were the contents:

Clinton, my dear Ellen, insists that I should join you at Beech Grove; but I cannot persuade myself to do so till I have your leave – till I have confessed my villainy, and besought your forgiveness, in addition to that of my noble-hearted boy, whom I devoted to ruin before his birth, and who has pardoned me. It is a hateful subject – unfit for your ears, my gentle, virtuous girl, and I must hurry it over. When I first knew Miss Towers, I had no idea of marrying her; for she was poor and of humble birth. We loved each other, and she was willing to become mine on my own terms. Our intercourse was betrayed to her parents; and to appease them, and please Matilda, I declared that we were married. My assertion was credited; Matilda assumed my name, and all the world, all her little world, was deceived; while at the same time I declared to my father that she was merely my mistress: he did not believe me. Thus I became entangled. A little before the birth of our second boy my father died, and my grandfather offered me two thousand a year on condition that I would secure the whole estate to my eldest son. I loved Matilda; my fears were dissipated by my father's death, and by this acknowledgement of my union by my grandfather. I married her; and three days after Vernon's birth signed the settlement of entail. Such is my story. Lady Gray's character necessitated the concealment from every human being of the period when the marriage was celebrated. My noble, beloved Clinton assumed the elder son's place. I dared not reveal the truth; nay, I fancied that I benefited him by allowing him to fill this false position till my death. He has undeceived me;

but he has not cursed me. From the moment I saw you, I designed that you should repair my faults towards him, as you alone could. I believed that you were formed for each other; I was not mistaken there. I meant to acknowledge all before your marriage, but I believed that if once your affections were engaged, you would not reject my son from base and worldly minded considerations. Am I not right also in this? Meanwhile, Clinton was abroad, and I became uneasy at observing the pains which Vernon took to ingratiate himself with you, and the intimacy which you encouraged. I forbade him to remain with you at Beech Grove – he defied me. Then I tried to entice him away from you; and, as a last bribe, disclosed the secret of his birth; he, in return, promised to leave the field open to Clinton. You know the rest. He never meant to give you up; he was my heir, and he grasped at your fortune besides – shall he succeed? Clinton is all kindness, and soothing angelic goodness – but he insists on no longer filling a situation to which he has no claim, and – is gone abroad. He fears to leave you exposed to Vernon's violence, and has made me promise to go down to Beech Grove, and to prevent his brother from seeing you without your free and entire consent. As I have said, I cannot prevail on myself to visit you till you are in full possession of all the facts. Now they are in your hands. You may expect me tomorrow. Do not fear Vernon; I will take care that he shall not commit further outrage on you, nor injure the interest which I fondly trust that you preserve for my godlike, my beloved Clinton.

I read and reread this letter a thousand times; my soul was in tumult. At first I could only think of the facts that it contained, and proudly and joyfully determined to compensate Clinton, as I believed I could, for every evil; and then again I read the letter, and many parts of it filled me with wonder and dismay. Clinton was gone abroad – against his promise – without a word, and there was something so indelicate in the way in which my uncle espoused his cause. It was strange – unlike any conduct I had expected on my dear cousin's part. Of course he would write – and yet he was gone, and no letter came! And then I dreaded to see Sir Richard, the wrongful, penitent father: the total indifference which he displayed to moral principle – not founded, like Vernon's, on selfishness, but on weakness of character and natural callousness to truth, revolted me. Where was my own dear father? He had thrown me from the sacred shelter of his virtue into a system of dissimulation and guilt, which even Clinton, I thought, deserting me as he did, did not redeem. I struggled with these feelings, but their justice confounded and overcame me. Yet, even in the midst of these disquieting reflections, a deep sense of happiness pervaded my soul. The mystery, the tyranny, which had enveloped me, was brushed away like a spider's web. I was free – I might follow the dictates of my feelings, and it was no longer sin to love him to whom my heart was irrevocably given. The hours of the day flew on, while I lived as in a dream, absorbed by wonder, hope, doubt and joy. At length, at six in the evening, a carriage drove up the avenue; a kind of terror at the expectation of seeing my uncle seized me, and I retreated hastily to my own room, gasping for breath. In a few minutes my servant tapped at my door; she told me that it was Lady Hythe who had arrived, and delivered me a letter. The letter was from Clinton; it was dated the same day, in London. I pressed it passionately to my lips and heart, and devoured its contents with eagerness. 'At length, dear Ellen,' he wrote, 'I am satisfied; I was long uneasy on your account. I besought my father to go down to you, yet even that did not content me – for you did not so much need protection as sympathy and true disinterested friendship. My thoughts turned towards my earliest and dearest friend, my sister Caroline. She was on the Continent – I set out immediately to meet her, to tell everything, and to ask her advice and assistance. Fortune befriended me – I found her at Calais – she is now with you. She is my better self. Her delicacy of character, her accurate judgement and warm heart, joined to her position as a woman, married to the best and most generous fellow breathing, render her the very person to whom I can entrust your happiness. I do not speak of myself – fortune cannot overcome my spirits, and my way is clear before me. I pity my father and family; but Caroline will explain to you better than I can my views and hopes. Adeiu, dear cousin! Heaven bless you as you deserve! Your fortitude, I am sure, has not deserted you; yet I am very anxious to hear that your health has not suffered by my brother's violence. Caroline will write to me, and rejoice me by telling me of your well-being.'

I hurried down immediately to welcome Clinton's sister; and from that moment my perplexities and sorrows vanished. Lady Hythe was a feminine likeness of Clinton; the same active kindness of heart, gentleness of temper and adorable frankness. We were friends and sisters on the instant, and her true affection repaid me for every suffering; none of which I should have experienced had she been in England on my arrival. Clinton had told her of his love, but left me to reveal my own sentiments, detailing only the artifices and jealousy of Vernon. I was without disguise, for we were all one family, with the same objects, hopes and pleasures. We went up to town immediately, and there I saw Clinton, and we exchanged our reserved, sad intercourse for a full acknowledgment of every thought and feeling.

The only piece of prudence that Sir Richard had practised was placing Clinton in the army, and purchasing promotion for him. He was so beloved by his fellow-officers that, on the discovery of his unfortunate birth, they all united in giving him the support of their friendship and good opinion. Clinton resolved, therefore, to enter at once on active service, and to follow up his profession with energy. Two years were to elapse before I could marry, and he expressed a wish that we should neither of us consider ourselves under any engagement. How vain are such words! Heaven designed us for each other, and the mere phrase of engagement or freedom could not affect a tie founded on affection, esteem or, beyond this, the passion that caused us to find happiness in each other only. He went with his regiment to Ireland, and we were a good deal divided during the two years that elapsed before I was twenty-one. I continued to reside with Lady Hythe, and enjoyed with her that peace of mind which true friendship affords.

At length the day came when I completed my twenty-first year. Sir Richard had wished to be present at our nuptials, but was unable from ill health. I went to him, and saw him for the first time since the fatal discovery; for, on finding that I was happily placed with his daughter, he had carefully avoided seeing me. His character, indeed, was wholly changed. While carrying on a system of dissimulation, he had appeared gay; he was extravagant, given up to pleasure and spending even beyond his large income, despite the ruin in which he knew that his son would be involved on his death. He made him indeed a princely allowance, as if that was to compensate him; while, in fact, Clinton was only thus habituated to expense. As soon as the discovery was made, Sir Richard, by one of those inconceivable changes which sometimes occur in the history of human nature, set his heart on saving a fortune for his beloved boy. He thought that I might be fickle; he feared his own death and the loss of power to benefit him. He gave up his establishment in town – he let Beech Grove – he saved every farthing that he could, and was enabled to settle twenty thousand pounds on Clinton on the day of our marriage.

I went to see him in a little lodging at Camberwell, whither he had retreated: he was emaciated and ill; his eyes brightened a little on seeing Clinton and me together.

'I would fain live a little longer,' he said, 'to increase my son's fortune; but God's will be done – you will make him happy, Ellen.'

We were inexpressibly shocked. He had concealed his penurious style of life and declining health all this time; and nothing but his illness, and our insisting upon seeing him, caused him to betray it now. Our first care after our marriage was to oblige him to take up his abode with us; and we devoted ourselves to calming his remorse and smoothing his path to the grave. He survived only four months; but he had the comfort of knowing that Clinton was satisfied and happy; and that we both from our hearts forgave the errors which he at last expiated so dearly.

We never saw Vernon again; nor can I tell what has happened to him, except that he lives the life of the rich in England, apparently attended by prosperity. Lady Hythe stood between me and him, and screened me from his violence and reproaches. He has never married. I have never seen him since the day when, in the park at Beech Grove, he unawares conferred on me every blessing of life, by releasing me from the ties that bound me to him.

The happiness of Clinton and myself has been unclouded. I at last persuaded him to give up his profession, and we live principally abroad. Lord and Lady Hythe frequently visit us; and every event of our lives – the unimportant events of domestic life – tends to increase our prosperity, and the entire affection we cherish for each other.

The Parvenue

W HY do I write my melancholy story? Is it as a lesson, to prevent any other from wishing to rise to rank superior to that in which they are born? No! miserable as I am, others might have been happy, I doubt not, in my position: the chalice has been poisoned for me alone! Am I evil-minded – am I wicked? What have been my errors that I am now an outcast and a wretch? I will tell my story – let others judge me; my mind is bewildered, I cannot judge myself.

My father was a land steward to a wealthy nobleman. He married young, and had several children. He then lost his wife, and remained fifteen years a widower, when he married again – a young girl, the daughter of a clergyman who died, leaving numerous offspring in extreme poverty. My maternal grandfather had been a man of sensibility and genius; my mother inherited many of his endowments. She was an earthly angel; all her works were charity, all her thoughts were love.

Within a year after her marriage, she gave birth to twins – I and my sister; soon after she fell into ill health, and from that time was always weakly. She could endure no fatigue, and seldom moved from her chair. I see her now; her white, delicate hands employed in needlework, her soft, love-lighted eyes fixed on me. I was still a child when my father fell into trouble, and we removed from the part of the country where we had hitherto lived, and went to a distant village, where we rented a cottage, with a little land adjoining. We were poor, and all the family assisted each other. My elder half-sisters were strong, industrious, rustic young women, and submitted to a life of labour with great cheerfulness. My father held the plough, my half-brothers worked in the barns; all was toil, yet all seemed enjoyment.

How happy my childhood was! Hand in hand with my dear twin sister, I plucked the spring flowers in the hedges, turned the hay in the summer meadows, shook the apples from the trees in the autumn, and at all seasons, gambolled in delicious liberty beneath the free air of heaven; or at my mother's feet, caressed by her, I was taught the sweetest lessons of charity and love. My elder sisters were kind; we were all linked by strong affection. The delicate, fragile existence of my mother gave an interest to our monotony, while her virtues and her refinement threw a grace over our homely household.

I and my sister did not seem twins, we were so unlike. She was robust, chubby, full of life and spirits; I, tall, slim, fair, and even pale. I loved to play with her, but soon grew tired, and then I crept to my mother's side, and she sang me to sleep and nursed me in her bosom, and looked on me with her own angelic smile. She took pains to instruct me, not in accomplishments, but in all real knowledge. She unfolded to me the wonders of the visible creation, and to each tale of bird and beast, of fiery mountain or vast river, was appended some moral, derived from her warm heart and ardent imagination. Above all, she impressed upon me the precepts of the gospel, charity to every fellow creature, the brotherhood of mankind, the rights that every sentient creature possesses to our services alone. I was her almoner; for, poor as she was, she was the benefactress of those who were poorer. Being delicate, I helped her in her task of needlework, while my sister aided the rest in their household or rustic labours.

When I was seventeen, a miserable accident happened. A hayrick caught fire, it communicated to our outhouses and at last to the cottage. We were roused from our beds at midnight, and escaped barely with our lives. My father bore out my mother in his arms, and then tried to save a portion of his property. The roof of the cottage fell in on him. He was dug out after an hour, scorched, maimed, crippled for life.

We were all saved, but by a miracle only was I preserved. I and my sister were awoken by cries of fire. The cottage was already enveloped in flames. Susan, with her accustomed intrepidity, rushed through the flames and escaped; I thought only of my mother, and hurried to her room. The fire raged around me; it encircled – hemmed me in. I believed that I must die, when suddenly I felt myself seized upon and borne away. I looked on my preserver – it was Lord Reginald Desborough.

For many Sundays past, when at church, I knew that Lord Reginald's eyes were fixed on me. He had met me and Susan in our walks; he had called at our cottage. There was fascination in his eye, in his soft voice and earnest gaze, and my heart throbbed with gladness as I thought that he surely loved me. To have been saved by him, was to make the boon of life doubly precious.

There is to me much obscurity in this part of my story. Lord Reginald loved me, it is true; why he loved me, so far as to forget pride of rank and ambition for my sake, he who afterwards showed no tendency to disregard the prejudices and habits of rank and wealth, I cannot tell; it seems strange. He had loved me before, but from the hour that he saved my life, love grew into an overpowering passion. He offered us a lodge on his estate to take refuge in; and while there, he sent us presents of game, and still more kindly, fruits and flowers to my mother, and came himself, especially when all were out except my mother and myself, and sat by us and conversed. Soon I learnt to expect the soft asking look of his eyes, and almost dared answer it. My mother once perceived these glances, and took an opportunity to appeal to Lord Reginald's good feelings not to make me miserable for life by implanting an attachment that could only be productive of unhappiness. His answer was to ask me in marriage.

I need not say that my mother gratefully consented – that my father, confined to his bed since the fire, thanked God with rapture; that my sisters were transported by delight: I was the least surprised then, though the most happy. Now, I wonder much, what could he see in me? So many girls of rank and fortune were prettier. I was an untaught, low-born, portionless girl. It was very strange.

Then I only thought of the happiness of marrying him, of being loved, of passing my life with him. My wedding day was fixed. Lord Reginald had neither father nor mother to interfere with his arrangements. He told no relation; he became one of our family during the interval. He saw no deficiencies in our mode of life – in my dress; he was satisfied with all; he was tender, assiduous and kind, even to my elder sisters; he seemed to adore my mother, and became a brother to my sister Susan. She was in love, and asked him to intercede to gain her parents' consent for her choice. He did so; and though before, Lawrence Cooper, the carpenter of the place, had been disdained, supported by him, he was accepted. Lawrence Cooper was young, well looking, well disposed and fondly attached to Susan.

My wedding day came. My mother kissed me fondly, my father blessed me with pride and joy, my sisters stood round, radiant with delight. There was but one drawback to the universal happiness – that immediately on my marriage, I was to go abroad.

From the church door I stepped into the carriage. Having once and again been folded in my dear mother's embrace, the wheels were in motion, and we were away. I looked out from the window; there was the dear group: my old father, white-headed and aged, in his large chair; my mother, smiling through her tears, with folded hands and upraised looks of gratitude, anticipating long years of happiness for her grateful Fanny; Susan and Lawrence standing side by side, unenvious of my greatness, happy in themselves; my sisters conning over with pride and joy the presents made to them, and the prosperity that flowed in from my husband's generosity. All looked happy, and it seemed as if I were the cause of all this happiness. We had been indeed saved from dreadful evils; ruin had ensued from the fire, and we had been sunk in adversity through that very event from which our good fortune took its rise. I felt proud and glad. I loved them all. I thought, I make them happy – they are prosperous through me! And my heart warmed with gratitude towards my husband at the idea.

We spent two years abroad. It was rather lonely for me, who had always been surrounded, as it were, by a populous world of my own, to find myself cast upon foreigners and strangers; the habits of the different sexes in the higher ranks so separate them from each other, that after a few months, I spent much of my time in solitude. I did not repine; I had been brought up to look upon the hard visage of life, if not unflinchingly, at least with resignation. I did not expect perfect happiness. Marriages in humble life are attended with so much care. I had none of this: my husband loved me; and though I often longed to see the dear familiar faces that thronged my childhood's home, and above all I pined for my mother's caresses and her wise maternal lessons, yet for a time I was content to think of them, and hope for a reunion, and to acquiesce in the present separation.

Still many things pained me: I had, poor myself, been brought up among the poor, and nothing, since I can remember forming an idea, so much astonished and jarred with my feelings as the thought of how the rich could spend so much on themselves while any one of their fellow creatures were in destitution. I had none of the patrician charity (though such is praiseworthy), which consists in distributing thin soup and coarse flannel petticoats – a sort of instinct or sentiment of justice, the offspring of my lowly paternal hearth and my mother's enlightened piety, was deeply implanted in my mind, that all had as good a right to the comforts of life as myself, or even as my husband. My charities, they were called – they seemed to me the payment of my debts to my fellow creatures – were abundant. Lord Reginald peremptorily checked them; but as I had a large allowance for my own expenses, I denied myself a thousand luxuries, to which it appeared to me I had no right, for the sake of feeding the hungry. Nor was it only that charity impelled me, but that I could not acquire a taste for spending money on myself – I disliked the apparatus of wealth. My husband called my ideas sordid, and reproved me severely when, instead of outshining all competitors at a fête, I appeared dowdily dressed, and declared warmly that I could not, I would not, spend twenty guineas on a gown, while I could dress so many sad faces in smiles and bring so much joy to so many drooping hearts by the same sum.

Was I right? I firmly believe that there is not one among the rich who will not affirm that I did wrong; that to please my husband and do honour to his rank was my first duty. Yet, shall I confess it? even now, rendered miserable by this fault – I cannot give it that name – I can call it a misfortune – it is such to be consumed at the stake a martyr for one's faith. Do not think me presumptuous in this simile, for many years I have wasted at the slow fire of knowing that I lost my husband's affections because I performed what I believed to be a duty.

But I am not come to that yet. It was not till my return to England that the full disaster crushed me. We had often been applied to for money by my family, and Lord Reginald had acceded to nearly all their requests. When we reached London after two years' absence, my first wish was to see my dear mother. She was at Margate for her health. It was agreed that I should go there alone, and pay a short visit. Before I went, Lord Reginald told me what I did not know before, that my family had often made exorbitant demands on him, with which he was resolved not to comply. He told me that he had no wish to raise my relatives from their station in society; and that, indeed, there were only two among them whom he conceived had any claims upon me – my mother and my twin sister: that the former was incapable of any improper request, and the latter, by marrying Cooper, had fixed her own position, and could in no way be raised from the rank of her chosen husband. I agreed to much that he said. I replied that he well knew that my own taste led me to consider mediocrity the best and happiest situation; that I had no wish, and would never consent, to supply any extravagant demands on the part of persons, however dear to me, whose circumstances he had rendered easy.

Satisfied with my reply, we parted most affectionately, and I went on my way to Margate with a light and glad heart; and the cordial reception I received from my whole family, collected together to receive me, was calculated to add to my satisfaction. The only drawback to my content was my mother's state; she was wasted to a shadow. They all talked and laughed around her, but it was evident to me that she had not long to live.

There was no room for me in the small furnished house in which they were all crowded, so I remained at the hotel. Early in the morning, before I was up, my father visited me. He begged me to intercede with my husband; that on the strength of his support he had embarked in a speculation which required a large capital; that many families would be ruined, and himself dishonoured, if a few hundreds were not advanced. I promised to do what I could, resolving to ask my mother's advice, and make her my guide. My father kissed me with an effusion of gratitude, and left me.

I cannot enter into the whole of these sad details; all my half-brothers and sisters had married, and trusted to their success in life to Lord Reginald's assistance. Each evidently thought that they asked little in not demanding an equal share of my luxuries and fortune; but they were all in difficulty – all needed large assistance – all depended on me.

Lastly, my own sister Susan appealed to me – but hers was the most moderate request of all – she only wished for twenty pounds. I gave it her at once from my own purse.

As soon as I saw my mother I explained to her my difficulties. She told me that she expected this, and that it broke her heart; I must summon courage and resist these demands. That my father's imprudence had ruined him, and that he must encounter the evil he had brought on himself; that my numerous relatives were absolutely mad with the notion of what I ought to do for them. I listened with grief – I saw the torments in store for me – I felt my own weakness, and knew that I could not meet the rapacity of those about me with any courage or firmness. That same night my mother fell into convulsions; her life was saved with difficulty. From Susan I learned the cause of her attack. She had had a violent altercation with my father: she insisted that I should not be appealed to; while he reproached her for rendering me undutiful, and bringing ruin and disgrace on his grey hairs. When I saw my pale mother trembling, fainting, dying – when I was again and again assured that she must be my father's victim unless I yielded, what wonder that, in the agony of my distress, I wrote to my husband to implore his assistance.

Oh! what thick clouds now obscured my destiny! how do I remember, with a sort of thrilling horror, the boundless sea, white cliffs and wide sands of Margate. The summer day that had welcomed my arrival changed to bleak wintry weather during this interval – while I waited with anguish for my husband's answer. Well do I remember the evening on which it came: the waves of the sea showed their white crests, no vessel ventured to meet the gale with any canvas except a topsail, the sky was bared clear by the wind, the sun was going down fiery red. I looked upon the troubled waters – I longed to be borne away upon them, away from care and misery. At this moment a servant followed me to the sands with my husband's answer, it contained a refusal. I dared not communicate it. The menaces of bankruptcy; the knowledge that he

Margate

had instilled false hopes into so many; the fears of disgrace – all rendered my father, always rough, absolutely ferocious. Life flickered in my dear mother's frame, it seemed on the point of expiring when she heard my father's step; if he came in with a smooth brow, her pale lips wreathed into her own sweet smile, and a delicate pink tinged her fallen cheeks; if he scowled, and his voice was high, every limb shivered, she turned her face to her pillow, while convulsive tears shook her frame, and threatened instant dissolution. My father sought me alone one day, as I was walking in melancholy guise upon the sands; he swore that he would not survive his disgrace. 'And do you think, Fanny,' he added, 'that your mother will survive the knowledge of my miserable end?' I saw the resolution of despair in his face as he spoke. I asked the sum needed, the time when it must be given. A thousand pounds in two days was all that was asked. I set off to London to implore my husband to give this sum.

No! no! I cannot step by step record my wretchedness – the money was given – I extorted it from Lord Reginald, though I saw his very heart closed on me as he wrote the cheque. Worse had happened since I had left him. Susan had used the twenty pounds I gave her to reach town, to throw herself at my husband's feet and implore his compassion. Rendered absolutely insane by the idea of having a lord for a brother-in-law, Cooper had launched into a system of extravagance, incredible as it was wicked. He was many thousand of pounds in debt, and when at last Lord Reginald wrote to refuse all further supply, the miserable man committed forgery. Two hundred pounds prevented exposure, and preserved him from an ignominious end. Five hundred more were advanced to send him and his wife to America, to settle there, out of the way of temptation. I parted from my dear sister. I loved her fondly; she had no part in her husband's guilt, yet she was still attached to him, and her child bound them together; they went into solitary, miserable exile. 'Ah! had we remained in virtuous poverty,' cried my broken-hearted sister, 'I had not been forced to leave my dying mother.'

The thousand pounds given to my father was but a drop of water in the ocean. Again I was appealed to; again I felt the slender thread of my mother's life depended on my getting a supply. Again, trembling and miserable, I implored the charity of my husband.

'I am content,' he said, 'to do what you ask, to do more than you ask; but remember the price you pay – either give up your parents and your family, whose rapacity and crimes deserve no mercy, or we part for ever. You shall have a proper allowance; you can maintain all your family on it if you please; but their names must never be mentioned to me again. Choose between us, Fanny – you never see them more, or we part for ever.'

Did I do right – I cannot tell – misery is the result – misery frightful, endless, unredeemed. My mother was dearer to me than all the world – my heart revolted from my husband's selfishness. I did not reply – I rushed to my room, and that night, in a sort of delirium of grief and horror at my being asked never again to see my mother, I set out for Margate – such was my reply to my husband.

Three years have passed since then; for these three I preserved my mother, and during all this time I was grateful to heaven for being permitted to do my duty by her, and though I wept over the alienation of my cruel husband, I did not repent. But she, my angelic support, is no more. My father survived my mother but two months; remorse for all he had done, and made me suffer, cut short his life. His family by his first wife are gathered round me, they importune, they rob, they destroy me. Last week I wrote to Lord Reginald. I communicated the death of my parents; I represented that my position was altered; that my duties did not now clash; and that if he still cared for his unhappy wife all might be well. Yesterday his answer came. It was too late, he said; I had myself torn asunder the ties that united us, they never could be knit together again.

By the same post came a letter from Susan. She is happy. Cooper, profiting by the frightful lesson he incurred, awakened to a manly sense of the duties of life, is thoroughly reformed. He is industrious, prosperous and respectable. Susan asks me to join her. I am resolved to go. Oh! my native village, and recollections of my youth, to which I sacrificed so much, where are ye now? tainted by pestilence, envenomed by serpents' stings, I long to close my eyes on every scene I have ever viewed. Let me seek a strange land, a land where a grave will soon be opened for me. I feel that I cannot live long – I desire to die. I am told that Lord Reginald loves another, a highborn girl; that he openly curses our union as the obstacle to his happiness. The memory of this will poison the oblivion I go to seek in a distant land. He will be free. Soon will the hand he once so fondly took in his and made his own, which, now flung away, trembles with misery as it traces these lines, moulder in its last decay.

The Pilgrims

THE twilight of one of those burning days of summer whose unclouded sky seems to speak to man of happier realms had already flung its broad shadows over the valley of Unspunnen, while the departing rays of a gorgeous sunset continued to glitter on the summits of the surrounding hills. Gradually, however, the glowing tints deepened; then grew darker and darker, until they finally yielded to the still more sober hues of night.

Beneath an avenue of lime trees, which, from their size and luxuriance, appeared almost coeval with the soil in which they grew, Burkhardt of Unspunnen wandered to and fro with uneasy step, as if some recent sorrow occupied his troubled mind. At times, he stood with his eyes steadfastly fixed on the earth, as if he expected to see the object of his contemplation start forth from its bosom; at other times, he would raise his eyes to the summits of the trees, whose branches, now gently agitated by the night breeze, seemed to breathe sighs of compassion in remembrance of those happy hours which had once been passed beneath their welcome shade. When, however, advancing from beneath them, he beheld the deep blue heavens with the bright host of stars, hope sprang up within him at the thoughts of that glory to which those heavens and those stars, all lovely and beauteous as they seem, are but the faint heralds, and for a time dissipated the grief which had so long weighed heavily upon his heart.

From these reflections, which, from the intensity of his feelings, shut him out, as it were, from the busy world and its many paths, he was suddenly aroused by the tones of a manly voice addressing him.

Burkhardt advancing beheld, standing in the light of the moon, two pilgrims, clothed in the usual coarse and sombre garb, with their broad hats drawn over their brows.

'Praise be to God!' said the pilgrim who had just before awakened Burkhardt's attention, and who, from his height and manner appeared to be the elder of the two. His words were echoed by a voice whose gentle and faltering accents showed the speaker to be still but of tender years.

'Whither are you going, friends? what seek you here, at this late hour?' said Burkhardt. 'If you wish to rest you after your journey enter, and with God's blessing and my hearty welcome recruit yourselves.'

'Noble sir, you have more than anticipated our petition,' replied the elder pilgrim. 'Our duty has led us far from our native land, being bound on a pilgrimage to fulfil the vow of a beloved parent. We have been forced during the heat of the day to climb the steep mountain paths; and the strength of my brother, whose youth but ill befits him for such fatigues, began to fail, when the sight of your castle's towers, which the moon's clear beams discovered to us, revived our hopes. We resolved to beg a night's lodging under your hospitable roof, that we might be enabled, on tomorrow's dawn, to pursue our weary way.'

'Follow me, my friends,' said Burkhardt, as he, with quickened step, preceded them, that he might give some orders for their entertainment. The pilgrims, rejoicing in so kind a reception, followed the knight in silence into a high vaulted saloon, over which the tapers, that were placed in branches against the walls, cast a solemn but pleasing light, well in accordance with the present feelings of the parties.

The knight then discerned two countenances of great beauty, the pleasing impression of which was considerably heightened by the modest yet easy manner with which the youthful pair received their host's kind attentions. Much struck with their appearance and demeanour, Burkhardt was involuntarily led back into the train of thoughts from which their approach had aroused him; and the scenes of former days flitted before him as he recollected that in this hall his beloved child was ever wont to greet him with her welcome smile on his return from the battle or the chase; brief scenes of happiness, which had been followed by events that had cankered his heart, and rendered memory but an instrument of bitterness and chastisement.

Supper was soon after served, and the pilgrims were supplied with the greatest attention, yet conversation wholly languished; for his melancholy reflections occupied Burkhardt, and respect, or perhaps a more kindly feeling, towards their host and benefactor, seemed to have sealed the lips of his youthful guests. After supper, however, a flask of the baron's old wine cheered his flagging spirits, and emboldened the elder pilgrim to break through the spell which had chained them.

'Pardon me, noble sir,' said he, 'for I feel that it must seem intrusive in me to presume to seek the cause of that sorrow which thus severely oppresses you, and renders you so sad a spectator of the bounty and happiness which you liberally bestow upon others. Believe me, it is not the impulse of a mere idle curiosity that makes me express my wonder that you can thus dwell alone in this spacious and noble mansion, the prey to so deeply rooted a sorrow. Would that it were in our power, even in the slightest degree, to alleviate the cares of one who with such bounteous hand relieves the wants of his poorer brethren!'

'I thank you for your sympathy, good pilgrim,' said the old noble, 'but what can it avail you to know the story of those griefs which have made this earth a desert? and which are, with rapid pace, conducting me where alone I can expect to find rest. Spare me, then, the pain of recalling scenes which I would fain bury in oblivion. As yet, you are in the spring of life, when no sad remembrance gives a discordant echo of past follies, or of joys irrecoverably lost. Seek not to darken the sunshine of your, I trust, unsullied youth, with a knowledge of those fierce, guilty beings who, in listening to the fiendlike suggestions of their passions, are led astray from the paths of rectitude and tear asunder ties which nature, by the holiest bonds, had seemed to unite to their very souls.'

Burkhardt thus sought to avoid the entreaty of the pilgrim. But the request was still urged with such earnest though delicate persuasion, and the rich tones of the stranger's voice awoke within him so many thoughts of days long, long past, that the knight felt himself almost irresistibly impelled to unburden his long closed heart to one who seemed to enter into its feelings with a sincere cordiality.

'Your artless sympathy has won my confidence, my young friends,' said he, 'and you shall learn the cause of that sorrow which gnaws my heart. You see me now, indeed, here, lonely and forsaken, like a tree shaken by the tempest's violence. But fortune once looked upon me with her blandest smiles; and I felt myself rich in the consciousness of my prosperity, and the gifts which bounteous heaven had bestowed. My powerful vassals made me a terror to those enemies which the protection, that I was ever ready to afford to the oppressed and helpless, brought against me. My rich and fertile possessions not only supplied my family with profusion, but enabled me, with liberal hand, to relieve the wants of the poor; and to exercise the rights of hospitality in a manner justly becoming my state and my name. But, of all the gifts which heaven had showered upon me, that which I most prized was a wife whose virtues had made her the idol of both the rich and the poor. But she who was already an angel, and unfitted for this grosser world, was too soon, alas! claimed by her kindred spirits. One brief year alone had beheld our happiness.

'My grief and anguish were most bitter, and would soon have laid me in the same grave with her, but that she had left me a daughter, for whose dear sake I struggled earnestly against my affliction. In her were now centred all my cares, all my hopes, all my happiness. As she grew in years, so did her likeness to her sainted mother increase; and every look and gesture reminded me of my Agnes. With her mother's beauty I had, with fond presumption, dared to cherish the hope that Ida would inherit her mother's virtues.

'Greatly did I feel the sad void that my irreparable loss had occasioned me; but the very thought of marrying again would have seemed to me a profanation to the memory of my Agnes. If, however, even for a single instant I had entertained this disposition, one look at her child would have crushed it and made me cling with still fonder hope to her, in the fond confidence that she would reward me for every sacrifice that I could make. Alas! my friends, this hope was built on an unsure foundation! and my heart is even now tortured when I think on those delusive dreams.

'Ida, with the fondest caresses, would dispel each care from my brow; in sickness and in health she watched me with the tenderest solicitude; her whole endeavour seemed to be to anticipate my wishes. But, alas! like the serpent, which only fascinates to destroy, she lavished these caresses and attentions to blind me, and wrap me in a fatal security.

'Many and deep were the affronts, revenged indeed but not forgotten, which had long since caused (with shame, I avow it) a deadly hatred between myself and Rupert, Lord of Wädischwyl, which the slightest occasion seemed to increase to a degree of madness. As he dared no longer throw down the gauntlet, I having always in single combat come off the victor, he found means, much harder than steel or iron, to glut his revenge upon me.

'Duke Berchtold of Zähringen, one of those wealthy and powerful tyrants who are the very pests of that society of whose rights they ought to be the ready guardians, had made a sudden irruption on the peaceful inhabitants of the mountains, seizing their herds and flocks, and insulting their wives and daughters. Though possessed of great courage, yet being not much used to warfare, these unhappy men found it impossible to resist the tyrant, and hastened to entreat my instant succour. Without a moment's delay, I assembled my brave vassals, and marched against the spoiler. After a long and severe struggle, God blessed our cause and our victory was complete.

'On the morning, that I was about to depart on my return to my castle, one of my followers announced to me that the Duke had arrived in my camp, and wished an immediate interview with me. I instantly went forth to meet him; and Berchtold hastening towards me, with a smile, offered me his hand in token of reconciliation. I frankly accepted it, not suspecting that falsehood could lurk beneath so open and friendly an aspect.

' "My friend," said he, "for such I must call you, your valour in this contest having won my esteem, although I could at once convince you that I have just cause of quarrel with the insolent mountaineers. But, in spite of your victory in this unjust strife, into which doubtless you were induced to enter by the misrepresentations of those villains, yet as my nature abhors to prolong dissensions, I would willingly cease to think that we are enemies, and commence a friendship which, on my part, at least, shall not be broken. In token, therefore, that you do not mistrust a fellow soldier, return with me to my castle, that we may there drown all remembrance of our past disunion."

'During a long time, I resisted his importunity, for I had now been more than a year absent from my home; and was doubly impatient to return, as I fondly imagined that my delay would occasion much anxiety to my daughter. But the duke, with such apparent kindness and in such a courteous manner renewed and urged his solicitations that I could resist no longer.

'His highness entertained me with the greatest hospitality and un-remitted attention. But I soon perceived that an *honest* man is more in his element amid the toils of the battle than among the blandish-ments of a court, where the lip and the gesture carry welcome, but where the heart, to which the tongue is never the herald, is corroded by the unceasing strifes of jealousy and envy. I soon too saw that my rough and undisguised manners were an occasion of much mirth to the perfumed and essenced nothings who crowded the halls of the duke. I however stifled my resentment, when I considered that these creatures lived but in his favour; like those swarms of insects which are warmed into existence from the dunghill by the sun's rays.

'I had remained the unwilling guest of the duke during some days, when the arrival of a stranger of distinction was announced with much ceremony; this stranger I found to be my bitterest foe, Rupert of Wädischwyl. The duke received him with the most marked politeness and attention; and more than once I fancied that I perceived the precedence of me was studiously given to my enemy. My frank yet haughty nature could ill brook this system of disparagement; and, besides, it seemed to me that I should but play the hypocrite if I partook of the same cup with the man for whom I entertained a deadly hatred.

'I resolved therefore to depart; and sought his highness to bid him farewell. He appeared much distressed at my resolution and earnestly pressed me to avow the cause of my abrupt departure. I candidly confessed that the undue favour which I thought he showed to my rival was the cause.

' "I am hurt, deeply hurt," said the Duke, affecting an air of great sorrow, "that my friend, and that friend the valiant Unspunnen, should think thus unjustly, dare I add, thus meanly of me. No, I have not even in thought wronged you; and to prove my sincerity and my regard for your welfare, know that it was not chance which conducted your adversary to my court. He comes in consequence of my eager wish to reconcile two men whom I so much esteem and whose worth and excellence place them among the brightest ornaments of our favoured land. Let me, therefore,' said he, taking my hand and the hand of Rupert, who had entered during our discourse, "let me have the enviable satisfaction of reconciling two such men, and of terminating your ancient discord. You cannot refuse a request so congenial to that holy faith which we all profess. Suffer me, therefore, to be the minister of peace; and to suggest that, in token and in confirmation of an act which will draw down heaven's blessing on us all, you will permit our holy church to unite in one your far-famed lovely daughter with Lord Rupert's only son, whose virtues, if reports speak truly, render him no undeserving object of her love."

'A rage, which seemed in an instant to turn my blood into fire, and which almost choked my utterance, took possession of me.

' "What!" exclaimed I, "what, think you that I would thus sacrifice, thus cast away my precious jewel! thus debase my beloved Ida? No, by her sainted mother, I swear that rather than see her married to *his* son, I would devote her to the cloister! Nay, I would rather see her dead at my feet than suffer her purity to be sullied by such contamination!"

' "But for the presence of his highness," cried Rupert wrathfully, "your life should instantly answer for this insult! Nathless,[226] I will well mark you, and watch you, too, my lord; and if you escape my revenge, you are more than man."

' "Indeed, indeed, my Lord of Unspunnen," said the duke, "you are much too rash. Your passion has clouded your reason; and, believe me, you will live to repent having so scornfully refused my friendly proposal."

' "You may judge me rash, my lord duke, and perhaps think me somewhat too bold because I dare assert the truth in the courts of princes. But since my tongue cannot frame itself to speak that which my heart does not dictate, and my plain but honest manner seems to displease you, I will, with your highness's permission, withdraw to my own domain, whence I have been but too long absent."

' "Undoubtedly, my lord, you have my permission," said the duke haughtily; and at the same time turning coldly from me.

'My horse was brought, I mounted him with as much composure as I could command; and I breathed more freely as I left the castle far behind.

'During the second day's journey I arrived within a near view of my own native mountains; and I felt doubly invigorated, as their pure breezes were wafted towards me. Still the fond anxiety of a father for his beloved child, and that child his only treasure, made the way seem doubly long. But as I approached the turn of the road which is immediately in front of my castle, I almost then wished the way lengthened; for my joy, my hopes, and my apprehensions crowded upon me almost to suffocation. "A few short minutes, however," I thought, "and then the truth, ill or good, will be known to me."

'When I came in full sight of my dwelling, all seemed in peace; nought exhibited any change since I had left it. I spurred my horse on to the gate; but as I advanced, the utter stillness and desertion of all around surprised me. Not a domestic, not a peasant was to be seen in the courts; it appeared as if the inhabitants of the castle were still asleep.

' "Merciful heaven!" I thought, "what can this stillness forbode! Is she, is my beloved child dead?"

'I could not summon courage to pull the bell. Thrice I attempted, yet thrice the dread of learning the awful truth prevented me. One moment, one word, even one sign, and I might be a forlorn, childless, wretched man, for ever! None but a father can feel or fully sympathise in the agony of those moments! none but a father can ever fitly describe them! My existence seemed even to depend upon the breath of the first passer-by; and my eye shrank from observation lest it should encounter him.

'I was aroused from this inactive state by my faithful dog springing towards me to welcome my return with his boisterous caresses and deep and loud-toned expressions of his joy. Then, the old porter, attracted by the noise, came to the gate, which he instantly opened; but, as he was hurrying forward to meet me, I readily perceived that some sudden and painful recollection checked his eagerness. I leaped from my horse quickly, and entered the hall. All the other domestics now came forward; except my faithful steward Wilfred, he who had been always the foremost to greet his master.

' "Where is my daughter? where is your mistress?" I eagerly exclaimed;

"let me know but that she lives. Yet stop, stop; one moment, one short moment, ere you tell me I am lost for ever!"

'The faithful Wilfred, who had now entered the hall, threw himself at my feet; and with the tears rolling down his furrowed cheeks, earnestly pressed my hand, and hesitatingly informed me that my daughter lived: was well, he believed, but – had quitted the castle.

' "Now, speak more quickly, old man," said I, hastily and passionately interrupting him: "What is it you can mean? My daughter lives; my Ida is well, but she is *not here*. Now, have you and my vassals proved recreants,[227] and suffered my castle in my absence to be robbed of its greatest treasure? Speak! speak plainly, I command ye!"

' "It is with anguish, as great almost as your own can be, my beloved master, that I make known to you the sad truth – that your daughter has quitted her father's roof to become the wife of Conrad, the son of the Lord of Wädischwyl."

' "The wife of Lord Rupert's son! my Ida the wife of the son of him whose very name my soul loathes!"

'My wrath now knew no bounds; the torments of hell seemed to have changed the current of my blood. In the madness of my passion I even cursed my own dear daughter! Yes, pilgrim, I even cursed her on whom I had so fondly doted; for whose sake alone life for me had any charms. Oh! how often since have I attempted to recall that curse! and these bitter tears, which even now I cannot control, witness how severe has been my repentance of that awful and unnatural act!

'Dreadful were the imprecations which I heaped upon my enemy; and deep was the revenge I swore. I know not to what fearful length my unbridled passion would have hurried me had I not, from its very excess, sunk senseless into the arms of my domestics. When I recovered, I found myself in my own chamber, and Wilfred seated near me. Some time, however, elapsed before I came to a clear recollection of the past events; and when I did, it seemed as if an age of crime and misery had weighed me down and chained my tongue. My eye involuntarily wandered to that part of the chamber where hung my daughter's portrait. But this, the faithful old man – who had not removed it, no doubt thinking that to do so would have offended me – had contrived to hide, by placing before it a piece of armour, which seemed as though it had accidentally fallen into that position.

'Many more days elapsed ere I was enabled to listen to the particulars of my daughter's flight; which I will, not to detain you longer with my griefs, now briefly relate. It appeared that urged by the fame of her beauty, and by a curiosity most natural, I confess, to youth, Conrad of

Wädischwyl had for a long time sought but sought in vain to see my Ida. Chance, at length, however, favoured him. On her way to hear mass at our neighbouring monastery, he beheld her; and beheld her but to love. Her holy errand did not prevent him from addressing her; and well the smooth-tongued villain knew how to gain the ear of one so innocent, so unsuspicious as my Ida! Too soon, alas, did his accursed flatteries win their way to her guiltless heart.

'My child's affection for her father was unbounded; and readily would she have sacrificed her life for mine. But when love has once taken possession of the female heart, too quickly drives he thence those sterner guests, reason and duty. Suffice it therefore to say she was won; and induced to unite herself to Wädischwyl, before my return, by his crafty and insidious argument that I should be more easily persuaded to give them my pardon and my blessing when I found that the step that she had taken was irrevocable. With almost equal art, he pleaded too that their union would doubtless heal the breach between the families of Wädischwyl and Unspunnen; and thus terminate that deadly hatred which my gentle Ida, ever the intercessor for peace, had always condemned. By this specious sophistry, my poor misguided child was prevailed upon to tear herself from the heart of a fond parent and to unite herself with an unprincipled deceiver, the son of that parent's most bitter enemy.'

The pain of these recollections so overcame Burkhardt, that some time elapsed ere he could master his feelings: at length he proceeded.

'My soul seemed now to have but one feeling, *revenge*. All other passions were annihilated by this master one; and I instantly prepared myself and my vassals to chastise this worse-than-robber. But such satisfaction was (I now thank God) denied me; for the Duke of Zähringen soon gave me memorable cause to recollect his parting words. He had attached himself with his numerous followers to my rival's party, and now both these powerful chiefs suddenly invaded my domain. A severe struggle against most unequal numbers ensued. But, at length, though my brave retainers would fain have prolonged the hopeless strife, resolved to stop a needless waste of blood, I left the field to my foes; and, with the remnant of my faithful soldiers, hastened, in deep mortification, to bury myself within these walls. This galling repulse prevented all possibility of reconciliation with my daughter, whom I now regarded as the cause of my disgrace: and consequently, I forbade her name even to be mentioned in my presence.

'Years rolled on, and I had no intelligence of her until I learned by a mere chance that she had with her husband quitted her native land.

Altogether, more than twenty, to me long, long years, have now passed since her flight; and though, when time brought repentance, and my anger and revenge yielded to better feelings, I made every effort to gain tidings of my poor child, I have not yet been able to discover any further traces of her. The chance of so doing was indeed rendered more difficult by the death of my faithful Wilfred, shortly after my defeat, and by the character of his successor, an individual of strict integrity, but of an austere temper and forbidding manners. Here, therefore, have I lived a widowed, childless, heart-broken old man. But I have at least learned to bow to the dispensations of an all-wise providence, which has in its justice stricken me for thus remorselessly cherishing that baneful passion which Holy Law so expressly forbids. Oh! how I have yearned to see my beloved child! how I have longed to clasp her to this withered, blighted heart! With scalding tears of the bitterest repentance have I revoked those deadly curses, which, in the plenitude of my unnatural wrath, I dared to utter daily. Ceaselessly do I now weary heaven with my prayers to obliterate all memory of those fatal imprecations; or to let them fall on my own head, and shower down only its choicest blessings on that of my beloved child! But a fear, which freezes my veins with horror, constantly haunts me lest the maledictions which I dared to utter in my moments of demoniac vindictiveness should, in punishment for my impiety, have been fulfilled.

'Often, in my dreams, do I behold my beloved child; but her looks are always in sadness, and she ever seems mildly but most sorrowfully to upbraid me for having so inhumanly cast her from me. Yet she must, I fear, have died long ere now; for, were she living, she would not, I think, have ceased to endeavour to regain the affections of a father who once loved her so tenderly. It is true that at first she made many efforts to obtain my forgiveness. Nay, I have subsequently learned that she even knelt at the threshold of my door, and piteously supplicated to be allowed to see me. But my commands had been so peremptory, and, as I before observed, the steward who had replaced Wilfred was of so stern and unbending a disposition, that, just and righteous as was this her last request, it was unfeelingly denied to her. Eternal heaven! she whom I had loved as perhaps never father loved before – she whom I had fondly watched almost hourly lest the rude breeze of winter should chill her, or the summer's heat should scorch her – she whom I had cherished in sickness through many a livelong night, with a mother's devotion, and more than a mother's solicitude, even *she*, the only child of my beloved Agnes and the anxious object of the last moments of her life, was spurned from my door! from this door whence no want goes unrelieved, and where the very beggar finds rest! And now, when I would bless the lips that even could say to me, "She lives," I can nowhere gather the slightest tidings of my child. Ah, had I listened to the voice of reason, had I not suffered my better feelings to be mastered by the wildest, and fellest passions, I might have seen herself, and perhaps her children, happy around me, cheering the evening of my life. And when my last hour shall come, they would have closed my eyes in peace, and in unfeigned sorrow have daily addressed to heaven their innocent prayers for my soul's eternal rest; instead of the hirelings who will now execute the mummery of mourning, and impatiently hurry me to an unlamented, a lonely and an unhonoured grave. To those children, also, would have descended that inheritance which must at my decease fall to an utter stranger, who bears not even my name.

'You now know, pilgrims, the cause of my grief; and I see by the tears which you have so abundantly shed that you truly pity the forlorn being before you. Remember him and his sorrows therefore ever in your prayers; and when you kneel at the shrine to which you are bound, let not those sorrows be forgotten.'

The elder pilgrim in vain attempted to answer; the excess of his feelings overpowered his utterance. At length, throwing himself at the feet of Burkhardt, and casting off his pilgrim's habit, he with difficulty exclaimed, 'See here, thine Ida's son! and behold in my youthful companion thine Ida's daughter! Yes, before you kneel the children of her whom you so much lament. We came to sue for that pardon, for that love, which we had feared would have been denied us. But, thanks be to God, who has mollified your heart, we have only to implore that you will suffer us to use our poor efforts to alleviate your sorrows and render more bright and cheerful your declining years.'

In wild and agitated surprise, Burkhardt gazed intently upon them. It seemed to him as if a beautiful vision were before him, which he feared even a breath might dispel. When, however, he became assured that he was under the influence of no delusion, the tumult of his feelings overpowered him, and he sank senselessly on the neck of the elder pilgrim; who, with his sister's assistance, quickly raised the old man, and by their united efforts restored him, ere long, to his senses. But when Burkhardt beheld the younger pilgrim, the very image of his lost Ida, bending over him with the most anxious and tender solicitude, he thought that death had ended all his worldly sufferings, and that heaven had already opened to his view.

'Great God!' at length he exclaimed, 'I am unworthy of these thy mercies! Grant me to receive them as I ought! I need not ask,' added he, after a pause, and pressing the pilgrims to his bosom, 'for a confirmation of your statement, or of my own sensations of joy. All, all tells me that you are the children of my beloved Ida. Say, therefore, is your mother dead? or dare I hope once more to clasp her to my heart?'

The elder pilgrim, whose name was Hermann, then stated to him that two years had passed since his parent had breathed her last in his arms. Her latest prayer was that heaven would forgive her the sorrow she had caused her father, and forbear to visit her own error on her children's heads. He then added that his father had been dead many years.

'My mother,' continued Hermann, drawing from his bosom a small sealed packet, 'commanded me, on her deathbed, to deliver this into your own hands. "My son," she said, "when I am dead, if my father still lives, cast yourself at his feet, and desist not your supplications until you have obtained from him a promise that he will read this prayer. It will acquaint him with a repentance that may incite him to recall his curse, and thus cause the earth to lie lightly on all that will shortly remain of his once loved Ida. Paint to him the hours of anguish which even your tender years have witnessed. Weary him, my son, with your entreaties; cease them not until you have wrung from him his forgiveness."

'As you may suppose, I solemnly engaged to perform my mother's request; and as soon as our grief for the loss of so dear, so fond a parent, would permit us, my sister and myself resolved, in these pilgrims' habits, to visit your castle and, by gradual means, to have attempted to win your affections, if we should have found you still relentless and unwilling to listen to our mother's prayer.'

'Praise be to that God, my son,' said Burkhardt, 'at whose command the waters spring from the barren rock, that he has bidden the streams of love and repentance to flow once more from my once barren and flinty heart. But let me not delay to open this sad memorial of your mother's griefs. I wish you, my children, to listen to it, that you may hear both her exculpation and her wrongs.'

Burkhardt hid his face in his hands, and remained for some moments earnestly struggling with his feelings. At length, he broke the seal and, with a voice which at times was almost overpowered, read aloud the contents.

'MY BELOVED FATHER (if by that fond title your daughter may still address you), Feeling that my sad days are now numbered, I make this last effort, ere my strength shall fail me, to obtain at least your pity for her you once so much loved; and to beseech you to recall that curse which has weighed too heavily upon her heart. Indeed, my father, I am not quite that guilty wretch you think me. Do not imagine that, neglecting every tie of duty and gratitude, I could have left the tenderest of parents to his widowed lonely home, and have united myself with the son of his sworn foe, had I not fondly, most ardently, hoped, nay, had cherished the idea almost to certainty, that you would, when you found that I was a wife, have quickly pardoned a fault which the fears of your refusal to our union had alone tempted me to commit. I firmly believed that my husband would then have shared with me my father's love, and have, with his child, the pleasing task of watching over his happiness and comfort. But never did I for an instant imagine that I was permanently wounding the heart of that father. My youth, and the ardour of my husband's persuasions, must plead some extenuation of my fault.

The day that I learnt the news of your having pronounced against me that fatal curse, and your fixed determination never more to admit me to your presence, has been marked in characters indelible on my memory. At that moment, it appeared as if heaven had abandoned me, had marked me for its reprobation as a parricide! My brain and my heart seemed on fire, while my blood froze in my veins. The chillness of death crept over every limb, and my tongue refused all utterance. I would have wept, but the source of my tears was dried within me.

How long I remained in this state I know not, as I at length became insensible, and remained so for some days. On returning to a full consciousness of my wretchedness, I would instantly have rushed to your abode, and cast myself at your feet, to wring from you, if possible, your forgiveness of my crime; but my limbs were incapable of all motion. Soon, too, I learned that the letters, which I dictated, were returned unopened; and my husband at last informed me that all his efforts to see you had been utterly fruitless.

Yet the moment I had gained sufficient strength, I went to the castle, but, unfortunately for me, even as I entered, I encountered a stern wretch, to whom my person was not unknown; and he instantly told me that my efforts to see his master would be useless. I used prayers and entreaties; I even knelt upon the bare ground to him. But so far from listening to me, he led me to the gate, and, in my presence, dismissed the old porter who had admitted me, and who afterwards followed my fortunes until the hour of his death. Finding that all my attempts were without hope, and that several of the old servants had been discarded on my account, with a heart completely broken, I succumbed to my fate and abandoned all further attempt.

After the birth of my son (to whose fidelity and love I trust this sad memorial) my husband, who, with the tenderest solicitude, employed every means in his power to divert my melancholy, having had a valuable property in Italy bequeathed to him, prevailed upon me to repair to that favoured and beauteous country. But neither the fond attentions of my beloved Conrad, nor the bright sunshine and luxurious breezes of that region of wonders, could overcome a grief so deeply rooted as mine; and I soon found that the gay garden of Europe had less charm for me than my own dear native land, with its dark, pine-clad mountains.

Shortly after we had arrived at Rome, I gave birth to a daughter; an event which was only too soon followed by the death of my affectionate husband. The necessity of ceaseless attention to my infant, in some measure alleviated the intense anguish which I suffered from that most severe loss. Nevertheless, in the very depth of this sorrow which almost overcharged my heart, heaven only knows how often, and how remorsefully, while bending over my own dear children in sickness, have I called to mind the anxious fondness with which the tenderest and best of fathers used to watch over me!

I struggled long and painfully with my feelings, and often did I beseech God to spare my life that I might be enabled to instruct my children in His holy love and fear, and teach them to atone for the error of their parent. My prayer has in mercy been heard; the boon I supplicated has been granted; and I trust, my beloved father, that if these children should be admitted to your affections, you will find that I have trained up two blessed intercessors for your forgiveness, when it shall have pleased heaven to have called your daughter to her account before that dread tribunal where a sire's curse will plead so awfully against her. Recall then, oh, beloved parent! recall your dreadful malediction from your poor repentant Ida! and send your blessing as an angel of mercy to plead for her eternal rest. Farewell, my father, for ever! for ever, farewell! By the cross, whose emblem her fevered lips now press; by Him, who in his boundless mercy hung upon that cross, your daughter, your once much loved Ida, implores you, supplicates you, not to let her plead in vain!

'My child, my child!' sobbed Burkhardt, as the letter dropped from his hand, 'may the Father of all forgive me as freely as I from the depths of my wrung heart forgive you! Would that your remorseful father could have pressed you to his heart; with his own lips have assured you of his affection; and wiped away the tears of sorrow from your eyes! But he will cherish these beloved remembrances of you; and will more jealously guard them than his own life.'

Burkhardt passed the whole of the following day in his chamber, to which the good Father Jerome alone was admitted, as the events of the preceding day rendered a long repose absolutely necessary. The following morning, however, he entered the hall, where Hermann and Ida were impatiently waiting for him. His pale countenance still exhibited deep traces of the agitation he had experienced; but having kissed his children most affectionately, he smilingly flung round Ida's neck a massive gold chain, richly wrought, with a bunch of keys appended to it.

'We must duly instal our Lady of the Castle,' said he, 'and invest her with her appropriate authorities. But, hark! from the sound of the porter's horn, it seems as if our hostess would have early calls upon her hospitality. Whom have we here?' continued he, looking out up the avenue. 'By St Hubert, a gay and gallant knight is approaching, who shall be right welcome – that is, if my lady approve. Well, Willibald, what bring you? a letter from our good friend the Abbot of St Anselm. What says he?

I am sure that you will not refuse your welcome to a young knight, who is returning by your castle to his home, from the emperor's wars. He is well known to me, and I can vouch for his being a guest worthy of your hospitality, which will not be the less freely granted to him because he does not bask in the golden smiles of fortune.

No, no, that it shall not, my good friend; and if fortune frown upon him, he shall be doubly welcome. Conduct him hither, instantly, good Willibald.'

The steward hastened to usher in the stranger, who advanced into the hall with a modest but manly air. He was apparently about twenty-five years of age; his person was such as might well, in the dreams of a young maiden, occupy no unconspicuous place.

'Sir knight,' said Burkhardt, taking him cordially by the hand, 'you are right welcome to my castle, and such poor entertainment as it can afford. We must make you forget your wounds, and the rough usage of a soldier's life. But, soft, I already neglect my duty in not first intro-ducing our hostess,' added the aged knight, presenting Ida. 'By my faith,' he continued, 'judging from my lady's blushing smile, you seem not to have met for the first time. Am I right in my conjecture?'

'We *have* met, sir,' replied Ida, with such confusion as pleasantly implied that the meeting was not indifferently recollected, 'in the parlour of the Abbess of the Ursulines, at Munich, where I have sometimes been to visit a much valued friend.'

'The abbess,' said the young knight, 'was my cousin; and my good fortune more than once gave me the happiness of seeing in her convent this lady. But little did I expect that among these mountains the fickle goddess would again have so favoured a homeless wanderer.'

'Well, sir knight,' replied Burkhardt, 'we trust that fortune has been equally favourable to us. And now we will make bold to ask your name; and then, without useless and tedious ceremony, on the part of ourselves and our hostess, bid you again a hearty welcome.'

'My name,' said the stranger, 'is Walter de Blumfeldt; though humble, it has never been disgraced; and with the blessing of heaven, I hope to hand it down as honoured as I have received it.'

*   *   *

Weeks, months, rolled on, and Walter de Blumfeldt was still the guest of the Lord of Unspunnen; till, by his virtues, and the many excellent qualities which daily more and more developed themselves, he wound himself around Burkhardt's heart, which the chastened life of the old knight had rendered particularly susceptible to the kindlier feelings. Frequently would he now, with tears in his eyes, declare that he wished he could convince each and all with whom his former habits had caused any difference how truly he forgave them and desired their forgiveness.

'Would,' said he one day, in allusion to this subject, 'that I could have met my old enemy, the Duke of Zähringen, and with a truly heartfelt pleasure and joy have embraced him, and numbered him among my friends. But he is gathered to his fathers, and I know not whether he has left anyone to bear his honours.'

Each time that Walter had offered to depart, Burkhardt had found some excuse to detain him; for it seemed to him that in separating from his young guest, he should lose a link of that chain which good fortune had so lately woven for him. Hermann, too, loved Walter as a brother; and Ida fain would have imagined that she loved him as a sister: but her heart more plainly told her what her colder reasoning sought to hide. Unspunnen, who had for some time perceived the growing attachment between Walter and Ida, was not displeased at the discovery, as he had long ceased to covet riches and had learnt to prize the sterling worth of the young knight, who fully answered the high terms in which the Prior of St Anselm always spoke of him.

Walking one evening under the shade of that very avenue where he had first encountered Hermann and Ida, he perceived the latter, at some little distance, in conversation with Walter. It was evident to Burkhardt that the young knight was not addressing himself to a very unwilling ear, as Ida was totally regardless of the loud cough with which Burkhardt chose to be seized at that moment; nor did she perceive him, until he exclaimed, or rather vociferated, 'Do you know, Walter, that, under this very avenue, two pilgrims, bound to some holy shrine, once accosted me; but that, in pity to my sins and forlorn condition, they exchanged their penitential journey for an act of greater charity; and have ever since remained to extend their kind cares to an aged and helpless relative but too little worthy of their love. One, however, of these affectionate beings is now about to quit my abode, and to pass through the rest of this life's pilgrimage with a helpmate in his toilsome journey in the person of the fair daughter of the Baron de Leichtfeldt, and thus leave his poor companion to battle the storms of the world with only the tedious society of an old man. Say, sir knight, will thy valour suffer that such wrong be done; or wilt *thou* undertake to conduct this forsaken pilgrim on her way, and guide her through the chequered paths of this variable life? I see by the lowliness with which you bend, and the colour which mantles in your cheek, that I speak not to one insensible to an old man's appeal. But soft, soft, sir knight, my Ida is not yet canonised, and therefore cannot afford to lose a hand,[228] which inevitably must occur if you continue to press it with such very ardent devotion. But what says our pilgrim, does she accept of thy conduct and service, sir knight?'

Ida, scarcely able to support herself, threw herself on Burkhardt's neck. We will not raise the veil which covers the awful moment that renders a man, as he supposes, happy or miserable for ever. Suffice it to say that the day which made Hermann the husband of the daughter of the Baron de Leichtfeldt saw Ida the wife of Walter de Blumfeldt.

*   *   *

Six months had passed rapidly away to the happy inhabitants of Unspunnen; and Burkhardt seemed almost to have grown young again; such wonders did the tranquillity which now reigned within him perform. He was therefore one of the most active and foremost in the preparations which were necessary in consequence of Walter suggesting that they should spend Ida's birthday in a favourite retreat of his and hers. This chosen spot was a beautiful meadow, in front of which meandered a small limpid river, or rather stream; at the back was a gorgeous amphitheatre of trees, the wide spreading branches of which cast a refreshing shade over the richly enamelled grass.

In this beauteous retreat were Burkhardt, Walter and his Ida passing the sultry hours of noon, with all that flow of mirth which careless hearts alone can experience, when Walter, who had been relating some of his adventures at the court of the emperor, and recounting the magnificence of the tournaments, turning to his bride, said: 'But what avails all that pomp, my Ida. How happy are we in this peaceful vale! We envy neither princes nor dukes their palaces, or their states. These woods, these glades, are worth all the stiffly trimmed gardens of the emperor, and the great monarch of France, to boot. What say you, my Ida, could you brook the ceremony of a court, and the pride of royalty? Methinks even the coronet of a duchess would but ill replace the wreath of blushing roses on your head.'

'Gently, my good husband,' replied Ida, laughing, 'they say, you know, that a woman loves these vanities too dearly in her heart ever to despise them. Then how can you expect so frail a mortal as your poor wife to hold them in contempt? Indeed, I think,' added she, assuming an air of burlesque dignity, 'that I should make a lofty duchess, and wear my coronet with most becoming grace. And now, by my faith, Walter, I recollect that you have this day, like a true and gallant knight, promised to grant whatever boon I shall ask. On my bended knee, therefore, I humbly sue that if you know any spell or magic wile to make a princess or a duchess for only a single day that you will forthwith exercise your art upon me; just in order to enable me to ascertain with how much or how little dignity I could sustain such honours. It is no very difficult matter, sir knight: you have only to call in the aid of Number Nip,[229] or some such handy workman of the woods. Answer, most chivalrous husband, for thy disconsolate wife rises not until her prayer is granted.'

'Why, Ida, you have indeed craved a rare boon,' replied Walter, 'and how to grant it may well puzzle my brain till it becomes crazed with the effort. But, let me see, let me see,' continued he, musingly; 'I have it! – Come hither, love, here is your throne,' said he, placing her on a gentle eminence richly covered with the fragrant wild thyme and the delicate harebell. 'Kings might now envy you the incense which is offered to you. And you, noble sir,' added he, addressing Burkhardt, 'must stand beside her highness, in quality of chief counsellor. There are your attendants around you: behold that tall oak, he must be your highness's *poursuivant*;[230] and yonder slender mountain ashes, your trusty pages.'

'This is but a poor fulfilment of the task you have undertaken,

Walter and Ida

sir mummer,' said Ida, with a playful, and arch affectation of disappointment.

'Have patience for a brief while, fair dame,' replied Walter, laughing;
'for now must I awaken your highness's men at arms.'

Then, taking from his side a silver horn, he loudly sounded the
melodious reveille. As he withdrew the instrument from his lips, a
trumpet thrillingly answered the call; and scarcely had its last notes died
away, when, from the midst of the woods, as if the very trees were gifted
with life, came forth a troop of horsemen, followed by a body of archers
on foot. They had but just entirely emerged, when numerous peasants,
both male and female, appeared in their gayest attire; and, together
with the horsemen and the archers, rapidly and picturesquely ranged
themselves in front of the astonished Ida, who had already abdicated
her throne, and clung to the arm of Walter. They then suddenly divided,
and twelve pages in richly emblazoned dresses advanced. After them
followed six young girls, whose forms and features the Graces might
have envied, bearing two coronets placed on embroidered cushions. In
the rear of these, supporting his steps with his abbatial staff, walked the
venerable Abbot of St Anselm, who, with his white beard flowing almost
to his girdle and his benign looks that showed the pure commerce of the
soul which gave life to an eye the brightness of which seventy years had
scarcely diminished, seemed to Ida a being of another world. The young
girls then advancing, and kneeling before Walter and his wife, presented
the coronets.

Ida, who had remained almost breathless with wonder, could now
scarcely articulate. 'Dear, dear Walter, what is all this pomp – what
does – what *can* it mean?'

'Mean! my beloved,' replied her husband, 'did you not bid me make
you a duchess? I have but obeyed your high commands, and I now
salute you, *Duchess* of Zähringen!'

The whole multitude then made the woods resound with the
acclamation, '*Long live the Duke and Duchess of Zähringen!*'

Walter, having for some moments enjoyed the unutterable amaze-
ment of the now breathless Ida, and the less evident but perhaps equally
intense surprise of Burkhardt, turning to the latter, said, 'My more than
father, you see in me the son of your once implacable enemy, the Duke
of Zähringen. He has been many years gathered to his fathers; and I, as
his only son, have succeeded to his title, and his large possessions. My
heart, my liberty, were entirely lost in the parlour of the Abbess of the
Ursulines. But when I learnt whose child my Ida was, and your sad
story, I resolved ere I would make her mine to win not only her love but

also your favour and esteem. How well I have succeeded, this little magic circle on my Ida's finger is my witness. It will add no small measure to your happiness, to know that my father had for many years repented of the wrongs which he had done you; and, as much as possible to atone for them, entrusted the education of his son to the care of this my best of friends, the Abbot of St Anselm, that he might learn to shun the errors into which his sire had unhappily fallen. And now,' continued he, advancing and leading Ida towards the Abbot, 'I have only to beg your blessing, and that this lady, whom through heaven's goodness I glory to call my wife, be invested with those insignia of the rank which she is so fit to adorn.'

Walter, or as we must now call him, the Duke of Zähringen, with Ida, then lowly knelt before the venerable abbot, while the holy man, with tears in his eyes, invoked upon them the blessings of heaven. His highness then rising, took one of the coronets and placing it on Ida's head, said, 'Mayst thou be as happy under this glittering coronet, as thou wert under the russet hood in which I first beheld thee.'

'God and Our Lady aid me!' replied the agitated Ida; 'and may He grant that I may wear it with as much humility. Yet thorns, they say, spring up beneath a crown.'

'True, my beloved,' said the duke, 'and they also grow beneath the peasant's homely cap. But the rich alchemy of my Ida's virtues will ever convert all thorns into the brightest jewels of her diadem.'

Euphrasia

A Tale of Greece

TWO years ago, that is at Christmas 1836, four friends left Brighton on their way to the seat of an acquaintance, about thirty miles distant, where they intended to pass this season of festivity. Anyone who was in Sussex at that time must remember the fall of snow on Christmas Eve which transformed Brighton into a town of Siberia, and held all its sojourners prisoner. The king's courier was stopped by the drift on his way to London; no letters were sent or received for three days; the Pavilion had no guests; the horses and carriages could not make their way through the blocked-up streets. It was a strange wild sight. Still, as this party was resolved to pursue its way, four horses were harnessed to their carriage and they set out. They arrived halfway to Lewes, when the carriage became blocked up; the postilions blinded by the drift; the horses unable to move. Night was drawing in, and they saw naught but one wide expanse of snow, which was scattered in thick showers by the winds. They looked from the windows; the horses were above their knees in drift, as the postilions urged them to wade on. What made it worse was that one of the party was a woman, a being ill suited to encounter the rude elements, whose father was overwhelmed with terror lest she should be chilled by the night air or forced to alight and wet her feet. Her spirit was high; she had insisted on accompanying him, and wrapped in fur, had braved the season; but now he wondered at his folly in bringing her, and looked at her little foot in its satin slipper with a sort of feeling that if she moved from the carriage she would be but a mouthful for the tempest and disappear on the instant. Meanwhile darkness gathered thick around; there was no hope of moving. The father of the lady had alighted to view the scene and then was afraid of getting into the carriage again, with a coating of snow round him, lest its thawing should give his daughter cold. She was not afraid; she was afraid of nothing; but he feared for her more than words can express. At length it was agreed that the father of the young lady and the postilions should mount the horses and make their way to Lewes, whence some sort of litter could be sent for her, and horses for the rest of the party, who remained to guard her.

They went, and those left behind continued looking wistfully on the scene, visible by its transcendent whiteness even now that night had closed round. For a few minutes they were silent; they thought on the road the travellers had to pass; they longed for their return – a few moments seemed an age. One of the gentlemen struck his repeater; the same sound was given as when he had struck it at the departure of his friend – a quarter past six.

'The hours will never pass!' exclaimed the anxious girl.

'Oh yes, they will,' said the other. 'I once passed a night more anxious than this promises to be, yet it had an end. It is strange that the scene I refer to should be vividly present now, being so different in scenery, in season, in personages and in country from this.'

Anxious to divert the mind of the daughter, and to lighten the slow pace of the hour, the third of this anxious party asked his young friend, Harry Valency, by name, what the events were that marked that long unforgotten night, and made him understand that he would do well to relate them, if the task were not a painful one. He understood the hint, and began. His tale was afterwards repeated to me, and as I heard it I wish to recount it now; yet, hearing it only at second-hand, I shall tell it lamely, and spoil the lively earnest interest he spread over every detail; while he who told it to me had but a vague recollection of dates and names of places, and even some of those of persons had entirely escaped him. However, such portion as reached me of the story I will set down.

*   *   *

It was not long after the breaking out of the Greek revolution[231] that Harry Valency visited Greece. Many an Englishman was led thither at that time by the spirit of adventure, and many perished. Valency was not nineteen; his spirit was wild and reckless; thought or care had never touched his brow; his heart was too light for love. Restless and energetic, he longed to try his powers, with the instinct that leads the young deer to butt against trees or to wrestle with each other in the forest dells. He was the only son of a widowed mother, whose life was wrapped in his, and he loved her fondly; yet left her, guided by a desire for adventure, unable to understand what anxiety and fear meant, and in his own person eager to meet even misfortune, so that it came in a guise to call forth manly and active struggles. He longed to have the pages of his young life written over by deeds that would hereafter be memories to which he could turn with delight. The cause of Greece warmed his soul. He was in a transport of ecstacy when he touched the shores of that antique land and looked around on mountain and mountain stream whose names were associated with the most heroic acts and the most sublime poetry man ever achieved or wrote. Yes, he was now in Greece. He was about to fight in her cause against the usurping Turk. He had prepared himself by a sedulous study of Romaic; he was on his way to the seat of government, to offer his services. To proceed thither from the spot where he had disembarked was a matter of some difficulty, the troops of the Pasha being then in possession of many of the passes. At length he heard that a band of about fifty Greek soldiers, headed by a young but brave and renowned chief, was about to pursue the same road; he asked and obtained leave to accompany them.

How delightful was the commencement of the journey! How beautiful the country – defile and steep hillside – by which they proceeded, where the grey olive clothed the upland, or vines, embracing elms, red now with late summer tints, varied the scene. The mountain tops were bare or crowned with pines, and torrents ran down the sides and fed a stream in the dell. The air was balmy, the cicala loud and merry – to live was to be happy. Valency was mounted on a spirited horse; he made it leap and caracole.[232] He threw a spear against a tree, and dashed after to recover it. He fired at a mark as he hurried on at full gallop; every feat was insufficient to tame his exhaustless spirits.

The chief marked him with eyes whose deep melancholy expression darkened as he gazed. He was known as bravest among the brave, yet gentle and kindly as a woman. He was very young, singularly handsome; his countenance was stamped with traces of intellectual refinement, while his person was tall, muscular and strong, but so gracefully formed that every attitude reminded you of some Praxitilean[233] shape of his own native land. Once he had been more beautiful: joy, as well as tenderness and a soldier's ardour had lighted up his dark eye; his lip had been the home of smiles, and the thoughts which presided in his brow had been as clear and soft and gladsome as that godlike brow itself. Now this was changed. Grief had become a master passion: his cheeks were sunken; his eye seemed to brood eternally over melancholy regrets; his measured harmonious voice was attuned to the utterance of no light fancy or gay sallies; he spoke only the necessary words of direction to his followers, and then silence and gloom gathered over his face. His sorrow was respected; for it was known to be well founded, and to spring from a recent disaster. If any of his troop desired to indulge in merriment, they withdrew from his vicinity. It was strange to them to hear the light laugh of the English youth ring through the grove, and to catch the tones of his merry voice as he sang some of their own gayest songs. The chief gazed with interest. There was a winning frankness in the boy; he was so very young, and all he did was in graceful accordance with his age. We are alike mere youths, thought the chief, and how different. Yet soon he may become like me. He soars like an eagle; but the eagle may be wounded and stoop to earth, because earth contains its secret and its regret.

Suddenly Valency, who was some hundred yards in advance, was encountered by a Greek, riding at full speed towards the advancing troop. 'Back! back! silence!' the man cried. He was a scout, who had been sent on before, and now brought tidings that a troop of three or four hundred of the Turkish army was entering the defile, and would soon advance on the handful of men which Valency accompanied. The scout rode directly up to the leader, and made his report, adding, 'We have yet time. If we fall back but a quarter of a mile, there is a path I know by which I can guide you across the mountain – on the other side we shall be safe.'

A smile of scorn for a moment wreathed the lip of the chief, at the word safety, but his face soon reassumed its usual sad composure. The troop had halted; each man bent his eye on the leader. Valency, in particular, marked the look of scorn, and felt that he would never retreat before danger.

'Comrades!' the chief thus addressed his men, 'it shall never be said that Greeks fell back to make way for the destroyers; we will betake ourselves to our old warfare. Before we entered this olive wood, we passed a thick cover where the dark jutting mountainside threw a deep shadow across our path and the torrent drowned all sound of voice or hoof. There we shall find ambush; there the enemy will meet death.'

He turned his horse's head, and in a few minutes reached the spot he named; the men were mostly eager for the fray – while one or two eyed the mountainside and then the path that led to the village, which they had quitted that morning. The chief saw their look, and he glanced also at the English youth, who had thrown himself from his horse, and was busy loading and priming his arms. The chief rode up to him – 'You are our guest and fellow-traveller,' he said, 'but not our comrade in the fight. We are about to meet danger – it may be that not one of us shall escape. You have no injuries to avenge, no liberty to gain; you have friends – probably a mother – in your native land. You must not fall with us. I am going to send a message to warn the village we last passed through – do you accompany my messengers.'

Valency had listened attentively at first; but as the chief continued, his attention reverted to his task of loading his pistols. The last words called a blush into his cheek.

'You treat me as a boy,' he cried; 'I may be one in aspect, but you shall find me a man in heart this day. You are also young, I have not deserved your scorn!'

The chief caught the youth's flashing eye. He held out his hand to him, saying, 'Forgive me.'

'I will,' said Valency, 'on one condition; give me a post of danger – of honour. You owe it to me in reparation of the insult you offered.'

'Be it so,' said the chief, 'your place shall be at my side.'

A few minutes more and his dispositions were made; two of the most down-hearted of the troop were despatched to alarm the village, the rest were placed behind the rocks; beneath the bushes, wherever broken ground, or tuft of underwood, or fragment from the cliff, afforded shelter and concealment, a man was placed, while the chief himself took his stand on an elevated platform and, sheltered by a tree, gazed upon the road. Soon the tramp of horses, the busy sound of feet and voices were heard, overpowering the rushing of the stream; and turban and musket could be distinguished as the enemy's troop threaded the defile.

*   *   *

The shout of battle – the firing – the clash of weapons were over. Above the crest of the hill, whose side had afforded ambush to the Greeks, the crescent moon hung, just about to dip behind; the stars in her train burnt bright as lamps floating in the firmament; while the fireflies flashed among the myrtle underwood and up the mountain-side; and sometimes the steel of the arms strewn around, dropped from the hands of the dead, caught and reflected the flashes of the celestial or earthly stars. The ground was strewn with the slain. Such of the enemy as had cut their way through, were already far – the sound of their horses' hoofs had died away. The Greeks who had fled across the mountain had reached a spot of safety – none lay there but the silent dead – cold as the moonbeam that rested on their pale faces for a moment, and then passed off, leaving them in shadow and death. All were still and motionless – some lay on the hillside, among the underwood – some on the open road – horses and men had fallen, pell mell – none moved – none breathed.

Yet there was a sigh – it was lost in the murmur of the stream; a groan succeeded, and then a voice feeble and broken – 'My mother, my poor mother!' – the pale lips that spoke these words could form no other, a gush of tears followed. The cry seemed to awake another form from among the dead. One of the prostrate bodies raised itself slowly and painfully on its arm; the eyes were filmy, the countenance white from approaching death; the voice was hollow, yet firm, that said – 'Who speaks? – who lives? – who weeps?'

The question struck shame to the wounded man; he checked his overflow of passionate sobbings. The other spoke again, 'It was not the voice of a Greek – yet I thought I had saved that gallant boy – the ball meant for him is now in my side. Speak again, young Englishman – on whom do you call?'

'On her who will weep my death too bitterly – on my mother,' replied Valency, and tears would follow the loved name.

'Art thou wounded to death?' asked the chief.

'Thus unaided I must die,' he replied, 'the blood gushes in torrents from a deep sabre cut – yet, could I reach those waters, I might live – I must try.' And Valency rose; he staggered a few steps, and fell heavily at the feet of the chief. He had fainted. The Greek looked on the ghastly pallor of his face; he half rose – his own wound did not bleed, but it was mortal, and a deadly sickness had gathered round his heart, and chilled his brow, which he strove to master that he might save the English boy. The struggle brought cold drops on his brow, as he rose on his knees and stooped to raise the head of Valency; he shuddered to feel the warm moisture his hand encountered. It is his blood; his life blood, he thought; and again he placed his head on the earth, and continued a moment still, summoning what vitality remained to him to animate his limbs. Then with a determined effort he rose and staggered to the banks of the stream. He held a steel cap in his hand – and now he stooped down to fill it; but with the effort the ground slid from under him, and he fell. There was a ringing in his ears – a cold dew on his brow – his breath came thick – the cap had fallen from his hand – he was dying. The bough of a tree, shot off in the morning's *mêlée*, lay near; the mind, even of a dying man, can form swift unerring combinations of thought; it was his last chance – the bough was plunged in the waters, and he scattered the grateful reviving drops over his face; vigour returned with the act, and he could stoop and fill the cap, and drink a deep draught, which for a moment restored the vital powers. And now he carried water to Valency; he dipped the unfolded turban of a Turk in the stream, and bound the youth's wound, which was a deep sabre cut in the shoulder that had bled copiously. Valency revived – life gathered warm in his heart – his cheeks, though still pale, lost the ashy hue of death – his limbs again seemed willing to obey his will – he sat up, but he was too weak and his head drooped. As a mother tending her sick first-born, the Greek chief hovered over him; he brought a cloak to pillow his head; as he picked up this, he found that some careful soldier had brought a small bag at his saddle bow, in which was a loaf and a bunch or two of grapes; he gave them to the youth, who ate. Valency now recognised his saviour; at first he wondered to see him there, tending on him, apparently unhurt; but soon the chief sank to the ground, and Valency could mark the rigidity of feature, and ghastliness of aspect, that portended death. In his turn he would have assisted his friend; but the chief stopped him – 'You die if you move,' he said; 'your wound will bleed afresh, and you will die, while you cannot aid me. My weakness does not arise from mere loss of blood. The messenger of death has reached a vital part – yet a little while and the soul will obey the summons. It is slow, slow is the deliverance; yet the long creeping hour will come at last, and I shall be free.'

'Do not speak thus,' cried Valency. 'I am strong now – I will go for help.'

'There is no help for me,' replied the chief, 'save the death I desire. I command you, move not.'

Valency had risen, but the effort was vain: his knees bent under him, his head spun round; before he could save himself, he had sunk to the ground.

'Why torture yourself?' said the chief; 'a few hours and help will come: it will not injure you to pass this interval beneath this calm sky. The cowards who fled will alarm the country, by dawn succour will be here; you must wait for it. I too must wait; not for help, but for death. It is soothing, even to me, to die here beneath this sky, with the murmurs of yonder stream in my ear, the shadows of my native mountains thrown athwart. Could aught save me, it would be the balmy airs of this most blessed night; my soul feels the bliss, though my body is sick[234] and fast stiffening in death. Such was not the hour when she died, whom soon I shall meet, my Euphrasia, my own sweet sister, in heaven!'

It was strange, Valency said, that at such an hour, but half saved from death, and his preserver in the grim destroyer's clutches, that he should feel curiosity to know the Greek chief's story. His youth, his surpassing beauty of person – his valour – the act, which Valency well remembered, of his springing forward so as to shield him with his own person – his last words and thoughts devoted to the soft recollection of a beloved sister – awakened an interest beyond even the present hour, fraught as it was with the chances of life and death. He questioned the chief; probably fever had succeeded to his previous state of weakness, imparted a deceitful strength, and even inclined him to talk; for thus dying, unaided and unsheltered, except by the starry sky, he willingly reverted to the years of his youth, and to the miserable event which a few months before had eclipsed the sun of his life, and rendered death welcome.

*   *   *

They – brother and sister, Constantine and Euphrasia – were the last of their race. They were orphans; their youth was passed under the guardianship of the brother by adoption of their father, whom they named father, and who loved them as his own soul. He was a glorious old man, nursed in classic lore, and more familiar with the deeds of men who had glorified his country several thousand years before than with any more modern names. Yet all who had ever done and suffered for Greece were embalmed in his memory and honoured as martyrs in the best of causes. He had been educated in Paris, and had travelled in Europe and America, and was aware of the progress made in the science of politics all over the civilised world. He felt that Greece would soon share the benefits to arise from the changes then operating, and he looked forward at no distant day to its liberation from bondage. He educated his young ward for that day. Had he believed that Greece would have continued hopelessly enslaved, he had brought him up as a scholar and a recluse, but assured of the impending struggle, he made him a warrior; he implanted a detestation of the oppressor; a yearning love for the sacred blessings of freedom, a noble desire to have his name enrolled among the deliverers of his country. The education he bestowed on Euphrasia was yet more singular. He knew that though liberty must be bought and maintained by the sword, yet that its dearest blessings must be derived from civilisation and knowledge, and he believed women to be the proper fosterers of these. They cannot handle a sword nor endure bodily labour for their country, but they could refine the manners, exalt the souls – impart honour, and truth, and wisdom, to their relatives and their children. Euphrasia therefore he made a scholar. By nature she was an enthusiast, and a poet. The study of the classic literature of her country corrected her taste and exalted her love of the beautiful. While a child she improvised passionate songs of liberty; and as she grew in years and loveliness, and her heart opened to tenderness, and she became aware of all the honour and happiness that a woman must derive from being held the friend of man, not his slave, she thanked God that she was a Greek and a Christian; and holding fast by the advantages which these names conferred, she looked forward eagerly to the day when Mahometanism should no longer contaminate her native land, and when her countrywomen should be awakened from ignorance and sloth in which they were plunged and learn that their proper vocation in the creation was that of mothers of heroes and teachers of sages.

Her brother was her idol – her hope – her joy. And he who had been taught that his career must be that of deeds not words, yet was fired by her poetry and eloquence to desire glory yet more eagerly, and to devote himself yet more entirely, and with purer ardour, to the hope of one day living and dying for his country. The first sorrow the orphans knew was the death of their father of adoption. He descended to the grave, full of years and honour. Constantine was then eighteen; his fair sister had just entered her fifteenth year. Often they spent the night beside the revered tomb of their lost friend, talking of the hopes and aspirations he had implanted. The young can form such sublime, such beautiful dreams. No disappointment, no evil, no bad passion shadows their glorious visions; to dare and do greatly for Greece was the ambition of Constantine. To cheer and watch over her brother, to regulate his wilder and more untaught soul, to paint in celestial colours the bourne he tended towards by action, were Euphrasia's tasks.

'There is a heaven,' said the dying man, as he told his tale; 'there is a paradise for those who die in the just cause. I know not what joys are there prepared for the blest; but they cannot transcend those that were mine as I listened to my own sweet sister and felt my heart swell with patriotism and fond warm affection.'

At length there was a stir through the land, and Constantine made a journey of some distance to confer with the *capitani* of the mountains, and to prepare for the outbreak of the revolution. The moment came, sooner even than he expected. As an eagle chained thrills when the iron links drop from him and with clang of wing and bright undazzled eye he soars to heaven, so did Constantine feel when freedom to Greece became the war cry. He was still among the mountains when first the echoes of his native valleys repeated that animating – that sacred word; instead of returning as he intended to his Athenian home, he was hurried off to western Greece, and became involved in a series of warlike movements, the promised success of which filled him with transport.

Suddenly a pause came in the delirium of joy which possessed his soul. He received not the accustomed letters from his sister – missives which had been to him angelic messengers, teaching him patience with the unworthy – hope in disappointment – security in final triumph. Those dear letters ceased; and he thought he saw in the countenances of his friends around a concealed knowledge of evil. He questioned them: their answers were evasive. At the same time, they endeavoured to fill his mind with the details of some anticipated exploit, in which his presence and cooperation was necessary. Day after day passed; he could not leave his post without injury to his cause, without even the taint of dishonour. He belonged to a band of Albanians, by whom he had been received as a brother, and he could not desert them in the hour of danger. But the suspense grew too terrible; and at length, finding that there was an interval of a few days which he might call his own, he left the camp; resting neither day nor night, dismounting from one horse only to bestride another, in forty-eight hours he was in Athens, before his vacant desecrated home. The tale of horror was soon told. Athens was still in the hands of the Turks; the sister of a rebel had become the prey of the oppressor. She had none to guard her. Her matchless beauty had been seen and marked by the son of the pasha; she had for the last two months inhabited his harem.

'Despair is a cold dark feeling,' said the dying warrior; 'if I may name that despair which had a hope – a certainty – an aim. Had Euphrasia died I had wept. Now my eyes were horn – my heart stone. I was silent. I neither expressed resentment nor revenge. I concealed myself by day; at night, I wandered round the tyrant's dwelling. It was a pleasure-palace, one of the most luxurious that adorned the enemies of our beloved Athens. At this time it was carefully guarded; my character was known and Euphrasia's worth, and the oppressor feared the result of his deed. Still, under shadow of darkness I drew near. I marked the position of the women's apartments – I learned the number – the length of the watch – the orders they received, and then I returned to the camp. I revealed my project to a few select spirits. They were fired by my wrongs, and eager to deliver my Euphrasia – '

Constantine broke off – a spasm of pain shook his body. After this had passed he lay motionless for a few minutes; then, starting up, as fever and delirium, excited by the exertion of speaking, increased by the agonies of recollection, at last fully possessed him, 'What is this,' he cried; 'fire! Yes, the palace burns. Do you not hear the roaring of the flames, and thunder too – the artillery of heaven levelled against the unblessed. Ha! a shot – he falls – they are driven back – now fling the torches – the wood crackles – there, there are the women's rooms – ha! poor victims, lo! you shudder and fly! Fear not; give me only my Euphrasia! – my own Euphrasia! No disguise can hide thee, dressed as

Conatantine and Euphrasia

a Turkish bride crowned with flowers, thy lovely face, the seat of unutterable woe; still, my sweet sister, even in this smoke and tumult of this house, thou art the angel of my life. Spring into my arms, poor frightened bird, cling to me – it is herself – her voice – her fair arms are round my neck – what ruin – what flame – what choking smoke – what driving storm, can stay me. Soft! the burning breach is passed – there are steps – gently – dear one, I am firm – fear not! – what eye glares? – fear not, Euphrasia, he is dead – the miserable retainers of the tyrant fell beneath our onset – ha! a shot – gracious Panagia,[235] is this thy protection!' Thus did he continue to rave – the onset – the burning of the palace – the deliverance of his sister, all seemed to pass again vividly as if in present action. His eyes glared – he tossed up his arms – he shouted as if calling his followers around him – and then, in tones of heartfelt tenderness, he addressed the fair burthen he fancied that he bore – till, with a shriek, he cried again, 'A shot!' and sank to the ground as if his heart strings had broken.

An interval of calm succeeded; he was exhausted; his voice was broken. 'What have I told thee?' he continued, feebly. 'I have said how a mere handful of men attacked the palace, and drove back the guards – how we strove in vain to make good our entrance – fresh troops were on their way – there was no alternative; we fired the palace. Deep in the seclusion of the harem the women had retreated, a herd of frightened deer. One alone stood erect. Her eyes bent on the intruders – a dagger in her hand – majestic and fearless, her face was marked with traces of past suffering, but at the moment the stern resolution her soft features expressed was more than human. The moment she saw me, all was changed; the angel alone beamed in her countenance. Her dagger fell from her hand – she was in my arms – I bore her from the burning roof – the rest you know; have I not said it? Some miscreant, who survived the slaughter, and yet lay as dead on the earth, aimed a deadly shot. She did not shriek. At first she clung closer to my neck, and then I felt her frame shiver in my arms and her hold relax. I trusted that fear alone moved her; but she knew not fear – it was death. Horses had been prepared, and were waiting; a few hours more and I hoped to be on our way to the west, to that portion of Greece that was free. But I felt her head fall on my shoulder. I heard her whisper, "I die, my brother! carry me to our father's tomb."

'My soul yearned to comply with her request; but it was impossible. The city was alarmed; troops gathering from all quarters. Our safety lay in flight, for still I thought that her wound was not mortal. I bore her to the spot where we had left our horses. Here two or three of my comrades speedily joined me; they had rescued the women of the harem from the flames; but the various sounds denoting the advance of the Turkish soldiery caused them to hurry from the scene. I leapt on my horse, and placed my sweet sister before me, and we fled amain through desert streets I well knew how to choose and along the lanes of the suburbs into the open country, where deviating from the high road – along which I directed my companions to proceed in all haste – alone with my beloved burthen, I sought a solitary unsuspected spot among the neighbouring hills. The storm which had ceased for a time, now broke afresh; the deafening thunder drowned every other sound, while the frequent glare of the lightning showed us our path; my horse did not quail before it. Euphrasia still lay clinging to me; no complaint escaped her; a few words of fondness, of encouragement, of pious resignation, she now and then breathed forth. I knew not she was dying, till at last entering a retired valley, where an olive wood afforded shelter, and still better the portico of a fallen ancient temple, I dismounted and bore her to the marble steps, on which I placed her. Then indeed I felt how near the beloved one was to death, from which I could not save her. The lightning showed me her face; pale as the marble which pillowed it. Her dress was dabbled in warm blood, which soon stained the stones on which she lay. I took her hand, it was deathly cold. I raised her from the marble; I pillowed her cheek upon my heart. I repressed my despair, or rather my despair in that hour was mild and soft as herself. There was no help – no hope. The life blood oozed fast from her side; scarce could she raise her heavy eyelids to look on me; her voice could no longer articulate my name. The burthen of her fair limbs grew heavier and more chill; soon it was a corse only that I held. When I knew that her sufferings were over, I raised her once more in my arms, and once more I placed her before me on my horse, and betook me to my journey alone, though still I bore her form in my arms. The storm was over now, and the moon bright above. Earth glittered under the rays, and a soft breeze swept by, as if heaven itself became clear and peaceful to receive her stainless soul, and present it to its Maker. By morning's dawn, I stopped at a convent gate, and rang. To the holy maidens within I consigned my own fair Euphrasia. I kissed but once again her dear brow, which spoke of peace in death, and then saw her placed upon a bier, and was away, back to my camp, to live and die for Greece.'

* * *

He grew more silent, as he became weaker. Now and then he spoke a few words to record some other of Euphrasia's perfections, or to repeat some of her dying words; to speak of her magnanimity, her genius, her love, and his own wish to die.

'I might have lived,' he said, 'till her image had faded in my mind, or been mingled with less holy memories. I die young, all her own. Those whom the gods favour, all die young.'

His voice grew more feeble after this; he complained of cold. Valency continued, 'I contrived to rise, and crawl about, and to collect a *capote* or two and a pelisse from among the slain, with some of which I covered him; and then I drew one over myself, for the air grew chill as midnight had passed away and the morning hour drew near. The warmth which the coverings imparted calmed the aching of my wound, and, strange to say, I felt slumber creep over me. I tried to watch and wake. At first the stars above, and the dark forms of the mountains mingled with my dreamy feelings; but soon I lost all sense of where I was, and what I had suffered, and slept peacefully and long.

'The morning sunbeams, as creeping down the hillside they at last fell upon my face, awoke me. At first I had forgotten all thought of the events of the past night, and my first impulse was to spring up, crying aloud, where am I? but the stiffness of my limbs and their weakness soon revealed the truth. Gladly I now welcomed the sound of voices, and marked the approach of a number of peasants along the ravine. Hitherto, strange to say, I had thought only of myself; but with the ideas of succour, came the recollection of my companion, and the tale of the previous night. I glanced eagerly to where he lay; his posture disclosed his state; he was still, and stiff, and dead. Yet his countenance was calm and beautiful. He had died in the dear hope of meeting his sister, and her image had shed peace over the last moment of life.

'I am ashamed to revert to myself. The death of Constantine is the true end of my tale. My wound was a severe one. I was forced to leave Greece, and for some months remained between life and death in Cefalonia, till a good constitution saved me, when at once I returned to England.'

The Heir of Mondolfo

IN the beautiful and wild country near Sorrento in the kingdom of Naples, at the time that it was governed by monarchs of the house of Anjou,[236] there lived a territorial noble whose wealth and power overbalanced that of the neighbouring nobles. His castle, itself a stronghold, was built on a rocky eminence toppling over the blue and lovely Mediterranean. The hills around were covered with ilex forests or subdued to the culture of the olive and vine. Under the sun no spot could be found more favoured by nature.

If at eventide you had passed on the placid wave beneath the castellated rock that bore the name of Mondolfo, you would have imagined that all happiness and bliss must reside within its walls, which, thus nestled in beauty, overlooked a scene of such surpassing loveliness. Yet if by chance you saw its lord issue from the portal, you shrank from his frowning brow, you wondered at what could impress on his worn cheek the combat of passions. More piteous sight was it to behold his gentle lady, who, the slave of his unbridled temper, the patient sufferer of many wrongs, seemed on the point of entering upon that only repose 'where the wicked cease from troubling and the weary are at rest'.[237] The Prince Mondolfo had been united early in life to a princess of the royal family of Sicily. She died on giving birth to a son. Many years afterwards, after a journey to the northern Italian states, he returned to his castle married. The speech of his bride declared her to be a Florentine. The current tale was that he married her for love, and then hated her as the hindrance of his ambitious views. She bore all for the sake of her only child – a child born to its father's hate: a boy of gallant spirit, brave even to wildness. As he grew up, he saw with anger the treatment his mother received from the haughty prince. He dared come forward her defender; he dared oppose his boyish courage to his father's rage. The result was natural: he became the object of his father's dislike. Indignity was heaped on him: the vassals were taught to disobey him, the menials to scorn him, his very brother to despise him as of inferior blood and birth. Yet the blood of Mondolfo was his, and though tempered by the gentle Isabel's more kindly tide, it boiled at the injustice to which he was a victim. A thousand times he poured forth the overflowings of his injured spirit in eloquent complaints to his mother. As her health decayed, he nurtured the project, in case of her death, of flying his paternal castle and becoming a wanderer, a soldier of fortune. He was now thirteen. The Lady Isabel soon, with a mother's penetration, discovered his secret, and on her deathbed made him swear not to quit his father's protection until he should have attained the age of twenty. Her heart bled for the wretchedness that she foresaw would be his lot, but she looked forward with still greater horror to the picture her active fancy drew of her son at an early age wandering forth in despair, alone and helpless, suffering all the extremities of famine and wretchedness – or almost worse, yielding to the temptations that in such a situation would be held out to him. She extracted this vow, and died satisfied that he would keep it. Of all the world, she alone knew the worth of her Ludovico – had penetrated beneath the rough surface and become acquainted with the rich store of virtue and affectionate feeling that lay like unmined ore in his sensitive heart.

Fernando hated his son. From his earliest boyhood he had felt the sentiment of aversion, which, far from endeavouring to quell, he allowed to take deep root until Ludovico's most innocent action became a crime; and a system of denial and resistance was introduced that called forth all of sinister that there was in the youth's character, and engendered an active spirit of detestation in his father's mind. Thus Ludovico grew hated and hating; brought together through their common situation, the father and son, lord and vassal, oppressor and oppressed, the one was continually ready to exert his power of inflicting evil – the other perpetually on the alert to resist even the shadow of tyranny.

After the death of his mother, Ludovico's character greatly changed: the smile that as the sun had then often irradiated his countenance now never shone; suspicion, irritability, and dogged resolution, seemed his master feelings. He dared his father to the worst, endured that worst, and, prevented from flying by his sacred observance to his vow, nurtured all angry and even revengeful feelings till the cup of wrath seemed ready to overflow. He was loved by none; his good qualities expired or slept as if they would never more awaken.

His father intended him for the Church, and Ludovico until he was sixteen wore the priestly garb. That period past, he cast it aside and appeared habited as a cavalier of those days, and in short words told his parent that he refused to comply with his wishes, that he should dedicate himself to arms and enterprise. All that followed this declaration – menace, imprisonment and even ignominy – he bore; but he continued firm, and the haughty Fernando was obliged to submit his towering will to the firmer will of a stripling. And now for the first time, while rage seemed to burst his heart, he felt to its highest degree the sentiment of hatred; he expressed this passion; words of contempt and boundless detestation were heaped upon Ludovico's head; the boy replied, and the bystanders feared that a personal encounter would ensue. Once, Fernando put his hand on his sword, and the unarmed Ludovico drew in and collected himself as if ready to spring and seize the arm that might be uplifted against him. Fernando saw and dreaded the mad ferocity his son's eye expressed. In all personal encounter of this kind, the victory rests not with the strong but the most fearless. Fernando was not ready to stake his life or even with his own hand to shed his son's blood; Ludovico, not as aggressor but in self-defence, was careless of the consequences of an attack. He would resist to the death, and this dauntless feeling gave him an ascendency his father felt and could not forgive.

From this time Fernando's conduct towards his son changed – he no longer punished, imprisoned or menaced him. This was usage for a boy, but the prince felt that they were man to man and acted accordingly. He was the gainer by the change, for he soon acquired all the ascendency that experience, craft and a court education must naturally give him over a hot-headed youth who, nerved to resist all personal violence, neither saw nor understood a more covert mode of proceeding. Fernando hoped to drive his son to desperation. He set spies over him, paid the tempters that were to lead him to crime, and, by a continual system of restraint and miserable thwarting, hoped to reduce him to such despair that he would take refuge in any line of conduct that promised freedom from so irksome and degrading a slavery. His observance of his vow saved the youth; and this steadiness of purpose gave him time to read and understand the motives of the tempters. He saw his father's master hand in all, and his heart sickened at the discovery.

He had reached his eighteenth year. The treatment he had endured and the constant exertion of fortitude and resolution had already given him the appearance of manhood. He was tall, well made and athletic. His person and demeanour were more energetic than graceful, and his manners were haughty and reserved. He had few accomplishments, for his father had been at no pains in his education; feats of horsemanship and arms made up the whole catalogue. He hated books as being a part of a priest's insignia: he was averse to all occupation that brought bodily repose with it. His complexion was dark – hardship had rendered it even sallow; his eyes, once soft, now glared with fierceness; his lips, formed to express tenderness, were now habitually curled in contempt; his dark hair, clustering in thick curls round his throat, completed the wild but grand and interesting appearance of his person.

It was winter, and the pleasures of the chase began. Every morning the huntsmen assembled to attack the wild boars or stags which the dogs might rouse in the fastnesses of the Apennines. This was the only pleasure that Ludovico ever enjoyed. During these pursuits he felt himself free. Mounted on a noble horse which he urged to its full speed, his blood danced in his veins and his eyes shone with rapture as he cast his eagle glance to heaven; with a smile of ineffable disdain, he passed his false friends or open tormentors and gained a solitary precedency in the pursuit.

The plain at the foot of Vesuvius and its neighbouring hills were stripped bare by winter; the full streams rushed impetuously from the hills, and their roar mingled with the baying of the dogs and the cries of the hunters. (The sea, dark under a lowering sky, made a melancholy dirge as its waves broke on the shore.) Vesuvius groaned heavily, and the birds answered it by wailing shrieks; a heavy sirocco[238] hung upon the atmosphere, rendering it damp and cold. This wind seems at once to excite and depress the human mind – it excites it to thought, but colours these thoughts as it does the sky with black. Ludovico felt this, but he tried to surmount the natural feelings with which the ungenial air filled him.

The temperature of the air changed as the day advanced; the clouded sky spent itself in snow which fell in abundance; it then became clear, and a sharp frost succeeded. The aspect of earth was changed. Snow covered the ground and lay on the leafless trees, sparkling, white and untrod. Early in the morning a stag had been roused, and, as he was coursed along the plain skirting the hills, the hunters went at speed. All day the chase endured. At length the stag, who from the beginning had directed his course towards the hills, began to ascend them, and with various windings and evolutions almost put the hounds to fault. Day was near its close when Ludovico alone followed the stag as it made for the edge of a kind of platform of the mountain, which, isthmus-like, was connected with the hill by a small tongue of land, and on three sides was precipitous to the plain below. Ludovico balanced his spear; and his dogs drew in, expecting that the despairing animal would there turn at bay. He made one bound which conducted him to the very brow of the precipice – another – and he was seen no more. He sprang downwards, expecting more pity from the rocks beneath than from his human adversary. Ludovico was fatigued by his chase and angry at the escape of his prey; he sprang from his horse, tied him to a tree, and sought a path by which he might safely descend to the plain. Snow covered and hid the ground, obliterating the usual traces that the flocks or herds might have left as they descended from their pastures on the hills to the hamlets beneath. But Ludovico had passed his boyhood among mountains: while his hunting spear found sure rest on the ground, he did not fear; or while a twig afforded him sufficient support as he held it, he did not doubt to secure his passage. But the descent was precipitous, and necessary caution obliged him to be long. The sun approached the horizon, and the glow of its departure was veiled by swift-rising clouds, which the wind blew upwards from the sea – a cold wind, which whirled the snow from its resting place and shook it from the trees. Ludovico at length arrived at the foot of the precipice. The snow reflected and increased the twilight, and he saw four deep marks that must have been made by the deer. The precipice was high above, and its escape appeared a miracle. It must have escaped, but those were the only marks it had left. Around lay a forest of ilex beset by thick and entangled underwood, and it seemed impossible that any animal so large as the stag in pursuit could have broken its way through the apparently impenetrable barrier it opposed. The desire to find his quarry became almost a passion in the heart of Ludovico; he walked round to seek for an opening, and at last found a narrow pathway through the forest, and some few marks seemed to indicate that the stag might have sought for refuge up the glen. With a swiftness characteristic even of his prey, Ludovico rushed up the pathway, and thought not of how far he ran until breathless he stopped before a cottage that opposed itself to his further progress. He stopped and looked around. There was something singularly mournful in the scene. It was not dark, but the shades of evening seemed to descend from the vast woof of cloud that climbed the sky from the west. The black and shining leaves of the ilex and those of the laurel and myrtle underwood were strongly contrasted with the white snow that lay upon them. A breeze passed among the boughs, and scattered the drift that fell in flakes, and disturbed at fits the silence around; or, again, a bird twittered or flew with melancholy flap of wing beneath the trees to its nest in some hollow trunk. The house seemed desolate: its windows were glassless, and small heaps of snow lay upon the sills; there was no print of footing on the equal surface of the path that led right up to the door. Yet, a little smoke now and then struggled upwards from its chimney; and on paying fixed attention, Prince Ludovico thought he heard a voice. He called but received no answer; he put his hand on the latch, it yielded, and he entered. On the floor strewn with leaves lay a person sick and dying – for though there was a slight motion in the eyes that showed that life had not yet deserted his throne, the paleness of the visage was that of death only. It was an aged woman, and her white hairs showed that she descended to no untimely grave. But a figure knelt beside her which might have been mistaken for the angel of heaven waiting to receive and guide the departing soul to eternal rest, but for the sharp agony that was stamped on the features, and the glazed but earnest gaze of her eye. She was very young and beautiful as the star of evening. She had apparently despoiled herself to bestow warmth on her dying friend, for her arms and neck were bare but for the quantity of dark and flowing hair that clustered on her shoulders. She was absorbed in one feeling, that of watching the change in the sick person. Her cheeks, even her lips, were pale; her eyes seemed to gaze as if her whole life reigned in their single perception. She did not hear Ludovico enter, or at least she made no sign that indicated that she was conscious of it. The sick person murmured, and she bent her head down to catch the sounds. She replied in an accent of despair: 'I can get no more leaves, for the snow is on the ground; nor have I any other earthly thing to place over you.'

'Is she cold?' said Ludovico, creeping near and bending down beside the afflicted girl.

'Oh, very cold,' she replied, 'and there is no help.'

Ludovico had gone to the chase in a silken mantle lined with the choicest furs. He had thrown it off and left it with his horse that it might not impede his descent. He hastened from the cottage, he ran down the lane, and following the marks of his footsteps, he arrived where his steed awaited him. He did not again descend by the same path. Reflecting that it might be necessary for him to seek assistance for the dying woman, he led his horse down the hill by a circuitous path; and although he did this with all possible speed, night closed in, and the glare of the snow alone permitted him to see the path that he desired to follow. When he arrived at the lane, he saw that the cottage, before so dark, was illuminated; and as he approached he heard the solemn hymn of death, as it was chanted by the priests who filled it. The change had taken place, the soul had left its mortal mansion, and the deserted ruin was attended with more solemnity than had been paid to the mortal struggle. Amidst the crowd of priests, Ludovico entered unperceived, and he looked round for the lovely female he had left. She sat retired from the priests, on a heap of leaves in a corner of the cottage. Her clasped hands lay on her knees, her head was bent downwards, and every now and then she wiped away her fast-falling tears with her hair. Ludovico threw his cloak over her. She looked up and drew the covering round her, more to hide her person than for the sake of warmth; and then, again turning away, was absorbed in her melancholy thoughts.

Ludovico gazed on her in pity. For the first time since his mother's death, tears filled his eyes, and his softened countenance beamed with tender sympathy. He said nothing, but he continued to look on as a wish arose in his mind that he might wipe the tears that one by one fell from the shrouded eyes of the unfortunate girl. As he was thus engaged, he heard his name called by one of the attendants of the castle; and throwing the few pieces of gold he possessed into the lap of the sufferer, he suddenly left the cottage, mounted his horse, and joining the servant who had been in search of him, rode rapidly towards his home.

As Ludovico rode along, and the first emotions of pity having as it were ceased to throb in his mind, these feelings merged into the strain of thought in which he habitually indulged and turned its course to something new. 'I call myself wretched,' he cried, 'I, the well clad and fed; and this lovely peasant girl, half famished, parts with her necessary clothing to cover the dying limbs of her only friend. I also have lost my only friend, and that is my true misfortune, the cause of all my real misery. Sycophants would assume that name, spies and traitors usurp that office; I have cast those aside – shaken them from me as yon bough shakes to earth its encumbrance of snow, not so cold as their iced hearts. But I am alone – solitude gnaws my heart and makes me savage – miserable – worthless.'

Yet, although he thought in this manner, the heart of Ludovico was softened by what he had seen, and milder feelings pressed upon him. He had felt sympathy for one who needed it, he had conferred a benefit on the necessitous, tenderness moulded his lips to a smile and the pride of utility gave dignity to the fire of his eye. The people about him saw the change, and not meeting with the usual disdain of his manner, they also became softened; and the alteration apparent in his character seemed ready to effect as great a metamorphosis in his external situation. But the time was not come when this change would become permanent.

On the day that succeeded to this hunt, Prince Fernando removed to Naples and commanded his son to accompany him. The residence at Naples was peculiarly irksome to Ludovico. In the country, he enjoyed comparative freedom; satisfied that he was in the castle, his father sometimes forgot him for days together; but it was otherwise here. Fearful that he should form friends and connections, and knowing that his commanding figure and peculiar manners excited attention and often curiosity, he kept him ever in sight; or if he left him for a moment, he first made himself sure of the people around him, and left such of his own confidants whose very presence was venom to the eye of Ludovico. Add to which, Prince Mondolfo delighted to insult and browbeat his son in public; and aware of his deficiency in the more elegant accomplishments, he exposed him even to the derision of his friends.

They remained two months at Naples and then returned to Mondolfo. It was spring; the air was genial and spirit-stirring. The white blossoms of the almond trees and the pink ones of the peach just began to be contrasted with the green leaves that shot forth among them. Ludovico felt little of the exhilarating effects of spring. Wounded in his heart's core, he asked nature why she painted a sepulchre; he asked the airs why they fanned the sorrowful and dead. He wandered forth to solitude. He rambled down the path that led to the sea; he sat on the beach watching the monotonous flow of the waves; they danced and sparkled; his gloomy thoughts refused to imbibe cheerfulness from wave or sun.

A form passed near him – a peasant girl who balanced a pitcher, urn-shaped, upon her head. She was meanly clad, but she attracted Ludovico's regard; and when having approached the fountain, she took her pitcher and turned to fill it, he recognised the cottager of the foregoing winter. She knew him also, and leaving her occupation she approached him and kissed his hand with that irresistible grace that southern climes seem to instil into the meanest of its children. At first she hesitated and began to thank him in broken accents; but words came as she spoke, and Ludovico listened to her eloquent thanks – the first he had heard addressed to him from any human being. A smile of pleasure stole over his face – a smile whose beauty sank deep in the gazer's heart. In a minute they were seated on the bank beside the fountain, and Viola told her story – of her poverty-stricken youth – her orphan lot – the death of her last friend; and it was now only the benign climate which in diminishing human wants made her appear less wretched than then. She was alone in the world – living in that desolate cottage, providing for her daily fare with difficulty. Her pale cheek, the sickly languor that pervaded her manner, gave evidence to the truth of her words, but she did not weep; she spoke words of good heart, and it was only when she alluded to the benefaction of Ludovico that her soft dark eyes swam with tears.

The youth visited her cottage the next day. He rode up the lane, now grass-grown and scented by violets which Viola was gathering from the banks. She presented her nosegay to him. They entered the cottage together – it was dilapidated and miserable. A few flowers placed in a broken vase was a type only of poor Viola herself – a lovely blossom in the midst of utter poverty; and the rose tree that shaded the window could only tell that sweet Italy, even in the midst of wretchedness, spares her natural wealth to adorn her children. Ludovico made Viola sit down on a bench by the window and stood opposite to her, her flowers in his hand, listening. She did not talk of her poverty, and it would be difficult to recount what was said. She seemed happy, and smiled and spoke with a gleeful voice which softened the heart of her friend, so that he almost wept with pity and admiration. After this, day by day Ludovico visited the cottage and bestowed all his time on Viola. He came and talked with her, gathered violets with her, consoled and advised her, and became happy. The idea that he was of use to a single human being instilled joy into his heart; and yet he was wholly unconscious how entirely he was necessary to the happiness of his protégée. He felt happy beside her; he was delighted to bestow benefits on her and to see her profit by them; but he did not think of love, and his mind, unawakened to passion, reposed from its long pain without a thought for the future. It was not so with the peasant girl. She could not see his eyes bent in gentleness on her – his mouth lighted by its tender smile – or listen to his voice as he bade her trust in him for that he would be father, brother, all to her, without deeply, passionately loving him. He became the sun of her day, the breath of her life – her hope, joy and sole possession. She watched for his coming, she watched him as he went, and for a long time she was happy. She would not repine. What though he replied to her earnest love with calm affection only – she was a peasant, he a noble – and she could claim and expect no more. He was a god; she might adore him; but it were blasphemy to hope for more than a benign acceptation of her worship.

Prince Mondolfo was soon made aware of Ludovico's visits to the cottage in the forest, and he did not doubt that Viola had become the mistress of his son. Yet he did not endeavour to interrupt this connection or put any bar to his visits. Ludovico indeed enjoyed more liberty than ever, and his cruel father confined himself alone to restricting him more than ever in money. His policy was apparent: Ludovico had resisted every temptation of gambling and other modes of expense thrown in his way. Fernando had long wished to bring his son to a painful sense of his poverty and dependence, and to oblige him to seek the necessary funds in such a career as would necessitate his desertion of the paternal roof. He had wound many snares around the boy, and all were snapped by his firm but almost unconscious resistance; but now without seeking, without expectation, the occasion came of itself which would lead him to require far more than his father had at any time allowed him; and now that allowance was restricted; yet Ludovico did not murmur, and until now he had enough.

For a long time Fernando abstained from all allusion to the connection of his son; but one evening at a banquet, gaiety overcame his caution – gaiety which ever led him to sport with his son's feelings and to excite a pain that might repress the smile that his new state of mind caused to make frequent visits to his countenance. 'Here,' cried Fernando as he filled a goblet – 'here, Ludovico, is to the health of your violet girl' – and he concluded his speech with some indecorous allusion that suffused Ludovico's cheek with red. Without replying he arose to depart. 'And whither are you going, sir?' cried his father. 'Take yon cup and answer my pledge, for by Bacchus none that sits at my table shall pass it uncourteously by.'

Ludovico, still standing, filled his cup and raised it as he was about to speak and retort to his father's speech; but the memory of his words and the innocence of Viola pressed upon him and filled his heart almost to bursting. He put down his cup, pushed aside the people who sought to detain him, and left the castle. Soon the laughter of the revellers was no more heard by him, though it had loudly rung and was echoed through the lofty halls. The words of Fernando awakened a strange spirit in Ludovico. 'Viola, can she love me? Do I love her?' The last question was quickly answered. Passion, suddenly awake, made every artery tingle by its thrilling presence. His cheeks burned as his heart danced with strange exultation as he hastened towards the cottage, unheeding all but the universe of sensation that dwelt within him. He reached its door – blank and dark the walls rose before him, and the boughs of the wood waved and sighed over him. Until now he had felt impatience alone – the sickness of fear, fear of finding a cold return to his passion's feeling, now entered his heart; and retreating a little from the cottage, he sat on a bank and hid his face in his hands, while passionate tears gushed from his eyes and trickled from between his fingers. Viola opened the door of her cottage; Ludovico had failed in his daily visit, and she was unhappy. She looked on the sky – the sun had set, and Hesperus[239] glowed in the west. The dark ilex trees made a deep shade which was broken by innumerable fireflies which flashed – now low on the ground, discovering the flowers as they slept hushed and closed in night; now high among the branches; and their light was reflected by the shining leaves of ilex and laurel. Viola's wandering eye unconsciously selected one and followed it as it flew, and ever and anon it cast aside its veil of darkness and spread a wide pallor around its own form. At length it nestled itself in a bower of green leaves, formed by a clump of united laurels and myrtles; and there it stayed flashing its beautiful light, which, coming from among the boughs, seemed as if the brightest star of the heavens had wandered from its course, and, trembling at its temerity, sat panting on its earthly perch. Ludovico sat near the laurel – Viola saw him – her breath came quick – she spoke not but stepped lightly to him – and looked with such mazed ecstasy of thought that she felt, nay almost heard, her heartbeat with her emotion. At length she spoke – she uttered his name, and he looked up on her gentle face, her beaming eyes and sylphlike form bent over him. He forgot his fears, and his hopes were soon confirmed. For the first time, he pressed the trembling lips of Viola and then tore himself away to think with rapture and wonder on all that had taken place.

Ludovico ever acted with energy and promptness. He returned only to plan with Viola the moment when they might be united. A small chapel amid the Apennines, sequestered and unknown, was selected and a priest easily procured from a neighbouring convent and easily bribed to silence. Ludovico led back his bride to her cottage in the forest, and there she continued to reside. For worlds he would not have had her change her habitation. All his wealth was expended in decorating her habitation, and his little wealth only sufficed to render it tolerable. But they were happy. The small circlet of earth's expanse that held in his Viola was the universe to her husband; and his heart and imagination widened and filled it, until it encompassed all of beautiful His father's taunts were unheeded, for he did not hear them. He no longer trod the earth, but angel-like, sustained by the wings of love, skimmed over it so that he felt not its inequalities and was not touched by its rude obstacles. And Viola, with deep gratitude and passionate tenderness, repaid his love. She thought of him only, lived for him, and with unwearied attention kept alive in his mind the first dream of passion.

Thus nearly two years passed, and a lovely child appeared to bind the lovers with closer ties and to fill their humble roof with smiles and joy. Ludovico seldom went to Mondolfo; and his father, still continuing his ancient policy and glad that, in his attachment to a peasant girl, he had relieved his mind from the fear of brilliant connections and able friends, even dispensed with his attendance when he visited Naples. Fernando did not suspect that his son had married this low-born favourite; if he had, his aversion would not have withheld him from resisting so degrading an alliance; and while his blood flowed in Ludovico's veins, he would never have avowed offspring who were contaminated by a peasant's less highly sprung tide.

Ludovico had nearly completed his twentieth year when his elder brother died. Prince Mondolfo at that time had spent four months at Naples, endeavouring to bring to a conclusion a treaty of marriage he had entered into between his heir and the daughter of a noble Neapolitan house, when this death overthrew his hopes, and he retired in grief and mourning to his castle. A few weeks of sorrow and reason restored him to himself. He had loved even this favoured elder son more as the heir of his name and fortunes than as his child; and the web that he had woven for him destroyed, he quickly began another.

Ludovico was summoned to his father's presence. Old habit yet rendered such a summons momentous; but the youth with a proud smile threw off these boyish cares and stood with gentle dignity before his altered parent.

'Ludovico,' said the prince, 'four years ago, you refused to take a priest's vows, and then you excited my utmost resentment; now I thank you for that resistance.'

A slight feeling of suspicion crossed Ludovico's mind – that his father was about to cajole him for some evil purpose. Two years before, he would have acted on such a thought, but the habit of happiness made him unsuspicious. He bent his head silently.

'Ludovico,' continued his father, while pride and a wish to conciliate disturbed his mind and even his countenance, 'my son, I have used you hardly; but that time is now passed.'

Ludovico gently replied: 'My father, I did not deserve your ill-treatment; I hope that I shall merit your kindness when I know – '

'Yes, yes,' interrupted Fernando uneasily, 'you do not understand, you desire to know why – in short, you, Ludovico, are now all my hope; Olimpio is dead – the house of Mondolfo has no support but you.'

'Pardon me,' replied the youth, 'Mondolfo is in no danger; you, my lord, are fully able to support and even augment its present dignity.'

'You do not understand – Mondolfo has no support but you. I am old, I feel my age, and these grey hairs announce it to me too glaringly. There is no collateral branch, and my hopes must rest in your children.'

'My child, my lord,' replied Ludovico. 'I have only one, and if the poor little boy – '

'What folly is this?' cried Fernando impatiently. 'I speak of your marriage and not – '

'My lord, my wife is ever ready to pay her duteous respects to you.'

'Your wife – Ludovico – but you speak without thought – how? who?'

'The violet girl, my lord.'

A tempest had crossed the countenance of Fernando. That his son, unknown to him, should have made an unworthy alliance convulsed every fibre of his frame, and the lowering of his brows and his impatient gesture told the intolerable anguish of such a thought. The last words of Ludovico restored him. It was not his wife that he thus named – he felt assured that it was not. He smiled, somewhat ghastly, yet still it was a smile of satisfaction. 'Yes,' he replied, 'I understand, but you task my patience. You should not trifle with such a subject or with me; I talk of your marriage. Now that Olimpio is dead and you are, in his place, heir of Mondolfo, you may in his stead conclude the advantageous, nay, even princely, alliance I was forming for him.'

Ludovico replied with earnestness: 'You are pleased to misunderstand me. I am already married. Two years ago, while I was still the despised, insulted Ludovico, I formed this connection, and it will be my pride to show the world how, in all but birth, my peasant wife is able to fulfil the duties of her distinguished situation.'

Fernando was accustomed to command himself. He felt as if stabbed by a poignard, but he paused till calm and voice returned, and then he said: 'You have a child?'

'An heir, my lord,' replied Ludovico, smiling – for his father's mildness deceived him – 'a lovely, healthy boy.'

'They live near here?'

'I can bring them to Mondolfo in an hour's space. Their cottage is in the forest, about a quarter of a mile east of the convent of Santa Chiara.'

'Enough, Ludovico – you have communicated strange tidings, and I must consider of them. I will see you again this evening.'

Ludovico bowed and disappeared. He hastened to his cottage and related all that he remembered or understood of this scene, and bade Viola prepare to come to the castle at an instant's notice. Viola trembled. It struck her that all was not so fair as Ludovico represented; but she hid her fears and even smiled as her husband with a kiss hailed his boy as heir of Mondolfo.

Fernando had commanded both look and voice while his son was within hearing. He had gone to the window of his chamber, and stood steadily gazing on the drawbridge until Ludovico crossed it and disappeared. Then, unrestrained, he strode up and down his apartment, while the roof rang with his impetuous tread. He uttered cries and curses, and struck his head with his clenched fist. It was long ere he could think; he felt only – and feeling was torture. The tempest at length subsided and he threw himself in his chair. His contracted brows and frequently constricted lips showed how entirely he was absorbed in consideration. All at first was one frightful whirl; by degrees the motion was appeased; his thoughts flowed with greater calmness; they subsided into one channel whose course he warily traced until he thought that he saw the result.

Hours passed during this contemplation. When he arose from his chair as one who had slept and dreamt uneasily, his brows became by degrees smooth; he stretched out his arm and, spreading his hand, cried: 'So it is, and I have vanquished him!' Evening came, and Ludovico was announced. Fernando feared his son. He had ever dreaded his determinate and fearless mode of action. He dreaded to encounter his passions with his own, and he felt in the clash that his was not the master passion. So subduing all of hate, revenge and wrath, he received him with a smile. Ludovico smiled also. Yet there was no similarity in their look: one was a smile of frankness, joy and affection – the other, the curled grimace of smothered malice. Fernando said: 'My son, you have entered lightly into a marriage as if it were a child's game; but where principalities and noble blood are at stake, the loss or gain is too momentous to be trifled with. Silence, Ludovico; listen to me, I entreat. You have made a strange marriage with a peasant, which, though I may acknowledge, I cannot approve; which must be displeasing to your sovereign, derogatory to all who claim alliance with the house of Mondolfo.' Cold dew stood on the forehead of Fernando as he spoke; he paused, recovered his self-command, and continued: 'It will be difficult to reconcile these discordant interests, and a moment of rashness might cause us to lose our station, fortune, everything. Your interests are in my hands. I will be careful of them. I trust, before the expiration of a very few months, the future Princess Mondolfo will be received at the court of Naples with due honour and respect. But you must leave it to me; you must not move in this affair; you must promise that you will not, until I permit, mention your marriage to anyone, or acknowledge it if you are taxed with it.'

Ludovico, after a moment's hesitation, replied: 'I promise that for the space of six months I will not mention my marriage to any. I will not be guilty of falsehood, but for that time I will not affirm it or bring it forward in any manner so as to annoy you.'

Fernando again paused; but prudence conquered, and he said no more. He entered on other topics with his son; they supped together, and the mind of Ludovico, now attuned to affection, received all the marks of love from his father with gratitude and joy.

A week passed thus in calm. Ludovico and Viola were perfectly happy. Ludovico only wished to draw his wife from obscurity, from that sensation of honest pride which makes us desire to declare to the whole world the excellence of a beloved object. Viola shrank from such an exhibition; she loved her humble cottage – humble still, though adorned with all that taste and love could bestow on it. The trees bent over its low roof and shaded its windows, which were filled with flowering shrubs; its floor shone with marble; and vases of antique shape and exquisite beauty stood in the niches of the room. Every part was consecrated by the memory of their first meeting and their loves – the walk of snow and violets; the forest of ilex with its underwood of myrtle and its population of fireflies; the birds; the wild and shy animals that sometimes came in sight and, seen, retreated; the changes of the seasons and of the hues of nature influenced by them; the alterations of the sky; the walk of the moon and the moving of the stars – all were dear, known and commented on by this pair, who saw the love their own hearts felt reflected in the whole scene around. And their child, their noisy but speechless companion – whose smiles won kisses, and whose bright form seemed as if sent from heaven to reward their constant affection.

A week passed, and Fernando and Ludovico were riding together when the prince said: 'Tomorrow early, my son, you must go to Naples. It is time that you should show yourself there as my heir and the best representative of a princely house. The sooner you do this, the quicker will arrive the period for which no doubt you long, when the unknown Princess Mondolfo will be acknowledged by all. I cannot accompany you. In fact, circumstances which you may guess make me desire that you should appear at first without me. You will be distinguished by your sovereign, courted by all; and you will remember your promise as the best means of accomplishing your object. In a very few days I will join you.'

Ludovico readily consented to this arrangement and went the same evening to take leave of Viola. She was seated beneath the laurel tree where first they had made their mutual vows; her child was in her arms, gazing with wonder and laughter on the light of the flies. Two years had passed. It was summer again, and as the beams from their eyes met and mingled, they each drank in the joyous certainty that they were still as dear to one another as when he, weeping from intense emotion, sat under that tree. He told her of his visit to Naples, and a cloud passed over her countenance; but she dismissed it; she would not fear.

Yet again and again, a thrilling sense of coming evil made her heart beat, and each time was resisted with greater difficulty. As night came on, she carried her sleeping child into the cottage, and placed him on his bed, and then walked up and down the pathway of the forest with Ludovico until the moment of his departure should arrive, for the heat of the weather rendered it necessary that he should travel by night. Again the fear of danger crossed her, and again she with a smile shook off the thought; but when he turned to give her his parting embrace, it returned with full force on her. Weeping bitterly, she clung to him and entreated him not to go. Startled by her earnestness, he eagerly sought an explanation, but the only explanation she could give excited a gentle smile as he caressed her and bade her be calm; and then pointing to the crescent moon that gleamed through the trees and chequered the ground with their moving shades, he told her that he would be with her ere its full, and with one more embrace left her weeping. And thus it is. A strange prophetic sense often creeps about, and the spirit of Cassandra[240] inhabits many a hapless human heart and utters from many lips unheeded foretellings of evils that are to be. The hearers heed them not; the speaker hardly gives them credit; and the evil comes which, if it could have been avoided, no Cassandra could have foretold. For if that spirit were not a sure harbinger, so would it not exist; nor could these half-revealings have place if the to-come did not fulfil and make out the sketch.

Viola beheld him depart with hopeless sorrow and then turned to console herself beside the couch of her child. Yet, gazing on him, her fears came thicker; and in a transport of terror, she rushed from the cottage, ran along the pathway calling on Ludovico's name, sometimes listening if she might hear the tread of his horse, and then again shrieking aloud for him to return. But he was far out of hearing, and she returned again to her cot and, lying down beside her child, clasping his little hand in hers, at length slept peacefully.

Her sleep was light and short. She arose before the sun, and hardly had he begun to cast long shadows on the ground than, attiring herself in her veil, she was about to go with her infant to the neighbouring chapel of Santa Chiara, when she heard the trampling of horses come up the pathway. Her heart beat quick – and still quicker when she saw a stranger enter her cottage. His form was commanding, and age, which had grizzled his hair, had not tempered the fire of his eye or marred the majesty of his carriage; but every lineament was impressed by pride and even cruelty. Self-will and scorn were even more apparent. He was somewhat like what Ludovico had been, and so like what he then was, that Viola did not doubt that his father stood before her. She tried to collect her courage, but the surprise, his haughty mien, and, above all, the sound of many horses and the voices of men who had remained outside the cottage so disturbed and distracted her that her heart for a moment failed her, and she leant trembling and ashy white against the wall, straining her child to her heart with convulsive energy. Fernando spoke – 'You are Viola Arnaldi, and you call yourself, I believe, the wife of Ludovico Mondolfo?'

'I am so' – her lips formed themselves to these words, but the sound died away.

Fernando continued: 'I am Prince Mondolfo, father of the rash boy who has entered into this illegal and foolish contract. When I heard of it, my plan was easily formed, and it is now about to be put into execution. I could easily have done so without coming to you, without enduring the scene which I suppose I shall endure; but benevolence has prompted me to the line of conduct I adopt, and I hope that I shall not repent it.'

Fernando paused; Viola had heard little of what he had said. She was employed in collecting her scattered spirits, in bidding her heart be still, and arming herself with the pride and courage of innocence and helplessness. Every word he spoke was thus of use to her as it gave her time to recollect herself. She only bowed her head as he paused, and he continued.

'While Ludovico was a younger son and did not seek to obtrude his misalliance into notice, I was content that he should enjoy what he termed happiness unmolested; but circumstances have changed. He has become the heir of Mondolfo and must support that family and title by a suitable marriage. Your dream has passed. I mean you no ill. You will be conducted hence with your child, placed on board a vessel and taken to a town of Spain. You will receive a yearly stipend; and as long as you seek no communication with Ludovico or endeavour to leave the asylum provided for you, you are safe. But the slightest movement, the merest yearning for a station you may never fill, shall draw upon you and that boy the vengeance of one whose menaces are but as the uplifted arm – the blow quickly follows.'

The excess of danger that menaced the unprotected Viola gave her courage. She replied: 'I am alone and feeble; you are strong and have ruffians waiting on you to execute such crimes as your imagination suggests. I care not for Mondolfo – nor the title, nor the possession – but I will never, oh never, never! renounce my Ludovico – never do aught to derogate from our plighted faith. Torn from him, I will seek him, though it be barefoot and a-hungered, through the wide world. He is mine by that love he has pleased to conceive for me; I am his by the sentiment of devotion and eternal attachment that now animates my voice. Tear us asunder, yet we shall meet again; and unless you put the grave between us, you cannot separate us.'

Fernando smiled in scorn. 'And that boy,' he said, pointing to him, 'will you lead him, innocent lamb, a sacrifice to the altar of your love, and plant the knife yourself in the victim's heart?'

Again the lips of Viola became pale as she clasped her boy and exclaimed in almost inarticulate accents – 'There is a God in Heaven!'

Fernando left the cottage, and it was soon filled by men. One threw a cloak over Viola and her boy, and, dragging her from the cottage, placed her in a kind of litter, and the cavalcade proceeded silently. Viola had uttered one shriek when she beheld her enemies; but knowing their power and her impotence, she stifled all further cries. When in the litter, she strove in vain to disengage herself from the cloak that enveloped her, and then tried to hush her child who, frightened at his strange situation, uttered piercing cries. At length he slept; and Viola, darkling and fearful with nothing to sustain her spirit or hopes, felt her courage vanish; and she wept long with despair and misery. She thought of Ludovico and what his grief would be, and her tears were redoubled. There was no hope, for her enemy was relentless; her child torn from her, a cloister her prison – such were the images constantly before her; they subdued her courage and filled her with terror and dismay.

The cavalcade entered the town of Salerno, and the roar of the sea announced to poor Viola that they were on its shores. 'O bitter waves,' she cried, 'my tears are as bitter as ye, and they will soon mingle.' Her conductors now entered a building; it was a watch tower, at some distance from the town, on the sea-beach. They lifted Viola from the litter and then led her to one of the dreary apartments of the tower. The window, which was not far from the ground, was grated with iron; it bore the appearance of a guard room. The chief of her conductors addressed her, courteously asked her to excuse the rough lodging: the wind was contrary, he said, but change was expected; and the next day he hoped that they would be able to embark. He pointed to the destined vessel in the offing. Viola, excited to hope by his mildness, began to entreat his compassion, but he immediately left her. Soon after, another man brought in food with a flask of wine and a jug of water. He also retired. Her massive door was locked. The sound of the retreating footsteps died away.

Viola did not despair; she felt, however, that it would need all her courage to extricate herself from her prison. She ate a part of the food which had been provided, drank some water, and then, a little refreshed, she spread the cloak her conductors had left on the floor, placed her child on it to play, and then stationed herself at the window to see if any might pass whom she might address; and if he were not able to assist her in any other way, he might at least bear a message to Ludovico, that her fate might not be veiled in the fearful mystery that threatened it; but probably the way past her window was guarded, for no one drew near. As she looked, however, and once advanced her head to gaze more earnestly, it struck her that her person would pass between the iron grates of her window. It was not high from the ground; the cloak, fastened to one of the staunchions, promised a safe descent. She did not dare make the essay. Nay, she was so fearful that she might be watched and that, if she were seen near the window, her jailers might be struck with the same idea, that she retreated to the farther end of the room and sat looking at the bars with fluctuating hope and fear, that now dyed her cheeks with crimson and again made them pale – as when Ludovico had first seen her.

Her boy passed his time in alternate play and sleep. The ocean still roared, and the dark clouds brought up by the sirocco blackened the sky and hastened the coming evening. Hour after hour passed; she heard no clock; there was no sun to mark the time; but by degrees her room grew dark, and at last the Ave Maria tolled,[241] heard by fits between the howling of the wind and the dashing of the waves. She knelt and put up a fervent prayer to the Madonna, protector of innocence – a prayer for her and her boy, no less innocent than the Mother and Divine Child to whom she made her orisons. Yet still she paused. Drawing near the window, she listened for the sounds of any human being. These died away, for with darkness came rain that poured in torrents, accompanied by thunder and lightning that drove every creature to shelter. Viola shuddered. Could she expose her child during such a night? Yet again she gathered courage. It only made her meditate on some plan by which she might get the cloak as a shelter for her boy after it had served for their descent. She tried the bars and found that with some difficulty she could pass; and gazing downwards from the outside, a flash of lightning discovered the ground not far below. Again she recommended herself to divine protection; again she called upon and blessed her Ludovico; and then, not fearless but determined, she began her operations. She fastened the cloak by means of her long veil which, hanging to the ground, was tied by a slipknot and would give way when pulled. She took her child in her arms and, having got without the bars, bound him with her sash to her waist; and then without accident she reached the ground. Having then secured the cloak and enveloped herself and her child in its dark and ample folds, she paused breathlessly to listen. Nature was awake with its loudest voice. The sea roared, and the incessant flashes of lightning that discovered solitude around her were followed by such deafening peals as almost made her fear. She crossed the field and kept the sight of the white sea foam to her right hand, knowing that thus she proceeded in an opposite direction from Mondolfo. She walked as fast as her burthen permitted her, keeping the beaten road, for the darkness made her fear to deviate. The rain ceased, and she walked on until, her limbs sinking under her, she was fain to rest, and refreshed herself with the bread she had brought with her from her prison. Action and success had inspired her with unusual energy. She would not fear – she believed herself free and secure. She wept, but it was with the overflowing emotion that found no other expression. She doubted not that she should rejoin Ludovico. Seated thus in the dark night, having for hours been the sport of the elements, which now for an instant paused in their fury – seated on a stone by the road's side, a wide, dreary, unknown country about her, her helpless child in her arms, herself having just finished eating the only food she possessed – she felt triumph and joy and love descend into her heart, prophetic of future reunion with her beloved.

It was summer, and the air consequently warm. Her cloak had protected her from the wet, so her limbs were free and unnumbed. At the first ray of dawn she arose, and at the nearest pathway she struck away from the road and took her course nearer the bordering Apennines. From Salerno as far south as the eye can reach, a low plain stretched itself along the seaside, and the hills at about the distance of ten miles bound it in. These mountains are high and singularly beautiful in their shape; their crags point to heaven, and streams flow down their sides and water the plain below. After several hours walking, Viola reached a pine forest which descended from the heights and stretched itself in the plain. She sought its friendly shelter with joy; and penetrating its depth until she saw trees only on all sides of her, she again reposed. The sirocco had been dissipated by the thunderstorm; and the sun, vanquishing the clouds that at first veiled its splendour, glowed forth in the clear majesty of noon. Southern-born, Viola did not fear the heat. She collected pinenuts, contrived to make a fire and ate them with appetite; and then seeking a covert, she lay down and slept, her boy in her arms, thanking heaven and the Virgin for her escape. When she awoke, the triumph of her heart had somewhat died away. She felt the solitude, she felt her helplessness, she feared pursuers; yet she dashed away her tears; and then reflecting that she was still too near Salerno, the sun being now at the sea's verge, she arose and pursued her way through the intricacies of the wood. She got to the edge of it, so far as to be able to direct her steps by the neighbouring sea. Torrents intercepted her path, and one rapid river seemed to impede it altogether; but going somewhat lower down, she found a bridge; and then approaching still nearer to the sea, she passed through a wide and desolate kind of pasture country, which seemed to afford neither shelter nor sustenance to any human being. Night closed in, and she was fearful to pursue her way; but seeing some buildings dimly in the distance, she directed her steps that way, hoping to discover a hamlet where she might get shelter and such assistance as would enable her to retrace her steps and reach Naples without being discovered by her powerful enemy. She kept these high buildings before her, which appeared like vast cathedrals but that they were untopped by any dome or spire; and she wondered much what they could be, when suddenly they seemed to disappear. She would have thought some rising ground had intercepted them, but all before her was plain. She paused, and at length resolved to wait for dawn. All day she had seen no human being; twice or thrice she had heard the bark of a dog, and once the whistle of a shepherd, but she saw no one. Desolation was around her; this indeed had lulled her to security at first. Where no men were, there was no danger for her. But at length the strange solitude became painful – she longed to see a cottage or to find some peasant, however uncouth, who might answer her queries and provide for her wants. She had viewed with surprise the buildings which had been as beacons to her. She did not wish to enter a large town, and she wondered how one could exist in such a desert; but she had left the wood far behind her, and she required food. Night passed, balmy and sweet night; the breezes fanned her; the glowing atmosphere encompassed her; the fireflies flitted round her; bats wheeled about in the air; and the heavy-winged owl hooted anigh, while the beetles' constant hum filled the air. She lay on the ground, her babe pillowed on her arm, looking upon the starry heavens. Many thoughts crowded upon her – the thought of Ludovico, of her reunion with him, of joy after sorrow; and she forgot that she was alone, half-famished, encompassed by enemies in a desert plain of Calabria – she slept.

She awoke not until the sun had risen high – it had risen above the temples of Paestum, and the columns threw short shadows on the ground. They were near her, unseen during night, and were now revealed as the edifices that had attracted her the evening before. They stood on a rugged plain, despoiled of all roof, their columns and cornices encompassing a space of high and weed-grown grass. The deep blue sky canopied them and filled them with light and cheerfulness. Viola looked on them with wonder and reverence. They were temples to some god who still seemed to deify them with his presence: he clothed them still with beauty; and what was called their ruin might, in its picturesque wildness and sublime loveliness, be more adapted to his nature than when, roofed and gilt, they stood in pristine strength; and the silent worship of air and happy animals might be more suited to him than the concourse of the busy and heartless. The most benevolent of spirits seemed to inhabit these desert, weed-grown areas. The spirit of beauty flitted between their columns embrowned by time, painted with strange colours, and rained a genial atmosphere on the deserted altar. Awe and devotion filled the heart of the lonely Viola. She raised her eyes and heart to heaven in thanksgiving and prayer – not that her lips formed words or her thoughts suggested connected sentences, but the feeling of worship and gratitude animated her; and as the sunlight streamed through the succession of columns, so did joy, dove-shaped, fall on her and illumine her soul.

With such devotion as seldom before she had visited a saint-dedicated church, she ascended the broken and crude steps of the larger temple and entered the plot that it enclosed. An inner circuit of smaller columns enclosed an inner area; she entered that and, sitting on a huge fragment of the broken cornice that had fallen to the ground, she silently waited, as if some oracle would visit her sense and guide her.

Thus sitting, she heard the near bark of a dog – followed by the bleating of sheep – and she saw a little flock spread itself in the field adjoining the farther temple. They were shepherded by a girl clothed in rags, but the season required little covering; and these poor people, moneyless and possessing only what their soil gives them, are in the articles of clothing poor even to nakedness. In inclement weather, they wrapped rudely formed clothes of undressed sheepskin around them; during the heats of summer, they do little more than throw aside these useless garments. The shepherd girl was probably about fifteen years of age; a large black straw hat shaded her head from the intense rays of the sun; her feet and legs were bare; and her petticoat, tucked up, Diana-like, above one knee, gave a picturesque appearance to her rags which, bound at her waist by a girdle, might have been the costume of a Greek maiden. Rags have even a costume of their own, as fine in their way, in their contrast of rich colours and the uncouth boldness of their drapery, as kingly robes. Viola approached the shepherdess and quietly entered into conversation with her, without making any appeal to her charity or feelings. She asked the name of the place where she was; and her boy, awake and joyous, soon attracted attention. The shepherd girl was pretty and, above all, good natured; she caressed the child, seemed delighted to have found a companion for her solitude, and, when Viola said that she was hungry, unloaded her scrip of roasted pinenuts, boiled chestnuts, and coarse bread. Viola ate with joy and gratitude. They remained together all day; the sun went down, the glowing light of its setting faded, and the shepherdess would have taken Viola home with her. But she dreaded a human dwelling, still fearing that wherever there appeared a possibility of shelter, there her pursuers would seek her. She gave a few small silver pieces, part of what she had about her when seized, to her new friend; and bidding her bring sufficient food for the next day, entreated her not to mention her adventure to anyone. The girl promised and, with the assistance of her dog, drove her flock towards their fold. Viola passed the night within the area of the larger temple.

Not doubting the success of his plan, on the very evening that followed its execution Prince Mondolfo had gone to Naples. He found his son at the Mondolfo palace. Despising the state of a court, and careless of the gaieties around him, Ludovico longed to return to the cottage of Viola. So after the expiration of two days, he told his father that he should ride over to Mondolfo and return the following morning. The conscious Fernando did not oppose him, but two hours after his departure he followed him and arrived at the castle just after Ludovico, leaving his attendants there, had quitted it to proceed alone to his cottage. The first person Prince Mondolfo saw was the chief of the company who had had the charge of Viola. His story was soon told: the unfavourable wind, her imprisonment in a room barricaded with the utmost strength, her incomprehensible escape, and the vain efforts that had subsequently been made to find her. Fernando listened as if in a dream. Convinced of the truth, he saw no clue to guide him, no hope of recovering possession of his prisoner. He foamed with rage and then endeavoured to suppress as useless the towering passion. He overwhelmed the bearer of the news with execrations; sent out parties of men in pursuit in all directions, promising every reward and urging the utmost secrecy; and then, left alone, paced his chamber in fury and dismay. His solitude was of no long duration. Ludovico burst into his room, his countenance lighted up with rage. 'Murderer,' he cried, 'where is my Viola?' Fernando remained speechless. 'Answer,' said

Ludovico. 'Speak with those lips that pronounced her death sentence –
or raise against me that hand from which her blood is scarcely washed.
Oh, my Viola! – thou and my angel child – descend with all thy
sweetness into my heart, that this hand write not parricide on my
brow!'

Fernando attempted to speak. 'No,' shrieked the miserable Ludovico,
'I will not listen to her murderer! – Yet, is she dead? I kneel – I call you
father, I appeal to that savage heart, I take in peace that hand that often
struck me and now has dealt the deathblow. Tell me – oh, tell me, does
she yet live?'

Fernando seized on this interval of calm to relate his story. He told
the simple truth; but could such a tale gain belief? It reawakened the
wildest rage in poor Ludovico's heart. He doubted not that she was
murdered; and after every expression of despair and hatred, he bade his
father seek his heir amid the clods of the earth, for that such he should
soon become, and rushed from his presence.

He wandered to the cottage; he searched the country round; he heard
the tale of those who had witnessed any part of the carrying off of his
Viola; he went to Salerno; he heard the tale there told with the most
determined incredulity. It was the tale, he doubted not, that his father
forged to free himself from accusation and to throw an impenetrable
veil over the destruction of Viola. His quick imagination made out for
itself the scene of her death. The very house in which she had been
confined had at the other extremity of it a tower jutting out over the
sea; a river flowed at its base, making its confluence with the ocean,
deep and dark. He was convinced that the fatal scene had been acted
there. He mounted the tower: the higher room was windowless, the
iron grates of the windows had for some cause been recently taken out.
He was persuaded that Viola and her child had been thrown from that
window into the deep and gurgling waters below.

He resolved to die. In those days of simple Catholic faith, suicide was
considered with horror; but there were other means almost as sure. He
would go a pilgrim to the Holy Land, and fight and die beneath the
walls of Jerusalem. Rash and energetic, his purpose was no sooner
formed than he hastened to put it in execution. He procured a pilgrim's
weeds at Salerno; and at midnight, advising none of his intention, he
left this city and proceeded southwards. Alternate rage and grief swelled
his heart; rage at length died away. She whose murderer he execrated
was an angel in heaven, an angel looking down on him; and he in the
Holy Land would win his right to join her. Tender grief dimmed his
eyes. The world's great theatre closed before him – of all its trappings,

his pilgrim's cloak was alone gorgeous, his pilgrim's staff the only sceptre – they were the symbols and signs of the power he possessed beyond the earth, and the pledges of his union with Viola. He bent his steps towards Brundusium.[242] He walked on fast as if he grudged all space and time that lay between him and his goal. Dawn awakened the earth, and he proceeded on his way. The sun of noon darted its rays upon him, but his march was uninterrupted. He entered a pine wood, and, following the track of flocks, he heard the murmurs of a fountain. Oppressed by thirst, he hastened towards it. The water welled up from the ground and filled a natural basin; flowers grew on its banks and looked upon the waters – unreflected, for the stream paused not, but whirled round and round, spending its superabundance in a small rivulet that, dancing over stones and glancing in the sun, went on its way to *its* eternity – the sea. The trees had retreated from the fountain and formed a circle about it; the grass was green and fresh, starred with summer flowers. At one extremity was a silent pool that formed a strange contrast with the fountain – that, ever in motion, showed no shape and reflected only the colour of the objects around it; the pool reflected the scene with greater distinctness and beauty than its real existence. The trees stood distinct, the ambient air between, all grouped and pictured with the hand of a divine artist. Ludovico drank from the fount and then approached the pool. He looked with half wonder on the scene depicted there. A bird now flitted across in the air, and its form, feathers and motion were shown in the waters. An ass came from among the trees, where in vain it sought herbage and came to graze near these waters; Ludovico saw it depicted therein and then looked on the living animal – almost appearing less real, less living than its semblance in the stream. Under the trees from whence the ass had come lay someone on the ground, enveloped in a mantle, sleeping. Ludovico looked carelessly, till he hardly at first knew why his curiosity was roused; then came an eager thought which he deemed madness yet resolved to gratify. Rapidly he approached the sleeper, knelt down, drew aside the cloak, and saw Viola – her child within her arms, the warm breath issuing from her parted lips, her love-beaming eyes hardly veiled by the transparent lids which soon were lifted up.

Ludovico and Viola, each too happy to feel the earth they trod, returned to their cottage – their cottage dearer than any palace – and yet, only half believing the excess of their own joy, by turns they wept and gazed on each other and their child, holding each other's hands as if grasping reality and fearful it would vanish.

Prince Mondolfo heard of their arrival. He had long suffered keenly from the fear of losing his son. The dread of finding himself childless, heirless, had tamed him. He feared the world's censure, his sovereign's displeasure, perhaps worse accusation and punishment. He yielded to fate. Not daring to appear before his intended victims, he sent his confessor to mediate for their forgiveness and to entreat them to take up their abode at Mondolfo. At first, little credit was given to these offers. They loved their cottage and had small inclination to risk happiness, liberty and life for worthless luxury. The prince by patience and perseverance at length convinced them. Time softened painful recollections; they paid him the duty of children; and cherished and honoured in his old age, while he caressed his lovely grandchild, he did not repine that the violet girl should be the mother of the heir of Mondolfo.

NOTES

In addition to the sources that appear in the Bibliography works consulted include William Cobbett's *A New French and English Dictionary in Two Parts* (Mills, Jowett and Mills, London, 1833), John Lemprière's *A Classical Dictionary*, Eleventh Edition (T. Cadell and W. Davies, London, 1820), Michael Sideri's *English–Greek Greek–English Dictionary*, Second Edition (Sideris, Athens, 1997), as well as on-line versions of the *Encyclopaedia Britannica*, the *Oxford English Dictionary*, the French and Italian *Oxford Language Dictionaries*, the *Merriam-Webster Dictionary* and the *Scottish National Dictionary*, and the website theoi.com.

MATHILDA

1 (p. 3) *it is as the wood . . . about to die*   In Sophocles' play *Oedipus at Colonus* (*c.* 406 BC) Oedipus dies in the sacred grove of the Eumenides (the Eumenides or Erinyes were born from the blood of Kronos' castration of his father Uranus) and his daughter Antigone expresses her futile wish to die in the same location.

2 (p. 4) *adamantine*   any especially hard substance

3 (p. 10) *there were none to praise/ And very few to love*   from lines 3–4 of William Wordsworth's poem 'She dwelt among the untrodden ways' (1800)

4 (p. 11) *ond' era pinta tutta la mia via*   Dante Alighieri, *Purgatorio* (*c.*1308–*c.*1321), 42, 28: Matilda gathers the flowers 'with which her entire path was painted' in the divine forest in the earthly paradise at the summit of Mount Purgatory; her role here is first to guide penitent souls to drink the waters of the Lethe so they forget their sins and then to drink of the River Eunoe to recall good deeds before entering heaven. Original quotation is 'sua via'.

5 (p. 11) *a translation of Livy and Rollin's ancient history*   Titus Livius Patavinus, author of *History of Rome* (*c.*27–*c.*20BC); Charles Rollin, author of *Ancient History* (1730–8)

6 (p. 12) *Rosalind and Miranda and the lady of Comus* Rosalind and Miranda are the female leads in Shakespeare's plays *As You Like It* and *The Tempest* (1623), and the lady of Comus was the female lead in John Milton's *Comus* (1637).

7 (p. 14) *rachan* usually rauchan, a plaid mantle or garment

8 (p. 15) *one of the seven sleepers, or like Nourjahad* The seven sleepers of Ephesus were persecuted Christians who slept for several hundred years; Nourjahad is the fabled sleeper of Frances Sheridan's *The History of Nourjahad* (1767).

9 (p. 15) *dingle* a small secluded wooded valley; a dell

10 (p. 16) *enchanted cup* In the legend of Tristan and Isolde the couple fall in love after drinking from a magically enchanted cup; Aristo's *Orlando Furioso* (1516–32) features an enchanted cup (borrowed from Sir Thomas Malory's *Le Morte Darthur* [1485]) that can only be safely drunk from by a faithful woman.

11 (p. 16) *a spirit . . . earthquake and volcano* Vulcan, the Roman god of fire, including volcano fire, is associated with fertility, while Poseidon caused earthquakes by striking the sea bed with his trident.

12 (p. 17) *Psyche* Cupid's beautiful human lover who is granted immortality after a period of wandering and the completion of a series of tasks; the enchanted palace is the location of Psyche's sexual encounters with Cupid that suddenly end when she violates his command never to look at him.

13 (p. 18) *silence and tears* from Lord Byron's poem 'When We Two Parted' (1816), lines 29–32: 'If I should meet thee/ After long years,/ How should I greet thee?—/ With silence and tears.'

14 (p. 18) *Proserpine . . . the abodes of death and misery* Proserpine (or Proserpina) was collecting flowers in Enna, Sicily, when she was abducted by Pluto to the Underworld where she had to remain as his wife for part of each year.

15 (p. 19) *for what should I . . . my poor heart life?* spoken by Lelia about Julio in Francis Beaumont and John Fletcher's comedic play *The Captain* (1647), 1, 3, 237–40. Lelia later attempts to seduce her disguised father, but after uncovering his identity she still wants to act on her desire: 'Though I know him now/ To be my Father, never let me live/ If my lust do abate' (4, 4, 157–9).

16 (p. 19) *like David . . . the evil spirit from him* I Samuel 16:23: 'And it came to pass, when the evil spirit from God was upon Saul, that

David took an harp, and played with his hand: so Saul was refreshed, and was well, and the evil spirit departed from him.'

17 (p. 19) *I thought Myhrra the best of Alfieri's tragedies* Vittorio Alfieri's tragedy *Mirra* (1785) was inspired by the Greek myth of Myrrha, who tricks her father into sexual intercourse, and is transformed by the gods into the myrrh tree.

18 (p. 19) *as a rainbow . . . tremendous sorrows* refers to Byron's comparison in *Childe Harold's Pilgrimage* (1812–18), 4, 71–2 of an iris by a cataract to 'Hope upon a death-bed'

19 (p. 21) *I took up Spencer . . . the halls of Avarice* In Edmund Spencer's *The Faerie Queene* (1590), 2, 7, Sir Guyon, the Knight of Temperance, is led into the Underworld by Mammon and confronted with a series of temptations.

20 (p. 26) *If there is a chasm . . . delight on the other side* reference to Apuleius' description in *Metamorphoses* of Psyche standing on the mountain cliff awaiting a marriage to Death when the West Wind gently lifts her and carries her down into the flowery and grassy valley below

21 (p. 27) *Now I have dashed from the . . . the fallen archangel* A possible reference to Pysche's sisters who, for the love of Cupid, leapt off a rocky cliff believing they would be borne up by the wind, but rather fell to their deaths; also, an allusion to Matthew Lewis's Gothic novel *The Monk* (1796) in which the villain Ambrosio is hurled from a height to his death on the rocks below by his demon-lover, Matilda.

22 (p. 28) *a whip of scorpions* carried by the Eumenides and mentioned in Byron's tragic poem 'The Siege of Corinth' (1816), 32, 546–9: 'her hated race/ Have felt the arm they would debase/ Scourge, with a whip of scorpions, those/ Whom vice and envy made my foes'

23 (p. 29) *as Boccaccio . . . the heart of Guiscardo* In Giovanni Boccaccio's *The Decameron* 4, 1, Ghismonda (called Sigismunda in John Dryden's 1699 translation and William Hogarth's 1759 painting) mourns her husband Guiscardo, who was murdered by her father. She commits suicide by pouring poison over Guiscardo's heart, sent to her in a goblet by her father.

24 (p. 31) *antipodes* the point on earth diametrically opposite a given place

25 (p. 33) *E quasi mi perdei gli occhi chini* in Dante's *Paradiso*, 3, 4, 143, Beatrice looks at Dante with eyes so full of love that he is powerless and 'with eyes cast down, I was almost lost'. Original quotation is 'con li' rather than 'gli'.

26 (p. 34) *as Anchises . . . if the sex had been changed* Anchises was the human lover of the goddess Aphrodite (or Venus), and their child was a son, Aeneas.

27 (p. 35) *Better have loved despair, and safer kissed her* In Beaumont and Fletcher's play *A Wife for a Month* (performed 1624, printed 1647), 1, 2, 156, 'Better have loved Despair, and safer kiss'd her!' is spoken by the tyrannical Frederick regarding his punishment of Evanthe's lover.

28 (p. 40) *the cavern of Antiparos* located on the island of Antiparos in the Greek Cyclades, famous for having the oldest stalactites and stalagmites in Europe and for being visited by Byron

29 (p. 41) *the poisonous simoon* violent and hot wind, laden with sand, of the Arabian and North African deserts

30 (p. 41) *Where is now . . . in the dust* Job 17:15–16: 'And where is now my hope? As for my hope, who shall see it? They shall go down to the bars of the pit, when our rest together is in the dust.'

31 (p. 42) *Whispered . . . soft and low* Samuel Taylor Coleridge's poem 'Fire, Famine and Slaughter' (1798), lines 17–18: 'Whisper it, sister! So and so!/ In a dark hint, soft and slow.'

32 (p. 42) *Constance* In Shakespeare's *King John* Lady Constance, widow of Geoffrey II, grieves for her husband and imprisoned son, Arthur, of whose fate she is unsure.

33 (p. 43) *the sight of the lovely water snakes . . . on my own soul* Coleridge's *The Rime of the Ancient Mariner* (1798), 4, 274–89 depicts the Mariner's response to the beautiful water-snakes, 'And I bless'd them unaware./ The selfsame moment I could pray,' as freeing him from the albatross.

34 (p. 43) *I tore my hair . . . if I might not* A reference to *King John*, 3, 4, 1428–60, where Constance responds to the accusation that she is mad rather than grieving, 'I am not mad: this hair I tear is mine,' claiming that it is her reasoning that makes her suicidal as she may never see her imprisoned son again.

35 (p. 44) *rack* thin mass of wind-driven clouds

36 (p. 45) *Before I see another day/ Oh, let this body die away!* from Wordsworth's poem 'The Complaint of a Forsaken Indian Woman' in *Lyrical Ballads with a Few Other Poems* (1798), lines 1–2, 'Before I see another day/ Oh let my body die away!'

37 (p. 47) *He was . . . bees had fed*   The ancient Greeks associated lips anointed with honey with the gift of eloquence and honey and bees generally with prophecy.

38 (p. 48) *Dr Darwin*   Erasmus Drawin's poem 'The Botanic Garden' (1791) aligns scientific progress with social advances and its depiction of 'sexual functions as the base of nature, freed from cultural determinants' (Teute, p. 168) became associated with the dangers of radicalism and revolution.

39 (p. 51) *a sylvan huntress by his side*   a reference to Wordsworth's poem 'Ruth, or, The Influences of Nature' in *Lyrical Ballads with a Few Other Poems* (1798), line 95, in which Ruth's lover imagines her as 'a sylvan huntress at my side'

40 (p. 56) *you are cruel . . . in this rough manner*   There are several possible sources for Shelley's use of this phrase, including Walter Scott's *Gortz of Berlingen* (1799), a translation of Goethe's *Götz von Berlichingen* (1773), in which Adelaide is told by her attendant 'you have ensnared his heart, and if he will tear it from the hook, it must bleed at every pore' (2, 43); Edwin's lines in Matthew West's tragedy *Ethelinda; or, Love and Duty* (1769), 'I mourn the sad necessity,/ And bleed at every pore!' (2, 31); or a reference to Luke 22:44: 'And being in an agony he prayed more earnestly: and his sweat was as it were great drops of blood falling down to the ground.'

41 (p. 56) *Gli occhi drizzo ver me con quel sembiante/ Che madre fa sopra figlioul deliro*   Dante's *Paradiso*, 1, 101–2: The original quotation, 'li occhi drizzò ver me con quell sembiante/ che madre fa sovre figlio deliro', describes how Beatrice 'directed her eyes on me with the look that a mother casts on her delirious child'.

42 (p. 58) *A little patience, and all will be over*   the last words of Mary Wollstonecraft's mother. Wollstonecraft used them in her unfinished novel *Maria; or, The Wrongs of Woman*: ' "Have a little patience," said Maria, holding her swimming head (she thought of her mother), "this cannot last long" ' (p. 147).

43 (p. 59) *What if some little payne . . . sleep in quiet grave?*   In Spencer's *Faerie Queene*, 1, 9, 40, Redcrosse is almost seduced into suicide by Despair when he is saved by Una, who reminds him that he can still experience mercy.

44 (p. 63) *bruna, bruna,/ Sotto l'ombra perpetua, che mai/ Raggiar non lascia sole ivi, nè Luna*   description of the river in the divine forest where Matilda picks flowers in Dante's *Purgatorio*, 28, 31–3: 'dark,

dark,/ beneath the endless shadows, which/ allow no ray of sun or moon to reach the waters'

45 (p. 64) *sul margine d'un rio* 'The Much Admired Air' appears in Tommaso Traetta's opera *Telemaco* (1777)

46 (p. 64) *gather a flower . . . where no flower grew* As well as being a reference to Dante's Matilda gathering flowers and Proserpine's abduction while collecting flowers (on the plains of Enna or on the Nysian plains, according to different versions of the myth) this also alludes to William Blake's 'Visions of the Daughters of Albion' (1793), lines 11–12, in which the female protagonist Oothoon 'wandered in woe,/ Along the vales of Leutha seeking flowers to comfort her'.

47 (p. 65) *The moon . . . small and dull* Coleridge's 'Christabel' in *Lyrical Ballads with a Few Other Poems* (1798)

48 (p. 66) *Rolled round . . . stones, and trees* Wordsworth's 'A Slumber Did My Spirit Seal' in *Lyrical Ballads with a Few Other Poems* (1800)

49 (p. 67) *magic lantern* a type of image projector popular in the late eighteenth and early nineteenth centuries used in séances and shows

50 (p. 68) *a being . . . return to her native soil* The reference reverses the traditional accounts of Proserpina's abduction by Hades into the Underworld that claim once there Hades tricked her into eating pomegranate seeds, thus forcing her to stay in the Underworld for part of the year.

51 (p. 69) *as the waters cover the sea* Isaiah 11:9

A TALE OF THE PASSIONS

52 (p. 71) *Corradino* Italian name for Conrad, Duke of Swabia (1252–1268), known as Conradin, who supported the Ghibellines against the Guelphs during the wars between these political factions in medieval Italy, and was executed by Charles of Anjou, King of Naples (Charles I).

53 (p. 71) *Piazza del Duomo* cathedral square

54 (p. 71) *Carroccio* an alter mounted on an ox-drawn cart that represented a city's honour. Often carrying a crucifix and flag, it was highly guarded during battle.

55 (p. 71) *anniversary of the first of May, 1268* In April 1267 Charles I and his troops entered Florence causing the Ghibellines to retreat.

56 (p. 71) *Vicare* Vicar-General of Tuscany, a role granted to Charles I in 1267

57 (p. 72) *fazioles* probably *facioli*, cloth headgear worn in medieval Italy by women; similar to a wimple

58 (p. 72) *minestra* light soup

59 (p. 72) *Piazza del Duomo* See Note 53.

60 (p. 72) *coloratio* Latin for colour or coloration. However, in the *The Liberal*, No. 2 (1823), in which the story first appeared, the word was given as 'calrasio' – raso or rasi (pl.) in Italian means satin – and could thus refer to the fabric of the dress.

61 (p. 72) *Arti Minori* minor arts and trades guilds. As a shoemaker Cincolo would have belonged to the Arte dei Calzolai guild.

62 (p. 72) *festa* festival or celebration; feast day

63 (p. 73) *when the castle of Pagibonzi was taken* Charles I and his army took the fortress of Poggibonsi in November 1267.

64 (p. 74) *Marzio the lion* The Guelphs banned the Ghibbelines' imperial eagle, using the lion on their heraldry and keeping live lions caged in the city centre.

65 (p. 74) *Monte Aperto* The Ghibbelines defeated the Guelphs in 1260 at the Battle of Montaperti.

66 (p. 76) *Cisalpines* the southern, or Italian, side of the Alps

67 (p. 78) *Ave Maria* refers to the Angelus or evening recitation of the Hail Mary, signalled by the ringing of church or cathedral bells

68 (p. 78) *Palagio del Popolo* palace of the Guelph leaders

69 (p. 80) *Palagio del Governo* Palace of Government

70 (p. 85) *Countess Elizabeth* probably Elisabeth of Bavaria (*c.*1227–73), mother of Corradino (Conradin)

71 (p. 88) *De Profundis* Psalm 130, often chanted as a dirge

72 (p. 90) *Stinchi* Le Stinche, prison in Florence

73 (p. 91) *contadini* farmers or peasants

74 (p. 91) *podesta* official or magistrate

75 (p. 92) *Vico Pisano* Vicopisano, the centre of the Republic of Pisa, located some 15 km east of Pisa

76 (p. 92) *the Arno* river that runs through Pisa and the Tuscany region of Italy

77 (p. 93) *Pope Clement IV . . . Viterbo*   an ally of Charles I who resided in the papal palace at Viterbo and, due to fears of Manfred's growing power, maintained the latter's earlier excommunication from the church

78 (p. 94) *Frederic of Austria*   Frederick I of Baden (1249–68), Conradin's friend with whom he was imprisoned and later publicly beheaded

79 (p. 94) *battle of Tagliacozzo*   the battle in which Charles I defeated Conradin's forces

80 (p. 94) *Robert of Flanders, the brother-in-law of Charles himself*   Robert III of Flanders (1249–1322) was, in fact, the son-in-law of Charles I, as he married Charles's daughter, Blanche of Sicily (1250–1269), in 1265.

THE BRIDE OF MODERN ITALY

81 (p. 97) *My heart is fixt:/ This is the sixt.* ELIA   Elia was the pen name used by the author Charles Lamb; this couplet may be from a poem of his which has not survived.

82 (p. 98) *Argus*   or Argos, a giant with one hundred eyes, set as a guard by Hera to keep her husband Zeus away from his lover, Io

83 (p. 99) *minestra*   See Note 58.

84 (p. 99) *bisogna d'amare*   necessity to love

85 (p. 99) *prie-dieu*   small prayer desk used for private devotions

86 (p. 102) *the Profession of Eloisa*   Héloïse d'Argenteuil, a brilliant scholar whose affair with and marriage to her teacher, Peter Abélard, caused her family to have him castrated. She became an abbess and he a monk; Alexander Pope's poem 'Eloisa to Abelard' (1717) describes the letters subsequently exchanged between them.

87 (p. 103) *Marry, this . . . means mischief*   Shakespeare, *Hamlet*, 3, 2

88 (p. 105) *corrèdo*   dowry

89 (p. 107) *fillet on her brow*   circlet or band worn around the head, usually to keep a wimple in place

90 (p. 107) *houris*   beautiful virgins described in the Qur'an

FERDINANDO EBOLI

91 (p. 109) *Murat, then called Gioacchino, King of Naples* Joachim Murat, in Italian Gioacchino Napoleone Murat (1767–1815), brother-in-law of Napoleon Bonaparte via his marriage to Napoleon's younger sister Caroline Bonaparte

92 (p. 112) *argine* riverbank

93 (p. 115) *briccone* rascal, rogue

94 (p. 116) *palazzo* palace

95 (p. 119) *duenna* female chaperone, usually elderly, of young girls

96 (p. 121) *Ave Maria* See Note 67.

97 (p. 122) *Ganymede . . . his natal Ida* the most beautiful mortal, abducted by Zeus from his homeland of Mount Ida to serve on Mount Olympus

THE SISTERS OF ALBANO

98 (p. 125) *And near Albano's . . . bard's delight* Byron, *Childe Harold's Pilgrimage*, 4, 174

99 (p. 125) *cicala* cicada

100 (p. 125) *aziola* or l'assiolo or assiuolo, the European scops owl (*Otus scops*)

101 (p. 126) *contadina* farmer; peasant; countrywoman

102 (p. 127) *podere* small farm

103 (p. 128) *contadino* farmer; peasant, countryman

104 (p. 129) *festa* See Note 62.

105 (p. 129) *ladri* thieves; robbers

106 (p. 130) *tabarro* cloak; mantle

107 (p. 130) *'Carissima, addio'* 'Goodbye, dearest'

108 (p. 131) *some baccalà under his pastrano* some salted codfish under his greatcoat

109 (p. 131) *scape-grace* scoundrel

110 (p. 132) *libeccio* westerly or south-westerly wind

111 (p. 132) *'Ecco il padre!'* 'There, her father!'

112 (p. 135) *holy father and some of his red stockings* refers to the Pope of the Roman Catholic Church and its cardinals, whose vestments included red stockings

113 (p. 136) *poltroons* cowards

THE EVIL EYE

114 (p. 139) *'The wild Albanian . . . man of Macedon'* Byron, *Childe Harold's Pilgrimage*, 2, 58

115 (p. 139) *Moreot* person from Morea, another name for the Peloponnese peninsula in southern Greece where the Greek War of Independence (1821–32) began

116 (p. 139) *the pashalik of Yannina* a semi-autonomous region of the Ottoman Empire ruled by the Ottoman Albanian Ali Pasha (1740–1822), comprised of Ioannina (also Janina or Jannena) and later much of Albania and Greece

117 (p. 139) *Klephts* groups of bandits and peasants, insurgents opposed to Ottoman rule, who fought for Greek independence and usually lived in the mountains or the countryside

118 (p. 139) *pobratimo* Shelley's explanation of this term as a ceremony in Greece conflicts with Owen Meredith's account that the term is 'peculiar to the Serbs [. . .] it constitutes a relationship voluntarily contracted [. . .] In the ancient Serbian liturgies are to be found prayers applicable to the consecration of this relationship by the priest' (Meredith, p. 65).

119 (p. 139) *Tepellenè* area in present-day Albania

120 (p. 139) *yataghans* short curved sabres

121 (p. 140) *Scio* Italian for Chios, a Greek island that due to its prominent trade was allowed near autonomy by the Ottoman Empire; when the island joined the Greek revolt in 1822 most of its inhabitants were murdered or enslaved.

122 (p. 140) *Mainotes* or Maniots, or Maniotes, people from the Mani (or Maina) Peninsula in the Peloponnese, known for piracy and fierceness, vital to the Greek fight for independence

123 (p. 140) *sacoleva* small merchant ship

124 (p. 140) *Arnaoots* a term used to describe Albanians

125 (p. 141) *caravokeiri* master of a ship

126 (p. 141) *Barbary corsair* pirate or pirate ship

127 (p. 142) *Fanariote beauty* beautiful woman from Fanar. See Note 130.

128 (p. 142) *Morea* See Note 115.

129 (p. 143) *cicala* See Note 99.

130 (p. 144) *Fanar* or Phanar, the Greek quarter of Constantinople. Those who lived there were generally well educated and wealthy, with political influence.

131 (p. 144) *Codja-Bashee* Greek governor or magistrate under Ottoman rule

132 (p. 146) *monoxylon* canoe or boat made from one piece of timber

133 (p. 147) *paramana* nanny or nurse

134 (p. 148) *papooshes* heelless slipper, typically oriental in style

135 (p. 150) *monastic Zitza* Byron, *Childe Harold's Pilgrimage*, 2, 48

136 (p. 150) *Caloyers* monks of the Greek or Eastern Orthodox Church

137 (p. 150) *Palikar* a Greek or Albanian soldier in the pay of the Sultan, or, later, a soldier in the Greek militia in the War of Independence against Turkey

138 (p. 152) *Belouk-Bashee* governor of an Ottoman town

139 (p. 155) *capote* long cloak, usually hooded

THE FALSE RHYME

140 (p. 157) *Come, tell me . . . at her feet* Thomas Moore, 'Come Tell Me Where the Maid is Found' (1801)

141 (p. 157) *Souvent femme varie,/Bien fou qui s'y fie!* Woman often changes,/mad the man who trusts her!

142 (p. 158) *Souvent homme varie,/Bien folle qui s'y fie!* Man often changes,/mad the woman who trusts him!

THE MOURNER

143 (p. 161) *One fatal remembrance . . . sting!* Thomas Moore, 'As a Beam O'er the Face of the Waters May Glow', in *A Selection of Irish Melodies*, *1* (1808); also quoted in Byron's 'The Giaour' (1813)

144 (p. 161) *more inspiring . . . the deed of ruin* Shelley likely means Timotheus rather than Tiresias; Dryden's poem 'Alexander's Feast' (1697) describes the effects of Timotheus' music on Alexander the Great.

145 (p. 162) *Belvidere* belvedere; structure, such as a summer-house, with a view

146 (p. 162) *no Cerberus untamable by sops*   Cerberus, the three-headed dog who guarded the gates of the Underworld, was fed drugged cakes by Aeneas in Virgil's *Aeneid*.

147 (p. 162) *In that sweet mood . . . sad thoughts to the mind*   lines 3–4 of Wordsworth's poem 'Lines Written in Early Spring' in *Lyrical Ballads with a Few Other Poems* (1798)

148 (p. 162) *'with sweet inland murmur'*   a reference to line 4 of Wordsworth's poem 'Tintern Abbey' in *Lyrical Ballads with a Few Other Poems* (1798), 'with a soft inland murmur'

149 (p. 163) *Bishopsgate*   the location of the Shelleys' first home

150 (p. 168) *avoid the stricken deer*   a reference to William Cowper's poem *The Task* (1785), 3, 108–16: 'I was a stricken deer, that left the herd/ Long since; with many an arrow deep infixt/ My panting side was charg'd, when I withdrew/ To seek a tranquil death in distant shades./ There I was found by one who had himself/ Been hurt by th'archers. In his side he bore,/ And in his hands and feet, the cruel scars./ With gentle force soliciting the darts,/ He drew them forth, and heal'd and bade me live.'

THE SWISS PEASANT

151 (p. 179) *the waters of Uri . . . for freedom*   William Tell was a Swiss folk hero who, according to legend, in the canton of Uri in the fourteenth century rebelled against the authority of an Austrian official and, after successfully shooting an apple from his son's head with a crossbow to avoid their executions, sparked revolutionary fervour by shooting the official.

152 (p. 179) *might as well . . . Wheel of Fortune*   Shelley refers to Richard Cumberland's comedic play *The Wheel of Fortune* (1795), but his *Memoirs* describe the view to which she refers: 'no other prospect from my single window but that of a turf-stack' (1, 271), as present during his composition of *The West Indian* (1771).

153 (p. 179) *The Prisoner of Chillon*   the noble author is Byron. The poem was published in 1816 following, as the narrator states, a stay at an inn necessitated by bad weather during his and Percy Shelley's sailing on Lake Geneva.

154 (p. 180) *coupée*   a four-wheeled, horse-drawn carriage

155 (p. 180) *wager a louis*   A louis (or a *louis d'or*) was a gold coin in circulation in France before the Revolution.

156 (p. 180) *aisance* affluence

157 (p. 184) *proud oppressors of the land* The 1777 edition of Arthur Murphy's play *The Grecian Daughter: A Tragedy* (1772) has a poetic dedication to Mrs Barry, the actress who played Euphrasia, including the lines: 'his extended hand menac'd the proud oppressors of the land' (p. 3).

158 (p. 184) *chamois* a goat antelope found in the mountains of Europe

159 (p. 187) *tree of liberty was set up in the neighbouring village* a pole with a cap on it that in the aftermath of Julius Caesar's assassination became a symbol for republicanism and freedom from tyranny and was subsequently taken up by proponents of the French Revolution

160 (p. 190) *charrette* cart

161 (p. 191) *'Mais, descendez . . . bien marcher'* 'But descend, therefore, ladies,' said a peasant; 'it would be better to walk.'

162 (p. 191) *'Grand Dieu! Nous sommes perdues!'* 'Great God! We are lost!'

163 (p. 192) *canaille* rogue, scoundrel

164 (p. 192) *'À bas les aristocrats!' – 'À la lanterne!'* 'Down with the aristocrats! Hang them from the lamp-post!'

165 (p. 192) *'Arretez-vous!'* 'Stop!'

166 (p. 193) *seigneurs* lords or sovereigns

167 (p. 193) *'Attendez-moi'* 'Wait for me'

168 (p. 195) *'Et toi, Louis – tu aussi es de retour'* 'And you, Louis – you also are back.'

TRANSFORMATION

169 (p. 197) *Forthwith this frame . . . within me burns* Coleridge, *The Rime of the Ancient Mariner*, 7, 578–85

170 (p. 198) *the poor king, Charles the Sixth* Charles VI (1368–1422), King of France (1380–1422), who suffered from bouts of insanity

171 (p. 199) *caparisons* richly ornamented coverings for a horse or its saddle

172 (p. 199) *The Duke of Orleans . . . pleasure was suspended* Louis I of Orléans (1372–1407), younger brother of Charles VI, was Duke of Orléans from 1392 until he was assassinated on the orders of John the Fearless, second Duke of Burgundy (1371–1419).

173 (p. 199) *Spanish jennet*   small Spanish saddle horse

174 (p. 200) *enfant gâté*   spoiled child

175 (p. 202) *Coriolanus*   According to legend, Gaius Marcus Coriolanus was a Roman general who, having been banished from the city, disguised himself before returning with an army to attack Rome.

176 (p. 204) *bright as the son of the morning*   See Note 239.

177 (p. 207) *'day began to grizzle its dark hair'*   Byron, *Werner* (1822), 3, 4: 'the grey begins to grizzle the dark hair of night'

178 (p. 210) *child of light and love*   from Percy Shelley's dedication to Mary in *The Revolt of Islam* (1818), 1, 9: 'thy beloved name, thou child of love and light'

179 (p. 212) *Guido il Cortese*   Guido the Courteous (or courtly)

THE DREAM

180 (p. 213) *Chi dice mal d'amore/ Dice una falsità!*   from Giovanni Simone Mayr's Italian air 'The Heart to Love a Stranger'; it translates as: 'Who speaks badly of love/ Speaks a falsehood'

181 (p. 213) *Henry IV of France*   Henry IV (1553–1610) converted to Roman Catholicism in order to reunite France, which he ruled as the first Bourbon king from 1589–1610.

182 (p. 214) *like the Lady Olivia . . . loneliness and weeping*   In Shakespeare's play *Twelfth Night*, Olivia declares a seven-year period of mourning for herself after the death of her brother.

183 (p. 218) *the tyrant . . . to a corpse*   In Virgil's *Aeneid*, 8, 483–6, King Mezentius is described as a tyrant: 'The living and the dead at his command/ Were coupled, face to face, and hand to hand,/ Till, chok'd with stench, in loath'd embraces tied,/ The ling'ring wretches pin'd away and died.'

184 (p. 219) *gaillard chevalier*   valiant knight or cavalier (horseman)

185 (p. 222) *an adept in the blind god's lore*   possible reference to Tiresias, blind prophet in Greek mythology

186 (p. 222) *suivante*   female attendant; waiting-woman or lady's maid

187 (p. 224) *what dreams . . . peopled her sleep?*   possible reference to Wordsworth's poem *White Doe of Rylstone* (1815), 6, 1432–6: 'No choice is left, the deed is mine – / Dead are they, dead! – and I will go,/ And, for their sakes, come weal or woe,/ Will lay the Relic on the shrine.'

188 (p. 225) *Paynim land*   heathen lands

THE BROTHER AND SISTER

189 (p. 227) *Foscari of Venice* Francesco Foscari (1373–1457), Doge of
Venice. Byron wrote the play *The Two Foscari* (1821) concerning
the events of his life.

190 (p. 232) *run a tilt with him* to fight at combat

191 (p. 242) *fabliaux, novelle* short, comic medieval tales; short narrative
tales

192 (p. 244) *timid as . . . the limed twigs* a type of adhesive used on
twigs or branches to capture birds

193 (p. 249) *crossing the Arno* See Note 76.

194 (p. 250) *bell of the Ave Maria* See Note 67.

THE INVISIBLE GIRL

195 (p. 253) *parroquet* parrot or parakeet

196 (p. 262) *with kid so fine* very soft leather made from the skin of a
young goat

197 (p. 264) *Hebe beauty* Hebe is the Greek goddess of youth.

THE POLE

198 (p. 267) *The Pole* published as a story 'by the author of *Frankenstein*' but likely written in large part by Claire Clairmont, who
asked Shelley to correct and complete it. The extent of her author-
ship is unknown.

199 (p. 267) *caleche* a light, horse-drawn carriage with a folding top

200 (p. 267) *Mola di Gaeta* present day Formia on the Mediterranean
coast halfway between Rome and Naples

201 (p. 268) *'Pann' . . . 'Ja pozwalam'* 'My Lord' . . . 'I will it.'

202 (p. 268) *grani* or grano, singular, a denomination of coin issued
in the Kingdom of Sicily and the Kingdom of Naples

203 (p. 269) *consigned Poland . . . Russian despotism* Poland was subjected
to the rule of the Russian Empire, to a greater or lesser extent, for
most of the period between the mid-eighteenth century until the
end of the First World War.

204 (p. 270) *'E vero, è verissimo'* 'And true, and absolutely true'

205 (p. 272) *the Corinna of the North* Corinna was an ancient Greek poet.

206 (p. 272) *conversazioni* a social gathering or meeting for discussion of the arts

207 (p. 274) *one of Kosciusko's unfortunate followers* Tadeusz Kosciuszko (1746–1817), Polish officer who fought in the American Revolution and led an uprising for Polish freedom before his capture and the further partitioning of Poland by Russia

208 (p. 275) *Cattivella!* naughty!

209 (p. 276) *'Mio ben quando verrà' . . . the 'Deh calma' from Otello* Marietta refers to a variety of musical numbers here, including two by the Neapolitan composer Giovanni Paisiello (1740–1816): the song 'My treasure when he will come' (It.: Mio ben quando verrà) and the 1789 opera *Nina, Driven Mad by Love* (It.: Nina pazza per Amore); the 'To Arms' (It.: All' armi) of the generals could refer to the patriotic Italian song or a number by the same name performed by the chorus of Giacomo Meyerbeer's opera *The Crusader in Egypt* (1824); 'O patria' from Gioachino Rossini's opera *Tancredi* (1813) and 'Ah Calm' (It.: Deh calma) from his opera *Otello* (1816).

210 (p. 276) *Santa Maria del Piè di Grotta!* expression of exasperation

211 (p. 276) *Maremma* large area in central-northern Italy

212 (p. 278) *Linternum of Scipio Africanus* Publius Cornelius Scipio Africanus (236–183BC), Roman general and statesmen who resided in and is believed to have died in Liternum

213 (p. 281) *rencontre* meeting

214 (p. 282) *calessino* small carriage or buggy

215 (p. 283) *desperate bravi* hired soldiers often operating as *banditti* or criminals

216 (p. 283) *Epicharis* In Tacitus's *Annals*, 15, 57, Epicharis is described as a Roman woman who withstood brutal torture without implicating those with whom she was accused of conspiring against Nero.

217 (p. 290) *if Wieprecht himself had presided* Wilhelm Friedrich Wieprecht (1802–1872), German composer

218 (p. 291) *stiletto* a small, slender-bladed dagger

219 (p. 292) *'But the Signora . . . a palfry?'* a palfrey is a saddle horse for a woman to ride. The Englishman is making a sexual joke about Idalie and Ladislas's absence.

THE MORTAL IMMORTAL

220 (p. 295) *The Wandering Jew*   legendary figure condemned to wander the earth until the second coming of Christ, as punishment for taunting Jesus on his way to the crucifixion; Percy Shelley used him as a figure in *Queen Mab* (1813), *Hellas* (1822) and 'The Wandering Jew' (1877)

221 (p. 295) *Nourjahad*   See Note 8.

222 (p. 295) *All the world ... destroyed by him*   Cornelius Agrippa (1486–1535), German occultist and alchemist; Robert Southey's poem 'Cornelius Agrippa' (1799) featured a young man who read Agrippa's books without permission, inadvertently conjuring a devil who ripped out his heart.

223 (p. 297) *alembics*   devices used to distil or process chemicals or liquids

224 (p. 300) *'Behold ... the vanity of human wishes'*   reference to Samuel Johnson's poem *The Vanity of Human Wishes* (1749)

225 (p. 303) *a sorry figure I cut among the Nestors of our village*   from the figure Nestor in Greek mythology; a venerable old man

THE PILGRIMS

226 (p. 348) *Nathless*   nevertheless

227 (p. 350) *recreants*   cowards or persons unfaithful to a belief

228 (p. 359) *my Ida . . . lose a hand*   a reference to the practice of severing a hand or other part of a saint's body after death for preservation as a relic

229 (p. 360) *the aid of Number Nip*   a giant of the woods popularised through several contemporary fairy tales in such as those in *The New Monthly Magazine*, 32, 446

230 (p. 360) *poursuivant*   servant; follower or attendant

EUPHRASIA

231 (p. 366) *the breaking out of the Greek revolution*   See Note 115.

232 (p. 367) *caracole*   turning manoeuvre on horseback used in military tactics to allow the cavalry to fire weapons

233 (p. 367) *Praxitilean*   in the style of Praxiteles, renowned fourth-century Greek sculptor

234 (p. 371) *my soul feels the bliss, though my body is sick*   possible allusions to Matthew 26:41: 'The spirit indeed is willing, but the flesh is weak'; and Byron's *Don Juan* (1819) 1, 63, 6: 'The flesh is frail, and so the soul undone.'

235 (p. 376) *gracious Panagia*   a term for Mary, mother of Jesus, used particularly in Orthodox Christianity

THE HEIR OF MONDOLFO

236 (p. 379) *governed by monarchs of the house of Anjou*   The House of Anjou ruled Naples from the 1266 victory at the Battle of Benevento until their defeat in 1442 following Alfonso V's siege of Naples.

237 (p. 379) *where the wicked . . . are at rest*   Job 3:17: 'There the wicked cease from troubling; and there the weary be at rest.'

238 (p. 382) *sirocco*   wind originating in the Sahara that reaches the Mediterranean, causing dry and dusty conditions in Africa and cold and wet weather in Europe

239 (p. 388) *Hesperus*   in Greek mythology, alternately known as the son of dawn (Eos) or the son or brother of Atlas; identified with the evening star and the morning star, the bringer of light (the planet Venus)

240 (p. 394) *Cassandra*   a figure in Greek mythology who has the gift of prophecy but has been cursed so that no one will believe her

241 (p. 397) *Ave Maria tolled*   See Note 67.

242 (p. 403) *Brundusium*   ancient name for the Italian city of Brindisi